D1052284

By Sara Douglass

DARKGLASS MOUNTAIN
The Serpent Bride

WAYFARER REDEMPTION
Wayfarer Redemption • Enchanter
Starman • Sinner
Pilgrim • Crusader

STAND-ALONES
Threshold (September 2003)
Beyond the Hanging Wall (July 2003)

TROY GAME SERIES
Darkwitch Rising • God's Concubine
Hades' Daughter • The Druid's Sword

THE CRUCIBLE SERIES
The Nameless Day
The Wounded Hawk
The Crippled Angel

THE
SERPENT BRIDE

DarkGlass Mountain: Book One

SARA DOUGLASS

An Imprint of HarperCollinsPublishers

This book is a work of fiction. The characters, incidents, and dialogue are drawn from the author's imagination and are not to be construed as real. Any resemblance to actual events or persons, living or dead, is entirely coincidental.

EOS
An Imprint of HarperCollins*Publishers*
10 East 53rd Street
New York, New York 10022-5299

Copyright © 2007 by Sara Douglass Enterprises
Excerpt from *The Twisted Citadel* copyright © 2008 by Sara Douglass Enterprises
Map design © Sara Douglass Enterprises Pty Ltd 2006
Cover art by Steve Stone/Bernstein & Andriulli, Inc.
ISBN: 978-0-06-088214-3
www.eosbooks.com

First Eos paperback printing: June 2008
First Eos hardcover printing: June 2007

HarperCollins® and Eos® are registered trademarks of HarperCollins Publishers.

Printed in the U.S.A.

10 9 8 7 6 5 4 3 2 1

For Snow

The Lands Beyond Tencendor

The Legend of Chaos (Kanubai)

In the beginning and for an infinity of time there was nothing but the darkness of Chaos, who called himself Kanubai. After a time Kanubai grew weary of his lonely existence and so he invited Light and Water to be his companions. Kanubai and Light and Water coexisted harmoniously, but one day Light and Water merged, just for an instant of time, but in that instant they conceived a child—Life.

Kanubai was jealous of Life, for it was the child of the union of Light and Water and he had been excluded from that union. He set out to murder Life, to consume it with darkness, but Light and Water came to the defense of their child. Aided by a great mage, Light and Water defeated Kanubai in a terrible battle, and interred his remains in a deep abyss. They stoppered this abyss with a sparkling, life-giving river, which combined the best both of Light and of Water, and they hoped that Kanubai was trapped for all time.

Trapped, but not extinguished. Every day Life was reminded of Kanubai's continuing malignant presence by the descent of the night, when for the space of some hours the dark memory of Kanubai blanketed the land.

Despite this daily sadness, Life prospered, and many creatures came into existence.

For eons Kanubai lay trapped, able to do little more than darken each light-filled day with the reminder of his presence.

But then, one day, something remarkable happened.

Infinity visited.

[Part One]

CHAPTER ONE

Margalit, the Outlands

The eight-year-old girl crouched by the stone column in the atrium of her parents' house. Clad only in a stained linen shift, she hugged her thin arms tightly about herself, her eyes wide and darting under her bedraggled and grimy fair hair.

The house was cold and still, and the girl's breath frosted as she hyperventilated.

The foul liquid of rotting cadavers streaked her face and arms. For many days now the girl had crept about the house, seeking out the bodies of her parents (almost unrecognizable, four weeks after their death), rubbing the stinking, viscous liquid that had leaked from their flesh over her body, sucking it from her fingers.

All she wanted was to die, too.

It had been a bad month. Four weeks ago everyone in the house—save the little girl—had died within a day of the first person falling sick. Thirty-four people—not just the girl's parents and siblings, but her three aunts, their husbands, their children, her grandmother, and the household's servants as well—all dead from the plague.

Just her, left alive.

Outside gathered a frightened and angry crowd, neighbors as well as sundry other concerned citizens and council members of Margalit. They had blocked off all entrances to the house as soon as they realized plague had struck the household.

In the initial days after everyone had died, the girl, Ishbel, screamed at the crowd outside for help, begging them to save her. She pressed her face against the glass of the windows and beat her small fists against the frames, but the hostile expressions on the faces of the crowd outside did not alter.

They would not move to aid her.

Instead, Ishbel heard cries demanding that the house be set alight, and all the corpses and their infection burned.

She screamed at them again, begging them to allow her freedom.

She wasn't ill.

She didn't have the plague.

Her skin was unmarked, her brow unfevered.

"Please, please, let me out. Everyone is dead. I want to get out. Please . . . please . . ."

The crowd outside had no mercy. They would not let her escape.

Ishbel begged until she lost her voice and scraped away several of her fingernails on the wood of the front door.

The crowd would not listen. No other house in Margalit had the plague. Just the Brunelle house. Its doors and windows would not be opened again. The house would never ring with life and laughter as once it had.

When the girl was dead, they would burn the house, and all the corpses within it. Until then they would wait.

Eventually Ishbel crept away from the windows and the cold, bolted doors. She could not bear the flat hostility in the eyes outside.

All she wanted was comfort, and so she crept close to the corpse of her mother and cuddled up next to it.

Her mother was very cold and smelled very bad, but even so Ishbel garnered some comfort from the contact with her body.

Until the moment it began to whisper to her.

Ishbel. Ishbel. Listen to us.

Ishbel recoiled, terrified.

Her mother's corpse twitched, and it whispered again.

Ishbel, Ishbel, listen to us. You must prepare—

Ishbel screamed, over and over, her hands pressed against

her ears, her eyes screwed shut, her body rolled into a tight ball in a corner of the room.

Then the corpses of two of her aunts, which lay a few feet from her mother's, also twitched and whispered.

Ishbel, Ishbel, listen to us, our darling. Prepare, prepare, for soon the Lord of Elcho Falling shall walk again.

A vision accompanied the horrifying whispers.

A man, clothed in black, standing in the snow, his back to her.

Darkness writhed about his shoulders.

He sensed her presence, and turned his head a little, glancing at her from over his shoulder.

Bleakness and despair, and desolation so extreme it was murderous, overwhelmed Ishbel's entire world.

The despair that engulfed her annihilated everything Ishbel had felt until now.

The loss of her family, and her entrapment with their corpses, was as nothing to what this man dragged at his heels.

Prepare, Ishbel, prepare for the coming of the Lord of Elcho Falling.

After her mother, and her two aunts, every other corpse in the house twitched in the same mad, cold, macabre dance of death, and whispered until the words echoed about the house.

Prepare, Ishbel, our darling, for the Lord of Elcho Falling shall walk again.

The twitching corpses and the constant whispering drove Ishbel to the brink of insanity. She didn't want to live. She had gone mad, here in this cold house of death, watching everyone she had ever loved putrefy before her eyes.

Listening to their never-ending whispers.

Prepare, our darling . . . for the Lord of Elcho Falling.

She tried to starve herself, but one day she had weakened, sobbing, stuffing her mouth with moldy pastries from the kitchen.

Then she found a knife, and drew it across her wrists, but was too weak to carve deeply, and too cowardly to bear the pain, so the blood just seeped from the thin cuts and Ishbel had not died.

Finally, frantic, crazy, Ishbel had stuffed her ears full of wadding and crept close enough to rub the foul effluent from the cadavers of her parents over her body and face. Then she licked the foulness from her fingers, just to be sure. It made her retch and sob and then scream in horror, but she did it, because surely, *surely*, this way the plague would manage to take a grip in her body and kill her as mercifully fast as it had killed everyone else in her life.

But all that had happened was that the scars on her wrists became infected, and wept a purulent discharge, and throbbed unbearably.

Ishbel survived.

Whenever she slept, she dreamed of the Lord of Elcho Falling, turning his head ever so slightly so that he could look at her over his shoulder, and engulfing her in sorrow and pain.

She grew thin, her joints aching with the cold and with malnutrition, but she survived.

Outside the crowds waited.

Every so often Ishbel called out to them, letting them know she still existed within, because, no matter how greatly Ishbel wanted to die, she did not want to do so within an inferno.

On this day, huddled in the atrium of the house, Ishbel began to dream about death. She looked at the great staircase that wound its way to the upper floors of the house, and she wondered why she'd never before thought that all she needed to do was to climb to the top, then throw herself down.

Very slowly, because she was now extremely weak, Ishbel crawled on her hands and knees toward the staircase. She was frail, and she would need to take it slowly to get to the top, but get there she would.

Ishbel felt overwhelmed with a great determination. Her death was but an hour away, at the most.

But it took her much longer than an hour to climb the stairs. Ishbel was seriously weak, and she could only crawl up the staircase a few steps at a time before she needed to rest, collapsing and gasping, on the dusty wooden treads.

By late afternoon she was almost there. Every muscle trembled, aching so greatly that Ishbel wept with the pain.

But she was almost there . . .

Then, as she was within three steps of the top, she heard the front door open.

A faint sound, for the door was far below her, but she heard it open.

Ishbel did not know what to do. She lay on the stairs, trembling, weeping, listening to slow steps ascend the staircase, and wondered if the crowd had sent someone in to murder her.

She was taking far too long to die.

Ishbel closed her eyes, and buried her face in her arms.

"Ishbel?"

A man's voice, very kind. Ishbel thought she must be dreaming.

"Ishbel."

Slowly, and crying out softly with the ache of it, Ishbel turned over, opening her eyes.

A man wrapped in a crimson cloak over a similarly colored robe stood a few steps down, smiling at her. He was a young man, good-looking, with brown hair that flopped over his forehead, and a long, fine nose.

"Ishbel?" The man held out a hand. "My name is Aziel. Would you like to come live with me?"

She stared at him, unable to comprehend his presence.

Aziel's smile became gentler, if that was possible. "I have been traveling for weeks to reach you, Ishbel. The Great Serpent himself sent me. He appeared to me in a dream and said that I must hurry to bring you home. He loves you, sweetheart, and so shall I."

"Are you the Lord of Elcho Falling?" Ishbel whispered, even though she knew he could not be, for he did not drag loss and sorrow at his heels, and there was no darkness clinging to his shoulders.

Aziel frowned briefly, then he shook his head. "My name is Aziel, Ishbel. And I am lord of nothing, only a poor servant of the Great Serpent. Will you come with me?"

"To where?" Ishbel could barely grasp the thought of escape, now.

"To my home," Aziel said, "and it will be yours. Serpent's Nest."

"I do not know of it."

"Then you shall. Please come with me, Ishbel. Don't die. You are too precious to die."

"I don't need to die?"

Aziel laughed. "Ishbel, you have no idea how greatly we all want you to live, and to live with us. Will you come? Will you?"

Ishbel swallowed, barely able to get the words out. "Are there whispers in your house?"

"Whispers?"

"Do the dead speak in your house?"

Aziel frowned again. "The dying do, from time to time, when they confess to us the Great Serpent's wishes, but once dead they are mute."

"Good."

"Ishbel, come with me, please. Forget about what has happened here. Forget—everything."

"Yes," said Ishbel, and stretched out a trembling hand. *I will forget,* she thought. *I will forget everything.*

She did not once wonder why this man should have been able to so easily wander through the vindictive crowd outside, or why that crowd should have stood back and allowed him to open the front door without a single murmur.

Two weeks later Aziel brought Ishbel home to Serpent's Nest. She had spoken little for the entire journey, and nothing at all for the final five days.

Aziel was worried for her.

The archpriestess of the Coil, who worshipped the Great Serpent, led Aziel, carrying the little girl, to a room where awaited food and a bed. They washed Ishbel, made her eat something, then put her to bed, retreating to a far corner of the room to sit watch as she slept.

The archpriestess was an older woman, well into her sixties, called Ional. She looked speculatively at Aziel, who had not allowed his eyes to stray from the sleeping form of the child. Aziel was Ional's partner at Serpent's Nest, archpriest to her archpriestess, but he was far younger and as yet inexperienced, for he'd replaced the former archpriest only within the past year, after that man had strangely disappeared.

Ional knew she would partner Aziel only for a few more years, until he was well settled into his position as archpriest, and then she would make way for someone younger. Stronger. More Aziel's match.

Now Ional looked back to the girl.

Ishbel.

"You said," Ional said very softly, so as to not wake the girl, "that the Great Serpent told you she would not stay for a lifetime."

"He told me," said Aziel, "that she would stay many years, but that eventually he would require her to leave. That there would be a duty for her within the wider world, but that she would return and that her true home was here at Serpent's Nest."

"She is so little," said Ional, "but so very powerful. I could feel it the moment you carried her into Serpent's Nest. How much more shall she need to grow, do you think, before she can assume my duties?"

"When she is strong enough to hold a knife," said Aziel, "she shall be ready."

Deep in the abyss the creature stirred, looking upward with flat, hate-filled eyes.

It whispered, sending the whisper up and outward with all its might, seething through the crack that Infinity had opened.

It had been sending out its call for countless millennia, and for all those countless millennia, no one had answered.

This day, the creature in the abyss received not one but two replies, and it bared its teeth, and knew its success was finally at hand.

Twenty years passed.

CHAPTER TWO

Serpent's Nest, the Outlands

The man hung naked and vulnerable, his arms outstretched and chained by the wrists to the wall, his feet barely touching the ground, and likewise chained by the ankle to the wall. He was bathed in sweat caused only partly by the warm, humid conditions of the Reading Room and the highly uncomfortable position in which he had been chained.

He was hyperventilating in terror. His eyes, wide and dark, darted about the room, trying to find some evidence of mercy in the crimson-cloaked and hooded figures standing facing him in a semicircle, just out of blood-splash distance.

He might have begged for mercy, were it not for the gag in his mouth.

A door opened, and two people entered.

The man pissed himself, his urine pooling about his feet, and struggled desperately, uselessly, to free himself from his bonds.

The two arrivals walked slowly into the area contained by the semicircle of witnesses. A man and a woman, they too were cloaked in crimson, although for the moment their hoods lay draped about their shoulders. The man was in middle age, his face thin and lined, his dark hair receding, his dark eyes curiously compassionate, but only as they regarded his companion. When he glanced at the man chained to the wall those eyes became blank and uncaring.

His name was Aziel, and he was the archpriest of the Coil, now gathered in the Reading Room.

The woman was in her late twenties, very lovely, with clear hazel eyes and dark blond hair. She listened to Aziel as he spoke softly to her, then nodded. She turned slightly, acknowledging the semicircle with a small bow—as one they returned the bow—then turned back to face the chained man.

She was the archpriestess of the Coil, Aziel's equal in leadership of the order, and his superior in Readings.

Ishbel Brunelle, the little girl he had rescued twenty years earlier from her home of horror.

Aziel handed Ishbel a long silken scarf of the same color as her cloak, and, as Aziel stood back, she slowly and deliberately wound the scarf about her head and face, leaving only her eyes visible. Then, equally slowly and deliberately, her eyes never leaving the chained man, Ishbel lifted the hood of her cloak over her head, pulling it forward so that her scarf-bound face was all but hidden. She arranged her cloak carefully, making certain her robe was protected.

Then, with precision, Ishbel made the sign of the Coil over her belly.

The man bound to the wall was now frantic, his body writhing, his eyes bulging, mews of horror escaping from behind his gag.

Ishbel took no notice.

From a pocket in her cloak she withdrew a small semicircular blade. It fitted neatly into the palm of her hand, the actual slicing edge protruding from between her two middle fingers.

She stepped forward, concentrating on the man.

He was now flailing about as much as he could given the restriction of his restraints, but his movements appeared to cause Ishbel no concern. She moved to within two paces of the man, took a very deep breath, her eyes closing as she murmured a prayer.

"Great Serpent be with me, Great Serpent be part of me, Great Serpent grace me."

Then Ishbel opened her eyes, stepped forward, lifted her slicing hand, and, in a movement honed by twenty years of the study of anatomy and practice both upon the living and the dead, cleanly disemboweled the man with a serpentine incision from sternum to groin.

Blood spurted outward in a spray, covering Ishbel's masked and hooded features.

As the man's intestines bulged outward, Ishbel lifted her slicing hand again and in several quick, deft movements freed the intestines from their abdominal supports, then stepped back nimbly as they tumbled out of the man's body to lie in a steaming heap at his feet.

The pile of intestines was still attached to the man's living body by two long, glistening ropes of bowel, stretching downward. The man himself, still alive, still conscious, stared at them in a combination of disbelief and shock.

The agony had yet to strike.

The man trembled so greatly that the movement carried down the connecting ropes of bowel to the pile at his feet, making them quiver as if they enjoyed independent life.

Ishbel ignored everything save the pile of intestines. Again she stepped forward, this time leaning down to sever the large intestine as it joined the small bowel.

Behind her the semicircle of the Coil began to chant, softly and sibilantly. "*Great Serpent, grace us, grace us, grace us. Great Serpent, grace us, grace us, grace us.*"

"Great Serpent, grace us, grace us, grace us," Aziel said, his voice a little stronger than those of the semicircle.

Ishbel had pocketed the slicing blade now, and stood before the intestines, her hands folded in front of her, eyes cast down.

Please, Great Serpent, she said in her mind, *grace me with your presence and tell me what is so wrong, and what we may do to aid you.*

The man's intestine began to uncoil. A long length of the large bowel, now independent, rose slowly into the air.

The man had bitten and masticated his way through his gag by now, and he began to shriek, thin harsh sounds that rattled about the chamber.

No one took any notice of him.

All eyes were on the rope of intestine now twisting into the air before the archpriestess.

It shimmered, and then transformed into the head and body of a black serpent, its scales gleaming with the fluids of the man's body and sending shimmering shafts of rainbow colors about the chamber. Its head grew hideously large, weaving its way forward until it was a bare finger's distance from Ishbel's masked face.

Then it began to speak.

When it was over—the serpent disintegrated into steaming bowel once more, the agonized man dispatched with a deep slash to the throat—Ishbel turned and stared at Aziel, dragging the scarf away from her face so he could see her horror.

"We need to speak," she said, then walked from the chamber.

CHAPTER THREE

A ziel followed Ishbel to the day chamber they shared, pouring her a large of glass of wine as she undid her cloak and tossed it to one side.

"Pour yourself one, too," she said. "You shall be glad enough of it when I tell you what the Great Serpent said."

"Ishbel, sit down and take a mouthful of that wine. Good. Now, what—"

"Disaster threatens. The Skraelings prepare to seethe south. Millions of them."

"But . . ."

"*Millions* of them, Aziel."

Aziel poured himself some wine, then sank into a chair, leaving the wine untouched. The Skraelings—insubstantial ice wraiths who lived in the frozen northern wastes—had ever been a bother to the countries of Viland, Gershadi, and Berfardi. Small bands of ten or fifteen occasionally attacked outlying villages, taking livestock and, sometimes, a child.

But *millions*? And seething as far south as Serpent's Nest?

"I know only what the Great Serpent showed me, Aziel," Ishbel said. "I don't understand it any more than you." She took a deep breath. "I saw Serpent's Nest overrun, the members of the Coil dragged out to be crucified on crosses. You . . ." Her voice broke a little. "You, dead."

"Ishbel—"

"There's worse."

Worse?

"A forgotten evil rises from the south," Ishbel said. "Something so anciently malevolent that even the bedrock has learned to fear it. It will crawl north to meet the Skraelings. They whisper to each other . . . the Skraelings are under its thrall, which is why they are so unnaturally organized. Between them they shall doom our world, Aziel."

"Ishbel," Aziel said, "there have been no reports of any unusual activity among the Skraelings. In fact, from what I've heard, they've been quieter than usual these past eighteen months. Are you sure you interpreted the Great Serpent's message correctly?"

Ishbel replied not with words but with such a dark look that Aziel's heart sank.

"I apologize," he said hastily. "I was shocked. I'm sorry." Aziel finally took a large swallow of his wine. "You are the most powerful visionary to have ever blessed the Coil, and what I just said was unforgivable." Then he gave a soft, humorless laugh. "I suppose that I am merely trying to find a means by which to disbelieve the Great Serpent's message. Did he show you the reason behind this disaster? Why it is happening? *How?* The Skraelings have never managed more than the occasional, if murderous, nuisance raid. A death or two at most. *Millions?* How can they organize themselves to that degree?"

"The evil in the south organizes them, Aziel," Ishbel said. "I thought I'd said that already."

Aziel did not reply. He understood Ishbel's irritability. By the Serpent, had he been the one to receive this message he was sure he would have snarled far harder than Ishbel.

Ishbel rose, pacing restlessly about the chamber. "There is more, Aziel," she said finally.

He, too, rose, more at the tone of her voice than her words. The irritation had now been replaced with something too close to despair. *"Ishbel?"*

She turned to face him, her lovely face drawn and pale. "The Great Serpent showed me the disaster which threatens, but he also showed me the means by which it can be averted."

"Oh, thank the gods! What must we do?"

"It is what *I* must do. I must leave the Coil, leave Serpent's Nest—"

Aziel stilled. Had not the Great Serpent told him twenty years ago, when he sent Aziel to rescue Ishbel from that house of carnage, that this would eventually come to pass?

"—and marry some man. A king." Ishbel paused, as if searching for the name, and Aziel had the sudden and most unwanted thought that he hoped Ishbel would remember the *right* name.

"A king called Maximilian," Ishbel said. "From some kingdom to the west . . . I cannot quite recall . . ."

"Escator," Aziel said softly. "Maximilian Persimius of Escator."

"Yes. Yes, Maximilian Persimius of Escator. Aziel . . . the Great Serpent wants me to *marry* this man! What can he be thinking? How can a marriage . . . to a *man* . . . avert this approaching disaster? I am not meant to be a *wife*, and I have no idea, *none*, of how to be a *woman*!"

Aziel stared at her lovely face, and saw the splatter of blood across one eyebrow that had penetrated her scarf's protection.

No, he could not imagine her a "wife," either. But, oh, the woman . . .

"We cannot hope to understand the Great Serpent's reasons," said Aziel, "nor the knowledge behind them."

He stepped over to Ishbel and took her face gently between his hands. "My dear, we always knew you would leave us. *You* knew you would need to leave us. It is why we marked you as we did." For a moment his hands slid into her hair, the tips of his fingers running lightly across her scalp. "Now," he continued, his hands sliding back to cradle her face, "the time is here."

"I do not know how to be a woman," Ishbel repeated, refusing to meet Aziel's eyes.

That statement, Aziel thought with infinite sadness, summarized Ishbel's life perfectly. In the twenty years since he had rescued her from that charnel house in Margalit, Ishbel had devoted her entire being to serving the Great Serpent. She had no idea of her beauty, nor of her allure. All the members of the Coil were bound by vows of chastity, but only loosely. Liaisons and relationships did develop, and were allowed to continue so long as they remained discreet.

Aziel would have given full ten years of his life if it meant Ishbel looked at him with eyes of love or desire.

But she had no idea of his true feelings for her, and Aziel often wondered if Ishbel could even grasp the concept of love.

He stepped away from her. "Marriage to Maximilian of Escator, eh? It is a small thing, surely, if it will save us from the disaster the Great Serpent showed you."

Ishbel looked at him as if he had committed an act of the basest betrayal. "Marriage? To some undoubtedly fat and ancient man who—"

"You do not know of Maximilian?" Aziel said. Surely *everyone* knew Maximilian's story—the news of his rescue eight years ago had rocked the Outlands, as well as all the Central Kingdoms and as far away as Coroleas. Had Ishbel listened to none of the gossip that infiltrated the walls of Serpent's Nest via tradesmen and suppliers?

Ishbel gave a small shrug. "Why should I know?"

Aziel sighed. *Because everyone else in the damned world knows.* "Sit down," he said, "and I shall tell you of Maximilian Persimius."

He waited until Ishbel had sat herself, her back rigid, her face expressionless, before he spoke.

"I shall be brief, as I am certain you shall have ample opportunity to hear this story from Maximilian himself."

Ishbel's face tightened, but Aziel ignored it.

"Eight years ago there was an uproar when the presumed long-dead heir to the Escatorian throne, Maximilian, suddenly reappeared. He told an astounding tale: stolen at the age of fourteen, thrown into the gloam mines—known as the Veins—to labor in darkness and pain for a full seventeen years until he was rescued by a youthful apprentice physician and a marsh witch. Yes, I know, stranger than myth, but sometimes it happens. It transpired that Maximilian's 'death' had been staged by his older cousin Cavor, who wanted the throne. Once free of the Veins, Maximilian challenged Cavor for the throne, won, and . . . well, there you have it. Maximilian has since led a fairly blameless life running Escator and, as luck would have it, looking for a wife. I have never seen him, nor met him, but I have heard good of him. He is respected both as a man and as a king."

"He was imprisoned in the gloam mines for seventeen years?"

"Yes."

"Then I hope he has since managed to scrub the dirt of the grave from under his fingernails."

"That was ungenerous, Ishbel."

"Don't lecture me," she snapped. "Maximilian may be of the noblest character, and patently has endurance beyond most other men, but I have no wish to be his wife. I do not wish to leave Serpent's Nest."

"Ishbel . . . the Great Serpent has said that—"

"Perhaps the Great Serpent is mistaken," Ishbel said, and with that she rose, snatched up her cloak, and left the chamber.

CHAPTER FOUR

Serpent's Nest, the Outlands

Wrapping the cloak tightly about herself, Ishbel walked quickly through the corridors until she came to the stairwell leading up to a small balcony high in Serpent's Nest. She was grateful she met no one, partly because she could not at the moment contemplate questions or small talk, but mostly because she felt deeply ashamed of her behavior and manner with Aziel.

Her shock and horror at the vision the Great Serpent had showed her—and then at the solution he had suggested—could not excuse her behavior toward Aziel. Ishbel owed the Great Serpent, the Coil, and even Serpent's Nest itself a great deal, but she owed Aziel so much more. *He* had been the one to rescue her. *His* had been the hand extended to lift her from the horror that assailed her. *His* had been the gentle smile, the soft encouragement, the friendship, over all of these years, which had helped her to put that frightful time behind her.

He hadn't deserved that face she had just shown him.

Ishbel sighed and began to climb the stairs. The eastern balcony was her favorite spot in Serpent's Nest, and she often came here to think, or simply to stand and allow the salt breeze from the Infinity Sea to wash over her face and through her hair.

The climb was a long one, and, as it progressed, the stone stairs became ever rougher and a little steeper. The increasing difficulty of the way did not bother Ishbel; rather, it comforted her, because it meant she approached the older part of Serpent's Nest.

The more mysterious part.

Serpent's Nest was a mystery in itself. Ishbel had begun to explore the structure in the first months after she had arrived as a child, completely fascinated by her new home. Serpent's Nest was not a town, nor even a building, but a series of interconnecting chambers and corridors hewn out of what Ional, the old archpriestess Ishbel had replaced, told her was the largest mountain in the world.

Inhabited once by giants among men, Ional had said, *and a legendary warrior-king who wielded magic beyond comprehension, but now left with only us to keep its empty spaces company.*

Ishbel could well believe that giants had once lived here. Well, many people, at the very least. The Coil only occupied a hundredth of the chambers that had been thus far explored, and there were yet more corridors and tunnels that led deep into the mountain through which no one had yet dared venture. No one knew who or what had once lived here. Ional had told Ishbel that the Coil had lived here for twenty-three generations, but that the mountain stronghold had been long empty when the Coil had first arrived.

The stairs suddenly broadened, and Ishbel felt the first breath of sea air wash over her face. She smiled, relaxing, and stepped onto the eastern balcony. Ishbel had found this place in her tenth year, and had come here regularly ever since. No one else ever used the balcony, and Ishbel was not sure that anyone else even knew how to reach it.

Perhaps, among the myriad stairwells and corridors and possibilities that Serpent's Nest offered, no one else had ever found this particular stairwell.

Ishbel leaned back against the stone face of the mountain, the semicircular balustrade of the balcony wall two paces before her, and looked out over the Infinity Sea.

By the Great Serpent, was there ever a more beautiful view?

The mountain that Ishbel knew as Serpent's Nest rose directly above the vast Infinity Sea, its eastern face, where Ishbel now relaxed on her balcony, plunging almost a thousand paces into the gray-blue waters of the sea. Ishbel loved the great vastness of the ocean stretching out before her, with its wildness, its unpredictability, its strangeness, and its unknowable secrets. Behind her rose the comforting solidity of the mountain, almost warm against her back.

Ishbel took a deep breath, forcing herself to think about what had happened today. The horror of the Great Serpent's vision . . . she shuddered as she replayed in her mind the sight of the ice wraiths with their huge silvery orbs for eyes and their oversized teeth, swarming over the mountain.

And the solution . . .

Ishbel shuddered again. Leave Serpent's Nest? Marriage? *Marriage?* Ishbel could almost not comprehend it. She struggled to remember household life in her parents' home. Her mother had been bound to the house, supervising the servants, the mending of linens, deciding what food should be served to her father for his dinner, being pleasant and hospitable to visitors. Her parents had been wealthy and important people, but Ishbel could remember that faint touch of servitude in her mother's manner to her husband—how the entire household revolved around *his* wants and needs—and even to those visitors that her husband needed to impress. She remembered how tired her mother had constantly appeared, worn down by the responsibilities of the house and her large family.

True, marriage to a king would be different, but not so greatly. Ishbel would still be his inferior, and would still need to subject herself to him, as would any wife.

Here she was Aziel's equal, respected by all other members of the Coil, and feared by those who came to the Coil seeking their visionary aid.

Even worse, Ishbel would need to subject herself physically to the man. Ishbel had led an utterly chaste life since her arrival at Serpent's Nest. She did not even think of any of the male members (or any of the female members, for that matter) in sexual terms. She could not imagine a man thinking he had the right to touch her, and to use her body in the most intimate sense. She could not imagine having to subject herself to such intrusion.

And to lose all the support she had at Serpent's Nest in

the doing. To lose everything she held dear, and which kept her safe, for such a life.

"The Great Serpent must be mistaken," she said. "This *can't* be the solution."

Ishbel straightened, squaring her shoulders, determined in her decision. "I will tell Aziel that I was mistaken, that I misinterpreted the Great Serpent's words, that—"

Ishbel, do as I have asked.

Ishbel froze in the act of moving toward the opening that led to the stairwell.

Very slowly, so slowly she thought she could hear the bones in her neck creak, Ishbel looked up toward the distant peak of the mountain.

An apparition of the Great Serpent writhed there: the setting sun glinted off his black scales and shimmered along the fangs of his slightly open mouth. His head wove back and forth, as if tasting the wind; then he slowly wound his way down the mountain toward Ishbel.

Do as I ask, Ishbel.

Ishbel could not move, let alone speak.

The Great Serpent wound closer, sliding between rocks and through cracks with ease until his head hung some ten paces above Ishbel.

Do as I ask.

Ishbel was recovered from her initial shock. The Great Serpent had occasionally appeared to her, but it had been when she was a young child and still wept for her mother. Then he had come to comfort her. Now, it seemed, he was here to ensure Ishbel did as he wished. Given that Ishbel had just spent some long minutes silently fuming at the idea she should have to subject herself to the wishes of a husband, the idea that the Great Serpent was here to force her to his will irritated her into a small rebellion.

"I cannot see how marriage to Maximilian would help, Great One. We need armies, warriors, magicians—"

I need you to marry Maximilian Persimius. Ishbel, do as I bid.

Ishbel's mouth compressed. "One of the other priestesses, perhaps. I—"

The Great Serpent's mouth flared wide in anger, and his tongue forked close to her hair. *Ishbel—*

Then, stunningly, another voice, a male voice, and one much gentler than that of the Great Serpent.

Ishbel, you need not fear.

Ishbel spun about, looking to the stone balustrading. An oversized frog balanced there, its body so insubstantial she could see right through it to the sea beyond.

A frog, but one such as she had never seen previously. He was very large, as big as a man's head, and quite impossibly beautiful. This beauty was mostly due to his eyes, great black pools of kindness and comfort.

He shifted a little on the balustrade—

Almost as if he balanced on the rim of a goblet . . .

—unconcerned about the precipitous drop behind him.

Ishbel, he said, *listen to my comrade, no matter how distasteful you think his directive. He is arrogant, sometimes, and uncaring of the fragility of those to whom he speaks.*

"I am not fragile," Ishbel said, almost automatically. This apparition was a god also: she could feel the power emanating from him, and she sensed that perhaps he was even more potent than the Great Serpent. It was a different power, though. Far more subtle, more gentle.

Compassionate.

For some reason Ishbel's eyes filled with tears. It was almost as if the frog god could see into her innermost being, where she still wept for her mother, and where she still shook with terror from the whisperings of her mother's corpse.

"Who are you?" she asked, her voice soft and deferential now, where she had been irritated with the Great Serpent.

Above her head the Great Serpent gave a theatrical sigh. *A companion through a long journey, Ishbel. My aquatic friend here keeps watch on the ancient evil to the south whereas I, it seems, must spend my time seeing that my archpriestess does her duty as she is bound.* There was a moment of silence. *I can't think what he does here.*

Ishbel felt amusement radiating from the frog.

I feared that if you got too dramatic, my serpent friend, the frog said, *Ishbel might be forced to throw herself from this balcony in sheer terror at your persuasive abilities.*

Ishbel bit her lip to stop her smile. For a moment the frog god's eyes met hers, and she felt such a connection with him that her eyes widened in surprise.

You are not alone, the frog said, into her mind alone. *We may not meet for a long time, but you are not alone.*

"Must I marry this man?" Ishbel said.

Yes, said the frog. *It shall not be a terror for you, for he is a gentle man. Do not be afraid.*

Your union with this man is vital, said the Great Serpent. *Allow nothing to impede it. You will do whatever you must in order to become Maximilian Persimius' wife.* Whatever *you must!*

He paused, then added in a gentler tone, *You will return to Serpent's Nest, Ishbel. It shall be your home once again.*

Then, as suddenly as both the frog god and the Great Serpent had appeared, they were gone, and Ishbel was left standing alone on the balcony high above the Infinity Sea.

She waited a moment, gathering her thoughts, still more than a little unsettled by the appearance of not one but two gods. Then she went down the stairwell to Aziel, to whom she said she had changed her mind, and that she would, after all, marry this man, Maximilian Persimius.

She did not tell Aziel of her meeting with the Great Serpent, nor of her encounter with the compassionate and hitherto unknown frog god.

In the morning Aziel met with Ishbel again. He would not have been surprised to learn she had changed her mind yet again, but to his relief, and his pride, she remained resolute.

"I will marry this Maximilian," she said. "I will do what is needed. After all, has not the Great Serpent said that I will return to Serpent's Nest eventually? This shall be a trial for me, yes, but marriage cannot be too high a price to pay for saving Serpent's Nest and the Outlands from the ravages of both Skraelings and ancient evils."

That was a pretty speech, Aziel thought, and well prepared, and he wondered if it was less for him than for Ishbel herself.

Perhaps Ishbel believed that if she repeated it enough times, over and over, the words would take on the power of prophecy.

"When the Great Serpent sent me to fetch you from Margalit," Aziel said, "he told me that you would eventually need to leave—perhaps even then he foresaw this disaster. And it is true enough he said you would eventually return." He smiled. "I hope you will not stay too long away, Ishbel."

"I also hope I shall not stay away long," she said, and Aziel laughed a little at the depth of emotion behind those words.

"Besides," Ishbel continued, "perhaps Maximilian of Escator will not accept me." She paused. "There would be few men willing to wed an archpriestess of the Coil, surely."

"Ah," said Aziel, "but I do not think we shall be offering him the archpriestess, eh? You are a rich noblewoman in your own right, and I think it is as the Lady Ishbel Brunelle that you should meet your new husband. We shall call you . . . let me see . . . ah yes, we shall call you a ward of the Coil. That should do nicely."

CHAPTER FIVE

The Royal Palace, Ruen, Escator

Maximilian Persimius, King of Escator, Warden of Ruen, Lord of the Ports and Suzerain of the Plains, preferred to keep as many of his royal duties as informal as possible. He met with the full Council of Nobles thrice a year, and the smaller Privy Council of Preferred Nobles once a month. Maximilian respected, listened to, and acted upon the advice he received from both those learned councils, but the council he leaned on most was that which he referred to as his Council of Friends—a small group of men that, indeed, made up Maximilian's closest circle of friends, but were also the men he trusted above any else, for all of them had been involved to some extent in his rescue from the gloam mines eight years earlier.

These men knew Maximilian's past, knew where he came from, had seen him at his worst, and they still loved him despite his occasional darker moments.

Today the king was in a lighthearted mood, and none expected any of his dark introspections on this fine morning. Maximilian sat in his chair, one long leg casually draped over one of its arms, his fine face with its striking aquiline nose and deep blue eyes creased in a mischievous grin, his dark hair—always worn a little too long—flopping over his brow. He was laughing at Egalion, captain of the king's Emerald Guard, who had hurried late into the chamber. Egalion was now making flustered excuses as he dragged a chair up to the semicircle seated about the fire that had been lit in the hearth.

"You must be getting old, my friend," Maximilian said, "to so oversleep."

"Out late, perhaps, with a lady friend?" said Vorstus, Abbot of the Order of Persimius. In his late middle age, Vorstus was a thin, dark man with sharp brown eyes and the distinctive tattoo of a faded quill on his right index finger. The Order of Persimius was a group of brothers devoted to the protection and furtherance of the Persimius family. Maximilian owed Vorstus a massive debt for aiding the effort to free him from the Veins, and sometimes, when Vorstus looked at Maximilian with his dark unreadable eyes, that debt sat heavily on Maximilian's shoulders. When first Maximilian had emerged from the Veins he had trusted Vorstus completely. Now he was not so sure of him, for he felt Vorstus watched him a little too carefully.

Maximilian ignored Vorstus' comment. "Perhaps you need the services of Garth, Egalion. A potion, perhaps, from the famous Baxtor recipes, to soothe you into an early sleep at night so that we may not be deprived of your company at morning council?"

That was as close to a reprimand as Maximilian was ever likely to deliver to any of these three men.

"I apologize, Maximilian," Egalion said. He was a tall, strong, fair-haired man who had served the Persimius throne for over thirty years, but now he reddened like a youth. "I have no acceptable excuse save that I did, indeed, oversleep, and no excuse for that—no woman or wine"—he shot a sharp-eyed glance at Vorstus—"save a need to compensate for a late night spent at the bedside of one of the Emerald Guard."

"And that late bedside vigil spent in my company," said Garth Baxtor, court physician and the fourth member of the group sitting about the fire. "One of the men developed a fever late yesterday afternoon, Maximilian, and Egalion and I spent many hours in his company until we were satisfied he was not in any danger to his life."

"Then *I* am the one to apologize," said Maximilian, all humor fading from his face.

"You were not to know," said Egalion. "The man, Thomas, asked that you not be disturbed."

"Nonetheless," said Maximilian, "I should have known."

"Thomas is well this morning," said Garth, "and after a day's bed rest should be able to recommence light duties tomorrow. I think his fever nothing more than a passing autumnal illness."

"But one that kept you and Egalion for hours at his bedside," said Maximilian. He studied Garth a moment, wondering at his luck that eight years ago the then seventeen-year-old should have believed in Maximilian so much that Garth had managed to persuade a diverse and powerful group of people to support his endeavor to free the king from the Veins.

Garth Baxtor was now a full-fledged physician, second only to his father in the use of the Touch, a semimagical ability to understand the precise nature of an illness and to help soothe away its horrors. He lived permanently at Maximilian's court, but, apart from treating Maximilian himself as well as other members of the court, Emerald Guard, and royal militia, he also spent two days a week treating the poor of Ruen for free. Garth, still only in his mid-twenties, was Maximilian's closest friend.

Garth grinned at Maximilian, his open, attractive face appearing even more boyish than it normally did. "It is too early in the day to succumb to guilt, Maxel. You didn't need to be there."

Garth and Vorstus were among the very few who used the familiar "Maxel" in conversation with the king. Egalion, who had permission to do so, only rarely managed to take such a huge leap into familiarity.

"Well, at least let me be cross," Maximilian said, "that you don't have any shadows under your eyes, Garth. Ah, the resilience of youth."

Garth laughed. "You are hardly old yourself, Maxel!"

"Almost forty," Maximilian said, his eyes once more gleaming with humor. "About to tip over the edge."

Now everyone laughed.

"Well, now," said Maximilian, "since we're all finally here, is there any business to discuss or can we give up governing as a bad idea this fine day and go visit the palace hawk house and admire my newest acquisition instead?"

Garth and Egalion brightened, but Vorstus glanced at a small satchel that lay beside his chair, and Maximilian did not miss it.

"My friend," the king said in a soft voice, "why do I fear that that satchel at your side contains dire news?"

Vorstus gave an embarrassed half laugh. "Well, hardly 'dire' news, Maxel." He paused, glancing at the satchel yet one more time. "A document pouch arrived late yesterday afternoon, from your ambassador to the Outlands."

"Another request for a swift return to civilization?" Maximilian said. The Outlands were not renowned for their creature comforts and Maximilian's ambassador to the region, Baron Lixel, had sent plaintive requests to return home at regular intervals over the past year. Maximilian knew he should allow him home soon, but there were so few men better equipped with such a smooth diplomatic tongue for dealing with the notoriously touchy Outlanders that Maximilian felt he could barely spare him from the duty.

"Among other things," Vorstus said. "And one of those other things . . ."

"Do we have to drag it out of you with blacksmith's tongs?" Maximilian said.

Vorstus took a deep breath. "One of those other things is a somewhat unexpected offer of a bride."

Garth and Egalion shot careful glances at Maximilian, gauging his reaction to this news.

Maximilian had been singularly unlucky in finding a bride. It was eight years since he'd been freed from the Veins, and he was still wifeless. Garth knew it niggled at him. It wasn't so much that Maximilian wanted a woman by his side, as welcome as that might be, but that he was desperate for a family. Maximilian had once confided to Garth that when he'd been trapped down the Veins, he'd occasionally overheard guards talking about their children. It had made him long for a family and children of his own, although, imprisoned in the Veins as he was, Maximilian could barely imagine a world where that might be possible.

Now that it *was* possible, it was proving difficult beyond anyone's wildest imagining.

"A bride?" said Maximilian. "How many negotiations have we opened and lost these past eight years? It must be all of . . . what . . . twelve or thirteen?"

"Fourteen," Vorstus muttered.

"Fourteen," Maximilian said. "All of them eligible, and all of them deciding for one reason or another that I wasn't quite 'right' for them."

His voice was so bitter that for a moment Garth more than half expected Maximilian to wave away the offer without even considering.

But then Maximilian sighed. "And here we have a new offer. From the Outlands, of all places. They're such a strange nomadic people, Vorstus. What manner of Outlander woman would want to spend her life as queen in my staid—and stationary—court? And why would *I* want her?"

Vorstus had by now retrieved a sheaf of papers from his satchel. "The lady in question's name is Lady Ishbel Brunelle, and she is the surviving member of an ancient family who for many centuries resided in Margalit."

"Margalit? The only place even faintly resembling a city in the Outlands?"

"Yes," said Vorstus. "It's the only place where families actually settle—as you say, everyone else lives a virtually nomadic life." He rustled through the papers. "Lixel has investigated the Brunelle family . . . let me see . . . ah yes, here it is . . . eminent and highly educated"—Vorstus looked up at Maximilian—"well, as highly educated as an Outlander family can get, I imagine." He looked back down to his papers. "Very distinguished. Somewhat cultured—I have no idea what Lixel means by that—and remarkably fecund." He chuckled. "Lixel patently thought that a point in the woman's favor."

"Yet this Lady Ishbel is the only remaining member of her family?" Egalion said. "That doesn't seem very fecund to me."

"A plague went through the Outlands twenty years ago," said Vorstus. "I don't even need to consult Lixel's report to remember that. Half the Central Kingdoms were affected by it as well, and Escator was damned lucky to escape its ravages. Anyway, the plague took out everyone in the Brunelle family except Ishbel, then an eight-year-old girl. So"—again Vorstus looked at Maximilian, but now with some humor twisting his mouth—"the Lady Ishbel comes with a considerable dowry along with her other attributes, which Lixel claims are a fair face and form, a decent education, and a pleasing manner of character."

"Why do I sense a 'but' coming?" said Maximilian.

Vorstus put down the papers, and sighed. "There *is* a problem."

"Yes?" said Maximilian.

"The Lady Ishbel is currently a ward with the Coil at their base in Serpent's Nest. It is the Coil who offers her to you, Maxel."

There was utter silence, everyone staring at Vorstus.

Egalion finally broke the quiet. "I thought the Coil was a myth! You can't tell me that the vile . . . *gut gazers* . . . actually exist!"

Vorstus looked down at his hands, now folding the papers over and over in his lap.

"Vorstus?" said Maximilian softly.

Vorstus sighed. "The Coil do exist. I have always believed them fact, and Lixel confirms it here."

"But they're nothing like the myth," said Garth. "Right, Vorstus?"

The abbot remained silent.

Maximilian gave a soft humorless laugh. "Do you—or Lixel—actually suggest I take to wife a woman who lives among those who slice open the bellies of the living in order to foresee the future?"

"And who in the doing turn the entrails of the still-living into *snakes*?" said Egalion. "I can't believe you—or Lixel—have actually thought to take this cursed offer so seriously as to bring it to the king's attention."

Maximilian waved a hand. "Vorstus must have a reason. Let's hear it."

"The lesser of the reasons is that the Lady Ishbel is not a priestess. She is not a member of the Order. The Coil took her in during the dark days when much of the Outlands was in turmoil. When Ishbel had no one, the Coil offered her a home."

"And a warm place to sleep amid the steaming entrails of their victims," muttered Egalion.

"The Coil's priests and priestesses never leave their Order, Maximilian," Vorstus continued. "The mere fact they offer her to you indicates that Ishbel has been their ward, but not their trainee."

Maximilian gave a shrug. "Why *should* I consider her? Gods, Vorstus, she comes tainted with all the vile reputation of the Coil . . . how could I take such a woman as my queen? No one would accept her."

"The Lady Ishbel comes with an added extra to her dowry, Maxel. The Brunelle family, as well as owning half of Margalit, also controlled vast estates in the principalities of Kyros and Pelemere in the Central Kingdoms, as *well* as the full manorial rights to Deepend. She would bring much-needed riches to Escator."

Maximilian said nothing, regarding Vorstus with unblinking eyes as he slowly stroked his chin with a thumb as he thought. Vast estates in Kyros and Pelemere. *And* full manorial rights to Deepend, the town and its land, which in turn controlled the trading and shipping rights to Deepend Bay to the south of Escator.

Riches indeed, particularly to a king who, in the very act of escaping and then destroying the rich gloam mines, had virtually crippled Escator's economy. Most of the past eight years had been spent, relatively unsuccessfully, trying to repair the country's finances.

What a difference this dowry could make.

"How is it a lady from the Outlands manages to control the rights to Deepend?" Maximilian asked. He'd known there had been an absentee lordship on the place—Escator had the right to use the bay for its shipping but each year Maximilian paid heavily for the privilege to the steward of Deepend—but had always believed it belonged to one of the more reclusive Central Kingdom families.

"The Brunelle family has lineage that stretches back many centuries," Vorstus said. "Lixel writes that they picked up the Deepend rights via a fortuitous marriage two hundred years ago."

"And now the Coil, via Ishbel, offers those rights to me," said Maximilian. "Why? Of what benefit can this be to them?"

"You're the least objectionable man on the aristocratic marriage market," said Vorstus bluntly, and Maximilian laughed, now with genuine amusement.

"Ah!" he said. "Now I see. The Coil doesn't want anyone from the Central Kingdoms getting them, eh?"

"Indeed," said Vorstus. "There's bad blood between the Outlands and the Central Kingdoms, as well you know—"

Maximilian grunted. The various kingdoms and principalities of the two regions had been posturing and threatening each other with war for years.

"—and perhaps the Coil, who Lixel says are closely allied with the Outlanders through blood and geography, think to establish an alliance with Escator so that they may have a friend on the rear flank of the Central Kingdoms."

"So we get to the heart of the matter," said Garth, silent until now as he studied Maximilian's reactions. "Is the thought of the economic advantage of the woman enough for Maxel to forget her more ghastly acquaintances?"

"There is no need for anyone beyond this room to know of the Lady Ishbel's 'more ghastly' acquaintances," said Vorstus softly. "She is the well-dowered Lady Ishbel Brunelle, of Margalit. An Outlander, to be sure, but one wealthy enough, and well-mannered enough, for that slight geographical stain to be conveniently forgotten. Maximilian"—Vorstus leaned forward—"*no one* need ever know of her time with the Coil."

"You really want me to consider this, don't you," said Maximilian.

"Aye," said Vorstus, "I don't think you can ignore it. Escator needs her wealth, and you need a wife to mother you a family. Damn it, all you need do is meet with her, talk, and if you don't like her, then walk away."

"How would I know," said Maximilian, "if she really is 'just a ward' of the Coil, and not some full-blooded member of their vile Order? I don't want some witch slitting open my belly in the middle of the night to see what the weather will be like for her tea party the following week."

Vorstus held out his right hand, showing Maximilian the mark of the quill on the back of its index finger. "If she was a priestess of the Coil then she would be marked with the sign of the Coil, the coiled serpent, somewhere on her body, just as I am marked with this as a member of the Order of Persimius. Just as *you* are marked with the Manteceros."

Maximilian absently touched his right bicep, where, just after his birth, the mark of the Manteceros—the semimythical protector of the Escatorian throne—had been tattooed in blue ink made from the blood of the creature itself.

"She *would* have to be marked, Maxel," Vorstus continued, "and if she isn't, then she is truly what the Coil claims her to be—a simple ward when no one else was left to ward her."

Egalion grinned. "Does that mean Maximilian gets to spend his wedding night going over her with a magnifying glass?"

Maximilian smiled politely, but his eyes were far distant.

The group broke up a half hour later. It was not a moment too soon for Maximilian, who needed to be by himself to think.

Egalion and Garth left, but Vorstus hung back a moment to hand Maximilian the sheaf of documents.

"Maxel," Vorstus said softly, "when you go through these papers, do be sure to cast your eyes over the map of the Outlands that Lixel enclosed most helpfully. I'm sure it will prove . . . interesting."

CHAPTER SIX

The Royal Palace, Ruen, Escator

Late that night Maximilian moved restlessly about his bedchamber. The palace at Ruen was a massive structure of dark red stone, rising more than five windowless stories from street level before splintering into fifty-three towers and spires. Maximilian could never quite decide whether it was the most beautiful structure he'd ever seen, or the ugliest, but he loved it. He'd been born within its walls, and raised here by loving parents for his first fourteen years before Cavor snatched him and condemned him to the Veins. Now, once more encased within its red stone walls, Maximilian appreciated the palace for the isolation it allowed him. Maximilian liked people, but he also loved solitude, and at night in his bedchamber, which rested at the summit of the highest of the palace towers, he could indulge that to the fullest.

There was something about living at the pinnacle of the tower, about being so high and having the castle stretch down beneath his booted feet, that sated some deep need within Maximilian.

But tonight that isolation irked him. He couldn't stop thinking about the Coil's offer of Ishbel Brunelle as a bride. His first instinct was to refuse her: he was repulsed by her association with an order as abominable as the Coil. Even if she had taken no part in any of their murderous ceremonies, nor even if she swore horror herself at their activities, Ishbel would always be tainted in his mind with their depravity.

But on the other hand she did come from a good family— Maximilian had spent an hour this afternoon poring over the information Lixel had sent . . . if not poring over the map that

Vorstus was so eager for him to read. Vorstus could annoy
Maximilian at times with his secretive eyes and his ambiguous
words, and Maximilian was in a perverse enough mood that
he did not want to immediately do what Vorstus wanted.

The documents kept Maximilian occupied enough. Gods,
this Ishbel came with such wealth trailing at her skirts! Escator's economy was virtually moribund. It had depended
so greatly on the gloam mines, and when they had been destroyed during Maximilian's release there was nothing to
take their place. Maximilian had worked hard to increase
trade, but he'd concentrated on trade alliances with Tencendor, and when that country had sunk beneath the waves five
years ago, then so also had Maximilian's hopes of an economic resurgence in Escator within his lifetime. The Central
Kingdoms to the east, his only other useful trading partners,
were locked in exclusive trading alliances with the far northern nations of Berfardi and Gershadi. The Coroleans were
too hopelessly unreliable and treacherous to consider as allies in anything, and as for the great southern lands beyond
the FarReach Mountains . . . well, they were so isolated by
reason of both the mountains and lack of ports, as well as
being totally uncommunicative, that Maximilian had never
even considered them as potential trading partners.

Besides, what did Escator have to trade with anyone? A
tiny surplus of agricultural produce and a surfeit of geniality
essentially encapsulated all Escator had to offer, and Maximilian honestly couldn't think of anyone desperate for a
bucketful of beans delivered with a smile.

Lady Ishbel Brunelle, ward of the Coil, offered Maximilian and Escator a lifeline. Perhaps some of the eastern
princelings would smile disdainfully at a handful of vast estates and the Deepend manorial rights, but to Maximilian
they represented salvation. The income would make all the
difference to the country.

They would make all the difference to Maximilian's guilt.
Although he knew he had no need, he did feel guilty about
the loss of the gloam mines. Yes, they were vile, but they
had kept Escator rich, and it was now Maximilian's task to
replace those lost riches.

A ring on Ishbel's finger would do it.

Ah! Maximilian paced restlessly about the chamber, his thoughts tumbling. Marriage to a woman tainted with the Coil to restore Escator's riches, or continued personal isolation and poverty for so many of his subjects?

"Damn it," he muttered. "Why couldn't I have found someone *else* with that kind of dowry who was interested in me?"

He paced about for a few more minutes, stripping off his jacket and shirt and tossing them over the back of a chair, running his hand through his too long hair and thinking he really ought to get it cut, rolling the Persimius ring around his finger, over and over.

Finally, coming to a decision, Maximilian walked to one of the high windows and opened wide the glass panes. He stared out into the night for a moment, then returned to stand by his bed, his back to the window, the fingers of his left hand absently running over the ungainly outline of the Manteceros on his right bicep.

He waited long minutes, finally relaxing when he heard the faint sound of movement in the window.

"How arrogant you are," she said softly, "that you were so certain I'd be crouching on a rooftop somewhere, waiting in hope that you'd open a window for me."

Maximilian smiled, slowly turning about. "And how glad I am, StarWeb, that you *were* sitting on that rooftop, waiting for me to open the window."

She crouched in the window, her dark wings held out gracefully behind her for balance, watching him with unreadable dark eyes. She had a mop of black curls, a fine-boned face, and a dancer's body, currently clothed in a short silken robe as dark as her hair and wings.

Maximilian slowly walked over to her and held out a hand. "StarWeb, I took a chance, knowing you often soar over the palace late at night. Arrogant assumption didn't open that window. Hope did."

StarWeb hesitated, then took his hand as she jumped down to the floor. She started to walk into the chamber, but Maximilian's grip on her hand tightened, and he pulled her close enough for a soft kiss.

"Smile for me," he whispered, drawing away fractionally.

"Why? What good news could you possibly have to make me smile?"

Still keeping her hand locked in his, Maximilian drew back enough so he could study her face. StarWeb was an Icarii, one of the race of bird people who had once ruled over the land of Tencendor to the west. StarWeb had also been one of the elite among the Icarii, a powerful Enchanter who could manipulate the magic of the Star Dance. But then Tencendor had descended into chaos, the ruling SunSoar family had imploded into tragedy; the Star Gate, through which the Icarii Enchanters drew the power of the Star Dance had been destroyed. Tencendor itself vanished into the waters of the Widowmaker Sea, taking all its peoples into doom.

But not quite *all* its peoples. Caelum SunSoar, who had ruled the land in its final years, had maintained strong diplomatic ties with both Coroleas and the continent over the Widowmaker Sea. During the final wars that had destroyed Tencendor, almost five thousand Icarii had been scattered about Coroleas and the eastern continent. More had joined them before the final cataclysm. Currently, StarWeb had told Maximilian, there was an expatriate community of almost six thousand Icarii scattered about the lands surrounding the Widowmaker Sea, as well as the Central Kingdoms. There were at least six hundred living in Escator alone.

The Icarii may have kept their lives, but the Enchanters among them had lost all their power, and Maximilian well knew from his relationship with StarWeb what that had cost them. It wasn't so much the *power* they resented losing, but the constant touch of the Star Dance, without which, StarWeb had once confided to him, their lives were but pale reflections of what had once been.

Maximilian pulled StarWeb closer again, and kissed her a little more lingeringly. They had been lovers for some months now, their relationship based almost entirely on a sexual bond rather than an emotional one, which suited Maximilian well, although he often wondered about StarWeb. He knew she disliked the fact he kept their trysts secret.

StarWeb pulled away. "What do you want, Maxel?"

He sighed. "To talk, to share some companionship. To make love, if you want. I don't want to be alone tonight."

She shrugged, moving deeper into the chamber, running a hand lightly over a table, then the back of a chair, folding her wings close in against her body—a sure sign that she remained annoyed with him.

"Is it only kings who want companionship completely on their terms, Maxel?"

"You're in a bad mood tonight."

She swung about to look at him. "That's because I hate it, Maxel, that I always come whenever you deign to open that window."

"I'm sorry, StarWeb. I am not what you need."

She studied that statement for any hint of sarcasm, and then decided the apology was genuine. "So what's up, Maxel? You're tense. Worried about something."

"I've been offered a bride."

StarWeb burst into laughter, her expression relaxing back into that of a delighted girl. "Well done, then! Are you going to take this one?"

"She's been offered to me by the Coil."

All StarWeb's amusement vanished. "I've heard of them."

"And not liked what you have heard, most apparently."

"You are truly considering taking a priestess of the Coil to your bed? As a *wife*?"

"She's not a priestess, merely a ward taken in after a plague wiped out her family and half the population of the Outlands. And she comes with wealth that Escator could well use."

"Oh, well. That makes it all right then."

"I don't need that sarcasm, StarWeb. If I were merely Maximilian Persimius, I would have winced and torn up the offer into a thousand pieces. But I am King of Escator as well, and with that comes a responsibility to my people. *Escator* needs that wealth."

"So shall you meet with her?"

He hesitated, then gave a nod. "Eventually, but—"

"But you want something from me first."

"I trust you, StarWeb. I trust your perception. I need someone to act as an emissary between me and the Coil. I need someone to meet her, and tell me what they think. *Will* we suit each other? *Is* she good enough for me to forget her association with the Coil?" He gave a shamefaced grin. "And I need someone who can do all this relatively quickly. This is not a decision I wish to linger over."

"Would you like me also to take her to bed, and see if she suits your needs?"

Maximilian smiled. "Would you?"

StarWeb laughed then, and the mood between them relaxed. The Icarii Enchanter walked over to Maximilian, running her hands slowly over his naked upper body, her fingers tracing the outlines of the scars left from his time in the Veins, kissing his neck slowly as she spoke. "How fortunate you are that I am not a jealous woman."

He took her face between gentle hands. "I am well aware how fortunate I am in you, StarWeb, and also well aware that I use you unmercifully. Whatever you want from me, you have it."

Your love? she wondered, and then discarded the thought. There had never been any expectation of love on either of their parts.

"Just you," she whispered. "For an hour or two tonight, so I can forget all I have lost."

While Maximilian lay with StarWeb, Vorstus sat at a table in his locked chamber in a distant part of the palace. On the table before him sat a small glass pyramid, about the height of a man's hand. It pulsated gently with soft rosy light, and its depths showed a man of ascetic appearance in late middle age who revealed, as he reached up a hand to rub thoughtfully at his nose, a serpent tattoo writhing up his forearm.

"Has Maximilian looked at the map yet?" said the man whose image showed within the pyramid.

"No, my Lord Lister," said Vorstus. "If he had, I am sure I would have heard the screech from here."

Lister smiled. "Will he be ready, do you think?"

"He had seventeen years battling the darkness in the Veins, my lord," said Vorstus. "He won't like it, but when he is needed, then, yes, I believe he will step forward. How goes the Lady Ishbel?"

"Resigning herself to marriage. She, also, will step forward when needed."

"If only she knew who had caused that plague to strike her family home in Margalit, my lord. Then perhaps she might not be so ready to 'step forward.'"

"Don't threaten me," Lister said. "Besides, what will Maximilian say, eh, when he learns who it was whispered to Cavor the plan to imprison him in the gloam mines for such a mighty length of time?"

"We have all done what was needed."

"Ah, we all have done what was needed," said Lister, "and we will do more, as the need dictates. Let me know what Maximilian says, why don't you, when he finally looks at that map."

The rose pyramid dulled, then died.

Lister stood in the central chamber of his castle of Crowhurst and stared as his own pyramid dulled into lifelessness on the table. He sighed, and turned away, walking to the open window to look out.

Beyond stretched a vast wasteland of frost and low, snow-covered rolling hills. The northern wastes were a desolate place, but they suited Lister's purpose for the time being, and for the time being he needed to be here. He shuddered, more from the cold than from any direction of his thoughts, and he reached out and closed the windows, revealing tattoos of black serpents crawling up both his forearms.

Kanubai's ancient foe, Light, had taken the form of Lister some forty-five years ago when it had become apparent to both Light and Water that Kanubai's prison had begun to fail. Light and Water needed mortal shape now, for the battle to come would be of the physical rather than the ethereal. While they had taken the flesh of men, Light also, from time to time, and as it amused him, took on the ethereal form of the serpent, while Water occasionally took the form of the frog.

Sometimes also, when it suited their purpose to manipulate those about them, they named themselves gods, and commanded ordinary men and women.

Ishbel had no idea what it was she truly served.

The move into the physical realm of men was dangerous. As flesh-and-blood men they might still command powers greater than those of most mortals, but were as vulnerable to the spear and the sword as any other.

There came a noise from the door, a footfall, and Lister turned about.

Three creatures of above man-height stood there. They were skeletal and vaguely man-shaped, but more wraith than flesh. The most substantial part of them was their oversized skull-like heads, dominated by heavy, great-toothed jaws and huge silver orbs set deep into their eye sockets.

One of them nodded at the table, which was covered at one end with the detritus of Lister's earlier meal.

"We've come for the leavings, Lord Lister," the Skraeling said, his voice more hissed whisper than spoken word.

"Take them," said Lister. "Did the kitchen hand out the scraps to your comrades earlier?"

"Yes," said another of the Skraelings. "Thank you. Lard and blood. Tasty."

"Tasty, tasty," whispered the other two.

Lister nodded at the table, and the three Skraelings crept forward, gathering plates into their awkward hands, licking each one clean as they picked them up. Then, silver orbs glancing at Lister, they crept back through the door, closing it behind them.

"Damned creatures," Lister muttered. He loathed them, but for the moment it was better to be their friend than their enemy.

Like his ally, Water, who stood watch over the ancient evil far to the south, Lister stood watch over the tens of thousands of Skraelings who gathered in the frozen hills about Crowhurst. He knew that Kanubai whispered to them from deep within his abyss, and that Kanubai was the Skraelings' only true lord. But Lister had wormed his serpentine way into the Skraelings' affections by feeding them scraps and leavings in order that he might live beside them, and watch their every move.

They were loathsome companions, but for the moment Lister must make do.

And at least they were not his only companions. Another footfall sounded at the door, and Lister looked up, smiling in genuine warmth as the winged woman entered.

CHAPTER SEVEN

The Royal Palace, Ruen, Escator

Maximilian lay in bed alone, wide awake, staring at the ceiling.

StarWeb had left an hour or more ago.

Since he'd returned from the gloam mines, Maximilian had taken a variety of lovers. He had spent his youth and early manhood trapped in the mines, and once free he did not hesitate to enjoy the comfort and excitement of a woman in his bed.

But they never stayed the night.

One of Maximilian's first lovers had been an accommodating lady of court. She was a sweet woman, and had taken it upon herself to teach Maximilian the skills that by rights he should have learned many years earlier. She had slept through the night at his side one time only (and that many months into their relationship), and in the morning had turned to him and said:

I think that the darkness is your true lover, Maximilian. I think you brought it with you out of the Veins. Perhaps you should wive the darkness, and not any flesh-and-blood woman.

That had stung Maximilian badly, and he'd never invited her back into his bedroom.

Now he lay on the bed, twisting the Persimius ring on his left hand over and over, thinking not so much about Ishbel, but about his parents. His father and mother had loved each other dearly, and their marriage had been strong.

But they had had separate bedrooms, and Maximilian suspected that his mother spent only a handful of entire nights with his father, and those, perhaps, only at the very beginning of their marriage.

Generally, she had preferred to sleep elsewhere than at her beloved husband's side.

Maximilian's lover had been wrong. It was not the Veins that had imbued Maximilian with his darkness, but something far older, and deeply embedded within the Persimius blood.

Maximilian sighed, finally admitting he could not sleep. He sat up and swung his legs over the side of the bed. He looked at his desk for a long time, then rose and walked over, lighting a lamp and scattering the documents regarding Ishbel Brunelle across the desktop with his fingers.

He paused as the folded map slid into view.

"By the gods, Vorstus," Maximilian muttered, "my life would be so much simpler without you."

Then he picked up the map and unfolded it.

At first glance the map was innocuous, showing the Central Kingdoms and the Outlands. Maximilian traced a finger over the Outlands, looking for Serpent's Nest. He knew it was a mountain, and had supposed it was one of the summits within the Sky Peaks, which ran down the western border of the Outlands.

He frowned as his initial scan of the map failed to reveal Ishbel's home.

Then, increasingly irritated, he looked farther afield, and finally spotted Serpent's Nest on the very eastern seaboard of the Outlands.

Maximilian dropped the map and stepped back from the desk, staring at the desktop as if it contained the most vile of monsters.

Serpent's Nest was what he knew as the Mountain at the Edge of the World.

It took Maximilian some minutes to bring his breathing back under control and to still his racing thoughts.

A coincidence, nothing more, surely. The Mountain at the Edge of the World must have been abandoned for thousands of years, it was not so strange that some others may have taken occasion to inhabit it.

But to be inhabited by an order devoted to a serpent god?

Maxel? said the Persimius ring. *Maxel? What is the matter?*

"Nothing," Maximilian said automatically, still staring at the desk.

Is it about Ishbel? said the ring.

"No," Maximilian responded, but wondered what it meant that this bride was coming to him from within the Mountain at the Edge of the World, now associated with a serpent.

No, no, surely not . . .

Maximilian turned on his heel and walked to one side of his bedchamber, which was clear of furniture. He stood, looking at the floor, then he leaned down.

As his hand approached the floorboards, a trapdoor materialized. Maximilian hesitated, then grabbed the iron pull ring and hauled the door open.

The Persimius Chamber lay directly under Maximilian's bedchamber. He rarely came here: several times when he was a boy and his father had been inducting him into the mysteries of the Persimius family; once, six months after he'd been restored to the throne and he'd felt he needed to check to ensure that all was still safe after seventeen years (Vorstus had told him Cavor had not been informed about the chamber); and once about a year ago, when some marriage negotiations had looked as though they might actually mature into fruition, and Maximilian had come to look at the mate to the ring he wore on his left hand that any wife of his would wear.

No one else ever came here. Only the king, his heir, and the abbot of the Order of Persimius knew of its existence.

The Persimius Chamber was oval in shape and relatively small. It contained two chest-high marble columns, each at opposing ends of the oval. Each column held a cushion, and each cushion cradled an object.

Maximilian walked first to the column at the western end

of the oval chamber. It held an emerald and ruby ring, worn by the wives of the Persimius king.

My lover, said Maximilian's ring, and Maximilian sighed, part in irritation and part in resignation, and, taking off his ring, laid it beside the emerald and ruby ring so they could chat for a while.

The Whispering Rings they were called, but only someone of Persimius blood could ever hear them, which Maximilian supposed was a good thing, as he knew his own cursed ring tended to mutter the most uncomplimentary things at the worst of moments.

What it had murmured about StarWeb tonight, just as Maximilian and StarWeb's lovemaking peaked, had very nearly distracted Maximilian completely.

He looked at the rings, tuning out their whispering as he thought.

Ishbel came to him from the Mountain at the Edge of the World now called Serpent's Nest. What did that mean? Coincidence? Or something deeper? Darker?

Maximilian knew the ancient legend of Kanubai, and he knew also, from his father's teachings, that Light often assumed the shape of the serpent, just as Water sometimes assumed the shape of the frog. He hadn't immediately connected the name of Serpent's Nest with Light, simply because then he had not realized that Serpent's Nest was the ancient Mountain at the Edge of the World.

The ancient home of the Lord of Elcho Falling, who had once allied himself with Light and Water in the battle to imprison Kanubai.

Finally, unable to ignore it any longer, Maximilian turned and looked at the other column.

Its velvet cushion held an object so ancient, and so cursed, that Maximilian felt slightly ill even looking at it.

It was the crown, simply made of three thick entwined golden bands, of a kingdom and a responsibility so ancient that its name had been forgotten by all living people, and which had never been recorded in any history book.

Living darkness writhed among the golden bands.

Very slowly, every step hesitant, Maximilian walked over

to it. He had never touched it, and hoped he never had to. His father had never touched it, nor his father before him.

If ever Maximilian had to lift that crown to his head, then it meant that the end of the world had risen, and was walking the land.

To Maximilian's profound relief, the crown looked just as it had every other time Maximilian had studied it. The darkness (that same darkness which writhed through the Persimius blood) lived, yes, but it did not seem aware, or awake. It merely waited, as it had been waiting for thousands of years.

Maximilian allowed himself a sigh of relief, his shoulders finally relaxing.

Perhaps Ishbel's connection with the Mountain at the Edge of the World and its current association with a serpent was coincidence merely. He should not worry.

But he should, perhaps, be highly careful.

Maximilian turned his back on the crown, and collected his ring, preparatory to leaving the chamber.

But just before he climbed back into his bedchamber, Maximilian turned and looked once more at the dark crown. He frowned, something stirring in his mind.

Cavor had never been inducted into the mystery of this chamber.

Why not? Everyone had believed Maximilian dead, so why hadn't Cavor been inducted into this mystery?

Maximilian stood there a long time, the rings silent, before he turned abruptly on his heel and left the chamber.

And the crown of Elcho Falling.

CHAPTER EIGHT

Serpent's Nest, and the Palace at Ruen

Ishbel sat in her bare chamber, staring unseeing at her hands clasped in her lap.

Tomorrow she was to leave for Margalit. The early negotiations with Maximilian had been successful. He was willing to consider the offer of the "ward" of the Coil—Ishbel's mouth curled slightly in a smile—as a wife. She'd entertained doubts that Maximilian would even come this far, but he had, and so now she must leave.

Maximilian was sending a deputation to Margalit to meet with Ishbel and to hash out more detailed negotiations. The negotiations could still break down—Ishbel could almost smell the wariness in Maximilian's initial interest—but they could just as easily progress further, and Ishbel needed to ready herself to commit to marriage.

Ishbel had indeed largely resigned herself to marriage with Maximilian. She still had no idea why the Great Serpent thought such a union would help avert the threatening disaster, but she would do as he (and as this curious frog god) wished. Ishbel had spent the last few weeks discovering all she could about her potential husband, but that was little enough. There had been more details about his harrowing seventeen years spent as a prisoner in the gloam mines, some interesting tales about how he'd been released and how he had defeated Cavor in battle, but very little information about the man himself. Ishbel discovered that Maximilian was respected across the Central Kingdoms, that he had a good relationship with the kings of Pelemere and Kyros, and that his small kingdom of Escator was, indeed, crippled by debt.

Ishbel had decided that Maximilian was likely harmless enough, and that his worst fault (apart from some as-yet-undiscovered socially embarrassing habit) was likely to be a mild dreariness engendered by his long imprisonment.

He certainly had done nothing to set the world afire since his restoration to the throne of Escator.

Ishbel had also steeled herself to accept the sexual intimacy of the marriage. She would endure, if that was what the Great Serpent needed of her.

Additionally, she would endure the necessity of deferring to her husband. She, the archpriestess of the Coil, who had hitherto bowed only before gods.

What Ishbel feared most was the actual leaving of Serpent's Nest. It had been her only home, her entire world, for most of her life. The mountain was her safety and her comfort, and it shielded her from the horror of the world beyond.

For an instant a memory resurfaced of her mother's whispering corpse, and Ishbel jerked a little, fighting to keep it at bay.

She was not looking forward at all to her journey to Margalit. Ishbel would be traveling only with a company of guardsmen from Margalit itself. No one from the Coil would be accompanying her. Ishbel understood the necessity for this. She needed to distance herself from them and become the Lady Ishbel Brunelle rather than the archpriestess of the Coil, and Ishbel could not do that if any of the Coil or their servants traveled with her.

There came a knock at her door, and Aziel entered. He came over to Ishbel and sat down beside her on the bed. Wordlessly he picked up her hand, kissed it, then kissed the side of her forehead.

"You will come back," he said softly, and Ishbel blinked away her tears, and nodded.

She would return.

Since the night he'd looked at the map, Maximilian had either avoided Vorstus, or had avoided speaking to him alone. Maximilian simply did not want to give Vorstus the satisfaction of a reaction.

It irritated Maximilian that Vorstus had not simply come to him and said, "Maxel, an offer of a bride comes out of the Mountain at the Edge of the World. A woman associated with a serpent god, no less. What do you think about that, then?"

Instead, Vorstus had decided to play games.

It took Vorstus eight days before he knocked one evening at the door to Maximilian's bedchamber as Maximilian was preparing for evening court.

Maximilian waved away the servants, then indicated Vorstus should take a chair. "What can I do for you, Vorstus? You are normally cloistered in your library at this time of night."

"What did you think of Serpent's Nest, Maxel?"

Maximilian tugged at the cuffs of his linen shirt, making sure they sat comfortably under his heavy velvet overjacket. "I'd wondered why you did not come to me directly, Vorstus, instead of cloaking this offer in mystery. You know more than you are saying. What?"

"All I know is what I have told you. No one was more shocked than I when I saw that Serpent's Nest is what was anciently called the Mountain at the Edge of the World."

Maximilian shot him a deeply cynical look. As abbot of the Order of Persimius, Vorstus was privy to almost all of its secrets.

"All I know is what I have told you," Vorstus repeated quietly.

"How coincidental that the Mountain at the Edge of the World is now dedicated to a serpent god."

"Perhaps just a coincidence."

Maximilian stopped fiddling with his attire and looked at Vorstus directly. "Is Elcho Falling stirring, Vorstus?"

"I don't know, Maxel."

"I am *sick* of hearing your 'I don't knows'!"

"I—"

"Listen to me, Vorstus. I know that you were instrumental in aiding my escape from the Veins, and for that you know I am grateful. But I am not going to spend my life mired in debt to you, nor am I going to put up with you stepping coyly about something that has the power to destroy this entire

world. Gods! Have I not had enough darkness in my life? Or
do the gods demand something *else* from me besides losing
seventeen years, *seventeen* years, Vorstus, to those damned,
damned gloam mines? *Have I not suffered enough*?"

"If Elcho Falling is waking, Maximilian Persimius, then
you must do what needs to be done."

The patronizing idiot, Maximilian thought. "Ah, get out
of here, Vorstus."

Maximilian waited until Vorstus had his hand on the door
handle before speaking again.

"One more thing, Vorstus. You know of the Persimius
Chamber?"

Vorstus gave a wary nod.

"You know what it contains?"

Another wary nod.

"But you never took Cavor there. You never inducted him
into the deeper mysteries of the Persimius throne."

Vorstus now gave a very reluctant single shake of his
head, and Maximilian could see that his hand had grown
white-knuckled about the door handle.

"I was standing in the Persimius Chamber the other night,
Vorstus, and a strange unsettling thought occurred to me.
Here you are, Abbot of the Order of Persimius, and the only
one apart from the king and his heir who knows what truly
underpins the Persimius throne. But for seventeen years,
when *everyone* save Cavor thought me dead, you never once
took the opportunity of inducting Cavor into the mysteries?
Should you not have done that? I can perhaps understand you
waiting a year or so, hoping for a miracle, but *seventeen*?"

"I always had faith that you—"

"You knew, for those entire seventeen years, Vorstus, that
I was alive. That is the only reason you did not induct Cavor
into the mysteries. You knew I was coming back."

"I—"

"Get out, Vorstus. Get *out*!"

When the door had closed behind him, Maximilian
walked to a mirror and stood before it, seeing not a reflection of himself, but of the bleakness that had consumed him
within the Veins.

"You knew where I was," Maximilian whispered, "and you left me there for seventeen years."

Much later that night, still unsettled and unable to turn his mind away from Elcho Falling, Maximilian sat in his darkened bedchamber, rested his head against the high back of the chair, and closed his eyes.

As he had visited the Persimius Chamber on a previous night, so now Maximilian visited another of the mysteries his father had taught him.

The Twisted Tower.

The crown of Elcho Falling carried with it many responsibilities, many duties, and a great depth of dark, writhing mystery. Each king of Escator, and his heir, had to learn it all in case they one day had to assume once more the crown of Elcho Falling.

There was an enormous amount of information, of ritual, of windings and wakings, and of magic so powerful that it took great skill, and an even better memory, to wield it. There was so much to recall, and to hand down through the generations, that long ago one of the Persimius kings, perhaps the last of the sitting lords of Elcho Falling, had created a memory palace in which to store all the knowledge of Elcho Falling.

They called it the Twisted Tower.

Maximilian now entered the Twisted Tower, recalling as he did so the day his father had first taught him how to open the door.

"Visualize before you," his father had said, "a great Twisted Tower, coiling into the sky. It stands ninety levels high, and contains but one door at ground level, and one window just below the roofline. On each level there is one single chamber. Can you picture it, Maxel?"

Maximilian, even though he was but nine, could do so easily. The strange tower—its masonry laid so that its courses lifted in corkscrews—rose before him as if he had known it intimately from birth and, under his father's direction, Maximilian laid his hand to the handle of the door and opened it.

A chamber lay directly inside, crowded with furniture that was overlaid with so many objects Maximilian could only stand and stare.

"See here," his father had said. "This blue and white plate as it sits on the table. It is the first object you see, and it contains a memory. Pick it up, Maxel, and tell me what you see."

Maximilian picked up the plate. As he did so, a stanza of verse filled his mind, and his lips moved soundlessly as he rolled the words about his mouth.

"That is part of the great invocation meant to raise the gates of Elcho Falling," said his father. "The second stanza lies right next to it, the red glass ball. Pick that up now, and learn . . ."

Maximilian had not entered the Twisted Tower since his last lesson with his father, just before his fourteenth birthday when he'd been abducted. That lesson had, fortuitously, been the day his father had taken him into the final chamber at the very top of the Twisted Tower. Despite it being well over twenty years since he'd last entered, Maximilian had no trouble in re-creating in his mind the Twisted Tower, and traveled it now, examining every object in each successive chamber and recalling their memories throughout the height of the tower.

As he rose, the chambers became increasingly empty.

It began at the thirty-sixth level chamber. This chamber was, as all the chambers below it, crammed with furniture, which in turn was crammed with objects, each containing a memory. But occasional empty places lay scattered about, marked by shapes in the dust, showing that objects had once rested there.

Maximilian turned to his father. "Why are there empty spaces, Father?"

His father shifted uncomfortably. "The memories held within these objects have been passed down for many thousands of years, Maxel. Sometimes mistakes have been made in the passing, objects have been mislaid, memories forgotten. So much has been lost, son. I am sorry."

"But what if we needed it, Father? What if we needed to resurrect Elcho Falling?"

His father had not answered that question, which had in itself been answer enough for Maximilian.

Now Maximilian entered the final chamber at the very top of the tower.

It was utterly barren of any furniture or objects.

Everything it had once contained had been forgotten.

Maximilian stood there, turning about, thinking about how the chambers had become progressively emptier as he'd climbed through the tower.

He was glad that he had remembered everything his father had taught him, and that he could retrieve the memories intact as he took each object into his hands.

But, contrariwise, Maximilian was filled with despair at the thought that if, *if*, he was to be the King of Escator who once again had to shoulder the ancient responsibilities of Elcho Falling, he would need to do so with well over half of the memories, the rituals, and the enchantments of Elcho Falling forgotten and lost for all time.

[Part Two]

CHAPTER ONE

Lake Juit, the Tyranny of Isembaard

Lake Juit, as old as the land itself, lay still and quiet in the dawn. The sun had barely risen, and broad, rosy horizontal shafts of soft light illuminated the gently rippling expanse of the lake, and set the deep reed beds surrounding the lake into deep mauve-pocked shadow.

A man poled a punt out of the reed beds.

He was very tall, broad-shouldered, and handsomely muscled, with a head of magnificent black tightly-braided hair that hung in a great sweep to a point midway down his back. He wore a white linen hipwrap, its simplicity a foil to the magnificent collar of pure gold and bejeweled links that draped over his shoulders and partway down his chest and back.

He was Isaiah, Tyrant of Isembaard, and the lake was surrounded by ten thousand of his spearmen, while on the ramshackle wooden pier from where he'd set out waited his court maniac, the elusively insane (but remarkably useful) Ba'al'uz.

Ba'al'uz narrowed his eyes thoughtfully as he watched his tyrant. One did not expect one's normally completely predictable tyrant to suddenly decamp from his palace at Aqhat, move ten thousand men and his maniac down to this humid and pest-ridden lake, saying nothing about his motives, and then get everyone up well before dawn to watch their tyrant set off by himself in a punt.

Ba'al'uz had no idea what Isaiah was about, and he did not like that at all.

* * *

Isaiah poled the punt slowly and steadily forward. He did not head out into the center of the shallow lake, but kept close to the reed beds. Occasionally he smiled very slightly, as here and there a frog peeked out from behind the reeds.

As Isaiah got deeper into the lake, he watched the dawn light carefully, waiting for the precise moment.

He poled rhythmically, using the regular movements of his arms and body to concentrate on the matter at hand. What he was about to do was so dangerous that if he allowed himself to think about it he knew he would turn the punt back to the wharf and the watching Ba'al'uz.

But Isaiah could not afford to do that. He needed to concentrate—

At one with the water.

—and he needed to focus—

On the Song of the Frogs.

—and he needed to draw on all the power he contained within his body—

And allow it to ripple, to wash, and to run with the tide.

—and he needed today to be successful, because without that which he'd come for, Isaiah knew the task of the Lord of Elcho Falling would be nigh to impossible, and the land itself would fail.

Besides, he knew this would annoy Ba'al'uz, and annoying Ba'al'uz always brightened Isaiah's day.

Above all, Isaiah was here because he needed something from the lake very, very badly, and he did not think the world would survive if he did not get that for which he'd come.

The sun was a little higher now, and nerves fluttered in Isaiah's belly, threatening to break his concentration. His hands tightened fractionally on the pole, and he forced himself to focus.

The air, clear a few minutes ago, was now damp with mist seeping out from the reed banks.

Frogs began to sing, a low, sweet melody, and one or two of them hopped onto the prow of the punt.

Isaiah closed his eyes briefly, overcome with the sweetness of their song.

Then, hands tightened once more, eyes opening, he drew down on the deep well of power within himself.

Isaiah spoke the words that were needed, and the moment the last one dropped from his mouth the air about the entire lake exploded in sound and movement as millions of pink- and scarlet-hued juit birds rose screaming into the dawn light.

On the wharf, Ba'al'uz crouched down, arms over his head, and shrieked together with the birds.

About the lake, ten thousand men thrust their spears into the air, and screamed as one with Ba'al'uz.

On the lake, Isaiah poled into the reed banks, into magic and mystery, and into the strange borderland between worlds. Then, while the air still rang with the harsh cries of bird and man, as the frogs screamed, and as the sun suddenly topped the horizon and flooded the lake and reed beds with light, Isaiah dropped the pole, reached down into the water, and lifted a struggling, naked man into the punt.

CHAPTER TWO

Baron Lixel's Residence, Margalit

The journey to Margalit took almost three weeks, longer than expected. The winter was closing in, and drifts of snow had forced Ishbel and her escort to spend long days idle in wayside inns, waiting for the weather to improve enough that they might continue their journey.

Ishbel had spent most of the idle days praying that the weather would close in so greatly she'd be forced to return to Serpent's Nest. Of course it hadn't happened. The snow had always cleared in time for her to move forward, and, by the time they reached Margalit, she had managed to convince herself that no matter the trials ahead, she would manage.

Ishbel hoped only that this Maximilian was tolerable, and that he would be kind to her, and that the Great Serpent had not lied when he'd said that she would return to Serpent's Nest, and that it would be her home, always.

She would be strong, because she had to be.

And, damn it, she was the archpriestess of the Coil, no matter how much she might hide that from Maximilian. She had courage and she had ability and she had *pride*, and she *would* endure.

Despite her carefully constructed shell of determination, it was a black moment for Ishbel when she first saw the smudge of Margalit in the distance. For an instant all the terrifying fear of her childhood threatened to swamp her, but Ishbel managed to bite down her nausea and panic, and maintain a calm exterior as they rode closer and closer to the city.

Then she took a deep breath, called on all her training and

courage, and the moment passed. Margalit held no horrors for her now. All that was past.

Ishbel was to stay with Baron Lixel, Maximilian's ambassador to the Outlands, in his house in Margalit. The house sat in one of Margalit's more desirable quarters. It was a large, spacious house, single-story like most of the Outlanders' buildings, with thick walls, high ceilings, and decorative woodwork around doors and windows. Lixel had rented the property from the Margalit Town Guild when he'd first arrived in the city, and Ishbel had no reason to suppose that Lixel knew that the house was, in fact, one of the properties in her not-inconsiderable inheritance.

Baron Lixel was there to greet Ishbel on her arrival, and he was not what Ishbel had imagined. Her fears had led her to expect a stern, forbidding man, uncommunicative and dismissive, but Lixel proved exactly the opposite. He was a pleasant man in middle age, very courtly, courteous, attentive without being fussy and with a charming habit of understatement in conversation, and Ishbel hoped it foretold well for Maximilian.

Ishbel spent a pleasant evening with him. Lixel seemed to intuit her anxiety and, surprisingly, managed to put Ishbel at her ease with his charming conversation and easy manner.

On the morrow Maximilian's party was to arrive, and the negotiations for the contract of marriage to commence.

Lixel knocked on the door of Ishbel's chamber at mid-morning, and bowed as she opened it. "Maximilian's delegation has arrived," Lixel said, offering Ishbel his arm. Then, as she took it, he added, "They won't eat you."

Ishbel gave a tense smile. "I feel very alone today, my lord. This is all most strange for me."

They walked down the corridor toward the large reception rooms of the house. "You do not wish to wed?" Lixel said.

"I am missing my home, my lord, as noxious as that home must be to you."

Ishbel was pushing Lixel a little too far with this statement, but she knew that his response would tell her a great deal about the man, and also, possibly, his master.

"A home is a home," Lixel said, leading Ishbel out the door and down the long corridor toward the main reception room of the house, "whatever its strangenesses. I do not think Maximilian will begrudge it in the slightest if you yearn for a home you have lost."

Not lost, Ishbel thought. *I will return to Serpent's Nest one day.*

"I would not have thought him so generous toward the Coil," Ishbel said, pushing just a little more.

"I was not speaking of the Coil," Lixel said quietly, and led her into the reception room.

Ishbel might have responded to that, she still had time before they met the gaggle of people standing at the far end of the large chamber, but just then she caught sight of the leading member of Maximilian's delegation, and she stopped dead, unable to repress a gasp.

It was a birdwoman. An Icarii. Ishbel had heard about them, and had heard about the land from which they had come, but had never seen one.

The birdwoman turned, looking directly at Ishbel with a discomforting frankness. She was clad all in black—form-fitting leather trousers and a top which allowed her wings freedom. She moved again, taking a half step forward, and Ishbel had her first glimpse of the stunning grace and elegance of the creatures.

The entire group had turned at her entrance now, and Ishbel tore her eyes away from the birdwoman long enough to see that several other Icarii were within the delegation.

Maximilian controlled Icarii?

Ishbel took a deep breath, hoping it wasn't obvious, set a smile to her face, and walked forward.

She was the archpriestess of the Coil, and she would manage.

"You were very surprised to see me," StarWeb said. "You paled considerably."

They were alone, standing on the glassed veranda that opened off the reception room. Everyone else was still inside, talking, drinking, negotiating, but as soon as practicable after the introductions and initial chat, StarWeb had requested Ishbel join her for a private word.

"I have never seen one of your kind," Ishbel said. "I was shocked." Her mouth quirked. "The Icarii are almost myth here in the Outlands."

StarWeb thought about being offended at the "your kind," but decided that for the moment she would accomplish more without assuming affront. Full-on confrontation would prove far more effective.

"Then in your marriage," she said, "you shall have to get used to us. There are many of 'my kind' at Maximilian's court."

"You know him well?"

"I am his lover." *There, Ishbel,* StarWeb thought, *make of that what you will.*

To StarWeb's surprise, Ishbel showed no emotion whatsoever. "That does not mean that you know him well."

"But I expect that," StarWeb countered, "should you become his wife, you shall come to know him well."

"*I* expect," Ishbel said, "that any man who has endured what Maximilian has experienced in life will be a man who lets only those he truly loves know him well. If he allows me that privilege, then I shall be honored."

"That was very good, my lady," said StarWeb. "You managed to be self-effacing and insult me all in one. You shall do very well at a royal court, but I do not know that it should be Maximilian's."

"Will all Escator welcome me as generously as you, StarWeb?"

"Let me be frank with you, Ishbel—I may call you Ishbel, yes?"

"I would prefer that you did not."

"Very well then, *my lady*, let me be quite frank with you. None of us here"—StarWeb gestured to the Escatorian delegation inside the reception room—"nor any back in Ruen among Maximilian's inner circle, entirely trust this offer. We don't trust who it comes from—the Coil are universally loathed—"

"Not by me," said Ishbel quietly. "The Coil took me in

when no one else would. They nurtured me, and were kind to me, and subjected me to none of the practices in which I hear rumored they indulge."

"Apparently so, my lady, for I believe your belly is still intact under that silken gown of yours. But allow me to return to the point, if I may. There are many about Maximilian who wonder about this offer and its timing. We wonder why a lady as lovely as you, and with such a dowry as yours, has only now decided to put herself on the marriage market, and to such a minor player—no, no, don't protest, Maximilian isn't the haughty kind—when she could have tempted a much nobler man, an emperor perhaps, or maybe even the Tyrant of Isembaard, for I have heard rumor he is looking for a new wife."

"My dowry," said Ishbel, her tone low, "would attract no emperor or tyrant. Particularly with, as you have been so kind to point out, such a home as I have enjoyed these past twenty years. Yes, the Coil is universally loathed, *but not by me*. I owe them a loyalty, StarWeb, that perhaps you cannot understand. It is one of love and gratitude. It is one of *family*. If you want a reason why I have not married in the past eight or nine years, when one might reasonably have expected me to take a husband, then it is because no man has interested me enough."

StarWeb looked at her carefully. "Yet Maximilian does."

"I think a man who has spent seventeen years in a black pit thinking his life at an end will have more understanding, more tolerance, than most." Ishbel paused, her eyes glittering. "Yet perhaps I am mistaken, if the kind of woman he takes as lover is any indication."

"Maximilian is a quiet man, of manner and mind," said StarWeb, "and you are a very unquiet woman, Ishbel. I do not know how I shall report you to him."

"Report me as a woman who can speak for herself," snapped Ishbel, "and who does not need an arrogant and threatened lover to speak on her behalf."

And with that she pushed past StarWeb and rejoined the reception.

CHAPTER THREE

Palace of Aqhat, Tyranny of Isembaard

Isaiah, Tyrant of Isembaard, walked along the wide corridor of his palace of Aqhat. He'd returned from Lake Juit a few days earlier, together with his maniac Ba'al'uz, his ten thousand men, and the man he had pulled from the lake.

It was this man that Isaiah now went to visit. He had not seen him since he'd deposited him, dripping wet, on the wharf of Lake Juit for his servants to attend.

He approached the entrance to an apartment, and the guards standing outside stood back, bowing as one and touching the tips of their spears to the floor.

Isaiah ignored them.

He strode through the door, through the spacious room that served as the day chamber of the apartment, then into the bedchamber. He stopped just inside the door, more than mildly displeased to see that Ba'al'uz hovered just behind the physician, who bent over the man lying on the bed.

Both Ba'al'uz and the physician bowed when they saw Isaiah, and the physician stepped back from the bed.

"His condition?" Isaiah said.

"Much better, Excellency," said the physician. "The nausea has subsided, and his muscles grow stronger. I expect that within a day or two he can begin to spend some time out of bed."

"Good," said Isaiah. "You may leave."

As the physician collected his bag, Isaiah switched his gaze to Ba'al'uz. "You also."

"I was here merely to sate my curiosity as to the health of

your guest," said Ba'al'uz. "I apologize if this has displeased you."

You were here to spy for your true lord and master, thought Isaiah. He did not speak, but merely regarded Ba'al'uz with his steady black gaze.

Ba'al'uz repressed a sigh, bowed slightly, then followed the physician from the room.

Once Isaiah had heard the outer door close behind them, he relaxed slightly and walked to the side of the bed.

The man who lay there was of an age with Isaiah, in his late thirties, but of completely different aspect. He was lean and strong, not so heavily muscled, and his shoulder-length hair, pulled into a club at the back of his neck, was the color of faded wheat. His close-shaven beard was of a similar color, while his eyes were pale blue, and as penetrating as those of a bird of prey.

His entire aspect had an alien cast, but that was not surprising, thought Isaiah as he sat down in a chair close by the man's bed, given his Icarii heritage.

"You do not like Ba'al'uz," said the man. His voice was a little hoarse, but not weak.

"I neither like nor trust him," said Isaiah. "He is that most dangerous of madmen, one whose insanity is so difficult to detect that most who meet him think him merely unpleasant."

"Yet I sense that he is a force at your court," said the man.

"You know who I am," said Isaiah.

"I have been asking questions."

Isaiah gave a small smile. "I would have expected nothing else from you. But as to your observation . . . Yes, Ba'al'uz is a force at my court. He is useful to me."

"I suspect he is too dangerous for you to move against."

Isaiah burst into laughter. "We shall be friends, you and I." He hesitated slightly. "Axis SunSoar."

Axis grunted. "I thought no one knew my name. I was reveling in the idea of such anonymity that I might invent my own past and name to suit."

"I wanted to be sure that you would live before I told anyone your name and history."

"Were you the one who pulled me from the afterlife?"

"Yes."

"Then you are far more than just a 'tyrant,' Isaiah."

Isaiah gave a small shrug. *That is of no matter at the moment.* "Tell me how you feel. There have been times since I pulled you from the water when my physicians feared they might lose you to death."

Axis rested back against the pillows, not entirely sure how to respond. He'd been walking with his wife, Azhure, along a cliff-top coastline in the strange Otherworld of the afterlife when he'd felt a terrifying force grab at his entire being. He'd gasped, grabbed at Azhure, and then pain such as he'd never felt before enveloped him, and the world of the afterlife had faded. All he could remember was Azhure, reaching for him, and then the utter shock of finding himself caught by tangled reeds at the bottom of a lake, unable to breathe, unable even to fight the grip of the reeds because every muscle in his body was so weak they would not, *could* not, respond to his needs.

"Weak," Axis said finally, "but improving. Eager to get out of this bed."

"Good," said Isaiah. "I am glad of it."

"Why am I here, Isaiah? Why drag me back from death?" Axis gave a soft, bitter laugh. "I do not think I made a great success at my last life, so I cannot think why you need me here now."

"Not a great success? You fought off an army of Skraelings, and resurrected an ancient land." Isaiah hesitated. "Skills that might possibly be useful again."

Axis shot Isaiah a sharp look, but did not speak. *Skraelings?*

"You became a wielder of great magic," Isaiah continued, "and discovered yourself a god. You—"

"Completely underestimated the problems in trying to unite ancient enemies together in the one land, made a complete mess of raising my own children, and then watched everything I had fought so hard for disintegrate into chaos and, eventually, death." Axis paused. "How long has it been since . . ."

"Since Tencendor vanished from the face of the earth? About five years."

"You know that I have no powers now. All the Icarii lost their powers of enchantment when the Star Gate was destroyed and we lost contact with the Star Dance. Isaiah, I am not a god anymore, I am not an Icarii Enchanter anymore, I am hardly even a man—I can barely feed myself my noonday soup. Why am I back? *Why do this to me*? I was at peace in death, curse you!"

"I apologize, Axis. I needed you."

"For what? For *what*?"

"For the moment, just to be my friend."

Axis fought back a black anger that threatened to overwhelm him. "You could not buy yourself a friend in the marketplace?"

"You have no idea how much I need a friend," Isaiah said very softly. "Someone I can trust. Perhaps you have mishandled much of your life, Axis SunSoar, but from what I know of you, you did know how to be a friend very, very well."

Axis closed his eyes. He did not know what to say. He did not want to be here, not back in this life, not back in a world where there was no Star Dance, nor any family.

"Am I a prisoner?" he said eventually.

"No," Isaiah said, "although you will notice guards about you. I seek only to protect you."

"Of course you do," Axis said.

"Get strong, Axis SunSoar," Isaiah said softly. "Get strong, and then we shall see."

Ba'al'uz may have been more than slightly insane, but he was no fool, he paid attention to world affairs, and he had a very good idea who the man was that Isaiah had hauled from Lake Juit.

So what did Isaiah want with a failed god?

From Axis' apartment Ba'al'uz wandered slowly through the palace complex of Aqhat until he entered a courtyard in its western boundary. From here he walked through a gate and down to the River Lhyl, the lifeblood of Isembaard.

Ba'al'uz stood at the edge of the river for an hour or more,

uncaring of the hot sun. He did not use this time to admire
the river, as beautiful and tranquil as it was, but instead stared
as if transfixed across to the far bank where, at a distance of
perhaps half an hour's ride, rose an extraordinary pyramid
clad in shimmering blue-green glass and topped with a capstone of golden glass that sent shafts of light reflecting back
at the sun.

DarkGlass Mountain.

Ancient. Unknowable.

Alive.

Twenty years ago it had suddenly whispered to Ba'al'uz.
Sweet whispers, very gentle at first, offering Ba'al'uz power
and friendship, the two things Ba'al'uz craved most.

Its name, it told him, was Kanubai.

Ba'al'uz knew a little of the history of DarkGlass Mountain. He knew it had been built some two thousand years
earlier by a caste of priests who had hoped to use the pyramid
to touch Infinity. He knew there had been a small catastrophe associated with the priests' attempts to open the pyramid
to Infinity, a catastrophe which resulted in the pyramid being
dismantled and the caste of priests disbanded and scattered
to the wind.

Dismantled.

Ba'al'uz looked at the pyramid, and smiled. What was once
dismantled could always, with some effort, be resurrected.

But Ba'al'uz had never heard the name Kanubai associated with the pyramid. So Ba'al'uz had spent many of his
free hours, over a period of almost a year, hunting down rare
scrolls and manuscripts in the tyrant's personal library (generally at night, when the tyrant was preoccupied with one of
his wives, and not likely to come to the library looking for
something to send him to sleep).

One day Ba'al'uz discovered a scroll which told of the
legend of Chaos—Kanubai.

That had not been a good day, for as he'd read the legend through, Ba'al'uz realized that the great being known as
Kanubai was preparing for escape. The damned incompetent
ancient priests must have unknowingly built their pyramid
atop the very abyss where Kanubai was interred, and when

they had opened the pyramid into Infinity . . . the stopper over the abyss had cracked.

Now Kanubai was seeking out helpers, for that great day when he would finally break free.

Like most of the insane, Ba'al'uz was a complete pragmatist. There was nothing he could do to stop Kanubai, and everything to gain if he aided him. Kanubai would be grateful when he finally stepped into the sunshine, and more than ready, perhaps, to repay those who had helped him.

Since then, Ba'al'uz had become the whisperer's devoted servant, willing to do all he could to aid him. For the moment, that was little more than keep his eyes and ears open.

Great Lord, Ba'al'uz whispered.

He felt Kanubai's interest, although the god did not speak.

An unusual event. Isaiah has brought back from the dead a man who I believe to be Axis SunSoar, former lord of the Icarii people in Tencendor. A man who was once of great power, but who is now powerless, and helpless. I do not know why Isaiah wants him, and I do not know how Isaiah managed to drag him out of death.

Isaiah is my enemy, Kanubai said. His voice sounded thick and a little muddled in Ba'al'uz' mind, but it was much clearer than it had been twenty years ago, when Ba'al'uz had struggled to understand the god. The fact that Kanubai's voice was now so much clearer meant that Kanubai was much, much closer than once he had been.

And mine, said Ba'al'uz. *I dislike him intensely. Shall I kill him for you?*

Kanubai did not respond, and Ba'al'uz could feel his interest seeping away.

I will watch for you, said Ba'al'uz. *Inform you, as needed.*

Do that, said Kanubai, and then his presence was gone, and Ba'al'uz blinked, and was once more aware of his surroundings.

CHAPTER FOUR

Baron Lixel's Residence, Margalit

The negotiations between Maximilian, King of Escator, and Lady Ishbel Brunelle took many days, the process not helped by the marked hostility between Ishbel and StarWeb. Lixel was beginning to wish Maximilian had never included StarWeb in his delegation, for the birdwoman was proving more than awkward to deal with. Coupled with this was the fact Ishbel was conducting her own negotiations, unheard of when generally a woman's parents or legal guardians did the negotiating on her behalf.

But then, this wasn't precisely a normal family situation, was it?

By the third day of the negotiations, Lixel had become painfully aware that without StarWeb they might have concluded the entire deal within a brief three hours, and that mostly spent deciding over which wine they'd prefer to settle the matter. He wasn't sure how much latitude Maximilian had given StarWeb, but was beginning to suspect the Icarii woman was overstepping the bounds.

The matter of the dowry, the lands, the manorial rights, the riches, and the marriage itself, all hung on one issue. According to StarWeb, Maximilian insisted that while a marriage ceremony could take place, the marriage would not be officially ratified, or made legal, until Ishbel produced a live child.

At that Ishbel had balked. "A marriage is between a man and a woman," she insisted. "It does not depend on children for legality."

"Nonetheless," StarWeb countered, "children are important to Maximilian, and the marriage will be as nothing to him without them."

"It is an insult to me," Ishbel said, "to suggest that I am nothing without the production of children. That I am nothing but a vessel in which to carry a child."

The talks had centered on this argument for almost three days, and Lixel was despairing of finding any way round it. He tended to side with Ishbel. It *was* insulting to her to hinge the marriage's legality on the production of live children; a marriage was far, far more than the children it created . . . it was an alliance between a man and a woman, between their families and their lands, and the children were incidental, if generally much desired and loved.

Lixel had also begun to half suspect that these demands made of Ishbel were in the manner of a test. Maximilian, through StarWeb, was pushing Ishbel as far as he dared, perhaps to see what manner of woman she was.

Or perhaps what manner of offer she truly represented.

"What Maximilian would like," StarWeb said for the hundredth time, "is that you meet and, if all is agreeable, that a civil marriage ceremony take place . . . between the man Maximilian and the woman Ishbel, if you like. Once a child is born, then the marriage becomes a legality, between the King of Escator and the Lady Ishbel Brunelle."

"The child would be a bastard," Ishbel said, as she had been saying for three days.

"Not so," said StarWeb. "There has already been a marriage ceremony . . . it just has not been ratified. The child would not be regarded as a bastard at all."

Lixel closed his eyes, trying to summon the strength to step in and try to mediate some compromise. But before he could do so, Ishbel spoke again.

"Perhaps if Maximilian would agree not to wait until the child is born to ratify the marriage, but to do so when it is clear that I carry Maximilian's child."

Lixel opened his eyes, astounded at this concession on Ishbel's part. There had been no hint of it until now, but to give way that much ground . . . even if the concession had been days in the arriving . . .

"Done!" said StarWeb. "Marriage shall be ratified when you are pregnant . . . and in Ruen."

"Accepted," said Ishbel. "Although the dowry won't be Maximilian's until the marriage is ratified, either. Until then, I remain in control of all properties and rights."

Lixel looked at StarWeb, sure she would object. To his surprise, she inclined her head. "Then I am sure Maximilian will be most keen to get you pregnant," she said. "You shall surely not lack any attention from your husband."

"That's going too far, StarWeb," Lixel put in, noting that Ishbel had colored faintly at that last. "You overreach yourself."

StarWeb shrugged, not in the slightest bit apologetic, and Lixel thought he'd best regain some control of the situation.

"It is a long and arduous journey between Margalit and Ruen, my lady," he said to Ishbel. "May I suggest, should Maximilian be agreeable to the terms mooted about this table, that you meet halfway? Perhaps at Pelemere? That way, it is not so far distant for either of you to return home if, at the eventual meeting, you don't suit each other."

Ishbel hesitated, then inclined her head. "Agreed," she said, and StarWeb smiled.

"Then I shall return immediately to Ruen," she said, "and put it to Maximilian. I am sure he shall agree."

She rose. "At Pelemere then, my lady," and with that she stepped to the window and lifted out into the gloomy sky.

Ishbel hoped she had done the right thing. She'd held out as long as she could, loathing StarWeb for her persistence, and for putting her, Ishbel, archpriestess of the Coil, into such a vile and humiliating position. She hadn't wanted to capitulate at all, but the Great Serpent had been so insistent the marriage take place . . . and if the only way that it was going to take place was to agree that it need not be ratified until she was pregnant, well then . . .

She had not been going to agree, but last night she'd

dreamed that the Great Serpent had appeared before her, on his knees (if a serpent could manage such a feat), reminding her that the marriage *must* take place. It must. So much depended on it.

Shaken and worried, Ishbel had capitulated as far as her own pride would allow her.

Ishbel sighed, her hand creeping over her belly, hesitating, then making the sign of the Coil. She would be unable to get pregnant—if Maximilian thought he'd get an heir out of her then he would be sadly disappointed—because she'd given up all her reproductive abilities when she'd been inducted into the Coil.

Would it matter?

No, she decided. A civil marriage would still take place—the marriage would be legal—but the formal union between her and Maximilian, between their lands and wealth and titles, would never eventuate. A marriage with the man would surely be enough for the Great Serpent. It was all he had wanted. Surely.

Ishbel wondered if she even need bed with him. Perhaps she'd manage to find a way around that, as well.

A thousand leagues to the southwest, Ba'al'uz sat cross-legged in the open window of his chamber in the palace of Aqhat, staring at the great pyramid across the River Lhyl.

Tonight Kanubai communicated less in whispers than in shared emotion. There was seething resentment directed toward Isaiah, which Ba'al'uz could understand, given his own seething resentment of the tyrant, although he did not yet understand why Kanubai should also resent him so much—and with the faintest undertone of fear.

Ba'al'uz also felt a dark hatred at imprisonment from Kanubai, as well as a cold, terrifying desire for revenge.

The cold desire for revenge was something Ba'al'uz understood very well.

And there was something else, a formless worry, that Kanubai enunciated more in emotion than in words.

Every so often, though, a whispered phrase came through,

although what Ba'al'uz was supposed to make of "The Lord of Elcho Falling," he had no idea.

The Lord of Elcho Falling stirs.

There was more hatred and worry underpinning that phrase, and so Ba'al'uz decided that he would hate and fear the Lord of Elcho Falling as well.

He would kill him, he thought, should he ever meet him.

CHAPTER FIVE

Palace of Aqhat, Tyranny of Isembaard

Isaiah, Tyrant of Isembaard, picked up the pyramid of glass, holding it in his hands as gingerly as if it contained the manner of his death. Then he raised his eyes and looked for a long moment into the shadowed depths of the chamber.

Axis sat there, hidden from the view of the pyramid. He had gained much in strength over the past days and was well enough to spend most of the day out of bed.

But Axis still didn't trust Isaiah, and was still angry at him for dragging him out of death.

Isaiah could understand that and he hoped that after today he and Axis might be a little closer to friendship.

Axis returned Isaiah's gaze, his face expressionless.

Isaiah studied the rose-tinged glass pyramid again.

"There are only a very few of these in existence," Isaiah said quietly. "I have one." He hefted it, as if Axis needed the visual reinforcement. "Ba'al'uz has one, and our ally has one. If there are more, then I do not know of them."

"Where did they come from?" said Axis. "I sense great power coming from the one you hold."

"They were a gift from my ally, Lister. One for him, one for Ba'al'uz—"

"What did Ba'al'uz do to deserve such a gift?"

Isaiah shrugged, choosing not to answer that. "And one for me. They make communication easier than it might otherwise be."

He paused, his attention now firmly on the glass pyramid in his hand. "I am going to speak to Lister now, my friend. It would be best for all concerned if you remained unobserved."

There was no answering sound or movement from the shadows.

Isaiah settled the pyramid carefully into the palm of his left hand, took a deep breath, then placed his right hand about it.

A moment later the glass glowed through the gaps of his fingers. First pink, then red, then it suddenly flared a deep gold before muting back to a soft yellow.

Isaiah slid his right hand away from the pyramid. "Greetings, Lister," he said.

While the glass pyramid still rested in Isaiah's hand, its shape was now so indistinct as to be almost indistinguishable. An ascetic, lined face topped with thinning brown hair now looked back at Isaiah from deep within the glass.

Isaiah was careful not to even suggest a glance toward the shadows.

"I hope all goes well?" Isaiah said.

"The negotiations between Maximilian and Ishbel proceed," Lister said. "Ishbel still does not like the idea of marriage, but intends to do as I, as *we*, wish, and Maximilian worries about the past rising to meet him. I hear he is stamping about his palace at Ruen in a right black temper. Maximilian and Ishbel are to meet in Pelemere, there to conduct a marriage if they find each other agreeable."

"That is good. How go your 'friends'?"

"My 'friends'?"

Isaiah sighed, trying very hard not to look at Axis watching keenly from the far recesses of the room. "The Skraelings," he said. "Are they massing?"

Axis made no sound, but from the corner of his eyes Isaiah saw him tense.

"Yes," said Lister, "although still not in quantities enough to seethe south. Not this winter, but next, surely."

"They pose no danger to you at Crowhurst?"

"I toss them scraps from my table, and speak kind words to them. They tolerate me. I do not think they will be a danger to me."

"Be careful."

In the pyramid Lister's shoulders rose in a small shrug.

"And what are you about, Isaiah?" Lister said. "How go your plans? Do you mass *your* army?"

"My forces accrue," said Isaiah, "as do the stores I will need for the march north. In addition, I am sending Ba'al'uz beyond the FarReach Mountains within the fortnight. He will prepare the way for our invasion. I admit myself pleased at the thought of getting him out of the palace."

"He could be more danger out of your sight than within it."

Now it was Isaiah's turn to shrug. "It is better, I think, to remove him from DarkGlass Mountain's presence for the moment."

Lister nodded. "We tread a dangerous dance here, Isaiah. Are you safe?"

Isaiah grunted. "From whom? My generals? I am never safe from them . . . but I will stay alive as long as it is needed, Lister. As must you."

"I was not thinking of your generals."

Isaiah did not respond.

Lister sighed. "Let me know when Ba'al'uz has departed."

"I will."

With that, the pyramid dulled, then resumed its usual rosy opaqueness.

"I cannot believe what I just heard!" Axis stalked out of the shadows, his gait not showing any signs of his former weakness. "You have allied with . . . with . . . with a lord of the *Skraelings*?"

"Axis, I know that in your time you battled long and hard with the Skraelings, and with their then terrible lord, Gorgrael. But I have my—"

"I cannot *believe* this!" Axis slammed his hand down on the table, and Isaiah's eyes slid toward the pyramid, grateful that Axis had not damaged it.

"What in the gods' names do you want from me, Isaiah?"

"Your aid and your advice, Axis. Your friendship."

"I lost tens of thousands of people to the Skraelings," Axis hissed. "I have *seen* what they can do! What the fuck do you think I will do, *ally* myself with you and the Skraelings to invade—"

"You will calm down and you will listen to me!" Isaiah rose to his feet. He was taller than Axis by a handbreadth, and now he used that slight advantage to stare down at Axis, holding the man's furious gaze with unwavering eyes. "Nothing is ever as it seems," Isaiah said, more moderately now. "Nothing."

He stepped away from Axis. "Wine?"

"Oh, for all the gods' sakes . . ."

Isaiah ignored him, walking over to a table and pouring a large measure of wine into a goblet. He brought it back to Axis, holding out the goblet.

Axis did not want wine. He lifted a hand to brush the goblet away, then froze, staring at what Isaiah held.

It was a large amber glass goblet of the most exquisite beauty. Completely forgetting his anger, Axis reached out and took the goblet into his hands.

It was truly the most extraordinary goblet he had ever seen. A craftsman of astonishing talent—*magical* talent— had carved an outer wall, or cage, of frogs gamboling among reeds about the inner wall of amber glass. When he held it up to the light, careful not to spill the wine inside, the outer caged wall of frogs shone almost emerald, coming to life in the light; the frogs seemed alive, leaping away from the goblet's inner amber wall as if they were about to take to life itself.

"Drink," Isaiah said softly.

Axis lifted the goblet to his mouth, but just before the wine reached his lips, one of the frogs about the outer cage lifted a toe pad and gently touched Axis' face.

Axis trembled so badly he almost dropped the goblet, and Isaiah had to reach out and take it from him.

"That is an object of great power," Axis said hoarsely. He was rattled, not so much by the fact that the goblet was of a powerful magic, but of the manner of power it represented.

Compassion.

Axis looked at Isaiah and saw in his black eyes, reflected

for just a moment, that same compassion he'd felt from the goblet.

"I found it one day," said Isaiah, somewhat diffidently. He took a draft of wine from the goblet. "Are you sure you want no wine?"

Axis shook his head. All his anger had vanished, and he was completely calm. He realized that this had been Isaiah's intention when he'd handed him the goblet, but Isaiah had not actually used any power to pacify Axis.

Instead, Isaiah had used the goblet to show Axis his true nature.

Compassion.

"Trust me," said Isaiah, and Axis nodded, still almost befuddled by what had just happened.

"Would you like me to tell you where I came from?" said Isaiah. "Where *Isembaard* came from?"

"Yes. Isembaard is such an unknown entity outside of its borders," Axis said.

Isaiah walked over to a cabinet and withdrew a large rolled map, which he spread over the table.

Axis came over. The huge map showed the known world in detail, and Axis was stunned by the size of Isembaard. It was three times, at least, the size Tencendor had been.

Axis' eyes drifted to the northwest of the map, where Tencendor should have been.

There was nothing there save a broken line showing where once the coastline had been, and the chilling label: *The Lost Land of Tencendor.*

"As you can see," Isaiah said, "my cartographers have produced a perfectly up-to-date map."

Axis nodded, not trusting his voice.

Isaiah tapped a small city on the east coast of Isembaard. "The original Isembaard rose from this small eastern city of the same name—the Tyranny takes its name from the city that gave it birth. When Isembaard was still a small city and not the vast empire it is now, the tyrants of Isembaard depended almost entirely on warfare for their reputation, and for the means to feed their people."

"How so?" said Axis. "Surely a state is the stronger the less it engages in war?"

"The city of Isembaard was small, surrounded by poor land," said Isaiah. "How else was it to grow, and strengthen, if it did not accrue lands unto itself? Isembaard needed to expand in order to survive. It needed its leaders, its tyrants, to be successful and ambitious war leaders, in order that the needed land be accrued."

"Ah," said Axis. "So over time Isembaard 'accrued' all the nations I have seen on your maps? The 'dependencies'? A city become an empire?"

"Yes," said Isaiah. "Bit by bit. It has taken us centuries."

Axis thought about the vast amount of territory within the Tyranny, and the different peoples contained therein. "It must be difficult," he observed, "ruling such an immense area and peoples."

"It is," said Isaiah, and Axis thought he saw that fleeting shadow cross the tyrant's face.

"Does the Tyrant of Isembaard still rely on the ancient methods of keeping people happy?" Axis asked. "Continual expansion? Warfare? Does your throne depend on victory in war, Isaiah?"

Isaiah turned his head to look at Axis fully. "You know the answer to that, Axis. Why else allow you to listen to my conversation with Lister?"

Axis looked back at the map. "You called Lister your 'northern ally,'" he said, "and from my own experience I know Skraelings prefer ice and snow above all else." He ran a hand slowly up the map, then tapped the area above Gershadi and Viland. "He's up here. In the frozen northern wastes."

Isaiah tilted his head in agreeance.

"And you want to invade 'north,'" Axis said. He fell silent, concentrating on the map.

"By the stars, Isaiah," Axis said eventually, "you have allied with Lister and the Skraelings with only one possible objective. The kingdoms above the FarReach Mountains: Pelemere, Kyros, Escator, perhaps even the Outlands. You intend to sandwich the Northern Kingdoms between you, yes? Two arms, two pincers, icy ghosts from the north, desert warriors from the south."

"A sound strategy, surely," Isaiah said.

"But such a risk," said Axis. "Not merely relying on an alliance with Skraelings, for the stars' sakes, but such a massive invasion into lands so far from your home." Axis studied the map once more. "Frankly, I would have tried for something more achievable that didn't necessitate a Skraeling alliance . . . the Eastern Independencies, for example." He tapped the map down in its lower eastern corner. "I can't think why you have not 'accrued' them already."

Isaiah did not answer, and Axis looked at him curiously. "By the gods," Axis said softly after a moment or two. "You *have* tried for the Eastern Independencies, haven't you?"

"I campaigned against the Eastern Independencies in my second year on the throne," Isaiah said. "The campaign proved to be . . . difficult."

Stars! Axis thought, recalling Lister's earlier remark about the generals. Isaiah was very uncertain of his throne. He had one military disaster behind him and he could not afford another—not with both a nation and some restless generals expecting a military victory resulting in the acquisition of yet more new territory.

"Why," Axis asked, "were the Eastern Independencies so hard to—"

"That is not the issue now," Isaiah said, his tone tight, and Axis knew this was not the time to push the point.

"So instead you ally with the Skraelings in the frozen northern wastes," Axis said. "An interesting alliance."

"It cannot fail," Isaiah said. "The Central Kingdoms, the Outlands, and their allies will not be able to resist us."

Axis was trying hard to reconcile this Isaiah with the one who had handed him the Goblet of the Frogs. He realized, very suddenly, that there was no contradiction at all. Isaiah was a man genuinely unsuited to tyranny, which made him immensely vulnerable, which in its turn made him even more determined to win for himself a great military victory that resulted in the conquering of vast lands.

The only question in Axis' mind was why Isaiah was so

determined to cling to his throne. Axis thought that Isaiah was not one who needed the magnificence of throne and title and power of life and death over millions in order to bolster his self-esteem.

So why the need to ally with the Skraelings in order to achieve military victory? Why embark on a course which would result in the death of tens of thousands?

"I need a friend here at court," Isaiah said, his eyes watching Axis carefully as if he could understand the train of Axis' thoughts. "I have none. No one I can trust."

"If you want me to be your friend, then tell me *why* you want this invasion so badly. The real reason, Isaiah."

Isaiah held his gaze for a moment. "And so I will tell you," he said, "when I am certain I can trust you."

Axis laughed softly, shaking his head. "Why do I find it impossible to remain angry with you, Isaiah?"

"Will you be my friend, Axis?"

"I will not aid you to invade the Central Kingdoms. I will not, under any circumstances, condone any action that sees you ally with Skraelings."

"Be my conscience then, if friendship is too difficult."

Isaiah's eyes twinkled, and Axis again shook his head in amusement. Isaiah was impossible to dislike.

"Your conscience, then," Axis said.

"Good," Isaiah said, taking Axis' hand, and Axis sensed that Isaiah was truly relieved.

"Now," said Isaiah, glancing at one of the windows, "it grows dark, and I fear I am late for an appointment with wife number fifty-nine. Can you find your way back to your apartment by yourself?"

Axis was struck firstly by the fact that at least Isaiah trusted him enough to allow him to wander the palace, and secondly by the casual mention of wife *number fifty-nine*.

"How many do you have?" Axis asked, aghast.

"Um, eighty-four, I think."

"So many?"

"I find myself displeased by a woman's body when she is pregnant. So as my wives fall pregnant, I send them back to the women's quarters and take to myself another wife. Also, many of the dependencies send me wives, hoping thus to garner my favor."

"And you love none of them." It was not a question.

"They are meaningless to me, Axis. I do not have an Azhure in my life."

The sudden mention of his wife upset Axis more than he'd thought possible. He was shocked to find his eyes filling with tears as a terrible ache consumed him.

"I am sorry, Axis," Isaiah said, the man of deep compassion now fully returned.

Axis nodded, then turned away.

Two hours later Axis lay awake in his chamber, hands behind his head, staring into the darkness.

Azhure.

He hadn't thought much about her since Isaiah had pulled him back into life, but Isaiah's words earlier brought home to Axis how much he missed her.

I do not have an Azhure in my life, Isaiah had said.

Neither, now, did Axis. She was dead, he was alive, and Axis had no idea if he would ever see her again. Who knew how many otherworlds there were? Who knew whether, once he died from this life, he would return to Azhure's side?

Besides, how *long* was he to live now?

The thought of enduring perhaps fifty years without his wife kept Axis awake throughout the night.

"Damn you, Isaiah," Axis muttered as the dawn light slowly filtered into his chamber, but there was no anger in his voice, only an infinite sadness.

CHAPTER SIX

Palace of Aqhat, Tyranny of Isembaard

Isaiah did not go back to his private quarters after talking with Axis.

Instead, restless and uncertain, he went down to the dark stables, saddled a horse (waving back to their beds the four or five grooms who hurried sleepy-eyed to serve their master), and rode the horse to the Lhyl.

He pushed the horse across the river, then rode south along the river road to where rose the great glass pyramid called DarkGlass Mountain. Isaiah did not once raise his eyes to look at it, but rode directly to a small door in its northern face, where he hobbled the horse, and entered.

He walked through the black glass tunnels of the pyramid to its very heart—a golden-glassed chamber known as the Infinity Chamber.

Here Isaiah sat cross-legged in its very center and meditated.

Kanubai—trapped deep beneath DarkGlass Mountain—and he were enemies. Bitter, terrible, lifetime enemies. Isaiah came here to expose himself to the beast, not only to test his own strength and resolve, but also to sense out his enemy and divine his strengths and weaknesses.

Time was when Kanubai's weaknesses outnumbered his strengths.

Now, the strengths were gaining.

Isaiah visualized the abyss that sank into the very heart of the world. He concentrated on that abyss until it formed his entire consciousness, until he knew nothing but the abyss.

Then, gathering his courage, he cast his eyes down into the darkness.

When he had first started doing this, he had seen nothing, although he had felt the horror that lurked in the pit of the abyss.

Kanubai, cast down an infinity of ages ago.

But over the past few years Isaiah had started to *see* as well as *sense* Kanubai. The gleam of an eye.

Or perhaps a tooth.

The wetness of a tongue.

Now, as he had over the past year, Isaiah's gaze managed to discern a blackened shape huddled against the walls of the abyss.

Kanubai was rising closer.

He was still far, far below, but every time Isaiah came here he could see that Kanubai was a little nearer.

Thin black fingers suckered into tiny cracks in the abyss.

A darkened face, staring upward, feeling the weight of Isaiah's regard.

Kanubai had once been stoppered tight in his abyss, but was no longer. Those ancient cursed magi who had built the glass pyramid, and then opened it into Infinity, had unwittingly cracked open the stopper Isaiah and Lister had placed over the abyss.

Kanubai had been inching his way through that crack ever since.

Hello, Isaiah.

Isaiah fought down his nausea. Kanubai had been whispering to him for many years now. At first nothing but unintelligible thick mutterings, but now almost every word was clear.

What do you, Isaiah?

Isaiah never replied. The last thing he wanted was to get into conversation with the beast.

Do you know what I will do to your river, Isaiah, when I rise?

Isaiah knew he had to break the connection. He had spent too long in here. He had to leave now before—

He went cold.

In his vision of Kanubai, Isaiah thought he had seen, just for a moment, something clinging to Kanubai's back.

Or something in his hands, perhaps.

Isaiah opened his eyes, then rose to his feet, stumbling a little in his foreboding as he made for the doorway out of the Infinity Chamber.

Something else rose with Kanubai.

CHAPTER SEVEN

The Royal Palace, Ruen, Escator

Maximilian stepped into the chamber where he met with his Council of Friends and saw that for once he was the last to arrive.

Egalion, Garth, and Vorstus regarded him a little warily. Egalion and Garth had been well aware of the tension between Maximilian and Vorstus, but had no idea of the cause. Both Garth and Egalion had, at different times, approached Maximilian cautiously, wondering what the problem might be, but Maximilian had waved away their gentle queries, saying there was nothing wrong save that he was suffering prewedding nerves.

Maximilian did not think Vorstus would be any more forthcoming with the two men if they were also to approach him.

Maximilian did not take his seat, but walked over to a window and leaned on the sill, looking out. "I have decided to depart for Pelemere, there to meet with the Lady Ishbel," he said. "Within the week."

Egalion and Garth looked at each other, but it was Vorstus who answered.

"But we have not yet heard if the negotiations StarWeb is conducting with the Lady Ishbel on your behalf have been successful."

"Oh," said Maximilian, turning about and looking Vorstus in the eye, "I am sure they will be successful, aren't you?"

Vorstus said nothing, holding Maximilian's eyes easily.

"Maxel," Garth said carefully, "how can you *know*?"

"Because I feel it in my bones," Maximilian said, but

mildly enough. *The serpent—Light—had sent Ishbel to him.* Maximilian had no real idea why, but he hoped it was because Light had decided only that the Persimius line needed a bit of strengthening and the Lady Ishbel's bloodlines would do nicely. Perhaps she might have some memories with which to refurniture his Twisted Tower.

The offer of this bride did not have to mean that Elcho Falling was needed.

"Besides," Maximilian continued, putting a disarming smile on his face, "I grow restless sitting here in Ruen. I want to be doing something, and even if the Lady Ishbel takes one look at my face and decides she'd rather marry a—"

Frog.

"—toad, then at least we'll have had the joy of many weeks on the road with the wind in our hair and the chance to meet up with Borchard and Malat in Kyros along the way. What say you, Garth, Egalion? Do you feel like a jaunt eastward?"

Garth laughed. "How can we refuse!"

Maximilian looked at Egalion. "We'll bring four or five units of the Emerald Guard. They shall keep us safe enough, and make a splendid showing for the Lady Ishbel."

"But to practical matters," Vorstus said. "Who shall govern Escator in your absence?"

Maximilian looked at Vorstus. *Not you.* "The Privy Council of Preferred Nobles have my authority to make what decisions are necessary. I shall not be gone too many months."

Vorstus gave a little smile and looked away. He was not surprised that Maximilian no longer trusted him.

No matter. Maximilian was doing precisely what Vorstus wanted anyway.

Over the next few days Maximilian busied himself with preparations for departure, as well as briefing the Privy Council. Maximilian was glad to be leaving Ruen. Ever since he'd had his confrontation with Vorstus he couldn't stop thinking about the fact that Vorstus may have left him down in the Veins deliberately.

Why, Maximilian had no idea, which itself made him question whether he was wrong about Vorstus, but he could not stop thinking about it.

Seventeen years in such horror . . .

Maximilian had reconciled himself long ago to the loss of those seventeen years. He had thought he'd reconciled himself to the horror he'd endured during that time—the beatings, the constant darkness, the never-ending swing of the pick, over and over, the dust and humidity and heat, the cave-ins, the pain . . .

The loneliness, the sheer mental desperation, year after year after year.

He thought he'd put all that behind him. Cavor, the man who had condemned him to the mines, was long dead.

Maximilian could walk away from the nightmare.

But what if Vorstus had also been aware of the plot to keep him incarcerated? What if the man who had guided his rescue had also dictated the timing of that rescue?

What if the nightmare was only in remission, not dead?

CHAPTER EIGHT

Palace of Aqhat, Tyranny of Isembaard

When there came a knock at the door, far earlier in the morning than usual, Axis was surprised to see Ba'al'uz waiting for him.

"Isaiah asked me to collect you today," Ba'al'uz said, "so that we might meet with him in his private chambers at the tenth hour."

"But that is two hours or more away," said Axis.

"I thought perhaps you and I might put those hours to good use," said Ba'al'uz. "For a chat, perhaps. Do you wish to come like that, or . . . ?"

Axis looked down.

All he had on was a towel from his morning ablutions.

Axis grinned. "You caught me early," he said. "Give me a moment."

And but a minute later, clad more respectably in light-colored trousers and waistcoat, with sandals on his feet, Axis set off with Ba'al'uz.

"Isaiah tells me you witnessed his communication with the Lord of the Skraelings," Ba'al'uz said without preamble as he led them along a corridor with huge, unglazed windows along one side.

"Indeed. It was most curious. I have many questions."

"It was why I came early for you. I thought you would want to know more."

"And you don't mind answering?"

"I have nothing to hide from you, Axis. Isaiah has requested that I indulge your every question, and so I will."

Axis doubted very much that Ba'al'uz had nothing to hide,

but hoped that, under Isaiah's directive, he might at least provide some answers to Axis' more pressing questions.

"Who are you, Ba'al'uz," Axis said. "*What* are you to Isaiah?"

"I am Isaiah's maniac."

"Yes, but what—"

"I am Isaiah's brother," Ba'al'uz said, grinning at the expression on Axis' face. "His elder brother by some dozen years."

"Then why is he tyrant, and not you?"

"Ah," said Ba'al'uz. "Thereby hangs a tale. Please, if you will, step through here."

Ba'al'uz indicated a doorway in the corridor, and Axis walked through into a magnificently tiled veranda commanding views over the surrounding countryside. Ten minutes' walk beyond the palace flowed the emerald waters and reed-covered riverbanks of the Lhyl, and just beyond that, on the far bank, rose the massive pyramid of DarkGlass Mountain. It was covered in blue-green glass and surmounted by a cap of gold.

Axis thought it the most beautiful and yet, somehow, the most deadly thing he had ever seen. He had questions about that, too, but for the moment he was intrigued more by the fact that Ba'al'uz and Isaiah were brothers.

"Do you know of the manner in which a tyrant comes to the throne of Isembaard?" Ba'al'uz said, leaning on the railing and looking out over the countryside.

"No. I'd assumed that Isaiah was his father's eldest son."

Ba'al'uz shook his head. "Isaiah was his father's twentieth son, and there were another eighteen after him. Thirty-eight of us, all told."

Axis thought that with all the wives Isaiah's father must have enjoyed, it was amazing he had so *few* sons. "By what process, then, is the tyrant chosen?" he said.

"You know the throne of Isembaard is a warrior throne?"

"Yes, Isaiah told me as much."

"Well, then, what better way to decide who to sit that throne than with individual combat bouts between the sons."

Ba'al'uz turned a little so he could see Axis' face. "To the death."

Axis could not speak for a moment. He'd battled with his brother Borneheld for Achar, and killed him, but to do that so many times over? Isaiah had seen thirty-six of his brothers die so he could assume the throne?

"Why are you still alive?" Axis finally asked.

"Me?" Ba'al'uz assumed an effeminate pose and an arch expression. "Can you imagine *me* with a weapon in my hand! No . . ." He laughed merrily. "There is a strain of madness runs through our family, Axis. In every generation there is one son . . . not quite right. Strange." He paused, then hissed, "*Crazed!* Such sons do not battle. Instead we become our successful brother's maniac. His court wit. His *weapon*."

Again he laughed, and Axis could indeed hear the faint strains of madness lurking deep within Ba'al'uz' being.

Genuine, or counterfeit? Axis wondered about a son who, knowing he did not have the skills to succeed in combat, might save his life by pretending madness.

"Weapon?" Axis said.

"A madman sees things, *hears* things, that no other can," said Ba'al'uz, and this time Axis thought he could recognize genuine insanity in the man's eyes.

"He dares things," Ba'al'uz continued, "that no other can. And he *knows* things that no other can comprehend. Madness is a gift of the gods, Axis, and I serve my brother well. Madness is *power*, yes? Not like that which once you wielded, but power nonetheless. I have my life, and I am grateful, and I do whatever I can to smooth Isaiah's path through tyranny. I slide through my brother's court like an evil wind, and in the doing I confound his enemies and scry out their secrets."

Axis gave an uncomfortable laugh. "What have you scried out from me, then?"

"That you are a burned-out hero, Axis, and that Isaiah has nothing to fear from you." He grinned as he said it, and with such malevolence that Axis actually leaned back a little.

Stars, how did Isaiah stand the man?

He couldn't, Axis realized. Isaiah may have sent Ba'al'uz to answer any questions Axis had, but the underlying purpose of Isaiah's request was that Axis see once and for all Ba'al'uz' true nature.

Ba'al'uz was a frighteningly dangerous man, and Axis wondered what his secret ambition was, how he meant to achieve it, and what it would mean to all about him. Maybe Isaiah hoped Axis could tell him.

"Well, then," said Axis, "why not tell this 'burned-out hero'"—he wished he had the control not to grind the words out—"the purpose of that pyramid across the river. It is most intriguing."

"Ah," said Ba'al'uz, "DarkGlass Mountain. It is intriguing, is it not?"

"Who built it? For what purpose?"

"Be patient, Axis, and I shall tell you what I know." He leaned on the balcony railing again, looking at the glass pyramid. "From what anyone can gather—and my forebears spent their lives checking records—DarkGlass Mountain was built about two thousand years ago."

"By whom?" asked Axis. The momentary antagonism between them had vanished, and Axis leaned on the railing as well, looking curiously at the massive pyramid.

"A group of men known as the Magi caused its construction. The Magi worshipped numbers, particularly the One. The Magi were mathematical geniuses. They used the power of the One in order to build a device by which they could touch more intimately the power of the One, and, by so doing, reach out to touch Infinity. Creation. Call it what you will."

Casual words for what made Axis' soul turn cold. *Touching the power of Creation. Was there anything more powerful, or more dangerous?*

"Then, the pyramid was not known as DarkGlass Mountain," continued Ba'al'uz. "It was called Threshold."

Threshold, thought Axis. *A doorway.* "Did the Magi manage it?" he said. "Did they touch Infinity?"

Ba'al'uz' lip curled. "Yes, they did. But when DarkGlass Mountain was first opened up to the power of Infinity, something went wrong."

Axis went even colder. *Something went "wrong."*

A catastrophe, more like.

"There was . . . a small rebellion, I believe," said Ba'al'uz, "initiated by those jealous of the Magi and the power they commanded. The Magi lost, and were all but slaughtered. DarkGlass Mountain was stripped of its glass, and left to be buried in sand drifts."

"But here it stands in all its glory."

"Yes," Ba'al'uz said very slowly. "Strange, is it not?"

Axis waited, refusing to ask the question, and Ba'al'uz pouted and continued. "Perhaps several hundred years ago, DarkGlass Mountain regrew itself."

"*What*?"

"After the rebellion, when the Magi were slaughtered and their knowledge condemned," said Ba'al'uz, "DarkGlass Mountain's glass was stripped away, its chambers blocked and its capstone buried. The glass was *supposed* to have been broken, but it was buried instead. For a thousand years and more, DarkGlass Mountain sat covered in hessian and sand, a mound only. Then, one day, some of the sand slid away, and a little more the next day, until over the space of two or three years the entire structure was revealed. Stone only, for DarkGlass Mountain had yet to reclad itself in glass and capstone."

"Someone must have been—"

"No," Ba'al'uz said softly, his gaze fixed on DarkGlass Mountain, "the tyrant at that time set men to watching. No one came near the pyramid. It simply . . . regrew. Once its stone structure was uncovered, the blue glass began to appear, growing up from the ground, gradually covering the pyramid's sides. It flowed up from the depths of burial. Very, very slowly, but the glass *flowed*.

"That process took five years to accomplish. Then the rest. The capstone, and all of DarkGlass Mountain's internal chambers."

"Internal chambers?"

"There are tunnels and shafts," said Ba'al'uz, "all of which lead to a central chamber of the most exquisite glass. The Infinity Chamber. You must ask Isaiah to show it to you someday. He sits there, on occasion."

Axis shuddered. "What *is* it, Ba'al'uz? What is its purpose?"

"No one knows. Isn't that amusing? Here it sits, a great beautiful glass pyramid, positively humming with power on some days, and no one knows." Ba'al'uz tapped his nose and assumed a conspiratorial look. "I can tell you this, Axis, because only I and Isaiah know. The tyrants, long ago when DarkGlass Mountain regrew itself, built their palace of Aqhat here so that it would appear they used the pyramid to bolster their power. 'Look at me, Great Tyrant of Isembaard, who controls the mysterious power of DarkGlass Mountain.' But between you and me and Isaiah, Axis, none of the tyrants have known anything about the pyramid, let alone how to use it. They use it as . . . oh, as a piece of stage. Every so often Isaiah embarks on a great ceremonial procession across the river, strides—alone—into the Infinity Chamber, sits there for an hour twiddling his thumbs, and then walks out again, proclaiming that he has had converse with the gods and they have shown him the way forward. Of course nothing of the sort has happened, but who is to know that? The tyrants have closely associated their throne and power with DarkGlass Mountain, and yet none of them has the faintest idea what it is!"

Ba'al'uz burst into a peal of laughter.

"How is it Lister also controls the power of the pyramids?" Axis said.

Now Axis had caught Ba'al'uz off balance. "What?"

"The glass pyramids that Lister gave Isaiah and yourself. They are powerful treasures, are they not? Perhaps Lister knows some of the secrets of the DarkGlass Mountain. Secrets that you have not yet learned."

Ba'al'uz frowned. "No. Surely not. Lister said he found them."

Axis laughed softly, disbelievingly, and Ba'al'uz flushed.

"He said he *found* them!"

"And you believed him. The Lord of the Skraelings. No wonder Isaiah needs my advice. Perhaps he and DarkGlass Mountain are in league, eh? Perhaps they spy on you with those pyramids, yes?"

"No. Lister knows nothing about DarkGlass Mountain. Nothing. It does not speak to *him*."

Oh, there was a question there begging to be asked, but

Axis did not think Ba'al'uz was aware of his slip, and he thought it best not to alert the maniac.

"How did Isaiah and Lister come to ally?" Axis said smoothly, leading Ba'al'uz away from what he'd just revealed. "I cannot imagine they met in a tavern, or on a chance walk along the riverbank."

"Lister approached Isaiah two years ago," said Ba'al'uz, his eyes narrowed, trying to work out how Axis had suddenly assumed the lead in the conversation. "A whispered word from a shadowed envoy. You were a king, you must know how these things work."

Axis shrugged. "And then Lister sent the pyramids to you."

"Yes," Ba'al'uz said slowly, then added a trifle hastily, "We don't trust him, you know."

"Good," said Axis, "for I doubt very much he is to be trusted. Now, the sun grows hot, and I am somewhat wearied of the view of DarkGlass Mountain. Shall we go to Isaiah?"

Ba'al'uz nodded. Reluctantly, and with a final glance at DarkGlass Mountain, he led Axis toward Isaiah's private apartments.

The palace of Aqhat was an amazing collection of buildings, spires, minarets, echoing audience and dining chambers, air walks, underground passages, hidden doors, soaring arches and windows, and, above all, of dazzling displays of wealth and power. Gold and jewels glittered on the walls and around the frames of doors and windows in every public chamber.

In stark contrast, Isaiah's private chambers were almost bare. The walls were unadorned, the furnishings simple if comfortable, and the few accoutrements present subtle. Isaiah allowed few people in here: not even his many wives, for Axis had heard he kept a special chamber for entertaining them in the evenings.

Apart from Ba'al'uz, Axis had never seen anyone else in the quarters, not even servants. While here, Isaiah served himself.

Isaiah beckoned them to a group of chairs set by a window to catch a cooling breeze from the Lhyl.

"You will not be surprised to hear," Isaiah said to Ba'al'uz as they sat down, "that Axis has agreed to advise me from time to time. I always think it best to have an independence of opinion about my decisions."

"I am indeed not surprised," Ba'al'uz said smoothly. "Axis SunSoar has a wealth of experience regarding the Skraelings. We would be wise to listen to him."

"And thus he sits in on this conversation," said Isaiah. "Ba'al'uz, I have talked to Lister, and he and I agree that you must go north within the week."

Isaiah looked at Axis. "As you have realized," Isaiah said, "Lord Lister and I mean to ally in an invasion of the north. Ba'al'uz is to go north for the next several months in order to, how shall I say this, sow the seeds for our success."

"Create mayhem and confusion," said Ba'al'uz with a decidedly cheerful air. "A small conflict or two as well, should I be lucky."

"You want to divide the Northern Kingdoms before you invade," said Axis. "Set them at each other's throats so they are less likely to notice you sneaking up at their backs, and far less able to respond well. Divide and conquer is surely the first maxim learned by all good tyrants."

Isaiah looked hard at him at the last, but did not comment on it.

"On the other hand," said Axis, "you will find the Northern Kingdoms with their forces already mobilized and battle-hardened. The ploy may work as much against you as for you. How good are their generals?"

"The Outlanders have some good leaders, but they are experienced only in intertribal warfare. I doubt they could manage a response to the kind of armies Lister and I can command."

No one can manage a good response to an invasion of Skraelings, thought Axis.

"Pelemere and Kyros have several good generals," Isaiah continued.

"Who I intend to take care of," said Ba'al'uz, studying the fingernails on one hand.

"And the kings and princes?" said Axis, regarding the

other two over steepled fingers. "You need only one charismatic leader to take a hopelessly divided muddle of peoples and turn them into victors."

"As you would know," said Isaiah. "But there are none who strike me as any potential threat." He paused. "Or is there someone you think I should know about . . . ?"

Axis thought about it. It wasn't so much that he needed the time to think of a name, but to decide if he should mention it to Isaiah and Ba'al'uz.

"There's a wild card," he said finally. "Maximilian Persimius, King of Escator."

Ba'al'uz smiled derisively. "Escator is a tiny kingdom, and all but ruined. It can hardly raise enough policemen to keep market-day traffic under control, let alone an army to repel forces such as Isaiah and Lister command between them."

"I am not talking of forces," said Axis. "I am talking of charismatic leaders."

"You know this Maximilian?" said Isaiah.

Axis shook his head. "I have never met him, but my son Caelum did, and Maximilian was for some time considered a match for my close friend Belial's daughter. He is highly, highly regarded. You know his story?"

"That he was imprisoned in Escator's gloam mines for . . . what . . . fifteen or more years?" Isaiah said. "And that he was released on the endeavors of several youths and a cohort of ancient monks, from what I can recall of the story. Maximilian has ever since been somewhat of a recluse. Axis, why mark him as a charismatic leader?"

"I think of him only as a possibility," Axis said. "The man survived seventeen years under conditions that killed everyone else within six months. That says something for his character and tenacity. It tells me that he is, to put it simply, a survivor, and that he has depths that should not be lightly disregarded. He is also liked by all who meet him. Highly regarded, as I said. The man has *something*."

"But not an army," said Ba'al'uz. "And unlikely to raise one anywhere. He is also stuck far away on the west coast of the continent. He is no threat."

Axis shrugged. "You asked, I told."

Isaiah studied Axis a moment, then looked to Ba'al'uz. "When shall you leave?"

"Within a few days," said Ba'al'uz. He smiled, all geniality and affability. "I do so like the idea of a vacation."

When Ba'al'uz was gone, Axis turned to Isaiah and said, "That man is your brother?"

"He terrifies me more than my other brothers did combined," said Isaiah. "The trouble is, I cannot know if he will be more trouble to me dead than alive. At the least he is traveling north and I shall be rid of the man for a few months."

CHAPTER NINE

The Road East, Escator

"Well?" said Maximilian. "Tell me of this strange offering from the Coil."

StarWeb flopped down on a stool in Maximilian's chamber in the wayside inn, trailing her wings to each side. She had arrived less than an hour previously, exhausted from the long, arduous flight from the Outlands, but Maximilian had not even allowed her time to wash and rest.

He wanted to know about Ishbel.

"She trails secrets like some women trail the scent of their perfume," StarWeb eventually said. "I don't trust her."

Maximilian crossed his arms and leaned against a window frame. "You don't like her," he said.

"No."

"Why not? Everyone trails secrets about them. It is a necessary condition of life."

"I do not think she would be a good wife for you. She is too unquiet."

"Hmmm. Unquiet is not good. Secrets I can tolerate, but not unquietness."

"You're making fun of me."

Maximilian grinned. "Not at all. So tell me, how went negotiations? Did you broker me a wife?"

"Yes. She agreed too readily."

"To all the conditions?"

"Not quite. She agreed that the marriage would not be ratified until she is carrying a child. She refused to wait until it was born. She also refused to hand over her dowry until the marriage was ratified. *I* said that would ensure her your immediate amorous intentions."

"You must have pushed her hard."

"I think it is fair to say she loathes me." StarWeb paused. "I told her I was your lover."

Maximilian went very still. "That was not wise, StarWeb, and most certainly not fair to Ishbel."

StarWeb shrugged, moving away from Maximilian. "I was honest with her. I hoped to startle some honesty from her in return, but was disappointed."

"I am surprised she conceded as much as she did," Maximilian said. "She must want me very much." *Or perhaps she is under strict instructions.*

StarWeb shot him a look. "I did not tell her you were a *good* lover."

Maximilian raised a small smile. "Nonetheless, she wants marriage with me badly, it seems. Perhaps tales of my attractions have spread."

"It is suspicious, Maxel."

"Yes. Perhaps."

StarWeb sighed. Maximilian was in one of his uncommunicative moods.

"What was she like, StarWeb?"

"Lovely, if you like the sharp-edged kind."

Now Maximilian smiled far more genuinely. "I like *you.*"

"Ha. Well, she *is* lovely, but curiously gauche. She is uncomfortable among people, constantly watching others as if she needs prompts on what to say and do. I think she has been hidden among the Coil for too long. God knows what they taught her, but social skills must not have been high on their list. Maximilian, if she is to be your queen, then she shall need some hasty lessons in the arts of conversation and etiquette once she reaches Ruen."

StarWeb paused, thinking. "She is not comfortable to be around, and I think that is mainly because *she* is desperately uncomfortable around others."

"I was not the world's best conversationalist when first I stepped forth from the Veins either, StarWeb."

"You are curiously defensive of a woman you have never met, Maxel."

Maximilian opened his mouth, then shut it again, and contented himself with a small shrug in answer.

StarWeb rose, weariness evident in her every movement. "I am going to take some rest, Maxel. Perhaps we can meet later?"

"Yes. Perhaps."

StarWeb looked at Maximilian a long moment, wondering why he'd decided to leave Ruen for Pelemere before hearing from her, then decided she was too tired and Maximilian was too uncommunicative to justify the question.

She turned and left the chamber without another word.

Maximilian did not move for an hour or more, leaning against the window frame, thinking.

He was not foolish enough to think that a bride sent to him from the heart of the Mountain at the Edge of the World from an order devoted to the Great Serpent was mere coincidence, but he *had* convinced himself that the only reason Light, in his guise as a serpent, had sent her was that he'd decided the Persimius line needed new, stronger blood.

Or that perhaps Maximilian was doing so badly at finding a bride on his own, when an heir was so badly needed, that he'd sent one himself.

Elcho Falling was not stirring. Maximilian was sure of it. He'd spent the night before he left Ruen standing in front of the crown, trying to see any chance, any sign of life.

But the crown of Elcho Falling was as it had been for millennia. Absolutely quiet.

Besides, there was no crisis, no desperation, no *reason* to think Elcho Falling was needed.

He need not worry.

He need not fret about the emptiness of the Twisted Tower. That would be for one of his descendants to worry about, perhaps, but not he.

Maximilian took a deep breath, consciously relaxing his shoulders as he exhaled. He had brought the emerald and ruby ring with him. He knew that he and Ishbel would marry.

They would live calm, settled lives, gradually building a marriage, and having many children.

All would be well.

Of course it will, said his ring. *Naturally. Just like your youth and early manhood was calm and settled and happy.*

Irritated, Maximilian pulled the ring from his finger and slipped it into the pocket of his outer robe.

CHAPTER TEN

Hairekeep, Tyranny of Isembaard

Ba'al'uz faced a long and arduous journey north into the Northern Kingdoms. The northern dependencies of the Tyranny of Isembaard themselves could be difficult at this time of the year, while the FarReach Mountains beyond were not well known for their winter bonhomie. Nonetheless, Ba'al'uz was looking forward to the experience. As much as he loved DarkGlass Mountain and Kanubai's whisperings, there was also knowledge to be gained and trouble to be caused in the Northern Kingdoms, and Ba'al'uz couldn't wait for either.

Isaiah and Lister might well think Ba'al'uz was laying the ground for their invasion, but in reality Ba'al'uz meant to prepare the ground for Kanubai.

But all that lay in the delectable future. For now Ba'al'uz was merely glad to remove himself from his brother's company. Ah, that Isaiah! Strutting about wrapped in his muscles and jewels and black, black braids, thinking himself lord of all, sneering behind Ba'al'uz' back.

Ba'al'uz could not wait to see Isaiah ground into the soil under Kanubai's heel.

Isaiah had always been irritating, but Ba'al'uz had discovered new depths of loathing and resentment toward his brother at the arrival of Axis SunSoar.

Axis' arrival dismayed Ba'al'uz, because, first and most important, Ba'al'uz had no idea how Isaiah had managed it. Isaiah was a tyrant, and he was a warrior, but surely he had not the skills or powers of a priest.

Yet no one *but* a priest, or the most remarkable of magicians, could have pulled Axis SunSoar from the Otherworld into this one.

Isaiah should not have been able to do it.

The fact that he *had* appalled Ba'al'uz, because it meant that Isaiah was harboring secrets from him, and secretive power.

Axis' arrival dismayed Ba'al'uz for a second reason—it meant that Isaiah meant to replace Ba'al'uz as his most intimate advisor.

Ba'al'uz loathed his younger, prettier brother, and the only thing that had made their close relationship bearable was the fact that Isaiah needed Ba'al'uz as his advisor and weapon within the volatile politics of Isaiah's court.

Now Isaiah had Axis and Ba'al'uz' jealousy and bitterness festered deeper with the passing of each hour.

Now he would do anything to ensure Isaiah's downfall.

With Kanubai's aid and the power of DarkGlass Mountain, then who knew? With Isaiah dead, then who knew . . . ?

The tyrant throne would be empty, and who better to sit it, eh, than Kanubai's best and most loyal friend?

Five days after his conversation with Isaiah and Axis, Ba'al'uz set out for his adventure in the kingdoms beyond the FarReach Mountains. He did not travel alone—Ba'al'uz had no intention of warding off brigands by himself, or of cooking his own lonely roadside meals—but with an escort of eight men, all of whom he had handpicked from the shadowy underworlds of Isembaard's cities. Ba'al'uz trusted them completely, for he had purchased their souls with bribes and obscene gifts many years ago. They were his factors, his apprentices in the arts and crafts of deception and treachery.

Ba'al'uz would have need of them in his journey. He called them his Eight, and he regarded them with an almost brotherly affection.

From the palace of Aqhat, Ba'al'uz and the Eight took a riverboat north and then east along the mighty Lhyl. They stopped each night, either at a riverside village or town, to commandeer the best accommodation and food possible, or to make their own encampment on the fertile floodplains of the river, setting up tents and comfortable beds, and roasting river lizards on spits beside cheerful campfires. There, at night, Ba'al'uz would entertain the Eight with twisted tales that sprang from the whispers in his mind.

Within days the Eight were more devoted to Ba'al'uz than ever. Their journey might be dangerous, and deceitful in the extreme, but the rewards at its successful conclusion were . . . entrancing.

The journey along the Lhyl was deceptively pleasant; Ba'al'uz knew that conditions would deteriorate from the moment they left the river. Normally, if he took the river journey north and then east with Isaiah to Isembaard's capital, Sakkuth, they would disembark where the Lhyl turned north once more so they could continue the journey to the city on horseback. Ba'al'uz liked Sakkuth. The city was a viciously immoral place and seethed with opportunity for such as Ba'al'uz. Indeed, he had found five of his Eight within its depraved depths. But on this journey Ba'al'uz embarked into the unknown, for he did not leave the river and ride east for Sakkuth at all, but continued on the river, drawing ever closer to the FarReach Mountains.

This far north the river journey was no longer pleasant. In its lower reaches the Lhyl was a broad, serene waterway, but close to its source the river narrowed and became an ever more unruly traveling companion. The travelers swapped their initial broad-beamed riverboat for a narrow and much smaller vessel, which depended on both sail and the raw brute force of rowers to enable them to continue against the current. There was little room, with both travelers and rowers crammed onto benches, and Ba'al'uz had to put up with the indignity of having the stench and grunting of the rowers in his face twelve hours a day.

It was a relief finally to disembark, pay the riverboat captain, and continue their journey by horseback.

After almost three weeks on the river, Ba'al'uz and his companions were now in the very north of the En-Dor Dependency, itself the northernmost of the Tyranny's dependencies. Directly north rose the foothills of the FarReach Mountains, and beyond them the soaring pink and cream sandstone snow-tipped peaks of the mountains themselves.

Ba'al'uz faced many days on horseback across a dry and barren landscape to reach Hairekeep, Isaiah's northernmost fortress, which guarded the entrance to the Salamaan Pass in the FarReach Mountains.

Once they'd left the Lhyl, water was hard to come by, and they needed to carefully plot each day's travel to ensure that they reached the next water source alive. The travel was a strain on both men and horses, and Ba'al'uz was heartily relieved to finally reach the fortress at the dusk of a particularly hot and uncomfortable day.

The fortress of Hairekeep had been built almost three centuries ago by one of the Isembaardian tyrants to control travel through the Salamaan Pass, which connected the lands of the Tyranny to the kingdoms north of the mountains. For travelers—apart from braving the treacherous sea passage between Coroleas and the Tyranny, or sailing down the Infinity Sea to the east (and in both cases there were no large ports on the Tyranny's coastlines at which trading vessels could dock)—the Salamaan Pass was the only dependable passage between the north of the continent and the south, and the soldiers stationed at Hairekeep ensured that it remained closed to all but the very few who had the necessary permissions.

Ba'al'uz thought the fortress resembled nothing less than a massive stone block rising vertically out of the rock-strewn landscape. For almost twenty paces from ground level there were no windows in those walls, then only slits for a further ten paces, and only after forty paces did windows punctuate the stone to allow light inside. The walls continued vertically for another fifty paces to parapets that commanded magnificent views, not only of the pass to the north, but of all the surrounding countryside. Despite its forbidding aspect, the fortress was stunning: built out of the sand and rose-colored stone of the FarReach Mountains themselves, it glowed with an almost unearthly radiance in the twilight, reminding Ba'al'uz of the small glass pyramids Lister had given him and Isaiah.

The fortress commander was expecting them, and treated them to a good meal and the promise of an evening of good company.

But Ba'al'uz was tired, and impatient to retire to his quarters, so he made his excuses as politely as he might, and made his way to his chambers set high in the fortress.

Here, having fortified himself with a glass of wine and washed away most of the grime of his journey, Ba'al'uz unwrapped his own rosy glass pyramid that he'd carefully stowed in his pack.

Ba'al'uz sat, fingering it for some time.

He didn't like Lister. He was a complication in Ba'al'uz' life. No one had been more surprised than Ba'al'uz at the arrival of Lister's offer to ally with Isaiah. Ba'al'uz was even more surprised at the gift to himself, from Lister, of one of the rosy pyramids.

Beautiful things they were, and powerful. Ba'al'uz had thought initially they were connected in some manner to DarkGlass Mountain, but use demonstrated that they were different entirely. The power associated with Lister's pyramids was colder, and far more horrid, than that which DarkGlass Mountain radiated. Ba'al'uz didn't particularly like using the pyramid, but it was useful, enabling him to discover what Lister was about and also to aid Lister's and Isaiah's plans to invade the kingdoms north of the FarReach Mountains.

There was nothing more Ba'al'uz wanted than to see Isaiah out of Isembaard.

So Ba'al'uz pretended to be Lister's ally, for at the moment it suited Ba'al'uz' purpose. He wondered, at times, if Lister thought he might use Ba'al'uz against Isaiah, and would smile at the thought of everyone plotting against everyone else.

Life sometimes could be so much fun.

Ba'al'uz took a deep breath, settled himself more comfortably on his bed, and wrapped his right hand about the pyramid.

As with Isaiah's pyramid, Ba'al'uz' glowed first a radiant pink, then red, then flared into sun-bright gold before subduing to a soft yellow.

Ba'al'uz removed his hand and there, waiting for him as arranged, was Lister, the Lord of the Skraelings.

"Where are you?" said Lister.

"Hairekeep. Well on my way to the north."

"You will need to negotiate the FarReach Mountains yet, my delightfully crazed friend."

Ba'al'uz grinned. "You know you can depend on me."

Lister laughed. "Yes, I know that. Now, tell me about Isaiah. He is hiding something. I felt it the last time I spoke with him."

"He has a new friend. Axis SunSoar. Perhaps you have heard of him?"

There was a brief silence, and Ba'al'uz could almost *feel* Lister's surprise, but then Lister spoke calmly. "Surely. The Skraelings curse with his name. But I thought Axis was long dead, sunk beneath the waves of the Widowmaker Sea along with his land. The Skraelings drank themselves silly with jubilation the day *that* happened, I can tell you."

"Some months ago Isaiah made a weekend foray down to Lake Juit. He took a punt out into the lake, and from its waters dragged forth Axis SunSoar. Remarkable, eh?"

"I imagine that you must have aided him in this," Lister said.

"I did not. Isaiah managed it all on his own. Do you know how he did it, Lister?"

"Me? How should I know? I cannot begin to imagine what Isaiah could want with the man."

"Surely you can work that one out, Lister. Isaiah doesn't trust you, and who better to tell him how to outwit the Lord of the Skraelings than Axis SunSoar."

Lister managed a small smile. "Then he is sadly mistaken if he thinks Axis can better *me*. I have far more secrets than the Skraelings to batter at Isaiah should he think to outwit me."

"Really? What? Do tell. You know you can trust me."

Lister waved a hand, dismissing Ba'al'uz' question. "Tell me, beloved friend, how goes DarkGlass Mountain?"

Ba'al'uz frowned. *What did Lister know?* "What do you mean?" he said.

"Just curious. I find myself fascinated with the mountain. It doesn't . . . chatter to you at all?"

"No! Never! Have you lost your senses, Lister?" Ba'al'uz

wondered if Kanubai was whispering to Lister as well, and felt a knot of jealousy in his belly.

Again that dismissive wave of the hand from Lister. "So. You travel north to create havoc and mayhem in order to prepare the way for Isaiah and myself?"

"Yes. Much havoc and mayhem."

"You are a good lad, Ba'al'uz," said Lister, "and in the new order, once Isaiah and I have succeeded, you can be assured of many and mighty rewards."

Fool, thought Ba'al'uz. *In the new order* you *can be assured of a swift and bitter end.*

"We shall keep in touch," said Lister, "just to let each other know what is going on, yes?"

"Of course," said Ba'al'uz.

Lister put his pyramid on the table in the central chamber of his castle of Crowhurst deep in the frozen north and looked at his companion. The man lounged back in his chair, snowy wings spread out to either side of him, one foot resting on the seat of another chair, frost trailing down one bare shoulder and arm to where a hand rested on the tabletop, and regarded Lister with gray eyes alive with amusement.

He was a strange creature, at first sight an Icarii, but at second . . . something *else*. His form was not completely solid, but made up rather of shifting shades of gray and white and silver, and small drifts of frost. Even his eyelashes were frosted, and when he lifted a hand from where it had rested on the table it left a patch of icy condensation, which quickly evaporated in the warmth of the chamber. He was of a race called the Lealfast, and they had, for their own reasons, closely allied themselves with the Lord of the Skraelings.

"Did you hear?" Lister said.

"Yes," said his companion, Eleanon. "DarkGlass Mountain has begun its infernal whispering, as much as Ba'al'uz tries to deny it."

"*And* caught Ba'al'uz in its clutches," said Lister. "The question is, my friend, do we continue to use the madman, or dispose of him here and now?"

Eleanon gave a small shrug. "He is moving away from

DarkGlass Mountain. He should still be malleable. Besides, you need him in the Central Kingdoms. Isaiah *has* to invade, and none of us wants to have an army waiting to meet him at the other end of the Salamaan Pass. Ba'al'uz can create the chaos to prevent that."

"True," Lister said, his fingers tapping on the table. "We will need to keep an eye on Ba'al'uz, though. One never knows which way his loyalties will dart next."

"I *loathe* it that he has one of the spires," said Eleanon, speaking of the glass pyramids. "If I'd known you would give one to that vile creature, then none of us would have consented to give them to you."

"He does not know what it is," said Lister. "He has no means at all to comprehend it. But to the real news. Isaiah has brought Axis SunSoar back from the Otherworld. All on his own." Lister gave a little laugh. "I'd never thought Isaiah would have the initiative to do something like that. How do you feel about it, Eleanon? The legendary StarMan back from the dead?"

"He means nothing to me."

Lister gave him a long look. "Of course not. And he is, after all, so far away. But what if, Eleanon—just suppose, if you please—one day Axis thought to command you?"

"I answer only to you, Lister."

Lister gave a small smile, and then a nod. "And, of course . . . ?"

"And, of course, to the Lord of Elcho Falling."

CHAPTER ELEVEN

Palace of Aqhat, Tyranny of Isembaard

Axis enjoyed Ba'al'uz' absence. Without Ba'al'uz' sly, insidious terror, the entire palace relaxed: servants smiled as they went about their daily duties, the frogs who lived on the reed banks of the River Lhyl sang more melodiously, the sun shone less fiercely, and Isaiah spent less time at his official duties and more time at leisure, when Axis could join him.

One of the first things Axis noticed was that, in the weeks following Ba'al'uz' departure, he was allowed far more liberty to move about the palace and its surrounds. Guards were either unobtrusive or utterly absent. Axis still could not ride out into the countryside by himself, but in all other respects he was given the freedom of Aqhat.

Axis did not abuse the privilege. There was nowhere he wished to "escape" to, anyway. His family, everyone he loved, existed in a world other than this, and Axis did not fret for them. They were safe, and he believed that Azhure would know something of where he was. She would not fret, either, although Axis was sure she missed him.

He most certainly missed her companionship and love. Not desperately, but it was a constant ache in his otherwise peaceful existence at Aqhat. To counter it, Axis spent hours each night writing Azhure long letters about what he'd done during the day, and his observations of Isaiah and of Isembaardian life in general. Axis had never been a great wordsmith. When he was BattleAxe and then StarMan, the pen had always been Axis' least favorite weapon of choice. Indeed, he'd hardly written anything save the occasional battle order, and he and Azhure had always been able to communicate by more magical means than letters during their occasional absences from each other. But now Axis found a great serenity in writing, and found himself enjoying playing with words, and expanding his literary skills.

Most of all, though, Axis found it beneficial to order his experiences and thoughts. The mere process of revising his day onto paper deepened his experiences: he remembered odd comments or sights that he might otherwise have forgotten, and was able to glean new insights in relating individual experiences to each other.

Once Axis had finished a letter, he carefully folded it, wondering what Azhure might think of what he'd written: how her interpretation of his experiences might differ from his, how she'd laugh over some amusing incident . . . or his cumbersome prose. The closing of the letter, and his imagining of Azhure's reaction to its contents, was the sweetest moment of the entire process, and one he looked forward to greatly.

Then, once it was folded and sealed, Axis left the letter on the table in his chamber and went to bed, accompanied by the agreeable chorus of the frogs coming in the window.

In the morning, every morning, the previous night's letter would be gone.

Axis didn't know where the letters went. Perhaps, by some magic, they were actually transported to Azhure's hand. More prosaically (and far more likely), Isaiah had a servant creep in during the night and remove the letter to Isaiah's hand. Axis often had a quiet laugh to himself, imagining Isaiah secreting himself away in a corner somewhere to read what Axis had written, and he wondered if Isaiah kept the letters, or burned each one once he'd read it.

Whatever the reason—Ba'al'uz' absence or Axis' letters—he and Isaiah were becoming closer. They spent many evenings together, and days were spent riding out across the plains to the east. More important, Isaiah began to include Axis into his public persona as tyrant.

One day Isaiah asked Axis to attend him in his privy chamber in the third hour after dawn. Axis was curious. Isaiah had kept Axis very much in his personal sphere to this point, but Axis knew that the privy chamber was where Isaiah met with his generals and governors, as well as other high-ranking officials, and where he conducted the day-to-day business of the Tyranny.

From his time spent with Isaiah, as well as occasional discussions with other household officials, Axis had gleaned that Isaiah, as all tyrants before him, governed his vast empire via the twin mechanisms of military generals and civil governors. Each dependency of the Tyranny was administered by a governor who reported directly to Isaiah, either in person three or four times a year, or via one of the governor's most senior and trusted aides. The entire tyranny was also coadministered by Isaiah's vast military. There was a similar number of generals to governors, and the generals played as important a role in the daily administration of each dependency as the governors.

Axis thought it an unwieldy system, and one designed to create frustrations between the governors and the generals, but he understood its necessity as far as Isaiah was concerned. Infighting between governors and generals meant that Isaiah could the more easily maintain control over men otherwise more than likely to challenge him.

The generals were there to keep the governors in order, the governors there to inform on the generals and their troop movements.

From what Isaiah had said to him—or, rather, from what Axis had inferred from what Isaiah had *not* said—a tyrant spent most of his reign trying to outmaneuver his generals. They were the main threat to his throne. Any perceived weakness on the part of the tyrant, and the generals might think themselves strong enough to move against him. Isaiah was already in a vulnerable position, having lost his initial campaign of conquest against the Eastern Independencies, thus his generals watched him with constantly speculative eyes.

Axis could only imagine how desperately Isaiah was needing to succeed in his invasion of the kingdoms north of the FarReach Mountains. Fail there, and he would lose both throne and life.

A soldier escorted him to Isaiah's chamber. It was set high in the palace, with airy views over the Lhyl and the plains beyond.

The one window that would have given view directly onto DarkGlass Mountain was kept shuttered.

Isaiah was already there, as were his five senior generals, and Isaiah introduced Axis.

"Axis SunSoar," said Isaiah, "of Tencendor. Its StarMan. I know you have heard his tale."

Axis repressed a grin as he nodded at each of the five men in turn. That single pronouncement of Isaiah's had rendered them speechless. Axis had no idea why the generals had been called to conference with Isaiah, but he wagered they had not thought to meet a redundant legend. As he made eye contact with each one, he tried to evaluate them.

The eldest and most experienced general was a white-haired but tall and fit man called Ezekiel, who had commanded for Isaiah's father as well. He had tight, watchful eyes, but Axis thought Ezekiel was possibly too old now to try for power himself. Nonetheless, he might prove an invaluable ally for someone else's attempt.

Axis thought that attempt was most likely to come from the three generals in mid-age: Morfah, Kezial, and Lamiah. They looked tough and experienced, but were young enough to hunger for power.

Axis wondered if they spent more time watching each other than eyeing Isaiah for any possible weakness.

He distrusted the youngest of the generals, Armat, the most. Axis had heard from Isaiah earlier that Armat had only recently joined the ranks of the generals, and had the least experience of the five men. He was also, judging by the calculation in his dark eyes, the most ambitious. That ambition was combined with inexperience meant Armat was potentially the most dangerous. Where the others might hold back, Armat might well leap forward.

It was Armat who stated what every one of the generals was thinking.

"I thought you were dead," he said.

"As I was," Axis said, knowing what Isaiah needed him to say, "until Isaiah pulled me out of my afterlife and back into this world. Your tyrant is a powerful man, gentlemen, with many hidden abilities."

As one, the generals all shifted their gaze to Isaiah, who shrugged as if the matter was not even worth the discussion.

"A small trick," Isaiah said, "taught to me by an old and wise man, many years ago."

Now the generals all exchanged glances between themselves, and Axis almost smiled.

Isaiah was a good manipulator.

"Why resurrect a dead man?" said Ezekiel. "One who has lived his life."

Axis repressed a grin. That last sentence of Ezekiel's translated directly to "an old and useless legend."

"I felt myself in need of an impartial advisor," Isaiah said, moving to a table where several maps and sheaves of documents were spread out. "One who could step into any of your shoes"—his eyes slipped over the five generals—"should I be so unfortunate as to lose any one of you. You are all, naturally, aware of Axis' stunning prowess as a military commander."

Stars, thought Axis, *now I shall have to look out for the knife in my back, as well!*

He happened to catch Ezekiel's glance, and was surprised to see amusement dancing there. Axis instantly revised his earlier estimation of him, thinking that the man might prove a worthwhile ally one day.

Ezekiel was true to Isaiah and would support no rebellion against the tyrant.

"To matters at hand," Isaiah said, waving the generals forward to the table. "We need to discuss our preparations for invasion. Reports?"

For the next half an hour each general gave a terse summary of the current state of readiness. At this point, approximately a year away from actual invasion, the emphasis was on gathering new recruits, training, and stockpiling equipment and supplies.

Axis was stunned by the size of the army that Isaiah was gathering—it would be at least half a million men, and probably much, much larger.

"I would also like to raise the subject of resettlement at this time," Isaiah said.

"Resettlement?" Axis said, then apologized for his interruption.

"Whenever a tyrant gathers to himself a new dependency," Ezekiel said, "he ensures its 'loyalty' by moving into its territories large numbers of Isembaardians to settle the new lands." He looked at Isaiah. "But this is not normally something we plan until our victory is assured."

"Consider my victory assured," Isaiah snapped, "and consider it time to begin the planning for resettlement *now*." He pulled a map toward him, then tapped the upper corner of it. "The northwest of the Tyranny—the FarReach and En-Dor Dependencies—are poor and their peoples struggling," he said. "They shall be happy to remove themselves to the gentler and more fertile pastures of the Outlands or the Central Kingdoms above the FarReach Mountains."

The five generals just stared at him.

"But—" Morfah began.

"You will be responsible for their organization, Morfah," said Isaiah, "together with Ezekiel. Unless you both feel yourselves incapable."

No one said anything, but again there were hurried glances among the generals.

"Or unless you wish me to bring someone *else* back from death to deal with it for you," Isaiah said.

"Your order," said Ezekiel in a smooth, calm voice, "is as always my command. Let us not disturb the dead any more than we need to. Morfah and I will see to it, Excellency. At what point after the invasion do you wish the peoples of En-Dor and the FarReach dependencies to begin the long trek north into—"

"They shall move *with* the invasion," Isaiah said. "Thus they shall need to be informed now that new lands await them and they need to begin making preparations for their journey north."

"*With* the invasion?" Lamiah said, adding almost as an afterthought, "Excellency?"

"The Outlands and Central Kingdoms are very far away from the main bulk of the Tyranny," said Isaiah. "They need to be settled as rapidly as possible. The peoples of the En-Dor and FarReach Dependencies shall follow directly behind the main military convoy."

"They are not going to be happy to be ordered from their homelands," Morfah muttered.

"Then your silver tongue shall be needed to persuade them," Isaiah said. "And persuade them you *will*, Morfah . . . Ezekiel."

They both gave small, stiff bows of acquiescence.

"Together with the army and the settlers," Axis said once the five generals had left, "how many people will there be in the convoy, Isaiah?"

"A million, maybe a little more."

Axis could say nothing for a moment. *A million people?* "The logistics . . ." he said.

"Are a nightmare," said Isaiah. "No wonder I needed you back from death to advise and aid me, eh? I cannot be every-where at once."

Axis just shook his head. *A million people.* He couldn't escape the feeling that Isaiah was heading directly for his second military fiasco.

Stars alone knew what the generals were thinking.

CHAPTER TWELVE

West of Pelemere, Central Kingdoms

They had been on the road for weeks, and Maximilian was enjoying the freedom. He appreciated the chance to catch up with old friends. He knew all the kings of the Central Kingdoms, some better than others. Malat, who ruled over Kyros, was a good friend, and his son, Borchard, an even better one. Maximilian had enjoyed his four-day stay in Kyros immensely, although the good-natured prenuptial ribbing of Borchard was something he was thankful to escape.

He worried a little about leaving Escator, but that worry was mainly engendered by guilt at enjoying his freedom so greatly. The Privy Council were capable enough of managing the kingdom's daily affairs, and all would manage nicely without him.

Some of Maximilian's enjoyment began to pall as they drew closer to Pelemere. Ishbel was near, an equal distance to the east of Pelemere, according to the report of a passing Icarii, as he was to the west, and now all of Maximilian's attention was focused on their meeting.

What would she truly be like, this serpent bride? What was her purpose: to become his wife and bear his children, or to deliver a darker message into his life?

Together with his increasing anxiety about Ishbel, Maximilian was also growing a little irritable with the constant company. Garth and Egalion were his close friends, and he knew the men of the Emerald Guard intimately. While he enjoyed their company, Maximilian was so solitary by nature, a trait exacerbated by his seventeen-year imprisonment, that he found the constant company trying. He found himself dreaming about pushing his horse into a gallop across a vast plain, seeing nothing but the gently rolling grasslands ahead of him, enjoying no company save that of his horse, having to respond to nothing more than the sun on his face and the wind in his hair.

And soon he would have a wife.

Six days out of Pelemere, Maximilian's rising anxiety and irritation combined to push him to a sudden decision.

"Egalion," he said, as they dismounted for the evening, "I am going to take a few stores, and a bedding roll, and ride off by myself for a few days."

"Maximilian—"

"I need to get away, Egalion. Just by myself. Just for a few days. You know how . . ."

Maximilian's voice drifted away, and Egalion nodded. Yes, he knew "how." Maximilian had spent seventeen years chained to a gang of men, and Egalion knew that sometimes it seemed to Maximilian as if those chains had never vanished.

"You need to keep safe," Egalion said.

"I don't need a guard." Maximilian's voice was sharp.

"I won't send men to shadow you, Maximilian. But *keep safe.*"

Maximilian tried a small smile, which didn't quite manage to warm into life. "What part of the world can be more boring, more *safe*, than the western plains of Pelemere, my friend?"

Garth had wandered over and had heard enough of the conversation to know what was happening. "Maxel?"

"The hanging wall," Maximilian said, referring to the ceiling of rock that had hung over him for so much of his life, "is bearing down on me, just a little too much. Let me go, Garth."

Garth and Egalion exchanged a glance, then Garth nodded. "Keep safe, Maxel."

"I will rejoin you a day outside of Pelemere."

Maximilian stepped back, his eyes holding those of Egalion and Garth for just a moment; then he vanished into the gloom of dusk.

* * *

Maximilian pushed his horse for five hours into the night, angling a little northeast of the route Egalion, Garth, and the Emerald Guard would take, until the animal was almost dropping from weariness. He halted in the shelter of a small grove, made his horse comfortable, then gathered enough dry wood for a fire.

Maximilian felt exhausted himself, but he knew he would not sleep.

There was something he wanted to do.

He just didn't know what Ishbel represented. Contentment, or the ruination of peace? Maximilian wasn't even sure that meeting her would solve the puzzle: Ishbel was likely to be an enigma not easily explained within the first five minutes of acquaintance.

Once the fire was blazing, Maximilian set out some food . . . then ignored it.

He would eat once he was finished.

Pushing the food to one side, he slid the Persimius ring from his left hand, then took the queen's ring from his cloak pocket. Holding them loosely in his hand for a moment, Maximilian took a deep breath, then set them down, slightly apart from each other, before the fire. The Whispering Rings could do more than just set his day on edge with their irritating chat.

Trying not to think too much about what he was about to do, Maximilian took a long stick, poked it into the fire, then scraped a goodly quantity of the bright coals over the rings.

They hissed, then hissed again, more violently than previously.

"Tell me what you see," Maximilian whispered.

For a moment nothing happened, then vision consumed his mind.

He strode through a corridor that appeared as if it stretched into eternity. Its walls glowed turquoise and white.

Behind him, he knew the corridor vanished into the darkness that trailed from his shoulders like a cloak.

Maximilian strode ahead, his steps determined.

He walked the hallways of Elcho Falling.

He turned a corner and halted, transfixed.

A woman sat in a bath, her back to him, her fair hair caught up about the crown of her head with pins, tipping water from an exquisite goblet encrusted with frogs over her shoulders so that it trickled slowly down her spine.

She turned very slightly as she became aware of his presence.

"My love? Is that you?"

He felt overwhelming grief at the sight of her, and could not understand it, for he knew also that he loved her.

He turned and resumed his walk down the corridor, brushing irritably at a weight about his brow.

After some time (hours, days perhaps), he became aware that something approached from behind him.

He turned, thinking (hoping) it might be the woman.

Instead, it was something so dark, so terrible, that Maximilian screamed, throwing his arms up about his face.

It was not a creature or person at all. Instead, Maximilian found himself staring into the open doorway of the Twisted Tower, and seeing that it was now entirely empty.

Not a single object remained in any of the chambers.

He had lost everything, every memory, every ritual, every piece of magic, that he needed to resurrect Elcho Falling.

He woke, his heart still thudding, just after dawn.

All he could remember for the moment was the horror of staring into the doorway of the Twisted Tower and realizing it was now entirely empty.

Terrified, but knowing he had to do it, Maximilian closed his eyes once more and called forth the Twisted Tower. Trembling, he laid his hand to the handle of the door and opened it.

The first chamber lay before him, groaning with the weight of its objects.

Relieved beyond measure, Maximilian opened his eyes, looking across once more at the fire.

The rings lay in cold, drifting ash.

Maximilian reached over and picked them up, sliding his

own ring on his hand, and slipping the queen's ring away in his cloak.

What was he supposed to make of what he'd dreamed?

He busied himself with some breakfast, discovering himself starving. He set aside the problem of the dream for the moment, instead concentrating on the simple tasks of breaking camp, grooming and saddling his horse, and riding out.

Toward the end of the day, when he was dismounting from the horse in order to make camp, Maximilian realized that there was something about the vision that he had not been conscious of while he'd been experiencing it, but of which he'd become aware, very gradually, in the past few hours.

As he'd been striding the corridors of Elcho Falling, he'd carried the weight of a crown about his head.

Maximilian had his answer.

Elcho Falling was waking.

He sank to his haunches, absolutely appalled, lowering his face into one hand.

Elcho Falling was waking, and he was the one who would need to assume once again the responsibilities of its crown.

For several minutes he crouched in turmoil, unable to order his thoughts. Finally, however, Maximilian managed a deep breath.

What should he do?

Carry on, put one foot in front of the other, until the way ahead became clear.

Taking another deep breath, Maximilian finally rose to his feet. Perhaps this Ishbel Brunelle would have some answers.

CHAPTER THIRTEEN

Pelemere, Central Kingdoms

The train of carts and horses and riders wound its slow, miserable way toward the city of Pelemere. Winter had set in and gray sleet drove down over the train, drenching horses and riders and even those Icarii sheltering inside the canvas-covered carts. Everyone huddled as deep as they could within cloaks, heads down against the driving rain, hands almost too cold and stiff to keep grip on reins. Horses plodded forward, heads down, tails plastered to their hind legs, eyes more than half closed against the rain. Mud splattered up from their hooves, coating their underbellies and the legs of their riders.

No one noticed the rider emerge from the shadows of a small wood and attach himself to the rear of the train. Within heartbeats he looked as though he had been there since the train had set out from Margalit weeks previously, face hidden beneath the hood of a sodden cloak, shoulders hunched against the cold.

A deputation from Pelemere met the train some four miles out of the city. It wasn't a very large deputation, for this was the train only of the possible wife of the rather poor King of Escator (when Maximilian arrived he would rate a slightly more ostentatious welcome), but it *was* a welcome, and Baron Lixel, riding at the head of the train, was pleased to see them.

If nothing else, the deputation meant food and shelter and a warm bed were nigh.

There were a few brief words of welcome, faces from the Pelemere deputation peering through the gloom to nod at the

Lady Ishbel sitting her mare five or six riders back, and then everyone headed as fast as they might for Pelemere. No one wanted to remain outside in this weather.

The city had almost entirely shut down for the night, but there was one gate left open and it was through this small, insignificant side gate that the Lady Ishbel Brunelle and her train were escorted to their residence in the eastern quarter of the city. The house was one which the king, Sirus, had lent to Ishbel for the coming weeks as a gesture of goodwill toward Maximilian. It was not particularly large, but it had a covered courtyard, and Ishbel was never so glad of anything as she was of that sudden relief from the wind and rain when she pulled her mare to a stop with cold-numbed hands.

A servant from the house hurried forward to help her to the ground, then left her to aid someone else.

Ishbel stood, alone in the milling activity of the courtyard, wishing only for someone to escort her to a bath and a bed.

For an instant a gap opened in the crowd of horses and riders, and Ishbel saw a heavily cloaked man watching her from the far edge of the courtyard.

There was a moment when Ishbel felt that their eyes met, even though his face was hidden beneath the hood of his cloak, and then a horse moved between them, the moment was broken, and Ishbel turned away.

Please, please, she thought, *let someone lead me away from this cold and misery soon.*

Then Baron Lixel was at her side, and a man who Lixel introduced as Fleathand, who was the steward of the house, and within moments Fleathand was leading her inside, and Ishbel could finally, gratefully, contemplate some solitude, some warmth, some rest, and, perhaps amid all that, a little bit of comfort.

Two hours later, fed and bathed and sitting alone in her chamber, Ishbel finally felt as if she could relax.

But she dared not. Relaxing meant Ishbel might weep with exhaustion and anxiety and overstrung emotion, and she was not quite ready to give in to tears.

She sat in her chair by the shuttered window, clad in her

night robe with an outer wrap pulled loosely about her, and tried to relax. The past weeks since leaving the Coil had been taxing; she was constantly on edge, alert for any stray word that might betray her, and the emotional wrench at her parting from everything she loved and trusted grew worse with each passing day. Well might Aziel, the Great Serpent, and the entire firmament, for all she cared, insist that she *would* return one day, but right at this moment Ishbel could not see that eventuality. She felt utterly lost and abandoned and, caught in her loneliness and melancholy, she simply couldn't believe that she would ever return to her home.

If only she knew why this marriage was so important. If only the Great Serpent would tell her. It was all very well to argue that this marriage was the only thing that would save her homeland from devastation, but Ishbel could not see *why*. It made no sense to her.

Ishbel thought about how she had been loved and valued and cherished by the Coil.

Then she thought about Maximilian, and about her humiliation at his insistence through StarWeb's demands.

She sighed, the sound ragged and heartrending. She tipped her head against the headrest of the chair, closing her eyes, and tried to think about something, anything, happier than her current situation.

It was only after long minutes that Ishbel came to realize she was not the only person in the chamber.

She jerked to her feet, staring wildly into the dimness beyond the lamp, and finally saw him.

He was standing in the shadows at the very rear wall of the large chamber, dressed in damp traveling leathers, leaning against the wall, arms folded, as still as the darkness itself, watching her.

Ishbel knew instantly who it was.

CHAPTER FOURTEEN

Pelemere, Central Kingdoms

Maximilian had traveled hard and fast once he'd left his first night's campsite to reach Pelemere at the same time as Ishbel. He was numb at the realization that Elcho Falling was probably waking, but as he had no idea what direction he should take, or what he should do, Maximilian simply continued on as he had originally planned.

Meet Ishbel, discover for himself what she was like.

The only thing that Maximilian knew was that, whatever else, Ishbel was somehow integral to Elcho Falling.

No one had spotted him as he slipped in at the back of Ishbel's train. Maximilian was dressed in clothes similar to those of Ishbel's escort, plus everyone's attention was on Pelemere and the necessity to get there as soon as possible, rather than on the actual number of men trailing along behind.

He dismounted in a quiet corner of the yard, looking about for Ishbel.

Maximilian had spotted her almost immediately, and his first thought was that she was the woman he'd seen in his vision.

The second was that he'd never seen anyone more alone than she was at that moment.

She had no retinue. No one. Not a maid, not a valet, not a single companion that she could trust and lean on for support.

Absolutely isolated, and looking lost and afraid because of it.

Maximilian had seen the look on her face and had recognized it instantly. He'd seen it on face after face of men condemned to the Veins—a hopeless, trapped expression that was impossible to fake.

She must truly be driven, then, to come all this way for a marriage she could not want.

Ishbel eventually vanished behind the milling horses and their dismounted riders, and Maximilian had taken the opportunity to slip into the house and merge with his old friend, the darkness.

He'd stood there, completely motionless, allowing the dark to curl about and hide him while Ishbel unpacked a single valise, ate a meal brought to her by a servant, and bathed in the hip bath set by the fire. He'd waited and watched, motionless, secreted, as Ishbel had dried herself, pulled on her nightgown and then the robe, summoned the servant to take away the bath, and then sat in the chair by the shuttered window, resting soft and silent and very, very still until the moment she tipped her head back against the chair and sighed with such misery that Maximilian felt his heart turn over.

It was the ultimate betrayal, this silent watching of a woman's most intimate moments, but Maximilian had needed to do it. He hadn't hoped to discover any of the secrets StarWeb had said Ishbel trailed behind her, nor had he hoped to discover the true reasons behind her journey to this point (whatever Ishbel thought they might be). What he'd wanted to do was discover, as best he might, the real Ishbel, the woman behind whatever intrigue she carried with her, and this was, he thought, one of the few times he would be able to observe her completely naked, physically, emotionally, and spiritually.

What he had discovered was that, no matter the exterior she showed to the world, Ishbel was very vulnerable and very sad.

He had discovered that she didn't have the mark of the Coil anywhere on her body.

And Maximilian had discovered that he wanted this woman for his wife.

It was not so much her physical beauty—Ishbel was a lovely woman with her mass of dark blond hair, her soft hazel eyes, translucent skin, and strong lithe body—but her quietness of movement that attracted Maximilian. StarWeb had said that Ishbel was very unquiet, but her movements about the room had been so soft, so simple, so contained, that Maximilian thought that she would be a very peaceful woman to have at his side.

If he could ever trust her, and if she could ever forgive him this inexcusable intrusion into her privacy.

He moved, breathed just a little more heavily, disturbed the shadows clinging to him, and Ishbel instantly realized his presence.

She leapt to her feet, staring at him, and Maximilian very slowly unfolded his arms, straightened up from the wall, and stepped forward.

"Ishbel—"

"You are Maximilian."

He came to a halt some three or four paces from her and gave a slow nod, his eyes not leaving hers. She was angry and hurt and frightened, and he was surprised by none of those. He was also intrigued: she had not taken a step back at his approach, and, even with her knowing who he was, he would have expected that.

"How long have you been standing there?"

"Since you entered," Maximilian said.

She drew in a long breath, her eyes huge, her face paling, then suddenly flaring in color.

"Yes," Maximilian said, "you may think all those things of me, and more. My behavior has been inexcusable, but necessary."

"Why?" The word was shot at him, almost hissed.

"Because I needed to see you for who you are, without any artifice."

"And for that *you* used all the artifice you could muster."

He tilted his head, conceding the point, his eyes still locked onto hers.

"I am sorry you are so very alone here," he said, and that sympathy accomplished what his previous words had not.

Her eyes flooded with tears, and her shoulders sagged. She half turned away from him, a hand over her mouth.

"Can we talk?" Maximilian said. He had taken a step closer to her.

"No. Go away."

"It is better we talk now, than be forced to talk before our assembled retinues at our 'official' meeting at my 'official' arrival' in three days' time. Far better we talk now, Ishbel." He took another step closer.

"*Go away!*"

"Ishbel . . ." Now Maximilian was very close, and she turned back, ready to throw off his hand.

But he was standing again as he had been when first she'd seen him, arms folded, leaning this time against the high post at the end of the bed.

"Why do you want to marry me?" he said.

"I don't." Ishbel was too tired, and still too shocked by Maximilian's appearance, to dissemble.

"Then why are you here?"

"Because the Coil told me to come. They were the ones who insisted I marry you."

"Why?"

A small hesitation. "I don't know." And that was only a small white lie, Ishbel thought. She had no idea at all why the Great Serpent thought marriage to this man would make a difference.

"They are prepared to offer me you and all your riches . . . just because . . ."

"I have never questioned the way of the Coil," Ishbel said, relieved that a measure of dignity had crept back into her voice.

He smiled, and Ishbel was taken aback by the difference it made to his face. He had striking looks with his aquiline nose and deep blue eyes, but was somewhat forbidding (not even considering the circumstances of his arrival into her room). But his smile lit up his face and made his eyes dance with mischievousness.

"You were honest," he said. "Thank you. But you do realize," he went on, "that once married to you, I will owe the Coil no debt? They have offered you, but I shall not be tied to them through that offering."

"They would not expect it."

"I am marrying you, not the Coil."

"I did not realize we had settled definitely on the marriage."

He smiled again, that slow, mischievous smile.

"And StarWeb?" Ishbel said, desperate to say something, anything.

He sobered immediately. "I apologize for StarWeb. She took matters too far. She—"

"She took matters as far as you gave her license."

"I wanted to push you. To see if—"

"You have almost pushed me too far," Ishbel said very softly.

"Then take my hand," he said, holding out his left hand, "and let me pull you back from the brink."

She waited a full five heartbeats, wishing she had the strength and the resources to clasp her hands behind her back and step away from him. Then, with a soft sigh of resignation, Ishbel offered up her hand.

Maximilian clasped it in his, then jerked a little, his eyes widening.

In that instant, as his flesh touched hers, Maximilian's entire world tipped on its axis. Gods! He had expected everything but this!

Ishbel might bear the name Brunelle, but she carried within her the ancient bloodlines of Persimius.

Maybe she did *carry with her the ancient, lost memories!*

While Maximilian's mind and heart were in turmoil, his calm exterior returned virtually instantaneously.

"I seem to have arrived most unexpectedly," he said, "and do not have a place for the night. May I sleep in your bed, my Lady Ishbel Brunelle?"

CHAPTER FIFTEEN

Pelemere, Central Kingdoms

Ishbel allowed him to do what he wanted, for two reasons. First, the Great Serpent had told her to allow nothing to stand in the way of this marriage, and Ishbel supposed that refusing Maximilian here might anger him enough to withdraw his offer. But the principal reason Ishbel allowed Maximilian to lead her slowly, gently, toward the bed was that he overwhelmed her utterly. She had expected to find a man who was . . . tedious. Someone she might regard with contempt. Nothing she'd heard had prepared her for the sheer presence and, she had to admit it, charm, of the man. She was tired and emotionally overwrought, but she could use neither of these states as an excuse.

Ishbel was simply incapable of refusing him.

Besides, when he'd touched her, something had happened. He had been shocked for a moment, and she . ... well, there had been something . . . enough, when combined with everything else, to strip Ishbel of all resistance.

He led her to the bed, took her face in gentle hands, and kissed her.

Ishbel struggled momentarily, then relaxed, again succumbing to whatever presence it was that Maximilian commanded. She allowed him to unclothe her (he had already witnessed her naked, what did it matter now?), and to run his hands and mouth over her body, and to bear her down to the bed and then, eventually, to mount and enter her.

It was not as abhorrent as she had expected. It was easier to relax and to allow his warmth and care to comfort her than it was to resist, or fear.

He was, she supposed, a good lover. She understood that he took great care with her, was infinitely gentle, and suffused their bedding with a self-deprecating humor that had her, unbelievably, smiling with genuine humor on one or two occasions.

There was some pain, a little discomfort, but mostly . . . an extraordinary sense of sinking into someone else's care. Ishbel had expected to feel used or violated, but Maximilian made her feel none of these things.

Everything about him was not what she had expected.

They lay in the dim light in silence for some time, then Maximilian propped himself on an elbow.

"You are such a mystery," he said. "Not what I expected."

"Neither are you what I expected," she said, a hint of dryness in her voice.

"Tell me about where you come from. Tell me about the Coil."

She tensed. "They took me in and cared for me when no one else would. I owe them everything."

"Save your loyalty, for that you shall shortly owe me."

She turned her head and looked at him. "Of course."

"Of course," he echoed. "Ishbel, I need to know that when you become my wife, then your loyalty will be *mine*, not left lingering with a . . . a . . ."

"With *what*? A bunch of murderous soothsayers?"

"They do not provide the best family for any bride, Ishbel. *Why* did they send you to me?"

"I don't know."

Maximilian wondered if she was lying. He didn't know her well enough to tell. Did she understand the ancient mysteries, or had she no knowledge at all? She sounded genuine, but . . .

"All your estates and inheritances," he said, "to be given to me, along with yourself. Why? Surely there were greater and better alliances the Coil—"

"All I know is that Aziel, the archpriest, told me that the Great Serpent instructed him that we would make a good marriage, and that it would be good for the land."

"Ah . . ." For a moment Maximilian tried to believe that the *only* reason Light had sent Ishbel to him was to strengthen the Persimius line. It was a seductive and reassuring idea—*that was the only reason Ishbel had come to him*—but Maximilian knew he could not ignore the vision he'd had on the way to Pelemere. "What about your family, Ishbel? The Brunelle family. Is Brunelle an Outlander name? Or an émigré from . . . somewhere else?"

"Outlander." Her voice and body were more relaxed now. "We have always been Outlanders."

"Hmmm. The family had no contact with Escator?"

"I was eight when I lost my family, Maximilian. I have no idea who my father corresponded with."

"I'm sorry. I am asking too many questions, but I want to understand you so much." He paused, one hand gently stroking her shoulder and upper arm. "Tell me about when you lost your family. When the plague struck and—"

"I'd rather not." Ishbel paused. "Not now. Sometime else, perhaps."

"Of course. We have, after all, a lifetime."

"And will you tell me about your time in the Veins, if I ask?"

"Yes, I will do that." Ishbel was very touchy, which Maximilian could understand given the circumstances of the night, and he also understood that further questions likely would not be a good idea, but he wanted desperately to know how much she understood about her bloodlines. Thus far she'd given no indication she understood anything, either about her Persimius heritage or about Elcho Falling.

"When I first received the offer of your hand from the Coil," Maximilian said, "I looked at a map of the Outlands to see where Serpent's Nest was. A mountain home, yes?"

"Yes."

"Right on the edge of the world," Maximilian said softly, watching Ishbel carefully.

"Serpent's Nest is on the east coastline of the Outlands," she said. "It is . . ."

"Yes?"

She shrugged. "I was going to say that it is my home."

"Was."

She did not reply.

"A mountain is a strange place for a home."

She sighed. "Maximilian . . ."

"I know, I'm sorry." He leaned over and kissed her softly. She did not return it, and he knew he had stayed long enough. Besides, it would be dawn soon, and he had a long ride ahead of him to rejoin Egalion and Garth and the Emerald Guard—all of whom were no doubt fretting about his continued absence.

"I have to go," he said. "I should be out of the house by dawn."

"You need to leave while the darkness still affords you cover," Ishbel said.

He hesitated a little before replying. "Yes. I shall tell you about that one day, if you want."

She nodded, not really knowing what to say, only wishing that having said he would go, he actually would. The thought of solitude brought her a rush of relief. Perhaps, then, she could finally relax and snatch a few brief hours of sleep.

As if in answer to her prayers Maximilian rolled away from her and rose from the bed. He hunted about in the dark for his clothes, dressed, then sat down on her side of the bed as he pulled on his boots.

Having buckled both boots, he sat still, looking at her. "I had no idea I would want you so much," he said. "I distrusted you and—"

"Still do," Ishbel said.

"Aye, yes, still do, although I distrust the motives of the Coil more. I shall be a watchful husband, Ishbel."

"We have not yet agreed on marriage, Maximilian."

He laughed, then leaned down and kissed her. "You *must* marry me, Ishbel. You have completely ruined my reputation with your seductions, and only marriage will save my name."

She smiled reluctantly, but with genuine humor.

Maximilian rose. "The King of Escator shall arrive with his full retinue in three days, Ishbel. He shall be gladder to see you than he had expected."

He took several steps to the door, hesitated, then strode

back to the bed and kissed Ishbel one more time, hard. "Three days, Ishbel," he whispered, then left her.

Maximilian cloaked himself once more in the darkness, walking through the house undiscovered. Once in the stable, he located his horse's stall, then stood for a long moment, his forehead resting gently against the horse's neck, thinking.

Elcho Falling was more likely than not about to stir, and Maximilian needed to marry this woman and return to Escator. There to . . . well, there to see what happened next. *If* Elcho Falling was about to stir, then Maximilian would need to be home in Escator.

Ishbel. Gods knows how they were blood-connected, or how many generations ago the Persimius family had splintered, but connected they most certainly were. Maximilian had not planned to seduce her. But having once taken her hand, he was unable to resist her. Partly this was their shared Persimius blood, but mostly it was the woman herself.

She was astounding. Maximilian replayed every moment of their lovemaking in his mind, remembering how she had felt beneath his hands and body, her scent and her taste. If, one day, she might respond to him with genuine passion . . . oh gods . . . what a day that would be.

His ring chattered softly, asking if they were leaving soon. It had been quiet all night, as Maximilian had instructed it when they'd entered the house, and now it was restless.

"Yes," whispered Maximilian. "Yes, we are leaving now."

After Maximilian had left, Ishbel slept.

She dreamed.

She walked through a hall that glittered with glass and color that spiraled in strange corkscrews far overhead.

She dreamed people filled this hall, tens of thousands of them, all standing back to allow her passage, all watching her.

She dreamed that she was filled with loss and sorrow, and in her dream she sobbed, because she knew what that sorrow portended.

In her hands she carried a goblet. It was heavy, made of exquisitely carved glass, with leaping frogs all about its outer rim.

It was a gift for the man who stood, his back to her, at the far end of the hall.

He was a dark man, and blackness seethed about him.

More than anything Ishbel wanted to turn and run, but her feet would not follow her command. Instead they carried her inexorably forward, until she stood before the man, and then her traitor legs bent beneath her, and she abased herself, and held out the Goblet of the Frogs to the Lord of Elcho Falling.

He turned his head a little, looking at her over his shoulder, and darkness and despair engulfed Ishbel's life.

[Part Three]

CHAPTER ONE

Pelemere, Central Kingdoms

Ishbel stood in the covered courtyard, listening to the approach of Maximilian Persimius, King of Escator. Maximilian had arrived in Pelemere the previous afternoon, received by King Sirus of Pelemere in two formal ceremonies: the first at the city gates, the second at the palace itself. Maximilian had then stayed at Sirus' palace overnight, being royally dined and entertained.

To none of these events had Ishbel been invited. She was still merely the Lady Ishbel Brunelle, prospective wife of the King of Escator, and until Maximilian formally accepted her as his bride, Ishbel was excluded from the royal receptions and entertainments. Today, however, having partaken of Sirus' hospitality and having also, presumably, slept the night away in a luxurious apartment within the king's palace, Maximilian was paying a visit to the Lady Ishbel's house in order to meet her and, should that meeting prove satisfactory, perhaps open more personal negotiations for a marriage.

What a farce all this is, thought Ishbel, listening to the sound of horses' hooves and jingling bits getting closer. *Four nights ago he spent the night in my bed, and here we must act as if we've never seen each other.*

Ishbel had expected Maximilian might appear in her bedchamber last night as well. She'd spent virtually the entire night awake, watching every shadow, listening, waiting. But Maximilian had not appeared, and Ishbel supposed Sirus had provided more amusing entertainments for Maximilian.

Perhaps StarWeb was with him.

Ishbel was far more nervous than she liked. She didn't

know how she would feel when she saw Maximilian again, and she had a tiny, niggling, horrible fear that when Maximilian rode into the courtyard it wouldn't be the same man she'd slept with a few nights ago.

Twisted in with all her anxiety and nervousness was a horrible sense of resentment: *Had* Maximilian spent last night with StarWeb? *Was* she going to have to share her husband with the birdwoman?

There were shouts from the guards at the gate now, and Ishbel barely had time to draw in a hasty, shaking breath before Maximilian rode into the courtyard at the head of a retinue some twenty strong. Dressed in a wine-colored velvet jacket quilted with seed pearls over dark leather breeches, he looked very different from the night he'd appeared in Ishbel's chamber. Very regal and, impossibly, even more certain of himself.

Ishbel's first emotion was one of profound relief—this *was* the man who had come to her bedchamber.

Her second emotion was one of overwhelming confusion at just how glad she was to see him again, and how desperately she hoped StarWeb wasn't in Pelemere.

Strangely, although Ishbel continued to resent everything to do with this marriage, as well as the marriage itself, Maximilian was the only thing she had resembling a friend within eight weeks' travel.

Maximilian pulled his horse to a halt, lifted his right leg over the horse's wither, and slid to the ground.

His eyes never left Ishbel the entire time.

She was very nervous. She held herself extremely still, watching him with apparent calmness, but he could see her nerves in the spots of color in her cheeks, in her overbright eyes, in her rigidity of bearing, and in the manner in which she pressed the palms of her hands too close to her silken skirts.

Behind him the rest of his entourage drew their horses to a halt. They would not dismount, not even move, until Maximilian had greeted Ishbel.

He walked up to her, very deliberately, slowly pulling the

leather gloves from his hands. The wind whipped his dark hair into his eyes, but he didn't blink, or make any move to brush it away.

"My Lady Brunelle," he said, coming to a halt before Ishbel. "How pleasant to finally meet you. I trust your journey to this point has been comfortable?"

She wanted to shout at him, he could see it in her face, and his eyes crinkled in amusement. Taking a final step forward he took her right hand and raised it to his lips. "Thank the gods I picked the right bedchamber four nights ago," he murmured. "All this time I've been terrified I might have seduced the laundress instead."

She relaxed. Her shoulders lost their tension, and she let out her breath on a shaky soft sigh.

"*Are* you all right, Ishbel?" he asked, serious now.

"Yes," she said, having pushed her dream of the Lord of Elcho Falling to the very back of her mind. "Yes, I am."

Baron Lixel now stepped up, greeted Maximilian warmly, and made the formal introductions. Then Maximilian turned and waved forward two members of his entourage: a young man who Ishbel thought was a year or so younger than herself, and an older man who was the captain of Maximilian's escort and who wore an emerald uniform jacket with a Manteceros outlined in brilliant blue on its front.

"Commander Egalion," Maxel said, introducing the older man first. "He captains my Emerald Guard, and is one of my closest friends."

Ishbel held out her hand for Egalion to take. "Commander," she murmured politely.

"And this is Garth Baxtor," Maximilian continued as Egalion stepped back to make way for the younger man. "Garth is court physician, another close companion."

Baxtor had an open, attractive face, very nonthreatening, and Ishbel liked him immediately. She smiled as she held out her hand for Garth.

"Physician Baxtor," she said as his fingers closed about hers.

Unlike Egalion, Garth did not immediately let go of Ishbel's hand. A strange, but not unpleasing, warm sensation passed through Ishbel's fingers and suddenly all the friendliness in Garth's eyes vanished.

"My Lady Brunelle," he said, dropping her hand before stepping back so abruptly it was almost rude.

Maximilian frowned, but then Lixel was ushering them all inside, and Maximilian contented himself with taking Ishbel's arm and asking her about her journey to Pelemere as they entered the house.

All the light had gone from Garth's day. All he wanted now was to speak with Maximilian urgently, but Maximilian was not leaving Ishbel's side. They had gone from the courtyard into the main reception room of the house, where to Garth's surprise (and Lixel's, and just about everyone else's except, he noted, Ishbel's), Maximilian pronounced an intention to get down to the nitty-gritty of the final details of the marriage contract between himself and the Lady Ishbel immediately.

"You have no objections, my lady?" Maximilian said to Ishbel.

She hesitated very slightly, then shook her head. "None, my lord."

"Well then, Lixel," Maximilian said, "to work! Do you have the necessary documents to hand?"

Still looking taken aback, Lixel showed Maximilian and Ishbel into a secondary chamber, where Maximilian closed the doors firmly on the entourage.

Garth and Egalion exchanged a look. "What was that all about?" Egalion said.

"I have no idea." Garth stared at the closed door, almost too shocked to be capable of coherent thought. For weeks and weeks Maximilian had been extremely wary. Over the past day or so, however, since his return from his time spent alone, his mood had changed, and he'd appeared far more confident and relaxed about the proposed marriage. Even so, Garth had hardly expected him to leap off his horse, take the lady's hand, and immediately drag her and Lixel into final conference about the matter.

"What do you think of her?" Egalion said. "I'd half anticipated a dumpy pockmarked crone . . . but . . ." He gave a soft laugh. "No wonder Maxel has hurried her off to sign what papers he must."

"I hope he doesn't sign them too fast," Garth murmured. "I need to speak to him. Badly."

Egalion looked at him, frowning. "What did you feel from her, my friend?"

As Maximilian and Ishbel sat down at the table, Lixel retrieved the marriage contracts from a satchel. He couldn't believe Maximilian was moving this precipitously. By gods, there hadn't even been the time for a convivial glass of wine first, let alone any time put aside for Maximilian and Ishbel to see if they liked each other or not.

As Lixel sat down at the table, sliding the contract toward Maximilian, he rather hoped that Maximilian had been so smitten by Ishbel at first sight that the king would grant Lixel immediate permission to return to Escator.

"I believe you have hashed out the contract with StarWeb, Ishbel?" Maximilian said.

"Yes," said Ishbel, and Lixel was not surprised to see a hardening of her expression and a tightening of her shoulders at the mention of StarWeb.

Maximilian nodded, running his eye over the document. "Are you prepared to sign?" He looked up at Ishbel then, and something passed between them that Lixel could not identify.

"If you are agreeable," she said softly.

"I am agreeable, Ishbel," Maximilian said. "Shall we make a marriage, then?"

There was a long pause, then Ishbel dipped her head. "Yes."

Lixel's mouth dropped open. Never had he witnessed such an unemotional, almost clinical assenting to a marriage. Why not spend time together, getting to know each other? Wasn't that what this entire exercise of meeting in Pelemere had been about?

"Lixel," said Maximilian, "can you fetch Garth and Egalion in to witness?"

Lixel closed his mouth, nodded, and did as he was told.

* * *

Garth had not answered Egalion's question truthfully. He couldn't. Not before he'd spoken to Maximilian. He'd fudged an answer, and was grasping about for something to say to distract Egalion when the door to the secondary chamber opened, Lixel appeared, and requested Garth and Egalion enter.

Garth could not believe what was happening. Maximilian was about to sign the contract within a few minutes of meeting the woman for the first time. *What in the name of all gods was he doing?*

Maximilian was running through the clauses, checking them, as Garth and Egalion entered.

"This one . . ." he said, tapping the document and looking between Ishbel and Lixel. "How did this come to be here?"

"StarWeb insisted on it," said Ishbel, her tone strained. "She said you would not ratify the marriage, declare it valid, until I was . . . um . . ." She glanced up at Garth and Egalion, clearly embarrassed.

As she has every reason to be, thought Garth, getting angrier by the moment.

"Until you were pregnant and in Ruen," said Maximilian. "Well, I think we can dispense with that, yes?" and with a single stroke of the pen he drew a thick black line through the clause. "Now, Ishbel, if you would sign here, if you please—"

"No!" Garth broke in. "No. Maxel, I beg you, a moment of your time, please."

Maximilian looked at him. "Explain yourself, Garth."

"Maxel," Garth said, "a moment of your time, *I beg you.* If you care or trust me at all, then grant me this moment. *Please.*"

Maximilian looked at Ishbel. "I apologize most sincerely for this unwelcome intrusion," he said, then rose, walked over to Garth, took his elbow in an ungentle hand, and ushered him out of the room.

"Garth!" Maximilian said. "What was the meaning of *that*?"

"Maxel, Ishbel is pregnant."

Maximilian went utterly still. *"What?"*

"Not much, perhaps a week . . . she has only just conceived. But she *is* pregnant. You know I can feel this."

Maximilian nodded. Garth had the Touch; determining an early pregnancy was but a trivial task for him. "And so," he said, "your point is . . ."

Garth was growing more astounded by the moment. Maximilian's anger had faded and he was now regarding Garth with an amused air.

"The Lady Ishbel is not as virtuous as you had hoped, Maxel," Garth said, wondering if he needed to put this into one-syllable words for Maximilian to comprehend. "Dear gods, my friend, you would take a woman to wife when she's carrying someone else's bastard?"

Maximilian grinned, the expression so surprising that Garth felt his mouth drop open. "It's my child, Garth."

Garth was now so shocked he could not speak.

"Where did you think I went," Maximilian said, "when I rode ahead of the main retinue and left you and Egalion to your own company for well over a week?"

Garth gazed at him, struggling to come to terms with what Maximilian had done. "You said . . . the forest . . ."

"Yes, yes," Maximilian said, waving a hand dismissively. Then he smiled, and actually winked. "Changed my mind. Thought I'd see if I couldn't make Ishbel's acquaintance under less strained circumstances than a formal meeting."

"Well, you surely made it very well," Garth muttered.

Maximilian laughed and clapped Garth on the shoulder. "She is well with the child?"

"Yes. Yes, she is well. There is no problem that I could feel."

"Good. Then perhaps you can come back in and apologize to my future wife for your behavior."

Garth wasn't going to allow Maximilian to get away with this entirely. "And perhaps, later, when your future wife is safely out of hearing range, you can apologize to Egalion and myself for your deception."

"A bargain," said Maximilian, and led the way back into the room.

* * *

Ishbel was growing more certain that her entire time as
Maximilian's wife would be spent in this terrible state of
feeling completely overwhelmed. Maximilian had arrived,
greeted her, swept her inside, asked for the marriage contract,
scratched out the clause StarWeb had fought so hard for, and
all within a relatively few short minutes. Ishbel doubted that
enough time had yet elapsed from his arrival for his entire
entourage to have completely dismounted.

Adding to this sense of feeling completely overwhelmed
by Maximilian was a stab of hurt that Garth Baxtor had so
obviously taken an immediate and deep dislike to her. Ishbel
had liked Garth—he had such an open, friendly attractive
face which invited instant trust—but then he'd taken her
hand and within a heartbeat his face had closed over and he
had turned his back to her.

And now he'd demanded that Maximilian talk with him
privately.

What had Garth discovered? Ishbel's heart was beating
fast, pounding in her chest, and her hands were damp where
she clutched them in her lap. Garth had felt *something* when
he'd touched her . . . *Great Serpent, please let it be that he
hadn't felt—*

Maximilian and Garth reentered the room, and Ishbel
jumped slightly in sheer nervousness.

Maximilian looked at her with amusement—and something else that she couldn't quite fathom—although at least
the amusement reassured Ishbel somewhat, but Garth's
change in attitude was nothing short of extraordinary.

"My Lady Ishbel," he said, dropping to one knee beside
her chair, his face alive once more with friendliness, "I must
beg your pardon for my behavior earlier. Sometimes I can be
a clump-headed fool, and too often I underestimate Maxel's
courage and daring. Will you forgive my former behavior? I
promise herewith that in future I shall ask before judging."

Ishbel had no idea at all what was going on about her.
She glanced again at Maximilian, more for reassurance than
anything else, then, at his slight nod, gave Garth a small and
somewhat uncertain smile.

"Of course," she said.

Garth's smiled broadened slightly, then he rose. "I beg everyone's forgiveness for my rudeness." He winked at Egalion, who was looking as confused as Ishbel felt, then stepped back a little from the table.

"'Maxel'?" Ishbel said to Maximilian, more to fill in the silence than out of any real curiosity.

"Maximilian is such a mouthful," he said. "Those closest to me always call me Maxel, and I hope you will, too."

Ishbel gave another uncertain smile, unable to stop herself imagining StarWeb calling out the name in the grip of passion, then cursing herself yet again for being weak enough to allow StarWeb to rattle her. *By the Great Serpent,* Ishbel thought, *what has happened to me? I am a stronger person than this.*

"Now." Maximilian sat down and spun the marriage contract toward him. He picked up a pen. "All we need decide on is a date for the marriage. I don't think we need wait, Ishbel. Shall the day after tomorrow be suitable?"

"I do not see the need to rush," Ishbel said. "I had thought this period in Pelemere was to be spent getting to know each other. I—"

"Ishbel," Maximilian said quietly.

Ishbel made the mistake of looking at him, and seeing the expression in his eyes. Seeing the *memory* in his eyes. *Why do I bother with this?* she wondered. *The Great Serpent wants me to marry him, after all.*

"The day after tomorrow," she agreed, and Maximilian smiled, then signed the document. He pushed the contract and pen over to Ishbel and, after the barest of hesitations, she signed as well, wishing she had the courage to list her true titles under her name.

CHAPTER TWO

Pelemere, Central Kingdoms

Ishbel's status changed the instant she signed the marriage
contract. Suddenly no longer the Lady Ishbel Brunelle, orphan of the Outlands and potential wife to King Maximilian
of Escator, now she was the affianced wife of Escator, due all
the respect and honor that position commanded.

As soon as Ishbel laid down the pen, Maximilian was
standing, requesting Egalion to send a member of the Emerald
Guard back to Sirus' palace and inform him of the upcom-
ing marriage. King Sirus, who had happily ignored Ishbel
to this point, would now allocate Ishbel quarters within the
palace for her use over the next two days, and would prepare
to regally welcome her as if she were only newly arrived into
Pelemere.

"You don't have much to pack, do you?" Maximilian
asked Ishbel. "Perhaps we can depart for the palace before
noon and have you settle in."

"I can be ready soon," said Ishbel, turning for the door.

"Ishbel."

She turned back, looking at Maximilian.

"Sirus has no idea of your association with the Coil," he
said. "No one outside this room does. I would prefer it stay
that way. You are the Lady Ishbel Brunelle of Margalit. Not
Ishbel of the Coil. Your association with them ends as of this
moment."

Garth Baxtor, watching, saw Ishbel's face mottle with
emotion, and he had his first intimation of how much loyalty she owed the Coil. He sympathized with that—they had,
after all, taken her in when no one else would—but he also

thought she must surely understand Maximilian's request. A Queen of Escator—a queen of *anywhere*—simply could not have any ties at all with something as controversial and abhorrent as the Coil.

"You know how much I owe the—" Ishbel began.

"I know it," said Maximilian, "but you must also know full well how reviled the Coil are beyond its front gates. For good reason. You are now my affianced wife, and soon to be queen. Your association with the Coil ends *here* and *now*."

Garth looked between them, intrigued by this clash of wills.

Ishbel was by now very pale, and holding herself absolutely rigid. Garth thought she was very close to losing her composure completely. He wondered if this was why Maximilian had chosen this very public time to have this conversation with Ishbel—she would likely be more circumspect in public than she would in private.

"Turn your eyes forward, Ishbel," Maximilian said very quietly, holding her furious gaze. "Look forward now to your new life. Forget the Coil. You'll never go back."

At that moment Garth saw something flare deep in Ishbel's eyes. She struggled with herself, managed to control her temper with a supreme effort, gave a jerk of her head, and left the room.

There was a silence, broken eventually by Baron Lixel huffing in embarrassment and gathering up the papers. "I'll, um, get these in order then," he said, and hurried from the room.

Maximilian looked over to Garth.

"Are you *sure* you want to marry this woman, Maxel?" Garth asked gently.

"I need a wife," Maximilian said, "and Escator needs wealth. I want children and she is pregnant. She will do."

Then he, too, left the room, leaving Garth staring after him.

Ishbel sat on her bed in her chamber, clothes scattered about her, trembling in absolute fury. She had never been so angry and so humiliated in all her life.

Who was *he* to tell *her* to forget the Coil?

She couldn't stop shaking, and she hated that. She beat her fists slowly on the bed, despising herself for capitulating to him.

Again.

What Ishbel hated most, though, was that she understood *why* Maximilian had said what he had. She was going to have to come to terms with the outside world's revulsion of the way of the Coil.

Slowly she managed to relax. She would never mention the Coil to Maximilian again. She would not defend it, nor allude to it. She would, to all intents and purposes, turn her eyes forward as he had commanded.

"But I will not turn my back on you, Great One," Ishbel whispered, and made the sign of the Coil over her belly with her right fist.

What Maximilian did not understand was that the Coil lay as much in her future as it did in her past.

She *was* the Coil.

CHAPTER THREE

Margalit, the Outlands

Ba'al'uz had been traveling north for many weeks. It had been tiresome, difficult, and very often dangerous, but he had enjoyed every moment of it. He'd never traveled beyond the borders of the Tyranny previously, and he found the exposure to different cultures and peoples exhilarating and rewarding.

He despised everyone he met, of course, but that only added to the serenity of his own world and to his belief that there were very few people in the world worth truly caring about. Late one night, lying wrapped in his blanket in the extreme northern reaches of the Salamaan Pass, watching crisp stars weaving their majesty through the sky, Ba'al'uz had a moment of absolute revelation: the lives of men and women were worthless. There was only himself, and Kanubai waiting inside DarkGlass Mountain, and the future that mattered.

Kanubai continued to whisper in his mind throughout the journey. He also whispered in the minds of the eight men Ba'al'uz traveled with, although never as clearly as in Ba'al'uz' mind.

The Eight were receptive. Ba'al'uz had, after all, chosen well in his companions. To augment Kanubai's whisperings, Ba'al'uz related to the men the powers and riches that could be theirs if they allied themselves with the powerful Kanubai.

Better allied with him, Ba'al'uz argued, *than set against him.*

The Eight agreed. Their lives were as nothing under Isaiah. Kanubai clearly promised better.

Ba'al'uz said to the Eight that an army would be theirs for the taking if they pledged Kanubai their loyalty, and with that army they would control the world.

"Kanubai," said Ba'al'uz, "wishes me to be his general and you his captains."

The Eight looked at him long and hard at that, but they agreed.

Better to be allied with He Who Approached, and his captains, than die as his enemy.

"There is nothing in this world but Kanubai," said Ba'al'uz one night, and the Eight nodded in complete agreeance.

"Everything," said Ba'al'uz, "must be subsumed to him."

"Everything," murmured the Eight.

"Including us," said Ba'al'uz.

There was a small hesitation. "Including us," the Eight eventually muttered.

"Although we, naturally, shall enjoy great rewards and privileges for our work on his behalf."

"Naturally," the Eight agreed, no hesitation this time.

"He needs to feed," said Ba'al'uz.

"Yes," said the Eight.

"It has been a very long time since he has fed."

"Of course."

"If we show Kanubai our devotion in this small matter," said Ba'al'uz, "then I am certain he shall be grateful."

Subsequently, on their passage northward through Adab and then through the Outlands toward Margalit, Ba'al'uz and the Eight, periodically, and very, very carefully and quietly, embarked on a campaign of murder. Not very much; just a life here and there and none who would be missed too greatly. These lives they offered to Kanubai, and to Dark-Glass Mountain itself. Whenever possible, Ba'al'uz and the Eight gathered about the dying victim, watching the light fade from his or her eyes, sensing that far, far away, Kanubai grew stronger for the food.

Besides, the odd murder here and there was good practice for what lay ahead.

At night, Kanubai whispered ever more clearly in Ba'al'uz' mind, and told him of an object he wanted.

Very badly.

The object, as strange as it seemed, was sure to cast Isaiah down into the bleakness of the abyss that Kanubai would shortly vacate. Delighted by the prospect, Ba'al'uz agreed to fetch the object once his business in the north was concluded.

Whatever loyalty he'd once owed Isaiah (not much, in any case) was now long gone.

Ba'al'uz was Kanubai's, through and through.

After many weeks of travel Ba'al'uz and the Eight arrived at Margalit. Here, once they were fed and settled and bathed and had enjoyed a few good nights of sleep in comfortable beds, they would embark on the initial stages of creating the chaos needed to pave the way for Isaiah's and Lister's invasion. The only reason they continued to act as Isaiah and Lister expected them to was because their purpose suited Kanubai as much as it suited Isaiah and Lister. It was for Kanubai's sake that Ba'al'uz and his Eight continued on with the plan.

But first, definitely, a bit of rest and recreation. A murder would have been vastly enjoyable, but Ba'al'uz was circumspect within Margalit. There was just one man they wanted to murder here, and that not for a few days; no point risking discovery for the sake of a moment or two of extra enjoyment. So, instead of hunting out a victim, the group took themselves off to a local tavern, where Ba'al'uz expected to derive abundant pleasure from a goodly intake of alcohol, and perhaps as much again from observing the Outlanders at recreation, which Ba'al'uz felt sure would further bolster his own sense of superiority.

Instead, he discovered something vastly more interesting.

Ba'al'uz and his companions did not wish to advertise their true origins, so they were dressed in the manner of Adab, and speaking with Adabian accents, which the power of Kanubai (which now infused all of them, if the Eight to a lesser extent than Ba'al'uz) allowed them to assume flawlessly.

They arrived at the tavern fairly early, and thus were able to find comfortable seating at the rear, where they would not be crowded and which was also conveniently close to the dispensing tap for the ale. The tavern keeper served them himself, then asked if they minded if he sat down with them for five or ten minutes to rest his aching legs and to share a glass of ale, and to gossip, which Ba'al'uz was soon to discover was the tavern keeper's primary reason for existence.

For a while the nine Isembaardians sat and drank as the tavern keeper chatted. There seemed to be no stopping him. They learned who was sleeping with whom within the entire Outlands; they discovered who had hobbled the favorite at the recent festive race meeting; they were quietly astounded to realize that Outlanders rather liked to expose their bottoms to people as a gesture of great rudeness.

"When the arses start flashing in here," the tavern keeper said, a righteous frown on his face, "then that's the time I start knocking heads together."

"Uh huh," said Ba'al'uz, incapable of further comment.

"It gets even worse when they add a fart or two to the insult," said the tavern keeper.

Ba'al'uz paused with his glass partway to his lips, appalled. By the great Kanubai, did any race more deserve to be completely overrun and obliterated than the Outlanders?

The tavern keeper sighed, despondent at the outrages he had to police. "I am just grateful that when the Lady Ishbel Brunelle stayed two houses down she did not think to visit my humble establishment. I cannot imagine what she would have thought had someone pushed his hairy arse into her face."

Brunelle? Brunelle?

Ba'al'uz froze. That had been Kanubai, whispering frantically in his mind. He looked at his companions. Without exception, they were all staring at the innkeeper in disgust. None of them had heard Kanubai's whisper.

The tavern keeper sniffed, wiping his nose with a corner of his apron. "Not that any of the high and mighty Brunelle family would ever visit with *me*."

"The Brunelle family?" Ba'al'uz said. Kanubai was still whispering madly in his head, now formless words of which Ba'al'uz could make neither head nor tail.

What he did know, though, was that this woman was of great interest to Kanubai.

The tavern keeper nodded. "Yes. The Brunelle family. Own most of Margalit, if you ask me, and I've heard they control vast fortunes in the Central Kingdoms as well. Ishbel was the surviving child of a terrible time. Plague took her entire family . . ."

As he continued prattling on about Ishbel's life story, one part of Ba'al'uz' mind was taking in everything the innkeeper said, while another part was trying to work out how he could use this information to further his cause with Kanubai.

"Someone took her in, don't know who," the innkeeper was saying, "but lo and behold she turned up at Baron Lixel's residence a couple of months ago . . . that's the big graywood house three down . . . had a really nice veranda put on it two years ago. If ever you need a good builder I can thoroughly recommend—"

"Ishbel Brunelle," said Ba'al'uz, desperately trying to return the conversation to the matter at hand.

The very, very important matter at hand.

"Ishbel—is she still in residence?" Ba'al'uz added.

The tavern keeper shook his head. "Left weeks ago, with Lixel and his entire entourage. Heard she's off to marry some high and mighty prince of the west." He shrugged. "Why she couldn't have picked a nice boy from her hometown, I don't know."

Possibly she didn't appreciate the flashing arses, thought Ba'al'uz. *Didn't want them with her soup at supper.*

Again he glanced about at his companions. They all watched him carefully, intuiting he'd experienced some kind of revelation at the name of the woman.

"Who?" said Ba'al'uz. "Which prince?"

"The Escatorian king. Maximilian. Lixel is his ambassador to the Outlands."

"She's gone to Escator?" Ba'al'uz said.

"To Pelemere, I think. Then on to Kyros. Leisurely journey. Maximilian is meeting her in Pelemere, and they're taking their time in getting back to Escator. Having a good honeymoon, I expect. Making happy friends with all the kings along the way in case Maximilian needs to borrow money later."

"You seem to know a great deal about their plans," said one of the Eight.

The tavern keeper shrugged. "I know a great deal about everything, don't I? But one of Lixel's men used to come in here and drink and gossip. That's how I know."

That night Ba'al'uz sat and meditated, opening his mind to Kanubai.

The whispers came, very faintly at first, but they gained in strength as the night wore on.

There was much incoherent muttering, but there were several concepts that stood out.

One was Kanubai's continual reference to Elcho Falling, which Ba'al'uz still did not understand.

The next was the name of Ishbel Brunelle, whispered over and over, which told Ba'al'uz that she was very important to Kanubai.

The third was more emotion and image than word, but Ba'al'uz understood it perfectly.

Sacrifice.

CHAPTER FOUR

DarkGlass Mountain, the Tyranny of Isembaard

The night lay very still about DarkGlass Mountain. The river lapped gently among the reed beds, birds shifted within their roosting places, a few cows wandered through a field a hundred paces away from the pyramid.

One of the cows looked up, watching the pyramid for a few minutes as if entranced, then shook its head and wandered off, the spell broken.

The cow was not what Kanubai wanted.

An hour or so later, when even the birds had stilled, a dog came wandering along the road that led along the river by DarkGlass Mountain. It was a brindle mongrel, with a barrel-shaped body and long spindly legs, and a long tattered tail that showed the scars of many street fights. The dog was hungry, for he had found no food in the streets of Aqhat the previous day, and so had swum the river in the hope of finding something in the fields.

Rats, perhaps, or some crumbs left from one of the field-workers' noon meal.

The dog trotted slowly along the road, stopping now and again to sniff at something on the verge, or within the reed banks, but always wandering off disappointed.

Then it caught the scent of gravy.

It instantly made the hungry dog's mouth water, and his ears pricked up. His pace quickened and he followed the scent of the gravy . . .

. . . without thinking, without any caution, straight through the dog-sized hole in the side of DarkGlass Mountain.

* * *

The brindle dog could think of nothing but the scent of the gravy. He trotted, and then ran, along the twisting corridors of fused black glass, not perturbed by the flickering streaks of fire deep within the glass.

There was only the food.

Within a few short minutes the dog arrived within a golden chamber. It was stunningly beautiful, but the dog's ears drooped in disappointment.

There was no food.

Dejected, he sniffed about the perimeter of the chamber, his cold moist nose brushing against the carved golden glass. He went about two walls in that fashion, but halfway along the third he yelped and tried to pull back.

But his nose was firmly stuck to the glass.

The dog growled and redoubled his efforts.

His nose stuck even more firmly.

And then it began to sink into the glass, dragging the dog with it.

The dog struggled, his breath coming in tight wheezes, more through fear than from his efforts.

Nothing helped. Within heartbeats his head was inside the glass, and then his shoulders and forelegs, and then, in one horrible moment, his entire body vanished behind the glass.

But not quite vanished completely. Shadows twisted behind the glass as the dog continued to struggle with whatever had trapped him.

Then everything went black. The entire chamber, constructed of pure golden glass, turned black.

Outside, for an instant, the massive shadow of a struggling dog appeared beneath the blue-green glass of DarkGlass Mountain.

And then everything was still.

The river lapped gently at the reed banks.

The birds shifted within their roosting.

And a brindle dog loped away from the glass pyramid, heading for the ford back to the palace of Aqhat.

Kanubai might still be trapped, but now he had eyes and

ears, and the recently attained knowledge that a Brunelle walked the land gave Kanubai hope that soon he would be able to breathe and walk within his *own* body.

If only Ba'al'uz would do what he needed of him.

CHAPTER FIVE

Pelemere, the Central Kingdoms

Ishbel stood in her finery by the open window of Sirus' palace in Pelemere. She had been at the palace almost two days. Today was her wedding day.

It was deep winter. Snow drifted in the window, scattering a few flakes over Ishbel's bare shoulders and neck and down the front of her ivory satin gown.

She didn't notice, nor seem to be aware of her goose-pimpled flesh. Ishbel stared into the palace grounds—half frozen and solid with snow—and thought about Serpent's Nest, making a promise to herself. She would endure. She would make this marriage, for this was what the Great Serpent demanded of her, and it was for this that he had saved her from the charnel house of her parents' home. When it was done, and the Great Serpent's purpose fulfilled, then she would turn and walk away. He had said that she would return home to Serpent's Nest, that it would be her home forever, and thus this marriage was not a life sentence.

Until then she would manage with dignity. Maximilian was a personable and charming man (if with a will of sheer steel). It would not be terrible.

Ishbel made the sign of the Coil over her belly with her right fist, then sighed and shivered, as if she had realized for the first time how cold she was. She closed the window, brushed away the few snowflakes that had settled on her shoulders and gown, and prepared to do what was needed.

The sooner it was done, the sooner she would eventually go home. Perhaps that might even be sooner rather than later. Ishbel had heard no reports to suggest that the Skraelings were massing in the north, nor any rumors of a great evil rising in the south. Perhaps her actions had already prevented the disaster the Great Serpent had shown her. She still needed to make the marriage, but perhaps in a year or so . . .

A knock sounded at the door, and Ishbel briefly closed her eyes, gathering her strength.

Ishbel did her best, and she thought she did it well enough until that moment Maximilian slid the ring on her finger. Sirus had put on a lovely reception for her and Maximilian, replete with many guests, much wine and food, and music and entertainments. Ishbel managed to smile occasionally, and take wine and, surprisingly, to look and act as if she was enjoying herself.

Then came the ceremony and the stilted words, and then Maximilian took a lovely emerald and ruby ring from his pocket, and slid it on her finger.

Ishbel's world turned instantly to mayhem.

Ishbel! Ishbel! We have waited so long for you! Oh, we are so delighted, and you are so delightful! We—

"Ishbel," Maximilian murmured, his grip tightening on her hand as her face went white with shock. "Ishbel, it is all right. Take a deep breath. *It is all right.*"

Nothing was "right"! Only the fact of Maximilian's grip on her hand kept Ishbel standing. She could barely breathe, and she was aware of nothing in the room save Maximilian and the whispers.

She was back in her parents' house, her mother's corpse gibbering and whispering.

"Be quiet!" Maximilian hissed under his breath and the ring fell silent.

"Ishbel, it is all right. Come on now, look at me, smile for me."

His fingers were very slowly stroking her hand, and Ishbel blinked, managing to focus on his face.

It was very reassuring, his eyes warm and concerned.

"Ishbel?"

Amid her confusion and all the lingering horror, Ishbel realized that everyone was staring at her. She summoned every particle of courage and determination she had, and croaked out the words needed to complete the ceremony.

When it was done and Maximilian leaned to kiss her, he paused with his mouth close to her ear. "I'm sorry, Ishbel. I didn't realize that would frighten you so much. If you put your mind to it you can block out the whispers."

She got through the rest of the afternoon's and evening's public events in a fugue of shock. She supposed she said what was expected of her, and she even allowed Maximilian to lead her onto the dance floor for a wedding dance.

Then, gratefully, it was over and she and Maximilian were alone in their chamber.

The first thing Ishbel did was to slip the ring from her finger and place it on a cabinet.

Relief washed through her, and she relaxed a little, and managed to smile for Maximilian, who was standing watching her.

There were no servants present. The chamber had been prepared but for this night they had been left alone. Now Maximilian came over to her, sliding his hands about her waist.

"I shall have to maid for you, as we have been left so solitary," murmured Maximilian, kissing her shoulder as he began, very gently, to unbutton her gown.

"I hardly need a maid. I was not used to one at . . . at the place I grew up."

"But you are a queen now. You need a bevy of servants"—Maximilian kissed her other shoulder—"and more finery than you can ever wear in a lifetime." The dress had fallen to the floor now, and Maximilian was unlacing her underclothes.

"I am a woman of abstemious nature," Ishbel said.

"Then I shall have to corrupt you."

She laughed, surprising herself. Perhaps she'd had too much wine, but more probably it was the sheer relief at finally losing the ring.

He turned her about to face him. "Was that a laugh, Ishbel? I have never heard you laugh before."

She was sober now, her hazel eyes very clear and calm. "I was raised to be serious and quiet."

"Then I shall have to teach you mayhem and ribaldry."

Her mouth twitched again. "Why can you laugh so much, Maxel"—this was the first time she had called him by his diminutive name—"when you have endured so much in your life?"

"Maybe you need to endure hardship in order to learn to appreciate laughter."

"But still . . ."

"Ishbel, this may surprise you enormously, but tonight is not the time I want to talk about the Veins. Perhaps when we are old and tired and can think of nothing else to entertain ourselves, eh?"

"When we are old and tired then, Maxel," she said, knowing that would never happen.

A few months, a year, and then she could go home. Surely.

He smiled, pulled her close, and kissed her with increasing passion, and she let him do with her what he wanted.

An hour or so later Maximilian lay by his wife, gently stroking her shoulder and arm. There was a lamp lit in a far corner of the chamber, and it cast a soft light over the room and its occupants. It was very late now, but Maximilian did not feel like sleeping. There was far too much to discuss.

The ring.

He ran his hand down to hers and lifted it.

"I am sorry the ring frightened you," he said. "I should have warned you. It was a shock."

She said nothing, but her entire body tensed into rigidity. She was terrified!

Maximilian had no idea why. Yes, the ring would have startled her, perhaps even frightened her, but he'd not expected this depth of reaction.

"It is just the Persimius rings," he said. "They mean no harm. They are irritating, but sometimes also they can be—"

"I do not want to talk about it."

"It is nothing to be frightened of, Ishbel. It—"

She whipped her face about to his. "I do not want it to touch me again."

"Ishbel—"

"I do not want it to touch me again."

Maximilian was glad at that moment that his own ring had kept its silence throughout this day—perhaps it understood Ishbel's fright.

"Ishbel, why so frightened? It *is* nothing of which to be scared."

She burst into tears, which disconcerted Maximilian so greatly he could say no more. He gathered her into his arms and cuddled her close until she finally began to relax, and her tears abated.

Why so frightened?

Eventually she leaned back a little, just enough to wipe her eyes. "What happened with Garth the other day?" she said, a little too brightly and in a patent effort to distract him away from talk of the rings. "We've not had a chance to talk about it since. What did he feel from me?"

Maximilian felt as if he were suspended over a great chasm of doom. How would she react to *this* snippet of news?

"Garth wanted to warn me against marrying you," he said. "He thought you a loose woman, a harlot, a—"

"What? Why should he think—"

"You're pregnant, Ishbel. Garth realized it. He had no idea that we'd already . . . 'met.'"

The chamber was only lit softly, but it was enough for Maximilian to see Ishbel go almost white with shock. She actually stopped breathing, her eyes wide and horrified.

"Ishbel . . . *breathe.*"

She drew in a harsh breath, then sat up suddenly in the bed, hugging her arms about her breasts. "No. I can't be. I *can't* be pregnant!"

"Garth has the Touch very, very powerfully, Ishbel, and he isn't mistaken. You're only a few days pregnant, a week or so, but you *are* pregnant."

"No."

"Yes," Maximilian said softly. "It is what sometimes happens, Ishbel, when a man and a woman lie together."

She glanced at him. "I'm sorry. I'd just not thought . . . a child . . . no."

"Ishbel . . ." He slid his hand over her belly, and she flinched. "Oh, for gods' sakes, Ishbel, what is wrong?"

"Everything," she whispered, then lay down and rolled away from him, and would not speak to him again.

CHAPTER SIX

Pelemere, the Central Kingdoms

Maximilian was surely irritated with her, at her reaction to the news of her pregnancy. Ishbel could understand why, but she had been so shocked, so appalled, so *terrified*, that she'd been unable to act any other way. By the Serpent, to have *that* little surprise dropped on her, on top of the horror of the ring.

Pregnant.

A child.

In her body.

She lay on the bed, Maximilian sleeping beside her, the fingers of one hand fluttering down to her belly, as if she could feel already the turmoil the child was about to create in her life.

She'd not considered the possibility of a child after the night Maximilian had come to her. Why should she? She should not be able to conceive. She had lost her ability to conceive the day she'd been inducted into her position as archpriestess of the Coil when she'd surrendered her reproductive ability to the Great Serpent in return for the blessing of his power. Since then she'd virtually forgotten she *had* a womb.

The only time she'd thought about her inability to conceive had been when StarWeb had been haggling the marriage contract and had insisted on the clause regarding a pregnancy being a required condition for ratification of the marriage. Ishbel had wondered then what excuse she might give Maximilian for her lack of ability to bear a child, and had thought that at least it might give her an excuse to get *out* of the marriage.

But, no, she'd conceived within the first hour of meeting the man.

It made her angry, mainly because she felt so out of control. Everything she had done as archpriestess of the Coil had been so ordered, so sure.

Now . . .

Ishbel lay her hand more firmly on her belly. The growing baby would surely disturb the Coil . . . and this, on top of the shock of the whispers.

Oh, Great Serpent, how could this happen? What should I do?

She must rid herself of the baby. Ishbel had no idea how to do this, but she knew women could manage it. She'd heard they took herbs. All she'd need to do would be to find someone to procure the right herbs and she could—

Suddenly Ishbel went rigid on the bed as the atmosphere in the chamber thickened.

She jerked her head over to look at Maximilian.

He remained asleep.

Then, her heart pounding, Ishbel very slowly turned her head to look at the side of the bed.

A great darkness was coalescing on the floor, at midpoint between the door and the bed.

Ishbel tried to control her breathing, tried to center herself, tried above all to *calm* herself so that she might be fit to greet the Great Serpent.

Very slowly the darkness resolved itself into a massive coiled serpent. It appeared to be made of the darkness itself, its scales so black they were more suggestion than reality, but glimmering here and there with faint rainbow colors as the serpent twisted in the dim lamplight.

The Great Serpent coiled about itself for a minute, then reared its head up so that it loomed over the bed.

Ishbel could not move, nor drag her eyes away from the enormous head that hovered above the bed. She'd been in the presence of the Great Serpent before, of course, but only rarely, and only when she'd been in control of herself and of the situation.

Not ever lying in a bed, with a man, and with a baby in her belly to corrupt the Coil.

The head moved, weaving back and forth, its forked tongue flickering out of its mouth as it tasted the night air. Its eyes were great dark holes with flashes of fire glimmering in their depths.

"Greetings, Great One," Ishbel said, making the sign of the Coil over her belly.

The Great Serpent ignored her. Instead its head wove ever closer to Maximilian, who lay fast asleep on the other side of the bed. It dipped low, then ran its glistening forked tongue slowly up Maximilian's body from his feet to his shoulders.

Ishbel stared wide-eyed, sure that Maximilian would wake.

But he slept on, his chest rising and falling in deep, slow breaths, unaware of the serpent's tongue coiling so intimately about his body.

The Great Serpent suddenly reared its head up, now directing its full attention to Ishbel.

It lowered its head once more, and ran its flickering tongue slowly, slowly, up Ishbel's body, until it coiled about her belly.

Do not disturb the baby.

"Yes, Great One," Ishbel whispered.

Do what Maximilian wants.

"Yes, Great One."

Wash with the tide for the time being. That will please me, and accomplish what I need.

"Great One, the whispers—"

Ishbel, just . . . wash with the tide. The whispers cannot harm you. Do not allow them to drive you from this man.

"Great One, please, how long must this marriage last? How long before I can go home to Serpent's Nest?"

The Great Serpent regarded her carefully for long moments before he answered.

You shall be home within a year, two at the most, Ishbel. It is not long to wait.

Ishbel relaxed in relief. A year, two at the most. She would manage.

"As it pleases you," she whispered.

The serpent's tongue flickered once more; then suddenly the chamber was free of its presence.

Later, when Ishbel slept, she once more dreamed of the Lord of Elcho Falling, standing in the snow, his back to her, then slowly becoming aware of her presence, his head turning, turning, turning, and then the torrent of despair and pain that engulfed her world as he laid eyes on her and opened his mouth to speak.

Ishbel rose in the morning, putting the dream from her mind, washed and dressed with the aid of a maidservant, then stood looking at the ring on the top of the cabinet.

"You need not wear it for the moment," said Maximilian, coming up beside her, "if that is what you wish."

Such profound relief washed over Ishbel that she gave him a brilliant smile. "Thank you."

"We do need to talk about the rings though, Ishbel."

"Later," she said.

"Yes. Very well. Later."

CHAPTER SEVEN

Margalit, the Central Kingdoms

Rilm Evenor was one of the three most important chiefs in the Outlands. For the past fifty-three years he had led the Evenor tribe and had for twenty-eight of those years also sat as High Chief on the Outlands Council, which governed the region. He was a strong man, of impeccable character and fair judgment, and there were few people within the Outlands who looked on Evenor with anything other than the deepest respect.

Evenor was also the Outlands' best war general. The Outlands had not been at formal war with any of its neighbors in over one hundred years, but there were always the niggling border territory issues with Pelemere and Berfardi. The Outlander tribes were largely nomadic for eight months of the year, and claimed the right to travel the pastures to the west and north of the Sky Peaks—rights to which Pelemere, Hosea, and Berfardi strenuously objected. There had been skirmishes every few years—nothing more than a few hundred men pitted against each other in a forgotten mountain pass or on barren pastureland—but Evenor's real military experience and renown had been in aiding the Outlands' northern neighbor, Viland, with their ever-present Skraeling threat.

Every few years, if their numbers had built up sufficiently that their normal feeding grounds could not support them, the Skraelings tended to drift south in small groups of twenty or so. They would attack outlying villages and farmsteads, making off with small animals and the occasional human child or small adult. They fed on fear and terror as much as they did on flesh, and all the northern nations loathed them. The Vilanders were well used to dealing with the creatures, but Viland was a small nation, and their men were out on whaling ships for long months of each year, and Evenor and his tribal army from the Outlands were welcome allies.

This year was one of the few Evenor was actually spending in the Outlands. He was growing older now, and had taken up residence in a town house in Margalit. Normally he hated the city, preferring a tent brittle with hoarfrost under frozen skies, but one of his daughters was unwell, and he had thought to spend the coldest months of the winter with her.

Evenor might be old, but he was still a strong man, and a cunning one, as well as experienced.

Thus it was that he was the first of the household to realize the presence of intruders. He rose from his bed silently, not disturbing the girl who slept next to him, and stole down the great central staircase of the house.

At the foot of the stairs he took a heavy walking stick from a rack, hefting it in his hand.

There were stealthy movements to his left, in the main reception area, and the very faint glow of a light.

Thieves, Evenor thought, who did not expect him to be in his daughter's house.

Taking a deep breath, he stepped quickly into the reception room . . .

And stopped in surprise.

A slightly built man stood in the center of the room, hands folded before him, his eyes downcast. He looked up as soon as he realized he had company.

"Ah," the man said, "Rilm Evenor. I'm sorry to disturb your night like this."

"Who are you?" Evenor had stopped several paces away. "How did you get past the guards?"

"Your guards shall be here soon enough," said the man, "but not soon enough to save your life, I am afraid."

Evenor moved. There was no time or reason for words now. He lunged forward and slightly to the right, striking out with the walking stick.

He didn't make it more than a pace.

A man loomed out of the shadows behind Ba'al'uz—
Zeboul, the most trusted among the Eight. He swung a great
wooden pole between his hands, stepping around Ba'al'uz
and smashing it into the front of Evenor's throat the moment
before Evenor struck Ba'al'uz.

Evenor crashed to the floor.

Ba'al'uz had not once flinched.

The remaining brothers moved out from the gloom, where
they'd been hiding.

"Are his guards coming?" whispered Ba'al'uz.

"Yes," said one of the Eight, "they have awoken in their
barracks and grabbed their weapons. They will be here
within a moment. Will we be safe?"

"Yes," said Ba'al'uz, and looked down.

Evenor was choking to death, unable to get air down his
windpipe. One hand clawed desperately at his throat, the
other scrabbled about uselessly for the stick that had rolled
away when he'd fallen.

Ba'al'uz murmured words whispered to him earlier by
Kanubai, and within the moment he and the Eight were
cloaked in dark power.

Footsteps sounded outside, and then eight or nine soldiers
burst into the room just as Evenor gave a final gasp, his body
arching in a death spasm.

The soldiers stopped momentarily, assessing the situation.

They saw their commander, apparently dead on the
floor.

They did not see Ba'al'uz and the Eight.

Instead they saw, and would swear to this for the rest of
their lives, Baron Allemorte of Pelemere and a mixed force
of armed men from Pelemere and Hosea.

"Tell your damned council," said Allemorte, stepping
away from the body, "to stay out of lands that don't belong
to them."

Then, suddenly, strangely, Allemorte and the foreign soldiers were gone.

Evenor's men would recall later that they'd had a bitter
battle with the murderous invaders, a battle they'd fought

long and hard, but that Allemorte and his band had finally managed an escape.

Residents in the houses adjoining Evenor's daughter's house would also report seeing the armed men escape down the street.

And when the Outlands Council, appalled, angry, and vengeful, investigated further, they discovered a trail of reports from innkeepers and road travelers from Pelemere to Margalit about Allemorte's band, who had traveled to Margalit and then escaped along the main Outlands highway to the west.

Ba'al'uz and the Eight returned to their inn, tired but satisfied. They were not so fatigued that they did not take the time and effort to murmur a prayer of thanks to Kanubai for his aid.

Three days later, much recovered, Ba'al'uz led his Eight toward Pelemere and thence to Kyros, well pleased to see the numbers of armed men gathering in Margalit.

CHAPTER EIGHT

Pelemere, the Central Kingdoms

Ishbel tried her utmost to settle into her role as Maximilian's wife. She thought of it only as a "role" and a pretense, not as any permanent reality, but ever since the appearance of the Great Serpent on her wedding night Ishbel did her best to accept her current situation.

She would *wash with the tide*, as the Great Serpent had commanded her. She would be whatever Maximilian needed in a wife, until the Great Serpent needed her elsewhere.

At least she did not have to wear the ring. Someone asked her a few days after the marriage why she did not wear it, and, while she hunted for an excuse, Maximilian stepped in smoothly.

"It fits poorly," he said. "Ishbel's finger is too slim. Once we return to Ruen I shall have it altered for her."

He looked at her as he said this, and Ishbel gave him a small nod of gratitude.

She was lucky, she realized, that the Great Serpent had not required her to marry some fat, intolerant fool. Maximilian was very bearable.

Ishbel became used to the sexual side of their marriage far quicker than she had ever anticipated. She'd always thought that she would find a man's touch and intimacies intrusive, perhaps even repulsive, but sharing a bed with Maximilian was neither of these. He made her laugh, he made her body thrum with unexpected sensation, and she found herself actually enjoying their intimate relationship.

What she did find difficult to accept was her pregnancy. *That* invaded, whereas Maximilian's sexual attention did not. The baby represented a complete loss of control—over her body and over her future—that Ishbel found extremely disconcerting.

Besides, Ishbel's life in the Coil had not prepared her in the slightest for a pregnancy. She had no idea what to expect, or what changes would occur in her body (apart from growing large and bulky, which she regarded with horror). She was not even too sure what *were* the early signs of pregnancy.

There was no one save Maximilian she could ask, or in whom she could confide. Garth Baxtor, with whom perhaps Ishbel could have talked, had left Pelemere on the day after her wedding to visit with a college of physicians in a town a few days' travel to the north.

Maximilian, however, not to Ishbel's surprise, had no idea what to expect either, and was faintly aghast that Ishbel was so unknowledgeable herself. She talked with him once about what she could expect, but received enough of a surprised and perplexed look that she didn't pursue the matter.

"Garth will help you when he gets back," said Maximilian, and Ishbel left it at that.

Meanwhile, Ishbel and Maximilian enjoyed the hospitality of Sirus. Sirus made Ishbel uneasy. He was old—at least seventy—but still hale and possessed of the whipcord strength of a man a quarter of his age. He was very tall and thin, and his head was crowned with an unruly mop of pure white hair over a hawk's nose. Maximilian liked him, but Ishbel simply didn't know what to make of the man. Half the time he appeared to be trying to make some very bad and crude jest, and the other half of the time he watched her with the silent, sharp eyes of a bird of prey.

Too sharp, and a little too intelligent, and Ishbel found herself either keeping conversation light, or avoiding the king's company altogether.

Her new role as Queen of Escator she found almost as difficult as her approaching maternity. Ishbel just did not know how to act as a wife, let alone as a queen. Since the age of eight she'd been cloistered within Serpent's Nest, undergoing strict training with the Coil. From the age of thirteen she'd been a priestess of the Coil, and from fifteen, archpriestess.

There had been no time for the fripperies of womanhood; there had only been time and desire for the strict isolationism of the Coil. Now Ishbel felt as if she was floundering along, trying to work out the correct demeanor for both woman and queen, and trying to manage court etiquette and expectations. The only time she could relax was at night, with Maximilian, in their chamber.

He didn't question too closely her lack of social skills and answered whatever questions she had, as well as guiding her throughout the day when he realized she struggled.

Ishbel knew she stood out like a sore thumb at Sirus' court, but a week after her marriage (during which week Ishbel had tried to avoid every social gathering she possibly could) she was largely saved from the horrors of the court when Pelemere was thrown into turmoil by the news that the Outlands Council had formally accused Sirus—as well as Fulmer of Hosea—of the murder of Rilm Evenor via the hand of Baron Allemorte. The Outlanders were outraged, they were mobilizing for retaliation, and amid all the fuss Ishbel could fade into the background and keep to her room much of the time.

Sirus was furious that the Outlanders had the affront to accuse Baron Allemorte of the murder, let alone concoct numerous false tales of Allemorte's ride from and to Pelemere for the murder, when Sirus had been entertaining Allemorte the entire time within Pelemere. There was a flurry of diplomatic activity and messages passed between Hosea and Pelemere. Maximilian spent some time cloistered with Sirus, but not too much. For the moment he wanted to remain as distanced as he could from the discussions: Escator could hardly afford to become involved in a war so far from home, and so far from Escator's own interests.

In the third week after the marriage, Garth Baxtor returned to Sirus' court. Ishbel learned of his return only when Garth appeared in her and Maximilian's chamber late one afternoon, when she was spending an hour or so alone before dressing for the evening dinner at court. He'd knocked at the door and Ishbel, expecting a servant with her bathwater, bid him enter.

"My lady," Garth said, bowing slightly as he paused inside the door, "I've startled you. I apologize."

"You're forever apologizing to me," Ishbel said.

"I have that habit with the ladies." Garth walked farther into the chamber. Ishbel was sitting with her back to the light, and he found it difficult to see her well.

"You had an enjoyable and profitable visit with your fellow physicians?" Ishbel said.

"Yes." Garth had advanced enough now to see her face more clearly. There were bright spots of color in her cheeks, and he wondered if she was embarrassed, or perhaps even shy in his presence. "It is always good to meet with others of my profession, and exchange ideas and experiences."

She smiled, a little distantly, clearly uncomfortable.

"My lady, Maxel suggested I come to see you. He said you have little idea as to what to expect with your pregnancy—and may I congratulate you on that, by the way, you must be thrilled—"

Ishbel's smile lost what little warmth it had.

"—and Maximilian thought I may be able to answer any questions you might have." Garth paused. "May I . . ." He gestured to the chair next to Ishbel's.

"As you wish."

That wasn't precisely a ringing invitation, but Garth sat down anyway.

"We got off to a poor start, my lady," he began. "I would do anything for Maximilian, and now I will do anything for his wife." He smiled a little. "He is besotted with you, my lady. I never thought to see the day."

Ishbel relaxed, her smile more genuine now, and for a few minutes they chatted about her pregnancy, what she might expect over the next few months, how she should eat, what precautions in her daily life she should take. Ishbel was guarded with him, but at least she was talking.

"I had never thought to be pregnant," she said, laying a hand over her belly. "I can still barely comprehend it."

Garth thought that a little strange. All other women he'd ever known had lived with the possibility of a pregnancy during a marriage, whether or not they desired a baby. Surely she must have given this *some* thought on her way to meet Maximilian?

"Perhaps I can set your mind to rest about the baby's health," Garth said, stretching out his hand to her arm. "And yours, as well."

"Don't touch me!"

Garth reeled back, stunned by the vehemence in her voice and face.

Whatever familiarity that had been between them had now vanished completely.

"It is a great intrusion," Ishbel said, her voice very cool, "that 'touch' of yours. Surely you ask permission of people before you scry out their innermost secrets?"

Garth sat back in his chair. "You're right. I should ask." Damn it, he was going to have to apologize again. "I apologize."

"Don't do it again, Master Baxtor. I do not like it. It is a *vast* invasion of any person's privacy, and look what a disaster you made of it."

"My lady—"

"You assumed all manner of things of me, and none of them correct. A harlot? A slut? Is that what you called me to my husband?"

Garth wished the floor would open up and swallow him. He couldn't believe Maximilian had repeated the conversation to Ishbel. He was angry, partly with Maximilian, but mostly with himself.

He was also curious as to what Ishbel had to hide. All this prattle of intrusion and privacy was surely nothing but a defensive screen for a secret.

"My lady," he said, rising, "I will not presume again."

Then, because he was sick of apologizing, Garth turned on his heel and left the chamber.

Garth and Egalion met privately with Maximilian after evening court. Ishbel had retired early, and Maximilian invited his two friends for a supper drink in a private chamber of the palace.

They talked for some time about the escalating crisis between Pelemere, Hosea, and the Outlands. Maximilian, as Egalion and Garth, could not understand how the misunderstanding—as it must be—could have happened.

"Could it have been someone pretending to be Allemorte?" Egalion said.

Maximilian gave a shake of his head. "According to the Outlands Council, they have obtained official likenesses of Allemorte, and Evenor's guards have identified him as the man they saw standing over their master's body."

"But how can that be?" said Garth. "Most of the court here at Pelemere can swear to Allemorte's presence every day for the past months. He cannot have gone to the Outlands."

Maximilian shrugged. "Perhaps the Outlanders are lying."

"Best not to say that within hearing of your lady wife," Garth muttered. Then, at Maximilian's look, "Maxel, I'm sorry, but I can't believe you told her what I'd said about her the day I first met her."

"She asked," Maximilian said, "I told her. I will keep no secrets from her."

Garth bit down irritation and, he was appalled to discover, just a little jealousy. He and Maximilian had been close ever since Garth had been instrumental in rescuing Maximilian from beyond the hanging wall, and Garth was now finding it difficult to consider the possibility that Maximilian might put a wife first.

This, of course, was precisely what Maximilian *should* do, and Garth felt he would have accepted it for any wife . . . but not Ishbel Brunelle.

"I don't like her," Garth said. "She's not . . . likeable."

Maximilian shrugged. "She has lived an isolated existence. She is not always good with people."

"I don't understand," said Egalion, "why you needed to rush into marriage with her. I don't like her either, I'm sorry. There is something hidden about her, something secretive. Something bleak. And her association with the Coil . . . Maximilian, I am sorry, but I find her a poor queen for such as you." He paused. "*Why* the rush, Maximilian? For all the gods' sakes, Escator can't be in such bad straits that you need money that badly."

Maximilian took a long time in answering.

"There are some things I cannot tell you," he said eventually, very slowly, "but I do owe you some explanation."

He paused again, drinking his wine.

"As you know, I managed to see Ishbel before my 'official' arrival in Pelemere. I watched her for an hour or two, unknown to her, and I liked what I saw."

"She is very lovely," Egalion offered.

"Aye, she is very lovely," Maximilian said, "but that was not the reason I liked her so greatly. She is . . . quiet. I thought I might find her peaceful to be about."

"There are many 'quiet' women about, Maximilian," said Garth.

"Who are prepared to marry me?" said Maximilian. "With such a large dowry at their heels? But there's something else. We talked, she didn't like me—for which I am not surprised, as I spied on her most intimate moments—and I discovered something."

Again a long pause, and again Egalion and Garth waited patiently.

"The Persimius family," Maximilian said, "is a very ancient family. We go back a long way."

Yet another lengthy silence as Maximilian struggled within himself.

"Ah," Maximilian said, "all I can say is that when I touched her for the first time, when I laid my hand to her skin, I knew that I had to have her as my wife, beyond any shadow of a doubt. She and I are meant for each other."

He gave a small, sad smile. "I know that—even if she refuses to believe it, and even though you doubt it—and for the moment that will need to be enough."

Ba'al'uz and his Eight were well on their way to Pelemere. They assumed the guise of traveling peddlers, and no one bothered them overmuch. It was spring, and the nights were either warm and damp, or crisp and cold, but they spent those nights camped out under canvas and blankets rather than in wayside inns.

They preferred it that way.

Kanubai was somehow clearer under the night sky.

He whispered into all of their minds, his words more lucid and purposeful with each passing day.

It became obvious that Kanubai regarded this Ishbel Brunelle with absolute loathing. His words about her were wrapped with the twin concepts of anger and sacrifice. It was plain to Ba'al'uz that Ishbel needed to die. Not only would this death please Kanubai's obvious wish for a sacrifice, but it also fitted neatly into Ba'al'uz' mission for Isaiah and Lister—to create chaos and confusion and enough angst to spark war between the kingdoms. What could be better than to murder the new bride of Escator while she was a guest at Pelemere?

Between his whispered loathings of Ishbel, Kanubai whispered of other things to Ba'al'uz. He talked more of the object that Ba'al'uz needed to obtain for Kanubai. This object was called the Weeper, and it rested over the sea in Coroleas. Ba'al'uz understood that Kanubai wished for the Weeper more than anything else (although Ba'al'uz thought Ishbel's sacrifice came a very close second).

Kanubai told Ba'al'uz that if he achieved both sacrifice *and* retrieval of the Weeper for Kanubai, Ba'al'uz would be rewarded with sovereignty over all the lands of this continent, and all its peoples would be his to order as he willed.

Just two things for me, Kanubai whispered over and over into Ba'al'uz' mind, *sacrifice and the Weeper . . . sacrifice and the Weeper.*

Easy, thought Ba'al'uz.

CHAPTER NINE

Palace of Aqhat, Tyranny of Isembaard

One morning Isaiah sent an invitation to Axis to join him in weapons practice.

As tyrant, Isaiah's reputation, his very tyranny, rose or fell on his success as a war leader. Already consumed with curiosity about Isaiah's competence as a military commander (he could find no one to ask about the mysterious failed campaign against the Eastern Independencies), Axis thought that at least in weapons practice he might learn more about Isaiah the warrior.

Axis was also glad of the invitation as a means to burn off his excess energy. When a young man, Axis had been devoted to war and military pursuits—and it was something he had missed desperately as one of the Star Gods. He hoped that he hadn't lost too much fitness since last he had trained seriously at war.

Axis had thought that Isaiah would hold weapons practice in the cool of the early morning . . . but, no. Their first session was held in the late morning, when the sun was already high and blazing.

Isaiah saw Axis' concerned glance at the sky as they entered the practice field.

"Too hot for you, my friend?" he asked.

Axis looked at him. Isaiah was dressed only in a hipwrap and sandals. He wore no jewelry, and the myriad tiny braids of his black hair were bound at the nape of his neck. He looked very fit, very strong, very comfortable in the heat, and was obviously amused at Axis' discomfort.

"I am surprised only," Axis said, taking the sword the weapons master handed him, "that you use the midday heat to acclimate yourself for a war that will most likely be fought in the driving snow."

Isaiah laughed, choosing a sword from the three the weapons master offered him. "When we have snow, Axis, then we shall fight in it. But for the moment I am at liberty to test you in whatever manner I choose."

"I did not realize this was a test."

"Then you are more out of practice than I realized," Isaiah said softly. "I need to know your skills, Axis."

The next instant the blade of his sword sliced through the air at Axis' neck.

Axis barely parried Isaiah's move, and then barely had time to recover from that before having to counter the next strike. Not only was Isaiah much faster and fitter than Axis (a sudden, galling realization), but Axis was unused to the type of sword with which they fought. The swords Axis had used in Tencendor had been straight and, to Axis' mind, well weighted, but the Isembaardian sword was curved, almost a scimitar, and Axis found it too light. He was constantly overcompensating, once or twice almost overbalancing, and Isaiah kept him permanently on the defensive.

Several guardsmen had gathered with the weapons master, witnesses to his humiliation.

"I had thought," Isaiah said effortlessly, now beating Axis back toward the compound wall, "that you'd be a better opponent than this. Perhaps the legends of your prowess were just that. Legends."

Axis knew he was being deliberately taunted, but he couldn't help a sudden spurt of anger. *How could he have allowed himself to be put in this position?* He summoned every remaining scrap of strength he had, trying to take the offensive rather than the defensive, but just when he thought he might have a tiny opening, sweat ran into his eyes and blinded him, and he thrust into thin air.

"We shall stop, I think," Isaiah's soft voice said to one side, and Axis wiped the sweat from his eyes, trying not to let his arms tremble as he lowered his sword.

Isaiah leaned forward, took Axis' sword, then tossed both swords to the weapons master.

"Come," he said, turning on his heel and striding away, and Axis had no choice but to mutter a curse and stumble after him.

There was a groom standing with two horses directly outside the weapons compound. The horses wore bridles only, no saddles, and Isaiah took the reins of the nearest horse and swung effortlessly onto its back.

Axis sent him a baleful glance (this was planned, surely) and managed, just, to order his still-trembling muscles to swing him up onto the other horse without landing in a pitiful dusty heap on the other side.

Isaiah grinned, easily and with no mockery. "I think you need to cool off," he said, and kicked his horse forward.

They rode out of the palace, through the outer gardens, then down to the River Lhyl, Axis keeping his horse very slightly behind that of Isaiah's.

It was only as they approached the water that Isaiah spoke again. "Death does little for a man's fitness, eh, Axis?"

Axis couldn't help a chuckle. "Would you believe me if I said that in my prime I could have sliced you off at the ankles?"

"No. But I'll grant you a nick or two."

"I need practice. I have lost my battle fitness." Axis hesitated. "Isaiah, can I—"

"Either I or my weapons master will partner you each day," Isaiah said, anticipating Axis' question. He looked at Axis directly. "I trust you with a sword, Axis, and I trust you with my life. If I have kept you somewhat hobbled to this date, then that was because of Ba'al'uz. I did not trust *him* with you. Now that he is gone . . . you are a free man."

Axis wondered if Isaiah was a trifle overobsessive about Ba'al'uz, or if the man was truly that dangerous. For the moment he let it go, however.

"You're very good, Isaiah. Who trained you?"

The horses were at the river edge now, and Isaiah nudged his into the water, motioning Axis to follow.

"All my father's sons were trained by his war master,"

Isaiah said, his horse now swimming out into the gentle current. He held the reins in one hand, and twisted the fingers of that hand into its mane to give himself some purchase before turning slightly to look at Axis. "Do you know how I came to the Tyranny?"

"Yes. Ba'al'uz told me. Isaiah, I can hardly believe that man is your brother."

"He has all of my father's worst qualities," Isaiah said, "and that compounded by madness."

"Do you think he is really mad, or just—"

"Sly? Cunning? Treacherous? Yes to all those, but I believe he is crazed as well. Perhaps not originally. When he was young he pretended madness." Isaiah looked ahead. "Now he worships this great pyramid, adores it as some might a lover. *It* has inspired madness in him, I think. Real madness."

"Ah," said Axis. "We're riding to DarkGlass Mountain, aren't we?"

"Indeed. I need to know what you think of it, Axis."

"Isaiah—"

"Leave your questions until later. Until afterward. Then I will talk."

Axis realized suddenly that Isaiah was apprehensive and he lifted his head and looked south to where DarkGlass Mountain loomed, brilliant in the sunshine. He had been curious about the pyramid ever since he'd arrived.

Now, perhaps, he would learn more about it.

Neither man looked back to the eastern bank of the river, where a brindle dog stood, half concealed by reeds, watching them with black, unnatural eyes.

From the far riverbank they turned their horses southeast, riding for perhaps an hour down a road that followed the course of the river. To their left, deep reed banks waved in the light breeze; to their right, flat grain fields stretched for miles, their borders marked by irrigation channels and pathways. Axis wondered a little that Isaiah would so happily ride unarmed through the countryside, then, after a quarter hour or so, he realized that they were utterly alone in the landscape.

Isaiah must have ordered the fields emptied earlier in the day.

It was now very hot, and even though there was a cooling river breeze, Axis was sweating in the blazing sun. He wore no shirt, and he could feel the sun burning his shoulders and back.

·   For a moment he was almost overwhelmed with a pang of nostalgia for the cooler climate of Tencendor.

They rounded a bend in the road and suddenly the thick reed banks came to an end. A massive stone wharf had been built into the riverbank: from this wharf a stone causeway moved in a direct line toward DarkGlass Mountain, rising almost a mile away in the desert plains.

Isaiah looked at Axis, and smiled a little at the expression on his face.

"This is the Great Processional Way," Isaiah said as they turned their horses onto the causeway for DarkGlass Mountain. "When the river is at its peak, the land to either side is flooded, and it is as if one rides across water to reach Dark-Glass Mountain."

Axis did not respond. He had attention for nothing but the glass pyramid rising in the distance.

The pyramid had looked large from the distance of Aqhat, but riding closer Axis realized its true size.

It was gigantic.

Graceful.

More beautiful than anything Axis had ever seen—and he'd been privileged to witness some astounding marvels. He'd thought it stunning when he'd viewed it from the balcony of Aqhat . . . but this close . . . no words any man could mouth could possibly do it justice. Even though there was still some distance to cover before they reached the pyramid, Axis was now close enough to see that the blue-green glass that coated the stone walls glowed with a preternatural light. The glass almost *throbbed*, and Axis could feel something deep within himself tug in response.

He raised his eyes to the very peak of the structure, his neck cricking a little painfully after his earlier exercise, his eyes squinting in the sun.

The capstone of golden glass reflected so much light it was almost impossible to make out any details. Axis narrowed his eyes even more, and for a moment thought he saw a pillar of blinding light ascend into the sky from the capstone.

They pulled their horses to a stop perhaps eighty paces away, and Isaiah watched the emotions play over Axis' face as he gazed at the pyramid.

"It stands almost two hundred paces tall, from foundations to capstone," Isaiah said softly. "Its four sides are perfectly aligned, perfectly square. Its builders must have been extraordinary. We could not do this today."

Axis managed to find his voice. "Ba'al'uz told me something of its history . . . built two thousand years ago by ancient mathematical wizards to touch the power of Infinity, abandoned after a rebellion. Dismantled, and then—"

"We will talk of that later," said Isaiah. "Not here, not now."

They were riding forward again now, very close to the pyramid, and suddenly Axis felt cold, as if the pyramid's shadow had swept over him, even though he could see it stretching out to the west.

"I want to take you into the heart of DarkGlass Mountain," said Isaiah. "I want you to see what lies there, and"—he swiveled on his horse a little so he could look directly at Axis—"I want you to tell me what you think of it."

Axis *loathed* it the moment they set foot inside the structure. He'd been growing progressively uneasier from the moment they'd dismounted outside (a groom appearing from a shadow to hold their horses) and stepped inside via a small door set unobtrusively into the pyramid's northern face.

The outside of the pyramid throbbed with beauty and reflected light.

Inside, the pyramid seemed to eat light and life and breath.

Isaiah led Axis along corridors lined on walls, ceiling, and floor with black glass that to Axis looked as if it had been melted, or in some manner otherwise fused, to the underlying stone. Every now and then he'd glimpse red light flickering through the glass, as if serpents lived under the glass, and spat their forked tongues at him.

There were torches set into the black glassed walls, but the light radiated only a handbreadth or two from its flames before being absorbed utterly by the glass. Axis and Isaiah walked down tunnels of darkness in which the only illumination was provided by the intermittent lamps and the odd flickering of red deep within the glass itself.

As they passed one lamp Axis peered at Isaiah, a pace or two ahead.

His shoulders and back were stiff.

Why has he brought me here?

"This is a strange place, Isaiah," Axis said softly, wanting to say, *This is a bad place, Isaiah*, but understanding, even after such a short time within the pyramid, that those would be unwise words to speak . . .

Within the pyramid's hearing.

"We do not have far to go now, Axis," Isaiah said softly, "until we reach this structure's golden heart. Be quiet until then."

By now every nerve in Axis' body was screaming at him to turn around and walk out—*if DarkGlass Mountain would allow him that privilege*—but just as he opened his mouth to speak, Isaiah stopped, and turned about.

"We're here," he said, his face barely visible in the gloom. "There's light ahead."

Somehow Axis doubted that—visual light, maybe, but he wondered if whatever lay at the heart of this structure could ever be characterized with a concept such as "light."

Isaiah turned about, touched something on the wall with his hand, and Axis heard the soft sound of a door sliding open.

CHAPTER TEN

Pelemere, the Central Kingdoms

The situation in Pelemere had deteriorated from the bad to the abysmal. The Outlands Council and King Sirus of Pelemere had ceased talking to each other—which was in its own way a relief, as their words had become ever more bitter and vengeful—and had moved instead to overt militarization. The Outlanders claimed Sirus, allied with King Fulmer of Hosea, had murdered Rilm Evenor as an initial strike in a planned invasion; Sirus and Fulmer believed the Outlanders had murdered Evenor themselves in order to invent a reason to war against the Central Kingdoms.

Maximilian felt increasingly uneasy as he became ensnarled in the middle of this diplomatic catastrophe. Sirus and Fulmer believed that Maximilian should be their natural ally . . . but Maximilian not only did not want to involve Escator in what he believed would be a fruitless and ultimately devastating war, but also felt it was the last thing he could do, given that his new wife was an Outlander herself. He was having enough trouble trying to work his way past Ishbel's outer reserve without alienating her by involving himself in a war against her home.

For the past ten days or more Maximilian had been engaged in a delicate dance of evasion; today he would not be so lucky.

Ishbel and Maximilian were lunching with Sirus. This involved not only eating with the king, but with half of Sirus' court, as well as servants and sundry hangers-on and curiosity seekers—Sirus kept, to Maximilian's thinking, a dangerously open court. They were all seated within the great hall of Sirus' palace, Maximilian and Ishbel at the high table on the dais closest to the huge fires used to heat the hall, everyone else seated according to rank at varying distances from both kings and fires, at long tables that ran at right angles to the high table.

Ishbel was seated next to Sirus' right hand, but was looking isolated and bored, which Maximilian knew meant she was intensely uncomfortable. He wondered if it was the baby—recently Ishbel had been feeling nauseous during the day—or Sirus' glowering face. Maximilian, seated two places farther down from Ishbel, was sandwiched between Baron Allemorte—supposed assassin of Evenor—who sat to Ishbel's right, and another of Sirus' barons, a man called Veremont.

Given the topic of conversation—the looming war with the Outlands—Maximilian thought it far more likely that it was the angry words surrounding Ishbel making her uncomfortable, rather than the baby.

At the rear of the hall a man slipped in, unremarked by the guards. He was of an unthreatening demeanor, true, and clad in the garb of a servant, but it was more likely Ba'al'uz' use of power that caused the guards' eyes to drift over him rather than anything else.

Ba'al'uz and his Eight had traveled hard and fast to reach Pelemere this quickly. Nonetheless, they'd spared time to inflame the burgeoning war between the Outlanders and the two kingdoms to their east by intercepting—and augmenting the inflammatory comment therein—many of the diplomatic messages flying via carrier bird between the combatants. Ba'al'uz was never one to miss an opportunity.

That was precisely why he was here today. He didn't think Maximilian and his new wife would long linger in Pelemere—not with Sirus glowering in such fashion—and he wanted an opportunity to study Ishbel, and gauge, if he could, the best way to murder her at the first opportunity.

Which might be today, were luck to fall his way. Kanubai wanted only two simple things from Ba'al'uz, sacrifice and this strange object called the Weeper from Coroleas, and the first of those Ba'al'uz hoped to accomplish today.

For a while Ba'al'uz lingered toward the rear of the hall, helping the servants fill goblets and refresh platters of food. After a while, confident that no one would remark on his presence, Ba'al'uz worked his way closer, very gradually, to the high table.

"I need to know your mind on this," said Sirus, King of Pelemere, leaning impolitely past Ishbel and looking in Maximilian's direction. "I need to know if you are willing to—"

"Sirus," Maximilian broke in, "I have no part in this, surely. I am moving through your territories only in order to collect a wife, and—"

"An *Outlander* wife," murmured Allemorte, who nursed his own private grudge against the Outlanders for accusing him of Evenor's murder.

"Horseshit," Sirus said, slapping a hand down on the table and making Ishbel flinch back in her chair. "Your damned wife is an Outlander herself, *you're* a damned, cursed king, and I want to know if you are going to back your new wife's people or me in this war."

"Sirus!" Maximilian said, appalled that Sirus referred to Ishbel as if she were not present.

Sirus leaned back a little and looked at Ishbel. "My apologies, my dear. Have I spoken my mind too true for comfort? Perhaps to reassure me, and perhaps even your husband, who must be wondering what murderousness he has married into, you can offer me your support in this little matter. Perhaps even a small revocation of loyalty to the Outlands themselves?"

"My lord—" Ishbel began, her face white, her voice very quiet, but Maximilian interrupted.

"There is nothing you need say, Ishbel," he said, catching her gaze. Then he looked back to Sirus. "Ishbel plays no part in this matter, Sirus. Leave her out of it, please. And me, too. *I* play no part in this matter. I am sorry that you and Fulmer have been caught up in this dispute with the Outlands, but I beg you understand that it is *your* dispute, and *not* mine."

Sirus opened his mouth, his face red with anger, but had to lean back momentarily as a serving man lifted away his platter.

Sirus glowered at him, but the man had already faded into the background.

"Easy words," muttered Allemorte, very low, "for a coward."

Ba'al'uz thought Maximilian might actually strike Allemorte at that. Ba'al'uz had just taken away Sirus' platter, and was hovering behind Ishbel's chair, about to reach for her virtually untouched platter, when Allemorte spoke so foolishly.

Maximilian went completely white, half rising from his own chair, and Ba'al'uz took a step back into the shadows by the chimney breast in anticipation of physical violence.

If he was fortunate enough, Maximilian would goad Sirus or Allemorte into murdering Ishbel for him, right here and now.

"Allemorte spoke a little too hastily," Sirus said, "but you can surely understand his level of ill feeling. Half of my country, including myself, can vouch to his presence here in Pelemere when the Outlander Council insist he was murdering Evenor, but still they insist."

Maximilian sank back into his chair. "Ishbel has *nothing* to do with this dispute, Sirus," he said. "She deserves none of your ill will. Leave her be."

Sirus glanced at Ishbel, who was leaning toward him as the serving man collected her platter. He thought she was looking very angry, and he wondered at it. Was her temper caused by his goading, or because, as an Outlander, she loathed him and his kingdom?

He distrusted all this pretty silence on her part. He distrusted even more the fact that she'd arrived just as news of the murder had broken in Pelemere. Was she a part of the plot? A spy, sent by the Outlander Council? An agent, perhaps, intent on harming Pelemere's interests in any way she could? Well might Maximilian champion her, but then he was sleeping with her, and Sirus had no doubts that Ishbel had enough bed tricks up her sleeve to keep her new husband quite besotted.

"I would like to hear from Lady Ishbel herself," Sirus said quietly, "of her views on this matter."

Ba'al'uz was almost beside himself with anticipation. No one was taking any notice of him, and now he hummed with the power of Kanubai. He could take Ishbel today, sacrifice her easily, and make it appear as if by Sirus' hand.

Gods, that would set the entire Northern Kingdoms aflame—Ba'al'uz was by now enjoying this exercise for its own sake rather than in the hope of pleasing Isaiah or Lister—*and* earn Kanubai's unending gratitude.

For a moment, hovering back in the shadows, he imagined what words of praise Kanubai would murmur in his mind tonight, what rewards he might have awaiting him on his return, but then, with supreme effort, Ba'al'uz managed to concentrate on the task at hand. He slipped a hand inside the pocket of his waistcoat, fingering the vial of poison he had secreted within. It was a special brew, something he carried with him always, and all it would take was a single brush against Ishbel's skin to have her dead within ten heartbeats.

He tipped the vial up and down, coating the stopper's tongue, then carefully withdrew the stopper, palming it in a well-practiced maneuver, and moved forward as if to refill Ishbel's wine goblet.

Ishbel was furious: with Sirus, with Allemorte, with Maximilian, with the damned servant who kept hovering about the back of her chair, and with the entire cursed situation. She hated these words against the Outlanders, even though she had been distanced from them for so long within Serpent's Nest. This was *her* blood they were cursing and deriding and plotting to spill, and this *her* heritage they insulted.

Maximilian was trying his best to fence-sit on the matter, and Ishbel could have screamed with frustration. *What in all gods' names did the Great Serpent think she could do here?* Married to Maximilian and forced to listen to this drivel from men who were less than any of the peasants and criminals she had sent to the grave? How, just half a year ago, could she ever have imagined that the archpriestess of the Coil could be sunk so low?

And with this damned baby in her belly, which even now was sending cold waves of nausea through her. Ishbel was terrified that if she so much as opened her mouth she'd spew forth the little she had managed to eat.

But no, here was Sirus leering at her, demanding that she say something to stoke even further the fires of his bigotry. That she *justify* herself.

The servant had now stepped forward again (what was *wrong* with the man, could he not stand still for more than five heartbeats?) and was making as if to reach for her wine goblet. Now irritated beyond measure, Ishbel waved a hand at the man, meaning to brush him away, as at the same moment she opened her mouth to put the damned Sirus in his place once and for all.

But all that came out from her mouth was a low moan of distress as Maximilian's ring suddenly screamed—

Danger, danger, darling Ishbel! Danger, danger! Murder, murder!

Two seats down Maximilian leapt to his feet, shoving Allemorte aside in his haste to reach his wife.

At the same instant the ring shrieked, Kanubai also screamed into Ba'al'uz' mind.

She is not the sacrifice, fool! It is her child I want!

Ba'al'uz cloaked himself in power the instant Kanubai spoke in his mind, shrinking back once more into the shadows of the great hearth, sliding the poisonous stopper safely into its vile home. He was safe for the moment, for no one's attention was on him. Sirus had thought Maximilian was lunging for Sirus himself (and Maximilian may well have been, for all Ba'al'uz knew), Ishbel did not have a single idea what was happening about her, Allemorte was still trying to recover from Maximilian's shove, and everything else was in confusion.

He *could* step forward again, step into the confusion, and wipe the stopper against the soft skin of Ishbel's neck.

But Kanubai wanted her child more than he wanted Ishbel (Ba'al'uz wasted a moment of indignation that Kanubai had left it until the very last instant to make this clear). Ba'al'uz understood that Ishbel would need to die as well, of course, but not just yet . . . not just yet.

So Ba'al'uz did not murder Ishbel as he had planned. But Ba'al'uz was primed to murder, he *wanted* it, he knew he wouldn't be able to settle if he didn't do it, and so, while Allemorte struggled to regain his footing amid the pushing and shoving, and as, to Ba'al'uz' perception, every guard within a hundred leagues rushed to protect Sirus, Ba'al'uz withdrew the stopper once more from its vial and wiped it gently, caressingly, against Allemorte's wrist as the baron tried to grab at the back of a chair for balance.

CHAPTER ELEVEN

Palace of Aqhat, Tyranny of Isembaard

Axis had thought the outside of the pyramid amazing, but it was as nothing compared to this internal chamber, shaped as a pyramid itself, and about fifteen paces square at the base. Both walls and floor were covered in intricately carved golden glass of such workmanship and beauty that Axis was dumbstruck. He walked over to one of the walls, running his hand softly along the glass.

"This is the Infinity Chamber," said Isaiah. "The golden heart of DarkGlass Mountain. Beautiful, eh?"

"It is . . ." Axis began, unable to find the words to continue.

"Extraordinary," Isaiah said. "No one now has the skills to carve glass like this."

Axis remembered what Ba'al'uz had said about the pyramid. *A doorway.* A means by which to touch Creation.

A means to touch the Star Dance again, Axis.

Axis went cold. He glanced at Isaiah, but the tyrant was walking slowly about the chamber, running several fingers over the carved glass.

That had not been Isaiah.

Wouldn't you like to feel the thrum of the stars through your body again, Axis? Wouldn't you like the power that once you enjoyed? This is a gateway, Axis. Just like the Star Gate, and if—

Axis blocked out the voice, turning to Isaiah just as the tyrant spoke.

"Tell me what you feel here, Axis."

It just spoke to me, Isaiah! But how can I speak that, here and now?

"Death. There has been a great deal of death here, although I felt it more strongly in the black corridors leading to this chamber. There is terror, and it is stronger in this chamber than elsewhere. There is fear. There is . . ."

"Opportunity?" Isaiah said, and Axis wondered if Isaiah had, after all, heard the voice that had spoken to Axis.

"Perhaps," Axis said. He wanted nothing more now than to get out of here. Stars, Ba'al'uz had said Isaiah came here and sat for hours at an end. *What did DarkGlass Mountain say to him then?*

"You want to leave," Isaiah said very softly.

"Yes," Axis grated. He could feel DarkGlass Mountain probing at his mind, feel its temptations—*I can realize all your dreams for you, Axis. Touch the Star Dance again, touch Azhure again, touch—*

Without another word Axis turned on his heel and strode from the Infinity Chamber.

"You didn't like the Infinity Chamber," said Isaiah. "Why?"

They had not spoken until they had ridden down the causeway and back onto the roadway running beside the river. They trotted along this for a little way, then, of one accord, pulled the horses to a halt and turned them so they could look back at DarkGlass Mountain.

More time than Axis could believe possible had passed since he'd entered the pyramid. It was now late afternoon, almost dusk, and the sun was sinking behind the pyramid, streaking the deep blue-green of the glass with long fingers of rust.

Or blood.

"Where will it be safe to speak, Isaiah?" said Axis quietly.

"In my chamber," said Isaiah, "away from its shadow."

They turned their horses for the river and did not speak again until they were, indeed, safe within Isaiah's most private chamber.

CHAPTER TWELVE

Pelemere, the Central Kingdoms.

It was, for almost an entire half hour, a time of the most exquisite joyousness.

Ba'al'uz sank back into the shadows by the hearth, concealed by the gloom, and watched mayhem erupt at Sirus' lunch table.

Evenor's murder had been enjoyable—but what Ba'al'uz experienced now was the most intense ecstasy normally only felt during the climax of sexual relations.

Ishbel, perhaps overwrought by all the anger about her, vomited what little lunch she'd eaten onto the snowy linen-covered expanse of the high table.

Guards rushed to surround the high table—members of Maximilian's Emerald Guard as well as Sirus' palace guard.

Maximilian had shoved Allemorte to one side in order to reach Ishbel. The baron had no time to recover his balance before Ba'al'uz had stepped smoothly forward from his shadow, wiped the poison over Allemorte's wrist as he tried to grab the back of a chair, and then retreated, unseen and unremarked by all as Allemorte slipped to his knees. He made as if to rise, but the next moment gagged, turned a horrible shade of gray-purple, clutched at his chest, then collapsed in convulsions.

Sirus lurched to his feet, his eyes initially on Ishbel and Maximilian, before turning in bewilderment to look at Allemorte writhing on the floor.

The hall erupted in shouting and cries and the sound of benches and chairs tumbling to the timber floor as people leapt to their feet.

Within a moment attention had turned from Maximilian and Ishbel to Allemorte. The poison had done its work in an instant, and where it quickly became obvious that Ishbel was well (apart from her sick stomach), it just as rapidly became obvious that Allemorte was in his final extremity.

Sirus was the first to reach him, leaning down and grabbing at the convulsing man's shoulder. "Allemorte!" he cried. "Allemorte!"

He was pushed unceremoniously aside by the arrival of a man Ba'al'uz could not name, but who was immediately recognizable as a physician. The physician grabbed at one of Allemorte's flailing hands, held it, an expression of deep concentration on his face, then looked up, first to Sirus and then to Maximilian, now holding Ishbel to one side.

"He has been poisoned," the physician said. "He is dying."

Ba'al'uz raised his eyebrows. The physician had uncommon skill—a depth of intuition that bordered on the magical. He was wrong in only one respect—Allemorte was not dying . . . by now he was very dead indeed.

"Murder!" cried Sirus, and turned instantly to Maximilian. "*You murdered him*!"

Ba'al'uz had to bite his inner cheek to keep himself from crowing out loud and betraying his presence. *This was too good to be true!* Now Ba'al'uz was torn between wanting desperately to stay and enjoy the continuing drama, or scurrying back to where the Eight waited and regaling them with the excitement.

The Eight could wait. The excitement here was too good to leave just yet.

As Sirus and Maximilian shouted, and as guards milled, Ba'al'uz studied Ishbel.

She was very pale, and Ba'al'uz thought he could see continuing traces of sickness about her eyes.

The baby.

Bring her to me, Kanubai whispered in his mind, and Ba'al'uz nodded.

Far away, on the banks of the River Lhyl, the brindle dog lay, head on paws, looking at the pyramid rising in the sunlight, but seeing nothing but Ishbel Brunelle reacting to the ring's call of danger.

The dog had no mind of its own now. Instead the shadows that chased about its skull were the thoughts of Kanubai, still waiting far below the pyramid.

Kanubai knew that bringing Ishbel to DarkGlass Mountain had its own dangers, but, oh, the strength that the sacrifice of her child would give him! The baby carried powerful bloodlines, *magical* bloodlines, and its sacrifice to enable Kanubai's rise would give him such power in life that he would be virtually unstoppable.

Never more would he be trapped.

Never again the bleakness of the abyss, but only that bleakness transferred to the light of day so that all joy and warmth might be murdered.

CHAPTER THIRTEEN

Palace of Aqhat, Tyranny of Isembaard

They rode back to the palace in silence, save for an odd comment about the strength of the river current or the evening chill of the air.

Once at the palace, Isaiah led the way at a brisk walk to his private chambers, waving aside the murmurs of courtiers and servants. He brought Axis to the large airy room that served as his dining and living chamber, checked to make sure all the windows were shuttered, then turned to Axis.

"Well?" Isaiah said.

"It spoke to me."

Isaiah drew in a deep breath. "Ah."

"You are not surprised."

"No. It has spoken to me, as well. Mumbled words at first, but now far clearer. What did it say?"

"It tempted me with the Star Dance . . . you know what that is?"

Isaiah shook his head. "Not truly. I have heard of it, but . . ."

"The Star Dance is the music the stars make in their dance through the heavens. That dance creates patterns, and those patterns can be manipulated by those with the ability—among the Icarii race it was the Enchanters—to achieve various ends. The more powerful the Enchanter, the more powerful the end. The Star Dance filtered into Tencendor via the Star Gate."

Axis thought back to his first sight of the Star Gate. Buried deep underground, the Star Gate had initially looked like a pool of blue light. But when Axis had looked deep into it he had seen the universe, the *real* universe, not the poor reflection that chased across the night sky. Galaxies and solar systems of rich, exquisite colors had chased each other through multihued stars . . . and the Star Dance, the music of the stars, had rushed out at him, engulfed him . . .

In a few quiet words Axis described the Star Gate for Isaiah. "It was astounding, Isaiah. The power it contained, its beauty . . . its allure . . . unbelievable. It was dreadful and frightening and irresistible, all in one. And it was our only connection to the Star Dance. The moment the Timekeeper Demons destroyed the gate, we lost the Star Dance. DarkGlass Mountain—or whatever it is that lingers in there—promised me the chance to touch the Star Dance again. Ba'al'uz said the original Magi who created DarkGlass Mountain made it as a gateway to Creation." Axis gave a small shrug. "There is no reason not to suppose that DarkGlass Mountain could not also be a gateway to the Star Dance."

"But—"

"But can you imagine what would happen to the Star Dance as it filtered through DarkGlass Mountain? Stars, it is a nightmare! It is so . . . *corrupt*. Darkness and filth."

"Axis, what does your gut tell you about DarkGlass Mountain?"

"What? Darkness and filth isn't enough for you?" Axis gave a small shrug. "It is toxic and dangerous beyond belief. And that . . ." Axis paused, thinking.

"And that . . . ?"

"I think that whatever is wrong with DarkGlass Mountain is far older than the pyramid itself, although that damned pile of glass is cursed enough. There's something there, Isaiah, something beneath the pyramid, a part of the very soil on which the Magi built. It is very ancient and very powerful. I don't know what it is, or what manner of thing it is: whether object or cavern or spirit or potential or sheer damned *memory*, but there it is. Isaiah, tell me what you know. Why do *you* go and sit inside it?"

"To test myself. To know my enemy. To try and discover his movements and his plans."

"*His* plans?"

Isaiah waved Axis to a low chair, poured them each a goblet of strong fortified wine, then sat down himself in a nearby chair.

"Let me tell you what *I* know of that pyramid, Axis. I agree with you. I think something dark and malignant lives far below the pyramid. For centuries DarkGlass Mountain was nothing but a great mound covered by sand, some rough grasses, and the odd scrap of rubbish. Then—"

"It regrew, Ba'al'uz said."

Isaiah gave a hollow laugh. "Yes. It uncovered itself, and then reclothed itself in its gown of glass. It fed on the bleakness waiting below it, and it just . . . regrew."

"That did not terrify people?"

"Terrify? For a year or so, when this first began to happen, the Tyranny of Isembaard was paralyzed. Ezela, the tyrant at that stage, did not know what to do. He had his army try to destroy it—instead, the army was crippled. Any soldier who touched it with intent to damage it was, oh gods, turned to stone. Fortunately no one lived in this area at that time, so there were no loose tongues to waggle, and Ezela himself made sure that not one of the soldiers who survived ever spoke of what had happened."

Axis winced, imagining only too well what Ezela must have done to those men.

"Ezela could not destroy it," continued Isaiah, "and he could not stop the pyramid's self-regeneration. So he did the next best thing. He watched it for years, until he was certain it would do little more than merely regenerate. Then, ever the innovator, he built the palace of Aqhat directly across the river from DarkGlass Mountain, settled himself inside, and claimed that DarkGlass Mountain was a testament to the power of the tyrant and that the tyrant himself drew great power from it and that it was a great talisman for the Tyranny. Nothing to be afraid of at all."

Now it was Axis' turn to produce the hollow laugh. "And thus for centuries the tyrants have sat in their palace listening to the damn thing whisper?"

"The 'damn thing' only started to whisper twenty years ago, and only a very few can hear it. Like you, I believe that something waits below the pyramid. That the pyramid itself, while noxious enough, is also being used by something far more powerful. Something *ancient*." He gave a slight shrug. "I refer to it as a 'he.' Somehow it helps to be able to personalize the nightmare."

Axis had every suspicion that Isaiah was not telling him everything he knew, but Axis also knew Isaiah well enough to understand that he could not be pushed. "For all the stars' sakes, Isaiah, you have this ancient monstrosity sitting directly across the river from your palace, stirring into gods-know-what witchery, and you've decided to invade the north in the meantime? Don't you think this is a somewhat bad time to abandon your realm to . . . *whatever* that thing is . . . and go invade somewhere else?"

Now Isaiah laughed more genuinely. "You can't think of a *better* time?"

"Isaiah . . ."

He sobered. "I have little choice, my friend. I told you about the Eastern Independences campaign."

"Yes," said Axis. *But you have not told me* why *it was you failed.*

Isaiah met Axis' eyes. "I have been living on borrowed time since then. My generals plot among themselves. If I do not manage a successful show of strength, of war, of *invasion*, within the next year or two, then I am a dead man. Lister offers me that chance. With my army, and his Skraelings, the kingdoms above the FarReach Mountains are ours. *Then* I can deal with DarkGlass Mountain, or whatever that nightmare really is."

"Isaiah, leaving that thing at your back—"

"What do you want me to do, Axis? If I stay here, if I stay actionless, then I die. But if I have the success of the invasion behind me, as well as the resources of the kingdoms to the north, then maybe I will have the strength and the chance to deal with whatever DarkGlass Mountain is plotting. Besides, the north has something I want," Isaiah added, almost as an afterthought.

He moved away to a map table, indicating Axis should join him. As Axis walked over, Isaiah unrolled a parchment map. It showed the full extent of the Tyranny of Isembaard, as well as the kingdoms to the north and Coroleas to the west.

Isaiah's fingers moved upward, tapping a drawing of a massive mountain. "This mountain is called Serpent's Nest, home to a rather vile little order of psychic murderers. It is fascinating. I have heard such intriguing rumors about it."

Axis waited, but Isaiah's silence forced him to ask the question. "What rumors?"

Isaiah gave a small smile. "Oh, treasures-buried-in-its-dungeons kind of rumors. You know the sort of thing. Just—"

"Just the usual thing that makes a man uproot a million of his people and invade a foreign land."

"It is just something I'd like to see, Axis. Perhaps something to obtain before Lister gets there, eh?"

And with that Isaiah rolled up the map and turned away.

"Why does Lister need to ally with you?" Axis said. "Why not just invade the north without you and take all for himself?"

"Because he and I are fools, Axis, and we cannot live without the other."

And to that Isaiah would not add any more.

[Part Four]

CHAPTER ONE

Pelemere, the Central Kingdoms

I shbel."

She didn't stir, so deeply asleep that Maximilian's murmur and his soft hand shaking her shoulder could not wake her.

"*Ishbel!*"

She moaned softly, and tried to roll away from his touch.

Maximilian leaned closer to her, put both hands on her shoulders, half lifted her up, and gave her another, more substantial, shake.

"Ishbel, *wake up!*" he hissed.

Her eyes flew open.

"Shush," he said, his voice low. "It is all right, there is no immediate danger, but we need to leave now."

He left her sitting, confused and blinking, as he fetched some thick felt and fur clothes from a nearby chest.

"Here," he said, "put these on. It is freezing outside—there has been a late, bitter snowfall—and we have a fair distance to ride."

"Maxel? What . . ."

He sat down by her side again. "We can't stay here, Ishbel. We barely got out of the great hall today without being tossed in Sirus' dungeons. I don't know what tomorrow will bring, but we can't be here for it. We need to be far away before this palace and city awakes."

"But . . ." Ishbel was still so sleepily confused she simply could not think. She'd been exhausted by the time they'd gone to bed last night, and ill both with the baby and the events of the day. She looked about their bedchamber.

It was still deep night.

"It is about six hours before dawn, Ishbel," Maximilian said.

"Where will we go?"

"I found somewhere on my way to Pelemere. It will do for the time being, but we need to get back to Escator as fast as we can. The Central Kingdoms are far too dangerous for me and for you now. Are you awake? Yes? Good. Now, use the bathroom—the gods alone know when next you'll have the chance—get dressed and we shall leave."

Maximilian sat on the bed, waiting for Ishbel, thinking that he felt as ill as Ishbel looked.

It had been an absolutely hellish day.

They *had* been lucky to have escaped Sirus' dungeons, and only the fact that no one could find any poison on either Maximilian or Ishbel had saved them.

Sirus was still convinced, however, that one or the other had murdered Allemorte. Furthermore, he was now absolutely certain that Ishbel was in league with the Outlanders, and that the Outlanders—for whatever reason—were planning further murderous attacks, if not a full-scale invasion, within his kingdom.

Whatever chance there had been for peace between the Outlands and Pelemere and its neighbors was now completely gone.

Maximilian rubbed a hand over tired eyes. He'd spent the two hours before he'd woken Ishbel with Garth, Egalion, and Lixel, arranging for them, as well as the Emerald Guard, to melt away into the night in ones and twos and to reassemble at a spot a suitable distance, and in suitable seclusion, from Pelemere.

Sirus might have his guard on high alert, but the Emerald Guard were almost as attuned to the darkness as Maximilian was himself—they had all come from the Veins—and would be able to slip past Sirus' guards without too much trouble. Maximilian thanked whichever gods watched over him that he'd brought only a relatively small retinue from Escator, and not a column of hundreds. *That* would have been impossible to sneak out of Pelemere.

Maximilian looked up. Ishbel had returned. Silently Maximilian helped her into the clothes he'd selected: thick felt underclothes and shirt, furred trousers, vest and hooded coat, and a heavy cloak.

Ishbel was a tall woman, but she looked lost beneath all the layers.

Maximilian tied the cloak around her shoulders. He needed to talk to Ishbel badly, but because of the turmoil of the day they had not yet discussed anything that had happened. Maximilian needed to confront Ishbel about the ring (why hadn't he had the courage to do this weeks ago?), *and* about why murder seemed to be trailing her every step.

Did it have anything to do with Elcho Falling? Was this part of the disaster that was eventually going to necessitate Elcho Falling's reawakening?

But for now, Maximilian felt tired and ill, and Ishbel looked even worse, and they were in mortal danger unless they could leave this palace and this city *now*.

Talk would need to wait.

They had gloves with them, but for the moment they kept their hands free so that Maximilian could hold one of hers in a firm grip, their fingers interlaced. Ishbel thought an observer might think it a result of affection, but in reality Maximilian needed close contact with her so that he could cloak her in his almost supernatural ability to move unseen through the dark.

Ishbel remembered how he'd managed to stand utterly unobserved in her chamber for hours, watching her. Now she, too, enjoyed the same degree of disguise and it made her wonder about him, about the depths within him she had not yet bothered to plumb and, again, why it might be that the Great Serpent wanted so badly for her to be married to this man.

Sirus had stationed guards, not directly outside their apartment but at the junction of the corridor that connected their apartment wing with the main part of the palace. This was the only means possible by which to leave their apartments, the windows being far too high from which to jump, and so Sirus had not needed to place guards closer.

The guards were awake and alert: Sirus had no doubt considered the possibility that Maximilian and Ishbel might try to escape. As they neared the guards, creeping along the wall, Maximilian's hand tightened briefly about Ishbel's, and he pulled her a little closer to him.

She felt a peculiar sensation creep over her: a heavy chill, oppressive, and yet humid. Ishbel's chest constricted, and she had to struggle to draw in a breath.

Maximilian stopped, watching her.

Ishbel struggled for a moment or two—not merely to breathe, but to do so quietly—then felt her chest relax somewhat, and her breath come easier.

Maximilian felt her relax, and he gave her a small nod and squeezed her hand again.

Then he led her past the guards.

Ishbel swore that two of them turned and looked at them directly. One of them blinked, but then he looked away again, while the other guard's eyes slid over them without pausing.

The cold grew denser, and Ishbel's shoulders sagged with its weight.

Again Maximilian's hand tightened about hers, but then the next step they were past the guards and about a corner, and, for the moment, were safe.

For an hour they crept through the palace and then the streets of the city. Ishbel's heart hammered in her chest, not merely with the constant fear of discovery, but also with the weight of Maximilian's oppressive concealment. She yearned for the spaces beyond the city, for any space, for *anything* that might give her relief from the pressure.

By the time they neared the city gates Ishbel was stumbling with fatigue. Maximilian had tried to pick her up, but Ishbel resisted. She murmured at him irritably, then blinked. They were standing *outside* the gates. How had that happened?

"Maxel?"

"I am almost as weary as you, Ishbel. Come. Not far to go now."

"Where? Where? Gods, Maxel . . ."

"This way." Again he took her by the hand and led her along a path by the city walls, north, then along a path that branched off to the northeast.

A period of time later—to Ishbel it felt as if half the night had passed, but she was sure Maximilian would claim the distance could have been measured in the space of a few minutes—they entered a small grove of trees.

A man stepped forward—Egalion.

"Maximilian! Thank the gods! We'd almost given up hope."

"We still have a way to go yet, Egalion," Maximilian said. "Do you have the horses?"

Egalion nodded behind him, and one of the Emerald Guard—Ishbel noted with some rancor that he looked as fresh as if he'd managed an entire night's sleep in a feather bed—led forward two saddled horses.

Maximilian looked at the horses, then at Ishbel.

"I'll carry Ishbel with me," Maximilian said to Egalion. "She's too tired to sit a horse by herself."

Ishbel wanted to protest, but Maximilian was right. She'd fall the instant they left her to balance herself, and the next moment Maximilian had mounted one of the horses, and Egalion was lifting her up to him, and Ishbel could finally succumb to the cold heaviness and lean against Maximilian, and sleep.

CHAPTER TWO

Pelemere, the Central Kingdoms

Maximilian wanted peace and he wanted quiet, and above all he wanted the opportunity to talk with Ishbel. They had been married some two months, and still she was a complete stranger to him—even more the stranger now, he felt, than when he'd first met her. Events were crowding in, and murders and wars piling up around them. What Maximilian had thought would be a simple business—the procuring of a bride—was now becoming ever more dangerously difficult by the hour.

He was growing increasingly concerned about the escalating crisis between the Central Kingdoms and the Outlands. This, combined with the vision he'd experienced on the way to seduce Ishbel, solidified in Maximilian's mind the certainty that Elcho Falling was about to wake.

Ishbel knew far more than she had admitted to him thus far, and Maximilian didn't think he could go on much longer, or farther, without prizing some of that knowledge out of her. She must have *some* of the answers locked within her. Not all perhaps, but many, certainly. She was of Persimius blood, she'd come from the Mountain at the Edge of the World, and she was somehow intimately connected with Elcho Falling.

But, oh, what a complicated woman she was! Her refusal to discuss matters that held any discomfort for her frustrated Maximilian beyond measure, yet at the same moment Ishbel endlessly intrigued him. Her reserve challenged him, her reluctantly awakening sexuality inflamed his desire for her, while her secrets angered and discouraged him and added to his ever-growing anxiety about Elcho Falling and what he needed to do about it.

At the grove of trees, Maximilian had given the Emerald Guard some brief orders, then, as was his wont, had turned his horse off in another direction, taking himself and Ishbel northwest. He was heading for one of the isolated woodsman's huts about which Borchard of Kyros had told him.

An hour after dawn, the new day's light almost lost amid the deepening snowstorm, Maximilian carried Ishbel inside the hut.

She slept through most of the day, waking only in the very late afternoon when Maximilian kicked open the door and stumbled inside, his arms laden with wood.

"Maxel? Where are we?"

"A woodsman's hut deep in a forest northwest of Pelemere." Maximilian dropped the wood onto the heap by the stove, removed his outer clothing, shook it free of snow, then stood before the fire, warming his hands.

"Why?" she said, swinging her legs over the side of the bed and sitting up.

"Because we needed to get away from Sirus."

"And the Emerald Guard? Garth Baxtor? Egalion? Lixel?" She dragged a blanket about her shoulders.

"They are secreting themselves deeper in the woods."

"But we're here. By ourselves."

"Does that bother you?"

"Maxel . . . why?"

"I needed to talk to you without the others about." *I need to wrest out into the open some of the secrets crammed into that beautiful head of yours.*

He could see her withdraw, see caution and anxiety shut down her face.

"And because I wanted time with you alone," Maximilian continued, "just to know you. You are my wife, and I your husband, and yet we are strangers to each other."

"That is not unusual in high marriage, surely."

He shrugged and moved to a small cupboard, from which he removed some dried provisions. "Hungry?"

She answered him with her own shrug, which Maximilian chose to interpret as an affirmative, and so he tossed some dried peas and beans and herbs into a pot of water and set it to the stove to simmer. "I am afraid that this king and queen shall have to eat as peasants," he said.

She gave a small smile at that. "I'm sure that it will be better fare than what Sirus would serve us in his dungeons."

Maximilian chuckled, cutting thick slices from a loaf of very stale bread and scooping out a portion of their centers so that they could be used as trenchers for the soup.

Ishbel had wandered over to the stove, still wrapped in a blanket, and was now looking curiously at the soup. "How did you learn to cook?"

"I often tend for myself." He nodded at the hut's basic interior. "In Ruen I abandon my kingly duties from time to time and spend a few days by myself in a woodsman's hut, similar to this, in the forests to the north of the city."

"Why? Why the need to be by yourself?"

"Because I find it impossible to be surrounded by faces all the time. Because I find my own company healing."

"Then it must be aggravating for you to have me here, now."

"I could have sent you on with Egalion, but I chose to bring you with me."

"Ah yes, to interrogate me."

"Ishbel, sit down at the table with me."

She hesitated, but finally did as he asked, taking a bench on the opposite side of the table.

"Ishbel, what do you think about the murders? Evenor, and then Allemorte, yesterday."

"I don't know anything about them, Maximilian. Why ask me?"

"I am asking for your thoughts, not for a detailed explanation."

She gave another small, disinterested shrug, and would not meet his eyes. "I have no thoughts on them. I was so isolated in Serpent's Nest that I am naive in the ways of the outside world."

Naive in the ways of the world. Maximilian really didn't know what to make of that. In many ways she was—that she'd been terribly isolated he had no doubt—but in other ways Ishbel appeared as old as the very land itself.

"Ishbel," he said gently, "yesterday a man fell dead at our feet, murdered with poison. How did it happen? Who did it?"

"It wasn't me."

"I wasn't accusing you, Ishbel, but, oh, murder *is* starting to follow you. Why?"

She dropped her eyes, and fiddled with a nonexistent particle on the tabletop.

"Ishbel?" Maximilian said as gently as he could. "Please . . ."

Again, a shrug. "I don't know, Maximilian. I don't."

He reached over and took her left hand. "Ishbel, all I want to do is to get home safely, with you and with our child. But at the moment I very much fear we're not going to get there, not safely or not ever. I hold you at night, and feel you drifting ever farther away from me. I want a marriage, Ishbel. I want *you*. I want a *family*. And I want to know why *you* were the target of that assassin yesterday, not Allemorte."

Her hand was very cold and still in his, and Maximilian wondered if that coldness and stillness extended all the way to her heart.

"Perhaps it was Sirus," Ishbel said. "He doesn't like me. He doesn't like any Outlanders."

"It wasn't Sirus. There was magic involved yesterday, and darkness swirling all about us. When my ring—"

"I don't want to talk about the ring. Not *any* ring."

Maximilian resisted the urge to pick something up and smash it against the wall. Instead, he contented himself with tightening his grip about her hand. "Ishbel, please—"

"I *don't* want to talk about the rings!"

"Well, I do. For all the gods' sakes, Ishbel, there is nothing to be afraid of about two chatty rings!"

She looked at him then, and Maximilian's heart turned over in his breast. He'd never seen anyone look so lost, or so afraid.

"I've heard them before," she said, so softly that Maximilian had to lean forward to catch her words, and even then he wasn't sure he'd heard correctly.

"What? The rings?"

"The whispers."

She was trembling now, and Maximilian slid around to her side of the table, sitting beside her on the bench and wrapping her in his arms. All his anger of a moment earlier was gone.

"Tell me," he said, very softly.

She was silent a long time, and Maximilian did not think she would answer.

Then, just as he was about to sigh and stand, she began to speak.

"When I was eight a plague came to my family's house."

Maximilian said nothing, but tightened his arms about her slightly, settling her more closely against his body, resting his cheek against the top of her head.

"My family all died within a day. Everyone in the house died, save me."

"The plague spread fast," Maximilian said.

"Yes. Too fast. The people of Margalit barricaded the house, refusing to allow me out in case I carried plague with me. They hammered shut all doors and windows, and did not listen to my pleas. I begged, over and over, beating at the closed door, but they turned their hearts against me."

"Oh, Ishbel . . ."

"It lasted forever. At least that's how it felt to me. Aziel later told me it was a month. I tried to kill myself. I thought that was the only way I'd escape. I rolled in the vileness excreting from my mother's body and . . . and . . ."

"Ishbel . . . sweetheart . . ."

That endearment, combined with the closeness and comfort of his arms and body, broke down Ishbel's final barriers.

She shuddered, leaning in as close to Maximilian as she could. "One day my mother's corpse began to whisper to me."

Maximilian stiffened, horrified. "Whispered?"

"It would not stop, Maxel. I ran all about the house, and it whispered and whispered, and I could not escape it! It spoke with the same voice as did the rings. Maxel . . ."

Maximilian could hardly force the words out. "What did the whispers say, Ishbel?"

"They told me . . . to . . . to . . . prepare, prepare, for the Lord of Elcho Falling shall rise again."

Maximilian froze. Nothing worked. His heart appeared to have stopped, his brain could not manage a single coherent thought, he could not force his breath in or out of his lungs.

The Lord of Elcho Falling shall rise again.

Even though he'd been steeling himself for this moment, the sudden, absolute confirmation of his worst fears threw Maximilian into utter denial.

"No," he finally whispered, "I don't believe you."

She tore herself out of his arms.

"Then stay away from me if you cannot believe me! *Stay away*!"

The next moment she had thrown open the door and had run outside, clad in nothing but her underclothes and a blanket.

CHAPTER THREE

Pelemere, the Central Kingdoms

She struggled through the snow, hardly aware of the cold penetrating her body, the ice about her bare feet, or of the fact that she had lost her blanket.

No. I don't believe you.

She sobbed, hating him. How could she have told him of the whispers? What a fool she was—to have believed his lie of comfort, only to hear him say, *No. I don't believe you.*

She had never told anyone. Never. Not even Aziel. What had possessed her to tell Maximilian?

She heard a step behind her and, not looking, lunged to one side, desperate to avoid him. She stumbled, her breath catching in her throat as she fell, and the next moment she was held tight in his arms, so tight she could almost not breathe, and she heard him sob as well, and kiss her face and forehead.

"I believe you, Ishbel. I *believe* you. Gods, I am sorry. It was such a shock, what you said. Come away inside now, come, I have you. I am sorry, so sorry . . ."

He kicked the door closed behind him and bore her straight to the fire, not letting her go, holding her as tight as he dared, saying he was sorry over and over and over.

"You have been through horror, sweetheart," he murmured against her hair, "no wonder you fought against the ring, why you will not wear it. It must truly have terrified you. Oh . . ." He cuddled her close, kissing her face and neck over and over, relaxing only once he felt her relax. "Are you warm enough now?"

"Yes."

"Please don't hate me for what I just said, Ishbel. Please."

"I don't hate you, Maximilian," Ishbel said, meaning it. She had not felt this safe in years. Twenty years, to be precise, since her mother had last held her, and told Ishbel how much she loved her.

"It was what you told me what the whispers had said, about the Lord of Elcho Falling rising—"

"You have heard of him?"

There was a slight hesitation. "There are legends in which he is mentioned."

"Then I do not want to hear them," she said. "I hate him. Over the years I've had visions of him, and always I know that if ever he catches me, then he will wrap my life in unbearable pain and sorrow, for pain and sorrow trail in the darkness at his shoulders like a miasma. I know he will ruin my life. He will ruin the *world*."

She stopped, leaning against him, finally allowing herself to feel comfortable, to feel safe, and not understanding his shocked silence.

"It *is* all right," she whispered, taking one of his hands and cradling it against her breast. "I hate him as well."

Maximilian did not speak for a long time. "What do you want, Ishbel? *Really* want?" he said finally.

"To go home to Serpent's Nest," she said. "To go back home. To be safe from the Lord of Elcho Falling. I will only feel safe from him there."

Maximilian closed his eyes and rested his forehead against the top of her hair. *All she wanted was to go home and be safe from the Lord of Elcho Falling, whom she hated, and who would wrap her life in unbearable pain and sorrow.*

What a damnable, cursed time, Maximilian thought, to realize that he loved her. He moved his hands over her body, feeling more hopeless than he had felt in—

More hopeless than he had felt in eight years, and as trapped and lost and desolate as he had felt when trapped in the Veins.

She was responding to his touch now, turning her body against his, lifting her face to be kissed.

If only you knew, Ishbel.

"Ishbel," he said, lifting his mouth from hers. "Let us make a pact, you and I. I know you did not wish to come to me, but only did as the Coil wanted. I know you do not truly want that child you are carrying."

"Maxel—"

"Let us make a pact—come home with me to Escator and stay a year. Give birth to our child. Let us see how we do. If you still want to go home to Serpent's Nest after that, then I will let you."

Give me a year, Ishbel. Please, just a year. Maybe at the end of that year you will not fear the Lord of Elcho Falling so much. A year of sleeping in his bed, Ishbel, please . . . please . . .

"Really?" She sat up, looking at him. "You mean it?"

"Yes, of course."

"I can leave the child with you and go home to Serpent's Nest after a year?"

She looked like a child herself, one who had been handed an unexpected treat, and Maximilian's heart turned to bleak despair that she could so easily smile at the thought of leaving him and their child.

"You have no idea how much I want that child," he said. "It means the world to me." *You mean the world to me.* "Whether or not you leave me after the year is your choice." His mouth quirked very slightly. "But if you wanted to stay, if you wanted to stay . . ."

"Thank you for understanding," she said, and leaned her body against his, and kissed him.

CHAPTER FOUR

Pelemere, the Central Kingdoms

Ishbel lay against Maximilian's body in their bed, relaxed but not sleepy. They had made love—a pleasure so intense Ishbel did not yet wish to slip into sleep and forget.

She was happy. Happier than she had been in months. Happy she'd told Maximilian about the terrifying whispers that continued to torment her, happy he'd suggested that he would allow her to go home after a year if she wished. A year with Maximilian would not be a trial, and perhaps she might even stay a few months longer . . . just to watch Maximilian with the child . . . just to see him smile.

Ishbel moved against Maximilian, running a hand softly down his side. He was deeply asleep, and did not move, and so she allowed her fingers to linger over some of the scars on his body.

Scars from his seventeen years spent in the Veins.

When they had first met, Maximilian had told Ishbel that if she asked him about that time, then he would tell her. Ishbel had, on several occasions since, asked a question about the Veins. Maximilian had answered, true to his word, but his answers had been brief and too unemotional, and Ishbel knew that he hid a world of pain behind them.

Her palm slid over a particularly ridged scar on his hip. She had felt it when they'd made love; now she allowed her fingers to travel up and down its length, wondering what had caused it. *What horror had befallen him in the Veins?*

She lay thinking a long time.

Eventually Ishbel came to a decision. As archpriestess of the Coil she had many skills, the very least of which was the slicing open of bellies to glimpse the future. She could use these skills now, to retrieve the memory of how Maximilian had come by this scar.

It would give her an insight into Maximilian she was sure he would never share with her, and Maximilian was fast asleep. He would never know.

Ishbel debated briefly whether or not to deepen his sleep with some of her power. She often granted unconsciousness to the victims of Readings, those who were there through no fault of their own—it was generally only the rapists and murderers she preferred to keep conscious throughout the entire procedure. But in the end Ishbel decided Maximilian was fast enough asleep anyway. Adding to that sleep magically could leave him groggy—and suspicious—in the morning.

Ishbel took a deep breath, steeling herself, for she would experience this memory as if it had happened to her, and allowed power to seep down her arm into the fingers lying over the scar.

Unwind for me, she whispered to it. *Show me the memory of your creation.*

After a long moment, memory began to uncoil from the scar, and Ishbel found herself transported to hell.

She had no name, and she had no identity, save that of her number: Lot No. 859. If she had ever had a name, she did not know it.

There was nothing in her existence save the rhythmic raising of the pick above her shoulder and the burying of it in the rock face before her, over and over, five swings over her left shoulder and five over her right before swinging back to her left shoulder.

There was nothing but the black tarry gloam collecting around her naked feet, nothing save the grunt of the anonymous man chained to her left ankle, and those of the seven other anonymous men in the chained gang.

Raise the pick, swing it, bury it. Breathe. Raise the pick, swing it, bury it. Breathe.

This was the entire sum of existence, nothing else. Occasionally when someone in the line of chained men died, and another brought in to fill his place, the new man would babble about sun and wind and children and happiness beyond the hanging wall—the rock face hanging over all their heads.

But Lot No. 859 knew there was nothing beyond the hanging wall, just a greater blackness, extending into infinity. Sometimes she thought she dreamed of something—an echoing memory, a glimpse of a rolling green sea, the scent of something called apple blossom—but Lot No. 859 knew these were figments of her imagination. Lies created by hopelessness to torment her.

She raised the pick, swung it, buried it in the rock face, feeling pain ripple throughout her entire body, but ignoring it because it was such a constant companion that it had ceased to have any meaning.

Something overhead groaned and then cracked.

The hanging wall, Lot No. 859's only hope for salvation.

She dropped the pick and looked upward, spreading her arms in supplication, baring her breasts to the inevitable rockfall, praying for the oblivion of death.

Beside her the men in her gang screamed, trying to scramble away.

Lot No. 859 knew it was too late.

In a breath the hanging wall collapsed. Rock fragments struck Lot No. 859, throwing her down to the gloom-covered floor of the tunnel, half burying her and wrapping her in thick, tarry, choking dust.

Lot No. 859 opened her mouth, sucking in the dust, praying that her lungs would drown in it, soon, please, gods, soon . . . this was her only hope, her only escape . . .

Pain exploded in her left hip, and she cried out, trying to wrench herself away, her hand fumbling down to feel what had happened.

It was the pick blade of the man next to her, hammered into her hip during his dying moments.

And worse, over the next terrible minutes, the knowledge that while everyone else in her team had been crushed or smothered into death by the rockfall and its dust, she was still alive, the Veins still had her, and there would never be an escape for her, not into death, not anywhere.

* * *

Ishbel woke out of the vision suddenly, gasping for air, bathed in cold sweat, absolutely terrified. For a moment she was completely disoriented, thinking that Maximilian's body next to her was that of the man who had died chained to her left ankle and that the darkness about her was that of the gloam mines. Only very gradually did she calm, and realize that the darkness was that of natural night, and that Maximilian's body was warm and alive.

She breathed in deeply, regaining her composure, grateful that her sudden waking had not disturbed Maximilian.

By the Great Serpent, Maxel had endured seventeen years of that?

What had struck her was his absolute hopelessness, and a despair so deep he had convinced himself that there *was* no world beyond that of the hanging wall, because to admit *that* would have been to go insane. She knew with absolute certainty that if she unwound the memories behind each of the scars on his body she would experience much the same thing.

How could anyone survive that and come out from it with as much compassion as Maxel?

"Oh, Maxel," she whispered. Seventeen *years*? "Maxel . . ."

She wrapped herself tightly about his body, wishing she could somehow comfort him. She ran her hands over his body again, with more pressure this time, deliberately meaning to awake and arouse him.

He moved slightly, then rolled into her arms, still more asleep than awake.

"Wake up, Maxel," she whispered into his ear, kissing his neck and then his collarbone, making him moan. "Wake up. There *is* a world beyond the hanging wall, and here it is, in my arms and in my mouth, and in my breasts and my belly. Here it is, here it is . . ."

To the south of them, on the main road between Pelemere and Kyros, Ba'al'uz led the Eight to the west. Despite the cold and snow, and the subsequent difficulty of travel, Ba'al'uz was in a high good humor. He knew that Maximilian and Ishbel had fled Pelemere, but he was content with that.

Ba'al'uz knew where they were going.

CHAPTER FIVE

*The Road from Pelemere to Kyros,
the Central Kingdoms*

The snowstorm that enveloped Pelemere and the surrounding countryside during the week that Maximilian and Ishbel escaped the city was winter's final blow. Two days after they had arrived at the woodsman's hut, Maximilian and Ishbel woke to find the sun shining and the snow melting.

Maximilian was anxious to leave. He would have preferred that the weather stay bad for a few weeks to come so that he and his retinue could more easily make their escape from Sirus (undoubtedly furious, and who would have sent soldiers to look for them), but they would make do with the sunshine. He roused Ishbel, fed her a hasty breakfast, then saddled the horse and mounted up, Ishbel behind him, heading west through the trees.

Maximilian left several gold coins for the woodsmen who used this hut to pay for his use of their stores and firewood.

Within two hours of their leaving, members of the Emerald Guard began to appear from the shadows of the forest, each one nodding silently to Maximilian before pulling their horse in behind his. Just after noon, Garth and Lixel joined them, exchanging a few words of greeting with Maximilian, and then, in midafternoon, Egalion and the final half dozen of the Emerald Guard fell in with the column.

Ishbel never heard an explanation as to where they'd been, but from the cold-pinched faces of Garth and Lixel, she thought they'd not had the same level of comfort that the woodsman's hut had provided her and Maximilian.

Thus began their hard ride home for Escator.

Escator was a long way distant, many weeks travel, and Maximilian wanted to get home as soon as he could. What Ishbel had said about the Lord of Elcho Falling had shocked him to the core. Since his vision he'd only slowly been coming to terms with the idea that Elcho Falling might be waking . . . and then to have Ishbel reveal to him how much she hated the Lord of Elcho Falling, how she believed that he would bring nothing but ruin and destruction to her life, to the entire world . . .

That had not been the kind of secret he'd hoped she would reveal.

Despite Maximilian's wish to travel fast, he was constrained by his concern for Ishbel and her baby, and did not push as hard as he truly wanted. For the next two weeks they traveled by night rather than during the day, Maximilian's sense for the darkness leading them through the countryside, enabling them to avoid roads and mainly use backcountry sheep and goat tracks.

One day, when they were resting and sat relatively apart from the others within their train, Maximilian dared ask Ishbel about the Twisted Tower.

If Elcho Falling was waking, then he needed, somehow, to rebuild what had been lost.

"Ishbel," he said as lightly as he could, wondering if this topic would terrify her as much as mention of the rings had, "have you ever heard of the Twisted Tower?"

Ishbel had no reaction save a mild puzzlement. "No. What is it, Maxel?"

"The Twisted Tower? Oh, a place where memories are stored." *Of he who you hate so much, Ishbel.* "Has there never been any stories in your family, or even within the Coil, of a tower filled with objects?"

"No."

"You don't ever dream of a tower with—"

"*No.* Maxel, what is this?"

"Nothing," he said, and sighed, and leaned back against a tree, pretending to fall into sleep.

Here he was, the poor fool who fate had decided would shoulder the responsibilities of Elcho Falling, whose wife had declared she had nothing but hatred for him, and to cap it all off, much of the lore needed to raise Elcho Falling had been lost. How could one man's life be dogged by such ill luck?

Ishbel spent the traveling time seated behind Maximilian. She wasn't a particularly good rider herself (she had not left Serpent's Nest for twenty years, and learning the skills of a horsewoman had been a low priority), and when Maximilian had insisted she continue to ride with him, Ishbel hadn't objected. She enjoyed the warmth and companionship of his closeness.

She felt markedly more relaxed around him after their talk in the woodsman's hut. Relieved. She had shared the burden of the whispers she'd heard as a child, and, after an initial misapprehension, Maximilian had understood. He would not force her to wear the ring, and he had allowed her the option of leaving him after a year. Ishbel wondered if those words had been placed in his mouth by the Great Serpent, for the serpent had told her that she would only be gone from Serpent's Nest a year, two at the most.

A year with Maximilian would be no trial. Ishbel had thoroughly resented the idea of being sent in marriage to this man, but now she found her heart beating a little faster when he looked up and smiled at her, and she enjoyed watching him move about their campsites when they rested. He was very quiet since leaving the woodsman's hut, and Ishbel thought it the product of his concerns for their safety. When they camped, Ishbel made sure she and Maximilian lay some way from the others, and she encouraged him to make love to her, finding herself more willing to be the one to initiate such intimacy.

There was another thing that increased her good spirits. Ishbel realized that her growing closeness to Maximilian irritated Garth. She'd heard enough from Maximilian to know that Garth had been Maximilian's closest companion until his marriage to her. Ishbel derived some pleasure from the idea that Garth was jealous of her. She didn't particularly like Garth; she had *hated* his intrusion on her body with his Touch, and she enjoyed the carefully neutral looks he gave her.

Ishbel was also enjoying—much to her surprise—the journey through the backcountry of the Central Kingdoms. Previously she had not traveled so much as a mile from Serpent's Nest, and this journey to marry Maximilian was literally her first foray into the wider world in her entire life. She had felt miserable and introspective on the journey from Serpent's Nest to Margalit, and from there to Pelemere, and she'd barely taken notice of the lands through which she traveled.

Now, however, feeling better and somewhat optimistic, Ishbel was interested in the world and discovered that she was endlessly fascinated by the country around her. She was seeing aspects of life that she'd only ever heard about previously: even the brief glimpse of a peasant's hut through the dark of the night, or the distant vista of a village at twilight, had her peering curiously over Maximilian's shoulder, or twisting about on the horse's back to soak it all in.

She peppered Maximilian with questions, and Lixel and Egalion also, until Egalion laughed and said even Maximilian had not been this curious about the workings of the world when he'd been freed from the Veins.

They ate as best they could, mainly the game that members of the Emerald Guard hunted as the column crept through the night. Occasionally Garth would add wild herbs to the pot, or Lixel would travel to a town to buy some grain, but they subsisted primarily on meat. Maximilian grew worried about the effect this might have on Ishbel and the child she carried, and asked Garth to examine Ishbel, but Ishbel refused, saying only that she felt well and that the nausea had subsided, which largely it had.

During the day they melted back into the forests, or into deep gullies, or, if they were very fortunate, abandoned barns with more roof left than not. It was a difficult existence, living hand-to-mouth, traveling as secretly as they were able, but do it they must.

Sirus did indeed have bands of soldiers out hunting them. Maximilian was well aware that their abrupt (and unexplainable) escape in the middle of the night would only have reinforced in Sirus' mind that they were responsible for Allemorte's death. From the moment he and Ishbel had left the woodsman's hut and started west, Maximilian and the Emerald Guard heard and saw evidence of scouting parties: campsites, tracks, the faint distant sound of many horses.

But they were never discovered. At times it was close—one night they sat their horses, utterly still under the branches of a clutch of trees, as a roaming band of soldiers passed within twenty paces of them—but manage to remain undetected they did. Ishbel supposed that Maximilian's—and his eerie Emerald Guard's—ability to merge with the darkness was largely responsible for this, but it still did not stop her heart thudding up into her mouth every time they had to blend into the landscape in order to avoid detection.

Three weeks after leaving Pelemere they drew close to Kyros. Maximilian was certain Sirus would have informed King Malat of Kyros of what had happened in Pelemere, and that Sirus believed Maximilian or Ishbel responsible for the murder of Allemorte. But Maximilian knew Malat far better than he'd known Sirus, and he thought that Malat would want to hear Maximilian's version of events before he tossed him in a dungeon. Nonetheless, while Maximilian was reasonably certain that Malat would give him a fair hearing, he didn't want to push his luck too far, or put Malat in the unenviable position of having to justify to Sirus why he hadn't instantly imprisoned Maximilian.

One morning, as they'd encamped after a night's travel, Maximilian drew Garth and Lixel to one side.

"My friends," he said, "today Ishbel and I will rest here with the Emerald Guard, but I would like you to travel ahead, and make our presence known to Malat."

"What do you think he'll do?" asked Lixel. The events of the past few months had aged the man considerably. He'd longed to return to Escator, but had never envisioned making the journey by the back roads and living off scraps as a fugitive. Once portly and florid, Lixel was a pale shadow of his former self.

Maximilian smiled. "Feed you first, I imagine. Then he

will ask you and Garth for your version of the events he has heard of from Sirus. Tell him what you know, *all* you know, and beg him to understand that neither myself nor Ishbel, nor any other of my party, had a hand in these murders. Tell him I will swear so on the bodies of my parents, and that if I lie I should be sent back to another seventeen years in the Veins. Beg him also for a town house somewhere within Kyros where Ishbel and I, as well as the Emerald Guard, may rest up for a week or so. My wife is pregnant, and all of us exhausted. We will not impose on his hospitality, and we will keep to ourselves so that no other may know of our presence, but, oh, for both his understanding and for some sweet, fresh beds, Malat will earn my undying gratitude."

They spent an uneasy (and somewhat wet, for it rained the entire time) three days waiting in the woods a league or so outside Kyros, but when Lixel and Garth returned, the smiles on their faces told Maximilian all he needed to know.

CHAPTER SIX

Kyros, the Central Kingdoms

They entered Kyros at night by a small gate set into the southern wall of the city. Someone had been stationed there to keep an eye out for them, for the normally locked gate swung open as soon as Maximilian and his party rode close, and, as Maximilian rode through, a man on horseback rode out of an overhang to greet them.

"Maximilian!" the man said, his tone welcoming, if hushed, and held out a hand as he pulled his horse to a halt before Maximilian's.

"Borchard," Maximilian said, taking the man's hand in his, and offering him a wide, unforced grin. Borchard was Malat's eldest son, heir to the throne, and a personal friend of Maximilian's. Despite the fact that Lixel and Garth had told him that Malat had been welcoming, Maximilian still had harbored doubts. To have Borchard here to greet him was the best indication he'd had yet that Malat would be more welcoming than judgmental.

Borchard turned his attention to Ishbel, sitting behind Maximilian, her hands lightly clasped to his waist. "And a wife," he said, an appreciative gleam in his eyes. "Maxel, you never said she was going to be so lovely."

He pushed his horse forward a pace, so he could take Ishbel's hand and kiss it. Borchard was not a conventionally handsome man, but he had an air of boyish fun about him, and a gleam of mischievousness in his eyes, that appealed to most women.

Ishbel did not resist his charm. She smiled as Borchard

kissed her hand, then glanced at Maximilian, her smile fading as she saw the sadness in his eyes.

Borchard caught the look and let go Ishbel's hand. "Maxel," he said, "we have heard some of what has happened in Pelemere, and in Margalit before that, and it beggars belief. My father and I are glad of the chance to hear your version of events. My father begs your understanding in not being here to greet you, nor even being able to grant you an audience . . . but, as I am sure you're aware, yours is a name spoken with a certain degree of frostiness these days. I and my companions"—Borchard inclined his head at a group of four or five armed horsemen waiting to one side—"shall have to provide you with all the company you need."

There was a perceptible coolness in Borchard's tone now, and Maximilian realized their welcome was not quite as guaranteed as he'd first thought.

"A meal and somewhere to rest our weary limbs," he said, "and we shall be grateful to relate anything you wish."

Borchard nodded, then turned his horse about and led them into the city.

He led them to a town house situated in a gated courtyard not far from where they entered (a fact closely noted by Maximilian, should, gods forbid, he need to make an escape quickly from this city as well). The town house was a good size, with enough stabling and dormitories for Maximilian's entire party, and the kitchens were lit and warm: the courtyard was redolent with the savory smell of roasting meat wafting out of the open kitchen windows.

"I can hardly thank you and your father enough," Maximilian said to Borchard as Maximilian helped Ishbel to dismount. "I've been so worried about Ishbel and the strain I've put her through."

"I have heard that you are expecting a child," Borchard said to Ishbel. "I hope that we can offer you good rest and comfort here in Kyros. Come, let me take you inside."

Borchard waited until they'd eaten, and then further, until Maximilian had seen Ishbel to the chamber and into bed, before he asked Maximilian about the events of the past few months.

They were alone now—Lixel and Garth having retired for the night; Egalion seeing to the settling of the Emerald Guard—and sharing a pitcher of warmed spiced wine by a fire.

Maximilian took a long draft of the wine from his glass, then held it out for Borchard to refill.

"To be honest, my friend," he said, "I have no idea where to begin."

"With Ishbel, perhaps, as she was the reason you traveled this far distant to begin with."

"With Ishbel, then." As Borchard sat listening and occasionally refilling Maximilian's glass, Maximilian related a reasonably full version of the events that had enveloped him ever since he'd left Escator. Some of them Borchard already knew, for Maximilian had stopped in Kyros on his way east to meet Ishbel, and many things Borchard, as his father, had heard from other sources. Maximilian did not relate everything, most particularly not that which had occurred between him and Ishbel in the woodsman's hut, but in all else he was frank with Borchard, knowing that the information would go directly back to Malat and that Malat would appreciate honesty and directness before all else.

"And so," Maximilian concluded, "here we are, finally in some comfort due to you and your father's generosity. Tell me, if you can, what news from Sirus? How badly is my name being bruited about?"

"As to your name, Maximilian, it does poorly, I am afraid. Sirus is certain that you, or your lovely wife, were responsible for Allemorte's death and that Ishbel is likely deeply involved in some Outlander plot to invade the Central Kingdoms. Maximilian, I hate to ask this of you, but are you *certain* of your wife?"

Maximilian did not know how to answer that. *Was* he certain of Ishbel? No, he wasn't. She harbored far too many secrets, and he was still uncertain of her true relationship with the Coil. She was somehow tied to Elcho Falling . . . but he had no idea how, or if she consciously concealed what she did know. He *wanted* to trust Ishbel unreservedly, but "wanting" did not help when so many doubts remained.

Maximilian became aware that he'd hesitated too long, and his mouth lifted wryly. "She has her secrets, Borchard, but I do not think them murderous ones."

"Perhaps," Borchard said. "Maxel, Sirus' accusations are serious. You and Ishbel were the only ones close to Allemorte when he was struck—"

"And Sirus."

"Sirus would hardly be likely to murder one of his own barons."

Maximilian contented himself with sending Borchard a deeply cynical look.

"Oh, Maxel, surely not!"

"No, I suppose I do not suspect Sirus of this. All I can say is that besides myself and Ishbel, there were countless servants and guards within two or three paces of us, and the deep stench of a black enchantment hanging over Allemorte's corpse. And as for Rilm Evenor—neither Ishbel nor myself were within a hundred leagues of that murder, and cannot, surely, be suspected of it."

"The 'deep stench of a black enchantment'? You did not mention this earlier."

Maximilian drained his wineglass and then waggled it before Borchard, asking for a refill. "I do not think Allemorte was the target. I think Ishbel was."

"*Ishbel*? Why?"

Maximilian had said nothing to Borchard about what the ring had screamed. How could he? Borchard would not have understood. "An intuition. I can explain it no further, Borchard."

Now it was Borchard who shot the deeply cynical look.

Maximilian shifted uncomfortably. He wished he could talk to Borchard about the secrets of Elcho Falling, but they were such deep secrets, mysteries only to be discussed among the initiated, and he could not speak of them to his friend.

"Borchard," he said, "have you heard any news, or even rumor, of troubles *apart* from those that ensnare the Outlands and Sirus and Fulmer?"

"You want more?" Borchard gave a small snort. "No. Praise gods. The trouble with the Outlands is bad enough."

"Nothing . . . no news from the south?"

"South?"

"From the Tyranny of Isembaard?"

Borchard frowned. "There is never any news from the Tyranny of Isembaard, Maxel! They keep themselves to themselves. We are too poor and uncultured to be of any concern to them."

Maximilian sipped his wine. He'd been concerned that the troubles in the Central Kingdoms had been somehow tied to the necessity for the Lord of Elcho Falling to wake, but if there was no problem in Isembaard, then maybe he could relax a little. Maybe there would be many months, perhaps even years, before he was required to do anything.

Maybe.

"Look," said Borchard, setting his own wine to one side and standing up, "perhaps we can continue this in the morning. I'm tired, and you look exhausted. I'll leave you to your rest now, and return midafternoon tomorrow. I ask only that you and yours do not leave the confines of this town house and its courtyard."

"Of course not," said Maximilian, now also standing. "Borchard, again I thank you for this welcome, and this town house. You are a friend indeed."

Borchard smiled, nodded, put a hand on Maximilian's shoulder, then left the room.

He opened the door to the dim corridor outside, and walked through.

Straight onto the blade of a sword.

CHAPTER SEVEN

Kyros, the Central Kingdoms

Maximilian froze, caught between disbelief and horror. Then he lunged forward, just as Borchard staggered back into the room.

There was a sword buried in his belly.

It was one of the Emerald Guard's distinctive weapons.

Maximilian caught Borchard as he lost his balance, breaking his fall before he reached the floor. He lay him down gently, unable for the moment to look at the sword, thinking only that he needed to be careful as at least half a handbreadth of the blade protruded from Borchard's back.

Borchard had his hands gripped about the hilt. His abdomen and thighs were soaked in blood, and now a thick stream of it bubbled from his mouth.

"Why, Maxel?" Borchard said, his hands scrabbling uselessly about the hilt of the sword. He spat out a great clot of blood. "Why?"

Then he died.

Maximilian could do nothing but kneel by his friend's body, now staring sightlessly. He was in deep, cold shock, unable to process the events of the last few moments, or to truly comprehend what had just happened.

He did not realize that he was kneeling on the floor, his back to the door, utterly defenseless against Borchard's murderer.

A step sounded behind him, then a soft gasp of shock. *"Maxel!"*

He turned his head, very slightly, just enough to see Ishbel standing there, clutching a shawl about her nightgown, huge eyes in a white face.

"Why are you out of bed?" Maximilian said. "What are you doing *here*?"

"I thought I heard something, and—"

"Go back to your bed, Ishbel."

"Maxel? What has happened?" Ishbel crept a little closer.

"I said to *go back to your bed*!"

She froze. "Maxel—"

"Get back to the bedchamber and *do not move from there until I allow it*!"

Ishbel went utterly still. Then, very slowly and very deliberately, she turned her back and walked away.

Egalion came within moments, closely followed by Garth.

"Ishbel called me," Egalion said, kneeling down next to Maximilian, who still had not moved.

Borchard remained as he had died, half on one side, his hands still wrapped about the hilt of the sword, his eyes staring sightlessly at the ceiling, blood still oozing very slowly from his mouth and belly.

"Garth," Egalion said, "get the Emerald Guard up, weaponed and surrounding this room. Then get Lixel. You can do nothing here."

Garth nodded, leaving the room.

"Maximilian," Egalion said softly. "What happened?"

Maximilian made a helpless gesture. "I don't know, Egalion. Borchard opened the door to leave, took a step out, then staggered back in, the sword in his body. He died within heartbeats. I didn't see who . . . I didn't see *anyone*, gods damn it!"

"Ishbel?" Egalion said, his voice still very quiet. "Why was she here? I thought she was abed and asleep hours ago. Was she here when Borchard was struck?"

"Yes. No. I don't know. I can't think."

"Death is following her everywhere, Maximilian."

Maximilian didn't respond.

"I will set guards about her bedchamber as well," Egalion said, and Maximilian did not countermand it.

"Maximilian, I am sorry, but I need to ask this. Do you think she was responsible for this?"

"I don't know. I can't bear to think about it. She was here immediately after, and I don't know why. How she knew."

Egalion looked at the body once more, then back at Maximilian. "Maxel, we need to get you away from—"

"No."

"Maxel—"

"I will not run from Borchard's death as I ran from Allemorte's. Borchard was my friend, and I owe it to Malat to remain."

"Gods, Maxel, don't you see what kind of sword it is sticking out of Borchard's belly? *No one* is going to believe your protests of innocence. You need to leave."

"No."

"Shit," Egalion muttered. He wiped a hand over his face, unable to think, unable to see a way out of this. *What in the name of all gods was happening to them?*

There was the sound of many feet, running quietly, coming closer. Garth returned, together with six or seven of the Emerald Guard.

Egalion rose from the floor, conferring quietly with the Emerald Guard, giving orders to secure the town house, guard Ishbel, and hunt for any other person within the compound who might possibly be a murderer.

"Borchard's companions are on their way," one of the Emerald Guard said. "They were in the kitchen. They know something is wrong."

"I wish they could have guarded their prince better than they did," Egalion said bitterly. "*Shit!*" he said again. Then he saw Baron Lixel hurrying along the corridor toward them.

"Lixel," Egalion said, and in a few terse words informed him of what had happened. "Maxel won't leave. He's decided to stay."

Lixel muttered a curse.

"I'm going to give you five of the Emerald Guard as escort," Egalion said, "and I want you to get out of this city and ride as hard as you can to Ruen. Let Vorstus and the Privy Council know what has happened, and that it will be a miracle if they ever see their king again. *Damn it*, Garth, why did you save Maximilian from the Veins, if this is what you saved him for?"

"No time for that now," Garth said. "Lixel, you have to go. *Now.* Egalion—"

"Yes, yes." Egalion gave one of the Emerald Guards hurried, urgent orders, then looked back at Lixel. "Be safe, Lixel. Let Vorstus know what is happening. Tell him *everything* you know. Now, *go! Go!* Borchard's men must surely be only moments away."

Lixel shot one anxious look at Maximilian, still by Borchard's body; then he hurried off with the Emerald Guard.

A moment later, Borchard's companions hurried around a corner from the opposite end of the corridor.

King Malat was a tall man, handsome and well built, but in the cold gray of the dawn he looked old and fragile. He sat in a chair in the chamber in which his son had died, his son's body laid out before him, the sword still in place, Borchard's cold hands still wrapped about its hilt, looking at Maximilian who sat in a chair the other side of the body.

"Why?" Malat said for the twentieth time. "Why is my son dead? For what reason?"

Maximilian waved a hand uselessly. It was a gesture he'd made countless times since Malat had arrived four hours ago.

They had spent that time as they were now, sitting in opposite chairs, Borchard lying between them.

The town house was now ringed with Malat's soldiers. Maximilian didn't know where everyone else in his party was, but he assumed they were under close guard.

"Who am I to blame if not you?" Malat said.

Another useless gesture on Maximilian's part.

"How can you say you did not see the murderer? The door was *open*."

"Malat—"

"I wish I'd listened to what Sirus had warned me. I wish I had not listened to the honeyed words of your friends Garth and Lixel and offered you rest within Kyros. Borchard"—his voice broke on the name of his son—"would still be alive if I had not capitulated."

"Malat, I am sorry. I—"

"I want you gone, Maximilian. I want you out of here. I don't know who murdered my son. I want to believe it wasn't you, but I just don't know. All I do know is that I want you *gone* from my house and sight and city and life. Leave me to grieve for my son without your corrupting presence. If, one day, I discover that you *were* responsible for Borchard's death, then I will come after you with everything I have. I will *destroy* your life as you have destroyed mine. Do you understand me, Maximilian?"

"I understand, Malat."

"Then *get out of here*. You have one hour to pack, get on your horses, and get you gone."

"Malat—"

"*Get out of here, get out of this room, now. Now!*"

Maximilian rose and walked for the door.

Just before he got there, Malat spoke again. "Maximilian? Please don't drop in on any more friends on your way home. I cannot bear to think that another father might have to go through what I go through now."

Maximilian stiffened, then he left without saying a word.

"Maxel?" Ishbel rose from where she'd been sitting on the side of the bed. "Please, tell me, what is going on?"

"You don't know?"

"No. I *don't* know!"

"Borchard is dead. Murdered. As is happening to too many people about me. And you."

"I am not responsible," she said softly, but with great feeling.

Maximilian walked over to her, staring for a long moment at her beautiful face. *What was happening to them?* "Borchard was gut struck, Ishbel. A belly blow."

"And your point?" Her face was very white now, and she clutched her wrap tightly about her.

Maximilian took a step forward and buried his fist in the material of the wrap. "Are you a priestess of the Coil, Ishbel?

Be honest with me now if you want me to retain a single shred of trust in you."

He was so angry, yet looked so lost. Ishbel didn't know what to do. She was terrified that if she revealed the truth now, then he *would* believe she was responsible for Borchard's death. Better to continue with the lies. He would never find out.

"No," she said, holding his angry gaze with unwavering eyes.

His fist tightened momentarily in the material of her wrap.

"You're lying," he said softly.

Then he let her go and turned, striding for the door.

"Get dressed," he said. "We're leaving. Now."

Ishbel stared after him, a trembling hand rising to her mouth, her eyes glistening with sudden tears.

CHAPTER EIGHT

The Road from Kyros to Escator,
the Central Kingdoms

They left Kyros within the hour, traveling in a largely un-speaking train. Ishbel rode her own horse: Maximilian had very pointedly not suggested she ride with him. Worse, Garth now rode at Maximilian's side, exchanging the very occasional soft word with him, while Ishbel was left to trail behind, several of the Emerald Guard close behind her, doubt and suspicion riding at her side.

Ishbel herself felt sick with fear and with regret. Fear that Maximilian suspected her; regret that she had so foolishly lied to him.

She wished beyond anything else she had not been stupid enough to lie to him. He was a generous man and would have understood, but Ishbel knew Maximilian well enough now to know that he did not tolerate lies.

How stupid she was! A fool!

She had no idea what was happening to them, why Allemorte and Borchard had died, and what purpose their deaths served anyone save to turn the entire Central Kingdoms against Maximilian, and Maximilian against her.

Was that the purpose? Ishbel shuddered, her hands entangled in the horse's mane to help keep her balance, wishing quite desperately she was safe behind Maximilian, clinging to his warm, strong body, listening to his occasional laugh as he pointed something out to her. She wondered if someone was trying to drive them apart, create a wall of suspicion between them, so that the Great Serpent's wishes could be thwarted.

She disentangled one of her hands, sliding it under her cloak to rest against her belly. She was almost four months pregnant now, and she could just, barely, feel the new hard roundness of her belly. It terrified her, this baby. It complicated everything, and with its growth Ishbel wondered if it drove the Great Serpent further and further from her perception as her swelling womb upset the delicate coil of her intestines. Without that, without the Coil perfectly aligned within her, Ishbel feared she would never sense the Great Serpent again.

Worse, she feared she'd never lie close to Maximilian again, wrapped in his arms, listening to him whisper endearments, and telling her how much he wanted the baby.

Ishbel didn't know what to think and was confused by her emotions. Losing Maximilian's regard was starting to appear as frightful as losing her life at Serpent's Nest.

Even worse.

Ishbel felt completely friendless in this world. Maximilian kept his back to her for most of the time, and his face and voice coldly neutral on those occasions when he couldn't avoid speaking to her. Garth was now back at Maximilian's side, and as careful as her husband not to look her way.

Ishbel didn't know what to do—she didn't know what she *wanted* to do.

They traveled westward for two days, stopping at wayside inns at night. Ishbel's nights were as friendless as her days. Maximilian still shared a bed with her, but he did not curl about her, keeping a vast physical and emotional distance from her within their bed.

On the second night out of Kyros, Ishbel tried to broach that distance.

They had eaten in the public room of the inn, and were now preparing for bed. They'd been completely silent since entering their chamber.

Ishbel had stripped down to her undershift when, heart thudding in mouth, she decided to speak.

"Maxel, please talk to me. What can I say to you? I had *nothing* to do with Borchard's death! I know nothing about why—"

"Then why were you there so soon after his murder? I'd left you asleep in bed, exhausted. Why, then, were you up and running about when Borchard lay dying?"

Because the Great Serpent woke me, Maxel, and said there was a murderer in the house. "I had a bad dream . . . I dreamed you were in danger. I . . . I had to—"

"I am sick of your lies, Ishbel. I am sorry, I am tired. I just want to sleep."

He turned away.

Ishbel wanted to scream at him; instead the tears spilled over and she turned her back as well, rubbing at her eyes. She waited until she heard Maximilian get into bed, then she blew out the lamp and slid in the other side.

They lay there for hours, both awake, staring up into the dark emptiness.

Maximilian had finally dropped off, and was lost in a deep, dreamless sleep when a noise disturbed his peace.

It sounded a little like Ishbel, crying out in fright.

He didn't immediately respond. He was too tired, too disheartened, too confused to leap immediately into wakefulness.

Ishbel cried out again, and this time he felt her body shift violently on the bed.

Finally, and now with some urgency, Maximilian roused himself.

The room was lit, something he would remember later as strange.

Armed men surrounded their bed, eight or nine of them, dressed in the colors and badges of Malat of Kyros.

One of the men held a struggling Ishbel in his arms.

"King Malat sends greetings," said this man. "He begs me to tell you that he wishes you to suffer the same pain as he suffers. He hopes that one day, as you remember the night you lost your wife, you also regret what you did to Malat, in Kyros. Take a long, hard look at your wife, Maximilian, for it is the last sight you will ever have of her."

Maximilian started to move, seeing only the terror and panic on Ishbel's face, and the brutal hand of her abductor gripping tight about her belly. But just as he swung toward the side of the bed, something came down hard on the back of his head, and he knew no more.

CHAPTER NINE

The Road from Kyros to Escator,
the Central Kingdoms

They enveloped her within a dark power that terrified Ishbel, and took her to a place that she could not comprehend, for it, too, was wrapped in dark power. She had thought the Great Serpent of infinite power, but he was a mere worm compared to the enchantment wielded by these nine men. She could not think nor act. All Ishbel could do was breathe, and try to hold on to life, and not panic—almost impossible given the circumstances.

She knew they were not Malat's men, whatever they'd said to Maximilian. The man who held her spoke with a voice that imitated the Kyrrian dialect, but which she recognized as a fabrication. The man's real voice, which she could hear shadowing the false one, was of an intonation utterly unknown to her.

He held Ishbel in a grip so tight, so strong, so implacable, she thought he would murder her. If not that, then she was sure he would crush the baby within her. In that first flush of sheer terror, Ishbel didn't care. She was in so much fear for her own life, which she was sure would be cut short within a moment, that she had no concern for anyone else, whether her husband or her child.

They took her to a dark place of power, and there they bound her and left her lying on a cold, unknown floor.

Even though Ishbel stared wildly into the darkness, she could see nothing. For an unknowable time she lay, her terror escalating with every breath, feeding her imagination until she began to believe that they did not mean to murder her, but to torment her into insanity.

Ba'al'uz drew his Eight aside, leaving the woman, Ishbel, for the moment, and they conversed in low tones so she could not hear them.

"Kanubai shall be pleased. We have the woman," said Ba'al'uz. "She and her child will make a lovely sacrifice."

Ba'al'uz was more than content with events. The murder of Borchard had been masterful, accomplished while Ba'al'uz was shrouded by Kanubai's power, and would be sure to drag both Kyros and Escator into the war that would soon consume the east.

And now they had Kanubai's sacrifice. Ba'al'uz almost floated on the glow of achievement.

"She'll be trouble," said Zeboul, the most senior of the Eight.

"We shan't have to worry about that," said Ba'al'uz. "I have just the thing." He held up a small vial. "Poison. Not enough to murder her—or her child—before Kanubai commands it, but enough to keep her quiet."

"And now?" asked another of the Eight, a man called Salim.

"Torment her," said Ba'al'uz, "just a little to amuse ourselves and to ensure complete compliance, and then we move down toward Deepend and the FarReach Mountains. You will need to take her back to Isaiah—I really don't care what he does with her so long as he keeps her alive and under some semblance of control—while I attend to the other little matter Kanubai requested."

Now all eyes glinted with delight.

"The Weeper," said Zeboul, for Ba'al'uz had told them about the object Kanubai desired.

"Yes," said Ba'al'uz, "the Weeper. Just think, my brothers. With that *and* the woman and her child . . . Kanubai shall reward us *most* handsomely, eh?"

CHAPTER TEN

*The Road from Kyros to Escator,
the Central Kingdoms*

Maximilian remained unconscious for a good six hours after Ishbel's kidnap and, because no one had thought to disturb the king and queen in their bedchamber, there was no alarm raised until Maximilian stumbled out of the chamber door, yelling for Egalion and the Emerald Guard.

There was instant commotion. Not chaos, for Egalion took command, directing the Emerald Guard to search the inn, all outbuildings, and the surrounding countryside.

"Are you *certain* these were Malat's men?" Egalion asked Maximilian, now back in the bedchamber, sitting on the edge of the bed, with Garth holding a compress against the swollen, broken skin at the back of his head.

Maximilian nodded, then instantly regretted it, groaning. "Yes. Yes, they wore Malat's livery and badges. *Shit!* They said . . . they said that Malat sent greetings, and that he wants me to suffer the same pain that he suffers. They said I would not see Ishbel again."

Egalion and Garth exchanged a look.

"Maxel," said Garth, "it might be that these were not Malat's men at all, but—"

"*Do not blame Ishbel for this!*" Maximilian seethed, wrenching himself away from Garth's hands. He stopped, taking a deep breath. "I apologize, Garth. I should not have spoken that way. I am racked with guilt at the way I treated Ishbel over the past few days . . . and you did not see her face as those men held her. She was terrified. Gods, *I* am terrified for her now."

Again a pause. "I find I do not much like the idea of never seeing her again," he said softly.

Garth gently put the compress back on Maximilian's head. "There was nothing you could have done, Maximilian. Do not blame yourself."

"Yes, I blame myself," said Maximilian. "What a muddle I have made of my marriage. How could I have mismanaged it so desperately?"

"Maxel—" Garth began.

"And I should have known better than to lie so unprotected in a public inn. The assassin who murdered Allemorte had been sent for Ishbel, I *know* this. Why did I not realize they would try again?"

Egalion squatted on the floor in front of Maximilian so he could look him directly in the face. "Maxel," he said, "almost seven hours have passed since they stole Ishbel. They could be anywhere. I have set the Emerald Guard to searching the inn and surrounding area, but I do not expect to find them. Whether Malat's men or others, they will be well away by now."

Maximilian said nothing, and Egalion and Garth exchanged another look.

"We need to decide what to do," said Egalion. "Whether to continue on for Escator, or . . ."

Maximilian winced as Garth moved the compress, then waved at him to take the thing away.

"Everything is going wrong," Maximilian said. "Too many things."

He stopped, and the other two waited.

After a long moment Maximilian sighed, gingerly stretching his upper back and shoulders. "I need to go back to Malat," he said. "Maybe they were his men, maybe not, but I need to see him. And . . . maybe he can give me some clue as to what is going *on*."

Maximilian's voice broke on that last, and Egalion stood up, and rested a hand on his shoulder.

"We'll find her, Maxel," he said.

"I doubt that very, very much," Maximilian said softly.

* * *

Malat could not believe it when he heard that his soldiers had apprehended the King of Escator a mile out of Kyros and that Maximilian was requesting to see him.

"He was heading *back*?" he said. "To see *me*? Does he have a death wish?"

"He has been injured in some fight," said the captain of the guard. "Perhaps he is looking for sympathy."

Malat cursed. "Then I wish well to whoever injured him, but they could have done a better job and stopped his heart entirely."

"What should we do with him, sire?"

"Is his entire retinue with him?"

"Several of his Emerald Guard," said the captain, "but none of his other companions. Maximilian said they waited for him at an inn some distance along the road."

"What the *fuck* does he want?" Malat muttered. "Why disturb me in this fashion? Oh, damn it, put him in a dungeon—the coldest, dampest one you can find—and tell him I will consider his request for an audience over my evening meal."

"Sire," the captain said, "Maximilian said the matter was desperate."

"Desperate is the state of my *heart*," said Malat. "Maximilian has no right to use the word." He fell silent, studying the captain of the guard, who was now looking decidedly uncomfortable. "Oh, very well, bring him in an hour to the smaller audience chamber—and empty it of any servants, guards, and courtiers beforehand. I will see him then."

"Sire, do you think it wise to talk with this brigand without protection?"

"If he so much as takes a step in my direction," Malat said, "I'll run him through with a sword. Now, go, and leave me in peace."

The smaller audience chamber was an unadorned room with few windows, paneled in dark wood, and with an air of such somberness that very few people had ever dared laugh in its confines.

It suited Malat's mood perfectly.

One of the double doors at the other end of the chamber opened, and the captain of the guard escorted Maximilian through.

At Malat's tip of his head, the captain retired, closing the door behind him.

"To what," said Malat, his voice underscored with venom, "do I owe this honor?"

"Ishbel has been taken," Maximilian said, walking forward from the far end of the chamber, "by your men."

"What!" Malat leapt from his chair. "How dare you—"

"They told me," said Maximilian, stopping halfway down the chamber, "that you wanted me to suffer the same pain as you suffered, and that I should never see Ishbel again. I want my wife, Malat. I did not murder your son, and now *I want my wife back*!"

Malat stopped a few paces away, studying Maximilian carefully. He was disheveled and dirty, his face tired and drawn with both physical and emotional pain, and the neck of his shirt appeared crusted with dried blood.

Malat walked forward, held Maximilian's eyes for a long moment, then slowly walked about him, noting the deep bruising and scabbed abrasion at the back of his head.

"What happened?" he said.

"Your men came, on your orders, and took my wife, beating me that I might not rescue her."

Malat was now back in front of Maximilian. Again, he spent a long moment holding Maximilian's eyes. "You don't believe that," Malat said.

"I am left to believe only what my eyes showed me and my ears told me," Maximilian snapped. "*Did* you send your men to take my wife and threaten her death?"

"No. Do you believe me?"

Maximilian took a deep breath, passing a trembling hand over his eyes. "Yes. If you'd sent men, their orders would have been to murder me, not take my wife."

"Correct. These men looked like mine?"

"They wore your livery, badges . . . perfect replicas of the uniform your guards wear."

"What is happening, Maximilian?"

"I . . . don't . . . know."

Malat sighed, then took Maximilian by the elbow and led him to a chair. He sat him down, then went to a sideboard and poured each of them a glass of wine.

"All right, then," Malat said, handing Maximilian his wine, then sitting down in a chair opposite. "Tell me what you *think* is happening."

"Someone has tried before to kill Ishbel. Someone is trying to implicate me in the deaths of Allemorte and Borchard. People are dying in a trail from the Outlands to Kyros, and the trail of death is following me. I don't know why. I don't *know* why, Malat." Maximilian was now almost certain that these deaths were tied in with Elcho Falling, or whatever was going wrong with the world that required Elcho Falling to stir into life, but *that* Maximilian could not discuss with Malat. "Now Ishbel has gone. I don't understand . . . why take *her*?"

Malat could think of several highly carnal reasons a group of men might want to seize Ishbel, but thought it best not to share his thoughts with Maximilian.

"Apart from Ishbel," Malat said, "the other three men share something in common."

Maximilian just looked at him. He was too tired and disheartened to speak.

"They're all highborn," said Malat, "but . . . they're all good generals. Some of the best."

Very carefully Maximilian put his wineglass down on the floor, then rested his elbows on his knees and his face in his hands. He should have seen that. Rilm Evenor had been the best war general in the Outlands, and the one with the most experience *and* the wisest head. Allemorte did not have the wealth of experience that Evenor did, but he'd proved himself on several occasions to have a cool head in battle and a superb eye for battle command. Borchard similarly. Malat had been at formal war with no one during his long reign, but Borchard had taken part in several campaigns in . . .

"Oh, gods," Maximilian murmured. "Borchard served as Evenor's lieutenant for a year, didn't he?"

"Yes, and you can be sure I was none too pleased about it

then, or now. But Evenor trained him well, and spoke highly of his ·capabilities." Malat paused. "I think you can thank your lucky stars, Maxel—"

Maximilian noted, somewhat numbly, that Malat was now using the familiar contraction of his name.

"—that you are not a highly skilled battle general yourself, or otherwise I think you, too, would be dead."

Hardly the best compliment, Maximilian thought, but true enough.

"Why Ishbel?" Malat said. "What part does she have to play in this?"

"Ishbel is a mystery to most people, including me," Maximilian said. "She was offered to me by the Coil—"

"*What*?"

"—as their ward. They'd raised her after she lost her family at the age of eight." Maximilian hesitated, wondering how much he could say, then decided he was tired of dissembling. Besides, Malat had lost a son, and deserved to hear as much as Maximilian could reveal. "But I think she might actually be a priestess of the Coil, not just a ward."

Malat swore, his face shocked. "Why send her to marry *you*?"

Maximilian phrased the response as best he could. It might not be the full truth, but it was still truth enough. "Our families were connected many years ago. The Coil apparently thought it would be a good thing to reunite blood and fortunes again." He gave a wry grin. "I was happy enough about the fortunes."

Malat ignored the poor attempt at humor. "By the gods, Maximilian, *what have you been dragging through the Central Kingdoms*? A priestess of the Coil? A—"

"I do not know if she is or not. Ishbel denies it, but I suspect it."

"Maximilian, my son died with a sword through his belly . . . are you trying to tell me now that he died, in that manner, with a priestess of the Coil close by, and that Ishbel was *not* involved?"

Maximilian now regretted telling Malat of his suspicions.

"*I* suspected her," Maximilian said, wishing he need not say this also, "and all but blamed her. I was a *fool*. When I woke to see her seized by brigands, when I saw her face as they threatened her life, I knew I'd been wrong. She was terrified, Malat. Genuinely terrified. I think she is as much a victim as—"

"No priestess of the Coil is a victim of anything."

Maximilian did not respond. There was nothing he could say to that.

Malat muttered yet another curse. "Sirus is moving ever closer to war with the Outlands, and dragging luckless Fulmer of Hosea with him. They should be stopped, but they are not going to believe what you've just told me. *I* don't know that I should believe what you've just told me. Gods, Maximilian, a priestess of the *Coil*? Of what were you *thinking*?"

"I don't know what to do, Malat. I don't know how to find her. I don't know *why* she was taken."

"Snap out of it, Maxel. You're a king and a husband. Do whatever you have to. Right at the moment, though, I'm just too tired and too old and too heartsick to help you."

CHAPTER ELEVEN

The Road from Kyros to Deepend,
Central Kingdoms

B a'al'uz and his companions moved south as fast as they could, which was not as fast as they wished. They needed to be circumspect, not so much lest they be suspected of the trail of murders across the Outlands and the Central Kingdoms, but because they had among them the wife of Maximilian, the Queen of Escator, a veritable nuisance who needed to be kept in a state of some lassitude in order to keep her quiet. This lassitude was accomplished by a combination of threats and the free use of the contents of the dark vial Ba'al'uz carried with him. Ishbel was drugged into insensibility, and Ba'al'uz did not care what harm the potent mixture he forced down her throat did to her or to the baby she carried, so long as both remained alive by the time she reached Aqhat. They only needed to be breathing. They did not need to be completely healthy.

They were fortunate in that the spring remained cold north of the FarReach Mountains. Ba'al'uz kept Ishbel heavily cloaked and largely concealed beneath canvas in the small cart he'd purchased from a farmer, as well as the donkey to draw it. They traveled as far as they could every day, using the power of Kanubai to speed their steps as well as those of the donkey.

But the Eight would be taking Ishbel home without Ba'al'uz. He had business to attend to in Coroleas. He would vastly have preferred to see to Ishbel's journey to Aqhat himself, but Kanubai needed him in Coroleas.

The Weeper resided in Coroleas, and Kanubai wanted it.

Very badly. More badly than he had wanted the woman.

On the night before they entered Deepend, where Ba'al'uz would leave for Coroleas, Ba'al'uz drew the Eight aside. Ishbel was bedded down in the cart in an abandoned barn, tied with physical restraints and heavily drugged.

"Tonight I will contact Isaiah," said Ba'al'uz, "to let him know that you and the woman shall be arriving at Aqhat. I shall tell Isaiah that she is the Queen of Escator, and that she would make him a good new wife. Before I depart for Coroleas, I shall hand the pyramid to you, Zeboul. I do not want Lister to know where I go. From now on, my life is devoted entirely to Kanubai. Keep the pyramid wrapped well, and do not respond if Lister tries to contact you through it."

"Why tell Isaiah about Ishbel?" Zeboul said. "Why present her to him as a new wife?"

"Because I want the woman kept safe at Aqhat. I want her kept as securely as possible." Ba'al'uz paused, and grinned. "And Isaiah keeps no one more safe than one of his wives. Especially one that he can claim as a 'hunting' trophy—the Queen of Escator. That might keep his generals in line for an extra half day or so."

The Eight laughed.

"You don't mind if he . . ." Zeboul asked.

"If he *what*?" said Ba'al'uz, his grin stretching to even slyer proportions. "So long as he keeps her alive for when I return to present her to Kanubai, then I really don't care how he plays with her in the meantime."

CHAPTER TWELVE

Aqhat and Crowhurst

Isaiah watched his rose pyramid dull back to its usual opaque inactivity. For a long time he sat motionless, staring at the pyramid, then very slowly the fingers of one hand began to thrum against the table.

Ba'al'uz had kidnapped Ishbel, Queen of Escator.

Ba'al'uz was sending her to Isaiah at Aqhat with his eight companions while he set off on some mysterious journey to Coroleas.

Ba'al'uz' excuse for stealing Ishbel was that Isaiah needed another wife and who better than the Queen of Escator when Isaiah was soon to invade the north? A trophy like Ishbel would be sure to impress, not only Isaiah's generals, but also the soon-to-be-subjected northern peoples. *It has added to my campaign of terror and chaos to confound the northern kings,* said Ba'al'uz, *and it will keep your generals from outright treason for a little while longer,* and Isaiah had nodded as if in complete agreement.

Of course, Ba'al'uz did have a point so far as the generals went.

Isaiah knew his five senior generals watched him constantly for weakness, for that moment when one among them might take the opportunity for a swift assassination and assumption of the throne for himself. Isaiah had many talents, and he was a very powerful man, but any one of those generals could ruin his, and Lister's, plans with that one fatal strike. For the moment, Isaiah needed to placate them.

A marriage to the captured Queen of Escator, a conquest not quite at the same level as invasion, but nonetheless not insignificant either, might keep that dagger sheathed a month or two longer. Long enough for Isaiah to shore up his own position with a successful invasion of the north.

Long enough for Isaiah to do what he needed.

But generals and treachery aside, Isaiah knew that Ba'al'uz had a far deeper reason for sending Ishbel to Aqhat.

He wanted her.

For a moment Isaiah's eyes slid toward the windows that looked over the river and DarkGlass Mountain beyond, then they slid back to the pyramid.

Then, as if to counteract that movement, they slid toward the Goblet of the Frogs, which, as usual at this time of evening, stood on the low table in the center of the room, a single lit reed taper behind it to set the glass afire. Isaiah looked at it for a long time, very still, thinking about Ishbel, Queen of Escator.

On her reluctant way to DarkGlass Mountain.

Isaiah drew a deep breath eventually, long and shaky. He needed to talk to Lister, but was far too disturbed to use the pyramid prop.

Instead, he used his power.

Lister, Isaiah whispered across the vast distance, *guess who is coming to visit?*

Lister was standing by the hearth in his chamber at Crowhurst, and the first that Eleanon and Inardle, another of the Lealfast and Eleanon's sister, knew of the communication with Isaiah was when Lister went very stiff for a moment or two, and then bent over slightly at his waist, rubbing his temples with the fingers of one hand and muttering, "Shit! Shit! Shit! Shit!"

"What is it?" said Eleanon, standing and moving to Lister's side, Inardle only a breath behind him.

"Ba'al'uz has kidnapped Ishbel," said Lister, "and he has sent her down to Aqhat. She is not there yet, but is on her way. Ba'al'uz just used his pyramid to contact Isaiah and let him know the fruits of Ba'al'uz' efforts in the north. Ishbel was his prized piece of information."

Eleanon and Inardle exchanged a shocked glance.

"Even worse," Lister said, "Isaiah thinks that Ba'al'uz

now works Kanubai's will exclusively. You can be sure that Ba'al'uz did not snatch Ishbel of his own accord. He doesn't have the wit or the length of coherent thought to be able to plan that."

"Ishbel shall need all *her* wits about her," said Eleanon.

"Ishbel refuses to acknowledge the time of day," muttered Lister, "let alone her true nature or talents. If Kanubai rose before her, she would simply refuse to see him. Witless, witless, *witless*!"

Inardle put a gentle hand on Lister's arm, knowing he referred to himself with those last words rather than Ishbel. "You could not have known Ba'al'uz would do something like that."

Lister contented himself by slamming a fist into the wall, then cursing as his hand bruised. "I could have predicted it!" he snarled. "By the wind-driven snow itself, *I should have thought Ba'al'uz might do something like this*! I knew Maximilian and Ishbel were traveling through the north, I *knew* it. I—"

"Lister," said Eleanon, "we must trust to the gods that—"

"Oh, you fool," said Lister. "We *are* the gods, and look what a mess we've got Ishbel into!"

He walked about the chamber, rubbing at his injured hand, pausing to look out a window at four or five Skraelings scurrying far below.

They're getting restless, he thought. *How much longer do any of us have?*

"Ba'al'uz has proved more nightmare than aid," Lister said eventually. "We should have had him murdered months ago."

"Perhaps now?" said Eleanon.

"Apparently he is off to Coroleas on some crazed expedition," Lister said. "I don't know what, but at least in Coroleas he cannot do *us* much more harm. We worry only if he returns, and we pray that the Coroleans have the sense to spit him the instant he sets foot in their empire."

"What is Isaiah going to do?" Eleanon said.

"Look after her, I hope," Lister muttered. "No, not hope. *Pray* to every benevolent being that he keeps her protected!"

CHAPTER THIRTEEN

The Tyranny of Isembaard

They had ridden out westward from Aqhat early in the morning, away from the River Lhyl and DarkGlass Mountain. Isaiah seemed to have something on his mind, for he was very introspective, and Axis did not push him for conversation. It was only when they'd reached the very edges of the Melachor Plains and had pulled their blowing horses to a halt that Isaiah finally looked to Axis, and spoke.

"Ba'al'uz contacted me last night."

"Yes?"

"His companions are on their way home," Isaiah said, "although Ba'al'uz has set off on a journey to Coroleas. Gods alone know why, but I for one don't begrudge his continuing absence."

Axis waited.

"Ba'al'uz and his companions have, apparently, accomplished their tasks better than expected in the north," Isaiah continued. "The Central Kingdoms and the Outlands are at each other's throats. Their best generals are dead. Disarray increases by the day."

"I don't like this, Isaiah. It is a miserable way to conduct a war, eh?"

"It is the successful way, Axis."

Axis shrugged, and turned his eyes forward, looking over the Melachor Plains. Any semblance of lushness and fertility had been long left behind at the river. Here the landscape was a rolling vast barrenness, carpeted with scrubby plants that clung to rock crevices and the shaded sides of dust bowls. It was a forbidding landscape, and Axis wondered that Isaiah should have ridden out to survey it. Did he find comfort here? Or challenge?

Comfort, Axis thought, and wondered that Isaiah needed such as this for comfort.

"There was something else," Isaiah said.

Axis looked back at him.

"Ba'al'uz has kidnapped the new wife of Maximilian of Escator and is sending her back to Aqhat."

"*What*?"

"Ba'al'uz said she would make *me* a fine wife."

Axis could do nothing now but stare, aghast.

Isaiah had been looking straight ahead over the landscape, but now turned his head to look directly at Axis. "She would be a fine conquest, Axis. Together with the territory, I take one of their queens. It would be a total emotional subjection. Ba'al'uz said she was of fair aspect, and that I would not find her displeasing."

"Isaiah—"

"Ba'al'uz has requested an escort for the lady from the FarReach Mountains back to Aqhat. He is worried that Maximilian might try to rescue his wife."

"Frankly, I'd be a bit worried about that as well," Axis muttered. Gods, what had Ba'al'uz done . . . and what in the world was Isaiah *thinking*?

"Axis, I ask that you lead a company of men north to the FarReach Mountains, there to meet Ba'al'uz' men and this woman, Ishbel, Queen of Escator, and escort her to me."

Axis was now rendered utterly speechless. The news that Ba'al'uz had kidnapped the new wife of Maximilian of Escator was startling, and the idea that Isaiah would take her as a conquest wife even more so, but that Isaiah should trust him to lead a company of armed men north . . . that was unbelievable.

And exciting. The idea of *doing* something was as heady as a draft of wine.

"Of course," said Axis, then he smiled. "So long as you trust me with her."

"You're the one man I do trust with her," said Isaiah. "I can't see you betraying Azhure for any other woman. Besides, the trip will be useful in another way, for you can check to see how well the resettlement plans are progressing. Ezekiel and Morfah have sent regular and very reassuring reports, but it doesn't hurt to have you cast your eye over their progress, does it?"

Later that night Isaiah sat in a chair in his private chamber, holding the Goblet of the Frogs in his hands. He rolled it gently between his palms, watching the light play through its beautifully crafted shape.

Ishbel, here at Aqhat. Oh, the dangers, not merely to her, but to everyone.

But, oh, the possibilities. Isaiah knew Lister would be worried—frantic, even—but Isaiah wondered if more was at play here than just what Kanubai might be whispering into Ba'al'uz' mind.

Ishbel coming back to Aqhat would be Ishbel coming home. Ishbel coming home could be an Ishbel awakened. From what Lister had said of her, Ishbel had shut herself off completely from her true nature.

She would need to wake, sooner or later.

Isaiah thought of what he'd sensed clinging to Kanubai's back . . . of his sense that something *else* was rising with Kanubai.

Ishbel might be able to see more clearly than he.

After all, she was the one with the blood for it.

"What of you, my friend," Isaiah murmured to the goblet. "Anxious, or pleased?"

The goblet responded, not with words, but with a wave of delighted emotion. Isaiah smiled, then raised the goblet to his lips and kissed it gently.

There were dangers, but Isaiah could protect her.

CHAPTER FOURTEEN

*The Road from Kyros to Escator,
the Central Kingdoms*

Maximilian had left Malat in Kyros without any clear idea what to do. He felt completely, stupidly useless. His wife had been taken from him, and he had no idea how best he might save her. Egalion had organized the Emerald Guard into a search of the area between Kyros and the inn, but they had discovered nothing. Maximilian was not surprised. Ishbel and her kidnappers must be far, far away by now.

But in what direction?

And *who*?

What could he do?

Nothing. *Nothing*, and that infuriated Maximilian more than anything. What a worthless husband he was! He could not protect his pregnant wife and keep her safe. He could do nothing to rescue her. He was leagues and leagues from home and friends, and, because of the series of events from Margalit to Kyros, no one wanted to lend him aid, or even a sympathetic ear.

And Ishbel didn't even have her ring.

If Ishbel had been wearing the ring, then Maximilian would have had a good sense of where she was, in which direction. The rings bound each other and their wearers.

But Ishbel had given hers back to Maximilian.

From hopelessness, Maximilian succumbed to anger. Why had he not *insisted* she wear the damned ring?

From anger, Maximilian swung back to guilt as he remembered how badly he'd treated Ishbel after Borchard's death. She had not been responsible. She had become yet another victim.

What memories would she have to carry her through her ordeal? His hard, judgmental face?

Everyone in his party left Maximilian alone as much as they could. Not even Garth dared engage him in conversation.

After three days of useless snarling and hanging about the inn from where Ishbel had been taken, Maximilian made the decision to return to Escator as fast as possible. He could do nothing here, and at least in Escator he'd have more resources, plus the advice of Vorstus, who Maximilian realized he needed to speak to very badly, as much as he disliked and distrusted the man.

And he'd be *home*.

If without his wife.

Maximilian and his party had just reached the western fringes of the Kyrrian lands when, at noon on a lovely warm day, eight Icarii landed on the road before them.

"StarWeb!" Maximilian cried, dismounting and striding out to meet her. He grabbed her shoulders, hugged her, then kissed her on the cheek.

"Thank the gods," he said.

"Maxel?" she said. "What has happened?"

"Ishbel has been taken. Gods, almost three weeks back. I have no idea where she is. StarWeb, I need you to—"

"Maxel! Stop a moment . . . what is going on? I am here because not a week ago Lixel rode into Ruen with a tale that none of us could believe. Murders, accusations against you . . . and now Ishbel? Taken?"

Egalion and Garth had now joined Maximilian, and both greeted StarWeb and the other Icarii warmly.

"Ishbel was kidnapped from my side almost three weeks ago," said Maximilian, "by men pretending to be Malat's soldiers. I have no idea where she is, but now that you're here—"

"That woman is nothing but trouble," StarWeb muttered.

"She's pregnant, StarWeb."

StarWeb glanced sharply at Maximilian at that, but did not comment.

"We can use your wings and eyes," Egalion said. "If you—"

"Almost three weeks?" said StarWeb. "She's likely to be dead by now."

Maximilian winced. He finally seemed to realize the presence of the other Icarii behind StarWeb, and greeted them, apologizing for his tardiness.

"You are distracted, Maximilian," said one of them, a blue-and-silver birdman called BroadWing EvenBeat. "Remembering your manners is surely a low priority right now." He looked at Egalion. "This is a mess."

"Aye," said Egalion. "Please, if you can aid us—"

"We will do what we can," said BroadWing, "and be glad of it. You have made a ground search of the area about Kyros, yes?"

"Yes," said Maximilian. "I do not think her anywhere near Kyros."

"Then where?"

"Either north or south," Maximilian said. "They would not take her toward Escator, and I think it unlikely they would take her back toward the troubles in the Central Kingdoms. But which? I can't decide which way to—"

"We will divide up," said BroadWing. "I will lead four of my fellows south, and EverNest can take two north. Maximilian, try not to worry. One of us shall find her."

"Ishbel is trouble," said StarWeb. "Too much trouble."

"For gods' sakes, StarWeb," Maximilian said. "She is pregnant. Does that mean nothing to you?"

Garth thought Maximilian's judgment of character had been severely clouded by his anxiety if he thought he could speak such words to his only-barely former lover. StarWeb didn't like Ishbel, was jealous of her, and would resent the fact she was pregnant. Icarii found it difficult to achieve a pregnancy, and that Ishbel had managed it so quickly would not endear her to StarWeb at all.

Suddenly Garth wondered if it was a good idea sending StarWeb to find Ishbel, after all.

"Maxel—" he began.

"We'll leave immediately," said BroadWing. "Maximilian, we will do all we can, I promise."

Maximilian nodded, but there was no hope in his eyes. "Thank you," he said.

[Part Five]

CHAPTER ONE

Palace of the First, Yoyette, Coroleas

Leave now," the Duchess of Sidon told the man sitting naked on the edge of her bed, and he rose silently, dressed, and did as ordered.

Salome lounged back on her pillow, sated with sex, glad the man had left without wanting to, of all things, talk.

She hated talkers. They invariably wanted something, or, even worse, thought they could mean something to her life.

Salome much preferred not having a man as a permanent fixture in her life. She loved sex and took lovers as she wanted them, or used some of the more attractive servants in her palace as she needed, but had no other need for men. Her husband, the late and never-to-be-regretted duke, had died within two years of their marriage, leaving her, a sixteen-year-old widow, to nurture an infant son, and to wield the political power that an enormous fortune and possession of the most powerful deity in Coroleas gave her.

His death had been a remarkable relief. Now Salome allowed no man to get near her emotionally, nor, apart from sex, physically.

Her son, Ezra, now Duke of Sidon (although held under the regency of his mother until his nineteenth birthday), was Salome's pride and joy. She meant him to be emperor one day, had schooled him in the alphabet and in intrigue, had loved and coddled him, prodded and encouraged him, bribed anyone who could aid her ambition, and smoothed the path forward to the emperor's throne with a few judicial murders along the way.

He would be emperor by the time he was twenty. Salome would let nothing stand in his (*her*) way.

It was close to dawn now, and Salome rose from the bed, the marks of her lover still on her, and went to stand naked by the open full-length window.

She was a striking woman. She had enormous strength to her face, an exotic lift to her cheekbones and eyes, and such long and glamorous (and, for Coroleas, unusual) white blond hair that men invariably found her irresistible. Naturally Salome was aware that her position as the most powerful woman in the empire (no one but a fool ever considered the current empress more powerful) also had its attractions, but men found it no hardship to be invited (or commanded) to her bed. Neither the marks of time nor childbearing had left their scars on her body, and it was still as straight and slim at thirty as it had been when the duke had first lusted for her as a fourteen-year-old girl.

Content with her world and her lot, Salome lounged against the window frame, as uncaring of any who might look up and see her as she was at the twenty-pace drop immediately below her feet.

The Palace of the First spread out below her: naturally Salome had one of the best apartments in the palace, high in the Tower of the Beloved, beneath only the emperor's apartment. Corolean society was divided into three castes: the Forty-four Hundred Families, also known as the First, who commanded the majority of the wealth and power in the empire—the emperor and nobles could only come from this caste; the Thirty-eight Thousand Second Families, or the Second, who made up the educated intelligentsia and traders and minor landowners of the empire; and the Third, the name given to the mass of men, women, and children who worked to serve the First and the Second.

Beneath the Third, living a life so wretched they did not even have a caste, were the slaves, who lived and died at the discretion of any who owned them.

Salome loved to stand at this window in the early morning, looking down over the Palace of the First (a sprawling complex of palaces and apartments that housed the members of the First when they were in Yoyette to attend the emperor's court), and reminding herself of her authority.

"Most powerful of all in this empire," she murmured, "save for the emperor himself, and then, within a few short years, not even he." Salome might love Ezra, but she wouldn't allow him to stand in her way. When Ezra commanded the vast Corolean Empire as its emperor, then she would command him. After all, the boy would have a vast debt to repay his mother.

The sun was well above the horizon now, and Salome stretched, catlike, in the window, before turning back into the room to prepare for her day.

As she did so, the sun caught her back and for an instant illuminated the faintest of scars that ran down her spine from the center of her shoulder blades to the crease of her buttocks.

The court of Coroleas at the Palace of the First in Yoyette was known over the entire civilized world for its elegance, its richness, its entertainments, its murderous intrigue, and its breathtaking, uninhibited immorality. That immorality did not merely encompass sexual conduct, but the way in which members of the First valued human life overall—generally with the utmost contempt. The court was a frightening, powerful, exhilarating, alive place in which to hunt or to enjoy oneself, and it drew to itself not only the members of the First (who could hardly imagine life without it), but also adventurers and fortune-hunters from countries across the Treachery Straits. The First tolerated them, allowing them generous access to the court, and accommodation within the palace. After all, it was the adventurers and fortune-hunters who provided the First with much of their amusement.

StarDrifter SunSoar had lived here, off and on, since the fall of Tencendor five years earlier. He loathed Corolean society, and was repelled by the manner in which the First mistreated everyone below them, but he had nowhere else to go. Somehow, during those cataclysmic events that had culminated in the loss of Tencendor beneath the waves of the

Widowmaker Sea, StarDrifter had found himself still alive, and inexplicably at the Corolean court.

To be completely factual, he'd found himself sprawled on the floor of a corridor just beyond the kitchens, bleeding to death from the terrible wounds in his back where the demonic Hawk Childs had torn out his wings.

He *would* have bled to death save that two male slaves had wandered by, discovered his barely conscious body, and had, without comment (finding the half murdered lying unattended in the corridors of the Palace of the First was hardly a remarkable event), dragged StarDrifter to a physician, who had managed to close his wounds and usher in their healing.

StarDrifter had not been grateful. He wished he *had* died. In the frenzy that had mutilated StarDrifter, the Hawk Childs had also murdered his granddaughter, Zenith, who StarDrifter had loved. Loved, that is, as a man loves a woman, for it was no sin in Icarii society for a grandfather to bed a granddaughter. They only balked at first blood: children or siblings. StarDrifter had lusted for Zenith for years, but she had continually rejected him, to his enormous frustration. It was that frustration, in the end, that had caused Zenith's death, for he had inadvertently set the Hawk Childs loose on her by his thoughtless words.

It was not just Zenith whom StarDrifter had lost. It was everyone and everything. Once a proud prince and Enchanter of Tencendor, and father of Axis, StarMan and Star God, StarDrifter had enjoyed privilege and honor. Now he was nothing but an amusement at the Corolean court. He drifted through the court, getting himself involved in some of the more minor and less bloody of its schemes, taking lovers here and there, getting drunk with various other adventurers and lost souls, and avoiding all the other Icarii at the court like the very plague.

They reminded him of everything he had lost. Most particularly, their ability to fly reminded him very painfully that he no longer had his wings. StarDrifter had spent two centuries soaring over the peaks and plains of Tencendor. Now he lived as a cripple: an Icarii with no wings was nothing, and he loathed those who could still soar. In truth he did not have to do much to avoid them, for there were relatively few Icarii at the court.

There were a thousand or so spread around Coroleas, at the universities and larger cities, and some haunting the Jai Alps to the south, but most were nauseated by the bloody immorality of the court and shunned it whenever possible.

Hate it as he might, StarDrifter could lose himself within the court, within its shadows and intrigues and its habit of never asking too many questions. He could drift and exist, hate and intrigue, and somehow hope to forget his empty life.

Today was one of the more interesting—and for the slaves in the Palace of the First, one of the most dangerous—days in the yearly cycle of court activities. It was Fillip Day.

One of the privileges that the First claimed for themselves was the right to play the ancient game of Fillip. The game epitomized everything StarDrifter loathed about the Corolean court—its blatant sexuality, its carelessness of life, its utter superficiality, its dark plots—but for his own terrible, bitter reasons, StarDrifter felt the need to attend.

Normally Fillip was played in the utmost privacy and, for Corolean standards, with great discretion. But on this one day of the year it came out of the closet and was celebrated in the Diamond Colonnade, the general gathering hall for the court (as opposed to the Emperor's Hall for more formal occasions), whose columns and vaulted ceiling were literally smothered with diamonds set in gold. The colonnade was massive, running almost two hundred paces east-west, open at both ends so that it caught both the rising and setting sun, and with star-shaped glassed openings in the vaulted roof that allowed in the noon light.

The colonnade glittered and sparkled every daylight hour.

StarDrifter thought it looked cheap.

He arrived in the colonnade at mid-morning, by which time most people who were going to attend had already arrived. Every one of the Forty-four Hundred First Families had several representatives present, and in some instances the entire family had decided to attend; members of the Second were only rarely invited. The emperor—an almost obscenely fat man clothed in several glaring shades of silk and far too much bulky lace for the warm morning—was in attendance, as was his empress and half a dozen of his official concubines. Most of the adventurers and hangers-on of the court were here, as were almost two thousand of the Third, to serve and indulge the First.

Yet even so, the Diamond Colonnade was not crowded.

StarDrifter strolled down one of the side aisles, hands behind his back, an expression on his face that discouraged any from engaging him in idle conversation. Despite the inapproachability of his demeanor he was a very striking man, almost beautiful. Tall and lean, yet of a muscular build, StarDrifter was clad in fitted cream breeches and shirt, which set off his close-cropped golden hair, high-cheekboned face, and blue eyes. He walked with a slow, lithe grace, rather like a dancer, yet with the calculated precision of a hunter.

His feet were bare save for plain gold rings about each of his big toes.

StarDrifter's clothing was in remarkable contrast to most of the other people in attendance. The Coroleans generally loved bright colors, floating fabrics, and as many jewels as they could fit on their bodies. Most of their gowns were belted, and from these belts hung small bronze figurines, each about the size of a woman's finger. The richer and more important the bearer, the more bronze figurines they had jangling about their waists; the colonnade was alive with the sound of jangling bronze.

They were small deities. The Coroleans collected them assiduously, believing that the more bronze deities they carried about their person the better protected they would be from life's mishaps, the better health they would enjoy (and the better able they would be to escape the various sexual diseases that infested the Corolean court), and the more luck they would bring upon themselves and their families. The more devout among them also collected half-sized deities that they inserted into bodily cavities, the better to warm the bronze figurines and engage their magical abilities. Looking at the crowd, StarDrifter thought he could see several people walking with that peculiarly pained gait which suggested they carried more bronze within their flesh than dangling from the outside of it; it was not unknown for Coroleans to die from perforated bowels and wombs due to crowding in one too many deities.

StarDrifter would have regarded the Coroleans' obsession with the bronze deities as little more than pathetic save for one thing: the manner in which the deities were created.

The Third contained within their number a subcaste of elite bronze workers whose guild was controlled tightly by the Thirty-eight Thousand of the Second. The bronze workers made the myriad small bronze shells to house the deities. These bronze shells were then transferred to the care of a caste of priests, known as the God Priests, within the Second, where they were offered up for sale to members of the First and the Second. As yet the bronze shells had no power associated with them at all—the purchaser also had to buy a deity to inhabit the shell. It was the responsibility of the God Priest to infuse the bronze shell with the god, which then created the bronze deity.

StarDrifter thought the entire thing epitomized everything he believed wrong with Corolean society: hopelessly complex and contrived, and mostly entirely morally valueless. But of everything, it was the manner in which the bronze shells were infused with the resident god that sickened StarDrifter and fed his contempt of everything Corolean.

The God Priests empowered the figurines by infusing them with the soul of a man, woman, or child. It was this soul that then gave the figurine its godlike powers. If the soul came from a man with great physical strength, then the deity would impart physical strength to its wearer. Whatever the most dominant trait of the soul-giver, thus the dominant trait of the bronze deity. StarDrifter had once heard that one of the most sought-after souls were those of assassins; every Corolean, it seemed, yearned for an assassin deity to work its deadliness on the bearer's enemies. Another soul greatly valued was that of the newborn baby—one who had not yet taken suck. This soul was treasured for its purity and strength, and Coroleans believed a bronze deity infused with this kind of soul imparted long, vigorous life to the bearer.

None of these souls were freely given. They were taken from the bodies of the living in horrific religious ceremonies conducted by the God Priests, who drew the soul from the living body in a process they extended over as many hours as possible, and which they made as painful as possible for the soul-giver. Only thus, they argued, would the soul retain all its strength for the bronze figurine it was to inhabit.

It was the mass of slaves and condemned criminals who provided the souls. The soul-givers were picked for their qualities, and wives never knew when their husbands might not return, or when their newborn infants might be snatched from the midwives' hands for the God Priest pits, or when they themselves might be selected as suitable souls for a bronze figurine. They were snatched from their homes, from the streets, from their beds at night, and they lived in such abject hopelessness that few of them ever struggled against their fate.

Today there was a huddled, miserable group of them set on a dais partway down the colonnade.

They were here to participate in the game of Fillip.

StarDrifter's carefully constructed mask of remoteness and inapproachability faltered as he stood to one side of the dais and looked at the wretched slaves. There were perhaps fifteen of them: one older man, several males in their prime, two heavily pregnant women, two male youths, three girls in their mid-teenaged years, two toddlers, and two swaddled babies laid on the floor.

Newborns.

StarDrifter's face went very still as he looked at them. Like all Icarii he loved children: partly because Icarii found it so difficult to fall pregnant themselves, partly because they simply loved the gaiety and innocence of children.

One of the teenaged girls kept looking at one of the newborn babies, and StarDrifter guessed she was its mother. Even so, even though she must have been desperate about both its and her fate, she did not move to touch it.

None of the slaves touched. They all stood alone, islanded by their total despair and subjection.

If he was honest with himself, these slaves were the reason StarDrifter had attended today. He felt he owed them this, at least. A witnessing of their suffering.

In his first year here, StarDrifter had been so appalled by Fillip Day he'd tried to help the slaves. He'd watched in stunned, heart-thumping disbelief as the God Priests started their hellish trade on the slave who had been picked to provide the soul for the bronze deity awarded to the victor in Fillip. StarDrifter had leapt forward, thinking only that he must do something to aid the slave.

He hadn't got three paces before he was seized from behind by two of the palace guards.

One of the God Priests (along with the entire massed presence of the First, amused by this unexpected interlude) had turned in StarDrifter's direction, a somewhat curious expression on his face as he listened to StarDrifter scream and desperately try to wrench himself away from the guards' grip, and then he'd laughed softly.

"Thank you," the God Priest had said. "You have given me the strength I need to extend this man's suffering that little bit longer. An extra hour, at least, I think."

StarDrifter had shut up, but he'd stayed there all that day watching as the slave suffered while the God Priest delicately, torturously, drew out the man's soul to inhabit the bronze shell.

When it was done, and the deity handed on to the victor of the game, the God Priest stepped down from the altar and walked slowly over to StarDrifter. He wore only a loincloth and a bronze necklet about his throat, from which hung a score of tiny, chiming deities.

He was covered in blood.

The God Priest had stopped before the Icarii, unflinching in the face of StarDrifter's seething hatred.

"You are a guest here," the God Priest had said in a flat, emotionless voice. "You are not one of us. You have no right to intervene in our practices. You may stay with us, but only if—"

"*You foul piece of dog shit!*" StarDrifter had hissed.

The expression on the God Priest's face had not changed. "I do my duty, and I do what is needed," he'd said. "*I* do not lust after my own flesh and blood and then arrange her murder out of spite and envy. Who is the foulest piece of dog shit between *us*, eh?"

And with that he'd turned his back and walked away. StarDrifter had collapsed to the floor, overcome with guilt and horror and self-loathing. While he had not deliberately arranged Zenith's murder, he was responsible for it by his careless words to that arch-bitch StarLaughter, who had set the Hawk Childs to murder Zenith.

After that, StarDrifter had been unable to interfere. He was as bad as the God Priests, and while he loathed the Coroleans, he loathed himself more. He had caused Zenith's death through his own selfish thoughtlessness, and he couldn't aid the slaves, not so much because he believed himself of worse character than the God Priests, but because he didn't want to be thrown out in the cold.

At least in the Palace of the First he had a good bed and decent food to eat and permission to while away his hours as he liked.

So, helpless, inadequate, self-loathing, StarDrifter never tried to aid the slaves again.

But he did come to Fillip Day every year to stand witness to their suffering.

CHAPTER TWO

Palace of the First, Yoyette, Coroleas

Salome strolled slowly through the colonnade, happier than she'd been in months. She adored Fillip Day. For the past six years she had contrived to have herself crowned Fillip Queen and, having put in the footwork, bribes, threats, and intrigue over the past few months, expected the same today.

She'd dressed for the part. Salome wore a filmy gown of pale blue that set off her coloring and features beautifully. It also revealed most of her body, for it was so diaphanous as to appear almost nonexistent. She wore very little jewelry—a spot of gold at her ears and about one ankle—sandals of the finest leather, and no bronzed deities at all.

That made the best statement of all: *Look at me, envy me, for I am the one who controls access to the greatest deity of them all, the Weeper. What need I a score of pathetic lesser deities?*

As she moved through the gathering, Salome made the best possible use of the light, walking in and out of pools of sunlight, appearing suddenly from shadows, and dazzling all who saw her virtual nakedness spotlighted in the golden light streaming down from the roof windows, before slinking off again into the shadows, making people glance nervously over their shoulders, wondering where she was, and what she might be plotting.

Everyone deferred to Salome, but no one loved her.

No one save her son, Ezra. Salome had been making her slow, dramatic way toward the emperor's dais at the eastern end of the colonnade when Ezra, standing just to the side of the dais, saw her. He gave a cry of glee, making the emperor wince, and walked down to greet Salome.

Ezra did not take after his mother in anything save her height. He was dark, somewhat heavy of feature and body, and had none of her grace.

Ezra and Salome kissed in the Corolean manner, touching foreheads before a decorous brushing of lips, then Salome turned and gave a light bow in the emperor's direction. "My Gracious Lord," she murmured, despising him as he looked on her with lust.

"I hear you are to be Fillip Queen this year, Salome," the emperor said. "Again."

"Will you fight for me, Gracious Lord?"

That was going too far, even for Salome, and for a moment the emperor reddened under her forthright gaze.

"Will you service me if I win?" he countered, and now Salome looked slightly uncomfortable before recovering.

"Fight for me," she whispered.

"I wouldn't lift a finger for you, bitch," the emperor hissed back.

Salome smiled, inclined her head, and turned back to the colonnade. There was an hour to spare yet before the fun began, and she could use that hour to her benefit.

StarDrifter watched her from the side aisle, where he'd taken a glass of golden wine to sip. He well knew who Salome was—there was no one who attended the court at the Palace of the First for more than five minutes without learning her identity—and had amused himself on many occasions in watching her from some shadowed corner.

He didn't like her—he didn't know of anyone who actually did—but she intrigued him. Salome's exotic looks and grace made him suspect a sprinkling of Icarii blood somewhere in her heritage. It certainly wouldn't be impossible, given that Icarii had been coming here for years even before the Tencendorian disaster, and, combined with the total immorality of the Corolean court, a few Icarii bastards on Corolean women might not be totally unexpected. Stars, even Axis had come down here as a young man, and it wouldn't have surprised StarDrifter to learn that he'd left a few by-blows scattered about the country. StarDrifter thought that few people other than himself would have picked up on Salome's Icarii heritage. It was only because of his familiarity with Axis and Azhure that StarDrifter had suspected Salome. Both StarDrifter's son Axis and Axis' wife, Azhure, were almost full-blooded Icarii and yet did not look it.

If it had been anyone other than Salome, StarDrifter wouldn't have cared less. He would have shrugged and lost interest immediately. But Salome . . . StarDrifter took a mouthful of his wine, his eyes still on the woman as she trailed treachery and sex through the gathering . . . Salome was virtually the most powerful member of the First, second only to the emperor. She commanded power and fear beyond knowing.

And yet the First had a rule, their most basic and rigid rule: the First admitted no new blood.

All members of the First could trace their ancestry back three thousand odd years to the original founders of their caste, and had admitted no new blood to the First since then. The instant a member was corrupted with outside blood, he or she (as well as any children of their body) was dropped into the Second. Outside blood was a total disaster.

Sometimes, in his most despairing moments, StarDrifter lifted his mood by imagining himself being able to prove the feathered shame in Salome's past and watching her and her son topple from their position within Corolean society.

He thought Salome would be dead within hours. She'd made so many enemies (virtually the entire population of Coroleas hated her) that the instant this dirty secret (should it actually exist) was made known, daggers would be sliding out of sheaths all over the empire.

"If only I knew," StarDrifter whispered, and took a new glass of the golden wine from the tray of a passing member of the Third. "If only . . ."

At that very moment Salome turned, and their eyes met.

StarDrifter lifted his glass to her—they had never talked, never made any connection until this moment—and was somewhat amused to see her eyes narrow speculatively at him for a moment.

Why? Was she pitying him? Marking him for seduction?

She moved away, the moment gone, but StarDrifter stood watching her for a long time, wondering what he would do if he received a command to her bed.

Eventually he shook himself out of his speculative mood. She had pitied him, no doubt. There would be no invitation.

And thank the stars for that, StarDrifter thought, *for I would not wish to risk my life refusing the vile woman.*

Some ten paces away a man watched StarDrifter with considerable interest. Ba'al'uz had arrived in Yoyette four days ago, and had wasted no time in acquiring an invitation to the Fillip Day celebrations. He'd wanted to come here to observe Salome, and to discover for himself the best and safest way to steal the deity known as the Weeper.

Ba'al'uz had realized he was staring at the solution to his dilemma.

StarDrifter SunSoar.

He could hardly believe his luck—or was it that Kanubai had arranged this for him? When Ba'al'uz had first entered the Diamond Colonnade earlier he'd spotted StarDrifter almost immediately. Then the Icarii man had only pricked at Ba'al'uz' interest. There'd been something about him, something that intrigued Ba'al'uz, but he couldn't quite put his finger on it . . .

So he'd asked a passing and more than half-drunk nobleman who the blond, wingless Icarii man was.

StarDrifter SunSoar.

Axis' father.

Ba'al'uz was not one to ignore coincidences. They were not accidents, they were chances handed you by fate, yours to seize or ignore as your abilities dictated.

Ba'al'uz was not going to disregard this coincidence.

StarDrifter was not only going to acquire the Weeper for Ba'al'uz; he was also, if Ba'al'uz could manipulate circumstances skillfully enough, the means by which to manage Axis.

* * *

The festivities began with a sounding of trumpets and a cry of delight.

The emperor lumbered to his feet, and took a card from a golden platter held out for him by a nobleman.

"Ahem!" the emperor called, his voice surprisingly strong and elegant for such a fat man. "I have before me the name of she who the First love before any other, and who they desire to be their queen on this special day!"

StarDrifter smiled around the rim of his wineglass. He could almost hear the stomachs curdling throughout the vast hall.

"The Dowager Duchess of Sidon!" the emperor cried, flinging his arms wide. "The Greatly Beloved Salome!"

Feigning surprised delight, Salome stepped forward, bowing at the scattering of applause that broke out (started, StarDrifter thought, by those too drunk to realize who they were applauding). He finished off his wine, then snatched yet another glass from a passing waiter.

Salome clapped her hands, once, twice, then a third time, demanding silence. "I thank the gracious emperor," she said, bowing now at the emperor, who was struggling to get back onto his throne without overturning it. "And," she continued, once more facing the masses crowding the colonnade, "I declare the Day of Fillip begun! Come now, who will compete for my hand?"

The game of Fillip was, so far as StarDrifter was concerned, as tasteless, as cheap, and as tawdry as was the rest of Corolean society. There was no finesse to it, nothing but the promise of violence and blood and sex and humiliation and pain—the five prime ingredients for a successful Corolean life.

Hated as Salome was, there were no shortage of takers for her challenge. The winner, after all, not only enjoyed the services of Salome for a night, but also won the bronzed deity of his choice, freshly made for him once the game was over. This was the aspect of Fillip that StarDrifter loathed above all else: the winner, often badly hurt, making his bloody way down to the slave dais to select a soul from the slave of his choice, who was then slowly murdered before the victor's eyes as the God Priest withdrew the slave's soul from his or her body into the bronze figurine.

Added to these two exquisite pleasures, the winner also won the admiration of the entire collected First, and could look forward to a year of privilege, free dinners and sex, and perhaps even a small fortune to be had from listening to the whispered secrets about the bedrooms and dinner tables of the First's most rich and fortunate.

The loser died.

Normally this did not happen in Fillip. Usually the loser was the one who lapsed into unconsciousness first, but this was just a very special day.

Salome slowly walked about the small throng of men who had stood forward, all high-ranking members of the First. There were elderly men and youths who had yet to beard up, thin men in the final stages of the wasting disease (no doubt hoping for a loss and a relatively quick exit from their suffering), and men as obese as the emperor. There were generals and diplomats, princes and scoundrels, assassins and cheats—men representing all the qualities for which the First were known. It was Salome's task to select from this menagerie two men to battle it out for her favors, the deity, and a year of delights.

Her reward came not only in the selection (which would clearly indicate her current bedroom tastes), but in the choice of weapon. The woman over whom the men battled always chose the weapon with which they tried to beat themselves unconscious (or into death, on this day). The weapon could be anything at all, not necessarily something of great value on the battlefield. Thus was derived Salome's greatest joy in this shambolic tragedy—choosing the weapon that would most humiliate her two suitors.

She stopped, her finger to her chin in a parody of thoughtfulness, then slowly smiled, seductive and murderous.

"You," she said, pointing, "and you."

The crowd gasped, the emperor mottled (thinking, correctly, that this was a gibe at him), and StarDrifter's jaw dropped open in a mixture of surprise and disgust: Salome had selected two of the most massively obese men he'd ever seen. The fact that she was going to have to sleep with one of these creatures at the end of the day appalled him, as did the idea that they would undoubtedly humiliate themselves during the process of the game.

He wondered again, briefly, at whether or not she had Icarii blood within her. If she did, then she'd managed to get only the worst of the Icarii heritage. StarDrifter could not imagine any Icarii ever acting like this.

What? whispered an unwelcome voice deep in his mind. *Not WolfStar? Not StarLaughter? Not some of the worst blood imaginable—and so much of it SunSoar?*

As the disappointed suitors melted back into the crowd, the two winners divested themselves of their clothing, leaving themselves naked. Great folds and rolls of flesh covered their arms and legs, their buttocks were doughy and pockmarked, and their bellies dewlapped down almost to mid-thigh, hiding their genitals.

Before them, Salome snapped her fingers, and a servant came forth bearing a large tray covered with a silver dome.

The weapons tray.

For a long, taunting moment Salome held everyone in suspense, then she oh-so-slowly lifted the dome and held up the two weapons.

Two lengths of silken cord.

StarDrifter frowned. That was almost too obvious, and too easy. Two lengths of cord—the victor would be the one who strangled the other first.

But just as the two men reached for the cords, Salome smiled, shaking a finger at them.

She picked up one of the cords and, moving to one of the combatants, tied his wrists loosely behind his back.

Then she tied the hands of the other behind his back.

"Use your teeth," she said. "*Gnaw* each other for my pleasure."

The men went pale, but StarDrifter had no doubt they would do it. There was no other possible outcome save that one of these two men would, somehow, manage to murder the other with his teeth to then take Salome, and the slave's soul of his choice embedded in a bronze figurine, in victory.

And everyone here would stay to watch, drinking themselves into a stupor in the process.

Sickened, StarDrifter put down his glass, turned, gave the slaves one last wretched glance of sympathy, and left the colonnade.

Deep in the shadows of the aisles, Ba'al'uz saw him leave, then followed.

CHAPTER THREE

FarReach Mountains, and the Northern Reaches
of the Ashdod Dependency

Ishbel existed in a fog of exhaustion, fear, and a drugged stupor that left her almost continually nauseated and headachy as her body fought to repel the drugs. She knew only that her kidnappers had dragged her south—the weather was warming considerably with every day's travel—and that they treated her with a level of contempt that terrified her. They mishandled her, not caring if they caused bruises, although they were careful not to hurt her excessively. Occasionally they remembered to offer her food and water. The food Ishbel did not care for, but whatever fluid they gave her she drank down greedily. She could not get enough to drink, and in times of better than usual clarity she knew it was an effect of the drugs they were giving her.

She had not washed in weeks, and her body and clothes stank of travel grime and sweat. She could not get privacy to attend to even her most basic bodily functions, and generally had to relieve herself under the unwaveringly contemptuous regard of the captors. During the day, when they traveled, she was either forced to stumble along shackled to one of her captors, or, when too exhausted or drugged, to lie on the bare boards of the tray of a small wooden cart pulled by an ill-tempered donkey.

Everything hurt: her muscles, her head (which pounded almost unceasingly), her belly. Ishbel did not know if that was the Coil unwinding within her, or the baby shrinking and dying from lack of nourishment, for she had not felt any movement, and she was sure Garth had said to expect some by this stage. She was now five months pregnant, but her belly had hardly swelled at all, another reason Ishbel thought the baby might have died.

Ishbel did not want her baby to have died. This was not for her sake, but for Maximilian's. She knew how much he wanted a child, knew how much this baby meant to him, and she did not want to be the one responsible for losing it. Not when he was already so angry at her.

Each day they struggled on, higher and higher into what Ishbel realized must be the FarReach Mountains, traversing icy mountain paths, sheltering at night in rocky canyons so cold that she could not sleep for shaking. Her captors sat around a fire, but she was left on the outer reaches, and received little of its warmth.

Days passed, each in a blur of exhaustion, drugged stupor, and desperation.

Axis was enjoying himself as he had not in . . . dozens of years before his death, he thought. Isaiah had given him command of a squad of some four dozen armed men, plus several cooks, numerous valets and grooms, two guides, and several spare horses for everyone. It all made Axis wonder how Isaiah traveled with an army, if he gave less than fifty soldiers this much support.

But he was glad of it. During the daylight hours they moved north, following the River Lhyl past the ruins of Setkoth to the west (which Axis would have loved to explore had they the time) and then the city of Azibar on the eastern bank. Because they had so many horses they traveled fast. Even the cooks' wagon was lightweight and strong, and was able to keep up with the riders. They covered many leagues each day, changing horses at noon and midafternoon stops. At night, when they camped, Axis appreciated the food and assistance of the cooks and valets and grooms. For once, he and the soldiers he commanded could just swing off their horses in the evening and allow others to set up camp, and provide food and beds, and feed and water the horses.

It was not just the freedom and exercise that Axis was enjoying, but the companionship of the soldiers as well. It made him realize, very forcefully, that of all the kinds of man he had once been—BattleAxe, Enchanter, StarMan, Star God—it was the first he had loved the most. The soldier and commander, man of war and action and of *doing*.

Isaiah had told Axis that the men under his command were among the best in Isaiah's army, and were from his own personal guard. Axis was certainly impressed with them. They were quiet, determined, disciplined, almost as good as Isaiah in weapons practice (which meant they were faster and better than Axis, who had still to regain full battle fitness), and yet humorous and friendly and warm in the evening while not losing, even in that warmth and friendliness, their discipline or deference to Axis. Axis had thought they might resent him, but he saw no trace of it. They were good soldiers, better men, and engaging companions, and if they were representative of Isaiah's larger army, then Axis envied Isaiah that army quite desperately.

It also made him regard Isaiah in a different light. Axis could see Isaiah, or at least a reflection of him, as a battle leader, and it intrigued him. If Isaiah's army was this good and this disciplined, then how was it Isaiah had failed so badly in the Eastern Independencies?

Axis relaxed into his long-forgotten life as soldier and commander faster than he could ever have imagined. At night, as he had done when he was BattleAxe, he pulled from his kit a small travel harp that he had managed to find in Aqhat and entertained the company of men with songs and ballads from lost Tencendor. Axis may have lost the Star Dance, but he had not lost his musical ability and his fine singing voice, and the evenings were filled with laughter and song and companionship.

So much so that Axis hardly remembered Azhure at all. When he did think of her, it was with warmth and affection, and a strange realization that she was fading further and further into his memory.

Now that he was on the move and fallen back into the companionship of men and weapons, Axis no longer wrote her letters.

When they reached the FarReach Dependency, Axis spent

several days with the general, Morfah, checking on behalf of Isaiah how the resettlement was going.

The generals might not have been very happy about it (and Axis himself still could not see the reason why Isaiah was preparing this massive resettlement program to follow hard on the heels of the invasion), but they had done a good job. Village after village had been evacuated and dismantled, people, livestock, and goods moved across the Lhyl in vast numbers to congregate on the eastern plains between the river and Sakkuth. The FarReach Dependency was almost deserted, and Morfah told Axis (somewhat reluctantly, as Morfah clearly neither liked nor trusted Axis, and resented his intrusion) that there were only a few remaining populated towns and villages and that they, within weeks, would be empty.

When Axis asked how the displaced people reacted to the news they were to be resettled in a foreign land, Morfah just shrugged.

"They do as they are told," he said. "They live resigned lives."

Axis raised his eyebrows at that, but didn't comment, and he wasn't sure who was the more relieved of the two of them when he took his leave of Morfah the next morning.

He was glad to leave the suffocating presence of the general. Back on the road, and back in the comfortable company of soldiers, Axis set thoughts of both Isaiah and Morfah to one side and enjoyed the sunshine and the vast open spaces, and the freedom of commanding his own fate, even if only for a short while.

Thus, happier than he'd been in many years, Axis led his men north, toward the FarReach Mountains and Isaiah's new, stolen bride.

CHAPTER FOUR

Palace of the First, Yoyette, Coroleas

"StarDrifter SunSoar, Prince of the Icarii, may I join you?"

StarDrifter turned on the garden bench, bristling with anger both at the salutation and at the intrusion. *Prince of the Icarii?* That was either sarcasm or flattery, and StarDrifter despised both.

A man stood a pace or two away. He was entirely nondescript, from his middling height to his middling features to his middling brown eyes, but there was something about him that StarDrifter instinctively disliked.

That hint of slyness in the man's eyes, perhaps, or those too casually clasped hands held before him.

"I came to the garden for peace," said StarDrifter. "Go away."

He turned his back on the intruder, not caring if he offended.

The man behind him drew a breath preparatory to speaking, and StarDrifter tensed. All he wanted was to be left alone, and if that man started to whine at him about wanting to know all about the Icarii race, then he was going to leap up from this garden bench and—

"I was having a noonday meal with your son Axis not a few weeks past," said the stranger, "and wondered if you'd like to know what he—"

"*What?*" StarDrifter exploded off the bench, so startling the man that he almost stumbled in his haste to step backward.

"What manner of cruel mischief is this, then?" StarDrifter

said, striding up to him and taking a fistful of the man's shirt
in his hand. "Who put you up to this?"

The man did not flinch in the face of StarDrifter's anger.
"I am sorry to so disturb you with the news of your son's
return," he said softly. "I apologize. I should have spoken
more circumspectly."

"Who are you?" said StarDrifter. "And what the fuck do
you want from me?"

"Merely a few moments of your time," said the man, who
seemed to be growing in confidence with every breath. "I
can offer you news of your son, and I can offer you a means
by which to regain the Star Dance, but if you're not interested
. . ."

StarDrifter almost hit the man. He was furious, not only
that this man had been sent, for whatever reason, to torment
him, but that he might actually be telling the truth. Axis *had*
returned, and there *might* be a means to once more revel
within the magic of the Star Dance, but, oh, to even think
about that was so brutally painful that StarDrifter did not
think he could bear it.

"Who are you?" he said, almost spitting the words out.

"My name is Ba'al'uz, and I come from the Tyranny of
Isembaard to the south of the FarReach Mountains. I understand your distress, StarDrifter, and once again I apologize
for my overdirectness in approaching you, but if you could
kindly release me . . ."

StarDrifter let the man's shirt go and stood back. His blue
eyes were brilliant with emotion, his face flushed, and anger
radiated out of him like a dangerous fever. Ba'al'uz thought
that StarDrifter exuded far more presence than his son, the
Icarii's anger being underscored by a powerful sensuality
and an undisciplined ego.

He would suit Ba'al'uz' purpose very well.

"I don't believe you," said StarDrifter.

"Of course you don't," Ba'al'uz said, "for I have not yet
had a chance to explain myself. May we sit?"

"No. Just tell me what you must, then leave."

"You are not going to want me to leave once you hear
what I have to say," Ba'al'uz said softly.

"*Just say it!*"

"In the land where I come from, we have a powerful structure. We call it DarkGlass Mountain, although in ages past it was known as Threshold. It acts in the same manner as your Star Gate once did, and, although it is infinitely more powerful than the Star Gate was, it is capable of being controlled and directed. It is perfectly possible that DarkGlass Mountain can filter the music of the Star Dance for you. If it does not do so already, then that is because no one has ever asked it to try."

StarDrifter did not know what to say. He stared at this man, almost hating him for what he was saying—*Was it true? Could it possibly be true?*—and wanting to have the strength to just turn his back and walk away from him.

"Perhaps a small demonstration?" Ba'al'uz said.

StarDrifter replied only with a flat stare.

Ba'al'uz gave a small shrug of indifference to StarDrifter's continuing hostility and gestured to a stone bench, where StarDrifter sat down, his every movement stiff.

"So far distant from DarkGlass Mountain," said Ba'al'uz, "I can only draw forth a fraction of the power normally available to me, but it shall be enough to give you an idea of the pyramid's potential."

He gathered some twigs from the ground and sat at the other end of the bench, leaving a clear stretch of stone between himself and StarDrifter. "Now, if you could hold these twigs here, like this, yes, thank you, and I take these and hold them so, then we have the most basic of structures, a pyramid, yes?"

StarDrifter made no response. His anger hadn't abated, but now he felt foolish also, for allowing this man to trick him into this—

"Watch," said Ba'al'uz, very softly. "Watch the pyramid."

The two men held between them a loosely constructed pyramid of twigs. As StarDrifter looked down, he felt the unmistakable aura of power emanating from the man Ba'al'uz. He glanced at the man's face, then looked down at the twigs again.

And gasped.

A moment ago the structure had been nothing but loose twigs held together in the vague semblance of a pyramid.

Now the twigs had vanished, replaced by lines of light enclosing a space that glowed with a very soft rosy radiance.

Ba'al'uz muttered something, and the rosy radiance dissipated, replaced with a view of a fair-haired and bearded man sitting under the stars by a fire, entertaining a group of soldiers with a harp.

StarDrifter's mouth dropped open.

That was Axis!

The vision faded, and a moment later the lines of light were replaced once more by twigs, which Ba'al'uz let topple slowly to the ground.

StarDrifter could not for the moment speak. He was still stunned at seeing his son. He did not doubt what he'd seen. That had not been a vision conjured from the far past, when Axis had been BattleAxe. For one thing, Axis had been wearing unfamiliar clothes, and for another, he'd worn the face that StarDrifter had last seen—tired and careworn—if now overlaid with something else . . . a sense of mischief, StarDrifter thought. His son was having fun, whatever he was doing.

"Why is my son back?" StarDrifter said. "How did he come back?"

"*I* brought him back," said Ba'al'uz, lying in order to secure StarDrifter's full cooperation, "using the power of DarkGlass Mountain. If it can do that, StarDrifter, it can touch the Star Dance for you as well."

"Take me to him," StarDrifter said. "Please."

Oh, gods, Axis was back!

Slyness slipped all about Ba'al'uz' face. "Of course," he said, "but in return I would ask that you do something for me."

"What?"

"I would like you to steal the Weeper from Salome, the Duchess of Sidon." Ba'al'uz smiled as StarDrifter looked shocked. "You can think of it as a parting gift to the Coroleans."

"I can't . . . no one can get near the Weeper. Stars, Ba'al'uz, that is the most closely guarded deity in Coroleas!"

Ba'al'uz noted that StarDrifter had not actually refused.

"Perhaps we can discuss this over a glass of wine some-where?" he said. "If you are willing, I can tell you just how easy it shall be to take the deity . . . and free its soul."

Ba'al'uz had noted StarDrifter's disgust during Fillip Day, and thought he understood the reason behind it.

"I want to free the Weeper," Ba'al'uz said. "Do you?"

CHAPTER FIVE

The FarReach Mountains

The group of five Icarii had been searching for weeks with no success save for rumors and some unsubstantiated reports. They'd flown to Deepend, to discover that, yes, a group of men had come through, and they might have had a woman with them, but no one could remember much detail. One man suggested that the group had continued farther south, perhaps aiming for the FarReach Mountains.

StarWeb had never liked Ishbel, and by now had come to loathe her. Without even trying, so it seemed, Ishbel trailed havoc, murder, and heartache behind her. StarWeb could not understand why Maximilian was so besotted with the woman.

Personally, she would have let the kidnappers do what they wanted with the cursed woman.

And why would anyone want her, anyway?

Oh yes, of course, she was *pregnant*.

Wasn't that a cunning move on Ishbel's part. She probably felt that Maximilian was slipping away from her and so had conceived. She had known from the marriage negotiations how much Maximilian wanted a child, must have thought to herself, *Ah yes, I can do anything with him once he knows I am carrying his child . . .*

Who knew if it was Maximilian's baby anyway?

Damn it! Why couldn't Maximilian have picked someone *else* as his wife?

StarWeb grew progressively more ill-tempered as the days and weeks dragged by. In the evenings, when they sheltered by a small fire, or were together at the dining table of a roadside tavern, she reasoned that they'd done enough, they should return to Ruen, and Maximilian would just have to get used to the idea that he'd lost his wife almost as soon as he'd found her.

But none of the others agreed with her. BroadWing Even-Beat was the most vocal. Maximilian was distraught, his wife had been taken from him, she was carrying his child, and Maximilian's life had already been too wrapped in tragedy to allow it to strike once more.

As if our lives haven't also been wrapped in enough tragedy, StarWeb always thought at the last argument, but she never spoke the words aloud, knowing BroadWing and her other companions could see it written all over her face.

Besides, it wasn't just altruism that drove the others onward in their search for Ishbel. It was also joy at having a purpose, joy at being allowed to soar over plain and mountain, joy at being able to discover new lands and skyscapes. It was either search for Ishbel and revel in life as they did so, or return to a useless existence in Ruen or wherever else they drifted.

Ishbel was an excuse, and they refused to let it go.

So they went on, day after day.

From Deepend they'd flown ever south, following a trail toward the FarReach Mountains. At that point StarWeb knew there was no holding BroadWing and the others back. The chance to soar over mountains almost as tall as the Icescarp Alps was irresistible, and as much as she hated to admit it, StarWeb enjoyed it as well. They had all missed the Icescarp Alps so much, and to feel once more the power of the thermals generated by the huge mountains . . . well, some days there was far more soaring done than searching.

Then, on the fifth day of the fourth week of the tenth month, they flew over a ravine, and they saw, far, far below, the thin trail of smoke from a fire.

Reluctantly, for the thermals were particularly enticing on this day, they spiraled downward for a closer look.

They crouched on a rock just below a peak that rose at least a thousand paces from the floor of the ravine.

It was cold here, and uncomfortable, but for the moment the five Icarii huddled close and peered down. Their eyesight was excellent, as good as an eagle's, and they could very clearly see the group of eight men . . . and the unmoving figure of a woman shackled to one of the men.

"It is her," said StarWeb, every word forced out. "See the color of the strand of hair fluttering from beneath the hood? It is Ishbel."

"Well, she's alive, at least," said ViewSky, one of the other Icarii. "She may not be moving, but they'd not shackle her if she wasn't still breathing."

"They're taking her into the Tyranny of Isembaard," said BroadWing. "Why, I wonder?"

StarWeb didn't care. All she wanted now was to get out of here. Even the mere *sight* of Ishbel made her almost nauseated with hatred.

"We'll need to report this to Maximilian," she said. "It'll be a long flight back to Ruen."

"No," said BroadWing. "We need to rescue her."

"No!" said StarWeb. "Stars, BroadWing! We cannot try to rescue her! There are more of them than us, and—"

"We don't fly away and leave her," said BroadWing. "Dear gods, StarWeb, she's pregnant! And they've shackled her! Stars alone knows what else they have done to her . . . look, they're eating, but Ishbel not. We rescue her."

StarWeb looked to the others for support, but they were all nodding at BroadWing.

Suddenly StarWeb felt very ill. They were going to risk their lives for that cursed woman?

"Imagine," said ViewSky, "Maximilian's face when we arrive back at Ruen with Ishbel."

StarWeb did not know how ViewSky, or any of the others, imagined the manner in which they were going to transport the fair and ailing Ishbel back to Ruen . . . if one of them wanted to carry her, then they could bloody well do it without her aid.

"I think I have a plan," said BroadWing.

CHAPTER SIX

Palace of the First, Yoyette, Coroleas

StarDrifter was more than slightly drunk. Not just with alcohol, although he'd surely had enough of that, but also with hope and purpose and joy. He didn't like Ba'al'uz, and he didn't particularly trust him, but he *appreciated* him.

Ba'al'uz was reinvigorating his life.

While the concept of once more touching the Star Dance was exhilarating, the other piece of news about Axis was the supreme joy for StarDrifter. Suddenly the universe seemed a much less lonely place. *His son was back!* StarDrifter could not wait to embrace him.

He wanted to be with Axis, desperately.

He wanted to escape the Corolean court, desperately.

All this Ba'al'uz offered him, with the added pleasure of not only being able to rescue at least one soul from its accursed imprisonment within a bronze shell (and that soul the most pitiful of all, the Weeper), but in the doing being able to destroy Salome. For StarDrifter, Salome epitomized the immorality, the cruelty, and the sheer horror of the life of the Corolean nobility. People had often criticized the Icarii for being arrogant, unfeeling, and selfish, but the Icarii were innocents in the arts of immorality and arrogance when compared to such as Salome and all she represented.

He and Ba'al'uz had retired to StarDrifter's tiny chamber in the bowels of the Palace of the First. StarDrifter had always hated this chamber, representing for him everything that had gone wrong with his life. It was deep underground, not having even a window, and there was nothing worse for an Icarii than to feel trapped underground, lacking the ability to soar. It was tiny, constantly reminding StarDrifter of all the grandeur he had lost. It was pitiful, constantly emphasizing StarDrifter's own pathetic existence. It was plain, utterly unadorned, and drab, when all Icarii gloried in color and vibrancy.

Ba'al'uz and StarDrifter both had to sit on the narrow bed pushed hard against one wall—there was no chair. StarDrifter had managed to purloin from the kitchen several jugs of rough ale, and they sat, drinking from the jugs—they had not even glasses or mugs.

"Tell me, then," said StarDrifter, "how easy *is* it going to be for me to steal the Weeper for you?"

The Weeper, the most desired deity in all of Coroleas, renowned for its ability to grant its owner almost anything he or she wished.

"Very easy," said Ba'al'uz. He had matched StarDrifter swallow for swallow, and now his eyes glittered, his cheeks glowed, and his mouth and chin were moist with spilled ale. "You seduce Salome—all know the Weeper is kept in her bedchamber—and then while she sleeps in postcoital abandonment, you take the Weeper, meet me outside, and we flee the palace for Isembaard."

StarDrifter laughed. "No wonder you need me, Ba'al'uz. You'd not have a hope of seducing a mouse, let alone the beautiful Duchess of Sidon."

Something shifted momentarily in Ba'al'uz' face, but then the addled, happy look slipped back into place. "You *can* seduce her, yes?"

StarDrifter remembered Salome's look of interest at him on Fillip Day, and he also remembered his speculation regarding her Icarii blood.

"Yes," he said softly, "I know precisely how to seduce her." He took another swallow of his ale. "But, tell me this, my newfound friend—Salome has been taking lovers into that bedchamber of hers for years. No doubt many of them have hoped she would slip into a postcoital slumber deep enough that they might risk dashing off with the Weeper. I appreciate that you think my lovemaking skills so extraordinary that I might exhaust the lady when none before have managed the feat, but still . . ."

"Ah," said Ba'al'uz, "I have a small pessary locked away

in my bag. It is a most potent pessary. It shall send her into a slumber so profound that she shall not wake for an entire day."

"Really. And this pessary goes . . . ?"

Ba'al'uz smiled, the expression cold and uncompromising, and told StarDrifter.

StarDrifter laughed again, a little uncomfortably this time. "Well, I suppose if I'm going to sleep with the woman anyway . . . But there is another problem."

"Then I shall solve it for you."

"I have heard also that no one can touch the Weeper without it . . . weeping. Not just weeping, but screaming, sobbing, and calling much unwanted attention to itself. Only its master or mistress can handle it without the deity calling down retribution upon its unwanted handler."

"I think I have the—"

"*Think*?"

"Well, neither of us will know until the theory is tested, will we?" Ba'al'uz paused, holding StarDrifter's somewhat incredulous stare. "But I am very sure that this will quiet the Weeper . . ."

"Yes?"

"Before you touch it, introduce yourself, then tell it that you want to take it home."

"And where might that be?"

"Tell the Weeper that you wish to take him home to the Lord of Elcho Falling. It shall want nothing more than to go home to Elcho Falling, StarDrifter. He will come with you then, of that I am sure." Kanubai had whispered this plan to Ba'al'uz the night before, and Ba'al'uz had no reason to doubt its efficacy, although he certainly doubted Kanubai would ever allow the Weeper anywhere near Elcho Falling or its lord.

"And you *can* free him?" StarDrifter said.

"Yes," Ba'al'uz said, his voice so gentle it brought tears to StarDrifter's eyes, "I can free him. We'll take him home to the Lord of Elcho Falling, and we'll take you back to your son. Two lives, regained. Two sorrows, erased."

"Then I'm your man," said StarDrifter.

CHAPTER SEVEN

*The Southern Reaches of the
FarReach Mountains*

Ishbel was not quite unconscious, drifting in that half-awake land where all sensations and perceptions are grossly distorted. Her eight captors were seated about a fire, eating, and their conversation filtered into Ishbel's mind as if it came through water. She could understand none of their words, and she made no attempt to understand. All Ishbel wanted was to sleep, to shut out the world and everything happening to her, to drift away, and just not know. They had given her drugs before they'd begun to eat, and even though her body was now becoming accustomed to their effect, she could feel the seductive pull of them as they coursed through her blood, and she willed herself to submit and sink deep into unconsciousness.

She was almost there, almost unknowing, then there was some manner of commotion. Several of the Eight started to their feet, their abrupt action making Ishbel open her eyes.

She could not see very well, but it appeared to her as if the men were all staring farther down the ravine.

Ishbel didn't care, and closed her eyes. It might have been a bear, or a pack of wolves or bandits, but she didn't care. Just so long as they allowed her to drift into—

One of the men shouted, a cry of pure alarm, and Ishbel jerked her eyes open once more. Two of the men had started down the ravine, but Zeboul, the senior of the Eight, had called them back.

Ishbel thought she heard something above her, and tried to shift her head so she could look up.

But, oh, it was so hard, and she was so tired.

More sound. Definitely something above her. Ishbel made a huge effort, and managed to turn over far enough that she could look up to the sky.

There appeared to be two shapes spiraling down toward her.

Eagles! Terror swept through Ishbel. She wasn't strong enough to fend them off, and they would peck at her face, her eyes . . .

More noise about the fire, and Ishbel thought she saw a faint shadow, but she was now staring, fixated, at the blurry but *huge* shapes spiraling closer and closer.

Sounds of fighting to her right, but Ishbel ignored them.

Oh, gods, gods, the shapes were Icarii!

Ishbel struggled to speak, to call out to them, to raise her hand.

To her right the sounds of fighting intensified, as also did the shadow—it seemed almost as if her immediate vicinity was being encased in a false dusk.

The Icarii landed at her side, and one of them bent over her.

"You have no idea what a trouble you have been, you bitch," StarWeb hissed, and then her head exploded in a mass of bone and tissue.

A heartbeat later, the male Icarii behind StarWeb, reeling back in shock at her death, also exploded, and Ishbel gave a great cry, only to choke on feathers and pulverized flesh.

Axis had been riding at the head of his column, heading for the opening to a ravine at the foot of the FarReach Mountains, when he heard the faint sound of fighting.

Adrenaline rushed through him. He pulled his sword from its scabbard, booted his horse into a gallop, and yelled at his men to do likewise.

Axis had only been some fifty paces from the entrance to the ravine when he'd urged his horse forward, and it had taken only moments for him to round the tumble of boulders that hid his view of the ravine.

The sight that met his eyes filled him with horror.

There were a group of men, who Axis recognized as those who had traveled north with Ba'al'uz, fighting with four or five Icarii—the whole encased in a writhing gray cloud that Axis instantly recognized as power. All his senses told him it was being used for a foul purpose.

Then, as he drew close, two of the Icarii, who had been standing over a bound figure lying on the ground, exploded.

Something cracked within Axis' heart.

Two more Icarii were struggling with Ba'al'uz' men, and then they, too, exploded.

Axis screamed, driving his horse directly into the melee.

There was a fifth Icarii, struggling to rise from the ground some distance away, but for the moment Axis ignored him. He raised his sword, and brought it down in a great arc, taking the head of one of Ba'al'uz' men.

Within the instant his men were with him, and the remainder of Ba'al'uz' men, stunned by the sudden attack, and losing whatever grip on power they'd had, dispersed and started to run.

Axis was overwhelmed, not only with the sudden, unexpected sight of Icarii, but with their almost simultaneous deaths. Right now, trying to catch the remaining men was not a priority, and he let them go. He jumped down from his horse, glanced at the woman lying some distance away, who he supposed must be Ishbel, then at the Icarii now rising to his feet.

The birdman was staring at him in complete disbelief.

"StarMan?" he said.

Axis walked slowly toward him, then halted as he saw the Icarii tense. For all he knew, Axis was a phantasm. Axis looked at him carefully, desperately trying to put a name to the face, which he'd recognized from his days of leading the Strike Force.

"BroadWing," he said. "BroadWing EvenBeat."

BroadWing relaxed, just a fraction, and nodded. "How is it you are here?" he said.

Axis gave a slight shrug. "By a magic I do not understand. No one else has come back. You?"

"I was stationed in Ruen when Tencendor collapsed, Star-

Man. There are some six thousand of us scattered about."

"Call me Axis, please. My title of StarMan is now useless."

The conversation was starting to feel surreal to Axis. What was left of the bodies of four Icarii lay about, and Ishbel, Queen of Escator, lay moaning to one side, grasping at thin air with one weak hand.

BroadWing saw the direction of Axis' glance. "We were trying to rescue her," he said. "She is—"

"I know who she is. Look, BroadWing, you cannot possibly take her back to Escator by yourself, and she looks too ill for us to linger here long enough for you to fetch aid. Furthermore, she is in no condition to attempt a journey back through the FarReach Mountains—and no Icarii could carry her that distance. I will take care of her. Tell Maximilian that. She will be safe. I promise it."

"When was any woman ever safe with you, Axis SunSoar?"

Axis gave a small smile. "She *will* be safe, BroadWing. Tell Maximilian not to worry."

"He loves her, Axis. He will tear the earth apart for her. Keep your word, I pray you. And . . ." He looked about, and Axis saw his face crumple in grief at the sight of his companions.

"I will farewell them, BroadWing," Axis said.

BroadWing hesitated, clearly torn about what to do. "Axis, what was that power those men used?"

"I fear very much it was something ancient and highly malignant," said Axis. "BroadWing, listen, I need to get Ishbel to a town and a physician as fast as I can. Do you want to come with us?"

He turned about as he said this, to indicate his armed escort, and realized for the first time how they stood, staring at BroadWing.

They'd never seen an Icarii before, and their expressions wavered between the hostile and the curious.

"I think I will report back to Maximilian," said BroadWing. "Axis, you *will* farewell my companions?"

Axis nodded. "Tell Maximilian I will take care of her."

BroadWing gave a small, cynical smile at that last. "He will come for her, Axis."

"I have no doubt," Axis said quietly.

With a final nod, BroadWing lifted off and spiraled rapidly into the sky.

CHAPTER EIGHT

The Southern Reaches of the
FarReach Mountains

He was no harm to us," Axis said to his men, and they slowly relaxed, murmuring between themselves.

"And the others?" said Insharah, who was the most senior of the men of Axis' escort. "They were Ba'al'uz' men?"

"Yes," said Axis. He looked around. "They will have fled by now and, frankly, I am not happy about that power of theirs."

"What did you mean," asked another of the men, Madarin, "when you said they wielded an ancient and malignant power?"

"I believe they used the power of DarkGlass Mountain," said Axis, "but we can't talk about that now. The woman needs aid, fast, and we also need to build a pyre for the remains of the Icarii—the winged people. It will not take long to build, and I can farewell them then properly, as I promised. Madarin, can you take five of the men to build the pyre? Insharah, take a dozen more and make sure Ba'al'uz' men are not lingering nearby, then search the belongings they left behind for anything that might be useful."

As the men turned to their tasks, Axis walked over to the two Icarii who had been struggling with Ba'al'uz' men when they'd exploded. There was almost nothing of them left—certainly nothing that Axis could recognize. He bent down by their remains, reaching out a hand to run his fingers over the curve of a wing.

He remembered, suddenly, horribly, how his daughter,

Zenith, and father, StarDrifter, had been torn apart by the Hawk Childs.

Blinded with tears, Axis rose and went to where the woman lay, the remains of two Icarii just beyond her. Axis brushed the tears from his eyes, then squatted down by Ishbel. He didn't look at her immediately, though, instead running his eyes over the tattered corpses just beyond her.

"I'm sorry," Ishbel whispered.

Axis took a deep breath, then looked down at her. What her features were like he could not tell, for she was covered in blood and tissue, with feathers stuck to her face.

"Help me," she whispered and, after a moment, Axis nodded.

Axis made Ishbel as comfortable as he could for the moment, giving her water to drink and placing her carefully in the tray of the cart, then helped his command gather the remains of the four Icarii; the corpse of the man Axis had killed he ordered to be tossed behind some distant rocks. Collecting what was left of the Icarii was a frightful task, and they did it in complete silence, placing the remains on a bed of timber. When it was done, Axis took a coal from the smoldering fire and placed it among the timber.

The Isembaardians watched in silence as the pyre burned, but Axis stood a little apart from them, and sang a beautiful song in a language the soldiers did not recognize. They did understand the emotion behind it, though, and its beauty, and knew that Axis was farewelling the birdmen and -woman into the Otherworld.

Once it was done, Axis gave the command to ride out. They needed to camp for the night, but he was damned if he'd spend the night in this place of death.

Now, as his men mounted up, Axis walked back to the cart, looking at Ishbel.

Only then did he realize the true extent of her illness. He'd wiped her face clean earlier, and now he saw that she was gray, her face sweating.

"Ishbel?" he said, calling her by her name for the first time. "What is wrong?"

She tried to speak, but her mouth was too dry, and Axis had to give her a drink of water from his canteen.

"The men," she said, her voice weak, "had kept me drugged for . . . oh, gods, weeks, I suppose. Now . . ."

"Your body is screaming out for more," Axis said.

She nodded.

He stood and looked at her, uncertain. He wondered if there were any drugs left in the packs that Ba'al'uz' men had left behind them and, if there was, if he should give Ishbel any more of it. He called Insharah over.

"Was there anything among the packs . . . any vials or drugs?"

Insharah shook his head. "If there were drugs, then one of Ba'al'uz' men must have been carrying them on his person."

He hesitated.

"Yes?" said Axis.

"There was one thing of interest," Insharah said. "A glass pyramid, small enough to sit in the palm of your hand."

Ba'al'uz' rose pyramid? "My goodness," said Axis softly. "Well, I have no time to study it now. Put it in my pack, will you, and I'll look at it later. For the moment we need to mount up and head for the nearest town. *If* we can find one still inhabited after Isaiah's push to move everyone west."

Insharah nodded and walked off.

"You will need to be strong enough to get through the next hour or two," Axis said to Ishbel. "We won't be able to make a town until tomorrow morning at least, but I'd like to make a start now. Can you wait that long?"

She nodded again.

"We will camp somewhere secure for the night, and then the cooks will make you something to eat. That might help."

It probably wouldn't, but it was all Axis could say.

"Thank you," she whispered, then, as Axis turned to go, reached out a hand and grabbed weakly at his sleeve.

"Who are you?" she said.

Axis smiled. "I'm sorry," he said. "My name is Axis Sun-Soar. As lost as you in this land, I think." He touched her face briefly. "Hold on just an hour, then we can make you more comfortable."

Then he was gone, and the donkey moved forward, pulling the cart after the men on horseback.

Ishbel lay in the lurching cart, feeling more ill than she could ever remember. She alternated between chills and fevers, and a constant nausea and throbbing headache compounded her misery. Everything was made worse by the fact that now the drugs had worn off she could *feel*, whereas before she had existed in a state of constant numbness and semiconsciousness. Everything ached: her limbs, her back, her chest, her abdomen.

What had happened to her child she had no idea. She'd run a hand over her belly, feeling the swelling there, but she did not know if the baby lived or had died.

If it lived, then it suffered as much as she.

Ishbel fought back the tears, not wanting Axis SunSoar to see them, nor wanting herself to succumb to the weakness. She thought a little about Axis. She knew the name, for she had heard the legend while at Sirus' court, but she did not think that this Axis could possibly be the same man. Ishbel did not worry overmuch about it, or even think too much about Axis. All she did was to lie as still as possible (and that was impossible in this lurching cart) and manage the pain as best she could.

Eventually, she heard Axis call to his men to establish camp. She did not know how long they had traveled, but now it was twilight, and very cold, and she was shaking uncontrollably beneath her wrappings.

The cart came to a halt suddenly, jolting her, and Ishbel screwed shut her eyes and cried out with the pain.

There was the sound of a horse, and then a muttered voice.

"Stars!"

The cart lurched, and Ishbel realized that someone had stepped onto the tray.

"Ishbel," Axis' soft voice said, and she managed to open her eyes.

He was squatting next to her in the tray of the cart, one hand resting on the coverings above her chest.

"Ishbel," he said, "I am going to lift you out of this cart, and down by a fire. I am sorry if I hurt you."

"I can get myself out, I think."

He smiled very slowly, and the pressure on her chest increased slightly. "I will lift you, Ishbel. Do not be afraid of me."

Ishbel wasn't, but she was mortified that she couldn't do more for herself. Axis lifted her very gently, causing her hardly any discomfort at all, stepped down from the cart, and carried her to where several of the soldiers had built a fire.

He set her down, made sure she was reasonably comfortable, then stepped aside for a murmured conversation with one of the soldiers. Once the soldier had gone—Ishbel heard him mount one of the horses and ride off at a gallop—Axis returned to her side.

"I've sent one of the men off to find better accommodation *somewhere* in this deserted land, and perhaps a herbalist or physician to help you. But in the meantime, Ishbel, what can I do for you? What do you need most?"

To return to my home, Ishbel thought. *Home to Serpent's Nest.* Her fever had taken hold once more, and she was shaking with its effects. Her throat was parched, her head throbbed unmercifully, and her nausea was getting worse with every breath.

"More water," she managed.

Axis lifted her up so he could put the canteen to her mouth, but Ishbel retched as soon as the water spilled into her mouth. She half fell out of Axis' supporting arm, and he had to grab at her to keep her steady, one hand on her belly.

"Stars," he muttered, "you're pregnant."

Then Ishbel heard him give a soft, ironic laugh. "Isaiah won't be happy about that."

"Who—" Ishbel began.

"Don't worry about that now," Axis said. "Ishbel, we will get you to a town and a physician as fast as we can. I don't want to keep you out in the open and away from better aid than I can provide any longer than is needed."

"I want to go home," she whispered.

"Escator is too far away," Axis said, and she could again

hear the smile in his voice. "One of Isembaard's border towns shall have to do for now."

Not Escator, Ishbel thought. *Home.*

Axis lay Ishbel down, wiping her face with a damp cloth, asking her if she wanted to try the water again. When she refused, he sat with her, unspeaking, until Ishbel drifted into a fevered sleep.

CHAPTER NINE

*The Town of Torinox, the Northern Borders
of the FarReach Dependency*

Ishbel slipped deeper into her fevered slumber, so that by
the time the soldier returned with news of a town that was
still partly inhabited some three hours ride to the southwest,
Axis was unable to rouse her. He frowned, worried, then
lifted her as gently as he could and, instead of putting her
back into the cart, propped her before him on his horse. The
donkey-drawn cart would be too slow—he needed to get Ishbel to aid as soon as possible.

Axis had not really thought about what he might find
when he met up with Ba'al'uz' men and their charge, but it
wasn't the slaughter he had actually encountered, and most
certainly not the sudden meeting with the Icarii. That sight of
them, the sight of them being *slaughtered*, had wrenched at
something very deep in his soul. He'd been living almost in
a state of unnatural serenity, almost a fugue, since he'd been
hauled back into this world.

Witnessing the death of those Icarii had propelled him
into full life.

*Stars! The spectacle of those Icarii, lying in almost un-
recognizable tatters of flesh and drifting, blood-spattered
feathers.*

As he rode through the night, Ishbel clutched before him,
Axis thought about the events of the day. The conversation
with BroadWing had unsettled him badly. It had felt as though
he were being dragged back into a world and a life that was
not completely welcome—or welcoming, for BroadWing had
certainly regarded Axis with some suspicion.

And how else was BroadWing supposed to react, eh? The Icarii who were left had been forced to manage with such great loss and tragedy that Axis had no idea how they had coped.

Suddenly he cursed to himself. Why hadn't he asked BroadWing about StarDrifter? Gods, if StarDrifter was alive somewhere then BroadWing may well have known about it.

What a lost opportunity.

Axis rode, one arm about Ishbel, his mind and heart in turmoil. Even though he'd now been riding for almost fourteen hours, he felt no exhaustion, only a terrible kind of nervous energy that, after an hour or two, he realized was a deep, unrelenting yearning for the man he had once been. Not the Star God, not even the StarMan, but those wonderful, intense years when he had been discovering himself as an Enchanter and as an Icarii prince. When he had been *doing* and *discovering*—two women he had loved beyond imagining; power beyond comprehension; excitement and life and energy and fear.

The sheer headiness of hurtling forward through life, of discoveries both wondrous and terrifying, of *doing*.

As a Star God, Axis had stopped moving forward. His extraordinary journey had come to a conclusion. He had stopped *doing*, and that had been the ruination of him.

Now here he was, hurtling through *life* once more, a company of fellow soldiers streaming out behind him, a stolen queen held tight in his arms, the stars whirling over his head, and the prospect of new discoveries, new challenges, new frontiers both glorious and dreadful before him.

Axis' arm tightened about Ishbel, his heels booted his horse into even greater effort, and he grinned, and wondered what adventures lay before him.

Ishbel knew almost nothing of that wild ride. In years to come she would remember flashes of it: the violent motion of the horse, Axis' arm tight about her, and the warmth and scent of his body, the glint of teeth as he grinned, the stars spinning overhead.

The pain.

Her fever was getting worse, and it sank dark fingers of agony into every single one of her joints. Any movement was a nightmare of hurt: not just her joints, but her head, which felt as if it wanted to explode, and her stomach, which now twisted and cramped as badly as if it had been flung onto a bed of hot coals.

She escaped as far as she could into unconsciousness, but even that held little relief for her. She dreamed, visionary nightmares that melded effortlessly into one another.

Her usual nightmare came to her first: the Lord of Elcho Falling, standing in the snow, his back to her, then slowly becoming aware of her presence, his head turning, turning, turning, and then the torrent of despair and pain that engulfed her world as he laid eyes on her and opened his mouth to speak.

This time it was worse than she'd ever experienced it before.

Then Ishbel dreamed of StarWeb whispering vicious hatred into her ear. Maximilian, turning on Ishbel in revulsion, and blaming her for the deaths of Evenor, Allemorte, and Borchard. StarWeb, exploding in a red mist of blood and bone and flesh. Maximilian, hearing the news of his lover's death, and breaking down in grief.

Maximilian, blaming Ishbel for StarWeb's death.

Herself, giving birth to a twisted, lumpen mass destroyed by Ba'al'uz' poisons.

Maximilian blaming her for his much-wanted child's death, too.

She was unaware that occasionally she called out his name—*Maxel! Maxel! Maxel!*—and that Axis' arm tightened fractionally about her every time she did so.

Worst of all, though, was the dream in which the Great Serpent appeared to her, hissing and spitting, cursing her for losing Maximilian, and any chance they had of preventing tragedy and annihilation.

What kind of foolish woman are you, the Great Serpent hissed, *to so lose Maximilian?*

And then, sometimes, dreams of Maximilian and the Great Serpent faded completely, and she was filled with a sense of total loss and foreboding, and she knew then that the Lord of Elcho Falling was close.

Torinox was more village than town, but it had an inn still open, and, blessed be to all gods, it had a physician called Zeboath waiting inside that inn. Apparently he'd been due to leave for the resettlement convoys gathering in the east the previous week, but his horse had needed rest to recover from a slight lameness, and he was still in the town. Zeboath had spent his time waiting, so far as Axis could see, sampling most of the innkeeper's remaining stocks of ale.

Still, Zeboath was a pleasant enough man, in both manner and aspect, and seemed competent despite his slight intoxication, giving Ishbel a quick examination as Axis carried her in.

"She's burning with fever," Zeboath said. "She needs to be put to bed immediately, given a bath, and she needs to have fluids."

"She tried to drink for me," said Axis, "but was unable to keep the water down."

"Fever?" said the innkeeper. "Fever? I am not so sure I want her to stay—"

Axis turned to the man, Ishbel still in his arms. "I hold in my arms the Queen of Escator, and your tyrant's future bride. If you want to refuse her aid, I am not entirely sure that Isaiah will understand."

The innkeeper shut his mouth with an audible snap, and hastened to show Axis to a room set aside on the ground floor.

Zeboath did what he could for Ishbel, but it was not very much. He and the innkeeper's daughter washed the filth of travel and sickness from her, and the physician managed to get some herbal medicine down Ishbel's throat, which he said would ease both her fever and her nausea. He also left pieces of juice-filled fruit in her mouth so that, even in her deep sleep, she could suck moisture and sweetness from them.

"But for the rest," Zeboath murmured to Axis as they stood by the door of Ishbel's chamber, "I can do little. I do not know what drugs she was given, so cannot counteract them. As for her fever . . ." He stopped, looking back through the door to where Ishbel lay motionless in the bed. "I cannot yet tell what has caused it, although I do not think it a plague or blight. More likely a result of weeks of little food and water, of sorrow and terror, if what you tell me about her circumstances is correct."

"And her baby?"

Zeboath shrugged. "Who can tell? She is about halfway through her pregnancy and the child is small. I cannot feel it move. She will either lose it, or manage to keep it until birth, but what damage may have been done to it, I don't—" He stopped suddenly, giving a shamefaced half smile. "And I should stop saying 'I don't know,' yes?"

Axis put his hand briefly on the man's shoulder, instinctively liking and trusting him. "You have done what you can." He glanced at Ishbel himself. "Until she wakes, and can speak, I doubt there's little anyone can do for her."

"Her husband?"

"I have no idea where he is," said Axis. "North of the Far-Reach Mountains, I assume."

He remembered what BroadWing had said—*Maximilian will tear the earth apart for her*—and he wondered how long Maximilian would stay north of the FarReach Mountains once BroadWing had reported back to him.

Zeboath was now looking at Ishbel with a degree of softness Axis found a little surprising. "If I had lost such a wife," Zeboath said, "I'd go mad trying to discover her again." Now he looked back at Axis. "Yet you say she is destined for Isaiah."

Axis hesitated to speak, wondering what he could say, then realized he had been handed a god-given opportunity to see just what Isaiah's subjects thought of their tyrant.

"You know what Isaiah is like," he said, with his own half shrug.

Zeboath gave a soft snort. "He is what Aqhat and his childhood have made him," he said. "He is better than his father."

"In what way?"

Now Zeboath looked at Axis curiously. "You're not from this land, are you? You speak the language well, but too precisely, and with a strange intonation."

"I come originally from the lost land of Tencendor," Axis said, "now earning my keep as a mercenary for Isaiah."

"And as his spy?"

"No. Whatever you say is safe. I ask questions only to sate my own curiosity."

"Perhaps. Well, Isaiah's father, Turmebt, was . . ." Zeboath sighed. "A man not given to understanding and tolerance. A man who was given to indulging his tastes, however repulsive they might be. Isembaard would have celebrated his death, save that people were terrified even of his ghost. Isaiah was like him when he was a young man, so reports have it, but then he changed, for which most of Isembaard is thankful."

"Oh? Changed? When, and how?"

"I live a long way from Aqhat, Axis, and I do not know the precise how. But it was within the first two or three years of Isaiah ascending the throne. Sometime after, or perhaps even during, his campaign against the Eastern Independencies."

That campaign again. Axis was more consumed by curiosity than ever, and wondered if he would one day become close enough to Isaiah to ask him about that campaign.

"Isaiah is not now the man his father once was," Zeboath finished.

"Indeed, that is warm praise for Isaiah."

"Aye, I suppose it is. I do not think people particularly like Isaiah, but they do not yet hate him, either. He has to prove himself."

"He has yet to conquer."

"If you say so," Zeboath said. Then, before Axis could query him on that comment, the physician went on. "You look exhausted, Axis. Go to bed. You can do no more for the lady tonight. I know I need my bed. Good night."

Rather than go to his room, Axis slouched down into a chair by Ishbel's bed, watching her for perhaps a half hour, and trying to go to sleep. But, even though he was desperately tired, it eluded him, and eventually Axis sighed and moved to drag his pack from where Insharah had left it, meaning to examine the rose pyramid.

He found it soon enough, wrapped in some oilcloth and stuffed into the center of the pack where it would be most protected, and he drew out the bundle and sat back down in the chair. He'd never handled the one that Isaiah had, and was curious as to what—

The instant his flesh touched the cool glass Axis gave a startled gasp, almost dropping the pyramid.

Stars, no! Surely not!

Trembling so badly he had to bite his lip and *force* his hands to move, Axis wrapped both palms about the rose pyramid.

It touched the Star Dance.

It touched the Star Dance.

Axis could barely breathe. His chest had constricted so much it hurt.

The Star Dance was filtering into his body via the pyramid.

Not much, a tiny amount, but . . . oh, stars, *stars*!

Far to the north, Eleanon stood by the open window of the main chamber of Crowhurst. Lister and Inardle had gone to bed hours ago, but Eleanon was enjoying standing in the frigid draft of air, watching it turn into ice as it passed across his body, and looking out over the frozen landscapes.

Suddenly his head whipped about and he stared at the spire—as he called the pyramid—sitting on a table to one side of the room.

Instantly he strode toward the table.

Axis sat in his chair, his entire body crouched over the pyramid. It had Enchanter power in it, but somehow *different*. It was Icarii-made, but yet *different*.

And it touched the Star Dance!

Almost panicked, Axis tried to remember the simplest enchantment he could. Perhaps something for warmth, this chamber was so damned cold, something to—

The pyramid glowed, and Axis had the sense of someone standing deep within it, but just out of sight.

Eleanon had both hands wrapped about the pyramid, and held it against his chest so that whoever had Ba'al'uz' pyramid (and it wasn't Ba'al'uz, never that) could not see him.

It was Axis. The StarMan. Eleanon could feel it, throbbing through the pyramid.

And Axis had just felt the Star Dance through it.

So, Axis, Eleanon thought. *Finally we touch.*

"Axis StarMan," he murmured. "My apologies . . ."

Then his hand tightened about the pyramid.

Axis cried out. Not in pain, but in loss. The pyramid in his hands had suddenly flared with an intense rose color—and then it had dulled into complete lifelessness, losing whatever color it had ever contained, to become a dull, pale gray.

All sense of the Star Dance had vanished.

Axis gripped the pyramid, willing it back to life, but nothing happened. The object he held in his hands was now as lifeless as if someone had closed the door on its power. He did not know quite what had happened, but he felt that someone had cut the flow of power to the pyramid the instant they realized Axis was using it.

Axis lowered his head over the pyramid and wept. Partly in loss, for to have lost even such a faint touch of the Star Dance was almost impossible to bear, but also in sheer joy.

It *was* possible to touch the Star Dance again. It was. This was an object of great Icarii (or Icarii-like) power, woven with enchantment that was foreign to Axis, but only barely so.

Wherever Lister had got these pyramids from, it had *not* been from DarkGlass Mountain.

The Star Dance was accessible again.

Axis was so focused on the glass pyramid and his own discovery that he did not realize Ishbel's eyes had opened briefly and had watched him.

When Ishbel woke it was well past dawn. The room was bright, and she had trouble focusing. For some time shapes in the room blurred in and out of focus, and when finally she did manage to bring her vision back under control, it was to see Axis SunSoar, sitting in a chair at some distance from her bed, watching her.

"Your fever has broken," he said. "Zeboath—the physician—came in not an hour ago. He said you were out of any immediate danger."

Ishbel did not directly respond, still a little disoriented. She lay quietly for a few minutes, looking at Axis, wondering about him. When he'd introduced himself yesterday (*was* it yesterday, or had she slept for weeks?) she had assumed that he could not possibly be the Axis SunSoar of legend, but now she was not so sure. He looked very much like the descriptions she'd heard of the Icarii StarMan: he had a tall lean grace, even slouched in the chair; wheat-colored hair pulled back into a tail at the nape of his neck; a clipped beard; and faded blue eyes. But it was his still watchfulness, and the aura of experience that hung about him, which made Ishbel revise her earlier conclusion. This was a man who had seen empires tumble and fall, who had *caused* their destruction, and who now tolerated her quiet regard with an infinite patience born, she thought, from a lifetime enduring cataclysmic events.

But mostly Ishbel reconsidered her original assessment because she was a priestess trained in the art and the world of gods, and this man stank of god power, even though he made every attempt to subdue it.

"Where am I?" Ishbel said finally.

"In a town called Torinox. I had to bring you here because—"

"Torinox? But what land, Axis? The men who took me told me nothing. I have no idea where I am."

"My apologies. We are in the northern reaches of a great empire called the Tyranny of Isembaard. Have you heard of it?"

Ishbel gave a weak nod. "It is to the south of my homeland. By the gods, Axis, I am so far from home."

"Maximilian will be searching for you." *Maximilian will tear apart the earth to find you.*

"I doubt it."

She saw Axis raise his brows at the bitterness in her voice.

"He thinks me responsible for a trail of death across the Central Kingdoms," she said, "and one of the Icarii who died yesterday—it *was* yesterday?"

Axis gave a nod.

"One of the Icarii who died, StarWeb, was his lover. He will blame me for her death as well."

Now Axis' eyes livened with interest. "Maximilian Persimius kept an Icarii lover?"

"Yes."

"Yet he cannot have found you too unattractive, Ishbel. You're some five months gone with child."

She moved a hand to her belly. "He wants the child. Not me, not anymore."

Axis started to say something, then caught himself. Instead he came over to the bed, sat down on its edge, and felt her pulse.

"The man responsible for that trail of deaths," he said softly, not looking at her, "was the man who captured you. A man called Ba'al'uz."

"Why?"

Axis gave a shrug, as if he did not know. Ishbel thought about pursuing the subject, but in the end was too tired and felt too ill to summon the energy.

"Are you truly Axis SunSoar of legend?" she said.

"Aye."

"I thought you were dead."

"So did I, but I seem to have a habit of rising from the dead."

"Axis?"

"Yes?"

"Thank you for yesterday. And . . . I am sorry for the Icarii. I wish . . ."

He nodded, but changed the subject when he spoke. "You need to breakfast," he said, "and regain your strength."

"Will you take me home, Axis?"

He looked her full in the eye then. "I am sorry, Ishbel. I cannot."

Ishbel turned her head away. "Where will you take me, then?"

"South, to a place called Aqhat."

Ishbel was silent a long moment, and when she spoke her voice was very quiet.

"Axis, what is the ancient evil that lives south? What is it that threatens our world?"

When Lister rose in the morning, Eleanon told him that Axis SunSoar had one of the pyramids.

"Which one?" Lister asked, a little sharply.

"That which belonged to Ba'al'uz," said Eleanon. "He must have left it with his men when he left for Coroleas."

"Well, I suppose it better that Axis have his than Isaiah's," said Lister. "Did he—"

"He felt the Star Dance, yes," said Eleanon. "I felt his gladness, his joy, here." He tapped his chest.

"Did he see *you*?" Lister said.

Eleanon gave a shake of his head.

"Did he *know* you?" Lister asked.

Again the shake of the head, and Lister relaxed slightly. "Well, that is something. I hope you shut the thing down."

"Yes."

"I don't like the fact that Isaiah brought Axis back," Lister said. "Why? What does Isaiah plan to do with him? And what is Axis going to say, my friend, if ever he meets *you*?"

"I have no desire to meet him. We cut our ties with the Icarii a long time ago, Lister. I owe Axis nothing, not friendship and certainly not loyalty. That belongs to you, as you know, and to the Lord of Elcho Falling."

CHAPTER TEN

Palace of the First, Yoyette, Coroleas

StarDrifter existed in a state of hope for the first time in years. That hope was fourfold: the chance that he would soon see Axis again; the hope that he would be once more able to touch the Star Dance; the hope that he would finally manage to free one of the lost souls trapped within the Corolean deities; and the hope that in the doing he would destroy a woman he loathed. He could not wait for that moment when he would begin his seduction of Salome. StarDrifter was beginning to see in Salome, in her cruelty and selfishness, all the women he'd hated—most notably StarLaughter, the ancient Enchantress who had come back from the dead and murdered the one birdwoman StarDrifter loved before any other: Zenith.

In doing what Ba'al'uz asked of him, StarDrifter saw redemption for himself. Revenge for Zenith, for all the slaves and children who were entrapped in their bronze deities, and for everyone who suffered at the hands of the Coroleans.

A revenge for five years of insults and sniggers at the Corolean court.

A revenge for the loss of his wings, and for his life of sheer, damned futility.

StarDrifter was determined not to fail, and he was arrogant enough to believe that he could *not* fail.

After all, who better than he to know the best way to seduce a woman?

StarDrifter pushed aside all sympathy for Salome. She was the worst of a corrupt society. She had murdered, indulged her love for cruelty, and trampled all who stood in her way. He was only doing to Salome what she'd done to countless thousands.

Tonight was Moonlit Night Court. StarDrifter might loathe much about Corolean society, but he always looked forward to the thirteen Moonlit Night Courts of the year. The emperor held court in the gardens of the Palace of the First on the night of full moon. While murder and intrigue and corruption still pervaded every moment of the evening, somehow the beauty of the gardens and the moonlight negated the pervasive cruelty of the Corolean court and made it, for just one night, something to be enjoyed rather than endured.

Moonlit Night Court did not get under way until a full two hours after dark. People filtered into the extensive topiary gardens of the Palace of the First in small groups, murmuring among themselves, accepting glasses of minted alcoholic julep and squares of sugared confections from servants, and wandering slowly among the fantastic topiary creations that stood over three paces high. Tens of thousands of topiaries dotted an area the size of a small town, created a mazelike tangle of paths and unexpected glades. Overhead drifted a galaxy of round paper lanterns, each lit from within by a small candle. StarDrifter had heard that there was an entire department of slaves within the palace devoted entirely to their production and deployment, and that throughout the night they would scurry about, launching fresh lanterns, retrieving those that had become caught among the tops of the topiary creations, and dampening any unfortunate fires.

StarDrifter arrived when the gardens were already humming with people and conspiracy. He'd spent the early part of the evening pacing the confines of his tiny room, not wanting to appear too early, and putting up with Ba'al'uz' murmured fretting about what might go wrong. StarDrifter had finally been forced to snarl at the man, and send him back to his own chamber, simply to get some peace.

But now he was here. StarDrifter had taken particular care with his appearance, using Ba'al'uz' coin to purchase an outfit that would, he hoped, be enough to make him stand out.

In a court renowned for its gaudy excess, StarDrifter had chosen well. Heads turned as he wandered slowly through the topiary maze, whispers trailing in his path.

StarDrifter wore a virtually skintight black ensemble that was remarkable for its subtlety and understatement. The material was of a fine matte silk, with a delicate, raised pattern woven into it that made the material shimmer very slightly in the moonlight. It covered StarDrifter from neck to toe, and even had gloves and shoes made of matching material. Its subtlety and color complemented his silvery-golden coloring perfectly, but it was StarDrifter's innate grace and elegance that turned an otherwise beautiful costume into the extraordinary.

StarDrifter only had to stroll through the garden, hands loosely clasped behind his back, for the entire court to become aware of his presence. He spoke to no one, inclined his head only very occasionally at someone, and refused all refreshment pressed on him by openmouthed servants.

Tonight, for the very first time since he'd arrived in Coroleas, StarDrifter felt truly like a prince of the Icarii.

Confidence and unavailability oozed from his every pore, and StarDrifter *knew*, without a shadow of a doubt, that every woman and half the men present desired him.

But only one woman mattered, only the one for whom this extraordinary showing was staged—and even if Salome managed to resist this display, StarDrifter had one trick left up his sleeve.

Something he was sure she would never resist.

It took StarDrifter almost an hour before he came across her, but he knew that she must have been aware of his approach for some minutes beforehand. The whispers he generated were spreading ahead of him like a wave.

He turned a corner, and there she was, the Duchess of Sidon, already staring at the gap in the topiary from which he emerged. Remarkably, Salome was dressed in black as well, although her costume revealed far more flesh than StarDrifter's. There were several other people standing with Salome, and they all stared wordlessly at him.

StarDrifter knew he had only two options, to nod at her

and then continue on his sinuous way and hope she was intrigued enough to send a sycophant scurrying after him, or to approach her directly, and reveal his interest.

He decided to take no chances.

StarDrifter approached her directly.

This was a risk, for as one of the most lowly members of the court, and one generally the butt of sarcasm and ill-meant humor, StarDrifter broke every rule of etiquette by so doing. But tonight he was not the bitter, hopeless man the court had become used to seeing skulking about in the shadows.

Tonight StarDrifter felt in every manner a prince, and one used to getting his own way.

Tonight Salome was his.

He stopped two paces away from her, his hands still loosely clasped behind his back, and nodded politely.

Then he looked up at the sky filled with myriad glowing lanterns and said very softly, "Do you know what this night reminds me of, Salome?"

One of her sycophants took a step forward. "Hold your tongue! *No one* approaches the great Duchess of—"

"And *no one* speaks to a prince of the Icarii in such a manner!" StarDrifter snapped back, wrapping himself in all the full arrogance and majesty of his birth. He moved slightly toward the man, as graceful and dangerous as a striking panther, then slid his eyes to Salome.

"Why surround yourself with such fools, Salome? Surely they are a detriment to your life."

"You are taking a huge risk," she said, her eyes brilliant as they watched him. "No one speaks to me like that."

"*Do* you know what this night reminds me of, Salome?"

She continued to stare at him, unreadable, and remained silent.

"In my land of Tencendor," StarDrifter continued, his attention now exclusively on Salome, "there was one special night every year. Beltide night. It was the celebration of spring, of the regeneration of the earth, of the great mother, of life and regeneration."

StarDrifter turned very slowly on his heel—making everyone in Salome's group, save Salome herself, shuffle slightly in alarm—and then moved in a small circle, his gloved hands floating out a little from his sides, one shoulder dipping.

It was the movement of a dancer.

He came to a halt, catching Salome's flat unreadable eyes again.

"The Icarii and the Avar peoples gathered in the groves of the mysterious Avarinheim," StarDrifter said, his voice so low all had to strain forward to hear it. "We danced, and drank, and we spent the night making love under the stars. It was a night of great power."

"And this pathetic little gathering reminds you of that?" Salome said, her voice heavy with disbelief.

"Not this gathering," said StarDrifter. "*You* remind me of Beltide's mystery and power."

Then he turned on his heel and left, feeling Salome's eyes boring into his back the entire way.

Hours passed. StarDrifter kept moving through the crowds, taking a glass of wine now and again, and sometimes drifting into a small clearing and dancing under the stars. When he did this his movements were very slow and deliberate, heavy with sorrow and memory, incalculably sweet.

Even among the Icarii, all of whom had exquisite grace and elegance, StarDrifter was renowned for the sheer beauty and power of his dancing. He might no longer command the power of the Star Dance, but StarDrifter nevertheless exuded such mystery, such sexuality, and imbued every single one of his movements, no matter how slight, with such extraordinary loveliness and bittersweetness that he reduced to tears most who paused to watch him.

People would gather at the edges of the clearing, silent, awestruck.

Most were Coroleans.

A few were Icarii, come to watch with tears in their eyes as the legendary StarDrifter danced.

Once the emperor and his wife stood there, open-mouthed.

On two occasions that StarDrifter was aware of, Salome watched as he danced.

He was careful not to look at her.

The entire evening, and his display, was meant for one purpose—to seduce Salome. But as the hours went by, StarDrifter discovered that he was enjoying the night for a very different reason.

Tonight he had returned to being a prince. Tonight he had once more embraced his full Icarii glory, even though he lacked his wings. When all the thousands went home to their beds, there was only one thing they would ever remember of this night.

StarDrifter, incalculably beautiful and full of grace, dancing under the drifting paper lanterns.

Toward dawn, when people were starting to return to their chambers and apartments, StarDrifter emerged from the shadows of a huge topiary tree.

Salome was standing across the clearing, talking in low tones with her son, Ezra, and one of the other nobles of the First.

She turned, intuiting his presence.

StarDrifter raised his hand in one of the most ancient and magical of Icarii gestures, and one designed to call to any of Icarii blood. He held his arm out at full length, his hand toward Salome, imperious, demanding. Slowly his fingers curled, one, twice, a third time, beckoning, commanding, in the traditional Icarii gesture of seduction.

Salome rocked on her feet, and StarDrifter knew he had won her.

Icarii blood would always out.

"I have rules in here," Salome said. "You will obey them."

StarDrifter did not answer. He wandered about her bedchamber, hands once again loosely clasped behind his back, inspecting the many objects of antiquity and beauty.

He stopped before the Weeper, staring at it. For all its value and power, it was only a small thing, standing about half a pace in height. It had been carefully fashioned by an ancient craftsman of great worth, for every detail of the deity's face was carefully and lovingly picked out, and even the weave of the cloth was apparent in its robe.

There was a faint trail of moisture down one cheek.

"You do not touch that," Salome said.

StarDrifter turned about. "One of your 'rules'?"

"You shall not speak to me. I have no interest in your thoughts. I shall use your body and then require you to leave."

StarDrifter gave her a cynical smile, then resumed his slow inspection of the room.

"I said—" Salome began.

"I heard what you said," StarDrifter said, now leaning over a collection of gems set into velvet and displayed on a low table. "I discover you have a hitherto unsuspected sense of humor."

Salome flushed. "I can destroy you," she said.

StarDrifter stood up and smiled at her, now with apparent genuine humor. "You cannot say that to a man who has lost everything he has ever held dear, and who longs only for death, and think to scare him with it. In fact, my dear"—he took a step closer to her—"you only entice him with such promises."

He drew off his gloves and tossed them back onto the gem-laden table. Then he walked forward and cupped her cheek in his hand.

She jerked away. "You do only what I—"

"Your skin is very soft," StarDrifter said. "Strange, for somehow I thought it would have a reptilian cast to it."

Her eyes glittered. "Leave."

"No."

She turned toward the door.

"You've never had an Icarii lover, have you?" said StarDrifter.

She turned back to him. "I've had thousands."

"Liar."

She stared at him, her breathing rapid. StarDrifter could see she wanted to order him to leave, or to order in the guards to *force* him to leave, but he could also see that she wanted him.

"Don't be frightened," he said, moving forward and again cupping her face in his hand.

She tensed, but before she could move away StarDrifter leaned down and kissed her.

What stunned him was not her response, but his own. The instant he felt her mouth open beneath his, he grabbed her to him, pressing her the length of his body, burying his hands in her hair, dragging his mouth to her jaw, and sinking in his teeth.

Then it was all movement. The tearing away of clothes, the grabbing of flesh, the hoarse breathing, the grunts, the sheer, unashamed arousal.

It wasn't pretty, or elegant, or clothed in any manner of regard or warmth. It was sheer, primitive sex, accomplished even before they managed the bed. When it was done, when StarDrifter managed to bring his breathing back from the fevered pitch of orgasm to something vaguely approaching normal, he rose from Salome's body, picked her up, carried her to the bed, flung her down, and began all over again.

He'd never felt this way when making love before. Not with his wife, Rivkah, not with any other of the many Icarii women he'd bedded, not with any other of his human lovers, such as Embeth, the woman he'd taken when first he'd arrived in the city of Carlon.

It was as if Salome was a drug, instantly addictive.

He hated the woman, but, oh, stars, his entire being screamed at him to take her just one more time, one more time . . .

CHAPTER ELEVEN

*The Town of Torinox, the Northern Borders of
the FarReach Dependency*

Did you manage all your breakfast this morning?" Zeboath asked.

"Yes," Ishbel said, wincing a little as Zeboath's fingers probed at the joints at the top of her spine.

"It still hurts a little," he said.

She nodded.

"But your body is expelling the poison faster than I had expected." Zeboath smiled, then stood back. "I think you will be well, my lady. You have a courageous constitution."

She smiled a little at that. "I did not realize constitutions could be 'courageous.'"

"Indeed. All good physicians know how to spot at first glance a courageous constitution, and an adventurous constitution, and even a glamorous constitution."

Now Ishbel laughed. "You are a likeable physician, Zeboath."

"I strive for it, my lady."

"Not all physicians are as likeable."

Curious, Zeboath was about to ask what had sparked that remark when Axis SunSoar entered the room.

"Ishbel," he said, nodding at her. "Zeboath, how is she this morning?"

"You may ask her yourself," Zeboath said. "I believe her voice has quite recovered."

Axis smiled and inscribed a small bow before Ishbel, seated at the small table in her room. "I apologize, Ishbel. I did not mean to speak as if you were not here."

"I am feeling much better, thank you. Zeboath's herbal drafts have done me much good."

Axis glanced at Zeboath and noted his flush of pleasure. "He is a good physician," Axis said, "and much wasted here at Torinox. Zeboath, once Ishbel has recovered sufficiently we shall need to ride to Aqhat. Would you accompany us? Isaiah provided my company all its needs, save for a physician. Or do you have ties with the resettlement peoples that you can't—"

"I'll come," said Zeboath. "Thank you!"

"You are hungry for the excitement of Aqhat, I think," Axis said, glad the man had accepted. Even in the short time they'd been at Torinox he'd grown to like Zeboath very much, and physicians were always useful around fighting men. "Now," he continued, keeping his tone light and bantering, "if you'd care to leave the lady and myself alone . . ."

"I don't know that I should," Zeboath said, responding to Axis' tone. "I fear for my lady's virtue."

"Come, come," said Axis, "if you're going to run with a band of unscrupulous fighting men, then you'll need to accept their dissolute ways."

Both men laughed, and Zeboath exited, bowing at Ishbel from the door.

Once the door had closed, Axis sat down at the table, and noticed with some surprise that Ishbel looked very uncomfortable at his and Zeboath's banter. That puzzled him. She might well have thought their exchange annoyingly juvenile, or she might have laughed with them—but to be made uncomfortable? It was not the kind of reaction Axis would have expected from a queen, or indeed any lady of court.

Ishbel intrigued him. There had been the remark she made last night about the ancient evil in the south, which at the time he'd not commented on because Ishbel had looked so tired and ill he'd thought it better she get some rest.

There was her relationship with Maximilian, which she appeared to believe was in dire straits. Here Axis had to partly agree with her, if it was true Maximilian had kept an Icarii lover, but on the other hand it didn't marry well with what BroadWing had said about Maximilian.

There was the very fact that Ba'al'uz had stolen her in the first place. Isaiah may have believed his brother's stated reason—to present Isaiah with a new bride—but Axis thought that Ba'al'uz likely had a deeper, far more secret reason for taking the woman.

Now this curious gaucheness, as if she had been kept secluded all her life.

Axis smelled a secret.

"You look far better today," he said. "A day or two's rest here, and then perhaps we can continue our journey south."

"Where are we going?"

"To Aqhat. It is a massive palace complex on the banks of the River Lhyl, home to the Tyrant of Isembaard, Isaiah."

"Why? What am I doing here? Why did this man, Ba'al'uz, take me?"

"Ba'al'uz took you in order to present you as a gift to the Tyrant of Isembaard, Isaiah," Axis said, wondering how Ishbel would react to this. "A trophy wife. A conquest, for a man who lives only for conquest."

She blanched, her eyes wide and brilliant, and for a moment Axis thought she had actually stopped breathing.

"Ishbel, don't worry. Isaiah has an unnatural aversion to women who are pregnant or who have given birth. Isaiah will take one look at you, be horribly appalled, and never want to set eyes on you again. You shall have the best apartment and care while you are Isaiah's 'guest,' but you shall not be harmed, nor touched."

"Axis . . ." Ishbel leaned forward a little on the table, half extending a hand over its surface toward him. "Please, let me go. Don't take me to Aqhat. I—"

"Where would you go?"

She leaned back in the chair, sliding her hand down to her lap. "I want to go home."

"Escator."

She shifted her eyes away.

Axis watched her, considering. *Not Escator.* "Where is 'home,' Ishbel? Where do you come from?"

"The Outlands. It is a province—"

"I know where it is. It is a very large area. From where in the Outlands?"

She looked back at him, lifting her chin, and Axis saw a flash of determination in her eyes. "A place called Serpent's Nest. You may not have heard of it."

Stars! That was the mountain that had so interested Isaiah.

Could *this* be the reason Ba'al'uz had snatched her? What was Serpent's Nest's secret?

"I have heard of it," he said, "but I have not heard well of the mountain." Axis paused, then decided to push a little. "Isaiah called it the home of a 'rather vile band of psychic murderers.'"

She blanched, but Axis could see he'd made her angry rather than fearful. "Tell me about Serpent's Nest," he said. "I know nothing other than what Isaiah told me. It was"—*is*, in her mind—"your home?"

Ishbel gave a jerk of her head. "Since I was a child of eight." She was so practiced now in her lies that they fell easily from her mouth. "I was an orphan, and the Coil took me in, caring for me. I was their ward."

"And you left there only to marry Maximilian."

"Yes."

"Tell me of the Coil."

"There is little enough to tell. They are an order who prophesy using the twists of a man's bowel. They worship a god called the Great Serpent." She shrugged. "I know little else save that they were good to me and that I owed them my utter loyalty."

She looked directly at Axis as she said this, and he knew that she would not be drawn further.

Later, he thought. *You have left too much unsaid for me to let this one go.*

"Was it the Coil who told you about the ancient evil?"

She hesitated, then nodded. "They are concerned."

"I have no doubt," Axis said. His fingers tapped lightly on the table as he considered her. She was such an enigma. She fascinated him and she attracted him, even as tired and disheveled and as pregnant as she was. Axis BattleAxe would most certainly have seduced her.

And Axis now?

"Tell me about Maximilian," Axis said. "He intrigues me. I have never met him, although I do know something of him. The daughter of a dear friend was once in negotiations to marry him, but the negotiations fell through."

Ishbel made a helpless gesture. "He flummoxes me. He overwhelms me. Sometimes I feel I can hardly breathe around him. He terrifies me."

You love him, thought Axis, remembering how she had called out to Maximilian during the long ride to Torinox, *but because you have no idea what love is, you don't recognize it.*

"Maximilian will have been glad to have lost me," Ishbel said.

"BroadWing, one of the Icarii who tried to rescue you, was sent by Maximilian. BroadWing said that Maximilian would tear the earth apart to get you back again."

Ishbel laughed bitterly. "That I cannot believe. This child, maybe, but not me."

"If that is true," Axis said, "then Maximilian is a terrible fool. And *that* I cannot believe of a man who won through the terrors of the Veins."

"He is a most strange man, Axis," Ishbel said. "Sometimes I think that he did not leave the terror *in* the Veins. Sometimes I think he may have brought it *out* with him."

CHAPTER TWELVE

Palace of the First, Yoyette, Coroleas

Where is the Weeper?"

StarDrifter did not even glance at Ba'al'uz as he closed the door to his chamber, then threw himself full-length on the bed. "Stars . . . I am *exhausted*."

"*Where is the Weeper*?"

"In Salome's chamber."

"But—"

StarDrifter rolled over, lacing his hands behind his head. "She was too alert, Ba'al'uz. Too nervy. I need to wait a night or two more, I think. Allow her to relax. It matters not a night or two more. Be assured. I will take it eventually."

Ba'al'uz took a deep breath, calming himself down. StarDrifter was right. A night or two would not matter.

"You *did* sleep with her."

A salacious grin on StarDrifter's face was all the answer Ba'al'uz needed.

"And you think she'll want you back?"

StarDrifter laughed softly. "Oh, she'll want me back."

Salome lay curled up in her bed, damp sheets twisted about her body. Her servant had come in earlier with her usual morning glass of tea, but Salome had snarled so viciously at her that the servant had dropped the glass and run.

All Salome wanted was to lie, and think.

Dear gods, what she'd done last night had been so dangerous. Taking an Icarii lover.

The risk was . . . incalculable.

No matter what she'd said to StarDrifter (and he had

known, curse him), Salome had never taken an Icarii to her bed before. Many had made their interest known. One had even used the same gesture of seduction to her that StarDrifter had used.

But Salome had resisted easily.

An Icarii lover had murdered her grandmother.

An Icarii lover had caused her mother to die of grief.

No cursed Icarii lover was going to cause *her* death.

Yet, last night, she had been unable to resist StarDrifter. Salome had no idea why. She didn't particularly like him and thought his beauty overstated. She *loathed* his arrogance and his discernible contempt of her. She had heard all the stories about the SunSoars and the women they destroyed.

She was strong enough to resist him, surely?

Yet she hadn't. He'd teased her, tempted her, danced before her, and then flung out his hand in that damned imperious gesture.

And Salome had simply capitulated.

No. She had not just "simply capitulated"; that made it sound far too innocent. Salome had cast aside her entire world for him. If she'd been given a choice at that moment between succeeding in placing Ezra on the throne and ruling through him, or having StarDrifter for one night, she would have cast aside every one of her carefully nurtured ambitions for that one night with StarDrifter.

Why? Why? Gods, he threatened her entire world. Even as lost in the throes of lust as she had been, Salome had remembered, throughout their protracted, sweaty, exhausting coupling, not to allow him to view her back. She hadn't even allowed him to caress it.

She hoped he hadn't noticed.

Salome lay in her bed for hours, the day warming outside, lost in her thoughts, terrified of the consequences, but knowing that she would allow him back.

Just for one more night, perhaps.

She'd be careful.

He'd never know.

CHAPTER THIRTEEN

The Royal Palace, Ruen, Escator

Maximilian had come back to Ruen because he had no idea what else to do. He couldn't find Ishbel on his own, and he knew he couldn't afford the time to scurry helplessly about southern Kyros in the hope of finding a clue. Somewhere. StarWeb and BroadWing and their companions were searching. Malat—after some persuasion—was searching for her via his network of agents and spies and guardsmen.

With that Maximilian had to be content.

He'd been away from Escator for almost seven months, and Maximilian couldn't ignore the fact he'd left his kingdom alone for all that time. Yes, the Privy Council had authority to do whatever they needed to keep life running smoothly, but Maximilian had his responsibilities to his kingdom even before his wife, and he'd simply had to return.

He felt keenly the embarrassment of returning without Ishbel. Escator had been preparing a grand welcome for the new queen, and instead their king had slunk home in the middle of the night, minus his wife, and with no idea where she was.

Maximilian had hardly been able to hold court, yet he'd had to, and had to bear the curious looks and whispers and muttered sympathies. He'd hated himself for feeling the embarrassment, knowing that Ishbel, wherever she was, was likely suffering far more than "embarrassment."

But most of all Maximilian hated himself for not being able to save her, or find her.

He prayed to all gods that BroadWing and StarWeb would have better luck.

At least he *was* home, and Maximilian took some comfort in that.

One of the first things he did, once he'd rested, was to talk with Vorstus.

"Elcho Falling is stirring," Maximilian said without preamble when Vorstus walked into the chamber.

"Truly?" said Vorstus, sitting down in a chair and folding his hands.

"How long have you known?" Maximilian said.

"A very long time," Vorstus said softly, holding Maximilian's gaze.

Maximilian turned on his heel, walked to a window, and leaned his hands on the sill to stare out.

A very long time? Had Vorstus—and perhaps Light and Water—been manipulating his life for *all* his forty years?

"You are the perfect man for it," Vorstus said.

Maximilian still said nothing. He was angry, so angry he was afraid that if he let go of the windowsill then he would physically attack the abbot. He didn't know what to do, about Ishbel or about Elcho Falling, but he did not trust Vorstus, and could not trust a single thing the man said to him.

All Maximilian wanted to do was to take control of his life, but he had no idea how.

"There is something you should know," he said finally, still staring out the window.

"Yes?" Vorstus said.

"Are you aware of something called the Twisted Tower?"

"Yes. The Persimius kings passed down the knowledge of Elcho Falling via a memory palace, a storage place for everything they needed to know. You would have been taught how to access the Twisted Tower at an early age."

"I was nine when my father first began to teach me." Maximilian turned about, looking at Vorstus steadily. "But did you know, Vorstus, that the Twisted Tower is all but empty? That I can do little more than raise Elcho Falling when it is needed, but that I no longer have access to the knowledge to enable me to wield it fully? Did you not ever consider the possibility that the Twisted Tower would have deteriorated over the centuries, and that knowledge would be forgotten?"

Vorstus rose to his feet. His face was tightly controlled, his eyes flinty. "Then what has been lost needs to be regained, my Lord of Elcho Falling. That shall be your responsibility."

With that Vorstus left the room, leaving Maximilian staring after him in silent, impotent rage.

Five days after Maximilian had arrived home, he was interrupted during a meeting with Egalion by the arrival of one of the Emerald Guard bursting into Maximilian's private chamber without even knocking.

"My lord, forgive me," the man said, sinking briefly to one knee, "but there is urgent news."

Maximilian had stood as soon as the man entered. "Yes?"

"BroadWing EvenBeat is home. Just now arrived. My lord, he—"

The man got no further, for Maximilian was now staring over his shoulder.

BroadWing was slumped in the doorway, barely able to maintain his feet.

"Dear gods," Maximilian muttered, knowing instinctively that BroadWing brought disastrous news.

Egalion and the Emerald Guardsman helped him to a chair.

"Send for Garth Baxtor," Maximilian said to the guardsman, and he nodded, and left.

"BroadWing," Maximilian said, sinking to his haunches beside the Icarii birdman's chair, "you need attention, and food and drink. Perhaps—"

"What I *need*," said BroadWing, "is to tell you what has happened. Everything else can wait."

Maximilian felt sick to the stomach.

"We found Ishbel," BroadWing went on without preamble. "She was being taken through the FarReach Mountains down to the Tyranny of Isembaard. Escorted by eight men. She was drugged, helpless. I am sorry, Maximilian, she did not look well."

"Gods . . ." Maximilian muttered.

"We decided—oh, stars, *I* decided, to try to rescue her. She looked so ill . . . so helpless . . ."

"BroadWing," said Maximilian, "don't blame yourself."

"Shit," BroadWing muttered. "I thought I had a brilliant plan. But it was shit, Maximilian. Shit. It killed StarWeb and the others."

Maximilian looked away.

"The men who had her commanded a frightful power. Dark and shadowy. None of us could withstand it. Star-Web and the others . . . exploded. There was nothing left of them."

Kanubai, thought Maximilian. It must have been Kanubai's power. *Shit! Kanubai had Ishbel? Had he risen already?*

Maximilian felt a moment of complete panic. *What should he do?*

"But you escaped," Egalion said.

"I would have died, too," said BroadWing, "save that just as these men turned toward me, a band of armed men arrived. They attacked the eight who had murdered my companions, and drove them away. They saved my life."

"A mercy," said Maximilian, "and one I am most profoundly grateful for. BroadWing, do not blame yourself. You did more than I could ever have expected of—"

"There's more," said BroadWing. "The leader of the armed men was Axis SunSoar."

For a moment there was complete silence as Maximilian and Egalion stared at BroadWing.

"No," said Maximilian, "that cannot be. You must be mistaken."

"I am not mistaken," BroadWing whispered. "Your wife, Ishbel—should she still be alive—is now secreted within the Tyranny of Isembaard, and she is in the hands of the StarMan himself, Axis SunSoar, returned from death."

"Oh, my gods," Maximilian muttered. "What *else* can go wrong?"

Garth Baxtor had arrived just after that, and had seen Broad-Wing taken to a room and given medication and food. Then he hurried back to Maximilian's chamber, where Maximilian sat with Egalion. A moment later Vorstus joined them, earning himself a dark look from Maximilian, who had avoided all contact with Vorstus since their conversation on Maximilian's return to Ruen.

They all looked stunned, unable to believe BroadWing's news. Maximilian looked particularly pale, and Garth thought that he'd taken the news of StarWeb badly.

"How could Axis SunSoar be alive, and in Isembaard, of all places?" Egalion said, and by the manner of his tone, Garth knew that question had been asked many times over the past half hour or so.

Maximilian shrugged. "From the legends of Tencendor that I have heard, Axis has escaped from death on a number of occasions. What is one more time?"

"But Isembaard?" Vorstus said.

"Has he been involved in the murders, do you think?" Garth said.

Maximilian gave a slow shake of his head. "Not if he fought for BroadWing's life against those who had stolen Ishbel, no. But what he is doing down there . . . who can tell?"

"What will you do?" Vorstus said.

For the first time in weeks, a look of determination and resolve lit Maximilian's eyes. "I am going to find my wife," he said.

"No," said Vorstus. "*No!*"

CHAPTER FOURTEEN

The Royal Palace, Ruen, Escator

It was a massive risk, leaving Escator so soon after he'd arrived home, but Maximilian knew he had to do it. He couldn't abandon Ishbel or their child. He needed to rescue her for purely personal reasons—he loved her and wanted both her and their child safe—and for darker reasons, as Ishbel had been sent to him for a purpose: she was somehow intimately connected with Elcho Falling and she could not be allowed to fall into the hands of Kanubai.

Kanubai wanted her. More than anything else, that fact reinforced in Maximilian's mind that she was somehow integral to Elcho Falling.

Well might Kanubai want her, but at least for the moment she was in the hands of Axis . . . and Maximilian thought Axis was the better bet than Kanubai.

Just slightly.

Maximilian lay awake at night, thinking of Ishbel, ill and alone, dragged through the FarReach Mountains. He lay awake, racked with guilt that the face he'd shown her in their last days together had been one of anger and accusation.

Maximilian grieved for StarWeb and carried a burden of guilt for her death, as well as the other three Icarii who had died trying to rescue Ishbel, but for the most part his thoughts were for Ishbel and her plight. This time he would not send others to do what perhaps he should have done in the first instance. This time he'd find her himself.

No one was happy with Maximilian's decision, whether the Privy Council of Preferred Nobles, or Egalion representing the Emerald Guard, or Garth Baxtor, or most particularly

Vorstus. The abbot of the Order of Persimius spent hours arguing with Maximilian, saying it was pointless to risk his own life when there were many others who could go. Others who were *trained* for this kind of thing, damn it! Maximilian was risking both his own life and Escator's well-being unnecessarily—not to mention Elcho Falling.

"Ishbel is intimately connected with Elcho Falling," Maximilian said to Vorstus as the abbot tried yet again to persuade him against mounting his own rescue effort.

"*You* are more important than Ishbel," Vorstus said. "Elcho Falling is more important than Ishbel!"

"Not to me," Maximilian responded quietly.

Vorstus was not the only one to try to persuade Maximilian against his plan.

"We can't afford to lose you," Baron Lixel said to Maximilian on a day that he, Egalion, Vorstus, and Garth met once more with the king to persuade him against this venture. "You are needed *here*. Only this morning we received word that the Outlands have declared formal war on Pelemere and Berfardi. Sire, I beg you, reconsider. Our world is disintegrating into war. We cannot afford to have you chase off after—"

He stopped, seeing Maximilian's eyes slide his way.

"Ishbel can be rescued as easily, *more* easily and with less risk, by someone else," Lixel finished.

"I'm sorry," Garth said, "but I don't like any of this. Is Ishbel worth risking your life, and Escator's peace, over?"

"I do not like you going after her personally," said Lixel. "I fear for you, and for Escator. I would prefer you sent Egalion, and the Emerald Guard. And what do any of us know about this land of Isembaard? Nothing! It is huge, and you have no idea where to search, and—"

"I will find her, Lixel," Maximilian said. "I am sure I know where she is going."

Lixel made a gesture of helplessness. "If you must, then go, Maximilian. But, please, gods, *return to us!*"

"I and the Emerald Guard will ensure that he—" Egalion began, before Maximilian raised a hand and stopped him.

"I'm sorry, Egalion, I do this with only a very small party.

Two of the best of the Emerald Guard. No more. Three of us all told. We can travel light and fast and undetected. My friends, if I could survive seventeen years in the Veins, I can survive a journey into Isembaard."

He shot Vorstus a dark look then, daring him to say something, but the abbot remained silent.

"Maxel," said Egalion. "I insist that you take with you—"

"Two of your very best men," said Maximilian. "But just two. Choose for me."

Egalion gave a tight nod, unhappy, but accepting Maximilian's decision.

"And I?" Garth said softly.

"I think it is better you stay, Garth. I am sorry."

Garth's face tightened, then he jerked his eyes away.

Maximilian watched him for a moment, then looked to Baron Lixel. "Baron, I hesitate to burden you with this, but I would that you act on my behalf while I am gone. I am meeting with the Privy Council in the morning, if you will join me."

Lixel nodded. "And to think I'd thought to enjoy my 'retirement' in Escator."

Maximilian managed a smile. "I have just made you a king, Lixel. Do not look so glum."

Vorstus remained behind when the others left. "This is madness, Maximilian," he said. "It is too dangerous. Elcho Falling needs you. You must not dash off on some *foolhardy* mission into utter danger. Maximilian, if your bloodline ends here, then our world dies."

"*I* need her, Vorstus, and I am certain that Elcho Falling needs her as well. I *am* going. Do not try to persuade me against—"

"Do you not know what awaits you down in Isembaard?"

"Kanubai? Is he risen already? If so, then we may as well lay down and die now, Vorstus, for at the moment I have not the heart, or the ability, to shoulder all the aches and pains of Elcho Falling."

"Then promise me one thing," Vorstus said, moving

forward with a speed and litheness that belied his years. "Promise you will not go near DarkGlass Mountain. Stay in the north if you possibly can, but do *not go near DarkGlass Mountain*!"

"I will do what is needed to retrieve Ishbel," Maximilian said, "and then I will come home to Escator, Vorstus. I promise you that."

Then he turned on his heel and was gone.

Vorstus stood and looked at the door through which Maximilian had vanished.

"Wrong," Vorstus whispered, his eyes glittering as if with madness. "You will never come home to Escator at all. Your time here is done, and Escator was doomed from the moment you rose from the Veins."

Then, closing his eyes and tipping his head back slightly, Vorstus sent an urgent message north to Lister.

Lister, disaster upon disaster. Maximilian now thinks to travel into Isembaard after Ishbel.

Vorstus thought about telling Lister what Maximilian had told him about the Twisted Tower, but decided against it. The Twisted Tower could wait—what everyone needed to do now was to ensure Maximilian's survival.

"Fool," Vorstus muttered one more time.

The day after Maximilian had left, accompanied only by two Emerald Guardsmen called Serge and Doyle, Vorstus went to Maximilian's bedchamber late one night.

He was dressed in traveling clothes, and he carried a leather satchel that hung loose and empty.

Vorstus went directly to that particular section of floor and made the same gesture with his hand that Maximilian had used to open the trapdoor.

Then he descended into the Persimius Chamber.

The column that had once held the queen's ring was empty save for its cushion.

Good. Maximilian had taken the ring with him.

Vorstus turned his eye to the crown.

It seethed with a darkness so profound that its three entwined bands of gold were all but hidden.

"I wonder if Maximilian came down here to see this before he left?" Vorstus muttered to himself, knowing that Maximilian probably hadn't—that he'd wanted no reason to abandon his foolish quest for Ishbel.

Vorstus walked over to the crown and, without any hesitation, seized it in both hands.

The crown hissed at him, the darkness writhing in agitation, but Vorstus took no notice. He thrust the crown into the leather satchel, secured it firmly, then left the chamber.

Within the hour he was on a horse and riding east.

CHAPTER FIFTEEN

Palace of the First, Yoyette, Coroleas

It was very dark, not a lamp lit anywhere in the apartment, and for that reason Salome was very relaxed.

StarDrifter could not see her back.

His hands were very soft and very sure on her body, and Salome allowed herself to drift into a state of sheer bliss.

She'd never had a lover like this. No wonder her mother and grandmother had succumbed.

But she would be careful. Yes, she would.

But no need to be careful now. He couldn't see. He wouldn't know. He didn't suspect.

He didn't talk, and Salome appreciated that.

He ran his hand down her flank, each individual finger touching her differently, each sending separate trails of ecstasy down her body.

Why had she denied herself an Icarii lover for so long? Who would want to deny themselves this?

He kissed her shoulder, and she felt his mouth smile against her flesh.

"You may stay the night," she murmured.

"I had no intention of leaving," StarDrifter whispered.

A moment's irritation engulfed her. StarDrifter refused to defer to her, laughed at her commands, ignored her demands.

Then his hand slid even lower, and her irritation vanished on her gasp, and was forgotten even before StarDrifter mounted her again.

She dozed. She was vaguely aware that StarDrifter had left the bed and used the washroom. She smiled as she felt his weight settle back on the bed, and stretched catlike as his arms wrapped about her once more.

He turned her face to his, and kissed her, slow and deep, making Salome rouse fully from her slumber and arch her body into his.

His hands were sliding slowly over her again, moving teasingly down her body. One slid over her sex, and she parted her legs for him, moaning with pleasure as his fingers slid deep within her, stroking and caressing.

He was murmuring in her ear. Not talk, just soft nothingness. His hand was now sliding up her body, stroking, stroking, and Salome realized his intent had changed. No longer was he arousing, but comforting, almost like a mother trying to lull her child to sleep.

And she *did* feel sleepy. Salome stretched once more, then yawned, and allowed StarDrifter to snuggle her in close to his body.

Within moments she was deeply asleep.

StarDrifter waited almost half an hour for the drug to have its full effect, then he rose from the bed and walked back to the washroom. He washed the smell of her from his body, then dressed, patting the pocket in his breeches where earlier had rested the pessary, now working its stupor deep within Salome's body.

StarDrifter lit a lamp when he came back into the bedchamber, partly so he could see what he was doing, partly to see if the light caused Salome to stir.

She slept on, her mouth now very slightly and unbecomingly agape. StarDrifter walked over to the bed, the lamp in his hand, and stood watching her for some minutes.

He might loathe her, but he could still manage to admire her beauty. Then, curious, he put a hand on her shoulder and rolled her over onto her belly.

She didn't stir.

StarDrifter sat down on the bed and brought the lamp closer . . . then muttered a soft oath of surprise. He lifted his free hand and lightly traced his fingers down the very faint outline of a scar down her spine.

Stars! She'd had wings taken out!

StarDrifter drew in a deep breath, thinking. She had far more Icarii blood in her than he'd originally thought. At least a half blood and possibly far more.

His fingers traced the scar again. It was very old, and StarDrifter suspected she'd had not wings taken out, but wing buds. Icarii didn't grow their wings until they were five or six, when the wings developed from nascent buds in their backs. Someone, her parents, had known she was likely to develop wings, and so had the buds removed when she would have been three or four.

Once more his fingers stroked down her back, this time more caressing than exploratory.

Her cruelty—was that Icarii arrogance more than anything else?

StarDrifter shuddered, finally drawing his hand away from her. Stars, he thought, anything but that.

He rose, stood for a long moment looking down at her, reflecting that by morning her entire world would have collapsed, and persuading himself that it was worth it; she had denied her Icarii heritage, refused to accept it, she deserved whatever ill came her way . . .

Giving himself a little shake, irritated that he'd fallen into such reflection, StarDrifter walked away from the bed and toward the shelf where stood the Weeper.

He stood before it, the lamp raised in his hand.

Then, very slowly, StarDrifter bowed before it. "I greet you well, Weeper," he said as he rose. "My name is StarDrifter SunSoar, a prince of the Icarii and a once-powerful Enchanter. I have come to take you to the Lord of Elcho Falling—"

He stopped there, horrified, for the bronze statue began to weep. Although there were always trails of moisture down its cheeks, now the bronze eyes began to flood with tears, so much so that the moisture ran down the deity's bronze body in rivulets, dripped off its toes, and puddled on the floor.

"Please," StarDrifter whispered, almost overcome himself by the Weeper's show of emotion, "allow me to take you in my arms, that I—"

The statue was weeping even harder now, and making soft, heartrending noises.

StarDrifter swallowed, "—that I may carry you to the Lord of Elcho Falling, so that he may release your tortured soul."

Stars! He didn't know what to do. The deity was now sobbing, StarDrifter could virtually see its shoulders shaking, although he knew that was not possible.

"Please," he whispered, risking resting his hand on the deity's shoulder.

What he felt from it was extraordinary: a loneliness so deep it broke StarDrifter's heart; a sadness so consuming it almost drove StarDrifter mad; a desperation for this man, this Lord of Elcho Falling, that was inconsolable.

StarDrifter did the only thing he could. He put the lamp down, then reached forward and took the deity from its shelf, cuddling it in his arms.

The deity was bronze, it was not capable of moving, but nonetheless StarDrifter thought he felt—or intuited—it snuggling against his body, almost as a small child would.

"I'll take you to he who waits for you," he whispered, "but for the moment you must be quiet."

Then, wrapping the deity in a bundle of Salome's clothes that she'd discarded by the bed, he left the bedchamber.

There were guards outside, but they were so used to Salome and her lovers that the sight of a man emerging from her chamber late at night was of no fuss to them.

Nonetheless, one stopped StarDrifter, asking what it was he held in his arms.

StarDrifter grimaced. "Her soiled linens," he said. "She demanded I hand them to the laundress."

The guards both laughed, waving him on his way. "At least she did not require you to wash them yourself!"

Ba'al'uz leapt up from the bed as StarDrifter entered, his eyes riveted on the bundle that StarDrifter carried. "You have it!"

"Aye, and it was easier than I'd thought," StarDrifter said.

He made as if to hand the bundle to Ba'al'uz, but the Weeper shrieked the instant he lifted it away from his body.

StarDrifter reflexively hugged it back to him, and the Weeper fell silent.

Ba'al'uz and StarDrifter looked at each other, and StarDrifter thought he could see flat hatred in Ba'al'uz' eyes.

"Looks like I'll need to carry it," said StarDrifter.

"At least until the ship is well embarked," Ba'al'uz muttered. "Tell me, how long do we have? When did you give Salome the pessary?"

"About an hour ago," StarDrifter said, then stopped awkwardly, as if he'd wanted to say something else but thought better of it.

"But?" said Ba'al'uz, his eyes narrowed.

"I had a close look at Salome's back," StarDrifter said slowly, wondering if he should tell Ba'al'uz this, but wanting to distract him from any thought of taking the Weeper.

"Yes? And?"

"She has a long scar down her spine. Very old. As a child she had wing nubs cut out of her back."

"*Salome is an Icarii*?"

"Yes. At least, she has Icarii blood in her. One of her parents, and probably one or more of her grandparents."

Ba'al'uz stared at StarDrifter, then gave a small nod and a smile. "Very well, then. Now, we must leave. The ship embarks at dawn."

An hour later, as they left the palace to hurry to the wharves, the Weeper still securely wrapped in StarDrifter's arms, Ba'al'uz took a moment to whisper to one of the men standing guard at the gates to the Palace of the First.

[Part Six]

CHAPTER ONE

Northern Plains of Isembaard

They left the next morning, Zeboath confident that Ishbel was well enough to travel. She was very quiet, and Axis wondered if it was because she still felt unwell, or if she feared what lay ahead. It was probably a combination, Axis thought, as he settled Ishbel on the quietest horse he could find for her. She could sit the horse well enough, but she had little confidence on it, and Axis thought he'd need to keep close by in case she experienced any troubles.

Axis nodded at Zeboath, who had brought his own horse, as well as a packhorse loaded with panniers and bundles. Zeboath had been prepared to leave Torinox in any case, and had needed only to load the packhorse to be ready to depart with Axis.

Axis' men had been up since dawn, readying for departure. He greeted Insharah and spent a few minutes quietly conferring with him about their plans and the route for the day. As they spoke, Axis noted one of the other men pausing as he saddled his horse, then resting his head momentarily against the horse's neck, as if he felt unwell.

"Is Madarin ill?" Axis asked Insharah.

Insharah looked over and grunted. "He has a bellyache," he said. "Ate too much of the landlord's eel pie last night."

"Ah," said Axis, "then a hard day's ride should iron out those knots, eh?"

They rode out of Torinox by midmorning. It was later than Axis had really wanted to leave (and if Zeboath had had his way then they would have been gone by dawn), but he hadn't wanted to push Ishbel. The most immediate route to Aqhat was directly south, but Axis thought it might be better if they rode southeast toward the Lhyl. He didn't think Ishbel should be made to ride the entire distance to Aqhat—it would be better by far to hire river craft for the majority of the journey.

Nonetheless, Ishbel managed fairly well. Axis did not force the pace, going only as fast as he judged was comfortable for her. The going was good. Even though it was high summer in Isembaard, this close to the FarReach Mountains the sun was mild, the breezes cool, and the ground soft underneath the horses' hooves. Axis enjoyed the day. Ishbel rode mostly in silence—Axis did not push her for conversation—but he, Zeboath, and Insharah rode together, just to one side of Ishbel, and laughed and chatted the day away. Zeboath was a good companion. He had a mischievous sense of humor and a witty turn of phrase, and was so palpably glad to have escaped Torinox that his zest infected both Axis and Insharah.

They stopped for a brief meal just after noon, then rode another four hours. By that time Ishbel was visibly wearying, and Axis knew they'd have to stop for the night. He'd hoped to find a village or small town, but there was nothing within three or four hours' ride.

For stars' sakes, Axis thought, irritated by the lack of anywhere comfortable to sleep, *I cannot understand Isaiah's wish to depopulate this region further!*

They would need to camp for the night, and as Ishbel had made it this far over the FarReach Mountains, Axis thought she would manage another night in the open.

It was close to evening by the time they'd unsaddled the horses and established a camp. Insharah had seen to the lighting of two campfires, one for the soldiers, and one for Axis, Ishbel, and Zeboath. Axis noted wryly that while he and the soldiers had shared the one campfire on the trip north, as soon as a woman (and a queen at that) and a physician had joined the troop, social distinctions had come silently into play, and Axis had been relegated to entertain the visitors while the soldiers maintained their own ribald campfire.

They settled down, eating a cold meal of bread and cheese

and pickles. As Axis chewed his food, he reflected on all the journeys he'd taken in his life, and all the people with whom he'd shared a campfire.

Zeboath saw Axis watching Ishbel speculatively, and asked him what he was thinking.

Axis gave a soft laugh, brushing his fingers together to rid himself of bread crumbs. "I was thinking of all the beautiful women I've shared a campfire with in my life," he said, "and of all the strange adventures and mysteries of which we were in pursuit. All the dangers, the terrors, and the ecstasies that we encountered."

"And all the magics," Ishbel said. "You were born for this kind of adventure, Axis. Not I."

Axis gave a small shrug of his shoulders.

"What did you mean yesterday," he said, "when you said Maximilian had brought the terror of the Veins *out* with him?"

Ishbel glanced at Zeboath.

"I am sure that Zeboath knows how to hold his tongue when needed," Axis said. "Eh, Zeboath?"

Zeboath nodded, his eyes round, and Axis repressed a grin. He'd never seen anyone enjoy an adventure as much as Zeboath.

"Maximilian has an affinity for the darkness," Ishbel said. She had a piece of bread and cheese in her hands, and she stared at it as she spoke, turning it over and over.

"In what manner?" Axis said.

"He becomes one with the darkness," Ishbel said, finally looking up and meeting Axis' eyes. "He can blend with it."

As Axis frowned slightly, she continued. "When first we met . . ." She gave a short, soft laugh. "When first we met he used the darkness to spy on me. It was in Pelemere. I had a chamber in a house belonging to King Sirus, and it was not especially large. I returned to it one evening, and bathed and ate, and for an hour or more I did not realize that Maximilian was in that chamber with me, until he drew a breath, and I heard him."

"He was not just lurking behind a wardrobe, or the shadow of the door?" Axis asked.

Ishbel shook her head. "He was standing against a wall, but I had clear sight of it. And yet, in all the time, I did not see him. And then, when we escaped the city—"

Axis made a mental note to ask her sometime why they'd needed to "escape" Pelemere.

"—he cloaked me in the same manner, and we crept past guards within touching distance, and they never saw us."

"That sounds an admirable skill," said Zeboath. "Imagine the ladies on whom I could spy."

Ishbel gave a small smile, but there was no amusement behind it. "Maximilian is very disconcerting."

Axis was becoming more intrigued with the man the more he heard about him, and wondered, somewhat idly, if Ba'al'uz had stolen the wrong person.

Ishbel looked at Axis directly. "As are you."

Axis jerked out of his reverie. "What?"

"I woke, the other night, and saw you holding a most strange object in your hand. It glowed . . . and, oh, the expression on your face. I have seen that expression before only ever on the faces of priests locked in god-power. So, Axis, what darkness are *you* carrying about in your pack and in your heart?"

Axis considered a moment, then decided to be frank. "Bear with me," he said. "I'll need to explain first some of my background, especially for Zeboath."

He looked to Zeboath. "I told you that I came from the lost land of Tencendor. My full name is Axis SunSoar, and once I was StarMan of Tencendor, and later one of the seven Star Gods of that land. Then came invasion and disaster, and I lost contact with the source of all my power, the Star Dance, and my son, DragonStar SunSoar, saved the land only by destroying it. Perhaps you have heard something of my life."

Zeboath managed to close his mouth and collect himself. "Ah, yes. Yes, I have."

"Well," said Axis, "when I was a far greater man than I am now, I drew power from the Star Dance—the music that the stars make in their dance through the heavens. It filtered through to Tencendor via the Star Gate, a magical gateway into the universe. From the Star Dance itself I could manipulate the dance and create enchantments out of it. When the Timekeeper Demons destroyed the Star Gate, they also cut off the flow of the Star Dance and I, supreme Star God, became once again a mere mortal."

His mouth twisted in deprecating humor. "It was a devastating blow. Not just to me, but to all Icarii Enchanters, all of whom drew strength and beauty and power from the Star Dance. It wasn't only the loss of power, but it was more the loss of the beauty that had underpinned our every breath and our every thought. That beauty . . ."

Axis sighed, rose, and fetched his pack. From it he withdrew a cloth bundle, which he unwrapped to reveal the glass pyramid, now a dull gray. He passed it first to Ishbel, who held it only a moment before passing it to Zeboath.

"One of my men found this in the packs of Ba'al'uz' men," Axis said, taking it back from Zeboath. "It belonged to Ba'al'uz himself, and I know what it is because Isaiah has one, as does . . . well, I know what it does. It is a communication device. I have seen Isaiah use his, but have never touched it myself. The first night I brought Ishbel to Torinox, while she slept, I pulled this from my pack and studied it." He paused, turning the pyramid over and over in his hand. "It did not look this gray then."

"It was a lovely rosy color, I think," Ishbel said. "I am sure I remember a rosy glow coming from it."

"Yes," Axis said, "normally it is an opaque rose color, and as soon as I touched it I felt the Star Dance. Just faintly, but, oh, stars, it was *there*."

He looked at the other two, willing them to understand the depth of his emotion at this discovery. "I—all Icarii Enchanters—thought the Star Dance lost forever. We were certain that the only means we'd had to access it was via the Star Gate, which was irretrievably destroyed by the Timekeeper Demons. We had thought . . . we had no idea . . ."

Axis had to stop. "You can have no idea what this discovery means to me."

"I think somehow I do," said Ishbel, very gently. She gave him a moment, then said, "But this pyramid is now gray and lifeless. What has happened?"

Axis smiled a little. "Ah. These are communication devices, although they may very well do other things. When I toyed with it, when I touched oh-so-briefly the Star Dance through it, someone *elsewhere* knew what I did. And they closed off all power to it, or shut this pyramid down. They did not want me examining it too closely. That was disappointing, yes, but this," he hefted the pyramid in his hand, "gives me so much hope. Partly because I know that if I can 'reopen' it, then I may be able to touch the Star Dance again, but also because this is not a natural object. Somewhere, someone has made it, and that someone *knows how to touch the Star Dance.*"

"An Icarii?" said Ishbel. "This is an Icarii object?"

"I am not sure. It stinks of Icarii, and I can't imagine who or what else could have made it, but yet there is something foreign about that sense. An Icarii . . . but not quite . . . Ah, I don't know. It is a mystery, and one I shall look forward to solving."

He gave a lopsided grin and packed the pyramid away again.

"You said it was a communication device," said Zeboath, "and you said that you knew of three. Isaiah has one, Ba'al'uz' one you now have, but who has the third?"

Axis glanced at Ishbel. "The third is in the hands of the Lord of the Skraelings, a man called Lister."

Axis had thought Ishbel might react to mention of the Skraelings and might have jumped to a conclusion about why Isaiah was communicating with the creatures' lord, but her reaction was far different to what he expected.

"Lister?" she said.

"You know him, Ishbel?" Axis said.

Ishbel hesitated, then opened her mouth to speak, but just then Insharah walked over to their campfire.

"Sir," Insharah murmured to Axis. "Madarin, the man you noted before we rode out, is sick nigh to death, I think. Can Zeboath the physician examine him?"

CHAPTER TWO

Palace of the First, Yoyette, Coroleas

Salome could not wake up. She was vaguely aware that the night had passed, and that she had slept right through the day, but, oh, she could not move, could barely breathe, could only lie, lost in a maze of dreams.

Icarii, tens of thousands of them, spiraling over an ice-clad peak so high it dwarfed an entire continent.

A woman, black-haired and beautiful, screaming in agony as wings were torn from her back.

StarDrifter, standing not in the topiary garden, but in a mysterious dark forest, holding out his hand in seduction.

Her own mother, standing at a window in the Palace of the First, waiting in the night for a shape to spiral down from the heavens.

StarDrifter again, screaming himself as terrifying creatures tore out his wings, and murdered a lovely birdwoman before him.

A woman that StarDrifter had loved before all others.

Salome's own back burned, and she moaned, remembering —even though she knew she should not be able to—that day when she was three and her mother had taken her down the back streets of Yoyette, to a man who specialized in . . .

Removing wing buds.

It must have hurt, even though the tiny child Salome had been given strong drugs to render her unconscious. In her dreams Salome imagined the pain she must have endured, imagined the days and nights spent twisting in agony as her mother applied soothing poultices to her back.

Imagined her screams and whimpers, and her mother

begging her to remain silent in case her husband, and the man Salome had always called "father," came to inquire the reason he'd not seen his daughter for days on end.

The pain in her back increased, and Salome drifted closer to consciousness. She was fighting to wake now, hating the sense of being out of control, not being able to move . . .

Oh, gods, she was lying on her belly, exposing her back to full sight!

She tried to roll over, but now the pain in her back was coupled with a great weight, as if someone leaned down on her.

"No need to struggle so, you contemptuous bitch. Your secret is out."

She recognized the voice. It was the emperor.

No, this must be a dream also. This could not be happening.

Someone hit her on the side of her head, hard and cruel, and Salome gave a great cry, and managed to open her eyes.

Someone—the emperor—was leaning over her.

Another man, no, two men, were holding her down at shoulders and hips so the emperor could trace his fingers down her back.

Down her scar.

"No!" Salome screamed, trying desperately to struggle, but was unable to move under the men's hands and the remaining effects of the drug.

She had been drugged. The Icarii bastard had drugged her!

Then the full import of her plight struck Salome.

Her outside blood had been discovered. She would be thrown out of the First. Her son would become a slave. Gods . . . *gods*! Everything was over.

Salome thought of all the people who loathed her, and quickly realized she would be very lucky to survive into the next day.

Her panic was indescribable. She had no anger, not at the moment, only an all-consuming desperation to survive, somehow.

"To think what we've been hiding in our midst all this

time," the emperor said, and Salome could hear the sheer joy underscoring his words.

His greatest enemy. Undone.

And undone so badly . . .

The emperor stood back, and Salome did not try to speak. There was nothing to say.

But, oh, where was Ezra? What had they done with her son?

"Toss her out on the midden heap," said the emperor, "and tie her to a stake, so that any who wish revenge for all her slights over the years may take it at their leisure."

The grip of the men holding her changed, and they hauled Salome naked from the bed.

Just as they dragged her toward the door, Salome managed to say something.

"Fools," she whispered hoarsely, "you have been distracted from the true crime enacted here. Look, he has taken the Weeper. StarDrifter has taken the Weeper."

CHAPTER THREE

Northern Plains of Isembaard

Axis and Zeboath rose at the same time.

"Madarin?" said Axis to Insharah. "I thought you said he had a bellyache from eating too much eel pie."

"That is all I thought it was," said Insharah, "and all Madarin thought it was. But he grew very quiet during the day's ride, and didn't eat anything at camp. Over the past hour his pain has become immeasurably worse, and he is gray and sweating."

"I'll look at him," said Zeboath, hurrying off to rummage in his pack for his physician's bag.

Axis followed him. He hated it when men under his command fell ill. He could deal with horrific battle wounds, but somehow the silent attack of disease and illness unsettled him far more. Even in his full power as StarMan, Axis had been unable to do anything for internal illnesses or raging fevers. He'd always had to leave it to women and physicians.

Madarin lay wrapped in blankets, curled about his belly. Even in the firelight Axis could see clearly that the skin of his face was gray and slick with sweat, and that his body trembled. He was biting his lip, trying not to moan.

Madarin was clearly very, very ill.

"Stars," Axis muttered, "I hope Zeboath can do something."

The physician arrived at that moment, bag in hand, shooing Insharah and Axis back, and asking one of the other soldiers to build up the fire.

"He's in shock," Zeboath said. "He will need the warmth."

"Shock?" said Axis. "Why?"

Zeboath held up a hand, silently asking for time. He knelt at Madarin's side, and very gently persuaded him to uncurl so that Zeboath might examine him.

For long, tense minutes, Zeboath probed at Madarin's chest and belly. At times, when Zeboath's fingers dug too deep, Madarin let out a shriek and Zeboath muttered an apology. Finally, Zeboath patted Madarin on the shoulder, told him he would mix him a pain remedy, and stood and motioned Axis and Insharah to one side.

The tight, anxious faces of the troop followed them.

"It is not good news," Zeboath said. "He has an obstruction within his bowel, and his bowel has gone into spasm and twisted about itself. Now Madarin's entire abdominal cavity is inflamed and, as you have seen, he has gone into shock. I need to give him some pain relief, fast."

"But you *can* fix it," said Axis.

Zeboath looked him directly in the eye. "It may resolve itself, Axis, but, no, I cannot 'fix it.' More likely he will develop such a massive infection within his belly from the inflammation and obstruction that he will die within days. I can relieve the pain and the spasms, but that is all I can do."

Axis stared at him, then gave a small shake of his head. So be it.

"There *must* be something else!" said Insharah.

"I'm sorry," Zeboath said. "I just can't—"

"Perhaps I can," said Ishbel, and all three men turned about in surprise.

She stood just a pace away.

"How?" said Axis.

"I have some skill in the, um, unraveling of intestines."

"Skill?" said Zeboath.

"Please," Ishbel said, "will you trust me? I can help this man, and even if not, what harm in allowing me to try?"

Axis and Zeboath exchanged a glance, then Axis nodded. "Very well."

Ishbel nodded and stepped over to Madarin.

Like Zeboath, she sank down on her knees next to the man. She put a hand on his shoulder—Axis thought she

might smile in reassurance, but her face remained grave—
and rolled the man fully onto his back.

"I need you to stay straight, and still," she said. "Can you
do that?"

Madarin's eyes were glassy with pain and shock, but he
managed a tiny nod.

"Good," said Ishbel, then she pulled back the blankets
covering the man, unlaced his breeches, pulling them down
to his hips, and ran a hand gently over his abdomen.

As she did so, the man's abdomen roiled, and he cried out
in pain.

There were gasps from about the circle, and many shifted
uneasily.

Ishbel's hand continued to move slowly over Madarin's
abdomen. She closed her eyes, bowing her head, concentrating, and her hand stilled.

No one moved. Every eye was fixated on Ishbel.

"You have not respected the Coil," Ishbel muttered, her
head still down, her eyes still closed. "It rebels."

"The eel pie—" Madarin began, his voice rasping.

"Be quiet!" Ishbel said. Then, suddenly, her hand dug
deep into Madarin's belly, and he screamed in pain, his back
arching so far off the ground his weight was supported only
by his shoulders and hips.

Everyone moved then, stepping forward; but Ishbel's head
jerked up and her eyes blazed. "Stay back!"

Axis raised a hand, stilling everyone's forward movement.
"Stay back," he said, "for the moment. Gods, Ishbel, I hope
you know what you are doing . . ."

She ignored him. Her hand continued to press into Madarin's
flesh, so deeply it appeared almost to disappear from view.

Then she released its tight grip and, very gently, very
quietly, began to rub her hand in a complex pattern over
Madarin's belly.

He was still shrieking, but his body had relaxed back to
the ground.

Ishbel's hand continued to move, slowly, gently, and now
her own body swayed back and forth, slowly, gently, following the movement of her hand.

Axis was fixated. He could not drag his eyes away from Ishbel, now weaving back and forth almost as if she were cradling a child, her eyes closed once more, her face peaceful, her hand moving, ever more slowly, ever more gently.

She was using a power he'd never seen before.

Madarin's shrieks eased back to moans.

"That is amazing," Zeboath whispered at Axis' side. "Astounding!"

Ishbel drew in a deep breath, and opened her eyes.

Her hand paused, then moved up to the bottom of Madarin's rib cage.

Then, very slowly, very deliberately, Ishbel traced out a serpentine path with her forefinger from the man's rib cage down to his groin.

"You are the servant of the Great Serpent now," Ishbel said to Madarin, who was completely quiet and staring at her with wide, shocked eyes. "Revere him."

Then she stood, slow and graceful, and walked back to the campfire she shared with Zeboath and Axis.

Far to the north, in Escator, Maximilian rode through the night. He'd led his party out of Ruen at noon, having convened a hasty meeting of the Privy Council of Preferred Nobles. He'd left his crown and his authority with the Council, Lixel as its head, and vowed to them that he would return.

As he rode, Maximilian often glanced to the east where the Outlands warred with Pelemere and Hosea, and imagined he could hear the opening clash of steel in battle and the screams of dying men.

With him rode two Emerald Guardsmen, Serge and Doyle. Egalion had recommended them highly, saying they were men of particular resource and skill.

At that, Maximilian's mouth had twisted wryly. In their lives before they'd been condemned to the Veins, Serge and Doyle had been assassins for hire.

But Serge and Doyle did not quite make up Maximilian's entire party. During the midafternoon Serge had gestured into the sky, and Maximilian looked up to see BroadWing and three other Icarii descending.

"We will come with you," BroadWing had said, refusing to listen to Maximilian's protestations. "You are not our king, so your commands have no force with us. We can help you, Maximilian. Do not refuse us."

Maximilian hadn't. The Icarii would be useful—more than useful—and he liked their company.

So now they rode through the night, their horses' pounding hooves eating up the miles, while the Icarii wheeled overhead. The traveling eased Maximilian's mind. He was *doing* something, he was taking control rather than being battered by circumstance, and he was traveling to snatch back the woman he loved.

Elcho Falling could wait until he had Ishbel again.

"Just a ward of the Coil, Ishbel," Axis said as he sat down. "Really? Perhaps you may now like to explain that a little more fully."

Ishbel sighed as Zeboath also sat. She felt drained from the energy expended in healing Madarin, but also, conversely, energized. She had always worried that the baby within her would disrupt her Coil and separate her from her powers as archpriestess.

But tonight had proved otherwise. Her Coil was as strong as it had always been.

"You are a member of the Coil?" Zeboath said, his eyes wide. "I have heard of them!"

"Well," said Axis, "according to Ishbel she is only—"

"Peace," said Ishbel, sighing again. She hesitated, reluctant to speak the truth even though it must now be blindingly obvious she was far more than just a ward of the Coil. But what would Axis and Zeboath say when they knew the truth? She liked both of them, and enjoyed their company, and wouldn't want to—

"Ishbel," said Axis, very gently, "I don't want to judge you. I am intrigued by you, and by what you said to me last night about the ancient evil. Tell me of Serpent's Nest, and of your life there. If you have heard anything of *my* life, then you must know some of my stupidities." Axis gave a small deprecating smile. "I am the last person to judge you, and I think that after tonight's little display Zeboath admires you far too much to even consider it. Trust us, Ishbel."

"Yet you were willing enough to taunt me the other night with your 'rather vile band of psychic murderers.'"

"I was wrong to say that, Ishbel, and I apologize to you for it. Tell us about Serpent's Nest. Tell us about *you*."

Ishbel studied her hands for a long time. Then, when she finally raised her head, she spoke calmly, and Axis had a glimpse of her inner strength and dignity.

"As you know, Serpent's Nest is home to the Coil, an order that worships and tends to the Great Serpent."

"The Great Serpent is a god?" said Axis.

"Yes. We only ever see him in visions during Readings, or on other very rare occasions when he reveals himself to us."

"You *are* a member of this order," Axis said.

"Yes." Ishbel tilted her chin slightly. "I am its arch-priestess."

Axis drew a soft breath between his teeth, and heard Zeboath do the same. He glanced at him, and saw that the physician's eyes were now almost popping out of his head.

"The knowledge of anatomy that you must have!" Zeboath said. "Would you mind, later, when you have the time and are strong enough, sharing some of that knowledge with me?"

Ishbel looked at him with some surprise, and Axis thought she must have been expecting judgment. Instead, she received breathless admiration.

Ishbel smiled, just very slightly. "Well, yes, Zeboath, I will gladly do that. I am sure there is much we can teach each other."

Axis was now a little irritated, as obviously Zeboath knew more about the Coil than did he. "Ishbel, tell me of the Coil, and what you do within it."

"We tend to the Great Serpent, and protect and honor him as best we may. We also conduct Readings, in which the Great Serpent speaks to us, and reveals . . ." She hesitated. "The Great Serpent is an oracle, Axis, of great mystery. He can reveal the future to us, or for any who desire to know it."

"What are these 'Readings'?"

"We take a living man, Axis, and we disembowel him to

reveal the Coil within—his bowel. His coil spills to the floor, then rises, taking on the form of the Great Serpent, who then speaks to us and reveals glimpses of the future or imparts information that we need to know."

"Your knowledge of anatomy *must* be superb," Zeboath muttered to one side.

Axis stared at Ishbel, wondering that so few words could describe such horror. "And the person you disembowel . . . ?"

"Dies."

"Sweet gods, Ishbel . . ."

"We take criminals destined for execution, and very rarely a man who offers us his life. In the latter instance, the Great Serpent blesses the man's family with good fortune, and we render him insensible during the Reading, so that he feels no pain."

Axis swallowed, dragging his eyes away from Ishbel. "You don't 'read' women?"

"No. Their coil within is too often disturbed by child-bearing, or by the waxing and waning of the womb with its monthly cycle."

"Yet you, a female, rank at the top of the Coil?"

"When I was inducted into the Coil I relinquished all reproductive rights and workings."

Axis nodded at her belly. "And that?"

"I cannot explain this pregnancy. I should not have been able to conceive."

"Maximilian is a man to be reckoned with, then," muttered Axis. "Tell me, does Maximilian know that you are the archpriestess of this order?"

"He suspects."

Axis looked back at her. "Then you cannot blame him for thinking you might be involved with the murders Ba'al'uz committed across the Central Kingdoms. Dear gods, Ishbel, you cannot blame *anyone* for reacting with horror at what you do."

"Are you repulsed, Axis?"

He sighed. "I have done many terrible things in my life, Ishbel. No. I am not repulsed, but I am saddened." He gave a small smile. "Zeboath, on the other hand, looks as though he shall be your student for life."

Ishbel smiled.

"Was it the Great Serpent who told you about the ancient evil?" Axis asked.

"Yes. He showed us Skraelings swarming over Serpent's Nest, and a terrible darkness rising from the south."

Whatever rests beneath DarkGlass Mountain, thought Axis. *Or perhaps even the cursed pyramid itself.*

"It is why I was sent to marry Maximilian," Ishbel offered.

"What? Why should marriage to Maximilian help?"

Ishbel shrugged. "I don't know." She paused. "I didn't want to marry him."

"And now?" Zeboath said.

"It matters no longer," she said, her tone bitter. "This marriage is over."

"Ishbel," Axis said eventually, very gently, "what is it about Maximilian that the Great Serpent felt was worth this?"

"I don't know. And now . . . now I have ruined everything. I have lost Maximilian. I have failed the Great Serpent. Oh, gods . . ."

"Ishbel, you were stolen. You couldn't help it that—"

"The Great Serpent wanted me to stay with Maximilian. He said I could come home eventually. I could leave Maximilian eventually. I told Maxel, we talked about this, he knew I was unhappy. He said to give it a year, and I thought I could give him that year, hand him this baby, then leave. Go home."

"You don't want the baby."

"No. Maxel wants it. I don't." Again, a pause to collect herself. "And now . . . now I worry that the baby has died, it doesn't move, and Maxel . . ."

What a complex woman, thought Axis. *She feels guilt for everyone. The Great Serpent. Maximilian. She may have been a brilliant archpriestess, but the god she served thought it better for her to be a woman, a wife, and a queen, all roles that Ishbel had no experience in and that terrified her.*

"Earlier," Axis said, "when I mentioned the name Lister, you reacted strongly. What do you know of him?"

"I have never met him," said Ishbel, "but I know *of* him.

He was once the archpriest of the Coil, serving at Serpent's Nest well before my time."

"*Lister* was an archpriest of the Coil?" Axis said. "Well, well. Go on, please."

"He vanished one day," Ishbel said. "Perhaps a year or two before I came to Serpent's Nest. Axis, why are Lister—whom you now style Lord of the Skraelings—and Isaiah in contact?"

"They are in an alliance to invade the Outlands and the Central Kingdoms," said Axis. "Isaiah from the south, Lister from the north."

"Oh, no," she whispered. "No . . ."

"Lister and Isaiah use the pyramids," Axis said, "to communicate. Lister either made these, or he has access to those who can. I admit myself highly curious about Lister, Lord of the Skraelings, and once archpriest of the Coil."

"Please, Axis," Ishbel said, "*please*—the Icarii are in the north, I have seen them, and you have talked to one of them. Let us, you and I, flee north. Dear gods, you *cannot* be involved in this invasion of innocent peoples! Have not enough Icarii died?"

Axis gave her a sharp look at that last. "I do not agree with Isaiah's plans for invasion," he said, "but I will do better here. With Isaiah. He is not a bad man." *He is a man full of mysteries himself.* "I like him. Besides, there are great puzzles to be solved here. DarkGlass Mountain, for one."

"DarkGlass Mountain?" Ishbel said, wanting to argue more with Axis about the invasion, but unable to resist the question.

"I think it is your ancient evil," Axis said, "or something associated with it. DarkGlass Mountain is a massive stone-and-glass pyramid far to the south, on the opposite riverbank from Aqhat. Zeboath, what do you know of it?"

Zeboath gave a small shrug. "Isembaardians know of it only as a great mystery to which only the tyrant has access."

Axis laughed. "Well, I shall disabuse you of that rumor here and now. The tyrants have no idea what it is, either."

CHAPTER FOUR

The Courtyard of the People, Yoyette, Coroleas

Salome supposed that there was an outcry over the loss of the Weeper, but it did not save her. The guardsmen who held her continued to drag her out of her bedchamber, out of her luxurious apartment, out of her privileged life, and down into a misery so extreme Salome wished beyond anything else for death.

They took her first to the guardroom, where they raped her, then handed her over to their fellows. A day or so later, when the entire guardroom had finished their fun, they dragged her bleeding body through the streets of Yoyette to the Courtyard of the People, where she was chained to a stake in one corner.

If Salome had thought she'd endured hell over the past day, it was nothing to what occurred now. Men and boys continued to rape her—at least while her body remained vaguely intact. The rapes stopped, however, once the countless rocks and pieces of wood thrown at her broke and tore her flesh to such an extent that not even rape became attractive.

The Coroleans did not stint themselves. The Duchess of Sidon was hated so violently that people from all the castes traveled in from the country to have their turn at her. They tried ever new and inventive ways of humiliating and abusing her. One man tried to persuade his dog to mount her, another the boar he'd brought in from his farm.

The dog refused, the boar was not so choosy.

Women spat at Salome and emptied chamber pots over her. Small boys poked at her flesh with hot coals held in iron pincers.

Salome wished for death, she *begged* for death, but it did not come.

Even death tormented her.

All this abuse was terrible enough, but it paled into insignificance when they dragged her son, Ezra, before her. Salome had hoped he'd escaped, or had at least been spared the emperor's vindictiveness.

But, no.

Ezra was too good an opportunity to torment Salome into hell itself to be ignored.

Guardsmen dragged him before Salome, tossing a bucket of icy water over her to rouse her.

Then they raped him, as violently and as viciously as they had raped Salome.

At one point, when she could no longer bear the screaming of her beloved son, Salome turned her head.

And saw to one side, through eyes bleary with agony, the emperor and half the court, hands laced over fat bellies, watching with satisfaction.

She tried to shriek to them to stop it, to save her son, but nothing came from her mouth save a faint croak.

When Ezra's rape became less amusing, the emperor gestured with his hand, and one of the guardsmen pulled forth a knife.

With long, slow strokes, he castrated the boy, tossing the severed genitals onto Salome's naked, battered breasts.

Then they dragged Ezra close to his mother, close enough that they could stare helplessly at each other as he slowly bled to death.

The last thing he whispered to her was, "You said I was to be emperor."

At that point Salome hated StarDrifter so greatly she thought her hate would become a living thing and rise from her body and hunt the birdman down on her behalf.

On the third night that Salome had been chained to the stake in the Courtyard of the People, she was finally left alone. She was close to death, and people had become tired of taunting her. Better for them to go home to bed, and resume in the morning, on their way to market.

Salome was largely incapable of coherent thought. All she wanted was to slide into death, and follow Ezra into whatever relief he'd managed to discover. As much as she was capable, she tried to concentrate on not breathing, and on making her heart stop.

But her body was too strong, and it did not want to give up on life just yet.

At some point when it had become very cold, Salome thought she heard a movement behind her.

She didn't care who it was, just so long as they had come to slide a merciful blade deep into her heart.

More footsteps, and murmured words.

Then a hand on her shoulder.

Salome almost screamed in shock. Then, before whoever had touched her could speak, she convulsed—caused by a combination of despair, shock, fright, and the sheer degree of physical damage done to her body.

"Stars," someone muttered, and the hands now moved faster and with more determination, cutting Salome free from her chains, and wrapping her in a blanket.

"No," she whispered. "No."

"We can't leave you here," said the voice, and then, horribly, terrifyingly, Salome felt herself lifted into the air and knew she was being carried by an Icarii.

She tried to struggle, tried to wrest herself free of the hated creature's grip so that she might fall mercifully to the ground and dash herself to death against its kindness.

But he was too strong, and she too weak, and so finally, gratefully, Salome slipped into unconsciousness, and knew no more.

Salome woke an indeterminate amount of time later. She was lying in a bed, in a plain, ill-lit chamber, and she was in agony.

She could feel every hurt and every injury done to her over the past few days as if it had been committed only moments earlier. She moaned, twisted a little on the bed, then cried out in pain as her body spasmed.

"Here," said a voice, "drink this."

A none-too-gentle hand gripped her hair and pulled her head up, and a cup was pressed against her lips.

A bitter liquid splashed into her mouth, and Salome choked on it. She tried to twist her head away, but the hands kept the cup to her mouth until she had gulped down all the liquid.

"That will keep you alive a little longer," the voice said, and Salome blinked, trying to bring the man into focus.

She could see by his silhouette against the lamp that he was an Icarii, and so she tried to spit at him and pinch him with her fingers.

But Salome was too weak to do more than purse her lips, and flutter her hand helplessly, and the Icarii gave a short, dry laugh.

"A little gratitude would be appreciated," he said.

"Who are you?" she managed. "Why . . ."

"Our names you are never likely to hear," said the Icarii, and Salome realized there must be more than one in the room. "Why reveal ourselves to such as *you*, when you would sell our souls to the highest bidder, even though we have saved your life?"

"And as to why," said another voice from somewhere to Salome's left. "We saved you because we could not let a fellow Icarii continue to suffer in that manner. Not at the hands of the Coroleans."

A fellow Icarii? thought Salome. *Gods, they called me an* Icarii!

Loathing for them rushed through her.

"But do not think we sympathize with you, or like you," said the first speaker. "You are foul in our eyes. What you have done in your life . . ."

"Me?" she managed, feeling stronger now that the pain-killing drink was taking hold. "Me? What about StarDrifter? *He* did this to me. And my son . . . my son."

"Ezra we do regret," said the Icarii to her left. "We would

have saved him had we the opportunity. But we didn't. Only your heart had the strength to hold fast."

"*Strong* Icarii blood," muttered the first Icarii.

"As for StarDrifter," said the other. "Well, we do not agree with what he has done, but we do not wonder at it. He would have hated you almost as much as we do."

She tried to move, but her body was so painful and stiff she could only wince. "What do you want from me?" Salome said. "Why save me if you loathe me this greatly?"

"For you to get strong enough that we can get you away from us," said the first. "We will make you stronger, then we will ensure you get out of this country. We will give you some clothes and some money, and after that your life is yours to rebuild as you will."

"After all," said the other, "if our Icarii blood is good enough to see you survive the brutality meted out to you over so many days, then you will surely live a long, long life. Five hundred years, at the very least."

Salome moaned. Nothing had hurt her so much as that. A life five hundred years long? No, no, she could not bear it.

Salome slipped back into unconsciousness.

The two Icarii males tended her over the next week. Salome never saw their faces clearly, nor learned their names. They stayed with her day in, day out. They washed her, rubbed salve over her wounds, and fed her food and herbal medicines.

After their first conversation they rarely talked to her, which suited Salome. She hated talkers, whether lovers or any others. She closed her eyes to them whenever they were near, as if in pretense that she slept, even though her mouth readily accepted any food they spooned in, or drank of any refreshment they offered.

Salome discovered that she wanted to live, after all. If she could not die, then she would do the next best thing.

Find StarDrifter.

Then ruin his life as he had ruined hers.

CHAPTER FIVE

The Widowmaker Sea, to the West of Escator

Ba'al'uz wished he'd thought to leave StarDrifter behind. He had come to loathe the birdman in the very few short days they'd been together on this cursed fishing vessel.

At night they lay in their tiny cramped cabin (and that they had a cabin at all was due entirely to Ba'al'uz' initiative in the use of some inventive and quite frightening threats), and in their narrow, uncomfortable, damp bunks, and pretended the other did not exist.

Neither was very good at it.

The trouble had started almost the instant they'd boarded the boat in Yoyette harbor.

StarDrifter had not liked the rank stink of the fish. Neither did Ba'al'uz, but under the circumstances (this was the only boat available and it was leaving immediately) he was prepared to put up with the fish stink in order to make a quick escape from Coroleas.

Then StarDrifter had objected to the way Ba'al'uz had made threats against the captain's wife in order that the captain evacuate his cabin for StarDrifter and Ba'al'uz.

Those objections had so irritated Ba'al'uz that the moment they were belowdecks and the boat had cast off from the wharf, he'd informed StarDrifter that he'd cast Salome to the wolves of the Corolean court.

"You did *what*?" StarDrifter said.

"What care you?" Ba'al'uz said, holding on to an overhead bulkhead in order to steady himself against the increasing motion of the vessel. "You have said yourself, countless times, what a cruel and selfish creature she is. Now she is reaping the rewards of a life lived at everyone else's expense. It would surprise me, frankly, if she was not already dead."

"It would have been enough that she will need to face the consequences of losing the Weeper," StarDrifter snapped, keeping his balance with an unconsciously graceful ease that did nothing for Ba'al'uz' irritation with the man. "You did not need to *ensure* her death!"

"I had not realized you'd developed an affection for her," Ba'al'uz said.

"I had not realized you were so fucking vindictive."

Ba'al'uz sneered, then looked at the Weeper. "Give it to me."

StarDrifter hesitated, then held the Weeper out for Ba'al'uz.

The instant it left the warmth of his arms, the Weeper shrieked.

It did more than shriek. It wept and wailed and sobbed until the cabin literally throbbed with sound and sadness.

Before Ba'al'uz could touch the Weeper, StarDrifter wrapped it in his arms again.

The noise ceased abruptly.

Now Ba'al'uz had a reason to not be merely irritated with StarDrifter, but to develop a considerable loathing for him.

"What have you done to it?" Ba'al'uz said. "Why won't it leave you?"

"I have done nothing to it," said StarDrifter, "and I can't even *begin* to imagine a reason why it might not want to go to you."

They'd stood there and stared at each other for a long moment, then StarDrifter turned aside and sat down on his bunk. He wrapped himself in a blanket, the Weeper beside him, and affected to go to sleep.

Ba'al'uz stood for a long time, watching StarDrifter's back, then he, too, lay down on his bunk.

Sleep did not come.

Over the next two days conditions on the fishing vessel grew ever worse. The ship's crew fed StarDrifter only the very worst of scraps from their galley (a fact that hardly surprised

StarDrifter, given Ba'al'uz' earlier threats), although he often found a better gruel in his bowl than that which appeared in Ba'al'uz', and a piece of good toasted bread secreted within a napkin.

While Ba'al'uz and StarDrifter wanted to go directly to the southern coast of Escator, the fishing boat was going on a circuitous route to get there. It did, after all, need to collect fish, and the best fish was always to be found in the Widow-maker Sea far to the north of Coroleas. Both this fact, and that the boat appeared to be heading into rough weather, did not improve Ba'al'uz' temper in the slightest.

To cap off all his woes, Ba'al'uz suffered badly from seasickness.

StarDrifter didn't get a twinge.

StarDrifter discovered that one of life's greater pleasures was standing over Ba'al'uz in his bunk, looking down at his green face while chewing voraciously on a piece of bread and fish, and asking, through his enthusiastic chewing, if there was anything he could get Ba'al'uz from the galley. It invariably drove Ba'al'uz into a hissing, spiteful fury, and gave StarDrifter an excuse to spend many hours on deck, the Weeper tucked comfortably under one arm, chatting to the crew as they went about their chores.

The crew had been wary of StarDrifter at first, but as Ba'al'uz' antagonism toward him grew ever more noticeable, so did his popularity with the fishermen.

They knew what the Weeper was, and they were intrigued by StarDrifter's acquisition of it, while at the same moment growing ever more anxious about whatever repercussions its theft might have for them back in Coroleas.

"Frankly," StarDrifter said one afternoon, as the crew paused for a break after spending hours cleaning their nets, "I'd advise you to seek sanctuary with King Maximilian in Escator. He has a good reputation for protecting his fishing fleets, and I've heard the harbor at Narbon has excellent facilities."

"But our families are back in Yoyette," the captain said, obviously still smarting over Ba'al'uz' threats.

StarDrifter was about to say something, but just then the

Weeper, tucked under StarDrifter's arm, went cold.

It did more than go cold—it became completely icy.

StarDrifter pulled it onto his lap and, along with the crew, looked at it in surprise.

Its contours were outlined in frost.

A sense of incredible peace pervaded StarDrifter. He looked up at the crew, and saw that they, too, had expressions of wonder on their faces.

StarDrifter, as did the crew (and none of them knew *how* they knew this, but know it they did), realized that the crew's families were safe . . . and no longer in Coroleas.

After that, StarDrifter began to eat and sleep with the crew, and left Ba'al'uz to the cabin.

Three nights after leaving Coroleas, while the fishing vessel was some two leagues from the Escatorian coast, a storm began to build.

CHAPTER SIX

The River Lhyl, the Tyranny of Isembaard

Ishbel opened the curtain that gave her tiny cabin on the riverboat some privacy, then moved toward the foredeck, where Axis and Zeboath were sitting in the twilight.

Ishbel had felt much more relaxed and at peace since the night she had healed Madarin. She now traveled with a group who knew precisely what she was—the archpriestess of the dreaded Coil—and who not only did not condemn her, but either regarded her with intrigued fascination or varying degrees of adulation (several of Madarin's comrades had asked her, hesitantly, if perhaps she might talk to them about the Great Serpent and enlighten them).

She was accepted and to some degree respected.

She no longer had to keep secrets, or listen to a husband who asked her to hide her origins and pretend to be something she was not.

And she still had the power of the Coil within her.

Ishbel had been so unsure of herself from the moment the Great Serpent had revealed he wanted her to leave Serpent's Nest and marry Maximilian. The realization of her pregnancy had distressed her, for she'd believed that it would disrupt the Coil within her, and separate her still further from the protection and the love of the Great Serpent.

She should have listened to the Great Serpent.

Wash with the tide.

He had not been upset by her pregnancy, and indeed had appeared pleased by it, while the experience with Madarin had demonstrated to all, and most particularly to Ishbel, that her connection with the power of the Great Serpent had not been lost at all.

Above all, having relaxed away from her fears and the draining need to constantly hide her true identity, Ishbel was beginning to enjoy herself. She found herself intrigued by the company with whom she traveled, and fascinated by the land and culture through which she moved.

It was all so different from her life within the Coil at Serpent's Nest. Ishbel knew she'd clung to her isolation, and to the enveloping, if suffocating, protection that the mountain and the Coil afforded her, because of the childhood terrors that continued, even now, to torment her.

But she was discovering that she might learn to deal with the terrors, that she was capable of dealing with *most* things, and that she had more courage and fortitude than she had thought.

She also trusted Axis and Zeboath to an extent she'd trusted few people in her life.

Maximilian's lack still managed to cause her some sleepless hours at night. She could hardly forget him, not with his baby growing inside her, but Ishbel wondered if Maximilian ever thought of her. She thought that he'd probably accepted her kidnapping with profound relief. No longer was he saddled with a wife who was not merely an embarrassment to him, but one who threatened to saddle him with the guilt of every murder and injustice committed throughout the Central Kingdoms over the last half year. Maximilian would likely annul the marriage and forget her.

Well might Axis have said that BroadWing had told him Maximilian would tear apart the earth for her, but Ishbel thought she knew the truth of her relationship with Maximilian far better than did BroadWing.

Maximilian would not care overmuch, she was sure.

Ishbel climbed the short steps to the top deck, lifted her head, and walked out to join Zeboath and Axis.

Ishbel decided she liked this hot, vast country. It was so different from anything she'd ever known previously. She appreciated the warmth of the evening wind, and the scent of distant spices it carried on its back. She enjoyed being able to wear loose, less restrictive clothes. She was fascinated by the vast aridness that spread beyond the fertile swathes of agricultural land that ran either side of the river. But of everything, Ishbel loved the River Lhyl the most. It was so peaceful and so beautiful, so calm and yet so strong, lined with deep reed banks that, at dusk and dawn, throbbed with the glorious song of the frogs and during the day erupted great clouds of brightly plumed river birds into the air.

The river was a world to itself. To Ishbel, it sometimes appeared to be so full of promise and sweetness that her eyes filled with tears.

She felt a wonderful serenity within herself every time she stepped from the lower decks of the riverboat and once again was enveloped by the sights and scents of Isembaard.

It felt almost as if she was coming back to a long-forgotten home.

It felt *right*.

"My lady," she heard Axis say, and she blinked.

He was standing before her, a gentle smile on his face at the expression on hers. He had his hand out, and she took it, and allowed him to lead her to where Zeboath waited among a group of chairs and low tables at the very prow of the boat.

With the authority of Isaiah, which he commanded, Axis had been able to requisition for them the most luxurious riverboat available.

Zeboath smiled and gave a slight bow as Ishbel and Axis approached, then sat down once Ishbel had made herself comfortable.

They chatted for an hour or more, often lapsing into comfortable silence as dusk settled about them. Servants came with lamps, and with food and drinks, and they busied themselves with their meal.

As the meal drew to a close, Zeboath patted at his mouth with his napkin, and addressed Ishbel.

"You look very content, my lady, for someone who has been kidnapped away from her home."

Ishbel gave a small smile, and decided to speak the truth.

"Sometimes I feel as if Maximilian did the kidnapping, and you two the rescuing." She paused. "I have never felt so relaxed with anyone, save for Aziel, archpriest of the Coil and a dear friend, as I do here, in this company."

She looked over the railing at the twilight vista before her. "And this land—it is so . . . intriguing. Listen to the frogs! Are they not beautiful? And the scent on the wind . . ."

Axis and Zeboath exchanged amused glances.

"Maximilian has some work to do, I think," said Axis, "if he is to win you back to his side."

"If he can," Ishbel said, still looking out at the view.

Then she turned her eyes back to her two companions. "Sometimes space—distance—can give you such perspective."

"And sometimes it can be very distorting," Axis said. "You and Maximilian met and married under pressure, and the start to your married life was not easy."

"Certainly not when he kept asking me to pretend to be something I was not," Ishbel said.

"You can understand his reasons, surely," Axis said.

"Neither you nor Zeboath have condemned me for who I am," said Ishbel, "nor any of the men who accompany us. Why did Maximilian?"

"Don't talk yourself out of this marriage," Axis said. "Not yet."

She gave a small shrug.

Axis frowned, leaning forward as if to say something more, but just then Ishbel gasped, and put her hand on her belly.

"The baby moved!" she said. "I am sure of it."

She looked at Zeboath. "Can you feel? Am I right? Oh, it moved again!"

Zeboath moved his chair closer to her, resting his hand on her belly. He felt in one place, then another, then grinned at her. "Yes, Ishbel, the baby is moving."

"Oh," Ishbel said on a long breath, "it is not dead, after all. I'd been so worried after the poisons Ba'al'uz gave me."

"Well," said Zeboath, sitting back in his chair, "I think that baby is making up for lost time now."

Ishbel sat for a moment, her face a welter of different emotions. Then she leaned over to Axis, took one of his hands, and put it on her belly.

"Axis? Feel?"

He said nothing, and Ishbel looked into his face and saw there, for the first time since she'd met him, the unmistakable darkness of desire.

It was a complete revelation, and Ishbel sat back slowly as Axis' hand slid away from her body, and allowed the world to open up about her.

CHAPTER SEVEN

The Widowmaker Sea, to the West of Escator

The captain of the fishing boat had set course for Narbon.

No one argued with him over the matter.

Fishing had become impossible the night previous as the storm had gathered and the sea arose in huge, rolling waves that made work impossible.

Even the crew began to feel queasy as the deck undulated back and forth, back and forth, rolling ever closer to the black, glassy surface of the sea.

Ba'al'uz suffered as he had never thought possible. He lay in the cabin, twisted among sweat-stained sheets, his head resting on the wooden sides of the bed, the deck beneath slippery with the thin fluid he vomited forth every few minutes.

No one came near him. Everyone had too much respect for their own life to risk his foul temper.

StarDrifter was unaffected, his stomach tranquil.

He sat on the deck, his back pressed against the timbers of the tiny bridge, knees drawn up, trying to make himself as small as possible so he would not trip any of the crew who ventured forth, the Weeper tucked in securely at his side, watching the rolling seas with distant eyes. He could not merely see the storm building—the dark, heavy clouds milling close to the sea then piling higher and higher until they completely obscured the sun—but *feel* it. The air was heavy, almost thick, uncomfortably humid.

Oppressive.

It was not just the storm. StarDrifter thought he could feel a sense of expectation slowly accumulating as the cloud mass thickened and darkened. A sense of power. Magic.

Something was happening.

Something was building.

StarDrifter did not know whether to anticipate or to fear.

So he sat through the morning and the early afternoon, his eyes fixed on some distant unknowable point far out to sea, watching the storm gather in strength and in power.

By midafternoon the wind had strengthened to almost gale force. It was not yet raining, but the sheer force of the wind blew spray over the ship's deck, slicking its timbers, and soaking StarDrifter. The captain, Prata, made his way out of the sheltered tiny bridge, grabbing handholds as he came, cursing once as he slipped to his knees and grabbed at StarDrifter's shoulder—as much for support as to get the man's attention.

"My friend, get belowdecks! This storm will hit us within the hour, and no one is going to survive out here then!"

StarDrifter looked up at Prata's concerned face, an amused glint in his eyes. "Then perhaps we should persuade Ba'al'uz that some open air would be good for him."

The captain chuckled. "StarDrifter, get below. Please. I can't be wasting energy worrying about you out here while trying to save the boat."

"Leave me be, Prata. I will go below soon. Do not worry about me."

Prata looked at him searchingly. "Then make sure it is soon, StarDrifter. Please."

StarDrifter nodded, and Prata struggled back along the deck into the slightly safer confines of the bridge.

StarDrifter returned his eyes to the sea, wrapping his cloak about him a little more tightly in a futile effort to keep some of the spray from his flesh.

He was fascinated by what was happening. Something, something *other* than the storm, was about to happen. Stars, the power gathering out to sea was sending electricity thrumming along his skin and making the hair on his head rise slightly.

Something was coming, and StarDrifter knew he would go insane if he were trapped belowdecks.

Even the Weeper felt different. It was growing colder, much like it had the day before when StarDrifter had felt the sudden explosion of power from the deity. But its current coldness could just as easily have been due to the increasing amounts of spray that soaked it, or to the fact that it may be expending small amounts of power merely in anticipation of the storm . . .

StarDrifter didn't really know. He knew he should heed Prata's warning to go belowdecks, but the storm looked a little way off yet, and surely he could sit here for a few more minutes.

Maximilian, Serge, and Doyle rode for Narbon. They were some two or three hours distant from the port city, and they wanted to get there as fast as they could.

To the west a massive storm was building over the Widowmaker Sea.

The atmosphere was heavy and oppressive, their horses skittish, too ready to shy at every gust of wind and every leaf blown across the road.

The road itself was deserted. Everyone had taken themselves inside and shut and bolted the doors, and Maximilian thought that he, too, should get himself and the two Emerald Guardsmen behind shelter.

Above them, treetops whipped to and fro, and leaves burst from shrubs in small, violent explosions.

How had the storm become this violent, so fast?

Maximilian pulled his horse to a halt, signaling the other two to stop as well.

The horses milled about on the road, unnerved by the violence carried on the wind, their heads tossing, their haunches bunched close to the ground, ready to bolt.

"We can't stay out in this," Maximilian said, having to almost shout to make himself audible above the howling wind. His hair whipped about his face, but it wasn't worth taking a hand away from the reins and risking what little control of the horse he had left to try to tuck it away.

Serge and Doyle nodded.

"We need shelter," shouted Doyle.

Maximilian looked up to the sky, squinting.

BroadWing and his three companions were still there, black dots high in the sky, riding a wild current that buffeted them about like leaves that tumbled across the roadway.

Maximilian momentarily waved an arm at them, hoping BroadWing would somehow intuit his meaning.

Find shelter.

His horse plunged to the left, and Maximilian grabbed at his reins again, pulling the horse up barely an instant before he totally lost control.

"Anywhere," said Maximilian between clenched teeth. "We need to find shelter *now*."

StarDrifter thought that he needed to get belowdecks very soon. The storm front was now only a few minutes away. The clouds hung like a thick veil before the ship, lightning forking through them in angry flashes of white and gold.

The sense of power was not only growing stronger, but far more unsettling.

Deciding he'd waited too long, StarDrifter began to move, slowly, trying to get to his feet without tangling his legs in the sodden cloak and slipping on the soaked deck, or being blown away by the increasingly violent gusts of wind.

A few drops of rain splattered across his face—a different feel to the spray: harder, more aggressive.

Icy. Sharp.

The wind threatened to unfoot him with every move he made, but StarDrifter finally managed to stand, clinging with one hand to the overhanging eaves of the bridge.

The Weeper whimpered.

"I've not forgotten you!" StarDrifter muttered, wondering how he was going to hold on to the bronze deity and still manage to reach the safety of belowdecks.

Perhaps if he could fashion a sling from his cloak . . .

The boat suddenly tilted down the side of a huge wave, and the Weeper slid toward the edge of the deck.

StarDrifter made a grab for it.

The Weeper shrieked.

StarDrifter managed to get one hand on it, then two, then cried out himself as he felt ice burn through his hands.

The boat tilted back the other way, and both the Weeper and StarDrifter slammed back against the bridge.

Prata partly opened the door, yelling something indecipherable.

StarDrifter tried to release the Weeper, but was unable to remove his hands from the frozen deity.

The boat, as suddenly as it had just moved, tilted the other way once more, just as a massive wave crashed over the deck.

StarDrifter and the Weeper were washed overboard.

Maximilian, Serge, and Doyle had given up trying to ride. It was almost impossible in this wind, and the horses were so frantic they were unrideable.

The last glimpse Maximilian had of the Icarii was of them tipping their wings, sliding through the air toward the ground, and Maximilian hoped they were able to find a safe harbor.

For himself and the two guardsmen, there seemed little likelihood of anything save a shallow and somewhat damp gully to the seaward side of the road. They'd been caught out on a particularly isolated stretch of the road into Narbon, one that led through the vast marshlands bordering the northern aspects of the city. There were no houses here. No villages, and the marshlands that stretched a few leagues inland were too risky for Maximilian and his men to venture, even in this storm.

The marshlands were known for their treacherous sands, and many were the tales of travelers who had sought shelter in them never to be heard from again.

"Come on," Maximilian yelled, pulling his reluctant and terrified horse down the slope into the gully. "We can wait it out here."

"So long as there's no storm surge," Serge said.

StarDrifter turned over and over in the turbulent water, eyes and mouth tightly closed, trying to fight his way to the surface.

The Weeper was gone, torn from his hands as they were dashed into the sea.

StarDrifter had no doubt at all that the Weeper had pulled them overboard. He was aware that the deity had expended a massive surge of power just before the fishing vessel had tilted that final, terrible time, and he'd felt both himself and the deity being *pulled* toward the sea.

StarDrifter had no idea why the Weeper might want him to drown in the Widowmaker Sea, and right now trying to drum up a reason was the last thing on his mind.

All StarDrifter wanted to do was survive.

His clothes—the cloak, his boots, his heavy jerkin and trousers—were pulling him ever downward, no matter his attempts to fight his way to the surface, and he tried to pull them off.

The cloak floated free fairly easily, although it tangled in his legs as it went, causing StarDrifter a moment of sheer panicky terror. His jerkin, a thick leather affair, and trousers, of similar material, were harder to dislodge, however, particularly when his lungs felt as if they were about to burst.

He started to sink, and he stopped struggling with his clothes and tried to work his way to the surface.

He sank farther.

It began to feel almost like flying.

StarDrifter stopped fighting altogether, overwhelmed by the sensation.

He'd missed flight so desperately. To re-create the sensation, even for a moment, would surely be worth death.

Wouldn't it?

Suddenly a powerful light blazed in the water before him, searing through his closed eyelids, and StarDrifter's eyes flew open. Something gripped his upper arms, and StarDrifter felt himself being drawn toward the surface.

Maximilian, Serge, and Doyle crouched in the lee of a boulder, trying to shelter themselves as best they could from the driving wind and rain.

Their best was pitiful little.

The horses had bolted almost as soon as they'd been tied to a strong hewen bush. So great was their fright, nothing could have held them, and Maximilian had signaled to the two guardsmen to let them go.

Trying to catch them in this storm was not an option, and all they could do was trust that their horses might find some degree of shelter rather than dash themselves to death in terror.

The three men huddled behind their boulder, faces turned away from the storm front, bodies crouched into as small a ball as possible, crowding themselves together for what little shelter and warmth they could provide each other. They did not talk—there was no point.

Maximilian hoped that BroadWing and his companions had managed to find shelter, and that he and his two companions would manage to survive.

He thought they could. They were in no danger so long as Serge had not managed to curse them with a storm surge through his pessimism. The night would be wild, and very wet and cold, but they were strong, and even though the boulder offered little comfort, it did shelter them from the worst of the weather.

Just as he'd managed to make himself feel a little easier, something twigged at Maximilian's consciousness.

Almost like a distant shout.

And then his Persimius ring screamed—so loudly that Maximilian himself shouted in shock, rolling away from Serge and Doyle into the full fury of the storm.

Maximilian heard one of them call out, the sound a thin and diminishing wail in the tempest, and then he was gone, the wind so vicious, so powerful, it rolled him over the lip of the gully toward the pounding surf on the beach.

Toward the beach? But that was against *the wind!*

Maximilian tried to grab at bushes, rocks, the occasional thin trunk of a stumped tree, but he was being pulled so fast toward the surf that his fingers did not manage to maintain a grip on a single thing.

He felt something tear in his shoulder, and he gave a hoarse cry of pain that was instantly lost within the maelstrom.

* * *

The blazing light—*the Weeper, StarDrifter knew that somehow, impossibly, it was the Weeper*—had somehow managed to drag him to the surface.

Here the danger felt even closer, for the waves loomed huge above them before crashing down on his head, and every so often he was dragged into the wrath below.

But now StarDrifter was almost entirely encased within the light, and whenever a rogue wave dashed him down, he bobbed back to the surface just at that moment when he thought his lungs would explode.

He was covered in scratches and bruises from debris in the water.

StarDrifter hoped it was not the wreckage of Prata's boat.

The coast! the Weeper said in his mind. *StarDrifter, look, the coast.*

StarDrifter blinked, but his eyes were blinded by the sea and spray and the mountainous waves, and he had no idea how the Weeper expected him to see any farther than his nose.

Maximilian will be there, the Weeper said. *Maximilian will be there for us.*

Maximilian managed somehow to hook the fingers of his left hand into the thickness of the damp sand at the surf's edge, then get his right hand wedged behind a boulder.

Thank the gods he hadn't slammed into that!

With his good arm he managed to pull himself farther and farther away from the sea, desperate to get himself as far away as possible.

Then, impossibly, he heard a faint shout coming from behind him.

From within the sea.

"No," Maximilian whispered, too tired, too cold, too desperate for shelter to even contemplate the idea that someone might be calling out to him for rescue from the raging waters.

His ring screamed again, *flared* as if in agony, and Maximilian cried and rolled to one side, the cry intensifying as his injured shoulder hit the boulder.

The shout came again, closer, and somehow Maximilian struggled to one elbow, and looked over his shoulder.

There was a man, struggling out from the surf, directly behind him. He was dragging something in his hand.

Another man, perhaps, or a log.

Then everything went black for an instant, and when he regained his vision, all Maximilian could see was a body being rolled over and over in the surf.

Almost crying with the effort, Maximilian managed to get to his knees, shuffled into the waves, then pushed forward with his feet as the water got deeper.

Waves crashed into him, blinding him, and he felt his feet give way.

The next instant the body collided into him, and Maximilian felt something very hard hit his head.

He blacked out for a moment, then something picked him up and thrust him forward. He found himself on sand, out of the water, a heavy body draped over him, almost suffocating him, and he felt the icy heaviness of metal against his injured shoulder.

He rolled away from it, onto his belly, raising his head a little to peer into the rain-swept gloom.

Then blinked, not believing what he saw.

A woman stood on the crest of the small hill that the wind had blown Maximilian over, her cloak wrapped about her, long dark hair streaming in the wind, but otherwise apparently unaffected by the storm.

CHAPTER EIGHT

The Marshlands Outside Narbon, Escator

Maximilian blinked, and she was gone.

He blinked again, and the driving wind and rain blocked any sight he may have had of the crest of the hill.

He blinked yet again, and the woman was standing before him, bending down to him, squatting at his side, her hand lifting back the sodden hair from his brow.

"Hello, Maxel," she said softly.

He stared at her, still too shocked by the events of the past half hour to comprehend what now was happening.

"It has been a long time," she said. "Perhaps too long. Don't you recognize me?"

Her hand continued to stroke back his hair, her fingers combing it into some order.

Maximilian still stared at her, trying to take her in. The one thing that instantly struck him, almost overwhelmed him, was that she was walking magic.

The second was that she was lovely—very long, thick, dark hair that, somewhat remarkably given the storm, appeared only slightly damp; an exquisitely structured face, pale skin, the lightest gray eyes he'd ever seen, ringed with thick, luxuriant dark lashes . . .

It was the eyes that were so different, Maximilian realized. They were far lighter than he remembered.

And her face was much stronger, and far more mature.

"Ravenna," he whispered.

Ravenna, the marsh girl who had helped Garth rescue him from the Veins.

Ravenna, the girl who rescued him from his madness, but

then left him, and Garth—with whom she was close—to run
with the Manteceros and Lord of Dreams, Drava, whose like-
ness Maximilian wore carved into his upper right biceps.

"You do remember," Ravenna said, and smiled. "What are
you doing here, Maximilian?"

"Pulled here by magic," Maximilian said, managing to
get to his feet with Ravenna's aid, and suppressing a wince
at the pain in his shoulder. "You?"

Ravenna shook her head, looking at the man still lying
half in the water behind Maximilian. The storm had abated
now. It still blew about them, and it still rained, but it was a
gentle and mild thing compared to what had enveloped both
sea and land only a few minutes earlier.

"It was magic that brought me here, too," she said. She
stepped past Maximilian and bent to the man lying at the
edge of the tide. "Who is this man, Maxel?"

"I don't know."

Ravenna rolled him over. "He has a strange aspect."

Maximilian stepped to her side, looking down. "He is Icarii," he said, "but with no wings."

"I have heard of the Icarii," Ravenna said.

"No doubt from Drava," said Maximilian.

She looked at him at that. "I heard about them while I was
with Drava, yes," she said. "Our lives together were filled
with the pursuit of mysteries."

"And now?"

"Now the dreamworld is waking, Maxel. The barriers between it and this world are cracking."

"So Drava sent you back?"

"I wandered back of my own accord. I am a marsh woman,
Maxel. I belong to no man, whether he be flesh and blood,
or dream."

This was, Maximilian thought, a bizarre place and time to
be having this conversation.

He looked back to the Icarii man, now softly moaning as
he regained consciousness. "Power dragged me here, to this
man. I have no idea why."

"Maxel?"

He looked at Ravenna.

She nodded at an object lying in the water a few feet behind the Icarii, almost obscured by the darkness and rolling waves. "What's that?"

Maximilian walked over, leaning down and grabbing at the object with his uninjured arm.

Almost immediately he swore softly, and jumped back.

"Maxel?" Ravenna said again, now at his side.

"You'll have to pick it up," Maxel said. He indicated his left shoulder. "I injured my shoulder. Can't use my left arm very well. Don't worry," he added. "It isn't dangerous."

She gave him a level look, then bent down and lifted the object gently from the water—it was an exquisitely worked bronze figurine of a young man.

It *reeked* with magic, which Ravenna knew Maximilian must have felt as well, but which, as he had, she instinctively knew wasn't dangerous to her.

Not dangerous, but Ravenna received the faint impression that the object didn't like her very much.

"It is very sad," she said, softly.

"He is the Weeper," said a weary voice from behind Ravenna and Maximilian, and they turned about. "And he is indeed very sad."

The Icarii man had lifted himself onto one elbow. "My name is StarDrifter SunSoar," he said, "and I beg your aid in finding me a dry and warm spot."

"StarDrifter SunSoar," murmured Maximilian. "Dear gods . . . are they *all* coming back?"

Ravenna looked at him, an eyebrow raised in query.

"His son, Axis," Maximilian said, his voice infused with weeks-old fatigue, "has also returned from the land of the dead, and now has my wife, Ishbel. I was traveling to rescue her when this," he waved his hand about, encompassing the storm and all it had wrought, "intervened."

"Well," said Ravenna, with a bright smile, "now you have Axis' father. I am sure, with your undoubted royal diplomatic skills, we can arrange a prisoner exchange."

"Axis has your wife?" StarDrifter said, having now struggled into a sitting position.

"You knew Axis was back?" Maximilian said.

"Look," said StarDrifter, "I have no idea who either of you are, and I don't really want to go through explanations and introductions sitting in this frigid water. Is it possible, do you think, that we can find some shelter, some *dry* shelter, and talk all this out there?"

"I have no idea where—" Maximilian began, but then Ravenna caught at his arm with her hand, and nodded at the crest of the hill.

Silhouetted against the night sky were the figures of Serge and Doyle, holding the reins of three horses.

"I know of somewhere," Ravenna said.

Venetia paced back and forth by the wooden table in her small ramshackle home deep within the marshlands.

Something was happening.

Something was coming.

She had felt this for many weeks . . . the sense of *something* happening. Over the past few days the sense had intensified, and had been infused with the pain and terror of a woman far distant.

A woman was in pain, and was being brutalized, and Venetia felt some tenuous connection with her, although she could not identify it.

Venetia inhabited the marshes beyond Narbon, a witch-woman, one who lived partly in the mortal world and partly in the Land of Dreams, a guardian of the borderlands between the dream world and the mortal. Generally Venetia was happy with her solitariness, but, as the sense of impending events crowded her, she'd become nervy, constantly on the alert.

Waiting for whatever it was to strike.

When the knock came at the door, Venetia gave a startled gasp, her body tensing, her eyes widening, one hand at her throat.

She should have detected someone approaching.

That she had not told Venetia that whatever waited outside for her was a power-wielder themselves.

Taking a deep breath, summoning her not inconsiderable courage, Venetia walked to the door and flung it open.

And then immediately enveloped the woman standing outside in a fierce embrace.

"Ravenna!"

Ravenna, her daughter, lost years ago to the seductive wiles of the Lord of Dreams.

Not lost, not totally, for Ravenna and Venetia still remained aware of each other, and on very rare occasions spent brief moments together within the Land of Dreams. But this was the first time in five years that Venetia had held a flesh-and-blood daughter in her arms, and she was not about to let her go too quickly.

Ravenna laughed, hugging her mother back.

Eventually Venetia stood back, her eyes shining. "How you've grown!" she said. "Your power, as well as your beauty. How could I have produced such a daughter?"

"I will never be the woman you are, Venetia," Ravenna said. "Look, I have brought people with me who need aid. Can you—"

"Of course," Venetia said, standing back slightly so she could see who was with her daughter.

She tensed. "Maximilian Persimius," she said softly. Venetia had never met Maximilian, but she knew him instinctively.

Venetia looked at her daughter, her eyes full of questions.

"There are many questions to be answered," Ravenna said, "and many tales to be told this night, I think. But they need to be spoken in some comfort and warmth. Maximilian is injured, and at least one other member of our group has been through extremity over the past few hours. May we come in?"

StarDrifter had been through many experiences in his vast lifetime, but he thought he'd never enjoyed anything so much as the wonder of being able to strip off his sodden clothes, wrap himself in a blanket, sit before a fire, and sip some of the wonderful ale the marsh witch-woman, Venetia, handed him.

Everything that had happened to him from the moment he'd been tossed overboard seemed dreamlike: the experience in the sea with the Weeper; meeting with a man who appeared to be the King of Escator, Maximilian Persimius (StarDrifter had heard of him, yes, but he'd never paid the story much attention); discovering Axis had apparently made off with Maximilian's wife (StarDrifter had to suppress a grin every time he thought about that. Axis had not changed, it appeared); and, finally, being escorted by one witch-woman to the home of another, deep in the marshlands.

From the beach Ravenna and Maximilian had helped StarDrifter (who had been given the Weeper to carry) up a hill to where two men waited with horses, and then Ravenna and Serge had led the others, riding the horses, deep into the marshes to Ravenna's mother's house.

Then there was apparently much discussion and catching-up to be done, but all StarDrifter could think about was the wonderful warmth of the fire, the delicious ale, the food that Venetia was spreading over the table, and the promise later of a bed . . . if bed this ramshackle establishment could provide.

The Weeper lay under his stool. It had been remarkably quiet ever since they'd been washed ashore.

Venetia kept casting him uncertain, and decidedly cool, glances, but StarDrifter had no idea why, nor did he particularly care. He could worry tomorrow about where he might go, and what he might do.

Tonight he was warm, and, he smiled around his mug of ale, he was free of the damned Ba'al'uz.

Eventually Venetia handed out the food as well—thick sausage encased in warm, fresh bread, and, as people ate, Maximilian Persimius began to tell his tale in between mouthfuls.

It entranced even StarDrifter. Tales of indifferent love and of wives lost were commonplace enough, but *who* this wife was (a priestess, perhaps, of an order that intrigued even someone as world-weary as StarDrifter) and the powers that Maximilian hinted she may possess, made this far more interesting.

"And you say my son, Axis, stole her from you?" StarDrifter eventually said, unable to keep quiet any longer.

Maximilian turned from his seat at the table to regard StarDrifter coolly. "He has possession of her now," Maximilian said, "but Ishbel was stolen by a band of men led by a man called Ba'al'uz—"

"Ah," said StarDrifter.

"Ah, indeed," said Maximilian, now regarding StarDrifter very keenly indeed. "I think perhaps we have heard enough of *my* sad tale. StarDrifter, perhaps you might enlighten us as to why you are here, washed up on the shores of Escator with that bronze statue."

Maximilian's eyes slipped to where the Weeper lay almost hidden beneath StarDrifter's stool.

"The Weeper is a bronze deity," said StarDrifter, "infused with the soul of a man I am trying to release. Let me explain . . ."

As clearly and succinctly as he could, StarDrifter related what had happened to him over the past few weeks: his meeting with Ba'al'uz, his seduction of Salome, the theft of the Weeper, and the adventures that led him to this hut this night.

He mentioned Salome only briefly, and only as the woman he'd needed to seduce in order to win the Weeper, but as soon as he'd stopped, Venetia leaned forward, interrupting Maximilian, who had begun to ask StarDrifter a question.

"This woman, Salome," Venetia said. "She is in trouble, I *know* it."

StarDrifter looked uncomfortable. "The Coroleans will be greatly angered at the loss of the Weeper," he said. "No doubt they have imprisoned Salome and—"

"She has been raped and brutalized," said Venetia flatly. "Treated with a contempt that is unimaginable. I have felt this, intimated it, over the past few days. It has unsettled me greatly. Now, as you have spoken, what has happened has clarified in my mind. Why, StarDrifter? Why has she been so cruelly treated? It is connected with you, somehow."

StarDrifter looked down at his hands, twiddling the empty mug of ale between them.

"Salome is almost pure Icarii," he said. "I have no idea from where she got the blood, but she has spent her life trying to hide her origins. She was a powerful member of the Forty-four Hundred First Families, and as a caste they allow no 'new' blood. Everyone must trace their ancestry back to an ancient group of families in pure and untainted line, or be cast from the First. Salome held the most powerful position within Coroleas, save for the throne itself . . . and she held it by lie and deceit. Once that lie and deceit was discovered . . . then Salome would have suffered for it."

"How was it discovered, StarDrifter?" Venetia asked.

StarDrifter raised his eyes to hers. "I told Ba'al'uz of her Icarii blood, and once we had left Coroleas he told me he'd informed a member of the emperor's court of the fact. Salome would have been seized within hours."

Venetia gave a slight nod. "You're speaking the truth. I can sense it, but even so . . ."

"I did not like the woman," StarDrifter said. "She had done things in her life that I abhor. But I would not have wished this on her. Her Icarii blood was no fault of hers."

"She may not see it so," Venetia said softly. Then she straightened, and looked around the table. "There is so much we need to discuss, but it is late. I need to look at Maximilian's shoulder, and we all need to get some rest. Perhaps—"

The Weeper sighed, stopping Venetia midsentence.

Then it gave a soft whimper.

StarDrifter put his mug on the floor, and lifted the Weeper into his lap.

"It seems to like me," StarDrifter said. "It would never go to Ba'al'uz, and when—"

The Weeper whimpered again, this time with such longing that tears sprang into StarDrifter's eyes.

"He wants to go to you now," StarDrifter said, and lifted the Weeper into Maximilian's arms. "Now you must carry him on his journey."

CHAPTER NINE

Crowhurst, the Far North

Crowhurst was a stunning castle, particularly given its position in the frozen northern wastes. Fashioned out of a pale turquoise rock, its battlements and edges coated in a dazzling white, it stood out from the snow-covered tundra like a jewel.

Lister had created it twenty years ago, using powerful magic that had left him tired for many months afterward, but even so, even given its stunning beauty, Lister knew it was but a pale imitation of the memory he had used to fashion it.

It was not Elcho Falling, as desperately as it tried.

For months now Skraelings had been gathering at its base. They drifted in from even farther north in small groups, their gray, wraithlike forms buffeted by the winds that cut across the tundra day and night, their huge silver eyes mournful, their tooth-ridden mouths hanging agape in longing and hunger.

They gathered at Crowhurst because it formed a convenient beacon for them—even the Skraelings thought it very pretty—and because the man inside was kind to them, and spoke soft words to them, and (far more important) fed them. He was also allied with the Lealfast, with whom the Skraelings had a love-hate relationship.

The Skraelings listened to what Lister had to say, and in return for the food and the kind words, they occasionally helped out in the castle (as much as Skraelings were capable of "helping out" anyone, but they did their best), but they owed him no particular loyalty.

Lister was not their master.

The Lealfast, as much as they tried to lord it over the Skraelings, were not their masters.

Their true lord lay far south, and every day his siren song grew stronger and stronger in their minds.

One day the Skraelings would go to him.

One day, when they were strong, they would swarm.

High in Crowhurst, Lister stood at a window looking down at the Skraelings. He was never too sure whether to be sorry for the creatures, or to be completely repulsed. For the moment he supposed he should be tolerant of them, for they tolerated him and gave him a stage on which to act.

"They're growing restless," said Inardle, standing at his side. She had a hand resting intimately on his lower back, caressing him through the soft fabric of his clothing.

"They will swarm this winter," said Eleanon, from where he stood farther back in the room.

Another of the Lealfast, a man called Bingaleal, who was older, more experienced, and somewhat harder in nature than the other two, moved up to Lister's shoulder. "They scare me to death," he said, earning himself a surprised look from Lister.

"*They* scare you to death?" Lister said. "But I would have thought you to be their friend."

He received no reply from Bingaleal save a slightly cynical twist of the man's mouth, and so Lister turned to Eleanon.

"Your brothers and sisters, your cousins and neighbors, your friends and comrades?" Lister asked the man, although he meant the question for all the Lealfast in the room. "Are *you* ready to swarm?"

"We are ready, Lister," said Eleanon. "All of us. We will do anything to ensure that Elcho Falling rises again."

Lister looked at Bingaleal, who held seniority over Eleanon and Inardle.

"*Anything* for the Lord of Elcho Falling," Bingaleal said in a quiet tone, and Lister nodded, satisfied.

"Then I, and *he*, are blessed indeed by the Lealfast," said Lister, giving Inardle a kiss on her forehead and smiling at

Eleanon. "Now, to business, eh? Ba'al'uz. I have heard or felt nothing from him, and I worry."

"Is he not in Coroleas?" said Inardle.

"The last I heard, yes," said Lister. "But now? I don't know. Until he makes himself known to us, we just won't know *where* he is."

"He must still be in Coroleas," said Inardle.

"I hope so," Lister muttered.

CHAPTER TEN

Venetia's Hut in the Marshlands, Escator

"Tell me what you know, Ravenna," Venetia said. "Tell me why you have left Lord Drava and returned to this world."

They were sitting at the table, conversing in quiet tones.

Everyone else was wrapped in blankets, and lying in various spots about the fire, but neither Ravenna nor her mother would be able to rest until they had spoken with each other.

"There is something coming," said Ravenna. "Something about to move between this world and . . . another. Not from the Land of Dreams, but from a far darker world. Drava spoke often of it, and I felt it, too. I think you have as well, Venetia."

Venetia nodded. "My dreams have been greatly disturbed these past months, and not just with my sense of the woman, Salome, who StarDrifter abandoned."

She paused, one hand rubbing at her forehead, as if to worry away her memories. "I feel as if the world is about to pull apart, Ravenna. Like dough that has been rolled and stretched too far on the pastry board. *Something* is stretching reality too thin in order that it might cross over. A terrifying, raging beast. I feel as if . . ."

Ravenna smiled, a little sadly. "I think it has come time for us to say good-bye, for the time being, to these comforting marshes."

They sat in silence for a little while, each lost in her own thoughts, then Venetia roused, and smiled a little.

"Tell me, Ravenna. Do I have a grandchild yet? I have often wondered. Did you give Drava a child?"

"No," Ravenna said, "I wanted no child. Not of his. He was not what I wanted." She gave a small shrug. "I had been thinking of leaving for a very long time. The darkness that now besets us finally gave me the courage to actually *leave*."

Venetia stretched her hand across the table, resting it on Ravenna's arm. "And I for one am glad to have your company again. It has been a lonely time here without you."

She gave her daughter's arm a pat. "And what a coincidence, my darling, that you should reappear just as Maximilian has lost his wife. Be careful, Ravenna. I sense deep sorrow about this, such abiding sadness, such *loss*, that I worry for you."

"Venetia, do not worry. Maxel is my friend. He cannot hurt me."

Maximilian lay wrapped in his blanket in a quiet corner of the hut, listening to Venetia and Ravenna's muted conversation. His shoulder still throbbed, but Venetia had rubbed an ointment into it earlier that had reduced both the pain and swelling, and Maximilian thought it would be well enough within a day or two.

He was tired, but for the moment he did not sleep.

Strangely, he felt content for the first time in many months.

The sudden appearance of Ravenna, a girl—now woman—to whom he'd once entrusted his life, he took as an omen of very good fortune. Maximilian had felt a distance between him and Garth, but Ravenna . . . he was glad to see her again, and he thought she would be a boon on his journey into Isembaard.

Maximilian knew without a shadow of a doubt that she, as her mother, would be accompanying him farther south.

More important, the Weeper accounted for his strange state of contentment. He'd known the instant he'd touched it on the beach that the bronze statue was somehow intimately connected with Elcho Falling and with himself.

That moment on the beach had been a shock, and he'd leapt back, asking Ravenna to pick up the statue.

But now . . . when StarDrifter had laid the Weeper into

his arms earlier, Maximilian felt as if an intimate part of him had been returned. He had no idea *what*, or even how, but the Weeper suddenly made him feel . . . vindicated. Doing something positive and riding after Ishbel had been the right thing, after all.

The Weeper was near his bedroll, not quite touching one of Maxel's hands as it lay outside the blankets. Maximilian knew his Persimius ring and the queen's ring, secreted away in a pocket of his jerkin, were communicating with the Weeper. Not in words, and not in any manner that Maximilian could understand, but communicating they were.

Somehow, they were old friends.

For the moment Maximilian felt contented, and he felt safe, and he felt optimistic, and none of these things had been close companions for many, many months.

Maximilian finally succumbed to his weariness and slept.

The rings and the Weeper chatted throughout most of the night.

CHAPTER ELEVEN

The Road Between Narbon and Deepend

Ba'al'uz had no idea how he'd managed to survive the storm. He'd crouched in a corner of that cursed cabin, holding on to anything he thought might give him purchase, screwed his eyes closed, and waited for that final, crashing wave that would send the fishing boat to the bottom of the sea.

It hadn't come.

The storm had grown immeasurably worse by the moment, the cabin had pitched and rolled until Ba'al'uz was covered in bruises and contusions from being tossed against chests and bunks, but the boat had not sunk.

Instead, incredibly, the storm calmed, the sea became unruffled, and everyone, apparently, was going to live at least another day.

Ba'al'uz had struggled on deck—only to discover that during the height of the storm, the captain had managed to lose StarDrifter overboard.

With the Weeper.

It had been a moment Ba'al'uz would never forget. Standing there on the now gently rolling deck, staring at the captain, trying to comprehend the words.

StarDrifter was lost.

The Weeper was gone.

Then the incredulity and incomprehension faded, and incandescent rage took their place. Ba'al'uz summoned every scrap of power that he could, meaning to strike the captain and the crew and even the entire damned, cursed fishing boat from the face of the sea (the fact that he needed captain, crew, *and* boat in order to reach safety himself just didn't occur to Ba'al'uz in his fury).

But something had quelled his power. Something about the captain, and the five crew standing in a semicircle behind him.

Something calm. Something . . . *protective*.

They'd been encased by a charm. Ba'al'uz could not see the precise nature of it, but he could smell the Weeper about it.

The Weeper had protected them.

Why it couldn't bloody protect itself and StarDrifter at the same time, Ba'al'uz didn't know.

So he had quelled his power, stamped back to the cabin, and sat there for the day it took to reach Narbon.

There he had disembarked with nary a word to the captain or crew, and set himself on the road for Deepend with no delay.

Ba'al'uz wanted to get back to Aqhat with the utmost alacrity.

The loss of the Weeper was a stunning blow. What would he tell Kanubai? How could he explain it?

StarDrifter. If it hadn't been for StarDrifter . . .

But he had time. It would take him weeks, at the very least, to get back to Aqhat. He could think of something to tell Kanubai.

But Ba'al'uz didn't get weeks.

Kanubai found him the night after he left Narbon.

Ba'al'uz had been riding the horse he'd purchased in Narbon. It was late, well after dusk, and he wanted to find a nice sheltered spot—or, better, an inn—to spend the night. The horse was ambling along and Ba'al'uz was peering into the night and muttering about his ill luck in finding suitable accommodation, when suddenly the horse shied to one side, tossing Ba'al'uz onto the road, before it galloped back the way they'd come.

Cursing, Ba'al'uz managed to get to his feet. Then, just before he turned about and trudged after the horse, a movement ahead caught his eye.

He stopped, squinting as he endeavored to make out what it was.

Again, a movement, and then something frightful coalesced into ghostly form two or three paces away from Ba'al'uz.

It was the spectral figure of a jackal-headed naked man, and Ba'al'uz knew instantly who it was.

"Great Kanubai!" he breathed, terror flooding his being as he abased himself full length, pressing his face into the grit of the road's surface. "Almighty One," he muttered, raising his face a finger's breadth from the dirt in order to get the words out. "How blessed I am that—"

You have lost the Weeper.

"Almighty One, I had a companion who—"

You have lost the Weeper.

"I shall retrieve it." Ba'al'uz dared a glance ahead, and saw that Kanubai, while frightening, was still only very spectral. The god's power was great, but not yet at full strength. Perhaps Ba'al'uz would manage to survive a little longer, after all.

Kanubai's head wove back and forth, back and forth, as if scenting this new land.

How you have disappointed me, Kanubai said.

"I *shall* retrieve it!" said Ba'al'uz.

It might be too late.

"No, I will—"

I need to grow strong, Ba'al'uz. I had hoped to do it with the Weeper.

Ba'al'uz wept. He wished Kanubai would stop accusing him. He'd done all he could, and how could he have known the Weeper would prefer StarDrifter to such an extent that it wouldn't allow Ba'al'uz to touch it?

Maybe it had known why Ba'al'uz wanted it.

"Ishbel travels to you," Ba'al'uz said, hoping to divert Kanubai.

It appeared to work.

Ishbel . . . she must reach me.

"She will, she will. Isaiah is desperate for her. He said he would dispatch men to fetch her safely to Aqhat."

I hope for your life that is the case.

"It *will* happen," said Ba'al'uz, knowing that if it did not, then he was a dead man.

And if it didn't happen, Ba'al'uz silently swore to himself that he'd murder Isaiah before Kanubai thought to murder Ba'al'uz.

I need the sacrifice, Kanubai said. *So badly.*

"You shall have it," said Ba'al'uz with as much confidence as he could muster.

"If I don't," Kanubai said, this time using a physical voice that grated through Ba'al'uz' entire being, "then I shall crush you." He paused, and Ba'al'uz could feel the weight of the god's eyes on him. "You need to reach me, Ba'al'uz. Fast. I shall give you a gift, I think."

For an instant indescribable pain flared through Ba'al'uz' body, and then both pain and Kanubai were gone, and Ba'al'uz was left weeping in frustration and anger in the dirt of the roadway.

The horse was gone, but as it transpired, its loss did not worry Ba'al'uz overmuch. Kanubai *had* given Ba'al'uz a gift, a new parcel of power that Ba'al'uz realized he could draw on to travel more quickly than otherwise physically possible. It would not allow him to fly, but it would shorten the journey by at least half.

Ba'al'uz made as much haste as he could. He knew he had been indescribably lucky in his encounter with Kanubai. The jackal god had been angry, and with every reason.

The Weeper had been so important.

There was a possibility it could be retrieved—perhaps StarDrifter was still close.

For now, however, the most important thing was to get back to Isembaard and make damn sure Ishbel had managed to get to Isaiah safely.

Ba'al'uz knew he wouldn't survive her loss as well.

So he traveled on foot, moving south to Deepend, aided by the extra power Kanubai had infused into his being so that he moved swiftly and remarkably effortlessly.

He could feel Kanubai's added power swarming about his

mind, twisting memories and thoughts, blurring them very slightly at the edges. There were moments when he felt but mildly disoriented, and moments when he felt utterly lost within the shadows that swirled through his mind.

There were memories there that shouldn't have been.

Stray thoughts that were not entirely his, but not Kanubai's, either. Reflections, almost, of other people about him, and possibly other people who had traveled this road.

Ba'al'uz began to chatter to himself far too much, and other travelers who encountered him on the road gave him wide berth.

CHAPTER TWELVE

Narbon, Escator

Maximilian gave it two days before he left Venetia's hut. Partly this was because his shoulder ached more than he'd thought, and he simply didn't want to ride. Partly it was because the horses themselves were tired and needed the rest (one had mildly injured a fetlock during its panic in the storm and needed time for it to strengthen). Partly it was because the weather had turned poor: the storm itself may have passed, but low clouds and icy rain set in, which made travel particularly unappealing. Partly it was because Maximilian wanted to reestablish contact with BroadWing and the other Icarii before they recommenced their journey—he had not heard from them since the day of the storm and he didn't want to leave without knowing their fate.

And partly it was because he had to arrange for three additional horses.

As he had thought the first night, Venetia, Ravenna, and StarDrifter would be joining his troupe.

Venetia and Ravenna he was glad of, and StarDrifter had brought the Weeper to him.

StarDrifter was also Axis' father, and Ishbel was now with Axis.

Maximilian felt very strongly that somehow they were being pulled together. He also believed this somehow necessary. The threads were being gathered: Elcho Falling was being rewoven, and for the moment Maximilian had no intention of trying to fight it. He could not stop what was about to happen.

He could, in the end, only do his best.

On the morning of the third day after the storm, Venetia told Maximilian she'd had word at dawn that four Icarii awaited him in Narbon.

Maximilian did not ask *how* she'd known, but just nodded his head.

"Then we ride within the hour," he said, and he picked up the Weeper, and settled it into the pack he slung on his back.

StarDrifter was happy to be on his way. Additionally, he was relieved to be out of Coroleas once and for all, he was happy to be rid of Ba'al'uz, and he was ecstatic at the idea of finally seeing Axis again.

He was far less enchanted with having to ride a horse. For his entire life, at least until five years ago, StarDrifter had never ridden a horse—why, when he could fly and soar into the heavens?

Now the necessity of depending on a horse for transport emphasized the loss of his wings. StarDrifter was actually a very good rider. His natural grace and strength, as well as an empathy with the animal, meant that the first time he'd had to ride a horse he'd done so with the apparent ease of one with forty years' horsemanship behind him, but that did nothing to quell his resentment.

Venetia had acquired the three extra horses, and the one she'd given StarDrifter was a lovely animal. A big horse, fully seventeen hands, with the strong build that suggested he'd been bred for hunting; he had a huge white blaze down his face and one startlingly blue eye that, surrounded by the blaze, gave him a perpetually crazed look.

StarDrifter mounted the horse and gave its neck a soothing pat as it skittered a little under his weight.

Narbon was a mere two hours ride south of Venetia's hut, and StarDrifter had assumed that the Icarii whom Maximilian had talked of would remain in the city for the king to arrive. He was somewhat taken aback when, a few miles out of the city, one of Maximilian's guardsmen, Doyle, gave a soft exclamation and pointed into the sky.

StarDrifter looked up.

Four Icarii were spiraling down from the clearing sky.

StarDrifter felt his stomach clench. He wasn't looking forward to meeting these Icarii. He'd avoided other Icarii assiduously while living in Coroleas, hating to be reminded of the loss not only of his wings, but of everything and everyone who had perished along with Tencendor.

He hoped it wasn't anyone he knew personally.

Unfortunately, within a few hundred feet of their approach (StarDrifter still had his excellent birdman's vision) he knew he was out of luck.

BroadWing EvenBeat had once been a member of the Strike Force under Axis' command, and subsequently had been a regular member of Caelum's court. StarDrifter did not know him well, but he knew him nonetheless, and he saw startled recognition in BroadWing's eyes as well.

The Icarii landed, and BroadWing greeted Maximilian. They spoke briefly, reassuring themselves that no one had been badly injured in the storm, then Maximilian turned slightly in his saddle and indicated StarDrifter and the two marsh women.

"We have new company," he said. He introduced Venetia and Ravenna, then looked to StarDrifter.

"You might remember—" Maximilian began, then stopped in amazement as BroadWing stepped near to StarDrifter's horse and dropped on one knee, his head bowed deeply, his wings spread out behind him on the ground in the traditional Icarii gesture of deep respect.

"Talon," BroadWing said, giving StarDrifter the title of the king of the Icarii. "I greet you well. I am yours, as are all under my command."

Maximilian's mouth dropped open, then he turned to StarDrifter.

The birdman looked as if he'd been hit with an ax. His face was bloodless, his eyes wide with shock, and his mouth opened, then closed, as he fought to find something to say.

"No," StarDrifter managed, finally. "I am not your Talon."

"Yes," BroadWing said, "you are. You are the rightful heir."

Everyone was now staring at StarDrifter.

"Axis is alive," StarDrifter said, his voice still hoarse with shock. "He should be the—"

"Axis was never Talon, and has never claimed the title," said BroadWing. "His bloodline was that of the StarSon over all Tencendor, *not* Talon over the Icarii. FreeFall is dead. You are his closest living male relative, his uncle."

The three other Icarii knelt behind BroadWing, offering StarDrifter their respect and loyalty as well.

"I don't want it," StarDrifter said, his voice tight.

"Nonetheless," BroadWing said, now rising to his feet, "the Icarii survive, and we need a Talon." His voice firmed. "You."

"I can't . . ."

BroadWing said nothing, holding StarDrifter's eyes in his cool, steady gaze.

"I am not worthy," said StarDrifter. "Not at all."

BroadWing smiled, very slightly. "Then you shall need to develop worthiness, StarDrifter. You are a SunSoar. I have no doubt you will manage it."

There was a long silence, broken eventually by Serge.

"Well, fancy," he said. "Now I find myself riding in the company of *two* kings."

Three days after Maximilian and his company had passed through Narbon, a woman alighted from a Corolean trading vessel at the city's wharves.

She was particularly striking, if a little gaunt and pale, but the expression on her face and the hardness in her eyes told anyone who looked upon her that she'd endured much adversity, and that recently.

The woman wasted no time in hiring a small escort and fast horses, and within two hours of her arrival in Narbon she had left the city, traveling west toward Deepend.

[Part Seven]

CHAPTER ONE

Palace of Aqhat, Isembaard

Ishbel stood on the deck of the riverboat under a gently undulating canvas canopy, using all of her self-control to present a calm, confident exterior, yet horribly aware that her constantly shifting eyes revealed her anxiety.

The long, slow, comfortable river journey had reached its conclusion. In the early hours of the morning the boat had docked at the wharf of the palace of the Tyrant of Isembaard, and now, midmorning, she was to disembark and meet, finally, her captor and the man who planned to destroy all the kingdoms north of the FarReach Mountains. She had dreamed the previous night of the Lord of Elcho Falling again, the dream more vivid and terrifying than ever, and she thought it boded ill for today.

She was dressed in the Isembaardian fashion for the day. She'd been wearing only her nightclothes when Ba'al'uz had snatched her, and for the terrible journey through the Far-Reach Mountains she'd been given only rough and functional garments. Once she'd fallen into the care of Axis, Ishbel's wardrobe improved, but had still been largely functional.

At breakfast, a servant had appeared, carrying over his arms a thick swathe of soft linen, saying that it was a gift from the tyrant, and he would be pleased if she were to wear it on this day.

Ishbel dressed hesitantly, unwilling to accept the gift, yet at the same moment glad of the opportunity to wear something elegant, comfortable, and flattering to her ever expanding figure. She did not know if Isaiah was aware of her pregnancy (had Axis sent word? Had he left the boat secretly, and met

with Isaiah?), but the robe of heavy white linen, draping softly
from a wide collar of multicolored glass beads that covered
her shoulders and upper chest and back, flattered both her
coloring and pregnancy, and in the warm humid air was far
more comfortable than something more closely fitted.

The tyrant, Isaiah, was clearly determined to make a
grand showing for her.

The riverboat was the only vessel docked at the expansive
stone wharf. The wharf was empty of all the paraphernalia
Ishbel would have expected: crates, ropes, casks, bundles of
sails, fishing nets. Instead, the vast area of cream stone had
been swept and scrubbed free of any stain so that it reflected
an almost blinding white light in the strong sunshine. Spear-
wielding soldiers, dressed only in white linen hipwraps,
sandals and glittering copper helmets, lined the wharf in
three rows, creating an avenue that stretched back at least
two hundred paces to the gates in the palace walls.

Further rows of armed men lined the tops of the palace
walls.

Aqhat glittered with the fire of copper and the lightning
flashes of steel.

Ishbel was not sure if this display was meant to impress
her or to intimidate her, but she had to confess to herself that
if Isaiah had aimed for intimidation, then he'd managed it
very well. The only thing that spoiled the perfect stillness
of the men, and the symmetry of their display, was an ugly
brindle dog that trotted slowly behind one of the lines.

The day was going to be hot. The air was very still, and,
save for the gentle lapping of water against the riverboat's
hull, it was completely silent.

Nothing moved. Ishbel had been standing here now for at
least half an hour and not once had any of the armed men
moved.

There was just the glittering light and ever-increasing
heat.

And Ishbel's own ever-increasing apprehension.

"What is this, Axis?" she said, very low, turning her face
only slightly toward Axis, who stood to her left and just behind her. "Why this display?"

Axis was clothed in clean shirt and trousers, his boots finely polished, his hair freshly washed and his beard trimmed close to his jawline. Among all this exotic landscape and peoples, he at least reminded her of the land of her birth.

He gave a small shrug at her question. "Isaiah must be bored," he said, "or perhaps, now that he is gathering his men for an invasion, he needs some duty to occupy the ever-increasing forces. A spot of ceremonial duty in the scorching sun will surely keep them out of mischief for the day."

"What does he *want* with me?" Ishbel hissed, unable to keep the anxiety from her voice.

"Not much, Ishbel," Axis said. "Remember that this was not his idea, but Ba'al'uz'. No doubt Isaiah wishes to impress you, but, the instant he sees that belly, any vague interest he may have in the idea of taking Maximilian's wife as his own bride will vanish in a rush of disagreeable revulsion. I am willing to wager that you will see him this morning, and then you'll barely ever see him again. He'll be no danger to you, Ishbel. Don't worry. Just enjoy the day. If nothing else, the Isembaardians know how to put on a display."

"Are you well, Ishbel?" said Zeboath softly from a few paces behind her. "You have been standing here for a time now, and the air is hot, even if we are shaded from the sun."

"I am well enough, Zeboath," Ishbel said, turning and smiling a little for him. "I haven't been too—"

Distant trumpets sounded, and Ishbel jerked her face back toward the palace gates.

They had opened, and a single figure emerged.

There was a sudden rush of sound as, in perfect harmony, every soldier lining wharf, avenue, and palace walls thrust his spear into the air.

The ugly brindle dog scampered off, his tail between his legs.

Ishbel drew in a quick breath, holding it an uncomfortably long time until she remembered to breathe again.

The man walking down the center of the avenue was as yet too distant for Ishbel to make out features, but amid all this glittering array and bright light, he appeared not only a man of considerable height and strength, but singularly dark. There was a mass of braided hair that swung over his shoulders and back, and the braids shimmered with each movement, as if he had diamonds threaded through them. He wore a black hipwrap and sandals, and little else save for a massive golden collar that draped over his shoulders and upper chest.

Golden bands shone at his wrists and ankles.

He strode ever closer, every movement measured and confident, and Ishbel saw that he wore no weapon.

All about him were weaponed, but Isaiah was confident enough of his power that he felt no need to arm himself.

When he'd come to within fifty paces of the docked boat, the men lining avenue and walls began to repeatedly thrust their spears into the air with extraordinary and almost graceful coordination, shouting their tyrant's name as he strode among them.

"Isaiah! Isaiah! Isaiah!"

Ishbel had to use every ounce of her self-control to keep her hands relaxed at her sides and her head held high.

"Be calm, Ishbel," Axis murmured. "This is a game, nothing else."

Isaiah now came to a halt ten or fifteen paces from the walkway connecting boat to wharf.

Ishbel had never seen any man—or woman, come to that—who commanded so much authority. He dazzled and intimidated with an easy command of that authority, and Ishbel thought that the Northern Kingdoms had very little chance indeed, if this man had set his mind to them.

"Ishbel," Axis murmured, holding out his arm for her.

She took it and, with thankfully confident steps, proceeded down the walkway to meet the Tyrant of Isembaard.

She noticed the instant he saw her belly. Something crossed his striking face, a shadow of disgust, probably, and Ishbel relaxed very slightly.

He would not bother her. He would set her aside in a chamber, and forget her.

Close up, Isaiah was taller and stronger than Ishbel had first thought. He was very handsome, and radiated such confidence and power that, despite her relief, Ishbel remained completely intimidated.

He regarded her with the steady black gaze of a hawk, his face now completely expressionless, his thoughts utterly closed to Ishbel.

Again as one, the troops fell silent, placing their spears back at their sides.

"Isaiah," Axis said, in what seemed to Ishbel to be a fantastically relaxed voice. "I have the honor to present to you Ishbel, Queen of Escator." His voice thickened with humor. "Your new bride."

"A somewhat used bride," Isaiah said, his voice devoid of any emotion, yet somehow managing to convey the utmost contempt.

All Ishbel's fear, intimidation, and nervousness vanished in a moment of blinding, consuming anger.

She stepped forward before any could stop her, and dealt the Tyrant of Isembaard a stinging slap across the face.

CHAPTER TWO

Palace of Aqhat, Isembaard

Axis supposed he'd had worse moments in his long life, but right at that moment they paled completely into insignificance at Ishbel's actions.

To hit Isaiah, in front of his troops; before so many witnesses, to so ridicule him.

"Stars, Ishbel!" Axis hissed, and grabbed at her elbow, wrenching her away from Isaiah. "You *fool*!"

That last he said a little louder, and more clearly, so that it would carry.

Axis glanced at Isaiah.

Isaiah had not moved.

His eyes had briefly shifted to Axis when he'd grabbed Ishbel, but now were back, steady and unflinching, on Ishbel.

Ishbel herself was flush-cheeked and glittery-eyed, and Axis did not know if it was due to remaining temper, or sheer fright at what she'd just done.

He hoped it was sheer fright, as that might, also, curb her tongue.

"I am assuming," Isaiah said, his voice chilling, "that your former husband must have shackled you on your wedding night, to get that child in you."

Then he looked at Axis. "Should I have chains and irons installed in *my* bedchamber, Axis, or do you think she can be tamed in time for our nuptials?" He paused. "Does she *bite*, do you think? Should I dare to hope for nails, as well?"

There was a ripple of amusement among the troops, and Axis saw Isaiah's shoulders relax fractionally.

Pray to all gods, he thought, *that Ishbel keeps her mouth closed.*

Just then he saw her open it to speak, and realized that the glitter in her eyes was indeed rage, and not fright.

"Ishbel," he hissed, his fingers closing a little more tightly about her elbow, "now is *not* the time!"

She whipped her face to his, furious, but Axis stared her down, and after a moment she dropped her eyes and looked to the ground.

Axis could feel her trembling with her anger. He looked to Isaiah, hoping that he, also, would now hold his tongue.

The man had a glint of humor in his eyes, which surprised Axis, but also relaxed him.

Ishbel had made her point, had then been suitably quelled, and Isaiah had regained with his pointed humor whatever he'd lost with her slap.

"Bring her inside," Isaiah said, "and I will decide what to do with her later."

"Forgive me, excellency," said Axis, now careful to be the essence of deference, "but the introductions are not yet quite complete."

Isaiah sent him a cold look.

"Ishbel, Queen of Escator," said Axis, "*and* archpriestess of the Coil, an order of prophets who reside within Serpent's Nest."

Axis had thought to have caused Isaiah some surprise with that last, but to his complete amazement Isaiah merely raised one eyebrow.

"Truly?" Isaiah said, now looking from Axis to Ishbel. "*I* had heard rumor she was priestess to the Lord of Elcho Falling."

Ishbel made a sound, half gasp, half moan, and went completely white. Axis, who had let her arm go, now grabbed at it again.

He felt completely bewildered. *Who was the Lord of Elcho Falling? And how did Isaiah know it would upset Ishbel so greatly?*

"Isaiah," Axis said, grating the words out, "we need to get inside."

"Then bring her inside," said Isaiah, "for I have grown weary with this extravagance of conversation. We shall dine tonight, all three of us, and share confidences over chilled wine."

With that, Isaiah turned on his heel, diamond-encrusted braids swinging, and strode back toward the palace.

Axis bathed, and dressed in fresh linens, then stood at the window of his chamber, head resting against the cool marble of the window frame, thinking about the scene on the wharf.

It had not played out quite as he'd imagined.

It had begun very much as he'd thought it would—all great dignity and arrogance on Isaiah's part, followed by a sarcastic comment regarding Ishbel's pregnancy, and then . . .

Axis had not thought Ishbel to have such a quick temper, although Isaiah had certainly earned that slap.

From that point on, though, something had been happening that Axis could not pinpoint. Isaiah's subsequent words, his sarcastic humor, had been vintage Isaiah . . . but Isaiah had been *genuinely* amused and, if Axis was not mistaken, very interested.

Perhaps Ishbel had ignited interest with that slap. Axis thought there could have been very few women who would ever have dared to slap Isaiah, even when he'd been just one prince among many competing for the throne of Isembaard.

Of everything, though, it had been Isaiah's comment about the Lord of Elcho Falling that had perplexed and intrigued Axis. Had Isaiah known Ishbel would react as she did?

Yes, Axis decided, Isaiah probably had known.

But how . . . *how?*

Damn the man! Axis had a feeling that anyone trying to plumb Isaiah's depths would drown within their complexity before they ever reached bottom.

And they were to dine together tonight. Axis grinned. It would be an interesting evening.

A servant—if that was a suitable word to describe a man so gorgeously appareled and with such an air of dignity—escorted Ishbel to Isaiah's private chambers just after dusk. She had spent the afternoon in a charming suite of rooms, full of beauty and coolness, a wonderful scent of spices drifting in the windows, gradually calming down after what Isaiah had said to her on the wharf.

Everything he'd said about her pregnancy, everything he'd intimated about his own bedding of her, was forgotten in that single, devastating phrase.

I had heard rumor she was priestess to the Lord of Elcho Falling.

At those words, a great tide of sadness and loss had flooded Ishbel's being, and she was washed momentarily back into the nightmare that had visited her the previous night.

Now she was to dine with Isaiah, and Ishbel was very, very tense and wished, yet once again, but with more desperation than ever, that she was home, and safe, in Serpent's Nest.

The chamber the servant led her to was not quite what she'd expected.

Anything but intimidating, the long room stretched from east to west with open floor-to-ceiling windows in each of its end walls. Soft lamps glowed on the walls, and gauzy drapes wafted gently in the open windows. Low, cushioned seats, each with low tables to either side of them, sat in a circle in the center of the chamber. A small round table stood in the center of the circle of chairs. Food and wine had been set out on yet another table, just behind the circle of chairs. The chamber was both intimate and airy, and furnished for comfort and relaxation rather than to awe.

There appeared to be no one about. Ishbel walked slowly into the room, stopping just before the circle of chairs.

She looked down at the table in the center of the chairs, and it seemed as if her heart stilled in her breast.

A goblet stood there, stunning in its beauty. Frogs capered about its cup and over the rim, and a single reed taper, lit and set just behind it, sent light glowing through its amber glass so that the frogs appeared almost as if they were alive, and moving.

It was the goblet she had seen in her dream, the goblet she had presented to the Lord of Elcho Falling.

Ishbel took a step backward, one hand on her chest as if to still her now wildly beating heart.

"It is known as the Goblet of the Frogs," said Isaiah, stepping out of the shadows, "and you have no reason whatsoever to be afraid of it."

She looked at him, still tense, still ready to run. He still wore the hipwrap and the diamonds in his braided hair, but the golden collar and other jewelry had disappeared.

Then she looked at his eyes, and her entire world changed.

His eyes were vast pools of compassion, and Ishbel suddenly, devastatingly, realized who he was.

The Great Serpent's companion, the god of the frogs and of the river.

She trembled, and made as if to bow, but Isaiah waved a hand. "No need," he said. "Not now."

"My lord—"

"Isaiah will suffice," he said, smiling, "although you might like to apologize for that little slap on the wharf."

"I—" Ishbel simply could not get her mouth to work.

Isaiah walked very close. She did not, could not, move.

Ishbel was mesmerized by those eyes, by their compassion and understanding, and by an almost instant renewal of the bond she'd felt when he appeared to her on the balcony of Serpent's Nest. She felt as if she had known him all her life, as if he were *part* of her life.

He leaned down, and kissed her briefly, and Ishbel closed her eyes and shuddered.

When she opened them Isaiah was offering the goblet to her. "There is no reason to be afraid of this," he repeated, "just as you have no reason to be afraid of who you are and of where you are going. Here, hold it."

Ishbel stared at the goblet, and did not move.

"I swear to you, Ishbel," Isaiah said softly, but with such intensity that she raised her eyes to his, "that if what you feel from this goblet frightens you then I will personally escort you back to Serpent's Nest, setting out in the morning. My oath, Ishbel, believe it."

She did.

She looked back at the outstretched goblet. "I might drop it," she said.

He gave a slight shrug. "Fate, then. Take it, Ishbel."

Very slowly she reached out a hand, clenching her fingers briefly as she realized how badly they shook, then slid them about the stem of the goblet, over Isaiah's own fingers.

"Do you feel?" he murmured.

She almost shook her head, because for a moment all she could feel, all she was aware of, was the warmth and strength of Isaiah's fingers, but then something else drifted through.

A soft whispering, but oh, so gentle, and oh, so soothing.
Hold me, soothe me, love me.

Ishbel drew in a deep, shaky breath.
Hold him, soothe him, love him.

Her eyes flew to Isaiah's, and he smiled at her, with such warmth that her own eyes flooded with tears. Gently, he slid his fingers from under hers, and Ishbel had to lift up her other hand to take the full weight of the goblet in both.

The tears spilled down her cheeks and she sank into one of the chairs, absorbed for the moment in the goblet and what it was saying to her.
Hold me, soothe me, love me.
Hold him, soothe him, love him.

Eventually, Isaiah came to her side, took the goblet from her, and placed it on a shelf on a side wall. Then Isaiah looked to the door, smiled, and said, "Welcome, Axis. I had wondered when you would arrive. We are both quite faint with hunger."

Axis was surprised to see Ishbel here before him. She was sitting with her back to him as he entered, and he thought he saw her wipe at her eyes.

What had they been saying? More of Isaiah's sarcasm?

Axis put the small satchel he'd been carrying to one side and stepped forward to greet Isaiah, then moved so he could see Ishbel, now looking up at him.

"Ishbel?" Axis said. "Are you well?"

"Yes," she said. "Better, now."

And she looked, then smiled, at Isaiah.

Axis felt a flame of interest, and not a little bit of jealousy. Isaiah waved him to a chair and both men sat down.

Axis wanted to ask what the other two had been talking about before he arrived, but before he could find the right words to phrase the question, servants came in a side door and began placing food and wine on the tables to the side of each diner's chair.

It was a pleasant way to eat, Axis thought, relaxing back in his chair, a white napkin spread over his lap, chewing a delightful concoction of rare meat minced with spiced nuts and dates. The conversation centered on easy generalities, servants hovered always to hand to proffer bowls of scented water to wash sticky fingers, or more food, or drink, or a clean napkin.

Eventually, when all had eaten to sufficiency, the servants cleared the tables, then set out small bowls of confectionery and ewers of iced wine. When they had done, Isaiah waved them away, saying that he and his guests would serve themselves.

"Tell me about your journey north, Axis," Isaiah said. "Where did you find Ishbel? In what manner?"

Axis briefly told Isaiah what had happened, leaving out nothing save his acquisition of Ba'al'uz' glass pyramid. Isaiah listened dispassionately, lifting his eyebrows only when Axis mentioned the Icarii, and BroadWing.

"Ishbel was cruelly treated by Ba'al'uz," Axis finished. "If it were not for the attention of Zeboath, the physician we found in Torinox—you might have seen him, he was standing just behind us on the riverboat—I fear we may have lost her. As it is, Zeboath continues to hold fears for the health of Ishbel's child."

Isaiah's gaze slid briefly to Ishbel's belly, then he shrugged. "She appears well enough now. This Zeboath, you like him? He is a good physician?"

"Yes. He is desperate for your patronage."

"Then he shall have due honor and regard in my court, and my goodwill besides. What other news, Axis?"

"Well . . . Ishbel does have some interesting news regarding Lister."

Isaiah raised his eyebrows at Ishbel.

In a low but steady voice Ishbel related what she'd told Axis and Zeboath. Lister had once been the archpriest of the Coil, but had vanished some twenty years since. No one among the Coil had seen or heard from him again.

"There had been uncertainty and loss in the year or two after he vanished," said Ishbel, "but with the rise of Aziel into the archpriesthood, life settled down, and so far as I remember, members of the Coil only rarely thought of Lister, or wondered where he was."

"And you became the archpriestess," Isaiah said, appearing completely uninterested in this news of Lister's origins. "Tell me the secrets of Serpent's Nest, Ishbel, if you will."

"Serpent's Nest has no secrets," Ishbel said, "but even if there were secrets, then I am not sure I should tell them to a man who plans to invade my homeland and destroy it."

She raised an eyebrow to Isaiah at this, as if asking a question.

"Ah," said Isaiah, giving the faintest shake of his head, as if he did not wish to answer Ishbel's unasked question. "Axis has told you all *my* secrets, then, and has got from you not a one."

"Axis does not know the extent of Isaiah's secrets," Axis said dryly, wondering again at what had happened between Isaiah and Ishbel before he arrived, "let alone the nature of them. I had thought you to be surprised at the news of Lister's former occupation, but no. I wonder what your interest in Serpent's Nest is, Isaiah. What has Lister told you?"

Isaiah made a vague gesture with his hand, as if to evade the question, but he was saved from any verbal response by Ishbel.

"Do not invade the north, Isaiah," said Ishbel. "Please." She paused. "I don't understand why *you* would want to—"

"Does your Great Serpent tell you his secrets, Ishbel? No? Then why should *I*?"

Ishbel almost shrank back into her chair, and turned aside her face.

There was a lengthy pause, Axis looking carefully between Ishbel and Isaiah.

"Ishbel," Axis said eventually, "has the Great Serpent never mentioned Lister? If Lister had been the god's archpriest, and then vanished, and then took up with the Skraelings, would not the Great Serpent have mentioned it at some point? After all, he warned you about the invasion of the Skraelings—"

And from the ancient evil from the south.

"He might not necessarily mention it," Ishbel said. "The Great Serpent speaks to us directly very infrequently, and then generally only in riddles. It is a habit of gods, I believe." There was a spot more color in her cheeks now.

"Still . . ." said Axis, wishing he knew what the hell was going on between Ishbel and Isaiah. "It is strange, nonetheless. He warned you about the Skraelings, but not about Lister. Very odd."

"And your Great Serpent did not mention *me*?" said Isaiah, refilling his wine goblet and lifting it to his mouth.

"Perhaps he referred to you when he spoke of the great and ancient evil rising from the south," Ishbel said, her tone somewhat tart.

Isaiah's mouth curved about the rim of his wine goblet, but he said nothing.

"There is something I have not yet mentioned," Axis said, having had enough of this bizarre conversation. He rose and fetched the small satchel he'd brought into the chamber with him.

He opened it, and lifted out the glass pyramid.

"Why, Axis," Isaiah said as Axis sat back down, "Ba'al'uz' pyramid. How strange you did not refer to it when earlier you related the adventure of Ishbel's rescue."

Axis sat down in his chair again, idly moving the pyramid from hand to hand.

"It really doesn't look very healthy, Axis," Isaiah continued. "I presume it was like that when you obtained it from Ba'al'uz' men?"

"No," Axis said. "It was perfectly healthy then, a lovely rose color, just like yours. I held it, Isaiah, and do you know what I felt?"

Another raised eyebrow from Isaiah.

"The Star Dance, Isaiah. I felt the Star Dance. You can have no idea how that felt to me . . . or perhaps you do . . ."

"I do not feel this Star Dance when I hold my pyramid, Axis," Isaiah said. "It feels warm, but nothing else."

"They are of Icarii magic, Isaiah."

"I do not know from where Lister obtained them," Isaiah said. "Perhaps they floated over the Widowmaker Sea after Tencendor's destruction. Maybe the Skraelings discovered them when they swarmed through Tencendor so many years ago, and the survivors of their army returned north with them. Perhaps—"

"And perhaps no more 'perhaps,' Isaiah," Axis said. "They are *powerful* Icarii magic. And now in the hands of the Skraelings, and Lister? I wonder how this could be possible."

"Well, two of them are no longer in the hands of the Skraelings or Lister," said Isaiah. "Two of them rest here now, in the palace of Aqhat. But explain, how did the pyramid lose its lovely translucence and dull to that insignificant gray?"

"Whoever held Lister's pyramid closed the link between it and this one the moment they felt my presence through it," said Axis. "Moreover, whoever it was closed its link with the Star Dance completely, so it turned gray and lifeless. Maybe Lister. Maybe someone else."

"Then we have another mystery to solve when finally we meet up with Lister," Isaiah said. "I know nothing of it, Axis."

Axis knew he was lying, but he could also tell Isaiah wasn't worried about Axis keeping the glass pyramid, either.

How many secrets *was* the man hiding?

Axis remembered WolfStar, who had masqueraded as so many different people during his life as StarMan of Tencendor. He remembered the secrets that man had kept, and remembered the harm and untold sadnesses he had wrought.

Yet every instinct in Axis told him Isaiah was not another WolfStar. He kept secrets, yes, and he was also manipulative (if not as much as WolfStar), but there was not the darkness or harm underpinning him as there had been with the renegade Enchanter-Talon.

"Perhaps," Isaiah said in a slow voice, "if these pyramids are such powerful Icarii magic, then this BroadWing you mentioned came to steal this pyramid, not Ishbel."

"They had come to rescue *Ishbel*," Axis said, starting to lose his patience with Isaiah. He felt as if he were being drawn along a long and pointless road just for Isaiah's amusement. "Sent by Maximilian Persimius, Ishbel's husband."

Something glinted then very deep in Isaiah's eyes, but it was gone in an instant.

"Her former husband," said Isaiah. "Maximilian has lost her now."

"You cannot discount him, Isaiah. BroadWing said he would tear apart the very earth for Ishbel."

Again, that strange glint in Isaiah's eyes.

"I, for one," continued Axis, "do not believe he is just going to shrug his shoulders and forget that once he had such a woman to wife."

"Perhaps," murmured Isaiah, and Axis almost threw the damned glass pyramid at him.

Toward midnight, when Ishbel and Axis had gone to their own apartments, Isaiah waved away his servants, called for a horse, and rode to DarkGlass Mountain, where he sat in the Infinity Chamber for an hour, thinking.

Trying to sense Kanubai—and whatever else accompanied him—crawling up the deep rent far below him. How far below? How far below? How much time left? How much?

The ugly brindle dog sat on the far bank of the river, looking at DarkGlass Mountain, and seeing straight through the glass and the stone to where Isaiah sat motionless.

Kanubai did not speak to Isaiah that night.

CHAPTER THREE

Palace of Aqhat, Isembaard

Ishbel had slept for a few hours, mostly from sheer exhaustion, but then her turbulent thoughts woke her. Knowing she would not be able to get back to sleep, she rose, donned an outer gown over her nightdress, and sat in the open window looking out over the vast inner courtyard of the palace.

In order to keep her thoughts at bay for a few minutes, she concentrated on the view. Aqhat—indeed, Isembaard itself—was so beautiful. Ishbel had spent her entire life until this past year in the cold, windswept north, and most of that in the even colder and more windswept Serpent's Nest. She was used to landscapes of blunted trees and tough grasses, cragged mountains and tired, rolling hills, gray mornings and dull days, underpinned by the constant pounding of the surf at the foundations of the mountain.

Here all was sweet, spiced warm winds and soft color, and a clarity and richness of the air which, Ishbel thought, could uplift the most jaded of spirits.

She leaned against the window, looking out into a wide courtyard. The courtyard was dotted here and there with tall palm trees and stands of thick broad-leaved lilies, which wound about the serpentine edges of a reflecting pool. Beyond the courtyard a broad path led down through lawns to the Lhyl. Ishbel could just make out the river's thick reed banks, and hear, very softly, the song of the frogs.

Her hand rested on her belly. The baby was moving, not much, just sweetly and gently, as if it were too languid to be bothered turning over completely in her womb.

She wondered where Maximilian was, and if he were

thinking of her, or of the child. He seemed very far away, almost a dream. If it wasn't for the child inside her, Ishbel thought it might be easy to forget him entirely, to let him go, let her memory of the marriage fade, just drift into the air . . .

She sighed, rousing herself slightly, thinking over the day, and finally allowing herself to think about Isaiah.

He was the god who had spoken to her atop Serpent's Nest. A companion god to the Great Serpent.

He was also a tyrant who planned an invasion of her homeland.

What was happening? *Was* he the great evil from the south that the Great Serpent had warned her about? But if he was, then why were the Serpent and Isaiah—a god of the waters as represented by the frog—so obviously close?

And what did he know about the Lord of Elcho Falling? Why refer to her as this bleak lord's priestess?

Ishbel did not know what to think. What she *felt* from Isaiah, once she got past that cold, arrogant exterior, was genuine warmth and incredible compassion, yet she could not reconcile that with the Isaiah who planned a massive invasion of the north, one which already, via Ba'al'uz, promulgated misery and death.

Ishbel's mind drifted as she sat, and she remembered the warmth of his fingers, and the sweet whispers of the goblet.

Hold me, soothe me, love me.

Hold him, soothe him, love him.

At that very moment Isaiah strode into view from the far side of the courtyard. It was late, almost dawn, and Ishbel wondered where he had been.

She leaned a little farther from the window, holding to its frame for safety, to watch his progress.

She was not surprised, nor particularly perturbed, when he lifted his eyes and saw her.

A few minutes later Ishbel heard the door to her chamber softly open and close.

She was still sitting in the window, and did not look at him as he walked over to her.

"Where have you been?" she said, and then wished she could snatch those words back, for they could be interpreted so many different ways.

"I have been sitting in DarkGlass Mountain," he said, coming to stand close to her and looking out the window. "Do you know of it?"

"Zeboath mentioned it, and Axis thought it might be the ancient evil rising in the south about which the Great Serpent warned me."

He laughed. "But you prefer to think the ancient evil is me."

"Isaiah . . . oh, I don't know what to *call* you . . ."

"Isaiah will do."

"Isaiah, what are you doing? You are the god who spoke to me atop Serpent's Nest, who embraced me with such compassion. Why *this* guise?" She gestured at his body, his attire. "Why the invasion? I cannot understand that of you . . . such cruelty."

"Trust me, Ishbel. Please. All is not as it seems."

"Axis does not know what you are?"

Isaiah gave a brief shake of his head.

"Why not?"

"I want Axis to distrust me slightly. He knows that I am far more than just 'tyrant,' and he knows I have great power."

"Why would you want him to distrust you? He could be a dangerous enemy to you, Isaiah."

"I do not think he will be my enemy. He *is* my friend, but I hope eventually that he will be a great friend to someone *else*. That is why I want him to distrust me, just that little bit. Someone else needs his entire friendship and trust far more than me. Someone else is going to need his advice and support far, far more than me."

"Who?"

Isaiah's mouth curved in a slight smile. "I cannot believe you slapped me on the wharf."

Ishbel accepted the change of subject, and that Isaiah did not want to tell her everything. "You were stupidly arrogant."

"I have an army and ambitious generals to control, Ishbel,

and this fleshed form makes me vulnerable. Perhaps better to keep your ire at my arrogance for more private admonishments, eh?"

There was an edge of rebuke in his voice now, and Ishbel dropped her eyes.

"But you are very courageous," Isaiah said, softly, the warmth back in his voice, "and that is good."

"Courageous? No, I think not. I have spent most of my life trembling at one thing or another."

"Like when people casually drop the name of Elcho Falling into the conversation. Ah, there you go again, tense enough to break should someone drop you."

"His name causes me such pain, and loss, and terrible foreboding."

"All emotions closely allied with the Lord of Elcho Falling."

"*Who is he?*"

"A legend, Ishbel. But . . ."

"But?"

"But a legend for which many yearn."

"Not I."

"Your future is tied to him. I think you know that."

"Isaiah, stop talking in riddles. Please, who is the Lord of Elcho Falling? What is his legend? And why should *I* be tied to him?"

Isaiah sat on the windowsill himself, facing her. "How brave *are* you, Ishbel? What if I said that to prove yourself courageous enough to hear the legend of the Lord of Elcho Falling, you should need to pass a test?"

"I am not a schoolgirl, Isaiah."

"In this matter you are very much the untutored schoolgirl," he said softly, holding her gaze.

Again she dropped her eyes from his, and Isaiah sighed, and changed the subject.

"Tell me about Maximilian. Tell me about your marriage."

"You want a report? I am not sure I am willing to give you one. Leave me my secrets, please, as you choose to keep yours."

"Does he love you, Ishbel?"

She wondered what to say to that. She could have lied, but she was too tired. "He blames me for the chaos in the Central Kingdoms. Ba'al'uz did not simply create the circumstances to favor your invasion, Isaiah, he destroyed my marriage. You and the Great Serpent sent me to marry Maximilian, but *you* also sent north the means by which our marriage has been destroyed. Maximilian hates me, Isaiah. For that blame either Ba'al'uz or yourself, I don't care which."

Isaiah sighed. "I apologize for Ba'al'uz, Ishbel. It was never my intention that he should attack either you or Maximilian, nor did I think Maximilian would blame you for the havoc Ba'al'uz wreaked. Maybe I should have thought more carefully before I sent Ba'al'uz. Maybe even gods make mistakes occasionally. But you are here now, and I confess myself glad. Isaiah the *man* is glad."

"Go away and leave me be, Isaiah. I am tired."

"And no wonder, for I must have caused you much disturbance on several levels today, Ishbel. I shall leave you be now and for the next few days. Then, perhaps, we shall test your courage, yes? To see if you are fit to hear the legend of Elcho Falling?"

CHAPTER FOUR

Deepend, and the Road from Deepend
to the FarReach Mountains

Salome had traveled quickly from Narbon to Deepend, desperate to reach StarDrifter, who she knew was only barely ahead of her. Salome was not quite certain how she knew, but sometimes at night, when she tossed and turned in sleep, she dreamed of the Weeper and heard it call to her.

During the day, she followed the trail of that call.

Just as she was not entirely certain of the precise nature of her knowledge of StarDrifter's location, neither was Salome entirely sure what she would do when she found him. Retrieve the Weeper, yes. Patently it wanted to return to her.

But StarDrifter. Salome blamed him for everything she'd lost. Her son, her life, her power. Everything.

And the degradation. The humiliation. They were what stayed with Salome the most during her long, silent trek east and then south. She could almost understand betrayal; after all, she had dealt enough of it in her lifetime, but the humiliation of herself and her son, their torture, her son's disgusting manner of death, and all accomplished to the laughter of the Corolean crowds . . . that she could not forgive.

Two guides traveled with Salome. The Icarii who'd rescued her had given her money enough for the passage across the Widowmaker Sea and then to hire these guides for several weeks, should she need them. After that, when the money ran out, Salome did not know. It just meant she had to catch StarDrifter sooner rather than later.

Then the Weeper would be hers again, and the world with it.

They'd traveled quickly from Narbon to Deepend, but on the day they arrived at the port town, Salome began to feel so fatigued she needed to sleep for over twelve hours.

The next day Salome felt a little better, but only a little. The day after that such great fatigue, and a queasiness in her stomach besides, encased her once again, and she found it difficult to move from her bed, let alone summon the energy to leave Deepend.

The guides kept watch over her, acquiring food and shelter for her, but they could do little else, and Salome refused a physician.

She knew what was wrong with her, and it only increased her determination to find StarDrifter.

She hated him more than ever.

He *would* pay. He would.

But, oh, it was so hard to find the motivation to get back on her horse and move onward.

Maximilian and his party, on the other hand, were making good time. Despite the disparate natures of the different members, they traveled well enough together, and kept each other good enough company at night that their spirits remained high. During the day BroadWing and his companions surveyed the route ahead from the air, and Maximilian made good use of their eyes and subsequent reports to move forward as fast as possible.

The situation among the Central Kingdoms was now critically grave. In Deepend, Maximilian had heard news of the wars raging between the Outlands, Hosea, and Pelemere. Kyros was being attacked, too, although by whom Maximilian did not know. There had been several major battles, two outside Hosea, one outside Pelemere, and thousands of men had perished.

A nightmare was engulfing the Central Kingdoms, and Maximilian prayed it did not reach Escator.

He wished, suddenly, he had brought the crown of Elcho Falling with him.

What if someone else laid hand to it? If Ruen was attacked, and fell to invaders, then the crown might well be lost.

On the day that the Icarii had scouted the foothills of the FarReach Mountains, seeking a passage through for those on horse, Venetia came to speak quietly to Maximilian at the evening's campfire.

"Maximilian," she said, "I know you have little cause to trust me, for you barely yet know me, but I have something strange to ask of you."

"What?" he said.

"That we wait here a week," she said. "There is someone coming behind us, a sad woman, and ill, who needs to catch us. *We* need her. I cannot say why."

"Who is she?"

Venetia hesitated. "She is this Salome, who StarDrifter has injured so greatly."

"She is behind us?"

"A week away."

This did not surprise Maximilian. It reinforced his sense that somehow everyone was being drawn together.

Salome was needed. Nonetheless . . . "A week is a long time, Venetia."

"That is how long it will take her to reach us. I'm sorry, Maxel, it is important she reach us. I *know* how badly you need to push ahead, but . . . perhaps BroadWing and his companions can use the time to scout a passage for us through the FarReach Mountains, and give them some time also to rest, as they have been doing so much work on your behalf, and—"

"Very well," Maximilian sighed. "Another mouth to feed, then." He gave a slight smile. "Look at what my realm has been reduced to, Venetia. A motley gathering of marsh women, reformed assassins, and crippled Icarii. Who would want to be king of this lot, eh?"

CHAPTER FIVE

At the Foot of the FarReach Mountains

"What do you think it is, Maxel?"

Ravenna sat down by him as he sprawled on his sleeping roll by the fire, the Weeper lying just before him, one of his hands resting lightly on it.

Maximilian gave a slight shrug. "I am not sure." He trusted Ravenna, but he did not wish to speak to her of Elcho Falling. Not yet.

"Aha, an evasive answer."

He smiled a little, and Ravenna took the opportunity to put a hand on his shoulder and lean over for a closer look. "May I touch it, Maxel?"

He was very conscious of her touch and wondered what to make of it. "Yes, of course."

The pressure of her hand lifted as she moved it to the Weeper, gently stroking it several times.

"What did you feel?" said Maximilian.

"Nothing save cool metal. What do *you* feel from it, Maxel?"

How to answer that?

"Contentment, mostly."

"Really?" she said. "How strange. I feel a slight irritation from it, as if it does not like me."

She leaned back from him then, watching him carefully. "I had imagined this wait would chafe at you."

"It does. Still . . ."

"Still?"

"Still, I would prefer this woman Salome to be among my party, and not haunting my back. She does not sound like a woman to cross." He sighed. "But I wish we could move. I spend these idle hours wondering about Ishbel, wondering if she is well, wondering where she is . . ."

"Maxel, what can I do to help?"

Maximilian felt a rush of affection for Ravenna. He took her hand, and kissed it softly.

"Thank you for asking, Ravenna. Tell me, if you will, that I am not in the habit of ruining everyone's lives."

"You have not in the least ruined my life," she said, very softly, "and I am sure everyone here would say the same. None of us were forced to join you. All of us would lose our right arms rather than lose you."

He gripped her hand tightly, then let it go. "I worry so much about Ishbel—this man who has taken her . . . why? Is he taking care of her, and the child? What if—"

"Maxel, stop. I have not met Ishbel but she sounds like a strong woman."

"She is lost, and very afraid."

"As you are lost, and very afraid."

Maximilian gave a slight shrug of his shoulders.

"Maxel . . . would you like me to stay with you tonight?"

For a moment Maximilian did not quite understand what she was saying. Where would she go *other* than staying in this miserable campsite?

Then the meaning of her words hit home, and, gods help him, he reddened.

She gave a soft laugh, then briefly touched his cheek with one finger. "I do hope, Maxel, that Ishbel is as true to you as you are to her. I do hope she deserves you."

"You should have offered when you rescued me from beyond the hanging wall, Ravenna. I would have accepted gladly then."

"Ah," she said, "but then I was young and foolish, and the Lord of Dreams filled my vision. I have come to regret that decision very greatly, Maximilian Persimius."

And with that she rose, and joined her mother sitting at a fire shared with Serge and Doyle.

Venetia had watched the exchange between her daughter and Maximilian from the moment Ravenna had sat down with him. She'd seen the hand on the shoulder, the hair left to brush casually against his face, the brief swell of breast against her robe as Ravenna adjusted her position now and again.

It disturbed Venetia, although she could not for the moment pinpoint why. No marsh woman was particularly monogamous, and they were not renowned for respecting it in others.

But Maximilian . . . there was trouble there, Venetia could sense it.

Still, when Ravenna rejoined her, Venetia said nothing, and the two women spent a companionable hour combing out each other's hair.

Her silence was something, much later, that Venetia would come to regret.

CHAPTER SIX

Palace of Aqhat, Isembaard

After that first, extraordinary day, Ishbel saw little of Isaiah for the next four. She spent the time with Axis and with Zeboath, and sometimes walking about the courtyard. She was escorted at all times by several of Isaiah's spearmen who managed, remarkably, never to intimidate her or make her feel as if her every step was being scrutinized, and the soldier Madarin often accompanied her also, a reassuring presence in the background.

On one of her walks in the courtyard, Ishbel glimpsed Isaiah in a shaded arcade some thirty paces distant, talking with two men. They appeared to be either arguing, or on the verge of it—the two men had assumed such threatening stances that it astounded her.

She turned to Axis, who walked with her on this occasion, and asked him who the men were.

"They are two of his generals," Axis said. "Kezial and Morfah. Very senior men."

One of the generals raised a finger and stabbed it several times at Isaiah, making a point, and Ishbel and Axis could hear the aggression in his raised voice.

"I had not thought Isaiah would allow such disrespect from anyone," Ishbel said. "But . . . he said something the other night, when we were alone, that makes me think Isaiah is vulnerable to his generals."

"Indeed, and may I compliment you on squeezing information out of Isaiah faster than anyone else I know."

Axis meant that as an invitation for Ishbel to speak further, for he was still curious about the underlying communication between them on the night they'd dined.

But Ishbel declined the invitation. "Tell me about the generals, Axis."

"I told you that the Tyrant of Isembaard relies on conquest to keep his generals—his entire tyranny—in line?"

"Yes. You mentioned it to me one evening on our journey down the Lhyl."

"There is always a general lurking in a tyrant's shadow, waiting for that chance to strike. The less successful a tyrant is at conquest, the more likely it is one of his generals will move against him. That man talking now is Morfah, the second most senior of the generals."

"And the other, Kezial, is the most senior?"

Axis shook his head. "No. Ezekiel is the senior general. Thus far he has been loyal to Isaiah, and that has helped to keep the younger generals in line. Isaiah needs a successful invasion of the north and he needs it badly. Ishbel, however you plead with Isaiah, he will not stop an invasion, not on your account."

"He is a strange man," Ishbel said softly.

Axis studied Ishbel carefully, wondering at her tone, and wondering again what had been going on between Isaiah and Ishbel.

"Yes," he responded, "Isaiah is a strange man indeed."

Later that day Zeboath spent some time with Ishbel. They chatted for a while, then Zeboath asked if he might examine her, to check the health of the baby. Ishbel did not mind, for she did not resent Zeboath as she had Garth Baxtor, and she had herself become increasingly worried about the child.

Zeboath spent some minutes feeling the child through the walls of Ishbel's womb, and sat back, his face clouded.

"Zeboath," Ishbel said, "what is wrong?"

"The baby . . ." Zeboath fiddled with his robe, buying time to think.

"What about the baby?" Ishbel said, too sharply.

"The child has not grown as much as I would have expected in the past two weeks, and responded only languidly to my probing. But perhaps that is just the heat, and perhaps the child will add more weight closer to the time of birth. Each pregnancy is different, and each child grows at a slightly different rate, and I do not want you to worry too much."

That was a foolish statement, Ishbel thought. No woman wants a physician, his face all wrapped in anxiety, to say the baby is not growing as it should and then tell her not to fret. She could not pretend to herself that she wanted this baby, and that she did not resent its intrusion into her life and the changes it made to her body, but Ishbel did not wish the baby harm, particularly knowing how much Maximilian wanted the child. She could not fail him in this.

But then, everything associated with her and Maximilian seemed destined for failure, and so perhaps she should not be surprised if this baby, too, failed.

Even that thought did nothing to ease Ishbel's concerns. When Zeboath had gone, she sat for hours by the window, her hand on her belly, trying to will her baby into life.

On the fourth morning after her arrival, Isaiah sent word that Ishbel should prepare herself for a short excursion.

My test, she thought, *to see if·I am fit to hear the legend of the Lord of Elcho Falling,* and felt both nervousness at what Isaiah might have in store for her and a warm delight at the thought of spending some more time in his company. She didn't know what to make of him, and she did not like his plans to invade the north, but the bond she'd felt when she'd looked into his eyes atop Serpent's Nest was still there, and it was too strong to ignore.

Isaiah arrived to collect her himself, walking her down to the courtyard, where waited his horse and a litter for her. His easy manner calmed some of Ishbel's nerves.

"Where do we go?" she asked as he aided her into the seat and bearers stepped forward to lift the litter to their shoulders.

"To a place called DarkGlass Mountain," Isaiah replied, and turned away to mount his horse.

At that, all of Ishbel's nerves returned. "Axis is not coming?" she said.

"No. I have sent him out with a patrol to the east. There are bandits menacing a village, and they need to be dealt with."

They accomplished the journey to DarkGlass Mountain in silence. Isaiah led the way on his horse, Ishbel's litter following and, after that, a squad of armed soldiers who fell into convoy as they left the courtyard. Ishbel's bearers carried her across the river without dampening her with a single drop of water, then along the river road and the processional way approaching DarkGlass Mountain, with smooth, well-practiced movements.

Ishbel should have been distracted from her worry about her baby, for the scenery was lovely, and the day warm rather than hot, cooled by a gentle, scented breeze. The closer her litter-bearers carried her to DarkGlass Mountain, however, the more apprehensive she became. She knew that Axis did not like the place, thinking it the source of the ancient evil to which the Serpent God had referred, but Ishbel had not yet had any cause to think too deeply on the pyramid.

There had been other things to occupy her mind.

But now, as they drew close, and even semireclined in the litter as she was—she had to crane her neck to gaze at the top of it—she felt a great sense of dread.

Images began to flash intermittently in her mind, of men being turned to stone, of spears of blue-green glass flying through the air to impale lovers, of loss so extreme that it became a reason for dying all in itself.

Of an entity, vile beyond comprehension, who lusted for life and warmth and revenge . . . revenge above anything else . . .

"Isaiah," she whispered as they drew to within fifty paces of the pyramid. Remarkably, he heard her, and turned his horse back.

"This will not be pleasant," he said, "but it will be good for you."

Ishbel doubted that very, very much.

* * *

She found it difficult to command her legs to swing over the side of the litter so she could stand up. Isaiah held out his hand, hesitated momentarily, then reached into the litter and helped her out.

"Do this for me, Ishbel, please," he murmured, and Ishbel gave a single, terse nod.

She wished she were anywhere else but here.

Isaiah led her to a small doorway set into the northern face of the pyramid. They stopped just outside, and Isaiah took her hand.

"Ishbel, listen to me. DarkGlass Mountain can do many things to you, but it cannot *harm* you. It cannot do that. It may wish to, quite desperately, but it cannot harm you. I am here with you, and I will protect you from any other dangers that may lurk."

Ishbel stared into the doorway, seeing what appeared to be a tunnel made of fused black glass stretching away into darkness. "I've changed my mind, Isaiah. I don't want to go in."

His grip on her hand tightened—comfortingly, rather than in any effort to further persuade her. "Ishbel, there is something inside I need you to see. I think you might be able to understand it where I can't. I—"

"If *you* are not strong enough, then how can *I* be?"

"Ishbel, you are so strong, and you have more understanding than I shall ever have." He paused. "Ishbel, you say that whenever you think of the Lord of Elcho Falling you feel overwhelming sadness and loss. What if I tell you that if you help me in this, then perhaps we can both avoid that sadness and loss."

She almost hated him then. "You have *no* idea what I have been through already, as a child, when—"

"I know what happened to you when you were eight, Ishbel. I know *exactly* what happened to you, while *you* live wrapped in false memories that have warped your understanding and your very being. Perhaps we will talk about this later. For now, Ishbel, I am *begging* you to come into this pyramid with me."

Ishbel stared at him. He knew what had happened to her when she was eight?

"Very well," she said, agreeing not so much because of anything Isaiah had said, but for the pleading in his eyes.

He smiled slightly, and nodded at her, then led her inside DarkGlass Mountain.

She could feel its hatred of her the moment she set foot to glass.

DarkGlass Mountain loathed her; she felt it running up her legs and her spine every time she moved forward a pace.

Isaiah kept a firm grip on her hand, and she kept very close to him, walking in the shadow of his warmth, and that gave her the fortitude to endure the visions that DarkGlass Mountain threw at her.

The visions she'd encountered on the way to the pyramid were as nothing compared to these.

She saw entire populations slaughtered, and other populations living in thrall to DarkGlass Mountain. She saw men and women and babies turned to stone, and then rise and walk, their souls weeping inside their shambling stone coffins.

She turned a corner, moving into another corridor within DarkGlass Mountain, and she saw her father, standing ten or twelve paces away, holding out his hand imploringly and calling her name as his flesh marbled into stone in a tide of death that swept up his legs and through his body.

Ishbel cried out, stumbling closer to Isaiah.

"That is not your father," he murmured to her. "That was Tirzah's father. Come now, not much farther."

I can do that to everyone you love, Ishbel. Everyone.

Ishbel moaned.

"An idle threat for the moment, Ishbel," Isaiah murmured. "He has not the strength for it. He relies on nightmares rather than actions. Come now, you are stronger than this. Be brave for me, Ishbel."

She nodded, straightened her back, and walked on.

* * *

He brought her, eventually, to a chamber of exquisite beauty. The hatred here was muted, and Ishbel allowed herself to relax, just a fraction, but enough to feel as if she could breathe again.

Isaiah gave her a smile, and squeezed her hand.

"Thank you," he said, and Ishbel was suddenly very glad she had managed to come this far.

"Was that the test?" she said, looking at the caged golden glass.

It seemed familiar, somehow.

"Mostly," said Isaiah. "What do you think of this chamber?"

"It is very beautiful, but . . . oh, the sadness here."

"This pyramid was once called Threshold, Ishbel—" He stopped as he saw her flinch.

So.

"This chamber was known as the Infinity Chamber," Isaiah continued, "because the men who built Threshold used it to open a doorway into Infinity."

Ishbel shuddered, and wrapped her arms about her shoulders. "It was a bad thing to do," she said.

"Yes," Isaiah said, "it was indeed. Ishbel . . ." He took one of her hands, and wrapped it in both of his. "Ishbel, I want to take you on a journey with me, share with you some of my sight. Will you trust me?"

She gave a reluctant nod of her head.

He took a deep breath. "It will be for a moment only, and when I pull you out of it I am going to ask you what you saw, what you *felt*. Your impressions are as gold to me. Will you do that?"

Another nod.

"Very well. Ishbel, watch with me."

Using his power, Isaiah opened up his senses to Ishbel, showing her what he saw.

Kanubai, far below them, his long, thin dark fingers inching ever upward, grasping hold of every crevice in the wall of the abyss that he could.

Ishbel gasped, and Isaiah increased the pressure about her hand, trying to reassure her.

Kanubai's eyes, shining red, malevolent, all-seeing. Seeing them.

And the something else that hovered about Kanubai, the something that Isaiah could not quite discern.

Ishbel took in a breath that was almost a shriek, and Isaiah broke the connection.

"Ishbel—"

We need to get out of here now!

Isaiah was so astounded that Ishbel had used hitherto untouched power to communicate with him that for an instant he did not react.

That instant almost cost them their lives.

The golden glass surrounding them turned black, then translucent, and then, unbelievably, hundreds if not thousands of faces and hands appeared behind the glass.

Anger and agony consumed every face.

Suddenly the glass walls began to rush toward Ishbel and Isaiah, converging on them as if the weight of the faces and hands was too much for it to bear.

Then the glass exploded, and Ishbel and Isaiah felt a blast of heat from the suddenly freed flesh waiting behind it.

Isaiah reacted instantly. He dragged Ishbel toward the door, feeling as they went through a hand grab at Ishbel's hair. He yanked at her with all his strength, pulling her through, and then they were running, running, running through the black tunnels, fingers and teeth snapping behind them at every step, until they tumbled forth into the sunlight beyond the pyramid, and peace once more returned to their world.

Satisfied that the danger was now past, Isaiah gathered Ishbel and held her until her shaking stopped.

"I am sorry," he said. "I had no idea it was that powerful."

Then, unable to help himself, he asked her what she had seen in the vision he'd shared with her.

"A being, darkness, crawling toward the surface," Ishbel said, very low.

Isaiah nodded. *Kanubai.* "There was something else—"

She leaned in against him, almost burying her face in his

chest so that he had to strain to hear her muffled words.

"He is being helped to the surface," she said. "He does not rise on his own power alone."

Isaiah went very cold.

"The pyramid is aiding him, Isaiah. The pyramid is angry. Consumed with hate. It wants revenge for some slight in its past. It . . . it has cast down to . . ."

"His name is Kanubai," Isaiah said softly.

"The pyramid has cast down to Kanubai a rope of knotted souls, souls of the pyramid's victims. That *being* below, Kanubai, rises partly under his own power, but he is aided far more powerfully by the pyramid. Isaiah, can we leave here now? Please."

CHAPTER SEVEN

The Palace of Aqhat, Isembaard

What have you done? Were you mad, to expose Ishbel like that?

Isaiah was not in the least surprised that Lister should contact him in such a fury. He was glad only that Lister had left it until Isaiah was back in his private quarters.

"She is the only one who can truly read the pyramid," Isaiah said. "We needed to know what was happening. We *needed* to, damn it! Ishbel was strong. In the end she survived."

"In the end she survived." Oh, what arrogance. You put her at such risk!

"And you put *us* at risk by communicating in this manner!" Isaiah snapped. "Is that not why we had the pyramids, so that Kanubai would not know—"

You berate me over such a detail when you have just returned from taking Ishbel into DarkGlass Mountain? Besides, you've used this method before. Stop trying to distract the conversation from your stupidity, Isaiah.

There was a silence.

Tell me what you learned, then.

Isaiah gave a soft laugh. "Really, you want to hear? After all this posturing about what a bad boy I have been?"

Tell me, Isaiah.

"The pyramid is as dangerous, probably more so, than Kanubai. It aids him to the surface. Ishbel said it has cast down a rope of lost souls to Kanubai, who uses it to haul himself upward. I think it possible the pyramid means to use Kanubai. We are going to battle two enemies, my friend, and

I think we may have been concentrating on the wrong one all this time."

Lister made a formless sound which Isaiah interpreted as part curse, part cry of frustration.

What can we do? Lister said eventually.

"Nothing more than what we have been. The invasion must go ahead. You cannot stop the Skraelings, and I . . . well, I need to attain the north."

How strong are they?

"They," Isaiah noted with a great weariness. Until today there had been but "one."

"Not so strong that they can strike yet. Kanubai needs to feed, and the pyramid . . . it is still waiting for something. Possibly Kanubai himself."

Where is Ba'al'uz?

"In Coroleas, I suppose. The man is not *here*, and that is all that matters. I have men set to guard Ishbel. She is safe."

We need to move soon, Isaiah. You are a laggard. I sense no great preparations for invasion.

"All is progressing smoothly."

You will need to move within a few weeks.

"Don't pester me, Lister! We dance a dangerous game here. One misstep—"

Such as today's adventure.

"—and all is lost."

Isaiah, you need to mobilize soon. I have heard reports that Maximilian has left Escator for Isembaard. He hunts his wife. Isaiah, he cannot get too close to DarkGlass Mountain—

"I will mobilize when I am good and ready, Lister! Autumn has barely set in, and surely the Skraelings will not move before winter."

I think today's adventure has shown that we need to move sooner than that. Isaiah—

"Leave me in peace, Lister. I am tired, and need to rest."

Ishbel sat in her chamber, curiously calm. After what she'd been through within DarkGlass Mountain she assumed she would have been rendered agitated, scared, emotional.

But, no.

What she had seen and intuited about the pyramid was terrifying. She shuddered every time she thought about those desperate, angry, agonized faces pressed against the glass.

About how they had broken through, reached for her, chased her.

She knew she'd been exposed to a malignant power this day, a power that for some unknown reason knew her and loathed her. But there was something else she'd felt, *heard*, that she had not told Isaiah.

The golden glass had spoken to her. Just before it had turned black, just before the faces and hands had appeared, the glass had said to her:

The strength of the malignancy's hatred of you is a direct reflection of your own strength, Ishbel. Use it.

Lister strode around in circles. Snow blew about him, ice crystals flew up from the impact of his boots, Skraelings drifted out of the mist to stare briefly at him, and then vanish.

Eleanon, Inardle, and Bingaleal stood to one side. High above, several more of the Lealfast rode the icy air currents, watching.

Lister was angry.

More, he was furious.

"I can't believe he put Ishbel in such danger," he said.

"Still," said Eleanon. "Now you have discovered that the pyramid—"

Lister swore, and Eleanon stopped speaking, his face assuming a martyred expression.

"He's not moving, and he should be, he *should*!" Lister said. "Especially now, especially after what he discovered today. Damn him, why doesn't he move?"

"Perhaps—" Inardle began, but Lister ignored her.

"I don't know *what* he is playing at," Lister continued. "What *is* he doing? *What*? Gods alone know where Ba'al'uz is, and I don't like that. I need to get Isaiah moving, damn it. *I need to get Ishbel out of Aqhat and further north!*"

He stopped suddenly, turning on his heel and striding over to the group of Lealfast.

"And can you imagine what will happen if *Maximilian* arrives down there?" Lister said, hands flung wide apart in an extravagant gesture. "Gods . . . *gods*, what game is Isaiah playing?"

He paused. "My friends, I need one of you to go to Aqhat for me. A small, but pleasurable task."

"Any of us," said Inardle. "I will go."

"Not you," Lister, Eleanon, and Bingaleal said as one.

"*I* will go," said Bingaleal. "I am stronger and more experienced."

Lister gave a nod. "I don't want to lose you, Bingaleal. Be careful."

"Most certainly," said Bingaleal. "What is it you wish me to do?"

"I need you to assassinate Isaiah."

CHAPTER EIGHT

The Palace of Aqhat, Isembaard

"Ishbel. Every evening I go to the River Lhyl to bathe. Will you join me on this occasion?" Isaiah gave a small smile. "I have a legend to relate to you."

Ishbel looked at Isaiah standing in the door of her chamber, a bevy of servants and attendants standing behind him carrying towels and unguents and perfumes and whatever else it might be that a tyrant needed for his evening ablutions. He looked so calm, so normal, it was strange to think that earlier today they'd been standing amid the malevolent darkness of DarkGlass Mountain.

Ishbel stood a moment, thinking, then decided that there was nothing to decide.

"Yes," she said, "I'll just fetch—"

"I have everything you need," Isaiah said very quietly.

Ishbel went very still for a moment; then she simply nodded, and took Isaiah's proffered arm.

Isaiah led her to a stone-paved area on the riverbank that was screened by reeds and a silken pavilion. The area was so enclosed that not only did it offer its occupants complete privacy, but also screened them from the outside world. Once Ishbel stepped into this area and Isaiah waved away all the attendants after they had deposited their loads, she felt as if she were enclosed in an entire world. She could see nothing of Aqhat, nor of DarkGlass Mountain (for which she was most grateful), and could hear only the gentle murmuring of the river, the breeze as it filtered through the reed banks, and the opening notes of the dusk chorus of the frogs. A lamp set to one side sent out muted scarves of light that wove their soft way about the reeds and water.

The stone platform sloped down to the water, where, just visible under the rippling water, it descended further in a series of broad steps.

"This is a special place to me," Isaiah said, picking up some towels from a pile and scattering them on the dry stone just above the river's edge. "The river is the land's lifeblood, its very soul."

"I know how special this must be to you, Isaiah," she said. "It is beautiful. So serene."

He gave her a soft smile at that. "Yes. Now, come, bathe."

He stripped off his linen hipwrap, kicked off his sandals, and stepped into the water, sitting down on one of the submerged steps so that the water came to his waist. He had a floating jar of soap with him, and he tipped some out and lathered up his face, chest, and arms.

Ishbel hesitated, then discarded her own robe and sandals, shook out her long hair, and joined Isaiah on the submerged step. She did not mind her nakedness with him, but hated her distended body—feeling a wash of guilt for that dislike—and breathed a sigh of relief as she sank into the warm water. The stone step was very smooth and, as the water took much of her weight, Ishbel relaxed, feeling more comfortable than she had in many days.

Isaiah pushed the floating dish of soap toward her. "Tell me what happened when you were a child, Ishbel."

Ishbel had reached for the dish of soap, but stilled as Isaiah spoke. "You said you *knew* what happened."

"Yes, but I would like to hear what you think happened. Somehow, I think that my understanding and yours differ markedly."

Ishbel soaped up her hands, then rubbed them slowly up and down her upper arms—not so much washing as forming a protective barrier between her and the outside world.

"When I was eight a plague came suddenly to my parents' house," she said, not looking at Isaiah, who had finished washing and was now leaning back on the steps, watching her. "Everyone within the house, the extended family and all servants, died within a day and a night. Everyone save me. Does that marry with your understanding, then?"

"Yes. That marries with my understanding. Go on."

"The city folk would not allow me to escape, fearing that I might carry the plague out into their number, so they blocked all doors and windows and remained outside, waiting for me to die so they could burn down the house. Does that marry with your understanding, Isaiah of Isembaard?"

"Not quite. Here is where I think our tales might begin to diverge. But continue, Ishbel, please."

"*I* wanted to die. You can hardly imagine what it was like in that house, Isaiah . . . or are you about to tell me that you can—"

"No," he said, very quietly, "I cannot even begin to imagine what it was like for you. I can only try to understand. Ishbel, continue, please."

Ishbel dashed a tear from her eye, wincing a little as the soap stung.

"I tried to die. I rolled in the pus draining from my mother's body. I . . ." Ishbel had to stop and take a deep breath. "Then, one day . . . oh gods . . . my mother's corpse began to speak to me, and then the corpses of everyone else in the—"

"Stop, Ishbel. This is where I cannot allow you to continue. You have lived with this horror all these years, and it has turned you in upon yourself as you shut out the world. But it is a lie. Their bodies did not—"

She rounded on him, distraught. "How can you say that! You were not there! You can have no idea what—"

"Ishbel—"

"—happened to me! How can you tell me that—"

"It was not the bodies of your parents and loved ones who spoke to you, Ishbel. It was their jewelry."

She froze, staring at him.

"That is why," he said, so softly, "you have spent your subsequent life avoiding jewelry of any kind and why, most particularly, you do not wear Maximilian Persimius' ring."

She remained silent, still staring at him, stricken.

Isaiah pushed himself over to her, ignoring her start as he put his hand on her shoulder. "Duck your head underwater a moment," he said, "and wet your hair. Then, as I wash it for you, I shall tell you the tale of Elcho Falling, of DarkGlass Mountain, and how both of these connect with your family. Hold your breath a moment . . . ah, good, now push me that dish of soap."

Ishbel could hardly breathe as his strong fingers began, very slowly, to massage soap into her scalp.

"Listen to me," he said, his voice soothing and rhythmical, "as I tell you the tale of Elcho Falling. It begins with a man named Avaldamon who lived in the Northern Kingdoms. Avaldamon was the younger brother of a man named Fledge. Fledge was an extraordinary man, a powerful mage, and he was also the Lord of Elcho Falling."

Isaiah felt Ishbel tense a little, but he continued on, his voice calm and soothing.

"But this is the tale of Avaldamon, not of Fledge. Avaldamon was also a powerful mage, although he could not match the power of his brother. He, as Fledge, were Elementals. Elementals, my love, are those who can hear the elements that comprise glass and metals and gems."

"Oh," Ishbel murmured, and she felt Isaiah lean forward very slightly, just enough to kiss the top of her head.

"And, yes, Ishbel," he said, "you are an Elemental, too. Elementals can not only *hear* the elements, they can often manipulate them. It was your family's jewels that spoke to you, *not* their corpses.

"Anyway, Avaldamon, a powerful Elemental mage, traveled very far south into this land, then called Ashdod. He married a princess, but soon after their marriage he was killed by a great water lizard. The princess gave birth to a son, Boaz, also a powerful Elemental mage, although he denied it for many years. Boaz became one of the Magi who built DarkGlass Mountain, and it was Boaz who opened it into Infinity and created the burgeoning disaster we have now: when Boaz opened DarkGlass Mountain to Infinity, then so was the crack opened to Kanubai, who you saw earlier.

"But Boaz was also the one who eventually managed to

quell the pyramid's power, and to have it dismantled. Boaz loved a woman called Tirzah, once a slave who had aided in the construction of that beautiful golden chamber we stood in earlier. Like Boaz, Tirzah was a powerful Elemental. It was she who carved the Goblet of the Frogs, and it was she who persuaded Boaz to accept his Elemental heritage. DarkGlass Mountain hates Elementals, because it was two powerful Elementals, Boaz and Tirzah, who caused its destruction."

"No wonder it hates me."

"No wonder. Now, duck your head under, that I might rinse this lather from your hair."

Ishbel held her breath as Isaiah pushed her under the water with gentle hands, using his fingers to rinse and comb out the soap from her long hair. When she emerged again, spluttering a little, he wrung out her hair, then put his arms around her shoulders, drawing her back against his body as he continued to speak.

Ishbel felt very much at peace, even though Isaiah related a tale that would normally have made her uncomfortable. This was due entirely to Isaiah's presence, to his soothing touch, to the depth of compassion that shone from his eyes, and due to that instantaneous bond they'd formed that first time they'd communicated atop Serpent's Nest. She felt very close to him, and at ease, and she could not, at any point previously in her life, have imagined feeling this close to anyone.

Not even with Maximilian, Ishbel?

"Oh no, Isaiah," she murmured, hardly even aware of either question or answer. "He makes me too uncomfortable."

I am not surprised.

"But where does my family fit into all of this?" Ishbel said.

"Boaz and Tirzah had three children. Their eldest was a girl, and in her adult life she traveled north, to what are the Outlands—but which then were called something entirely different—and she married a man called Imreen Brunelle."

"Oh!"

"Aye, Ishbel, you are descended from the line of Boaz and Tirzah and, like them, you are an Elemental. You are also, through Avaldamon, Boaz's father, of the line of the Lords of Elcho Falling, who are powerful mages, and powerful Elementals. DarkGlass Mountain hates you for two reasons, Ishbel. You are not only an Elemental, but you are directly descended from the two people who caused its dismantling thousands of years ago."

"May I ask a question?" Ishbel said.

"Of course," Isaiah said.

"Maximilian can also hear the elements. He talked to me about the rings." She gave a soft laugh devoid of humor. "I didn't want to listen."

"Then he must also be an Elemental, Ishbel." *Gods, he thought privately, don't you yet realize, Ishbel? How can you be so blind?* "The ability to hear the elements was not confined to one family, nor even to one race. It appears in many families of this continent."

"You are an Elemental, besides being a river god?"

He laughed. "Yes. I am truly multitalented."

She smiled, and Isaiah almost cursed Ishbel for her easy manner in moving so smoothly past Maximilian in their conversation.

"Why do I sense such foreboding and loss whenever I think of the Lord of Elcho Falling?" Ishbel asked. "I dream of him constantly, and my dreams always terrify me. I had thought that he was a lord of despair, but from what you say . . . not?"

"Most definitely not, Ishbel. He is a mage of such power that the very stars themselves would bend knees before him, if they met. He is a man who, once he assumes his full power, shall command me, and even your Great Serpent. DarkGlass Mountain loathes him because he is the most powerful Elemental in existence, and thus is capable of destroying it. Kanubai hates him . . . well, because a very long time ago the Lord of Elcho Falling was partly responsible for his imprisonment. As to your vision of foreboding and loss . . . well, it is not for me to explain that."

"I have also had a vision of handing to the Lord of Elcho Falling the Goblet of the Frogs. Is that because he is such a powerful Elemental mage?"

"Yes. It truly belongs with him. In the right hands it might become a weapon." *And sometimes, Ishbel, you need to open your eyes, and your ears, and your damn heart, and just accept.*

This thought also he kept from her, and Isaiah sighed, and gathered Ishbel a little closer. She and Maximilian clearly had caused a rift in their relationship, and Isaiah wondered if they'd be able to close that rift by themselves.

Sometimes lovers needed a little help.

Sometimes they needed to be shown just what they had lost.

And sometimes hopeful lovers, Isaiah thought ruefully, thought up any reason they could to justify their own actions. He was more than a little in love with Ishbel himself, and most assuredly attracted to her. Sitting here so close together had set his entire body afire.

Maximilian might tear apart the earth for her, but he wasn't here now.

"I have no real idea why Ba'al'uz sent you to me," Isaiah said, "but the excuse he gave me was that you would make me a good wife. A wife stolen from a northern king makes a good trophy. Such a wife would consolidate my position as tyrant, Ishbel. My generals mutter, and my throne is often not as secure as I would like. Water god I may be, but when I am incarnate in flesh I am as vulnerable as any man, and the swords of my generals beckon. If you became my wife, then my position would be strengthened. You would be a help to me. It can be whatever manner of marriage you wish—a true marriage or a pretense, I do not care. Either way you will help consolidate my position."

"I do not want a husband, pretend or otherwise, who will invade my homeland," she said. "I still do not understand why you do that. It is not like the being I know you are."

He gave another small shrug. "I have my reasons, Ishbel, and for the moment I cannot share them with you."

"And this baby?" she said.

There was regret in her voice, and confusion and pain, and Isaiah was glad to hear it.

"Perhaps we can give it back to Maximilian when it is born, yes?"

That was a suggestion so close to the pact that she and Maximilian had made between them that it left Ishbel wordless.

"We shall make a marriage soon, then. I shall arrange a Spectacle, which is a somewhat grand and pretentious word for holding a high court, very formal, and announce to all and sundry—making sure my generals are present—that we were married, um, shall we say, in the heart of DarkGlass Mountain? Yes? That will give the marriage so much more importance. So much more *mystery*."

Ishbel smiled, partly at his words, partly at his teasing tone.

"I do not know that I want another husband," she said.

Isaiah laughed, very soft and low, and one of his hands strayed to her breast. "Maximilian had his serpent bride, and lost her. Now, perhaps, I shall take what has slipped through his fingers."

Ishbel sat up and moved away from him, crossing her arms over her breasts.

"I understand you have wives already. I do not wish to be your . . . what? eighty-fifth? eighty-sixth? That is no honor."

"I shall set aside my other wives, for they have never interested me. You shall be my only wife. My Favored Wife."

Ishbel sat in the gentle, warm waters of the Lhyl, and listened to the growing chorus of the frogs in the evening.

"We can marry now," Isaiah said to her, his eyes black in the gloom, "and, should you wish to, consummate our marriage only after the child is born."

"Why are you so afraid of your generals?"

"Because I failed badly once, and cannot afford to again. Help me, Ishbel."

"Put aside your lust for war, I beg you."

"I cannot, for otherwise we all die. Marry me, Ishbel."

"I am already married."

"You would not wear your husband's ring, and he lost you. Marry me, yes?"

Ishbel sat, the water lapping away all her doubts, the song of the frogs soothing her wariness, and thought about how easy and comfortable she had felt with Isaiah, and how easy

and comfortable he made her feel about something that had
only ever frightened her with Maximilian.

"I am not a good wife," she said, "and I am an even worse
woman."

"I am a good teacher," he said, and for some reason that
made sense to Ishbel, and clarified her path for her.

"Very well," she said, and hoped that the seductive touch
of both Isaiah and the River Lhyl had not deprived her of
all common sense. She glanced toward where she knew
DarkGlass Mountain rose. "Isaiah, are we in danger from
DarkGlass Mountain, and what lurks beneath it?"

"Not just yet. We have some time."

"When can we leave here?"

"Soon, my darling. Soon."

They eventually walked back to the palace, the servants and
attendants falling in behind them as they left the riverbank,
and no one among them, not even Isaiah, saw the ugly brindle dog crouched down within the reed beds.

It watched the procession all the way back to the palace,
but it had eyes for nothing but Ishbel's belly.

There lay power and, finally, *finally*, life and breath.

And revenge.

At DarkGlass Mountain, unseen by any living eye, shadows started to move under the glass that plated the entire
pyramid as, deep in the abyss, Kanubai moved toward wakefulness, hand over hand, up the knotted rope of souls.

North, Ba'al'uz stumbled through the ruins of Setkoth, bumping and bruising his way through the tumbled
masonry.

He no longer had much of a mind left, but what there was
of it concentrated on one matter only.

Ishbel, her baby, and the rewards of final union with
Kanubai.

CHAPTER NINE

The Palace of Aqhat, Isembaard

Axis stamped his feet as he drew off his riding gloves, trying to get some circulation back into his lower legs after a long ride home. He was standing in the large courtyard that served the main stable area of the palace, and about him men and horses milled in the lamplight as almost three hundred soldiers tried to dismount and get their horses unsaddled at once.

"Axis?" It was Insharah, who had again served as his second-in-command on this expedition. Axis was growing to like and respect him very much, and had enjoyed his week away with the man and the four hundred strong column of spearmen and swordsmen.

Had enjoyed a week away in the saddle again, fighting.

"Insharah. Time to get home to your wife, eh? We were away a little longer than anticipated and she will be anxious. It is too late at night now to hang about here. Go home."

Insharah grinned at him. "If I go home now she will berate me for waking her. Some of the men propose a game of Kus, and a barrel of barley wine. Join us?"

Axis grinned. "I must be getting old, my friend, for all I want at the moment is my bed. I'll check with you tomorrow. Make sure those men who are injured receive proper care from the physicians."

Insharah nodded, and walked off. Axis turned and headed for the archway that led through to the palace proper, lost in thought. The expedition *had* been good for him. There had been real fighting—the bandits who had been harrying the villages to the east belonged to a group almost one hundred and fifty strong, and they'd built themselves a good base in nearby mountains. There had been two days of hard fighting, several men lost, many injured, but Axis' sword had been bloodied, and his battle lust fully ignited.

Coming back to Aqhat had caused him some gut-draining disappointment.

He wondered what Isaiah was preparing him for. Would Isaiah want to give him a large command for the invasion? And what would Axis do if this was the case? Bandits were one thing, but the last thing Axis really wanted to do was lead fighting men against the armies of the Northern Kingdoms, with whom he had no quarrel.

"Perhaps I could divert to one side," he muttered to himself, "and skewer me some Skraelings. I wonder if Isaiah would notice."

"That would be an interesting maneuver," said a dry voice, and Axis jumped, then instantly felt annoyed for allowing himself to be caught unawares.

No soldier should ever relax.

Ezekiel, the eldest and most senior of Isaiah's generals, peeled himself off a shadowy wall and walked into a faint pool of light cast by the moon.

"And I am quite sure Isaiah would both notice *and* disapprove," the general said, coming to a halt a pace or two away from Axis.

"Then I shall have to be careful to learn your skill at shadowy movement," said Axis, even more annoyed at himself for the sharp tone in his voice.

Now Ezekiel knows for certain he caught you off-guard.

This was the first time Axis had ever talked alone with Ezekiel, and he studied the general with undisguised frankness. What reason had the man for seeking him out?

"May I ask how your expedition went?" said Ezekiel. "Most of the men you led were once commanded by me. I have . . . how shall we say this, a—"

Proprietary, thought Axis.

"—fatherly interest in them."

"We rode to the village of Mentara," Axis said. "You know it?"

"I was born there."

Axis felt as though he was walking over needles of glass laid down on a bed of hot coals.

"Bandits, well over a hundred strong," Axis said, "had established a base in the mountains nearby, and were harrying villages along the road from Mentara to the Lhyl. We had to draw them out of their stronghold, then double back and clean out their camp. They were good fighters. It is a shame they didn't want to join Isaiah's army."

"Isaiah loses many of his men to the lure of the mountain encampments," Ezekiel said, and continued talking before Axis, patently curious, asked why. "Axis, let me walk you to your quarters. There is something I'd like to ask of you."

Axis wondered if he were about to be offered a place within a cabal plotting against Isaiah, and wondered further how long he would live if he declined it.

They walked into the center of the courtyard, talking generalities, before Axis asked what was on his mind.

"Isaiah has called a Spectacle in three days time," Ezekiel said, coming to a halt and forcing Axis to do the same. "You know what that is?"

Axis frowned. Ezekiel had drawn him into the very center of the courtyard, which the windows of Isaiah's private quarters gazed upon. Their conversation might not be heard, but the odds that Isaiah would see them standing here talking quietly, or have someone report to him that Ezekiel and Axis had been plotting away at midnight, were astronomical.

Axis put his hands on his hips. "Yes. I know what it is. What do you want, Ezekiel?"

"I want to know what he is up to, Axis."

"For the stars' sakes, Ezekiel, I have been away this past week. I have no idea."

"I have heard rumor it is to marry Ishbel. Or at least to announce the *fact* of their marriage."

"Isaiah is always taking new wives," Axis said, although the news disturbed him. He wondered what Ishbel thought about it, and wondered also that Isaiah had apparently managed to set aside his famous dislike of pregnant women.

"The palace chamberlain told me," Ezekiel said, "that

Isaiah took Ishbel deep into DarkGlass Mountain last week, while you were away, and there they married amid powerful dark magic. Is this possible?"

Axis just stared, unable for the moment to process all this information.

"Ah . . ." he said, stalling for time. *What was Isaiah up to? Was this why Axis had been sent away for a week? So Isaiah could play?*

Ezekiel was watching Axis very carefully. "How powerful is Ishbel's husband, Maximilian?"

"Well, that I can answer readily enough," Axis said. "Maximilian is a very quiet man, one who keeps many secrets. He is charismatic and resourceful and has survived what kills most men. You have heard his story?"

Ezekiel shook his head.

Axis briefly told the general of Maximilian's seventeen years trapped beneath the hanging wall, and of his rescue.

"He does not control great wealth, nor great armies," Axis concluded, "but—"

"He is a dangerous man."

"He is a man to be watched, yes."

Ezekiel chewed the inside of his cheek, thinking. "So if Isaiah had truly won his bride from Maximilian, then Isaiah is stronger than many believe," he said eventually. "But if Maximilian regains her, well then . . ."

Axis shrugged his shoulders. "Is that all you wanted to talk to me about?" he said. "I am tired, and long for my bed."

Ezekiel's eyes gleamed. "The only reason I wanted to talk to you, Axis," he said, "was to get your measure."

And with that he turned on his heel, and was off.

Axis looked after him for a long moment, then glanced upward to Isaiah's windows.

The tyrant was standing there, looking down.

Axis thought for a moment about going to see him, but then decided he was too tired, so he, in turn, spun on his heel and strode for the stairway to his apartment.

Isaiah would have to wait.

CHAPTER TEN

Northern Isembaard

*B*a'al'uz? Ba'al'uz? Where are you?
  Ba'al'uz had been driving himself for weeks now, feeding on little more than the power infused into him by Kanubai.

He had not eaten in over two weeks, and had not drunk any liquid in ten days. He had not slept in five days. By rights, his body should have shut down, if not died, but Ba'al'uz kept on walking, eyes wide and staring in a face leathered and battered by deprivation and the elements. His gait was uneven, his clothes tattered, his mind occupied with only two thoughts: to gain Aqhat, and regain Kanubai's favor.

Those that saw him stared, then stumbled away, desperate not to come to his notice.

Ba'al'uz appeared not merely crazed, but as if gray shadows of sorrow, or maybe retribution, trailed behind him.

Ba'al'uz? Ba'al'uz? Where are you?

"Setkoth," Ba'al'uz managed to get out on his fifth attempt at mouthing the word. "Setkoth."

Not far from Aqhat then.

"Three days, Great One, no more."

Excellent. Ba'al'uz, you do need to hurry. I should not want to have to use someone else to carry out my desires.

"I will hurry, Great One. I will."

You must, you must. Nearer and nearer draws the time.

Ba'al'uz lurched on, one insane footstep after the other.

CHAPTER ELEVEN

The FarReach Mountains, Southern Kyros

They'd made good distance over the past few days, mainly because Salome was no longer feeling quite so fatigued. The two guides traveling with her were palpably relieved, to Salome's grim amusement.

What man ever liked a weak woman?

Gods, she hated them, too.

StarDrifter was not far ahead. Salome could sense it. She wasn't sure why, or how she knew this—perhaps that extraordinary sexual magnetism somehow communicated itself to her, even now—but just ahead he most certainly was.

The weather was sliding deeper into autumn. The mornings were frosty, the nights had that edge of ice to them associated with winter, and made sleeping uncomfortable. Salome was glad that StarDrifter was still this side of the FarReach Mountains. At least she could deal with him now, finish what lay between them, without having to voyage through the mountains in ever-deteriorating weather.

On this day they were traveling at a brisk trot along a little-used path, heading directly for the mountains that rose perhaps a day's ride away; pink and purple massifs that wore tangled clouds about their snowy peaks and promised enormous hardship for those foolish enough to risk the passes. The guides had told Salome that few people dared to try— the FarReach Mountains effectively cut off Isembaard from the Northern Kingdoms.

Salome didn't care about the mountains.

All she wanted was her chance at StarDrifter.

In the midafternoon, when she was tired enough that her

attention had begun to lag, one of the guides murmured a caution.

"Someone approaches."

Salome jerked to full attention, looking ahead.

A lone rider, a man, approached them on the road. He was bare-headed and unarmed, and did not appear surprised to see the three travelers halting their horses.

He pulled his own horse to a stop a few paces away from Salome and her guides.

"My name is Maximilian," he said. "Of Escator."

Salome frowned, trying to remember where she'd heard that name. It may not have come to her so quickly, had not she noticed the sudden servile demeanor of the guides.

"Oh," she said, "you're the King of Escator."

He smiled very slightly. "Yes. I am the King of Escator."

Salome's frown deepened. There'd been some trouble with the King of Escator. In fact, there had always been trouble, of one sort or another, associated with this man's life. Salome tried to remember the details, but her life had been so centered on Coroleas and on her own schemes that she'd paid scant attention to what happened elsewhere in the world.

"I'm sorry," she said vaguely, and hoped that would cover most eventualities in this man's history.

His smile widened, his dark blue eyes danced, and Salome suspected she had just made a complete fool of herself.

"That is very good of you," he said, and Salome *knew* she had made a fool of herself.

She opened her mouth to make a tart comment (for the gods' sakes, this man was a nobody king of a nothing kingdom!), but Maximilian continued speaking, addressing the two guides.

"I assume you are here to guide the Lady Salome?"

Salome's mouth, already open, hung a little wider in her shock. How had he known who she was?

One of the guides nodded. "She hired us in Narbon, sire, to bring her south. She's looking for a man."

"StarDrifter SunSoar," said Maximilian. "Yes, I know." He looked directly at Salome. "He is back at my camp, Salome, waiting for you. An hour's ride away."

Then he addressed the guides again. "The lady has paid you? Yes? Then your task is done, my good men. She and I thank you, and I shall take over the lady's care from this point. You may return to Narbon."

Salome had managed, by this stage, to wrench her mouth shut. She was torn between irritation with this Maximilian who had just ridden into her life and decided to take it over, and the continuing bewilderment she felt as to how he'd known who she was and who she hunted (and what was the King of Escator doing out here, anyway?). She was also torn between a thrill of excitement and a growing self-righteous anger now she knew StarDrifter to be so close.

Finally, she would get her hands on him.

She'd drifted off again, and realized suddenly that the two guides had turned their horses and were cantering back down the track.

Maximilian was still smiling at her.

"They did say good-bye," he said, "but your thoughts had wandered."

"I'm sorry," she said again, and then flamed in humiliation. What had happened to her famous poise?

"You do not have to apologize for everything," Maximilian said. "Come, ride on. We have a way to go, and we can talk as we go."

"How did you know who I was?" said Salome, kicking her horse after Maximilian's. "And who I hunted? And how it was that I was *here*?"

"I am traveling into Isembaard," said Maximilian, "hunting my wife, who was stolen from me. I have a somewhat disparate group of individuals within my group. StarDrifter, who you seek—"

"Does he still have the Weeper? I want it back."

"Yes, we have the Weeper, but I doubt you will 'get it back.'"

"It is *mine*."

Maximilian gave a small shrug, his eyes on the road ahead. "I think the Weeper chooses his own companions. Now, please, allow me to finish."

Salome gave a curt movement of assent with her head,

wondering how it was that this man could make her feel so small with such a simple statement.

"I also have in my group four Icarii—I assume you know of the Icarii?"

"Yes," Salome said, "of course. They fluttered uselessly about Yoyette from time to time."

That earned her an unreadable look from Maximilian, but he made no comment on her words.

"I also have two marsh women with me," he said. "Witch-women who walk the boundaries between the dream world and this one. Their names are Venetia and Ravenna, mother and daughter. Venetia knew you were coming, and asked me to wait for you. She knows you hunt StarDrifter, and—"

"Does she know *why* I hunt him?"

Maximilian's look of sympathy at that point almost undid her.

"Yes," he said. "At least we know some of it—of what happened after StarDrifter stole the Weeper and left you to suffer the hatred and revenge of the Corolean court."

"They murdered my son!" she hissed. *"Murdered him!"*

"And you were poorly treated, too," Maximilian said. "*I* am sorry, Salome. You have our sympathy for it, know that. Although I will not allow you to physically harm StarDrifter, I am prepared to stand back and watch whatever else you deal to him."

Salome humiliated herself yet further by bursting into tears. She had been deeply angry and emotionally over-wrought for many weeks. Maximilian's unexpected sympathy caught her so unawares she could not prevent the emotion spilling over.

"I want to kill him so badly," she managed to get out be-tween the sobs. "I want to . . . but I can't . . . I can't."

Maximilian pulled his horse to a halt across the path of Salome's horse, making it stop as well. He didn't say anything, but he reached out a hand, resting it on her shoulder, and Sa-lome dropped her reins, lowered her face into her hands, and cried as she'd never allowed herself in her life previously.

StarDrifter rose to his feet as he saw the two riders ap-proaching.

Nerves fluttered in his belly.

Everyone else—the Icarii, Maximilian's two guardsmen, Venetia and Ravenna—stood slightly apart from him, distancing themselves both physically and emotionally.

The sound of the horses' hooves grew louder, and StarDrifter forced himself to look at Salome.

She was still lovely, but the suffering she'd experienced at the hands of the vengeful Coroleans (*at his hands*) showed clearly on her face and in the brittleness of her eyes.

She and Maximilian pulled their horses to a halt, Maximilian dismounting and then helping Salome off her mount.

Salome's eyes did not leave StarDrifter for one moment.

She was dressed in men's clothes, leather trousers and boots, and a jerkin over a thickly woven undyed linen shirt, but StarDrifter could still see that she'd lost a lot of weight.

Maximilian bent down and said something very quietly in Salome's ear.

She gave a tight nod, then walked over to StarDrifter.

The atmosphere was so tense that StarDrifter could barely breathe. The sheer weight of the guilt he felt was almost too much to bear.

All he'd wanted was to snatch the Weeper and walk away. He didn't really want to know about what Salome had endured after he'd taken the Weeper, and he very much didn't want to be faced with it now.

She didn't say anything. Not at first. She stood before him, regarding him with such a passion of hatred that StarDrifter was forced to drop his eyes.

"Do you have any idea?" she whispered finally. "*Any* idea, StarDrifter, what you did to me?"

There wasn't anything he could say. He wanted to say that it hadn't been him, that it had been Ba'al'uz, but he knew he couldn't say that.

In the end, he was as guilty of what had happened as Ba'al'uz.

StarDrifter forced himself to meet Salome's eyes again.

They were brilliant with emotion.

"They murdered Ezra," she said, her voice close to breaking. "They brought him before me and, not enough that they'd raped me, they raped him, five men, or perhaps ten. I lost count. They brutalized him so badly . . ."

Her voice broke, her entire body shook, and for a moment StarDrifter thought she would fall over.

He reached out a hand, but she flinched away from him.

"Don't touch me!" Salome took several huge breaths, managing to bring her emotions under control enough to resume speaking. "They raped and brutalized him, before the entire court, then took a knife and cut off his penis and his testicles, and they let him bleed out in front of me, *over me* . . . I still feel his blood all over me, StarDrifter! It stained me, *it stains me*, to this day, and it stains you, too . . . can't you *feel* it, can't you *see* it? Can't you . . . can't you . . ."

She burst into sobs. StarDrifter knew he should do something, but didn't know what, then in a moment Maximilian was beside her, an arm about her shoulder, pulling her against his body, murmuring something into her hair.

StarDrifter wanted to sink into the ground. He wanted one of Gorgrael's Ice Worms to appear right now and swallow him. He wanted a gryphon to drop down from the sky and seize him in cruel talons and carry him to a mountaintop where he would be torn apart and released from this damned, cursed *misery* of guilt.

He thought he could have weathered a Salome accusing him of the hurt done to her, but this broken woman before him now, accusing him of the hurt and harm and death done to Ezra, who StarDrifter had never meant to hurt, against whom he had held absolutely no grudge at all . . .

"I'm sorry," he murmured, and Salome tore herself out of Maximilian's arms.

"Do you have any idea what it is like to watch your child die before you?" she screamed at him.

StarDrifter's eyes filmed with tears—not tears of pity for himself, but for Salome. "Yes," he said, very softly, remembering watching his granddaughter Zenith being torn to pieces before his eyes.

He'd been responsible for that death, too.

"Yes," he said, "I do know, Salome. I am so sorry, I don't know what I can do to—"

"I don't want you to do anything!" she shouted. "Nothing! I want nothing from you! I want . . . I want . . ."

Suddenly she wheeled to one side, almost leaping the two or three paces between herself and Doyle. The movement shocked and surprised everyone, and before Doyle could stop her Salome had seized his sword, and was back before StarDrifter again.

She shrieked, lifted the sword above her shoulders, and, even as Maximilian grabbed frantically at her, hit StarDrifter across the cheek with the flat of the blade with all the strength she could muster.

StarDrifter staggered back several paces. He raised a hand to his cheek, watching Salome, now held firmly about the waist by Maximilian.

He pulled his hand away from his cheek. It was slick with blood. Salome had hit him with only the flat of the blade, but even so the twin edges of the blade had cut into his flesh, and now he had two parallel cuts along his cheek.

"I want to murder you," Salome said in a voice half hiss, half whisper. "I want to stick this into your belly, and make you suffer the way Ezra suffered, but I can't . . . I can't . . . I can't kill you . . ."

She bent half over, still holding the sword, the point of the blade now resting on the ground, and sobbed again, once, twice, then she looked up to StarDrifter, her eyes swollen with emotion and grief.

"I can't kill you, StarDrifter, because I am pregnant with your baby. An Icarii baby, and I know more than anyone that if a woman bears an Icarii baby without its Enchanter father there to sing it out, then the baby will tear her to pieces, and I don't want to die like my grandmother died, screaming and bleeding as her child was born . . . I don't want to die like my grandmother died . . ."

StarDrifter already felt as if his world was falling apart—*his child? She was pregnant with his child?*—but then Salome uttered the words that exploded his entire life into a million jagged, terrible pieces.

"I don't want to die like Embeth died," she whispered.

CHAPTER TWELVE

The FarReach Mountains, Southern Kyros

Something terrible had happened. No one was quite sure what, but as soon as Salome had mentioned the name of her grandmother—Embeth—StarDrifter had let out a choked cry and sunk to the ground, his face contorted, his fingers clawing into the earth.

Maximilian was tired. Tired of all the complications the SunSoars brought into everyone's lives. They just couldn't lead normal, straightforward, blameless lives. Instead, the SunSoars demonstrated a remarkable talent for destroying everyone within flesh-touching distance.

It was dusk, and they were all now sitting about the campfire. Maximilian had introduced Salome to everyone—she was very quiet now, clearly emotionally and physically exhausted—and they had sat down. Ravenna, Serge, and one of BroadWing's companions, SongFlight, handed about food and flasks of wine.

Maximilian thought they'd all needed the wine.

StarDrifter had joined the circle about the fire, but he refused the food, and had taken only a couple of sips of wine from the flask being handed about.

He looked completely wretched, and Maximilian sighed, supposing it would be up to him to find out what now had gone so wrong in StarDrifter's life.

Doubtless it would affect them all sooner or later.

"Who was Embeth?" Maximilian said, looking at StarDrifter.

His face tightened. He did not speak, and it was Salome who answered.

"My grandmother," she said, her voice quiet and lacking in any emotion at all. "The birth that killed her produced a daughter, Hasweb, who was my mother."

"Hasweb," StarDrifter murmured, and passed a hand over his eyes.

Maximilian glanced at him, but addressed Salome. "You said she died giving birth?"

Salome sighed, more from weariness than anything else. "Yes. She was not a Corolean. She came from Tencendor—"

Maximilian had a sudden terrible premonition of where this tale would lead.

"—but married into a noble Corolean family. She was pregnant at the time. Everyone thought it was her new husband's child, but . . . she had a terrible labor. The child would not be born. It tore my grandmother apart. My mother, Hasweb, survived, but Embeth did not.

"Hasweb was an Icarii child. But she was a *wanted* and loved child, and Embeth's husband forgave the fact she'd come into their marriage pregnant with an Icarii child, for he had loved Embeth, and raised the child as his own.

"When she was five they sent her to a specialist, who cut from her back her wing nubs."

"Oh, gods!" StarDrifter said. "No! How could they—"

"StarDrifter, you will say no more until Salome has finished," said Maximilian. "You will say *nothing*, do you understand?"

StarDrifter gave one tight nod.

"It was done cleanly and kindly," said Salome, "as it would later be done to me. Hasweb was given a powerful drug that rendered her unconscious. There was only a little pain from the incisions later, when she awoke, and the scarring faded within a year or two. As it faded with me." She paused, then continued. "Hasweb was married into the First. Embeth's Corolean husband was a member of the First . . . and he passed Hasweb off as the child of his former wife, who had died only weeks before he'd married Embeth while he'd been on a diplomatic mission within Tencendor. So no one knew that Hasweb was not a born and bred child of the First. No one knew that I was not, until . . ." She shot a vicious glance at StarDrifter.

"So that is how you came by your Icarii blood," said Maximilian. "From your mother's unknown father."

Salome grimaced slightly. "Not all of it. My mother Hasweb had married into the First, but . . . she took an Icarii lover herself. *My* own father was Icarii. I am almost full blood Icarii."

"And did Hasweb die in your birth?" Venetia asked.

Salome shook her head. "No. Her lover came back for my birth, for he had loved my mother, and he sang me out of her womb."

"Is Hasweb . . . is Hasweb still living?" StarDrifter asked, ignoring Maximilian's injunction to keep his silence.

Salome did not appear to notice who had asked the question. "No. She died when I was fourteen, pining for her lover, I think."

"Who was your father, Salome?" Maximilian asked.

She gave a little shrug. "I don't know. Not really. My mother would only say that he was the loveliest man she had ever met, with copper hair and violet eyes, and a power so extraordinary that—"

"No!" StarDrifter cried. "I can't believe this!"

Maximilian ignored him. "And Hasweb's father?"

Again that shrug. "I have no idea. Embeth never said."

Now Maximilian looked at StarDrifter. "Well?"

"How do you know?" said StarDrifter, his voice hoarse with emotion.

"Because the SunSoars destroy lives so effectively that I cannot imagine that you have not had a greater hand in the destruction of Salome's life than what has occurred only in the past few weeks."

StarDrifter did not reply immediately, and by now every eye about the campfire was trained on him.

"I was Embeth's lover," StarDrifter said eventually. "I was Hasweb's father. I had no idea Embeth was pregnant when she left Carlon. Salome, I'm sorry. I had no idea."

"You are my *grandfather*?" she said.

StarDrifter made a helpless gesture with a hand. "I had *no* idea, Salome. I am sorry."

"But she was your lover!" Salome said. "How could you leave her pregnant and not know and not care?"

Maximilian thought of several highly cynical comments he could interject at this point, but thought it better to remain silent. This was now between Salome and StarDrifter only.

StarDrifter was too emotionally drained to couch the truth in palatable words. "I didn't love her. Perhaps I liked her. I can't really remember. She was just someone to have in my bed at night. It was during the heady days of Axis' first wave of great success. He'd taken Carlon and defeated his brother, Borneheld. Life was about celebrating. About getting drunk on song and wine and success and taking to bed the woman you wanted. But the woman *I* wanted, Azhure, was wedded to Axis, and so instead I took Embeth, Axis' old lover. It seemed fitting, somehow."

He paused, and didn't seem to realize the silence about the fire was thick with horror.

"She left Carlon at some point," StarDrifter continued. "With Faraday, I think. I never thought of her again."

"Faraday being *Axis'* rejected lover, also pregnant at that stage with *his* child," BroadWing put in for the benefit of the non-Tencendorians among them who were not familiar with the twists in the tale.

Maximilian closed his eyes momentarily. He couldn't believe it.

"And *my* father?" said Salome. "Who was he?"

"Your father could have been no one else but the fabled Enchanter-Talon WolfStar SunSoar," said StarDrifter. "The description fits him perfectly. And WolfStar would have *known*, somehow, that Embeth had left Carlon pregnant with my child. He would have known Hasweb was my daughter. She was of SunSoar blood. He wouldn't have been able to leave her alone, and her seduction would have amused him. He would have known that at some point it would cause havoc—and causing havoc was what WolfStar did best. The instant he laid eyes on Hasweb he would have known her

SunSoar blood. All SunSoars are pulled to each other. *We* felt it, Salome. That's why—"

"Just get on with it!" Salome hissed.

"I am your grandfather, Salome. WolfStar SunSoar, the greatest Enchanter the Icarii has ever known, was your father. You are not only virtually full blood Icarii, but you are also virtually full blood SunSoar. I don't know what to do, Salome. I don't know how to atone for what I have done to your family. Hasweb , . . gods, I had another daughter, she would have been an *Enchanter*, and I had no idea . . . no idea . . . nor that you . . . Salome, I don't know what to say. I'm sorry."

For a long time no one said anything.

Then BroadWing gave a short laugh. "Trust the SunSoars to survive the destruction of Tencendor in virtual full force. You are the heir to the Icarii throne, StarDrifter. You are our Talon—an Enchanter-Talon. And now you have made an heir to succeed you, *and* on a hitherto unknown granddaughter of yours and a daughter of the renegade WolfStar. I don't know whether to congratulate you, or to curse you."

CHAPTER THIRTEEN

The FarReach Mountains, Southern Kyros

StarDrifter sat numbed. It was late at night, and he stared across the campfire to Salome's blanketed form. Everyone was asleep—or pretending sleep—save himself, BroadWing and Maximilian, both of whom sat with him, conversing in low tones as they shared a flask of wine.

Earlier Maximilian and Venetia had spent some time with Salome. StarDrifter did not know what they had said to her, but she'd eaten some food before lying down on the mattress of heath that SongFlight had made for her, and pulled a blanket to her shoulders, and StarDrifter supposed she was now asleep.

"Salome will be accompanying us," Maximilian said.

"Maximilian—" StarDrifter began.

"What else do you suggest?" Maximilian said. "That we leave her here?"

"I wasn't going to suggest that," StarDrifter snapped. "Only that I take responsibility for her. That I can do for her, at least."

"If she will accept it," BroadWing muttered.

"Good," said Maximilian, "that's one less problem I need to worry about." There was a glint of white as he smiled. "And I admit to feeling relieved that Salome is now your responsibility, StarDrifter. Do try to keep her from murdering you."

StarDrifter touched his cheek gingerly. "If she was going to murder, I think she would have done so already."

"Today has been quite the day for surprises," BroadWing

said. "If WolfStar is Salome's father, then should we fear her?"

WolfStar had caused mayhem, misery, and destruction among the Icarii, and even though now everyone believed him dead (finally), even the mention of his name caused most Icarii to shudder in horror.

StarDrifter gave a slight shrug. "I doubt it. Azhure was also WolfStar's daughter, and she was not to be feared."

"And you are Salome's grandfather," Maximilian said. "I have heard that the Icarii do not regard incest with the same degree of approbation as other races . . . but even so, StarDrifter, to sleep with your granddaughter, and to father a child on her . . ."

Both BroadWing and StarDrifter looked at Maximilian in some mild surprise.

"Well, neither knew at the time," said BroadWing.

"For gods' sakes," said Maximilian. "You know *now*! It doesn't give you any pause for thought?"

"It is not a problem for us," said BroadWing, glancing at StarDrifter before he spoke, almost as if he wanted permission to respond. "Only sexual relations between first blood—parents and children, and between siblings—is forbidden."

Maximilian gave a somewhat bewildered shake of his head. "Still . . . I find it strange. And what is this baby to you, StarDrifter? Child . . . or great-grandchild?"

"Child," said StarDrifter. He paused, thinking. "Salome was willing, Maximilian—"

"But she had no idea then that she slept with her *grandfather*!"

StarDrifter gave a faint smile. "And even had she known then," he said, "it would have given her little cause for hesitation, save to add a certain tang to proceedings."

And how different Salome was to Zenith, StarDrifter thought, remembering how he'd pursued Zenith, and yet she could never overcome her own repulsion at sharing flesh with her grandfather. *Maybe it was WolfStar's blood in Salome.*

His smile widened, just fractionally, remembering that first time he and Salome had coupled. *That* frantic, desperate union had been the mad, bad SunSoar blood roiling to the surface. They had not been able to resist each other.

Then StarDrifter's smile faded. *And how sad that Zenith had not shared either the madness or the badness.*

"Do you know," said BroadWing, "that today has given me more hope for our future than any other day in the past five years. The Icarii have drifted directionless for all these years. We have lost the majority of our people. We have lost our homeland. We have lost our enchantment. We have lost the Star Dance. We have lost all purpose. And now? Now suddenly the SunSoars are back. We have our Talon, and his—"

"For the stars' sakes, BroadWing," StarDrifter said. "Let this go, I beg you. I am no more your Talon than—"

BroadWing leaned over and gripped StarDrifter's forearm. "*You are our Talon, StarDrifter!* Accept it! You have enjoyed the benefits of SunSoar blood all these centuries, and you will now accept the responsibility of it. The Icarii are desperate. *Desperate!* You—yes, curse it, *you*—now have the responsibility, the blood, and the experience to give the Icarii direction and purpose and leadership and a home. *Your* responsibility, StarDrifter. Yours."

StarDrifter wrenched his arm free. "Me? *Me?* Look at me, BroadWing. I've never accepted responsibility. I am just feckless StarDrifter—and, oh, how my parents named me well, drifting aimlessly, taking pleasure in nothing but pleasure, and sowing aimless seeds of destruction as I went. Have you forgot who fathered Gorgrael? Who—"

"Who fathered Axis," said BroadWing, his voice calm and even.

"Axis was no savior," StarDrifter said. "He was a golden hero who restored the Icarii and Tencendor, but who then allowed everything to slide into bleakness again."

"And that is why I am here now, arguing with you," BroadWing said. "Axis was never the man to lead the Icarii, but I think you are."

StarDrifter gave a soft, hollow laugh.

"I have seen you at your very best and at your very worst," BroadWing said. "I know to what extremes of dissipation you can sink, and the heights to which you can rise."

"And today you have seen me at my very worst," StarDrifter said. "How then can you sit here and argue so passionately that I have the qualities for Talon?"

"I think today he has seen you at your very best," Maximilian put in quietly.

"Maximilian is right," BroadWing said. "You stood there before Salome and accepted responsibility for your actions. I know enough about what happened in Coroleas that I am well aware that you could very easily have shifted blame onto Ba'al'uz, but you didn't. You accepted whatever Salome chose to deal you. That was the action of a mature man, StarDrifter. Not some feckless, uncaring dissipate. And I have seen you in . . ."

BroadWing's voice broke, and he had to pause and clear his throat. "I was present in the Assembly Chamber of Talon Spike that day, so many vast years ago, when you addressed the assembled Icarii race. Do you remember it, StarDrifter? Do you remember that day?"

StarDrifter took a moment to answer. "I sang for you. I sang of the Wars of the Axe, of how the Icarii had come to be imprisoned in the Icescarp Alps."

"And you sang of hope, and of how the Icarii could rise again, and regain that which was lost. Stars, StarDrifter, you had the entire Icarii race in tears, you held them in the palm of your hand, *you owned us*. That day was when you and RavenCrest, your brother, and our Talon at the time, persuaded us to accept Axis as our StarMan."

BroadWing's voice dropped very low. "But you were so astounding, so powerful, that we would have done anything that day, StarDrifter. Anything for *you*. You were extraordinarily beautiful and powerful, and you reminded us of how extraordinarily beautiful and powerful *we* could be. You can do that again." An infinitesimal pause. "You *must*."

StarDrifter said nothing.

"You take Salome," BroadWing said, "and you take that child, and you rebuild the SunSoar dynasty, and you rebuild the Icarii pride and race. You lead us to a new homeland, and back into the Star Dance, StarDrifter, or else we will *all* perish in hopelessness."

"I am a hopeless messiah," StarDrifter said.

"You are all we have," BroadWing said, and he smiled. "And you will be more than enough."

"And Salome," StarDrifter said, his words argumentative, but his voice now resigned. "She is hardly likely to—"

"Salome is the best wife you could ever hope for," Broad-Wing said. "I have heard of her cruelty and dissipation, but today we saw the better part of her, too. Salome did not accuse or attack you for what happened to her, for what *she* had lost, but for her son—the loss of his life and future."

"She has great strength," put in Maximilian, earning himself a black glance from StarDrifter.

"And I think she has great compassion," Maximilian added, softly, daring StarDrifter to throw him another look.

"Salome is a far better mate for you than Rivkah ever was," said BroadWing, naming the Acharite princess on whom StarDrifter had fathered Axis, "or Azhure, or her and Axis' daughter, Zenith, or any other of the women you have thought to have loved. Fate . . . no . . . I am prepared to say stronger here, the *Star Dance*, has led her to you, and you to her, and then the both of you back to the Icarii people. Take a deep breath, right now, StarDrifter, and accept both Salome and the Talon torc of leadership."

Maximilian watched StarDrifter curiously, wondering what he would do.

The Icarii prince sat in silence for a long time, staring across the fire to where Salome lay; then, without looking at BroadWing, he held out his hand to the birdman, and Broad-Wing gripped it.

They held the grip for a long moment, then both let go and sat back, and Maximilian passed them the flask of wine.

So passed the leadership of the Icarii to StarDrifter SunSoar.

The three men sat there for another hour in silence, occasionally taking sips of wine.

Finally StarDrifter rose, and went to Salome.

CHAPTER FOURTEEN

The FarReach Mountains, Southern Kyros

Salome was too emotionally and physically exhausted to sleep. She lay there, drifting between wakefulness and drowsiness, listening to the murmur of voices coming from across the campfire, and turning over in her mind the events of the day.

It had not eventuated quite as she'd expected.

Salome wasn't quite sure *what* she had expected, for she'd never been precisely clear in her own mind about what she would do to StarDrifter when she found him, but today's events hadn't fitted any of her imagined scenarios.

She had expected StarDrifter to justify and excuse and evade, and he'd done none of those things.

She'd expected him to strike back at her, to be angry and judgmental, and he'd done none of those things, either.

She had never imagined, *never*, the revelations the day would bring.

He was Embeth's unknown lover.

StarDrifter was her grandfather.

That had numbed Salome as nothing else could have.

StarDrifter was the lover who had deserted Embeth, who had left her to die birthing his child.

Salome felt as if this should make her hate him even more.

But, astoundingly, it didn't. Perhaps that was because all her emotions appeared utterly dead.

The naming of her father meant nothing to her. Salome supposed she'd heard the name WolfStar somewhere, but she'd paid so little attention to the world beyond the intrigues of the

Corolean court that she could not recall what she'd heard.

"Would you like me to tell you about WolfStar?" StarDrifter said softly behind her, and Salome jumped, her heart pounding painfully.

"I'm sorry," he said, for what must have been the hundredth time that day. "I startled you. I thought you were awake."

He sat down on the ground beside her. "Do you mind if I share the blanket, and your hearth bedding?"

Salome couldn't believe he'd ask that. She struggled to rouse some indignant anger, but she was so spent that she couldn't raise the effort, and so when StarDrifter took her silence for assent and lifted the blanket and crawled under beside her, pulling her back against his body, all she could manage was an affronted stiffness.

At least she had her back to him, but all that meant was that StarDrifter could curl the more effectively about her own body.

"WolfStar lived many thousands of years ago," StarDrifter said, very softly. Salome thought he was infusing his voice with something else. A melody perhaps. Was he trying to fool her with some Icarii trickery?

Trickery or not, as StarDrifter continued speaking the gentle melody in his voice soothed away both her irritation and stiffness, and she gradually relaxed against his warmth.

This wasn't how she'd envisioned ending this day, either.

"He was then, and remains to this day, the most powerful Enchanter the Icarii had ever produced," StarDrifter continued.

"He was a SunSoar?" Salome asked, surprising herself with her interest.

"Yes. And Talon. An Enchanter-Talon." StarDrifter laughed very softly, washing warm breath over the back of her neck. "Enchanter-Talons have ever been the most troublesome to the Icarii people. I can't think why BroadWing now wants another one."

The last meant nothing to Salome, but she did not comment.

"WolfStar developed a fascination with the Star Dance,"

StarDrifter continued. His arm, where it lay about her waist, tightened fractionally. "Do you know what that is, Salome? Have you ever felt it?"

"No," she said, and StarDrifter sighed, fanning more breath against her neck.

"You are an Enchanter as well, Salome," he said. "Hasweb was undoubtedly one, too. Your lives should for many years have been dictated by the Star Dance—the music the stars make in their dance about the heavens. That music infiltrated every aspect of our lives, our very *souls*, and Enchanters used it to weave such magic . . .

"Ah, but all that was lost during the devastation of the wars of the Timekeeper Demons. They destroyed the Star Gate, through which the music of the stars filtered, and we lost the Star Dance. That happened some five or six years ago, so you *must* have lived for twenty-five years or more with the Star Dance washing about you. Are you sure you have never—"

"I have never felt a thing. It means nothing to me."

"Well, anyway, WolfStar wanted to step through the Star Gate and allow the music of the Star Dance to consume him completely. To cut a long story short, he did. He vanished through the Star Gate, and for thousands of years the Icarii people assumed he'd died. But, no. He came back, more powerful and dreadful than ever before, and created mayhem and disaster among the peoples of Tencendor. If the land perished, then it was largely due to his machinations."

"You are afraid of him."

"Yes, I am."

"And now? Is he dead? Wandering about?"

"Dead. I hope." Again StarDrifter gave a soft laugh. "But one never assumes that death can hold WolfStar forever."

"I have a powerful father, then." *There,* thought Salome. *A powerful father, but* not *a powerful grandfather.*

"Aye," StarDrifter said, and did not sound affronted at all. "Very powerful indeed."

"Then should you be afraid of me?"

"Very much so," StarDrifter said, and Salome frowned at the teasing note in his voice.

"Salome," StarDrifter said, before she could speak, "I have been a wandering, dissipated fool most of my life. I have loved women, and destroyed women. I have failed many people. Perhaps with you I can make a fresh—"

"Don't try to pretend we have a—"

StarDrifter's hand slid under the loosened waistband of her trousers and then over the warm skin of her slightly rounded belly.

"*This* is not pretense, Salome. Tell me, did you not think to discard the child? I am sure you must have known how."

She was silent.

He sang a little snatch of melody, very softly, and she drew in a sharp breath.

A sense of peace had washed over her with that melody, and as she exhaled the breath, she relaxed entirely against his body.

"I knew as soon as you said you were pregnant," StarDrifter said, his mouth now almost against the skin at the back of her neck, "that this child would be my get, and not the product of your rapes. BroadWing said fate bound us together, Salome. I think BroadWing has a somewhat remarkable perceptivity."

Again, that snatch of melody, and Salome closed her eyes as they filled with sudden tears.

"It is a son, Salome," StarDrifter said. "An Enchanter. And," Salome could feel his mouth curl in a smile against her neck, "a peaceful and happy child. An heir to everything we have both lost."

Salome thought StarDrifter was being terribly presumptuous with that last remark, but now she was so comfortable, so warm, and so peaceful, that drowsiness was finally achieving dominion over her body.

"Mmmm," she murmured—and then shivered as StarDrifter kissed the back of her neck.

"Sleep," he whispered.

The Weeper lay a few feet away, forgotten by both Salome and StarDrifter.

As they fell into sleep, StarDrifter still curled about Salome's body, the Weeper began to ice over.

It spent all night encased in ice, engaged in such a powerful magic that even the ground beneath it froze solid.

In the morning, when the camp stirred, the Weeper lay in a small puddle of water, condensation sliding down its body.

No one paid any attention.

When Salome awoke—the last of the camp to rise—it was to find that StarDrifter had left a mug of tea and a wedge of warmed bread slathered with butter and red beet and onion chutney by her side.

Salome sat up and ate the food.

It was the best breakfast she could ever remember having eaten.

When she rose to her feet, brushing away the remaining crumbs of the bread, she winced as something caught in her back.

A muscle, she thought, grown cold and stiff during her long night's unmoving slumber.

CHAPTER FIFTEEN

The Palace of Aqhat, Isembaard

Today Isaiah was holding his Spectacle. Axis knew of two other occasions Isaiah had held a Spectacle since he'd been in Isembaard, but Axis had not been invited to either of those formal courts. They had been held during his early days in Isembaard when Isaiah had tended to keep Axis very much in his private sphere. Today, however, Axis had received a request to attend.

It was, after all, the day on which Isaiah meant to announce his marriage to Ishbel.

Axis had not seen Ishbel since his return from flushing out the brigands from the eastern mountains. He'd tried to see her, but either she had been asleep, or resting, or bathing with Isaiah in the River Lhyl in the evening (and since when had she started doing that, Axis wondered), or simply not in her apartments when he'd called, so that by now Axis suspected she was avoiding him.

Or perhaps her servants and guards had been well instructed by Isaiah in how to deflect Axis SunSoar should he come to visit.

Well, at least Axis would see Ishbel at the Spectacle, and probably even get the chance to speak with her, as he'd been given to understand he was to sit with Isaiah and Ishbel on their dais.

Despite being worried about Ishbel, Axis was curious about the Spectacle itself. He had gathered, from various conversations with Insharah, Zeboath, and the palace chamberlain, that the Spectacle existed to remind the generals and the governors of the various dependencies who it was controlled the reins of power, to impress various visiting diplomats, nobles, and ambassadors, and to make it perfectly clear to the entire population of Isembaard, via subsequent gossip and reports, the extent of Isaiah's power and prestige.

Today, Isaiah was using the Spectacle to present his new "conquest," Ishbel, Queen of Escator, to the Tyranny.

Look what a great and fearsome leader I am, Isaiah would say to his peoples via the Spectacle. *I have captured for my own both the northern king's queen* and *his heir. The northern kings are weak indeed, and they shall lay down before me, and submit themselves to Isembaard.*

The Spectacle was held at midday in what Insharah had somewhat caustically called the sunroom. Insharah had not explained that comment, but its memory was enough to add further fuel to Axis' already well-developed curiosity about the day's proceedings. By the time his escort knocked at his chamber door, just before noon, Axis was pacing about in a state of high anticipation.

He'd dressed carefully for the occasion, wearing black leather trousers topped with an airy lawn linen shirt. He'd abandoned the sandals he normally wore in the heat for well-tooled leather boots, topped the shirt with a tightly fitted vest of gold silk, and then carefully trimmed his beard and dressed his hair, clubbing it into a queue at the back of his neck.

Isaiah had sent one of the captains of the Spear to escort him, and they chatted amiably as the captain led Axis higher and higher into the palace.

Finally Axis' curiosity got the better of him.

"Just where *does* Isaiah hold his Spectacle?" he asked.

The captain shot him an amused glance as they approached yet another graceful, winding staircase. "In the sunroom, of course."

"Yes, but where—"

"On the roof, Lord Axis. In the sun."

A slow smile spread across Axis' face. He was starting to realize the nature of Isaiah's Spectacle.

"Should I have brought a broad-brimmed hat?" he said.

The captain laughed. "You shall be among the shaded, Lord Axis. Be grateful."

The captain finally led Axis into a vast chamber which Axis realized acted as the anteroom for Isaiah's "sunroom." It was thronged with people, all of whom glanced every few minutes toward a massive flight of steps that rose to an equally impressive doorway beyond which Axis could see only blinding light.

"We don't go that way," the captain murmured to Axis. "Come with me."

He led Axis around the side of the room, avoiding the throng (almost all of whom glanced away from the flight of steps long enough to look curiously at Axis), through a small doorway and up a flight of stairs much less grand than those in the anteroom. These steps led in turn to a doorway, again much less grand than that which awaited the throng in the anteroom, but leading into the same rectangle of blinding light.

The captain led Axis straight through.

Then stopped, grinning at Axis as he gaped.

The "sunroom" was, to Axis' eyes, the most spectacular and the most stunningly beautiful chamber he'd ever seen . . . and Axis had lived to see some amazing buildings and chambers.

The rectangular space covered the entire roof area of the palace—a vast acreage of beauty that was stunning in its simplicity.

There was no roof—the space was entirely open to the vivid blue Isembaardian sky.

The area was floored in a polished stone of a deep emerald hue, glasslike in its sheen. Axis had never seen anything like it: more translucent than marble, it was similarly veined with silver and gold through its emerald depths. Axis could not see a join anywhere—it was as if the entire floor had been laid down in a single piece. Neither could he see anything beneath the translucent stone. It appeared to sink down forever, although Axis knew that was impossible.

"It represents the River Lhyl," the captain said softly, "the lifeblood of the Tyranny."

Axis nodded, unable to speak.

He looked up, studying the rest of the space.

Eight rows of columns, fully twenty paces high and five in

diameter at the base, arranged in four sets of twinned rows, ran down either side of the central space.

The columns were as remarkable as the floor.

They were composed of what looked like an almost translucent glass. Virtually clear at their base, they gradually became more opaque as they rose to dizzying heights, until, at their summit, where they blossomed into open-petaled water lily flowers, the glass became solid colors of the faintest pinks and blues and greens.

"I have never seen anything so beautiful," Axis said very softly.

"No one ever has," said the captain. "One never gets tired of the sight."

"Did Isaiah build this?"

The captain shook his head. "It was constructed over several generations, I believe, and was only completed during Isaiah's grandfather's time. Come. Isaiah is waiting."

The captain led Axis down the central open space, flanked on either side by the rows of twinned water lily columns.

At the far end of the open space was a shaded pavilion where, Axis could just make out, stood a raised dais.

By the time he and the captain had made the halfway point, Axis was beginning to understand the reason the Isembaardian tyrants had created this particular arena for their Spectacles.

It was damnably hot.

In fact, anyone who had to spend any time at all in this "sunroom"—and that would be most of those who attended the Spectacle, for Axis assumed it would take Isaiah some time to work his way through whatever ceremony he had planned—would be at a disadvantage to Isaiah within a very few minutes. The combined effect of glass floor and columns and the sun made the space a furnace.

There were shaded areas to either side, and Isaiah's covered pavilion at the head of the space, and Axis thought it would all be reserved for the favored.

Anyone in disfavor, or as yet uncategorized in Isaiah's list of who he trusted and who not, would be forced to stand in the sun.

Isaiah rose from his throne—made of the same glasslike substance as the floor and columns, but comfortably cushioned—as Axis approached.

Isaiah waved away the captain with a nod of thanks, then gestured to Axis to join him on the dais.

"In the shade, my friend," he said, with a smile. "What think you?"

Axis shook his head in admiration. "I think you are a cruel man, Isaiah. How many are you to keep waiting in the sun today?"

Isaiah smiled, but did not otherwise respond to the question. He was accoutred in the most magnificent finery Axis had yet seen—jewels of various hues gleamed among his braids and studded the golden collar he wore about his shoulders. Bangles adorned his wrists and ankles, but Isaiah had kept his hipwrap to plain linen, and had no sandals on his feet—to all the more display the wealth of his gems, Axis thought.

He wore no weapon, but hardly needed to: the dais was surrounded on three sides by rows of spearmen.

Axis caught sight of Ishbel, sitting on an ornate chair to Isaiah's right.

She was beautifully gowned, and her hair almost as impressively styled as Isaiah's, but Axis thought he saw lines of strain about her eyes and mouth, and she barely smiled at his greeting.

"Ishbel?" Axis murmured as he kissed her hand. "How are you?"

"Just a little tired," she said. "I find it difficult to sleep in this heat."

"The baby?" Axis said.

She replied only with a slight shrug, and a tightening of the worry lines about her eyes.

"You should not be here," Axis said, "but in your chamber, resting. Isaiah—"

"No, Axis," Ishbel said, "I will be well enough, and I have little to do here but sit and nod and smile."

"And you *will* nod and smile?"

"I am happy enough, Axis. I like Isaiah, and feel comfortable with him. Maximilian is a long way in my past."

Axis studied her, wondering. She seemed genuinely relaxed about Isaiah's announcement of marriage, but she most certainly did not appear well.

"Isaiah," he said, turning back to the tyrant.

"Later, Axis," Isaiah said. "This will take little time, and will be no strain on Ishbel. Will you sit now?"

That last was said in a tone that clearly indicated Isaiah was not prepared to receive a negative response, and so, with a further worried glance at Ishbel, and a silent promise to himself to keep an eye on her, Axis took his appointed seat just to one side of Ishbel's.

Isaiah nodded at him, then returned to his own throne. As soon as he was seated, a haunting melody of horn music filled the air.

Axis was used to blaring trumpet clarions for ceremonial events, but this haunting melody was, to his mind, even more unsettling and unnerving for the participants outside than an overpowering clarion would have been.

The music wound in and out of the columns, skimming over the floor, wafting gently between the assembled dignitaries on the dais and the spearmen standing about it.

It strengthened just a little, and then Axis saw people slowly entering the Spectacle Chamber from the massive rectangular doorway at the head of the flight of steps from the anteroom.

They were guided into the space in no particular order, which Axis thought must have been even more unsettling for them. All had to find their own place.

After a moment's hesitation and disorientation as they first entered, most headed straight for the shaded areas to either side of the sun-filled columned space.

There awaited a cordon of Isaiah's aides.

Some, a very few, were allowed through to wait in the pleasant shade, but most were directed back into the sun. The generals and their senior captains arrived, and Axis was glad to see them waved through to the shaded area.

He did not think it would have been a very good idea to keep the generals in the sun.

Gradually the central space filled up, people managing

to stand in ordered groups (which groupings themselves revealed alliances and enmities).

Most people had attired themselves in their best raiments,
which meant much heavy draping of silks and linens topped
with encrusted jewelry. In the heat and the brilliant sun, people became uncomfortable very quickly.

Axis glanced at Isaiah.

He had a tiny smile on his face.

Axis wondered about the wisdom of leaving the participants in such discomfort. They were, after all, important
people in their own right, and would not appreciate this obvious manipulation.

But then, perhaps, it was all a part of the game, and the
instinctive groupings did, after all, reveal to Isaiah better
than anything else where lay loyalties and alliances.

The music increased in intensity for a moment, then faded
away to nothing.

The door at the back of the chamber closed.

Isaiah stood.

He did not, as Axis expected, remain in the comfortable
shade, but strode to the very front of the dais where lay a belt
of savage sun.

It illuminated him—the jewels in his hair, and the golden
collar about his shoulders—until his form shimmered.

Axis thought that the assembled throng would either see
him as a god, standing there in the light . . . or as an intensely
irritating and manipulative bully.

There was movement to either side, and Axis looked
around.

The majority of the spearmen, while leaving a cordon of
warriors on the dais, were now moving down the sides of the
chamber, ready to act should anyone get too hot-tempered
from discomfort.

Isaiah began to speak to the throng. His voice was very
strong, and very confident, his body language reflecting all
the power and arrogance of his office.

Axis grinned. Isaiah was spinning a fantastic tale about
the capture of Ishbel . . . a tale in which Ba'al'uz did not
figure at all.

Isaiah continued with the news that Ishbel was to become his new wife, and was to bear the newly created title of Favored Wife.

Axis glanced at Ishbel at that, and she smiled slightly and rolled her eyes at him, making him grin.

Isaiah continued on, describing Ishbel's acquisition almost as he would a successful invasion. Maximilian, the Escatorian king, had been "humbled" by the loss of his wife to Isaiah and was now a recluse, unable to act through sheer inadequacy. The Escatorian nation itself was now virtually a satellite to Isembaard and wanted only Isaiah's imminent invasion to capitulate completely.

Ishbel represented Isaiah's potency, his might, his success.

Axis sincerely hoped that Maximilian wasn't going to ride into Aqhat at the head of an avenging army (unlikely, but Axis wasn't about to discount Maximilian quite as completely as Isaiah appeared to be doing), which event would severely damage Isaiah's presentation.

Isaiah turned slightly, gesturing to Ishbel to join him.

She rose, hesitated slightly as she got to her feet, then regained her composure and walked forward to Isaiah.

Axis leaned forward in concern. Ishbel did not look well at all.

Isaiah's eyes crinkled at Ishbel a little—Axis was relieved to see he was laughing at himself—then took her hand, presenting her to the throng.

It was right at that moment that the bowman rose from the center of the gigantic lily flower at the top of the nearest column, and fired the arrow into Isaiah's chest.

A second's worth of horror, then Axis moved. He lunged forward, grabbing Isaiah by the arm and pulling him to one side.

He wasn't fast enough. Just as he grabbed Isaiah's arm, the arrow thudded into Isaiah's chest.

The force of the impact sent Isaiah sprawling, knocking Ishbel to the ground as well, and the next moment the chamber was in an uproar.

Axis stumbled, managed to gain his balance, then looked up at the top of the column.

The bowman was standing there in full view, and even from this distance Axis could see the small smile of satisfaction on the man's face.

But that wasn't what shocked Axis.

What completely appalled him was that the bowman was an Icarii.

Bingaleal let the bow droop slowly to his hip as he stared into the eyes of the StarMan.

Greetings, Axis SunSoar, he thought, then allowed a small derisive smile to form.

Axis had looked away now, and was kneeling by Isaiah's blood-covered form, lying partly atop that of the sprawled woman, her face twisting in shock and perhaps some pain. Axis was shouting for help, trying to staunch Isaiah's bleeding while at the same time trying to take the woman's hand, as if to comfort her.

Bingaleal didn't care what Axis tried to do, for whatever it was, it was too late now. Lister's purpose had been served. He looked at the milling confusion, and at the generals striding forth, waving forward spearmen and archers, calling for ropes so soldiers could scale the column, ordering that should the birdman assassin lift off then he should be feathered out of the air with several score of arrows.

As if I would fly out of here, Bingaleal thought. *You have not seen my like, although one day we hope to rule over you.*

He allowed the bow to drop completely, and he sank to his knees in the great flower that sat atop the column. Ignoring the frenetic activity below him, the spears that rattled every moment or two against the column and occasionally flew in a deadly arc over his flower shelter, Bingaleal curled into a tight ball, wrapping his wings about him entirely.

Within moments ice formed along the ridged outlines of his wings and body. Despite the hot sun, it spread rapidly, so that by the time the soldiers had fetched their ropes and prepared to mount the column, ice entirely encased Bingaleal.

As a noose of rope caught one of the petals, and the more

daring among the soldiers began the treacherous ascent of
the column, the ice enshrouding Bingaleal's body clouded
over, then became completely opaque.

Then the ice faded. Bingaleal's body did not shrink, it
merely disappeared slowly, until, by the time the first of the
soldiers had gripped the outer rim of the flower with his
hands and peered cautiously over, there was nothing left but
a single tiny snowflake, rising into the streaming sun and
vanishing in a breath of air.

The palace was in an uproar, all attention centered on the
sunroom, and so no one noticed the thin, tattered figure that
tottered into the palace complex from one of the river gates.

Ba'al'uz stopped long enough to drink a great draft from
the fountain in the great courtyard, then he made for the
doorway that led into the private quarters of the palace.
As he drank, an ugly brindle dog crept to his heels, and
then followed as Ba'al'uz completed his journey across the
courtyard.

When he entered the palace, Ba'al'uz and the dog went entirely unnoticed, encased as they were in Kanubai's power.

The activity and consternation in the palace meant that
one other activity also went unremarked. Atop DarkGlass
Mountain, thin rivulets of blood had begun to flow down
the glass sides of the pyramid from under its gigantic golden
capstone. They trailed to about halfway down the pyramid,
then, strangely, veered sideways so that, after some time, the
rivulets of blood entirely enclosed the central portion of the
pyramid.

Then they turned black, as if girding the pyramid's waist
in bands of iron.

CHAPTER SIXTEEN

The Palace of Aqhat, Isembaard

An Icarii? An Icarii? What the fuck have you done to me, Axis?"

"Isaiah—"

"I trusted you. *I trusted you*! And this is how you—"

"Isaiah, I am not to blame, I—"

"Don't tell me that. I saw you talking with Ezekiel the other night. What were you plotting, eh? I can't imagine you wanted my throne. What then? Ishbel?"

"I had nothing to do with it, Isaiah!"

The two men glared at each other, bodies rigid with anger and shock, faces tight with emotion, then Isaiah turned away, muttering an obscenity.

He'd known that Axis had nothing to do with the attempt on his life (and he was almost certain who *had* ordered it), but Isaiah was angry, *furious*, and he'd needed someone at whom to lash out.

His chest was still streaked with blood from his wound, which was now stitched and daubed with antiseptic. He'd been lucky. The arrow had struck him square in the chest, but it had hit a section where the golden collar draped down from his shoulders.

Although the arrow had penetrated the metal links, it had only superficially wounded Isaiah.

Without the collar he would have been dead.

It almost did not matter. Aqhat was in crisis.

Such a brazen assassination attempt, in the middle of a Spectacle, with every high-ranking witness Isembaard could produce, was a disaster for Isaiah. He relied on his image of total strength and invulnerability to maintain control over the military and over the vast and disparate elements of his empire.

To have an assassin penetrate into the very heart of his power, to have an assassin so brazenly and so easily evade all security, utterly undermined Isaiah's credibility.

Everything was made so much worse by the fact the assassin had not been caught. He had simply . . . vanished.

Within moments armed men had hustled Isaiah, Ishbel, and Axis off the rooftop and down into Isaiah's private chambers via a back entrance, Isaiah having recovered enough from the shock of the arrow strike in his chest to shout orders at his generals.

It was there, in Isaiah's private quarters, as Zeboath stitched and cleaned his chest wound, that Axis told him the assassin had been an Icarii bowman. Ishbel had since gone to her own chamber to rest, and Isaiah had angrily pushed Zeboath aside, telling him to get out of the chamber.

"I was not responsible," Axis said.

"It was an *Icarii*," Isaiah said, although his voice had lost much of its accusation. "One of *your* people. Is that what you did when you went north to fetch Ishbel, eh? Make contact with the Icarii? Suggest they might like to assassinate me?"

"If I'd wanted to assassinate you," Axis snarled, "I would have done it privately and I would have done it *well*."

Isaiah stared at him, then his body subtly relaxed. It wasn't much, but it was enough for Axis to relax slightly, too.

"It wasn't me, Isaiah," Axis said.

Isaiah made a gesture with his hand, as if to wave away the fact he had accused Axis in the first instance, then poured himself a goblet of wine, draining it in a couple of swallows.

"Why an Icarii?" he said, wondering what Axis would say. "Why would an Icarii hunt me? Are they assassins for hire now?"

Axis hesitated.

"I'm not entirely sure it *was* an Icarii," he said.

Ishbel had dismissed her attendants, and now sat in a chair, rubbing at her aching back.

She felt dreadful. She hadn't been feeling well all day—nauseated, headachy, weak—but all those troublesome irritants had magnified fivefold after Isaiah had fallen atop her in the Spectacle Chamber. Her legs were now so wobbly they could scarcely hold her, and her head throbbed as if the arrow had cracked her skull instead of Isaiah's chest.

But, thank the gods, he was alive and relatively well. For a long, terrible moment immediately after that arrow had struck Isaiah, Ishbel had thought he was dead.

She decided to rise and fetch herself some iced wine, but as soon as she moved she gave a gasp as a band of fire encircled her body.

Her hands instinctively clutched at her belly, then she tried once more to rise in order to walk the fifteen or so steps to the bellpull to summon aid.

But the instant Ishbel tried to put weight on her legs she collapsed to the floor, unable even to shriek as agony of incredible magnitude encircled her body.

At DarkGlass Mountain, the black bands encircling the pyramid throbbed and glittered, as if they rhythmically expanded and contracted.

"What?" said a voice. "Has someone managed to get in before me?"

Ishbel thought she vaguely recognized the voice. She managed to roll over, toward the voice, grateful that someone was here, then gasped once more, this time in mingled pain and horror and shock.

Ba'al'uz stood a few paces away.

She almost didn't recognize him. His clothes hung in dusty tatters, and likewise his skin—as if the man had been exposed to so much sun his skin had dried and then shredded away from his face and the exposed parts of his limbs.

There appeared to be an ugly cur skulking about his heels, but surprised as she was to see Ba'al'uz and in such a state, Ishbel gave it no notice.

Already in shock from the continuing viselike bands of agony contorting her abdomen, Ishbel's mind couldn't quite

make sense of what she was seeing. Ba'al'uz? Here? Why?
And what had happened to him to—

More viselike agony, and Ishbel screwed her eyes shut
and moaned.

"Are you giving birth?" Ba'al'uz asked, quite pleasantly.

"I need help," Ishbel said. "Can you fetch me aid, please.
I beg you, Ba'al'uz, please, I need—"

"I am the only aid you will ever see," said Ba'al'uz, "and
even that not much aid at all, I think."

Indescribable pain gripped her. Ishbel wanted to scream.
Her mouth hung open, but even breathing was impossible
with this much agony consuming her, and to make a sound
was utterly beyond her.

The fingers of one hand scrabbled desperately at the cold
floor.

She felt the baby shift within her.

She heard Ba'al'uz laugh, softly and pleasantly, and mutter something, as if he were talking to someone else in the
room.

Then she heard the unmistakable sound of a sword being
drawn from its scabbard, and she looked up.

"What do you mean, not an Icarii?" Isaiah said. "You have
just finished telling me that—"

Axis made a gesture of frustration. "It looked like an
Icarii—but there was something . . . wrong. Something different. Gods, Isaiah, I saw him for an instant only, and that
from a distance. I can't give you anything more than that.
I'm sorry."

"You are of little help to me, Axis."

"I am trying my best for you, damn it!"

"What I need, Axis, is—"

Right at that moment the Goblet of the Frogs, sitting on
the low table in the center of the chamber, screamed in formless terror.

Isaiah heard it, and Axis sensed it, and both felt it to the
core of their beings.

Isaiah stopped midsentence, staring at Axis.

Then he blinked.

"Ishbel," he said, and ran for the door.

* * *

Ishbel supposed she had managed to rack in a little air, for otherwise she should now be dead, but breathing was of little matter to her now.

The baby was being born too rapidly for her body to cope. She was rendered virtually soundless save for the occasional gasp, and incapable of moving save for her desperate writhing.

All Ishbel wanted to do was to get away from the frightful apparition of Ba'al'uz, now standing over her, his eyes gleaming, his sword held ready. All she wanted was for someone to rush in and discover her, and save her, and make this pain stop, make this pain stop, oh, gods, make this pain stop . . .

She tried to reach out for the Great Serpent, tried to use the power of the Coil, but Ishbel had not so much as thought about either the Coil or the Great Serpent for what seemed like weeks now, and in her current extremity both seemed very far away, and untouchable.

Then, suddenly, the baby was being born, and Ba'al'uz was reaching down.

At DarkGlass Mountain, the bands of black encircling the pyramid now raced for the shafts which fed light into the Infinity Chamber.

Within moments, every one of the bands of black blood had slithered into the shafts, and were sliding toward the Infinity Chamber.

Isaiah didn't even pause to order the armed men waiting outside his chamber to follow him. He ran, using every particle of strength and speed and agility he commanded, through the corridors toward Ishbel's chamber.

Axis was a step behind him, and then a bare step behind Axis came the dozen or so armed men whose commander's desperation had been order enough.

Isaiah reached Ishbel's chamber in a matter of moments. There was a guard standing outside, clearly alarmed by the sudden arrival of Isaiah, Axis, and the soldiers.

"Your sword, fool," Isaiah snapped, then snatched it from the guard without pausing to wait for him to react.

Then he was inside, and staring at a tableau that, for the rest of his life, he would never be able to forget.

Ba'al'uz—a terribly disfigured Ba'al'uz, but Ba'al'uz nonetheless—straightening up from a bloodied Ishbel sprawled on the floor, a baby in one hand and a sword in the other.

A dog at his heels, an ugly street cur, baying and yapping as if it wanted the baby for its own.

Isaiah ran for him, but it seemed as if every step he took was in slow motion.

He took one step, and Ba'al'uz raised the child before him.

He took another step, and Ba'al'uz lifted his sword.

He took yet another step, hearing a distant roaring, which he only very dimly realized was himself, and Ba'al'uz took the baby's head off with one clean sweep of the sword.

Another step, and Ba'al'uz was turning toward him, an expression of half surprise, half pleasure on his face.

"I did it," he said. "Kanubai is born."

And then Isaiah took his final step, and he raised his own sword, and he smote Ba'al'uz' head from his shoulders with such force it flew across the room and smashed against a far wall.

Isaiah took off the dog's head with the return swing of the sword.

CHAPTER SEVENTEEN

DarkGlass Mountain, Isembaard

The Infinity Chamber rang with blackness and death and blood. Manic shadows writhed about the shattered chamber, and as, firstly, Ba'al'uz' sword struck, then the two strikes from Isaiah's sword, blood spattered in great, terrible gouts across the walls of the chamber.

There came a roaring, as if a giant, far, far below, was taking a massive intake of breath in order to bellow.

The room began to stink. Gaseous fumes and malodorous clouds billowed through the chamber, and the blood staining the walls appeared to thicken and then coagulate, before slumping to the floor in sickening, gelatinous masses.

Then, from far below, the giant bellowed, and the crack opened into a rent, and the abyss opened into the Infinity Chamber.

In the River Lhyl, the frogs cowered, and Isaiah, bending over Ishbel in his palace, looked up briefly, the tragedy deepening in his eyes.

The shadows continued to writhe, gaining strength and thickness with every frenzied turn about the Infinity Chamber. The formless, soundless bellow came once more, this time stilling the shadows.

As one, they fell to the floor and were absorbed by the masses of coagulated blood.

All was still.

Then, something . . .

The separate pools of blood were now one, and now were no more.

Instead, there lay on the floor of the darkened Infinity Chamber the form of a dog-headed man.

Kanubai.

He rolled over onto his back, still weak, but far, far stronger than he had been in an infinity of time.

And *flesh*! Flesh! The blood of the child, the dog, and Ba'al'uz had all combined, and Kanubai was now infused with the matter and power of all three.

Best of all, most *delicious* of all, he was now made flesh with the blood of his enemy, so that he could *become* his enemy, and his enemy could no longer have any power over him.

Kanubai raised his muzzle, and sent a thin howl shrieking about the chamber.

Thousands of leagues to the north, the Skraelings heard, and wept for joy.

Kanubai whispered to them, and his whispers were magic, and the Skraelings began to alter.

About Kanubai, as he lay on the floor of the Infinity Chamber, the glass mountain gloated.

Finally, it had the tool of its revenge.

Many leagues to the north, Maximilian suddenly awoke from his sleep. He stared into the night, riddled with cold and shock.

Kanubai had just risen.

Maximilian had been fast asleep when something in the Twisted Tower shifted, fell over, and shattered. It had been a simple glass vase, but Maximilian had learned that it was an object to be feared.

Its death would herald Kanubai's rise.

Gods, Maximilian thought, *how can I ever manage? How can I ever be what is needed to defeat Kanubai? And where are my helpers, my servants? Where Light, and Water?*

He did not sleep again that night.

CHAPTER EIGHTEEN

The Palace of Aqhat, Isembaard

Ishbel refused to believe what she had just witnessed.

That could not have happened.

No. She was in agony from the birth, she had lost much blood, she was in shock.

She could not have just seen what her eyes insisted she had seen.

Maximilian's baby was safe. She would find it in a moment, on the floor perhaps, cold and bruised but alive.

Maximilian's baby was alive. It must be. It must be, oh, gods, it must be alive . . .

Isaiah was shouting . . .

At Axis, who had just appeared behind Isaiah's shoulder.

Shouting something about Zeboath, and Axis, after giving her one long appalled look, turned and ran, shouting in turn at the armed men who had crowded into the chamber.

Yes. Zeboath. That's who she needed. That's who her baby needed. Zeboath was good. Ishbel felt an overwhelming rush of affection for Isaiah. Isaiah knew what to do. He had killed Ba'al'uz. She was very grateful to him.

Now, if he could just help her to sit up. If he could just hand her the baby, then all would be well.

"Ishbel . . ." Isaiah dropped the sword, and Ishbel winced at the noise of it clattering to the floor.

He bent down to her, gathering her into his arms and lifting her as easily as if she had been the baby.

"My baby," she said. "Please, Isaiah, give me my baby."

He turned about so that she faced away from Ba'al'uz' body and that of . . .

Ishbel began to moan, and Isaiah held her close, and

rocked her back and forth, murmuring to her as gently as if she were a baby herself, and Ishbel began to weep.

Zeboath passed a trembling hand over his eyes.

He had just spent an hour with Ishbel, now settled in a chamber distant from the bloodied mess where she'd given birth, and he felt drained and barely able to talk.

"Well?" said Isaiah.

They were standing outside the closed door of Ishbel's chamber, he, Isaiah, and Axis.

"Ishbel is well enough," said Zeboath, "considering what she has just gone through. The birth was sudden, and thus very painful, but it did her surprisingly little damage. Often, you see, when babies come this quickly, they—"

"Yes, yes," said Isaiah. "Ishbel *is* well?"

"Well enough in body," said Zeboath. "But in spirit . . ."

They stood in silence a moment, each remembering the frightful, bloody scene where Ishbel had given birth.

"She keeps asking me for the baby," Zeboath said. "She says she wants to hold the baby. But how can I give it to her? Gods, I can't sew that head back on! And I can't give her . . . I can't give her the . . . headless . . . I can't . . ."

Axis put a hand on Zeboath's shoulder. "You have done more than enough, Zeboath. Thank you."

Zeboath took a deep, shuddery breath. "If it is any consolation, I do not think the baby would have lived, anyway. It was early, yes, even though by a month only, but its lungs had not formed, and its body was severely malnourished. Both Ishbel and I had been worried about its lack of movement over these past weeks. I think perhaps the drugs and poisons Ba'al'uz gave Ishbel during the journey through the FarReach Mountains . . ."

"You told her this?" Isaiah said.

Zeboath nodded. "She needed to know, Excellency."

Isaiah sighed. "Yes. She needed to know. I thank you as well, Zeboath. You have done your best for both of us today. Axis, can you supervise the clearing of Ishbel's chamber? Take away Ba'al'uz' body and that of the damned dog and *burn* the damned things. And, ah, speak to the palace chamberlain about a burial for the baby. Tell him that I want a full ceremony at dawn tomorrow. The least we can do for Ishbel is to farewell the child in full due. Then meet me back in my private chamber. We need to talk."

Axis nodded, and left.

"Is Ishbel awake?" Isaiah asked Zeboath.

"Yes. I have given her an herbal draft to sedate her, but she is still awake."

"Good," said Isaiah.

Ishbel lay completely still on her bed in the darkened chamber, weeping great silent tears that rolled down her cheeks and soaked into her pillow.

For the first time in weeks she was thinking about Maximilian. All she could think about was how much he'd wanted this child.

A family of his own. Children of his own, when for so many long, terrible years that concept had been a dream beyond reach.

He'd loved her growing belly, had been so proud of it and of her.

So cherished a hope, shattered with such callous madness.

Ishbel wept for Maximilian, not for herself. The baby had been a girl. A daughter. Ishbel could imagine Maximilian with a daughter, imagine his face creasing in a delighted smile as the girl played before him, imagine him swinging her high in the air in his arms, imagine his face, the *wonder* in his face, as he watched her grow.

And she'd lost the baby. Lost her.

Nothing Zeboath had said to her had eased her guilt. Ba'al'uz may have been the hand by which the child had died, whether by poison or by that single, devastating sword stroke, but Ishbel felt as if she had killed the child herself, through lack of interest.

She'd never really cared for her pregnancy. She'd regarded it with distaste or disinterest or outright resentment.

Today her daughter had paid for that disinterest and resentment.

"Ishbel?"

Isaiah was standing by the side of the bed, looking at her. He hesitated, then sat down carefully on the bed.

He lifted one of her hands into his, interlacing their fingers, and he sat there for an hour in silence, holding her hand in his, and kept her company until she finally succumbed to Zeboath's herbal draft and slid into sleep.

Isaiah sat, his fingers interlaced with Ishbel's, and watched her sleep.

This was his fault. His alone.

He'd ignored the risk of Ba'al'uz, and had assumed the man was simply off wandering in some deranged manner about Coroleas.

Ba'al'uz *had* been wandering, deranged, but in the end his steps had been guided and purposeful.

Isaiah had assumed that placing guards about Ishbel would keep her safe, and they had not.

Ba'al'uz had come wrapped in Kanubai's power, and no mortal man would have seen him.

Gods, what would Lister say when he heard?

Isaiah lifted his head and looked out the window. He could not see DarkGlass Mountain, but he could *feel* it, and he knew Kanubai had finally wormed his way free of the abyss.

Via the blood of the sacrificial child, the child of Maximilian and Ishbel.

And that rope of tortured souls? What part had Dark-Glass Mountain itself had to play in today's tragedy? Had it whispered to Kanubai the means? Had it whispered to him a *plan*?

Shit . . . shit . . . *shit*!

Maximilian and Ishbel's child, sacrificed to Kanubai.

Kanubai, born of Maximilian's flesh.

It was a disaster.

They had no time to waste now. Kanubai was still very weak, and would be so until the Skraelings reached him, but Isaiah did not think he'd be having any more meditative sessions inside DarkGlass Mountain.

He had to move north, and he had to return Ishbel north. No one was doing any good here.

But for now, he sat and held Ishbel's hand, watching her sleep.

CHAPTER NINETEEN

The Palace of Aqhat, Isembaard

Isaiah walked back to his own chambers, leaving Ishbel's chamber surrounded by armed men.

As he walked he stared into the faces of the palace guards, trying to see in their bland expressions any hint of disloyalty, or treason.

He could almost hear the whispers seething about the entire tyranny.

The tyrant is weak. Now is our time.

All Isaiah wanted was to concentrate on Ishbel, and then on whatever was now growing inside DarkGlass Mountain, on the damned glass pyramid itself, but he could not afford to. If he didn't shore up his hold on the throne *right now* then there would be no invasion, and if there was no invasion . . .

Then there would be nothing left.

All he wanted was to spend the night watching Ishbel sleep, but what he *needed* was to get back to his private quarters and call the generals to attendance and order the invasion of the north *now*.

Isaiah had to admire Lister's tactics. He was almost certain that the assassination attempt had been Lister's doing—the bowman had surely been one of the Lealfast, and the man could have killed him as easily as he had wounded him. Lister had wanted to spur Isaiah into action and, by the gods, he'd managed it.

But Lister could *not* have predicted the true disaster of this day . . . could he?

Damn it, now Isaiah was beginning to see treachery lurking in every shadow.

* * *

Isaiah strode into his private chamber in a black mood, ready to shout for his chamberlain to fetch his generals, when he stopped dead, appalled and angry, and horribly frightened to see Axis sitting at the table leaning back in the chair, legs crossed comfortably at the ankles, feet resting on the table, and chatting apparently quite amiably to Lister through Isaiah's glass pyramid, which sat in the center of the table.

Isaiah slammed the door shut behind him, hitting one of the approaching servants in the face.

He didn't give a damn.

"Why, Axis," Isaiah said softly, "what do you now?"

Axis straightened up in the chair, putting his feet back on the floor, and nodded at the pyramid. "Lister intuited that there was a fuss. He opened the communication, Isaiah. Not I. He wanted to know what was happening."

"And you told him?"

"Most of it, yes," Axis said, and Isaiah had to physically restrain himself from bunching his fists. *Had he lost control over the entire world on this day?*

He looked into the glass pyramid and went cold. Always before, when he had communicated with Lister, the man was within his palace of Crowhurst. Now, however, Lister was garbed in a hooded black cloak, gusting in the wind, and he was standing on what appeared to be a ridge overlooking a vast snowy plain.

Over which flowed an army of Skraeling wraiths.

The Skraelings were on the move.

A movement at the corner of his eye caught Isaiah's attention.

It was Axis, looking intently at Isaiah and then moving his eyes fractionally toward the pyramid.

There was something in there Axis wanted Isaiah to see.

Isaiah looked at Lister, who was smiling amiably and waiting patiently for Isaiah to greet him, and then looked more clearly behind the man.

There was something else behind Lister other than seething wraiths and snowy plains.

Something in the sky.

Something flying, and then alighting in the distance behind and below Lister.

"Where are you, Lister?" Isaiah said, growing cold at the realization of what he'd just seen.

"I've left home," said Lister. "The wraiths decided all this waiting was terribly tedious, and just like that they decided to head south. Swarm. They claim a deep hunger."

"Where are you?" barked Isaiah.

Lister made a pretense of rubbing his hands together and blowing out his cheeks, as if surprised to find himself out in the cold. "Oh, somewhere just above Gershadi, I believe," he said. "Nasty weather, eh?"

Then he dropped all pretense and looked very directly at Isaiah. "It is time you moved, Isaiah. More than time, considering what Axis has just told me. An assassination attempt. And then that scoundrel, Ba'al'uz, murdering your beautiful new bride's child."

Lister hesitated there, staring through the pyramid into Isaiah's eyes, and while he did not speak verbally, Isaiah could hear Lister's screaming thoughts.

He murdered Maximilian and Ishbel's child. He sacrificed it! Have you got any idea what that child has been used for, Isaiah? Do you realize what—

"I know, Lister," Isaiah whispered, and Axis looked strangely at him.

"What a trouble, eh?" Lister carried on, conscious that Axis was listening. "Best to leave Isembaard behind and embark on your conquest of the northern world, yes?" His voice hardened. "It is time to *save* something, Isaiah, or else lose everything."

And then he was gone, and the pyramid dulled into lifelessness. Isaiah picked it up, looked at it a moment, then put it away in a box.

"What did Lister mean, Isaiah?"

Isaiah gave a shrug.

Axis' eyes narrowed. There had been a great deal more to that conversation than mere words. "Did you see the creature alighting behind Lister, Isaiah?"

"Yes. Was it an Icarii?"

"Possibly. And possibly not. Isaiah, that assassin was sent by Lister."

Isaiah hesitated. Then, grudgingly, he answered, "Yes."

"Why?"

"Lister wants me to invade. He thought I was delaying. Therefore he created the circumstances under which I would *have* to invade. If I don't, one of the generals will be sitting on my bloodstained throne within a week."

And in a month after that . . . Kanubai?

"When, Isaiah?"

Isaiah looked at him for a long moment. "Invade. Now. In six short weeks I can be in the Outlands." He paused. "Did you enjoy using the pyramid, Axis?"

"Yes. I could *smell* the Star Dance oozing from it. Who are those almost-Icarii, Isaiah? I feel sure that you know."

Isaiah was saved from a response by a servant, entering the room, bowing, and announcing the arrival of Isaiah's generals.

Lister put his glass pyramid down in the snow, staring at it as if he would have liked to kick it all the way to Isembaard.

"Peace, Lister," Eleanon said, coming up behind him. "Do not destroy it now. It may yet come in useful. Now, tell me, what has happened?"

"The assassination attempt went well."

"Yes, I know that. Bingaleal is already well on his way home."

"Ba'al'uz appeared from nowhere, back from Coroleas. He attempted to assassinate Ishbel."

"*What*?"

"There is worse," Lister said very softly, staring south as if he could see into the very heart of Aqhat. "Ba'al'uz might have failed at Ishbel, but he has taken the life of Maximilian and Ishbel's child. She is dead. Her head smote from her shoulders."

"*The baby is dead?*"

"And Kanubai risen, no doubt, on the strength of that blood sacrifice. Curse it, Eleanon, I can *feel* Kanubai in my blood and every sinew of my being. Damn Isaiah for not saving that baby. *Damn him!*"

Eleanon thought about pointing out that Isaiah had likely been somewhat distracted by the assassination attempt, but thought it politic not to say that to Lister in his current mood.

"Lister," Eleanon said finally, "what are you going to do? What are *we* going to do?"

"Pray for a miracle, my beloved friend." Lister paused, staring south as if he could will that miracle. "Move, Isaiah. *Move*, damn you! Save what is left before we all die!"

CHAPTER TWENTY

The Palace of Aqhat, Isembaard

The generals, five of them, filed into Isaiah's chamber. They carried no weapons, but that did not lessen the danger Axis felt emanating from them.

He regretted the lack of his own weapon.

Axis glanced at Isaiah. He appeared outwardly calm and composed, confident, but Axis knew he had to be worried.

The generals could make or break him, here and now. After today's—Axis glanced at the open window, seeing with some surprise the first staining of dawn at the horizon— *yesterday's* assassination attempt, Isaiah's vulnerability was now at a critical level.

"Axis SunSoar shall stay for this conference," Isaiah said, waving a hand vaguely in Axis' direction.

Axis nodded at the generals.

Isaiah wasted no time on preliminaries or niceties. "We move," he said. "When you leave me this morning you return to your commands and prepare for my order to march for Salamaan Pass."

Armat, the youngest and, Axis thought, the most dangerous of the generals, looked at the other four generals, but the older men kept their faces expressionless.

Axis moved very slightly, putting himself to one side and between Isaiah and the generals. It was a symbolic gesture only. He did not think the generals would—if in the mood and if they thought the time right—attempt to murder Isaiah here and now.

That would come later. In the darkness of full night, when the assassin's face might not be seen.

"Are you certain we are strong enough for an invasion, Excellency?" Ezekiel said.

Are you certain you *are strong enough?*

"My strength," Isaiah said softly, looking at each of the generals in turn, "depends on your strength. I do you the honor, my friends, of trusting that you are each strong enough, and prepared enough, to do Isembaard proud."

Kezial made a moue. "It is just there are whispers, Excellency. People are . . . anxious . . . after yesterday's unfortunate events. All of Isembaard now knows the tyrant suffered yesterday, was brought to his knees by an assassin's arrow."

"And all of Isembaard is worried," said Lamiah, "that the assassin escaped so cleanly. Who knows when he might strike again?"

Axis looked at Isaiah. The generals were probing, and they were not hiding the fact.

"The responsibility for the regrettable fact of the assassin's escape," Isaiah said, "I lay at your feet. As I blame his entry. If Isembaard worries about its tyrant, who is not to say the tyrant does not worry about the capabilities of his generals, who cannot keep a single bowman away from their lord? Perhaps," he continued, turning away a little and strolling about the chamber, as if supremely relaxed, "I should consider retiring my current generals and replacing them with more experienced command."

He glanced pointedly at Axis.

Axis gave a soft laugh, startled and not a little annoyed by Isaiah's insinuation. Stars, now he had most certainly leapt to the top of the generals' assassination list!

He shot Isaiah a significant look, but Isaiah had averted his eyes and was now toying with the Goblet of the Frogs, which he had lifted from its table.

"We are not responsible for assassination attempts from magicians!" snapped Ezekiel.

"Magicians?" said Isaiah, turning about and looking directly at Ezekiel.

"No one but a magician could have escaped our spearmen," said Morfah. "We must be frank with you, Excellency. We do not relish a confrontation with an army of magicians."

"Especially after what happened with the Eastern Independencies," said Lamiah, very softly.

To a man the generals were now standing aggressively, shoulders thrown back slightly, bodies rigid, eyes hard and confrontational. Axis may not have been in the chamber, for all the attention they gave him.

Axis tensed himself, wishing for what must have been the fiftieth time he knew why it was that Isaiah had failed so dismally in the Eastern Independencies.

Of everyone, Isaiah still appeared relaxed and sure of himself. "Who needs magici—" he began.

"People think you are weak, Isaiah," Armat said.

Not "Excellency" now. Just "Isaiah."

"Who needs magicians," Isaiah said again, his stance also confrontational, "when I command the land itself?"

Ezekiel, as did Lamiah and Armat, opened his mouth, and then closed it, his eyes wide, as he stared at the Goblet of the Frogs.

It was . . . moving.

Axis stared himself, unable to believe what he was seeing. A shaft of the dawn light had hit the caged glass goblet, illuminating it as if it were filled with blood. Spectacular as that effect was, it was not what had so startled everyone watching Isaiah.

The glass frogs attached to the reeds set into the side of the goblet were now moving. They clambered playfully up and down the sides of the goblet, jumping in and out of the cup, croaking cheerfully.

The reeds themselves wafted, as if caught by a breeze.

And the glass of the inner wall of the goblet shifted and rippled, as if it were water.

One of the frogs crawled over the back of one of Isaiah's hands, then dropped into the bowl of the goblet.

Isaiah had not moved his eyes from his generals. "Imagine," he said softly, "if I can make this simple glass goblet come to life and do my bidding, what I might do to a sword at a man's hip, if that man annoyed me. The elements themselves obey me, my friends, and I would beg you to consider your wives' and children's tears and do similar."

Axis could not speak. He was stunned. He'd always suspected Isaiah of some kind of supernatural power. But to see this, now . . .

Ezekiel stiffened. "My life and my command is yours at your will, Excellency. You need not doubt my loyalty."

Isaiah's mouth moved in a small cynical smile.

"And mine," said Morfah, and the other generals tripped over their tongues, hastening to assure Isaiah of their respective loyalties.

"Then do as I bid," Isaiah said softly, "and do as I say. Ready your commands—and the families who wish to partake of the riches of the kingdoms beyond the FarReach Mountains—at the head of the Salamaan Pass for me to join you. The Northern Kingdoms shall not be another debacle. I can assure you of that."

The generals looked, nodded, then left.

"Well," said Axis, "I had been dozing off there until you produced that little surprise. I had no idea, Isaiah."

Isaiah put the goblet back on the table. "It was a trick of the light, Axis, nothing more. Generals are so easily fooled, so easily manipulated."

Now it was Axis who allowed the cynicism to flower on his face, but he said no more on the matter.

But, oh, gods, who could he ask about the Eastern Independencies campaign?

"I would like to give you command of ten thousand men, Axis," Isaiah said.

"No," said Axis, "I will not fight the Northern Kingdoms for you, Isaiah. I don't agree with this invasion and I do not like your alliance with Lister."

"Are you refusing me?"

"I am refusing you, but I am not rebelling. There is a difference."

"Yes. I *am* aware of the difference, Axis. Very well then, if you will not fight for me, will you at least act as my . . ." He paused, looking for a suitable term.

"Adjutant," said Axis with a smile, using a rather archaic word for a general assistant to a military commander. "Adjutant" covered a myriad of ills.

Isaiah laughed softly. "Adjutant, then. Yes. That would

please me. And, as my adjutant, if you might keep a sword
by your hip at all times from this point on, that would also
please me."

"The generals are restless, Isaiah. This campaign needs
to go well."

"Perhaps I should reconsider and give you my entire army
to command."

"Isaiah," Axis said, hesitantly, "have you considered the
possibility of *not* invading?"

"That is not a possibility."

"Isaiah—"

"It is *not* a possibility, Axis."

Axis held Isaiah's eyes for a long moment, then he nodded, and left the chamber.

Once Axis had gone Isaiah wasted no time in contacting
Lister.

You fool! he hissed, more angry than he had been in countless years. *What did you think you were doing, eh? Trying
to force my hand? Look what happened! The palace was in
uproar, Ishbel was left unprotected, and Ba'al'uz murdered
her and Maximilian's child!*

You were not moving fast enough, Lister said. *You needed
to be pushed. Now you will need to move, if only to keep your
throne for the time it takes you to get you and yours into the
Outlands. Kanubai has been born. You shall need to leave
in the morning.*

Isaiah's temper had quieted, but only to a deeper, colder
anger than previously.

You want me to move from Aqhat in the morning—

You need to, Lister said. *Kanubai has risen! DarkGlass
Mountain writhes! You cannot possibly remain there—*

*I cannot move, not for ten days or so. If I move in the
morning then all will say I am unsettled and frightened,
weakened, by the assassination attempt and am fleeing. I'll
be dead by evening by one of the generals' swords. Then
where will our little "invasion" be, eh? I need to be alive
and in control to lead this land to safety and, after your little
stupidity of today, that means I will need to remain here for*

a time yet. Kanubai cannot act immediately. Not without the lifeblood of the Skraelings. Where are they?

Still distant. But don't leave it any longer than two weeks to leave for the north. Please, please, Isaiah, be careful.

Isaiah did not reply for a moment. Gods, the damned, cursed *stupidity* of Lister!

Have you discovered Maximilian's whereabouts? Isaiah finally asked.

There has been a rumor that he was seen in the FarReach Mountains. There have been some Icarii closely associated with him hanging about Deepend and transferring supplies south. I think he is in the FarReach Mountains, Isaiah. Perhaps even in Isembaard by now. You need to get out of Aqhat or else Kanubai will have Maximilian to swallow, too!

[Part Eight]

CHAPTER ONE

The FarReach Mountains

StarDrifter leaned back against the rock face in the gully Maximilian had decided would shelter them for the night and tried not to sigh too deeply. He felt exhausted, and was both ashamed and concerned by the depth of his fatigue. He'd always been so fit, so strong. To now hardly be able to manage a day's travel through mountain passes, even if that journeying could be difficult, was humiliating. He had no idea what was wrong with him. He thought he would shout in frustration if he had to brush off yet another murmur of concern from Ravenna or Venetia or Maximilian, and all he ever wanted was to eat—*stars, he was so hungry!*—and then sleep.

He shifted uncomfortably. He'd neither washed nor changed his clothes in the two weeks they'd been traversing the mountains, and the linen of his shirt was stiff with sweat and dirt and scratched uncomfortably at his back.

He'd managed to pick a damnably lumpy piece of rock to lean against, too. StarDrifter raised himself enough to lean forward a bit, easing his aching back, and glared at the rock. It *appeared* perfectly smooth, but he knew it contained myriad jagged edges, because, by the gods, they had dug into every plane of his spine.

Salome was sitting a pace or two away. She looked as bad as StarDrifter felt himself, but at least she had her growing baby as an excuse for her weariness.

There was the soft, whispering sound of wings, and StarDrifter looked up.

BroadWing and his companions were landing, laden with bundles of food.

Without the four Icarii, StarDrifter seriously doubted any of them would have managed the mountain traverses. The Icarii scouted ahead for the best route, and they ferried in food from the northern borderlands of the mountains. Their efforts meant those confined to the ground needed to carry much less with them, and could travel faster.

Well, they could have traveled faster had not StarDrifter and Salome held them back.

StarDrifter's mouth watered, and he tried to avoid looking too desperately at the food bundles. BroadWing and the others did a magnificent job, but it was hard on them. The deeper Maximilian led his party into the mountains, the further they had to fly every few days for food supplies. Maximilian did not want them flying into Isembaard. The Tyranny had no contact with Icarii so far as anyone knew, and Maximilian did not want to put the Icarii into the possibly dangerous position of being mistaken for flying demons and skewered by a terrified peasant or guardsman.

"StarDrifter," said BroadWing, handing the bundle he carried to Venetia. "You look—"

StarDrifter waved away the query. "I am well enough, BroadWing. Just a little tired."

BroadWing did not need to say anything—the expression on his face registered his concern well enough.

"We'll be out of these mountains within two or three days," Maximilian said. He'd built a fire, using pieces of the coarse heather that dotted the more sheltered parts of the mountain passes. The heather smoked horribly, but it burned, and it produced heat, and for that everyone was grateful.

Maximilian looked at StarDrifter as he spoke, and StarDrifter realized there was a connection he should be making . . . some decision he should be announcing. He tried to marshal his thoughts . . . oh, yes . . .

"It will soon be time for you to leave us, BroadWing," StarDrifter said, smiling for the man. "Head back into the safety of the north."

"Hardly 'safety,'" BroadWing muttered, sitting down beside StarDrifter. During their trips back to buy food, the Icarii had heard snatches of gossip about the escalating wars between the Central Kingdoms. The Outlands had invaded Pelemere, the fighting stretching to the borders of Kyros. Maximilian was desperately worried about Escator. Although he barely spoke of it, the others could see his concern in the tightness about his eyes and mouth every time the Icarii came back with more news.

They were not to know Maximilian also knew of the birth of Kanubai, and lay awake many nights, going through the Twisted Tower, trying to *guess* what objects might fill the empty spots, and what they might mean.

"But you *will* go," StarDrifter said. Since his somewhat reluctant acceptance of the title of Talon, the Icarii scouts had looked to him, rather than Maximilian, for direction. StarDrifter had initially found that difficult—the years spent as a bitter exile at the Corolean court had undermined his prior easy acceptance of his status within Icarii society— but very gradually princely command had returned, and the Icarii's deference felt less strange.

"Yes, we will go," BroadWing said. His mouth crooked. "We will stand out a little too much, I think, for an easy passage in Isembaard. We will go back to Kyros, or perhaps even Pelemere, and wait for you there. Stars alone knows where you will come *out* of these mountains again, once you have rescued Ishbel."

"BroadWing," Maximilian said, leaning forward slightly, "if there are any troubles—"

"Then we will let you know," BroadWing said. "Somehow."

Maximilian nodded, leaning back. It was the best he could hope for.

Venetia and Serge prepared a meal while everyone sat watching and unspeaking, lost in their thoughts.

The traverse through the mountains had been difficult and wearying for everyone, not just StarDrifter and Salome, but it had not been fraught with too many hardships. The mountains *were* traversable, it was just that people without benefit of winged companions who could scout ahead for the best and most direct routes, or who could also fetch and carry for them, tended to lose themselves within the ten thousand gullies and valleys between the peaks and starve before they ever managed to find their way out. The FarReach Mountains were a maze of blind gullies and valleys, difficult to move through and impossible to climb out of.

Without the Icarii, Maximilian was sure they would have found the journey almost impossible.

He finished his meal, once again grateful to the Icarii for their help, and studied Salome and StarDrifter.

They looked terrible. Both appeared to have lost weight (although that was difficult to gauge, given their bulky warm clothing), their faces were pale, and smudged under their eyes were deep circles of weariness.

What was wrong with them?

"Salome," Maximilian said, "I want Venetia to have a look at you and StarDrifter. We need to know what's wrong."

"There's nothing wrong," both said together, glanced at each other, then as quickly looked away again.

They had largely traveled as a pair, StarDrifter staying close to Salome and helping her if she needed. At night they bundled down very close. They did not argue, nor express any particular emotion toward the other. In fact, they barely passed a word between them. Maximilian did not know if that was merely a by-product of their exhaustion, or if they had arrived at some silent companionship that was not friendship, but a resigned acknowledgment of their ties.

Personally, Maximilian thought it was likely a combination of both.

"Look, Maxel," StarDrifter said, "I don't think anything is—"

"If Venetia could look at my back, I'd be grateful," Salome put in. "The past few days it has been so sore . . . perhaps I have pulled a ligament."

"Then a rub may help it," Venetia said, moving over to Salome's side. She tried to aid Salome in removing her jacket, vest, and shirt while preserving the woman's modesty, but, irritable, Salome shrugged off her attempts to cover her chest.

"I doubt anyone here has not seen a pair of breasts before," she snapped, and StarDrifter smiled. If Venetia had seen Salome parading about in her completely transparent finery in Coroleas then she would not have worried about preserving the woman's "modesty."

Salome shot StarDrifter an irritated look, and he managed to suppress the smile.

Venetia ran her hands over Salome's back, frowning. "There's something wrong with your back," she said. "I don't know . . . Ravenna?"

Her daughter moved over, frowning as well once she saw Salome's back.

"Perhaps it is an infection," Venetia said.

"Venetia?" Maximilian said. "What is it?"

"I don't think it is an infection," Ravenna said quietly. "BroadWing, can you . . . ?"

He came over, and leaned down for a look.

"Stars!" he exclaimed, and almost fell over as he stumbled back a pace. "I cannot believe it!"

"*What is it?*" Maximilian said.

BroadWing did not answer him. Instead he looked to StarDrifter. "StarDrifter . . . is *your* back troubling you?"

"Yes, but it is just weariness, perhaps, and—"

"StarDrifter," said BroadWing, "please have a look at Salome's back."

"Oh, for all the gods' sakes," snapped Salome, as StarDrifter sighed and rose. "Just give it a rub, Venetia, and let me be. I wish I'd never asked you to look at it."

"Oh, dear gods," StarDrifter whispered, also taking a step back as he saw Salome's back.

"*What is*—" Maximilian began, then stopped, astounded, as StarDrifter literally ripped his upper clothes off.

He had never seen such a look of sheer desperation on anyone's face before.

The other Icarii had rushed over by now, and the four of them were standing back, looking between Salome and StarDrifter with expressions that ranged from the incredulous to the awestruck.

"BroadWing," StarDrifter said, his voice tight. "Is . . . is . . ."

BroadWing was looking at StarDrifter's back, then laid a hand softly on it.

"Yes," he said, and StarDrifter moaned, and sank to his knees, his face in his hands.

"Will someone tell me what is going on!" Maximilian snarled, now also on his feet, and looking between Salome's and StarDrifter's backs.

They did look inflamed, and curiously lumpy, as if something had burrowed under the skin on either side of their spines.

Suddenly Maximilian knew what was happening, and did not need BroadWing's quietly spoken confirmation.

"They are regrowing their wings," he said.

"That's impossible," Ravenna said. "I thought you'd both had everything removed . . . wings . . . their roots . . . everything."

"I don't . . . I can't . . ." StarDrifter said, looking up at everyone standing about, tears staining his face. "I can't explain . . . oh, gods, thank you, thank you, *thank you*!"

BroadWing was weeping as well, and he squatted down by StarDrifter and hugged the man.

"Wings?" said Salome. "I don't want wings!"

"Nonetheless," said SongFlight, one of BroadWing's companions, "you shall have them soon enough. See, Maximilian, the wings are forming on either side of their spines, under the skin." Her hand traced down Salome's back, outlining the nascent wings. "They will break through within a few weeks, and grow from there."

"No wonder you both have been so exhausted, and so hungry," said BroadWing. "Your bodies have been putting most of your energy into the development of the wings."

"And Salome's baby?" said StarDrifter, on his feet again. He'd regained some of his composure, and for the first time since he'd met him, Maximilian had a glimpse of the sheer charismatic power of the man.

"Well," said Venetia, "once all the gentlemen here can give us a little privacy, and Salome and I might manage a bit of peace, perhaps I can answer that for you."

"The baby grows well enough," said Salome. "It—"

"He," said StarDrifter.

"—has been moving and wriggling for all *he* is worth. I

doubt he's much fussed about the wings." She paused, looking at StarDrifter as if it was his fault. "I *really* don't want wings."

StarDrifter laughed, the sound one of pure joy. "Welcome to your full heritage, Salome. Welcome to the wonder of Icarii life."

Maximilian smiled, enjoying StarDrifter's happiness.

Then he glanced over to his spot by the fire. For a moment he'd been sure he'd heard the Weeper laughing softly.

CHAPTER TWO

The Palace of Aqhat, Tyranny of Isembaard

Ishbel sat by one of the open windows in her chamber, enjoying the peace and beauty of the night. A breeze wafted in, rippling her lawn nightgown and the hair she'd left loose about her shoulders. The warm air was scented with a hint of faraway spices, and the sound of frogs, and of children playing somewhere, could be heard from the riverbanks.

The river had come to mean so much to her.

From the day after the birth, and murder, of her baby, Isaiah had been taking her down to the river to bathe. For the first three evenings they did this, Ishbel could only sit in the water and weep. Isaiah said nothing, but he would wash her down with gentle hands, and massage her scalp, and soothe her misery. During the day there was always hustle and bustle, people moving and shouting, soldiers and horses milling as Isaiah pushed forward his invasion, but at dusk, everything would quiet, and Isaiah would come for Ishbel, and walk her down to the Lhyl.

There she bathed, and passed some brief and gentle conversations with Isaiah, and healed. Ishbel decided the waters of the Lhyl must hold some magical properties, because their gentle lapping had healed both her body and spirit from the travail and loss of her daughter.

She no longer wept, and every day she waited for the dusk, when Isaiah would come.

Memories of her previous life, more than ever now the baby was gone, slipped further and further away with each day's ending. She never thought of the Great Serpent or her former life in the Coil. She no longer harbored any ambition to return to SerpentNest. Only two weeks had gone by since that terrible night when Ba'al'uz had killed her daughter—and attempted her murder as well—but even that shocking night seemed to be a long-ago dream.

She did think of Maximilian. Not an hour of any day passed that she did not find her mind returning to him. Ishbel did not like this, for thoughts of Maximilian brought such a confusing welter of emotions to the surface that she did not think she could bear it. Prime among these emotions was guilt at the loss of the baby, but there was also a regret that was so sharp it may as well have been a dagger for the degree of pain it caused, and an anger at him for turning such a cold back to her, and an anger at herself for not being honest with him.

She wanted desperately to forget him, and buried herself in Isaiah as a means by which to accomplish this. Isaiah offered her nothing but comfort, and Ishbel needed comfort so badly . . .

Ishbel sighed, wondering where Isaiah was. Preparations for invasion were almost complete. Tomorrow they would leave for Sakkuth, where Isaiah's main army gathered. Ishbel would go with him. Ishbel was ambivalent about returning to the north at the head of an invading army, but she did not wish to be separated from Isaiah, and she could not bear to be left behind at Aqhat, with that pyramid—she glanced in the direction of DarkGlass Mountain—looming over her.

DarkGlass Mountain now exuded a clear and malevolent threat. It was not only she who could feel it, or Isaiah, but everyone. Servants went about their appointed tasks, abnormally quiet, eyes glancing every now and then in the pyramid's direction.

The days seemed somehow darker, and colder.

There was something so ominous, so malignant, about DarkGlass Mountain, that Ishbel felt as if it snatched her very life from her body every time she glanced at it. She tried not to think about what Isaiah had shown her crawling up from the abyss below, nor about how the pyramid seemed to hate her very personally.

Ishbel wanted to leave this place. All the joy of the land

had gone since the death of her child and the growing malevolence throbbing across the Lhyl from DarkGlass Mountain.

There came a soft sound from the corridor outside her chamber, and Ishbel's head tilted slightly in that direction, glad to be distracted from thoughts of the pyramid.

Soft voices. Isaiah, talking with the guards.

Ishbel smiled, pleased. He had come to take her to bathe.

The door opened, and she looked at him. "Isaiah."

Unusually for Isaiah, he was wearing very little jewelry—just some small gold hoops in his ears and a bangle about one wrist, and his great mass of black braids had, like her hair, been left to swing freely about his shoulders and back.

He smiled, just a little, and it struck Ishbel then that Isaiah was a sunshine man, a man of the light, whereas Maximilian had always been so much of the shadows.

"I had hoped you'd still be awake," Isaiah said. "I'm sorry I am so late. We can still go to bathe, if you like, or . . ." He sat down on the low couch with her, their bodies touching in a score of small places, and Ishbel knew then that his "or . . ." held a number of possibilities.

What should she do? Isaiah had always left open the possibility that their "marriage" could be whatever she wanted, and he had never hidden his desire for her.

"It has been dark for hours," she said.

"I'm sorry. Invasions are finicky things to arrange." He reached out a hand, tucking a stray tendril of hair behind one of her ears, and let his fingers linger a moment on her skin, caressing.

Ishbel hesitated, then leaned her head, very slightly, against the pressure of his fingers. *Maybe he would be a comfort for her.*

"We will be leaving in the morning," he said.

"Yes."

"I know this journey back to your homeland will be difficult for you. It is possibly not the way you'd hoped to return. I'm sorry it must be at the head of an army, at my side."

"I am not so sorry to be going home at your side," she said, very softly. She wondered if she was doing the right thing, if succumbing to Isaiah's seductions would cause more problems than it might solve.

But he was so comforting, and she found herself longing very much for the reassurance of a man's arms about her, and the solidity of his body curled about hers at night.

Perhaps if she went to Isaiah, she would forget Maximilian.

He, surely, had forgotten her.

"Then I am most pleased at that," he said, and cupped her face in his hands, and kissed her.

This night, when his hand encircled her breast, she moved in toward him, rather than away.

"Frankly, I thought Isaiah would have put you in complete command of all his forces by now," Ezekiel said, draining his wine cup. "It is a wonder I have a job left at all."

Axis laughed, and refilled both their wine cups. They were in Ezekiel's quarters, and had been for the past hour, sinking ever more deeply into a slight inebriation. Although Axis had spent time with Ezekiel and several other of the generals previously, this was the first time he'd spent such a companionable evening with him.

Companionable, but they were both still wearing their swords.

"Isaiah offered me a command," Axis said. "I refused."

"Really? Why?"

"You thought it might be a stepping-stone for me to greater things? A generalship, perhaps?"

"The thought had crossed my mind."

"And the minds of Morfah and Kezial and Lamiah and Armat, too, no doubt."

"Indeed. Why did you refuse the command?"

"It was tempting, Ezekiel, I won't deny that, but I did not want to lead men against the kingdoms to the north."

"A conscience, then."

Axis smiled. "And that's not a good thing for a general, eh?"

Ezekiel tipped his head in a vague response. "And so you will be moving north with us?"

"Yes. I may not wish to command, Ezekiel, but I do not want to be left behind."

"Then watch your back, Axis. Lamiah and Armat particu-

larly resent you. *And* fear you, which is even more dangerous.
You are too close to Isaiah, and they worry about your connection to the Icarii assassin."

Axis wasn't quite sure where to start with that little
speech—there was so much to think about, and address,
within it. "You *don't* resent me, Ezekiel?"

"A little, but not fatally."

Axis laughed in genuine amusement, and decided he both
liked and trusted this man. "I was not responsible for that
assassin. I am not even convinced he *was* Icarii. There was
something about him . . ."

Ezekiel arched an eyebrow.

"Ah, I don't know," said Axis. "I can't put a finger to it. Just
a . . . strangeness. Ezekiel, will you tell me something?"

Ezekiel retreated only a little into wariness. "Perhaps."

"I have been here a year now, and I have yet to hear of
the debacle of the Eastern Independencies. What happened,
Ezekiel? I know enough of Isaiah to know he is a more than
competent commander. Considering the forces he has to
command and what I have heard are the inadequacies of the
Eastern Independencies . . ."

"The campaign to take the Eastern Independencies," said
Ezekiel, "was Isaiah's first major campaign. It *should* have
been a walkover."

"But . . ."

"All went well. Isaiah led a vast army toward the Independencies. There were a few skirmishes. Then, on the night
before what would have been a—and probably the only—
major battle with the deeply inadequate forces of the Eastern
Independencies, Isaiah disappeared."

"Disappeared?"

Ezekiel gave a small shrug. "Was taken. Kidnapped, if
you like. It was a massive embarrassment for his security
guard. He was in his command tent, late at night. Alone. The
tent was ringed with armed men, all awake and alert. The men
later said they'd heard the sound of a scuffle inside the tent,
and as some tightened the ring about the perimeter of Isaiah's
tent, others rushed inside.

"Isaiah was gone. Vanished. It was *inexplicable*. Ah . . .

shetzah!" Ezekiel cursed, waving a hand about in the air as if somehow the air could explain it all, and Axis could see that the kidnap still troubled the general.

"You couldn't find him?" Axis said.

Ezekiel grunted. "We searched, the entire *army* searched, and we could not find him. He was gone a month."

"And the Independencies' army? They . . ."

"Laughed at us. I swear we could hear them from several miles distance. Then they packed up and went home. They did not fear us."

"*They* didn't have him?"

"We sent emissaries, but their generals swore they hadn't taken Isaiah, and we were forced to believe them."

"You didn't attack?"

Ezekiel hesitated. "No. We didn't. The Independencies' generals said the ground itself was infested with evil spirits, and that if we attacked them then we'd vanish as Isaiah had."

"And you *believed* them?"

"You weren't there!" Ezekiel snapped. "And it wasn't so much a matter of attacking the Independencies to see if we could recover Isaiah . . . ah, Axis, you know us, and you know the way our society works. Everyone with claim to a fistful of power lusts for the throne. So . . . once we'd established that Isaiah was well and truly gone . . ."

"The Eastern Independencies were forgotten for the moment as various generals vied for the throne."

"Yes. We fought among ourselves. It was not our proudest moment, Axis. There we were, in the middle of a vast, arid, gods-forgotten plain, and Isaiah's army descended into madness as general fought against general and company against company. Scores were settled, rivalries decided, and one of my comrades, General Thettle, finally managed to seize control. It was a bloody, stupid, inexcusable mess. Tens of thousands died."

Axis was so astounded he could not comment. How could such undiscipline, such *sheer stupidity*, have not witnessed the fall of the Tyranny well before now? He had to silently congratulate whoever had taken Isaiah . . . they'd known just how easily the Isembaardian army could be brought to its knees.

"It took a month," Ezekiel continued, "but Thettle got what he wanted. We were in desperate straits, almost out of supplies, vulnerable, but at least we had a tyrant again. Thettle had himself crowned and anointed in the middle of the bloodstained plain. I . . . I . . . was the one to slip the golden collar of command about his shoulders. I stood back, and Thettle walked forward to receive the acclaim of the as-sembled soldiers, and . . ."

"And . . ." Axis was on the edge of his seat by now, his wine forgotten.

"Isaiah appeared out of nowhere . . . out of *nowhere*, Axis, and walked up to Thettle and struck his head from his body with his sword. Then he took the blood-soaked golden collar from Thettle's corpse, draped it about his own shoulders, and announced we were going home."

"I . . . what . . . where . . ."

Ezekiel grinned wryly. "That just about mirrors the reac-tion of the entire army, Axis. We were all stunned, speechless, desperate to know what had happened, where Isaiah had been, who had taken him . . . and he told us nothing. He sim-ply ordered the army home . . . and home we came. He has never spoken of that month since, where he had been, what had happened, who had taken him."

"Do you think he'd managed it himself? Scared of the impending battle, perhaps?"

"Isaiah has never been a man to be scared of battle, Axis. Besides, there was no escape from that tent. Whoever took him had power of some sort."

"Isaiah . . . the other night . . . with the Goblet of the Frogs . . ."

"Isaiah came back changed, Axis. He is a different man to what he was once. *Before* the Eastern Independencies campaign Isaiah was a mirror of his father, short-tempered, brutal, viciously ambitious. Everyone was terrified of him. But that's not the man you know, is it?"

"No."

"I don't know what happened to him, Axis, but Isaiah

now is vastly different to the Isaiah who first took the throne. And, to be frank, I think I am even more scared of this one." Ezekiel gave a grunt of humorless laughter. "Sometimes we probe him, Axis, as you saw, but then he does something, and it reminds us of the look we saw in his eyes when he strode out of thin air and took Thettle's life, and we back off."

He paused. "Armat is the only one who wasn't there. Who didn't see that look. He is the one to watch, Axis. He is the one who will make the move on Isaiah eventually."

They had made love, somewhat cautiously, and very gently, and now Ishbel lay sleeping in Isaiah's arms. Isaiah eased himself away from her, and then out of the bed.

He lifted his head and, as he had done so much this past fortnight, and as he had done ever since he had come to live at Aqhat, he looked out the window to where he knew Dark-Glass Mountain rose on the far side of the river.

Then, not pausing to clothe himself, Isaiah left the chamber.

Ishbel opened her eyes as soon as he had gone.

She lay there for all the hours that Isaiah was away, and wept very softly. She wished she hadn't slept with him, for all she had been able to think about while they had made love was that he was not Maximilian.

She had thought sleeping with Isaiah would be a comfort to her, but in reality all it had done was drive home to her how much she missed Maximilian. How much she wanted him.

It was, she thought, a truly pitiful time to realize just how much she had loved Maximilian.

Too late now. Too late for everything.

He went down to the river, knowing this would be the last chance in a very long time—perhaps forever.

He bathed ritually, as he always did, cleansing himself within the pure waters of the Lhyl.

Then, still wet, he crouched in the shallows and looked up at DarkGlass Mountain in the distance.

Kanubai was within. Not yet strong, but *born*.

When he did grow strong, as he surely would within a few months at the very least, Kanubai would be *viciously* strong.

He had been born of the blood of the child of the Lord of Elcho Falling, the only one now who could save this world, but whose task was now grown infinitely more difficult.

And as for DarkGlass Mountain itself, Isaiah swore he could feel it watching him. Like Kanubai, it also needed to grow strong, but once it *was* strong . . .

Isaiah didn't like running away from Kanubai, or Dark-Glass Mountain, but he also knew he had no choice. No one was ready to confront either Kanubai or the pyramid. No one, not even himself or Lister, had the power.

Not this time around. He and Lister had exhausted themselves when first they'd pushed Kanubai down into the abyss. Chaos would not allow himself to be trapped so easily as he had the first time. Now Chaos had an ally who completely altered the balance of power between him and Light and Water.

Sighing, Isaiah looked down to the river water. He spoke to it gently, wishing it well, saying good-bye, and promising to return if and when he could. He begged it to be strong, and to endure, and to hope that with fortune and fortitude it would again one day ring with the Song of the Frogs.

Isaiah paused a while, weeping, then he reached out both hands, cupping them just above the surface of the river, and he spoke a phrase in a strange, guttural language.

For a moment, nothing.

Then a frog broke the surface of the water, and sprang into Isaiah's cupped hands. Another one broke surface, and likewise leaped into Isaiah's hands, and then another, and another, and another.

Soon the surface of the water was boiling with frogs as they leaped frantically into the river god's hands. As soon as they had made the leap successfully, they bounded up his arms where, one by one, they faded and vanished as they were absorbed into Isaiah's body.

* * *

When Isaiah finally made his way back to the palace, the river was empty of the Song of the Frogs.

He went to Ishbel's chamber, kissed her, apologized for not being there when she woke, then went back to his own quarters where, reverently, he packed the Goblet of the Frogs into the saddlebags he would carry with him.

CHAPTER THREE

The Eastern Plains, Gershadi

Jelial, Lord Warden of the Eastern Plains Province of Gershadi, could not credit what he saw. His mind simply would not process the information. He sat his horse, growing colder by the moment, staring ahead at what had been his home base, the castle and town of Hornridge.

It lay in smoking ruins. These tumbled ruins *might* have been a stark black scar against the snow-covered plains save for one thing—it was covered in something gray, and red, which undulated as if it were a sea of pale insects.

"Skraelings," muttered his lieutenant, sitting his horse alongside Jelial.

He and his party of fifteen armed men had been away for six weeks, attending court at Hosea to discuss the escalating military conflict with the Outlands. Jelial had returned to Hornridge mainly to marshal his forces to join Fulmer in his push south against the cursed Outlanders, who were pushing north and threatening to lay siege to Hosea.

Now it looked very much as if Jelial might not have any forces *left* to marshal.

In fact, it looked as if there was not very much left at all.

"Skraelings?" Jelial whispered. He could *see* it was Skraelings. There was a small herd of them not fifty paces away, snuffling around in the remains of a pig herder's hut and pens, but his mind still could not comprehend the enormous numbers of them that it must take to completely cover Hornridge *and* the surrounding countryside for miles about.

It reminded Jelial of something he'd seen as a boy when his father had taken him to hunt the snow deer that lived in the borderlands of the Frozen Wastes. Every year the snow deer migrated south to the rich pasturelands of the lower Sky Peaks in massive herds of million upon millions of animals.

That was what this sight reminded him of, save the migration consisted of million upon millions of Skraelings.

And they were heading south.

"My lord!" his lieutenant hissed, and Jelial looked to where he pointed.

Out of the mass of Skraelings investigating the pigpens came a man. Dressed entirely in black, and with a black cloak billowing out behind him, he appeared to be crossing the snow toward Jelial and his party with supernaturally long strides.

Jelial—as did all his men—drew his sword.

"I will not harm you," said the man, halting a few paces away from Jelial.

He was of striking appearance, exuding power and confidence, and even though he appeared unarmed, Jelial knew that if it came to blows, even a thousand men at his back, bristling with weapons, would not protect him against this being.

"My name is Lister," said the man. "I am Lord of the Skraelings." His mouth twisted a little, and his light brown eyes glinted. "As you can see, I command considerable strength. Hornridge is gone, Jelial. Your family is gone—"

Something tore apart in Jelial's chest, and he thought it was probably his heart, breaking.

"Eaten," Lister said. "Consumed. The Skraelings are hungry, I am afraid."

Jelial tried to speak, but couldn't. Incomprehension and grief had utterly swamped any anger he may have felt.

"Everything is very bloodied at Hornridge," Lister said, his voice quiet now, his eyes fixed on Jelial. "Quite congealed, in fact. I wouldn't even attempt an entry, if I were you. My boys remain hungry, and Hornridge could get bloodier still."

"I . . ." Jelial said, and could get no further.

"We're heading south," Lister said, one arm sweeping out in that direction, making his cloak billow and heave in the wind. "As far as we can go. I have a massive army—"

Jelial wondered why he called it an army and not a herd. His mind, now utterly shocked, kept trying to return to the memory of the migrating herds of snow deer.

"—and it is so very, very hungry. It will eat everything in its path, Jelial. *Everything*. I suggest you return the way you came, and spread the news."

Then he was gone, and Jelial and his men were left sitting their horses in the cold wasteland, looking at the great mass of Skraelings heaving and swelling over what was once their home.

And their families.

Lister, Eleanon, and Inardle stood to one side of the pigpens, cloaked from the vision of Jelial and his party, watching as, eventually, they turned their horses' heads away from Hornridge.

"Thank the gods," Eleanon said. "I thought they might have actually tried to enter Hornridge."

"Grief is a strange beast," said Lister, watching the group as they rode away, "and when coupled with shock it can make men do foolish things."

"I wish we could have saved Hornridge," Inardle said. "No one deserved to die as those people did."

They fell silent, remembering the horror as the Skraelings overwhelmed the castle and town, tearing terrified men and women to shreds.

No one had escaped.

"The entire world is going to be destroyed in far more horrific circumstances," Lister said eventually, "if we cannot manage the impossible."

"Do you think the southerners will listen to Jelial?" said Eleanon. "Do you think they will heed your warning?"

"I hope so," said Lister, "for there is little else I can do to save them. It is not as if I have ever controlled the Skraelings, is it?" He gave a bitter little laugh. "My title of Lord of the Skraelings is completely useless, although I suppose it has served me well to this point. But, oh, gods, how glad I shall be when I can slough it off my shoulders, and leave these disgusting creatures far behind me, and assume my true face."

CHAPTER FOUR

*The Dependency of En-Dor,
the Tyranny of Isembaard*

Maximilian's party emerged from the FarReach Mountains into the very northern reaches of the Dependency of En-Dor. Here Maximilian and StarDrifter and the rest of their group farewelled BroadWing and the other three Icarii. It was an emotional good-bye, particularly for Maximilian and StarDrifter, but everyone had come to like the Icarii and would miss them.

It was too dangerous for the Icarii to remain with the rest of the party. No one knew what kind of reaction they would elicit in Isembaard, and neither Maximilian nor StarDrifter wanted to risk it, no matter how useful the Icarii would have been.

"We will go north," BroadWing said, embracing first StarDrifter, then Maximilian, "and wait for news. Be safe, and snatch back that bride of yours, Maxel. Stars, she will be making you a father soon!"

Then he had grinned at StarDrifter and Salome. "And hide those growing hunchbacks of yours under cloaks. The next time I see you, I expect it to be among the clouds."

Travel through En-Dor was easier than anyone had expected. Maximilian had not exactly known quite *what* to expect— Isembaard was such an unknown quantity—but the northern parts of the dependency were sparsely populated (indeed, many villages were completely deserted)—and those very few occupied small homesteads they did happen across were relatively friendly.

Language was not a problem. Like the kingdoms north of the FarReach Mountains, the Isembaardians spoke a version of the ancient common trading tongue. They spoke a different dialect, and their intonation was very different, but neither presented an obstacle to understanding.

When they did meet with Isembaardians, Maximilian let Venetia and, to a lesser extent, Serge do the talking. Both were fairly dark, and both had come into contact with Isembaardians in the past: Venetia from her conversations with Isembaardian witch-women she'd met in the borderlands of the Land of Dreams, and Serge in his younger and wilder days, when he'd been an assassin for hire, and had spent time in Isembaard.

Whenever their party neared a homestead, Maximilian sent Venetia and Serge in to buy or barter for food, while the rest of them hung back. Maximilian supposed Venetia used a little of her witch-woman skills in order to obtain the co-operation of the villagers, but he did not inquire too closely, and was grateful for whatever food and information Venetia and Serge brought back with them.

One day, a week after they'd farewelled BroadWing and his companions, Venetia and Serge came back with some disturbing news.

"Isembaard is gearing up for war," Serge said, sitting down cross-legged at the fire while Venetia, Ravenna, and Salome, who was feeling far less fatigued than she had in the mountains, handed about fresh bread and goat's cheese. "The tyrant, Isaiah, is marshaling his forces at Sakkuth for a push through the Salamaan Pass into the Outlands. And we've learned the reason why this land is so deserted. Apparently Isaiah wants the people from these parts of his land to resettle in the Outlands. The settlers are gathering with the army near Sakkuth. Isaiah himself is even now, apparently, moving up the Lhyl from his palace in the south toward Sakkuth and is expected there within days."

Serge paused at that point, and Maximilian looked at him keenly.

"What *else* have you heard?" Maximilian said. He wondered who this Isaiah was truly. Kanubai? Already preparing for his push on Elcho Falling? No, surely not . . . surely not . . .

Serge and Venetia exchanged a glance, then Serge continued. "Maximilian, the rumor among the Isembaardians, started by soldiers who were recently in this area, is that Isaiah of Isembaard plans to meet with an army of Skraelings that are in the process of swarming south. An army of *millions* of Skraelings, heading into the Central Kingdoms."

Everyone stared at Serge, StarDrifter muttering a shocked obscenity.

"No . . ." Maximilian whispered. "Oh, *gods*!" To hear this now, when they no longer had the winged Icarii among them who might have been able to warn the Central Kingdoms.

Skraelings? Millions? Maximilian ran a hand over his eyes, aghast.

How?

He did not need to answer that. Kanubai.

Would Escator be safe? Maximilian didn't know, and he felt physically sick.

"There is yet more news," Venetia said, very softly, looking at Maximilian.

"Any worse than this I have just heard?" Maximilian said, and Venetia shrugged a little.

"The homesteaders passed on some more gossip they'd heard from Isaiah's troops," she said.

"And?" said Maximilian.

"Isaiah has abandoned and forsaken all his eighty-odd former wives," said Serge, "for a new and Favored Wife, as she is styled. A new bride. Ishbel, former Queen of Escator."

There was a complete silence about the campfire as everyone fought not to look at Maximilian.

"Then this Isaiah has good taste," said Maximilian, his voice now very tight, "and poor judgment, to think Ishbel's Escatorian husband so willing to abandon her."

"I am sure that Ishbel wouldn't—" Ravenna began.

"I don't think any of us can count on what Ishbel would or wouldn't do," said Maximilian, very quietly, "or where her loyalties lie. I just want her and our child. I have not come this far to turn back now."

No one said anything.

"But, by gods," Maximilian said, "I cannot *wait* to quit this land and get back home. Skraelings! Ah . . . Serge, do you know how far distant Sakkuth is? And in what direction?"

Serge gave a nod. "It will take us a week to travel there. East, and slightly south. But we will be traveling into a war zone, Maximilian, and life will not be easy for us once we approach Sakkuth . . . not the least because, according to the villagers, Isaiah has at least half a million men gathering in and about Sakkuth. And then more, for many of them have their wives and families. Perhaps close to a million people, all to move north."

Maximilian opened his mouth, then closed it again. It was too much to assimilate all at once: invasion, Skraelings, Ishbel now Isaiah's "Favored Wife," and now this.

"Sakkuth it is then," he said after a moment. "We free Ishbel, then we head home as fast as we may. Ravenna, Venetia, we will need your skills, as well as my penchant for the shadows, to get us close to this Isaiah."

He paused. "And then to get us out again."

Maximilian found it difficult to accept this much abysmal news. He set aside the terrifying news of the Skraeling invasion, and even that of the forces that Isaiah mustered, for at the moment he could do nothing about either.

Instead he thought about Ishbel.

He sat apart from the others for a while, the Weeper in his lap, his fingers gently stroking its cool surface. He hoped that it might say something to him, impart *some* understanding, but there was nothing. Maximilian had once or twice asked his Persimius ring what it knew of the Weeper, and the ring had only replied that the Weeper was very old and very sad and entirely lost without his employment. That last confused Maximilian even more, and the ring steadfastly evaded any attempt to get it to explain itself.

Ishbel. This Isaiah's Favored Wife.

Maximilian hoped that she'd been taken unwillingly, and that the relationship was purely theater and not actuality. What else? Ishbel was now virtually full-term in her pregnancy and could surely not be sharing her body with this man.

Isaiah . . .

Maximilian still had the sense that people were being drawn together, all being drawn toward Elcho Falling. Even though he was now desperate to get home to Escator, Maximilian had the powerful sense that he *must* get to Ishbel first. Perhaps she would know more of what was happening.

Perhaps she might even be prepared, now, to share some truths with him.

A week and he would have more answers.

A week, and perhaps he would have his wife and maybe even a child.

A week, and then he could take his family home to Escator.

"Maxel?" Ravenna sat down next to him in his solitary spot a little distant from the fire. "Such bad news we have heard this day, and poor news regarding Ishbel indeed. I am sorry for the hurt it has caused you."

Maximilian made a gesture with his hand, not truly wanting to discuss Ishbel with Ravenna.

"Perhaps she is not such a good wife for you, Maxel."

Maximilian sighed. He set the Weeper to one side and began to strip off his outer coat, then his shirt, meaning to change into something fresher, and hoping that perhaps Ravenna would take the hint and move away. As much as he liked Ravenna, for the moment he just wanted to be alone.

"Maxel, what will you do if she has gone to Isaiah willingly?"

"Ravenna, we will know soon enough. I really do not feel like roaming into conjecture here and now. I just want to get Ishbel and our child, and go home."

"Of course, Maxel. I'm sorry, I shouldn't have pried." Ravenna started to rise, then halted, staring at Maximilian's right biceps.

"Maxel?"

"What is it?"

Ravenna had laid a hand on his shoulder, and Maximilian felt his flesh quiver at its warmth and pressure.

"Your mark . . . the Manteceros."

Maximilian twisted his head to look at the bright blue tattoo of the Manteceros, the supernatural creature that was both symbol and protector of Escator, that had been engraved into his skin as a baby.

It had faded into almost nonexistence.

Maximilian went cold. He was being prepared for a greater throne indeed—Escator was literally fading from his grasp.

Perhaps he would never return to Escator . . .

"What is going on?" Ravenna hissed. "What sorcery erases this mark?"

Maximilian studied her. She both looked and sounded angry, almost affronted. The Manteceros, in his true guise as Drava, Lord of Dreams, had been Ravenna's lover for many years, and Maximilian supposed that she saw this fading as an affront to Drava himself.

I wonder where your true loyalties lie, my lady, he thought. *Are you here for me, or to watch me on behalf of your supernatural lover?*

"The world is turning upside down, Ravenna," he said, shrugging off her hand and pulling on a fresh shirt. "Perhaps the mark of the Manteceros is being lost in the confusion."

After she'd left Maximilian, Ravenna went for a walk into the darkness. She was disturbed deeply by the fading of Maximilian's mark. Everything had gone wrong in Maximilian's life, and it had all gone wrong from the moment he'd met this woman, Ishbel.

"I do not think I like you, Ishbel," Ravenna whispered, "but I think you are going to play right into my hands."

CHAPTER FIVE

Sakkuth, Isembaard

In the end it took Maximilian and his party a mere six days to get to Sakkuth, and that accomplished only with effort, physical as well as magical. For the first two days they traveled relatively unhindered, but then, having crossed the River Lhyl, they entered the territory just to the west of Sakkuth.

It was here that Isaiah's army gathered, together with the settlers from the northwest of the Tyranny.

Maximilian, Serge, and Doyle stood together on a small hillock at dawn on the day they encountered the gathering army, hidden by a small stand of trees and some of Maximilian's ability to meld with the shadows, and stared eastward.

"That is not an army," Doyle said softly. "That is a nation."

"An ocean," said Serge, "gathering for a storm."

"When did you two become so poetical?" Maximilian said, but any humor in his voice was overwhelmed by the shock of the sight before him.

Thousands, no . . . *hundreds of thousands* . . . of men gathered in encampments spreading as far as the eye could see. The original rumor of a million men, Maximilian decided, was wrong. There were far more, particularly when the numbers were engorged by settlers.

"The north will fall within weeks," said Serge. "Days."

"Thank you for your revised estimate," Maximilian said, then he paused. "*Shit!* I cannot *believe* this!"

Serge and Doyle looked at Maximilian with some surprise—the man rarely swore.

"Can we get around them?" Serge said.

"We have no time," Maximilian said. "Getting 'around' them will take weeks, and weeks we don't have."

"Through them, then?" Doyle said, his voice soft.

"That is our only option," Maximilian said. "Venetia, Ravenna, and I have some skill in the arts of disguise . . . we will need all of that and then some luck, but we shall have to manage it."

"You don't want to announce yourself to the nearest senior officer and demand to be taken to Isaiah in the style of a king?" Serge said.

Maximilian gave a soft laugh, and indicated his grubby clothing, far the worse for the wear and tear of his journey through the mountains and northern Isembaard.

"Who would believe *this*?" he said. "No. We do this secretively, and we do it as fast as possible. Come."

Manage it they did, but only at the cost of exhaustion for Maximilian, Venetia, and Ravenna, as well as the drain of nervous energy on the rest of the party. StarDrifter and Salome also battled continuing fatigue from the development of their wings—now large, twin raised ridges hunching out almost four handbreadths from either side of their spines.

They managed it only with the aid of the Weeper. When one or more among Maximilian, Venetia, or Ravenna began to flag while moving the group quietly through the ranks of the army, then the Weeper began to hum, and bolstered not only the concealing shadowy cloak that the two marsh witches and Maximilian had constructed, but its constructors' strength as well.

The days spent creeping through the ranks of what everyone had come to refer to as the gathering storm drained emotional energy as well as physical and magical.

Everyone was appalled at the enormity of what Isaiah would throw at the north. No one had ever seen anything like it, nor heard of it.

At night, when they crouched in whatever shelter they could find, relying on the Weeper by that stage of the day to conceal them, they talked in low tones about what they had passed through.

"StarDrifter," Serge asked one night, "did you ever see the like during the wars you witnessed in Tencendor?"

StarDrifter took some time to answer that, dredging up the memories of the wars with considerable reluctance. "No," he said eventually. "I saw seething Skraeling armies—and to think that such are gathering again, to bolster Isaiah's forces!—but nothing like this. No one in Tencendor could have managed such sheer *numbers* of soldiers." He shook his head slightly. "It is inconceivable."

"Salome?" Maximilian said. "Did Coroleas ever raise such a force?"

Salome gave a cynical laugh. "No, Maximilian. Coroleans practice war by stealth. The single, highly paid assassin, with a dagger in a crowd of frivolity. A drugged glass of wine. Or drugs administered by other means." She sent a single dark glance at StarDrifter. "But not armies. No. Never. We were far too indolent."

"I wish BroadWing and his companions were with us still," Maximilian said, "if only so I could use their wings to report this nightmare. I am sure my fellow princes are still engaged in a futile struggle with each other. Not looking south."

"Or north toward the Skraeling homelands," Doyle muttered. He turned to his friend and fellow former assassin. "What do you think of the Isembaardians' weapons, my friend?"

Serge thought a few minutes, every eye in the group on him.

"They're not intending much close hand-to-hand fighting," he said. "Spears and arrows predominate. I imagine Isaiah plans to send a storm of metal raining down upon the forces opposing him, decimating them within an hour at most. Then, if needed, Isaiah could send in a few swordsmen to finish off those still left alive."

"*If* they could get through the bristling crop of spears and arrows littering the corpses on the ground," said Venetia. "Why do you men do this? Why propagate such vile death?"

"It is not *us*," Maximilian said sharply. "All *I* want is my bride and child returned to me."

"I apologize, Maxel," Venetia said. "The question was rhetorical only, and born of my fright and fatigue more than anything." She looked at her daughter. "Methinks you should have remained with the Lord of Dreams, Ravenna. I am sure that this"—she gestured vaguely at the encampment of soldiers not fifty paces distant—"was not something to which you wanted to return."

"I returned because I was needed, Venetia," Ravenna said, but she looked at Maximilian rather than her mother as she replied.

A day later they arrived in Sakkuth.

Here they did not need to use magical disguise as much, for the city was bustling with people, come to aid the gathering forces. Merchants, traders and craftsmen, prostitutes, cooks, tailors—countless differing skills and hopes paraded on the streets every twenty paces. StarDrifter and Salome did, however, need to keep cloaks hunched over their backs to disguise their growing wings. Fortunately Sakkuth was in the midst of an unnaturally cold snap—even in winter the city rarely slipped below the balmy—and thus the cloaks caused no comment on the streets.

By some miracle of comradeship, Venetia found them two small rooms in the basement of a bakery. The baker's wife was a covert witch-woman whom Venetia had met previously in the borderlands of the Land of Dreams. They recognized each other instantly, and the baker's wife just as instantly intuited their need for shelter and rest. Her husband was not so enthusiastic about a band of strangers occupying two of his bakery's storerooms until Serge took out a bag of coin and casually moved it from hand to hand; then he grudgingly agreed.

"And so it has come to this," Maximilian said, sitting on a sack of grain and idly swinging one leg back and forth. "A king, a talon, two witch-women, two assassins, and . . . what would you call yourself, Salome?"

"The single sane member of this group."

Maximilian smiled. "And the single sane one among us, hidden in the basement of a bakery, in a strange land, surrounded by the largest army creation has ever seen, looking for a woman and a child. What do you think our chances of success are?"

"Fairly high," said the baker's wife, who had just entered the room, "for the streets are abuzz with the news that the tyrant himself is now entering the city. There are stairs inside the bakery to the roof. You should have a good view there."

Maximilian's humor had vanished, and his face was now tight with emotion.

"To the roof, then," he said.

CHAPTER SIX

Sakkuth, Isembaard

Axis was almost as astonished at the size and complexity of Isaiah's forces as, had he known it, were Maximilian and his party.

He'd never seen anything like it.

For the past week they'd ridden from the Lhyl where they'd left their riverboats, across territory undulating with soldiers. Their encampments had stretched as far as the eye could see.

Axis had been as impressed with the tight discipline of the horde as much as he was with its size. After what Ezekiel had told him about the chaos that had ensued after Isaiah had been kidnapped on the Eastern Independencies campaign, Axis had more than half expected a mass of undisciplined and slothful soldiers.

But perhaps they sank to such depths only once a tyrant's throne was vacant, for the army that Axis saw was under tight control and exhibited extreme discipline.

His admiration for the Isembaardian generals, as well as for Isaiah, notched up yet another degree.

Sakkuth was everything Axis had expected. It was a stunningly beautiful, walled, and multispired city constructed predominantly of pink and cream stone quarried in the Far-Reach Mountains. As they rode through the main gates and into the wide avenue that led through the heart of the city to Isaiah's official palace, Axis wondered why Isaiah didn't spend more time here. Axis had been with him for a year, and yet not once in that time had Isaiah left Aqhat.

What kept him in Aqhat? The serenity of the river . . . or DarkGlass Mountain?

The avenue was crowded with people, mostly ordinary city dwellers going about their daily business. Soldiers had crowded people back against the buildings in order to give Isaiah room to pass, and in order to give him the room to pass in splendor.

Axis noted their response to Isaiah and his two hundred strong escort with as much curiosity as he'd marked the army beyond the city's walls.

Generally the crowds displayed a mix of deference, genuine awe (or perhaps fear), and a decided reluctance to look directly at the face of Isaiah, or any of his closest companions—among which included Ishbel, who rode directly behind Isaiah, the pair of them kept closely guarded by several squadrons of heavily armed men.

This morning, when Axis had gone to mount his horse, he'd noted that Isaiah and Ishbel, who had regained all her strength and vitality after the baby's birth, had attired themselves in great majesty. Both wore great golden and bejeweled collars that draped over their shoulders, robes of fine embroidered silks, and two or three golden bands on each of their bare arms.

Isaiah appeared calm and relaxed, Ishbel a little less so, and Axis thought he saw slight lines of strain about her eyes and mouth.

Axis was ambivalent about their relationship. He knew they were now sleeping together, and was honest enough with himself to admit there was a small kernel of jealousy there. But he didn't know what Ishbel wanted. Did she truly wish to be Isaiah's wife? Was she just marking time until she could manage a means to leave him? How did she actually feel about arriving back in her homeland on the tide of a massive invasion and on the arm (and in the bed) of the invader?

To none of these questions did Axis have an answer, and he hadn't had the opportunity of asking Ishbel. He'd not seen her alone for weeks—a situation he realized was fully managed by Isaiah as well as by Ishbel herself—and any time he did spend with her was in the company of Isaiah, who deflected any conversation away from Ishbel if he felt it too personal.

Ishbel was now clearly out of bounds to Axis.

Ah! What did it matter to him? Ishbel was her own woman, and old enough to know what she was doing with her life.

But still . . . Axis wondered if she had really thought through what she did.

He dismissed the thought the next moment as ungenerous and undoubtedly born of his own jealousy.

Stars, would he have refused if Ishbel had come to him?

No. He wouldn't.

Axis sighed, looking about. He was some four or five riders behind Isaiah and Ishbel, and enjoying not being the center of attention for once. It gave him so much opportunity to observe freely.

He looked at Isaiah, sitting his horse with such confidence and such natural arrogance that it appeared he could fear nothing.

Axis suddenly thought of the assassination attempt on Isaiah at Aqhat and, his heart thudding in his chest, glanced upward at the roofline.

Straight into the eyes of his father.

Maximilian had been transfixed by the sight of Ishbel. She looked so beautiful, and very obviously no longer pregnant.

His eyes quickly scanned back through Isaiah's column, looking for the nursery litter, a wet nurse cradling the child, anything, then decided that perhaps the baby would come into the city later, when everything was calmer, or that, gods forbid, Ishbel had left it behind from wherever she had come.

Would she have done that? Why?

Then, four or five horsemen back from Isaiah, a man had looked up directly at the roof where Maximilian and his party stood, and StarDrifter had cried out, softly and heart-achingly, *"Axis!"*

Maximilian acted instantly. He grabbed StarDrifter, now stepping forth to the very edge of the building, and hauled him backward toward the trapdoor that led from the flat roof down into the bakery.

"Everyone back, now!" Maximilian hesitated. "Save you,

Serge. Watch as carefully as you can. Let me know if you think Axis has reported us."

"Axis will keep his mouth *shut*!" StarDrifter hissed.

"Yes?" said Maximilian, angry with frustration at being so near Ishbel and yet so damned distant, and angry also that he hadn't thought to use either his power or that of Venetia and Ravenna to cloak them from prying eyes. Gods, what had he been thinking? Had the thought of seeing Ishbel so addled his wits?

And where was their child?

"Really?" Maximilian continued, his grip tightening about StarDrifter's arm. "He's been living in Isembaard with Isaiah for many months at the least, and he didn't look a reluctant captive to me just then, eh? Downstairs. *Now!*"

Axis couldn't think. He could not manage a single, damned coherent thought. He sat his horse in a state of shock, riding forward with Isaiah's train automatically, trying to marshal some sense from his brain.

StarDrifter. StarDrifter. *Stars, his father was here in Sakkuth!*

Axis had not thought of StarDrifter in many, many weeks. To see him now, *here*, of all places, left him breathless not merely in shock, but in joy as well.

His father.

Oh, gods . . . what should he do?

Axis managed to glance behind him again, trying to see the roof where he'd seen StarDrifter, but they'd ridden forward too far, and around a slight curve in the avenue, for him to be able to make it out.

His brain, finally, managed to send out a few cautious observations.

The darker man who had grabbed at StarDrifter, pulling him away.

"Oh no," Axis whispered, knowing intuitively who that must be. He had no reason at all to know it was Maximilian, but somehow he just knew. Axis' hands, which to his amazement he discovered were trembling, tightened about his reins, making his horse jitter a little.

What should he do?

He looked ahead.

Isaiah had turned on his horse and was smiling at Ishbel, then laughed at something she said.

Axis' face lost all expression. Isaiah and Ishbel had underestimated Maximilian. Very badly.

He glanced upward again, although he knew he had no hope of seeing StarDrifter.

What should he do?

Nothing. Watch. And wait for his father.

Axis knew StarDrifter had seen him as well, and he knew his father well enough to know that StarDrifter would seek him out.

And what was Maximilian going to do?

He looked ahead once more to Isaiah and Ishbel, revising his opinion that he should say nothing. But *what* to say? If he told Isaiah that Maximilian was in Sakkuth, would Isaiah then close down the city while soldiers searched door to door? Was that fair to Maximilian? To StarDrifter?

Was it fair to Ishbel *not* to tell her that her husband was in town?

"Stars," he muttered, "what should I do?"

Once more safely ensconced in the storerooms under the bakery, Maximilian finally let StarDrifter go and turned to Ravenna.

"Tonight," he said. "You and me only. Isaiah's palace."

"Maxel—" StarDrifter began.

"Ravenna and me *only*," Maximilian snapped, and such was the expression on his face that no one argued the point.

CHAPTER SEVEN

Sakkuth, Isembaard

T he supply column?" Isaiah said.

"Already heading through the Salamaan Pass," said Morfah. He tapped the map on the table about which Isaiah, Axis, and the five senior generals were standing. "There are already supplies of food positioned here, here, and here." His finger stabbed down at locations in northern Isembaard between Sakkuth and Salamaan Pass, and then once at a point a third of the way through the pass. "And the supply train will encamp just before the pass widens into the plains leading to Adab. The army will move smoothly, Excellency, and shall not lack for food, equipment, or weapons."

Axis stood to one side, still in a quandary about Maximilian and StarDrifter. He'd not had a chance to speak privately either to Isaiah or Ishbel, and could hardly say something in front of the generals. With luck, he might manage a word once the generals had left.

"Good," said Isaiah. "And the settlers?"

"They are traveling in a convoy just behind the army column," said Ezekiel. "They are well provisioned and tightly organized. No laggards among them. Several Rivers"—a River was a unit of ten thousand soldiers—"come behind."

Axis set aside his quandary about Maximilian for the moment, thinking instead about the resettlement issue. It seemed extraordinary to him that Isaiah would want to weigh down the invasion column with women and children and great-aunts, plus their belongings and livestock, but Isaiah was insistent. The Outlands were to be colonized with native Isembaardians as rapidly as possible.

Axis wondered how the settlers felt about this—ordered from their homelands into the unknown—but from all the reports he'd heard they appeared resigned. He remembered what the country had been like in the northwest when he'd ridden to meet Ishbel, and thought that perhaps they might even be a little glad to leave a land of arid and poor soil.

"This is a huge column," Axis said, keeping his thoughts about the settlers to himself. "You are not concerned that its existence, lurking just inside the northern entrance to the Salamaan Pass, will not be reported to the Outlanders?"

"No one is being allowed through the pass to discover the column," said Morfah. "We keep the pass so tightly closed that few people ever attempt its passage in any case, and the few stray peddlers who try are either turned back or, if too persistent, otherwise stopped."

Axis grimaced at the "otherwise stopped," but said nothing.

"No one will realize until it is too late," said Ezekiel.

"Besides," said Isaiah, "the latest intelligence puts the majority of the Outlands' armed forces up here." He pointed to an area halfway between Pelemere and Hosea. "No one in their command will realize until too late just *what* it is comes up the Salamaan Pass."

He sighed, rubbing his eyes. "It is late, and I am tired. I thank you," he said to the generals, "for these reports. All goes well. By tomorrow—"

He turned as the door opened, then smiled as Ishbel walked in.

In contrast to the men, all of whom looked weary, she looked refreshed and lovely, her hair left in a long loose plait over one shoulder, wound about with a thin bejeweled gold wire, and wearing a simple white linen robe that accentuated her figure and coloring.

Axis froze. His reaction was not at Ishbel's entrance as such, but at what he'd felt *from the shadows in the back of the room at her entrance.*

Everything Ishbel had told him about Maximilian suddenly roared to the forefront of his mind.

Stars . . .

Ishbel went directly to Isaiah, who laid a hand on her shoulder, and pulled her close for a slow kiss.

The generals all looked on impassively.

Axis watched Isaiah and Ishbel, then, so briefly most would have missed it, glanced toward the shadows at the rear of the large chamber.

"Well," said Isaiah, still smiling down at Ishbel's face, "tomorrow is another day and, right now, I would rather think about the rest of this night."

Axis suppressed a wince.

Taking the hint, the generals murmured their good-nights, and left.

"I'm sure," said Isaiah, as the door closed behind the departing men, "that you also need your rest, Axis."

"Isaiah—" said Axis, then got no further.

"Ishbel," said a voice, *"what have you done?"*

Axis looked to the back of the chamber as Isaiah and Ishbel spun about, Isaiah pushing Ishbel a little way behind him.

A man and a woman had stepped forth from the shadows.

The man, tall, dark, and with a face marked by pain and tragedy, registered briefly in Axis' mind—*Maximilian of Escator, it could be no other*—but his attention was almost immediately and completely caught by the woman.

For a single heart-stopping moment he thought it was Azhure, then realized that she was far younger and, while as tall as Azhure had been, slighter. She shared Azhure's long and almost blue-black hair, but her face was finer, and her eyes . . . they were the most extraordinary eyes Axis had ever seen. Pale gray, the irises ringed with black, they were startlingly beautiful.

Then Ishbel gave a cry, and Axis looked at her directly.

He'd never seen such a look of utter devastation, such all-consuming *guilt*, on anyone's face as he saw now on Ishbel's.

It was, she thought, the most terrible moment she could ever possibly suffer. She'd thought that Maximilian would have gone home to Escator, and stayed there. She'd thought him to have forgotten her.

But no, he'd come all this way—a hard, terrible journey, if his appearance was any indication—and she did not know how she could possibly tell him about their child, or explain Isaiah.

Isaiah had grabbed a sword from the table, but Ishbel reached out one shaky hand and waved him away.

"No," she said, "not that."

Isaiah let the sword droop, but did not step away from Ishbel's side.

"That was a poor way to announce yourself, Maximilian Persimius," Isaiah said, softly.

Maximilian ignored him. He stepped forward, walked toward Ishbel, stopping two or three paces from her. "Ishbel?"

She realized that he was as shocked as she, she could see it in his eyes.

Along with such astounding pain that each successive breath she took became harder and harder.

I have caused that pain, she thought. *Oh, gods, what can I do?*

Ishbel became aware that everyone in the room was incredibly tense, and that no one knew what to do or say.

"I would like," she said, holding Maximilian's eyes and speaking with as much dignity as she could, "to speak with Maxel alone."

"The baby is dead, isn't it?" said the woman, who, to this point, had hardly even registered on Ishbel's consciousness. "The baby is dead and you have fallen gratefully into the bed of a man who seeks to invade your homeland. Maxel, you are well rid of this woman. I think we ought to—"

"Be quiet, you fool!" Isaiah snapped at the woman.

"Dead?" Maximilian said at the same time, and Ishbel's eyes filled with tears. She did not know how she could keep standing. She wished everyone would just *go* so that she could speak to Maximilian.

She wished . . . oh, she wished that everything had been different.

"Will she be safe with you, Maximilian Persimius?" Isaiah said, and Ishbel saw Maximilian look at him.

Something altered in Maximilian's face, even more shock, if that were possible, piled atop everything else he must be feeling.

Recognition.

"What have you done?" Maximilian whispered, still staring at Isaiah.

"Nothing but prepare the way for the Lord of Elcho Falling," Isaiah said, and then Maximilian stepped forward and hit him.

Axis' first thought was to wonder if it were some northern trait, this ritual of face-striking on first acquaintance.

His second was one of astonishment at Maximilian's strength, for the power of his blow sent Isaiah—a big man— sprawling back several paces.

Axis grabbed at Maximilian, pulling him back, although it was apparent that Maximilian had no intention of continuing the assault.

"Let me go," Maximilian said, and Axis did so. The dark-haired woman was by his side now, taking his arm.

"You are Axis," she said. "My name is Ravenna."

Axis' sense of disorientation deepened. Social introductions? Now?

Isaiah slowly rose to his feet, one hand rubbing at his jaw, his eyes wary.

"Will everyone *please* leave Maximilian and me alone," Ishbel said. Her voice was strained, her entire body stiff, and Axis noticed that she held her head slightly to one side so that she did not have to look anyone in the eye.

"I will not leave you with—" Isaiah began, but Axis interrupted.

"Isaiah, out, now. Maximilian will not hurt Ishbel. Ravenna, come with me."

Within a moment, Ishbel and Maximilian were left alone as Axis hustled the other two out the door.

CHAPTER EIGHT

Sakkuth, Isembaard

A xis turned to Ravenna the moment they were in the corridor. "My father is with your party. Where is he?"

"*What?*" said Isaiah. "How do you know this?"

"I saw Maximilian and my father, StarDrifter, today,"
Axis said. "While we were on your grand procession into
Sakkuth. They watched from a rooftop."

"And you thought this was not important enough to tell
me, or Ishbel?" Isaiah said. "Damn you! Did you not think
enough of *Ishbel* to tell her that her husband was close? Did
you not have the *courtesy*?"

He whipped about to Ravenna. "Who are you?"

"I don't think I need to—" Ravenna began.

"Tell me your name, curse you!"

"My name is Ravenna," she said. "I am a marsh woman,
one who patrols the pathways between this world and the
Land of Dreams."

"Very pretty," said Isaiah. "Unfortunately I am not impressed with your pretensions." He took a step forward,
jabbing a finger in Ravenna's face. "How *dare* you interfere
between Maximilian and Ishbel! You have no right."

"That is hardly an accusation *you* can toss about lightly."

"My father . . ." Axis said, desperate to edge the conversation back into civility.

"He is well, Axis," Ravenna said. "More than anxious to
see you."

Axis smiled. "And I him."

"Oh, for the gods' sakes," Isaiah muttered. "Ravenna,
who *else* do you have in 'your party'? Who *else* can I expect
to find emerging from the shadows?"

"My mother, Venetia," said Ravenna. "StarDrifter's wife,
Salome"—she sent an apologetic glance to Axis as she said

this—"and two men-at-arms. Not an invasion force. Not the kind *you* feel you need to carry about with you."

Axis broke in before Isaiah could speak. "Isaiah, I apologize to you, and I will humble myself before Ishbel when I have the chance. I should have said something and it was wrong of me not to do so. The fact was, the sight of my father stunned me so much, roiled my emotions so deeply, that I was unable to think clearly, and—"

"You were one of the greatest military commanders this world has ever seen," said Isaiah, "and I do not believe for a moment this excuse that the sight of your father upset you so much you forgot to mention to me you had seen both him *and* Maximilian."

Now he addressed Ravenna again. "I knew Maximilian was in that room, hiding in the shadows. What I am most angry about is not so much his presence, but the manner of it. That degree of slyness does not suit a man of his station and responsibility—and I know that it is not the first time he has practiced it. Oh, I know, you do not need to tell me, *always* with the best possible reasons, of course. I gave Maximilian the opportunity to act honorably, and he did not take it. Spare me your indignation, girl. I find it as unjustifiable as Maximilian's righteous anger."

Axis thought that Ravenna was the kind of woman who would very rarely be put in her place, but he thought Isaiah had just managed it. Ravenna kept her tongue still, but her eyes glittered, and Axis wondered if Isaiah had just made himself a bad enemy.

"Axis," Isaiah continued, "you will go with Ravenna and you will fetch to this palace the rest of Maximilian's party. I am sure that you will be glad to see your father again."

"Are we to be captives?" Ravenna asked, bright spots of color in her cheeks.

"You will be treated with the honor I am not sure you completely deserve," Isaiah said, "but the conditions of your time at Sakkuth remain to be negotiated between myself and Maximilian. Not with you."

Isaiah injected enough derision into that last that Axis glanced worriedly at Ravenna.

The spots of color in her cheeks were, if anything, much

brighter. "You have no idea," she said, rather quietly, "to whom you speak."

"And you can have no idea either, you petty little marsh woman, to whom *you* speak."

Ignoring her gasp, Isaiah looked at Axis. "See that Maximilian's party gets back here safely," he said. "Assure them I mean them no enmity, and see that they are quartered comfortably. If I get the chance, I will speak with Maximilian myself later tonight."

And with that he turned on his heel and stalked off.

Maximilian and Ishbel sat at opposite sides of the table, neither looking at the other.

"The baby?" he said, his voice wooden and cracked, an echo of how he felt inside.

Ishbel made a helpless gesture with her hand, then brushed away a tear that had crept down one cheek.

Her hand trembled badly.

"There was a man called Ba'al'uz," she said. "He was responsible for the deaths in the Outlands and Central Kingdoms and for taking me from your side. He—"

"*The baby?*"

"Ba'al'uz killed the baby, Maxel. Just after she was born. I'm sorry."

She, he thought. *A daughter.*

He sat in silence for a long time, unable to look at Ishbel, and unable to accept even the concept of the death of the child he'd wanted so badly.

A daughter.

He had his hands clasped in front of him on the table, and they turned over and about themselves as he tried to unmuddle thought and emotion.

"Maxel," Ishbel said softly, "I am so sorry."

"I came so far for you, Ishbel. For you and our child. It has been so hard. So difficult."

Her heart tore apart at the pain in his voice, and she clasped her hands to her face in a useless attempt to stem the tears.

"I'm so sorry," she whispered again. "I didn't think . . . I thought you'd just go back to Escator, forget me."

"*Forget* you?"

"I thought you hated me. Maxel, I'm sorry. I—"

"*Stop telling me you're sorry!* I don't *ever* want to hear that again! For months I have abandoned my kingdom, all my responsibilities, brought trusted friends into danger with me, and for what? For *what*? A wife who has been disporting herself with a man in the very process of *invading her homeland*?"

"I thought you *hated* me, Maxel."

"Don't call me that. You have abandoned the marriage and you have abandoned me. Do not think to address me so familiarly."

Ishbel closed her eyes, taking a shaky breath before re-opening them and forcing herself to look at Maximilian.

"Isaiah offered me comfort and compassion," she said, her voice low. "If I had known that you had wanted me, were coming for me . . . oh, gods, Maximilian, why is life so full of 'ifs'?"

He said nothing, refusing to look at her.

Ishbel began to babble, wishing she didn't feel the need to speak further excuses, but unable to stop herself.

"I was so upset when our daughter died. I wept for days. Isaiah . . . he was so good to me. He has such compassion. He offered me comfort, not judgment. He did not even want to judge me for being the archpriestess of the Coil—"

Ishbel stopped, appalled at what her babbling had brought her.

"Oh, what lies you have told me," Maximilian said, looking directly at her now. "I tore the earth apart for you, and for what? For what?"

He stood.

"I will say this to you one time," he said, "and then I will never, *never* allow these words to pass my lips again. I loved you, Ishbel. *You*. The loss of you wounds me more than the loss of the child."

There was an infinitesimal pause. "You have broken my heart, Ishbel, and in the doing ruined my world."

He stared at her a long moment, then left the room.

CHAPTER NINE

Axis and Ravenna walked through the ill-lit and largely deserted streets. A squad of ten armed men followed them at a distance of about twelve paces.

Axis did not try to evade them, and did not particularly resent them. If he'd been Isaiah he would have done the same thing and, frankly, he thought it remarkable that he and Ravenna were walking the streets at all after this night's debacle.

He wondered how Maximilian and Ishbel were doing.

"I remember you from the tales told of Maximilian's rescue from beyond the hanging wall," Axis said quietly to Ravenna as she led them to where StarDrifter and the remainder of Maximilian's party waited.

"And I, naturally, know of you from the many tales circulating of Tencendor."

"Isn't legend such a wonderful social introduction aid," Axis said, and Ravenna laughed softly, a lovely, low, seductive sound.

Axis glanced at her. "If I was Ishbel, I'd be worried that Maximilian has had such as you for company all these weeks and months."

"She has no reason at all, as yet, to be jealous of me. *Maxel* has remained true to her, if not she to him."

Axis noted that "as yet," and also noted, from the tone of Ravenna's voice, that perhaps Ishbel was a subject best left alone for the time being.

Besides, there was something else, far more wonderful, awaiting him.

"My father," he said. "StarDrifter. Is he well?"

Ravenna smiled at the repressed excitement in Axis' voice. "Yes. He is well. And regrowing his wings."

"What? How?"

"Ah, we carry our own mysteries with us. And, as you heard, StarDrifter also has a wife, if a somewhat reluctant one."

"This I cannot believe! Who can have managed to nab my father? Tell me, who is this Salome?"

"Well . . . they, ah, met in Coroleas. I will leave it to StarDrifter to tell you about her."

There was a mischievous glint in her eye as she said this, and Axis had to bite his tongue from peppering her with questions.

"StarDrifter is an extraordinary man," Axis said. "I remember the first time we met . . . at the base of the Icescarp Alps . . ."

His voice faltered, and Ravenna touched his arm briefly in empathy.

Axis brought his emotions under control. "And the other members of the party? Not many, from what you said."

"My mother, Venetia, and Serge and Doyle. I think you will like them. They once worked as assassins, but now are Maxel's loyal men."

"Assassins?" Axis laughed. "Never tell Isaiah that!"

"Look, we are here. Let me go down first, Axis, for Serge and Doyle will be as nervous as cats and you'll like as not meet the blades of their swords before ever you meet them if you enter first."

"Axis!" StarDrifter hugged his son to him, so tight that Ravenna, standing to one side, later swore she had heard Axis' bones creak in protest. Tears streamed down his face, as they did down Axis', who returned his father's embrace with equal ferocity.

Venetia met her daughter's eyes, and smiled. She had rarely seen StarDrifter smile, let alone display this magnitude of joy, and she was glad for him, that finally he had his son in his arms and his life again.

She glanced at Salome. The woman was standing against

a wall, almost in the shadows, looking both distant and cautious, and Venetia wondered what she made of this arrival.

Axis SunSoar, the great legend, of whom even Salome in her time at Coroleas must have heard.

And now a close relative.

Axis and StarDrifter were still embracing, laughing, tears flowing freely down both their faces. Finally, Axis pulled away a little, one hand patting at StarDrifter's back as he did so.

"What is this then, StarDrifter? *Wings?*"

StarDrifter sobered. "You know how—"

"How you lost them. Yes. Gods, StarDrifter, no one knew what had become of you. Where you had gone. We had lost Zenith, only to rediscover her in the world beyond death, but you . . . No one . . . oh, sweet stars in heaven, I can hardly believe you are *here*. I saw you this morning, and thought you an apparition . . . and this evening, when Maximilian and Ravenna appeared—"

"Please," interrupted Serge, "what of Maximilian? Is he safe?"

"Yes," said Ravenna, "for the moment I believe he is safe enough in body if not well in spirit or heart, Serge. Ishbel has abandoned her wifely vows for the Tyrant of Isembaard, and the daughter she bore Maxel died at birth. Murdered, I believe, by the maniac Ba'al'uz."

His hand still on StarDrifter's shoulder, Axis turned to face the rest of the group.

"We all have much news to share," he said, "and we need somewhere better than this to share it. Isaiah, the tyrant, has offered Maximilian and all of you shelter within his palace. He—"

"Oh, come now!" said Doyle. "Surely you don't expect us to believe that!"

"Isaiah is not the great evil warlord of the south," Axis said. "He is a good man. And I think you will be no more imprisoned within his palace than you are"—he glanced about the dismal bakery cellar—"here, and far more comfortable, although you may have to relinquish your weapons at the door."

Serge's and Doyle's hands both tightened reflexively about the hilts of their swords.

"And I shall return them to you within your quarters as soon as I might," Axis said. "A deal?"

Serge and Doyle exchanged a nod. "A deal," Doyle said.

"So then," said Axis, "now that we've sorted out the difficulties of accommodation, perhaps some introductions?"

"Ah, I am sorry," said StarDrifter. "Where are my manners? Serge and Doyle," he said, nodding in turn at each man, "are Maxel's men."

"And former assassins, I hear," said Axis, stepping forward to take each man's hand. "Please don't mention that to Isaiah. He has just survived an assassination attempt, by an Icarii—"

"What?" said StarDrifter.

"StarDrifter, I will talk to you about it later," said Axis. "Serge, Doyle, your former employ shall have to remain quiet for the moment, I think. Agreed?"

They both nodded. "Agreed."

"This is Venetia," said StarDrifter. "Ravenna's mother."

Axis smiled at her. She was as lovely as her daughter, with the same coloring and strange gray eyes, but whereas Ravenna's beauty was that of the freshness of youth, Venetia's was that of the mature woman. Axis felt immediately attracted to her—experience was always the more seductive beauty than youthful freshness.

And when combined with her obvious power . . .

As with Serge and Doyle, Axis took Venetia's hand, but did not immediately let go of it.

"I have never met such as you and your daughter," he said quietly, holding her level gaze. "Maximilian is a lucky man to have you as his allies."

"He is a man who attracts such luck," said Venetia. She started to pull her hand from Axis', but he tightened his grip fractionally, keeping it trapped a moment longer.

"I shall have to ask him his secret," Axis said, then let Venetia's hand go with a slight widening of his smile, and turned to where Salome stood.

"You are Salome," he said, taking her hand as he had everyone else's. "An Icarii . . . and also growing wings, I see. There is a story here."

Salome said nothing, looking uncomfortable.

Axis looked to his father.

StarDrifter looked even more uncomfortable.

"Salome is a SunSoar, Axis," Venetia said, irritated by all the hesitation, "and now carrying StarDrifter's child. The SunSoars are to be congratulated, I think, for their skill in re-kindling their dynasty. The rest I should leave for StarDrifter or Salome to explain to you."

Axis was aware he was gaping unbecomingly, but for the moment he could do little else. The instant Venetia had said Salome was a SunSoar he had recognized it in her face. *But how? Whose child was she?*

StarDrifter had come over and gently disengaged Salome's hand from Axis'. "We have a great deal to share, Axis," he said softly, "but as you said, this is not the place to do it."

Axis finally managed to regain his composure, and turned to Salome fully.

"Have you been welcomed into the House of SunSoar, Salome?"

She frowned, flickering a glance at StarDrifter.

"No," she said, "what do you mean?"

"Although my father has very obviously been an attentive man, Salome," said Axis, "he has also been somewhat neglectful of his duties." He gave a little shrug, remembering how he had shunned his son DragonStar for far too long. "As we have all been, from time to time."

He stepped closer to Salome, placing both of his hands on her shoulders.

"These are words, Salome, that are usually spoken to a newborn baby, as StarDrifter and myself, and you, too, will speak them to the child you are carrying at his birth. But I sense you have had a difficult life, and have only come recently into your heritage, and I think you need to hear these words very much indeed."

He leaned forward, kissing her softly on the forehead.

"Welcome, Salome, into the House of SunSoar and into my heart. My name is Axis SunSoar, and I am your kinsman.

Sing well and fly high, and"—here Axis hesitated, wondering whether he should speak redundant words, then quickly revised the traditional greeting—"may all of creation work to ensure that one day your feet will tread the path of the Star Dance."

But still, he thought, remembering the lifeless glass pyramid he still had in his safekeeping, *there is hope that one day you, as all Icarii, may set foot once more on the path of the Star Dance.*

CHAPTER TEN

Sakkuth, Isembaard

The palace chamberlain met Maximilian as he strode out of the room where he'd talked with Ishbel, informing him that Axis and Ravenna had gone to fetch the rest of the party and they were to be accommodated with all honor in Isaiah's palace.

Maximilian was so angry, so hurt, and so overwrought at that moment he couldn't have cared less had the palace chamberlain informed him he was to be escorted to the dungeons, so he'd simply followed the man wordlessly.

The chamberlain led him to a door, saying that his apartment lay beyond it, and Maximilian had just laid a hand to the door handle when a voice spoke.

"Maximilian."

Maximilian realized he was going to have to wait a little while yet for the peace he craved. He turned slightly.

Isaiah stood, arms folded, leaning in the frame of another doorway a few paces down the corridor.

He hadn't been there when Maximilian had walked past a moment ago.

"Isaiah," Maximilian responded, his voice dull.

"Can we go inside?" Isaiah said, nodding at the doorway leading into the apartment. "I do not wish to speak to you in the corridor."

A muscle flickered in Maximilian's jaw, then he gave a terse nod.

"You know who I am," said Isaiah the moment the door closed behind him.

Maximilian said nothing. They were in the first room of what appeared to be a suite of spacious and well-appointed chambers, and he marched over to a side table, poured himself a glass of wine, and gulped it down.

"My Lord of Elcho Falling—" Isaiah began.

Maximilian whipped about. *"Don't call me that!"*

"Wake up, damn you!" Isaiah said. "Kanubai is risen, and it is time for you to assume your responsibilities. You *must* know that!"

Maximilian decanted himself another glass of wine, drinking it down as fast as he had the first.

"*I* walk," said Isaiah, "and Light walks as a man named Lister. Kanubai is risen." Isaiah thought about telling Maximilian that Kanubai had used the blood of his daughter to attain flesh, but thought better of it—another time, but not now. "Elcho Falling is stirring. I don't care what you *want*, Maximilian Persimius, but you must have known from the moment you met Ishbel, from the moment you heard from *where* she came, that Elcho Falling stirred. The time has come, my lord."

Maximilian poured himself a third glass, stared at it, then slammed it down so hard on the table that red wine spilled over its glossy surface, and sank into a nearby chair.

"Why take her from me?" he said, his voice weary. "Why sleep with her? What purpose did that serve save to break hearts?"

"You had lost her, Maximilian, turned your back on her. I am a man, and Ishbel is a lovely woman."

"I had expected a more noble excuse. Surely there were other lovely women about you could fuck for recreation."

"Maximilian—"

Maximilian leapt to his feet. "Don't you *ever* step in my way again, you shitty little piece of frog spawn!" He took a step toward Isaiah, who moved backward.

"Maximilian—"

"Don't you ever step in my way again!"

Isaiah gave a little nod, and the faintest suggestion of a bow from his shoulders.

Maximilian stared at him, then turned back to the side

table and downed what was left of the wine in the glass. "Get out," he said.

"We leave within days for the north, Maximilian. You know why we head north."

Maximilian sloshed some more wine into the glass. The last thing he wanted to do now was talk about Elcho Falling.

"Travel with us, you and your party. There is no point in your breaking away to travel independently. After all," Isaiah added softly, "we head in the same direction. North, to Elcho Falling."

"And the Skraelings you go to meet? Your *allies*?"

"They are under the control of Kanubai. Neither I nor Lister can do anything about them, Maximilian. I am sorry."

Maximilian drank the glass of wine in one gulp, spilling a little of the liquid down his chin. He wiped the dribble away with the back of one hand. "Get out."

"While with me, you will be treated with all honor and—"

"Get out!"

Isaiah turned on his heel and left.

Axis escorted StarDrifter and the rest of the group back to the palace, StarDrifter carrying a blanket-wrapped bundle that piqued Axis' curiosity, although for the moment he kept his questions to himself. Isaiah's armed men trailed them, closely enough to earn black looks from Serge and Doyle.

There were even more black looks at the palace where Serge and Doyle reluctantly handed over their weapons, before the palace chamberlain, polite and unquestioning, even though the night's events must have been extraordinary to him, escorted them to their various apartments. Axis left StarDrifter and Salome in their apartment, to bathe and refresh themselves, before heading to the guards' main equipment room and securing two swords for Serge and Doyle. He liked and trusted the two men instinctively, knowing he would have been glad of them in any command of his, and knew also that they would fret constantly until they had weapons with which to guard Maximilian.

Axis was pleased to see that Maximilian had been allocated what amounted to a small wing of the palace with at least five bedchambers and four reception rooms. Serge, Doyle, Venetia, and Ravenna were all staying in Maximilian's quarters. Once Axis had delivered the swords to the relieved and grateful Serge and Doyle, he stood in the anteroom looking at the closed door to Maximilian's private bedchamber, wondering how Maximilian was, but knowing that the last thing the man needed now was a stranger prying into his heartache.

After a quick glance up and down the corridor—Isaiah had stationed guards at several points—Axis left Maximilian and his companions and went to rejoin his father and whoever Salome might prove to be.

"Maxel?"

His bedchamber was lit with only a single lamp left to burn low, and it had taken Ravenna a few moments after she'd closed the door behind her to make him out as he sat on the floor, hunched into a corner.

Her heart almost stopped. Maximilian looked as lost as he had when she and Garth rescued him from the Veins.

Ravenna walked over to sit beside him. Now that she was closer she could smell the wine on him.

"Maxel," she said softly, and he tipped his head and looked at her.

"Oh, Maxel," she said, appalled at the haggard lines running down from eyes and nose, and the tears in his eyes.

He sighed, picking up one of her hands. "I was unutterably cruel to her, Ravenna. I couldn't help myself. What is it, then, about the human spirit that makes us act so?"

"I wish I had left the Lord of Dreams earlier," she said, "and married you myself, Maxel. I would never have left you."

He laughed, softly, and a little bitterly. "Marsh women marry no men, Ravenna. And they stay with men even less time than Ishbel stayed with me. They need men to sire their babies, and then they abandon the men who love them and take their babies with them. How much better are you than Ishbel, Ravenna?"

She froze, appalled at being compared to Ishbel even more than the personal attack.

"Oh, gods, I am sorry, Ravenna. You of all people did not deserve me to say that to you. I'm sorry. I'm *sorry*. Don't go. Please, don't go."

She relaxed a little. "Ishbel has hurt you, Maxel."

"And I have hurt her, and now you. I have come out of this night the worse, I think."

They sat silently a little while, their hands still loosely interlinked.

"Are Serge and Doyle here? And your mother?" Maximilian said eventually.

"Yes. They are settled outside, all nervy at the thought of being ensconced in Isaiah's palace."

Maximilian smiled a fraction at that.

"StarDrifter and Salome are here, too, and settled in their own quarters."

"Was Axis happy to see his father?"

"I have never seen two men happier to see each other."

"Then I am glad some joy has come out of this day."

"Well . . ." Ravenna smiled. "Now StarDrifter has the task of explaining to Axis how he managed to sire Salome's mother on Axis' old lover."

Maximilian managed a more genuine smile. "Ah, those SunSoars. I hope they manage to somehow complicate Isaiah's life, as they complicate everyone else's. That might be some small punishment for him for stealing away my wife."

"Maxel, what are you going to do?"

"I don't know, Ravenna. I just don't know. Here I sit, huddled on the floor of the palace of the man who is about to invade the Northern Kingdoms. I don't even *know* what is happening in Escator. What the fuck *am* I doing, Ravenna? I—"

"You are doing the best you can, Maxel."

"Oh, don't try to placate me, please. If only . . . if only I'd not dreamed of a family. If only I'd not set out on a quest for a dammed, damned bride. If only . . ."

"And that is futile, stupid talk. But you are tired, and tonight has not been pleasant for you, and so I shall forgive you."

Maximilian chuckled. "Did you treat the Lord of Dreams with this much contempt, Ravenna?"

"Yes. He grew tired of me and asked me to leave."

"And *that* I do not believe." He squeezed her hand, turning his head once more so he could look at her directly. "He would have gone down on his knees and begged you to stay."

She smiled, hesitated, then leaned forward and kissed him softly on his forehead.

"Ravenna . . ."

"Let me stay with you tonight, Maxel."

"I would be poor company for you, my sweet marsh woman. My breath stinks of wine, and my heart aches for—"

"Don't say her name again, not tonight." Ravenna kissed him again, this time softly, on the mouth.

There was a part of Maximilian that knew he should pull back. He understood that tonight, blackened as it was by strong, bitter emotion, and by the shock of meeting directly with the embodiment of Water, was the worst time of all to succumb to Ravenna's seductions.

But then there was also a part of him that thought that, as Ishbel had abandoned him for another, while he had abandoned a *kingdom* for *her*, then perhaps he should no longer deny himself the comfort that Ravenna offered.

Surely he should be allowed a little revenge. Just this once.

Her fingers and mouth were trailing over his face and neck now, and Maximilian allowed himself to sink into their promises and comforts.

"Skip, trip, my pretty man," she murmured in his ear, recalling the song she had once used to summon the Lord of Dreams to her side. "Skip, trip, into my hand."

He shuddered, and took her shoulders in his hands, and kissed the angle of her jaw, and used the wine as an excuse for what he was doing.

Skip, trip, into my heart.

* * *

Isaiah went straight to the apartment he shared with Ishbel.

She sat on the floor, against the wall, arms about knees, unwittingly echoing Maximilian's distress.

"Did you know Maximilian was coming for me?" she asked quietly.

"Yes," Isaiah said.

She raised her head and looked at him, her eyes full of black bitterness. "How can I ever trust you again?"

CHAPTER ELEVEN

Sakkuth, Isembaard

Axis was sitting on a wooden chair at the table in StarDrifter's and Salome's apartment. He'd tipped the chair back, balancing himself with one foot, and was now staring aghast between Salome and his father as StarDrifter finished his tale of who Salome was, and how she'd come to be with him now *and* bearing his child.

"Embeth," Axis finally managed. "Oh, stars, I'd never thought of her once I'd married Azhure. She is as much my guilt as yours, StarDrifter. I hadn't even realized she was your lover at Carlon. And to think that she bore a child, and died in the doing . . .

"Salome," he continued, "you have been cruelly treated by the SunSoars indeed. I am sorry for it, for the loss of your grandmother and for that of your son particularly. We are not an easy family."

She sighed, looking down at her hands interlaced over her stomach. "These past few months have been like a dream, Axis. I never wanted to leave Coroleas. I *loved* my life there." She paused. "At least, I thought I did. Now it seems so far distant. A dream. I still wake at night crying for Ezra. *His* loss is real enough, but as for my life in Yoyette . . . I am not sure I want *this* in its place, though."

She indicated her back, although Axis was aware she meant her sudden inclusion into the Icarii race and the Sun-Soar fold. He knew how she felt—he'd had enough problems coming to terms with his Icarii heritage when first he'd learned of it.

"Can I have a look?" Axis said, nodding at her back. "Or my father's, if you'd prefer me not to—"

"I don't care," Salome said with a slight shrug, and unfolded the robe she wore, revealing not only her back, but her breasts as well.

Axis repressed a smile, glancing at his father as he rose and walked about the table to where Salome sat. *SunSoar blood.*

And he could feel it, as soon as he got to within a pace of her. The pull that all SunSoars exerted each to the other. No wonder she and his father . . . Axis saw StarDrifter glaring and he grinned at him, and concentrated on the matter at hand.

Salome's back both repelled and excited him. It looked horrendous, with twin massive cartilaginous ridges protruding from either side of her spine. They were barely covered with skin, and Axis realized that very soon the wings would break free. Very gently he ran his fingers down one of the ridges, feeling the wing within folded back on itself.

It felt hot, and Axis knew it must be very painful.

"Is it worse, StarDrifter," he said, "now, than when you were a child?" Icarii children generally developed their wings when they were five or six, and apart from some grumbling and whining about the ache, as when they'd teethed earlier in childhood, they generally did not suffer much pain.

"Yes," StarDrifter said, "much worse. Our bones are set now, and our muscles and bodies complain about the growth. I will be glad once they have broken free, and can grow beyond the confines of our backs."

"Salome?" Axis asked.

"It is agony," she said, "and all for something I don't want."

"I will remind you of that remark one day," Axis said, "when you have returned flushed of cheek and exhilarated of spirit after soaring a league into the sky."

He lifted the robe over her back again, then stood looking at her.

"Yes?" she said.

"Sorry," Axis said. "You have been reminding me of

someone, and I have only just remembered." He looked at his father. "You don't see it?"

"No. Who?"

"There are none so blind," Axis murmured. Then said, louder, "Salome, you are the spitting image of my grandmother, your great-grandmother and StarDrifter's mother—MorningStar SunSoar. Not only in features, but you have something of her flair and directness as well. I remember the day she tried to seduce me—"

"My *mother* tried to seduce you?" StarDrifter said.

Axis laughed. "And you seduced your granddaughter, StarDrifter. Perhaps we can lay the blame for this entire grandparent-grandchild attraction at her feet, eh? Now, let me look at your back."

If anything, his father's back looked even worse than Salome's. "Gods, StarDrifter . . ."

"I don't complain," StarDrifter said. "I rejoice in every twinge."

"I am sure you do," Axis said, knowing how his father must have hated living flightless. "But I don't understand, how is it that you are growing your wings? I have never heard of anything like this before."

"I told you that I'd seduced Salome in an effort to steal the deity known as the Weeper," StarDrifter said.

Axis nodded.

"Well," StarDrifter continued, "Maxel thinks, and I agree with him, that the Weeper has done this. It is the only possibility I can think of."

"Is the Weeper the bundle you carried from the bakery?" Axis said.

"Yes," said StarDrifter. "Usually only Maximilian carries the Weeper, but for the journey from the bakery it accepted me as an old friend, if only because I would return it to Maxel's side."

"Salome," Axis said, "what *is* the Weeper? I mean, what soul went into its creation? It must have been powerful indeed."

"All I know," said Salome, "is what legend tells us: the man who gave his soul into the deity was a man from a dis-

tant land, and very, very powerful. Stunningly so." She gave
a slight shrug. "That would explain the power of the Weeper,
of course."

"I think the Weeper has only ever wanted to get to Maximilian," StarDrifter said. "These"—he indicated his back
and Salome's—"are thank-you gifts to Salome and myself."

"But Ba'al'uz knew about the Weeper," said Axis, "or, at
the least, he knew about its power. He abandoned his quest
of chaos in the Northern Kingdoms, and abandoned Ishbel,
to retrieve the Weeper. So perhaps the Weeper has some connection with Isembaard."

"Perhaps this DarkGlass Mountain told Ba'al'uz to fetch
the Weeper," StarDrifter said.

He leaned forward a little, looking keenly at Axis. "Axis,
one of the things that made me agree to do what Ba'al'uz
wished, apart, that is"—he glanced at Salome—"from the
opportunity to sleep with the lovely Duchess of Sidon, *and*
the fact you were in Isembaard, was that he said DarkGlass
Mountain could reconnect us with the Star Dance. Do you
know anything about—"

"Ha," said Axis. "I have been in this DarkGlass Mountain, StarDrifter, and, yes, the possibility exists that it *could*
connect us back to the Star Dance."

"But . . ."

"But to do so would be to invite catastrophe. DarkGlass
Mountain is death itself. I think that if the Star Dance filtered through DarkGlass Mountain then the Dance would be
contaminated with such horror . . . so, not DarkGlass Mountain, StarDrifter, but I think maybe something else."

StarDrifter leaned forward, eyes gleaming. "What?"

Axis told StarDrifter and Salome about the glass pyramid
he'd taken from the packs of Ba'al'uz' men. "I will show
it to you later," he concluded. "Tomorrow, perhaps, when
we are rested. Isaiah has one of these glass pyramids, and
this strange Lord of the Skraelings as well, Lister. Recently
I touched Isaiah's while it was active, and again felt the Star
Dance through it. Faintly, and not enough for me to catch.
But it *was* there."

"But how?" said StarDrifter. "Where do these glass pyramids come from? Who made them? *Axis?*"

Axis would have smiled at his father's eagerness if he didn't understand the desperate longing that lay behind it. How must his father feel, to be so close to the two things he'd missed desperately?

"Lister, this Lord of the Skraelings, has some interesting creatures as his allies," Axis said. "A few short weeks ago he sent one of them to stage an assassination attempt on Isaiah to push him forward in his invasion plans. They are Icarii . . . and yet not Icarii."

"In what way?" said StarDrifter.

"This assassin looked like an Icarii—features, wings, bearing, elegance, arrogance, everything. But . . . ah, I can't explain it. There was *something* about him, an air . . . and he escaped a rain of spears and arrows when he simply should not have done. He attacked Isaiah in a hall crammed with marksmen. Wings or not, he should not have been able to get away. But he did. He vanished."

"He used the Star Dance?" StarDrifter said.

Axis gave a slight shrug. "Perhaps, although if he did, then I did not feel it. I just don't know who or what he could be. There are no other winged races you know of, StarDrifter? Nothing from legend? No cousin race to the Icarii?"

"No," said StarDrifter. "There's nothing that . . ." He stopped suddenly.

"And then again, perhaps there is," said Salome, looking at him carefully.

"During the initial Wars of the Axe," StarDrifter said, speaking slowly, thinking as he went, "when the Icarii were being pushed back into the Icescarp Alps, there was a conflict among the Icarii leadership."

"And?" said Axis.

"Some among the Icarii thought that the Icescarp Alps would not be enough to keep the Acharites at bay. There were some families, led by a senior Icarii, who fled still further north. Perhaps fifty or sixty Icarii all told."

"They fled into the frozen wastelands?" Axis said. "They must have been terrified, indeed."

"Yes. I think everyone assumed they had died—we never heard from them again, and the frozen wastelands were so inhospitable, and populated with Skraelings, and—"

Axis swore, making his father stop and raise a disapproving eyebrow.

"Of course!" Axis said. "Of *course*! There we have it! The assassin, the almost but not quite Icarii, was sent by Lister, the Lord of the Skraelings, Isaiah's 'ally.' StarDrifter, you never heard from the Icarii families again because they traveled far further than anyone had thought—right across the ice bridge between Tencendor and this continent, which also has a massive Skraeling population in its extreme frozen north. That's where they survived."

"But why did you sense a difference in the assassin?" said StarDrifter.

Axis hesitated a long moment before he responded.

"Because over the past few thousand years," he said eventually, "they interbred with the Skraelings. That's the only reason they survived. They interbred with the Skraelings."

Axis had gone, and StarDrifter and Salome were alone in their apartment.

They had bathed, and now sat on the bed, both naked in the early dawn light.

StarDrifter was rubbing an unguent that Venetia had given them into Salome's back, and she was sighing in pleasure at the relief it brought from the ache of the emerging wings.

"Tell me," she said, "that these wings are going to be worth the pain and disfigurement they bring me now."

StarDrifter thought of how lovely she had been in Yoyette, how lithe and graceful, how sensual and beautiful. Now her back humped in ghastly forms, red and angry with the inflammation caused by the growing bones and sinews of her wings.

"The world will be at your feet," he said. "Literally. Salome, you have no idea how wonderful it will be to fly."

His hand slipped from her back and under her arms to her collarbones, their outer edges lightly resting on the swell of her breasts.

"You shall have to tone these muscles, though," he said.

"It will likely take you many weeks before you are able to lift more than a pace or so off the ground."

"And I thought I should be soaring to the sun within moments of combing flat my feathers!"

StarDrifter wondered what he should say. He opened his mouth, and then realized she was teasing him.

He smiled, and very softly kissed her shoulder. They had not made love at all since Coroleas. There had been no opportunity on the journey through the FarReach Mountains, and both had been either so weary, or in such pain, or still so emotionally drained after that day they'd met at the foot of the mountains, that neither had felt the desire.

And he hadn't known what he had wanted. Nor what she wanted.

Now . . .

Now they were warm from their shared bath, and, due both to the hot soak and to Venetia's unguent, their backs felt better than they had in weeks.

Now there was both the opportunity and, certainly on StarDrifter's part, the desire.

But he didn't know Salome well enough, or feel sure enough of her, to know what *she* felt at this stage.

His hands slowly moved down over her breasts—he felt her shudder, and knew that she felt desire, at least—and then to her very softly rounded belly. Like most Icarii, Salome would not grow very large with her pregnancy. Icarii babies were healthy and strong at birth, but smaller than human babies.

She leaned back against him, turning slightly so that her cumbersome back slid to one side.

"Tell me about the baby," she said.

"He is safe and very warm and comfortable," said StarDrifter. "He loves you, and is also glad I am near. He knows your wings grow, and is curious, but saddened by your pain."

"If we made love, would he know?"

StarDrifter kissed her shoulder again, more firmly this time, and his hands moved back to her breasts. "Yes."

"Would it trouble him?"

StarDrifter smiled against her flesh. "He is an Icarii. It will not trouble him at all. He will merely dream more deeply of us later, when he sleeps."

"StarDrifter, I hated you so much."

"I know. You had every right to."

"You don't seem to trouble me so much now, though."

He laughed. "Good."

"I can't believe I am about to say this, and I didn't realize it until very recently . . ."

"Yes?"

"I am very glad you came into my life, StarDrifter. I wish I had not lost Ezra. I wish *I* had not done many things. But I am glad you came into my life."

StarDrifter took a very deep breath, sudden emotion bringing tears to his eyes. He tilted her head, and kissed her, gently at first, then with more desire.

"You know," he said eventually, "I think we may be the only reasonably happy couple in this damned palace right now."

"StarDrifter, tell me, if you can, how shall we manage this lovemaking, with our backs so sore and awkward?"

Again he laughed, and he thought that he had not laughed this much in many years.

"You are no granddaughter of mine, Salome, if you cannot solve such a simple problem."

"I thought I might give you the opportunity to appear wise. That expression appears so rarely on your face."

StarDrifter grinned, pulling her onto his lap. "Axis was right. You *do* take after my mother."

Later, when the rest of Sakkuth was rising and donning their invasion clothes, StarDrifter lay in bed, Salome asleep beside him, thinking about what Axis had said.

The lost Icarii families had interbred with the Skraelings.

StarDrifter couldn't believe it. Rather, he could not bring himself to believe it. How could *any* Icarii lie down with a Skraeling?

Axis must be wrong.

Surely.

If he *wasn't*, then StarDrifter dreaded to think what this half-breed Icarii race was like.

Skraelings, with wings.

He inched a little closer to Salome, running a gentle hand over her stomach.

The baby was asleep inside her, lulled by their earlier lovemaking.

A son. StarDrifter had sired two other sons. One, a horror—Gorgrael, the former Lord of the Skraelings. One, a wonder—Axis, StarMan and savior of Tencendor.

What would this son prove?

StarDrifter moved his thumb slowly, backward and forward, softly rubbing Salome's skin.

She opened her eyes, and looked at him.

He rested his head on her shoulder, his thumb and hand still gently stroking her belly, and they lay like that for another hour before rising for the day.

CHAPTER TWELVE

The Borderlands of Hosea

*G*ood *news.*
  Lister had been sleeping soundly, Inardle warm against his body, when Isaiah spoke in his mind and woke him.

"What?" he whispered, feeling Inardle stirring.

Maximilian is with me in Sakkuth. I have him. Ishbel drew him like a lodestone.

"Oh, praise all gods!" Lister said, sitting up and snatching at a cloak to wrap about his shoulders. He would be more than glad when he could swap this tent for more salubrious surroundings.

At his side Inardle opened her eyes, watching her lover carefully, while outside the never-ending stream of Skraelings continued south, south, south.

"You shall not lose him?" Lister added, a little anxiously.

I hope not—I will not hold him prisoner, Lister. I do not think he will try to escape.

"He knows about the baby?"

Yes. He knows. He despairs.

"As should we all," Lister said. "Did you speak of Elcho Falling?"

Yes. But tonight was not the time to speak of it in depth.

"Soon, perhaps. Tell me, when do you leave for the Salamaan Pass?"

Within a few days. Where are you?

"Approaching Hosea. Isaiah . . . the Skraelings are changing."

In what manner, Lister?

"They are growing dogs' heads."

[Part Nine]

CHAPTER ONE

Sakkuth, Isembaard

Maximilian woke slowly, reluctantly. His night had been filled with violently colored, fragmentary dreams—partly of Ishbel, partly of the vision he'd had while on the way to meet Ishbel in Pelemere.

Maximilian did not want to wake. Once he was awake he'd need to cope with the loss of Ishbel and their child, as well as the knowledge that he would need to face what all kings of Escator before him had dreaded facing: the terrifying responsibilities of their far more ancient and frightening title . . . the Lord of Elcho Falling.

Intertwined through all these dreams and fears and thoughts was the knowledge that he'd drunk far too much, and that he'd need to face the coming day's trials with a hangover of monstrous proportions.

Maximilian roused, moving a little more firmly against the body in his bed, wrapping one arm about the woman's waist, feeling the delight of her naked back pressing against his flesh, thinking that his dreams and memories had duped him and that Ishbel had been here all along, and that she—

"Maxel?"

He leapt into wakefulness, recoiling away from Ravenna.

"I'm sorry," he stuttered. "I woke you, I didn't mean to. Go back to sleep, Ravenna."

He rolled out of bed, hastily pulling on some clothing and painfully aware of Ravenna watching his every move. It was still early, barely light, and he mumbled something about getting some fresh air and fled the chamber.

* * *

Maximilian more than expected to find guards outside the main door to his apartment, but the corridor was empty. Feeling nauseated, both from the effects of the wine and the shock of discovering Ravenna in his bed, Maximilian wandered through the palace into the central courtyard where he sank down on a cask, resting his head in his hands as he allowed the rising sun to warm him.

Oh, gods, what had he done?

He liked Ravenna, but he didn't love her, or really particularly desire her. He was grateful to her, as he was to Garth, and had once been to Vorstus, for their efforts in rescuing him from the Veins, but over the past year Maximilian was very much aware that he'd been growing distant from these three friends. Vorstus because Maximilian now suspected him of manipulating his early life, perhaps even of causing him to be interred in the Veins in the first instance, and Garth and Ravenna because . . . well, they now belonged to an earlier part of his life, and while he liked them, he wanted to move on.

Ishbel had made all the difference. She had opened that massive gap between what he had once been and where he was now going.

Maximilian had been barely living before Ishbel had come into his life. She had brought great pain, and frustration, and fear when Maximilian had realized that she trailed Elcho Falling at her heels, but she also brought love.

Gods, he shouldn't have slept with Ravenna. Maximilian would have liked to blame the wine, or even Ishbel for driving him to such desperate distraction, but in the end it had been his error of judgment, and his weakness, for not pushing her away.

Gods only knew to where it would lead.

"Maximilian? You look like you could do with some of this."

Maximilian jerked his head out of his hands, squinting into the bright sun.

It was Axis, holding out what looked like two mugs of

tea in one hand and a plate of bread and fruit preserves in the other.

"I saw you from the kitchens," said Axis. "Thought I'd bring you some breakfast." He paused. "You look dreadful."

"Thank you," Maximilian said, surprising himself by meaning it. There were few people he would like near him at the present moment, but he thought Axis might be one of them.

"It was a bad day for you yesterday," Axis said, sitting down on a neighboring cask and handing Maximilian the tea and plate.

Maximilian answered only with a grunt, taking a tentative sip of the tea, then a longer drink. "You have seen your father?" he said after a moment.

Axis smiled. "Yes. *Yes*."

"He was desperate to see you. Longing for you."

"He means the world to me, Maximilian. Thank you for bringing him to me."

"What did you make of Salome?"

Axis laughed, stretching his long legs into the sun. "She is a true SunSoar. I am glad my father found her first, for I think she would have been too much for me to manage."

Maximilian almost smiled. "I have heard about the Sun-Soar attraction to each other."

They sat in companionable silence for a few minutes, sipping their tea, sharing the bread and preserves. Maximilian found that the tea, the food, and the company were making a surprising difference to how he felt. The tea and food soothed his stomach and head, and Axis soothed his nerves. From all he knew of Axis, Maximilian understood that he would be very unlikely to judge.

"Can you tell me what happened to my daughter?" Maximilian asked finally, very softly, looking ahead rather than at Axis.

"Yes," Axis said and, in a low voice, told Maximilian not only about the manner of his daughter's death, but of the relationship between Isaiah and Ishbel.

At the end of it, Maximilian put his empty mug down,

lowered his face once more into his hands, and wept. Axis put a hand on his shoulder, and for ten minutes or more they sat there, two men sharing grief, companionship, and understanding.

"Isaiah keeps on about this Lord of Elcho Falling," Axis said eventually. "Who is he, Maximilian?"

Maximilian gave a deep sigh, releasing the last of the emotion spent over the past minutes. "I am the Lord of Elcho Falling," he said and, at Axis' surprised look, continued. "The title of King of Escator is the far lesser of the Persimius titles. Elcho Falling is an ancient kingdom that encompassed virtually the entire continent above the FarReach Mountains. As a kingdom it broke up into many individual independent realms well over two thousand years ago. The ancient line of Persimius, which controls the hereditary titles of Elcho Falling, retains the crown and the ancient rings of office. We do not like to anticipate the day when we shall be required to wear the crown once more."

"Why not?"

"Because it is a thing of darkness," Maximilian said, his tone now short. He rose, handing his mug back to Axis. "I thank you for both the tea and the companionship, Axis. Perhaps we shall have time for more of both over the coming days. Now, do you know where I might find Isaiah? Without Ishbel, if you please."

Isaiah turned from the two generals with whom he'd been consulting, saw Maximilian waiting just inside the door of the chamber, and waved the generals away.

"Well," Isaiah said as he walked over, "it is easy to see that you did not spend a good night."

"Don't preach to me, Isaiah. We need to talk."

"Indeed, but I thought I'd tried last night to—"

"That was a shitty time to approach me, Isaiah, as well you know."

"So tell me," Isaiah said, "to whom do I speak today? The somewhat bedraggled King of Escator . . . or the Lord of Elcho Falling?"

"I do not yet wear the crown, Isaiah."

"But you are prepared to accept it."

There was a long pause, in which Maximilian would not meet Isaiah's eyes.

Then, finally, Maximilian shifted his gaze back to Isaiah's. "Yes," he said.

Isaiah's shoulders visibly slumped in relief. "Thank the gods," he mumbled.

"What is happening?" Maximilian said. "Can you show me?"

Isaiah led the way to a large map unrolled across a table. "The Skraelings spent the past eighteen months massing in the north. Currently they are swarming south, heading . . ."

"For the FarReach Mountains," Maximilian said. He paused a moment, one finger tapping idly at the map. "This isn't an 'invasion' force you command at all, is it, Isaiah?"

"No," said Isaiah, "it is an evacuation. See . . ." His finger traced a path through the FarReach Mountains, then down the territory to the west of the River Lhyl. "The Skraelings will seethe down through the western parts of Isembaard toward where Kanubai waits, there to form his army. I have emptied that part of Isembaard as best I can . . . and encouraged families of the army to travel north with their husbands and fathers."

"Then why not just simply call it an evacuation?"

"An 'invasion' was the only means I could manage an evacuation, Maximilian. If I had suddenly announced that my tyranny was to be invaded by an army of wraiths, flocking to their newly risen ghastly commander, I would have been dead within a day by the hand of one of my generals. An invasion they can understand, an evacuation not. They would have seen it as a weakness on my part."

"And Ishbel? Why bring her here, Isaiah? Why—"

"No one planned for her to come to Isembaard, Maximilian. Believe it or not, all I and Lister have ever wanted was to see her safe with you."

"But still you managed to seduce her."

"Maximilian—"

Maximilian waved a hand. "Leave it."

"She is not happy with me, Maximilian."

"*Leave it,* I said!"

"Then stop bringing it up!" Isaiah snapped. He took a deep breath, and inclined his head slightly. "I apologize."

Maximilian was not sure what it was that Isaiah apologized for—seducing Ishbel or for snarling his response—but inclined his own head in acknowledgment of the apology. He wondered if they were going to spend their entire lives alternatively snapping and inclining their heads at each other.

"I will go north with you," Maximilian said. "It makes sense. We are, I suppose, headed for the same place."

Elcho Falling.

"Maximilian," Isaiah said. "Can you do it? Can you assume the mantle of the Lord of Elcho Falling?"

Maximilian thought about all the empty spaces and chambers within the Twisted Tower, all the lost knowledge. "Who cares what I answer, Isaiah? I am all that you—and Elcho Falling—have."

On his way back to his apartments, trying to work out in his head what he could say to Ravenna, Maximilian literally walked into Ishbel as he turned a corner.

They sprang back from each other.

There was a stunningly awkward moment.

"Sorry," Maximilian and Ishbel both said at the same time, then both reddened, looking away.

The moment had passed where they could have just walked away from each other. Now they were going to have to pass a few words, at the very least.

"I said some cruel things last night," Maximilian finally said, taking all his courage in hand to look Ishbel in the face. "I should not have done. I apologize."

It was the day for apologies, he thought.

"What you heard and saw would have tested anyone's patience, Maximilian. I, ah, I just . . . I can't believe you came all this way for me."

"There was no reason for you *to* believe it. Not the way I'd treated you after Borchard's death."

There was another awkward silence.

"I suppose you'll be leaving soon," said Ishbel, her voice now slightly strained.

"No. I will be traveling north with Isaiah's army."

"Oh."

"I'm sure there will be enough room for us to avoid each other."

"Yes."

Silence.

"Ravenna seems a nice girl," Ishbel said, both her color and her tone revealing her desperation to find *something* to say.

Ravenna seems a nice girl. If it had been under any other circumstances Maximilian would likely have smiled at Ishbel's distracted attempts to keep conversation going. He might even have laughed.

But not after last night.

Guilt swept through him, stronger than ever before. "Yes," he said, "Ravenna is a nice girl."

Then he turned on his heel and walked away, leaving Ishbel staring after him.

CHAPTER TWO

Salamaan Pass, Northern Kingdoms

Axis had led some massive armies in his time, but nothing like what Isaiah now commanded, nor had he ever managed to trail behind such an army with half of their wives and children and great-aunts, not to mention livestock and worldly goods. He would not have liked to lead this number of people (*almost a million, by the stars!*) and he most certainly would not have liked to be responsible for its organization. Isaiah, however, managed it without apparent effort, or concern, or a single worry line down the center of his tanned forehead.

The running, organization, and movement of this unbelievable column of people certainly kept his generals busy, and it most definitely kept Axis running from the time he rose in the morning until that blessed hour when he could hit his sleeping roll late at night. Isaiah had ordered the march forward three days after Maximilian and his party had arrived in Sakkuth. Getting the army (and its innumerable followers) on the move had been like trying to waken a vast, grudging, sleepy monster—but once wakened, it was seemingly impossible to stop. Axis was not sure that the entire column ever *did* halt. There always seemed to be some part of it snaking forward. Ten thousand may stop here for a meal and a rest, but somewhere else ten thousand rose from their sleeping rolls, and stretched, then picked up their packs and weapons and trudged forward yet once more.

Isaiah traveled in a relatively small convoy of commanders. He lived as one of the soldiers, and moved his convoy between others within the greater column. Isaiah's convoy was Axis' "home" within the vast mass marching forward, but he tended to see Isaiah only once every two or three days as Isaiah constantly had him traveling between different sections, probing, delivering orders, chatting to commanders, receiving reports, laughing, shouting, and sometimes sitting down for a few minutes with his harp, entertaining men grouped about fires with songs and tales from the myth and reality of Tencendor. Axis spoke with generals and foot soldiers alike, and covered leagues of territory every day as he moved about his appointed tasks.

Each day was hectic and tiring beyond belief, but Axis loved it. He gained a sense of the army, of its structure, its abilities, its heart and soul, which would otherwise have been virtually impossible.

Nonetheless, it surprised him when, a few days after they'd entered the Salamaan Pass, and about ten after they'd left Sakkuth, a group of men in a section he passed on his horse called out to him, and cheered him as he went, as if he were their chief instead of Isaiah.

His father, StarDrifter, and Maximilian and the others of their party, traveled in their own convoy, which kept to its strictly appointed place in the overall army. They were not guarded as such, but Axis was aware that Isaiah had set men to watching them.

Maximilian had mostly kept to himself since he'd arrived in Sakkuth. He had spoken with Isaiah on several occasions that Axis knew about, but Axis did not think he'd seen Ishbel. StarDrifter had told Axis that Maximilian spent a great deal of time alone, that he appeared preoccupied with something, whether Ishbel or some other worry, and that only Ravenna had any real contact with him.

Axis knew that Ishbel and Isaiah now spent their time apart. Ishbel traveled with Isaiah's convoy, but Isaiah had made a great show of saying that he now slept on the ground with his troops rather than in a softer bed. Axis interpreted that as meaning Ishbel did not want him near her.

Unhappiness prevailed, and Axis wished that Isaiah, Ishbel, and Maximilian could sort out the mess among them.

He was, to be frank, surprised that Maximilian remained with Isaiah's column, but supposed that traveling with this massive convoy, which was, after all, heading directly north, was the most direct route home for Maximilian. He would hardly want to scramble his independent way back through the mountains with little food and support.

It must, nonetheless, be galling for him to travel with the invader.

There was something going on that Axis did not understand, and he found that unbelievably frustrating.

On this day, a half hour or more after Axis had been surprised by the cheer that went up for him from some of Isaiah's soldiers as he'd ridden past, he saw StarDrifter and Maximilian riding up ahead. His father's wings, as Salome's, had emerged about a week ago, accompanied by much moaning and groaning (according to Salome, who swore it wasn't anywhere near as painful as childbirth and she didn't know what StarDrifter was complaining about) from StarDrifter and a few choice swear words that had surprised even Salome.

While their wings had now emerged completely from their backs, they were yet to fully fledge and muscle, so thus far neither could fly. Both of them grew similar wings—once fully feathered, they would be a silvery white, their feathers tipped with gold.

Airborne, both would be spectacular.

Axis knew that Zeboath had examined StarDrifter and Salome on several occasions, fascinated by their wings. StarDrifter and Salome were apparently philosophical about Zeboath's interest, and Axis thought it indicative of Zeboath's tact that he'd managed more than one examination.

Publicly, Salome was less enthusiastic about her wings and the possibility of flight, but Axis thought she was growing not only more curious about her wings, but also hid a growing eagerness to try them out. Sometimes, when she thought no one was watching her, Axis would catch her looking skyward, wondering . . .

Salome was good for his father, he decided. StarDrifter had loved Axis' own mother, Rivkah, deeply, but she had been an Acharite, a human, and she'd not been able to hold his interest as she aged. She'd also been too *nice*, too good, much as Zenith—Axis' own daughter—had been. StarDrifter had an arrogant bad streak in him that could light up a moonless night as if it were day, and Salome, just as arrogant, just as bad, was his perfect match. They were rarely publicly affectionate toward each other, but Axis sensed a deep bonding between them that had never been present between StarDrifter and his mother, and certainly not between StarDrifter and Zenith.

Watching his father ride, Axis could see him stretching and flexing each wing, one at a time, and knew it would not be long before StarDrifter would be able to take to the thermals.

Axis grinned. He'd hardly seen his father for more than a chance to exchange a few hasty words since leaving Sakkūth, and, while he still had a thousand things he needed to do today, he could spare a half hour for a chat.

He rode up behind them quietly, his approach masked by the sound of a thousand horsemen nearby. StarDrifter and Maximilian were riding along easily, both men relaxed, Maximilian actually smiling a little, their horses at a loose-limbed trot.

It gave Axis heart to think that Maximilian *could* smile. It changed his face completely, all the darkness sloughing off to reveal charm and charisma.

Axis suddenly spurred his horse forward, pushing in between the mounts of both men and making their horses shy a little in surprise.

"Axis!" StarDrifter exclaimed, reining in his horse and pulling it close enough to that of his son's to give Axis a welcoming slap on the shoulder.

Maximilian smiled as well, looking genuinely pleased to see Axis.

"Such guilty expressions!" Axis said, still grinning. "What were you two planning? Tell me, that I might report it to Isaiah."

"We were talking about my wings," said StarDrifter. "About how splendid they are." He stretched both of them in a luxurious manner, the sun catching the glints of gold at the point of each emerging feather.

"And I was just remarking to your father," said Maximilian, "that he shall be fully splendid by the time he stands before his people as Talon."

"*Talon?*" Axis said.

"You didn't know?" said Maximilian. "BroadWing pressed StarDrifter to accept the throne of Talon. StarDrifter was reluctant, but finally accepted."

"Axis," StarDrifter said, looking a little unsure. "I know that you—"

But Axis was smiling, and he kneed his horse close enough to that of his father's that he could briefly embrace him. "This is the *happiest* news, StarDrifter! You have been a long time coming to the Talon's throne, but I think it was always, *always* yours."

"You don't want it?" StarDrifter said.

"Me?" Axis said. "No! It was never mine." He sobered a little. "This *is* the happiest news, StarDrifter. Until this moment I had doubted the Icarii could rise again. Now I know they can."

Again he kneed his horse close to StarDrifter's, and, controlling his horse only with his knees and balance, reached out and grasped his father's left hand in both of his.

"StarDrifter SunSoar," Axis said, "as my father you have my heart and my love, but as my liege lord you have not only my heart and my love, but my hands and my loyalty and whatever power may be mine to command. I am yours, Talon, heart and soul and mind. Command me as you will."

Then he kissed his father's hand, and laid it very briefly on the top of his head.

"Axis . . ." StarDrifter had tears in his eyes, and he had to blink them back before he could continue. Axis had done so much in his life that was noteworthy, but StarDrifter wondered if he had ever said or done anything that had affected him as deeply as this heartfelt pledge of love and loyalty.

Their hands clasped again, just for a moment, but with a fierce intensity.

"Soon you must begin to garner your nation to you,"

said Axis. "The Icarii are scattered. You must find them a home."

"Ah, and I thought you were here to cheer me," StarDrifter said. "But as soon as you have flattered me with attention, you hand me the task impossible. Find the Icarii a homeland, indeed."

"The world is being torn apart," said Maximilian. "I have no doubt that you can find five or six thousand Icarii a home somewhere among the tatters."

"It must be difficult for you," said Axis, "seeing how every day this force grinds its way toward your homelands."

Maximilian shot him an unfathomable look as his only answer.

"We were curious, Axis," StarDrifter said, "to know what your relationship with Isaiah is. Tell us of him, and what you do riding with . . . this." He, in his turn, waved about. "Frankly, I would not have thought you so willing to ride with such an invasion."

Axis ignored the last comment. "Isaiah was the one to bring me back from the Otherworld," he said. "He has reserves of power that he rarely, almost *never*, shows to any other. That intrigues me. *Fascinates* me."

"What do you mean?" StarDrifter said.

"Isaiah is using his face as tyrant as a disguise," Axis said. "He hides tremendous power beneath it. Why need so powerful a disguise? What *is* he hiding? I would be fearful of it, save that I like Isaiah. Immensely. And I respect him as I respect few people."

Axis gave a short laugh. "We have our disagreements, and snipe at each other, but I would trust him with my life, and he would trust me likewise, I think."

"Sometimes trust can be entirely misplaced," Maximilian said.

On that same day, Salome—bored witless by the never-ending travel, and irritated with StarDrifter for leaving her to go and bond with Maximilian—made the effort to escape the wagon in which she traveled with Ravenna and Venetia to find Ishbel.

On the face of it, the task was a nightmare. Ishbel traveled in Isaiah's group, and on any given day that might be at any given spot within the convoy.

In the end, Salome had simply commandeered a horse, ridden up to the less than subtle military escort that accompanied them at all times, and asked two of the men to take her to Ishbel.

"After all," she said, "you must know in which direction your master's party lies, as you must report to him daily. Yes?"

The men looked at each other.

"I am not about to slaughter her," said Salome. "You may search me for a weapon, if you wish . . . and as thoroughly as you wish."

They did, to Salome's complete amusement. They took her to one side, one man holding up a blanket for some privacy while the other searched her as thoroughly as Salome had invited.

At the end of the search, having rearranged her clothes, Salome dealt the man a stinging slap across the cheek. "You have heard of me, no doubt," she said. "The vile, murdering Duchess of Sidon? Yes? Then, believe me, should I ever hear of sniggering tales regarding this incident being passed about fires at night, you and he"—she inclined her head at the other man, now folding up the blanket—"shall be dead by nightfall of the following day. Not even Isaiah can save you. You understand? Yes? Good, then help me to my horse, and let us be on our way. And be careful of that wing, it is still tender."

Ishbel was traveling as alone as anyone might in this vast mass of people and horses. She rode her horse to one side of Isaiah's personal party of wagons and riders, isolated and introspective. Isaiah was busy elsewhere, and although he spent time with her each day, Ishbel often felt as if she were traveling by herself. She did not feel the same isolation as she had when leaving Serpent's Nest to marry Maximilian, but it was a similar sensation, and kept her wreathed in sadness for most of the time. Ishbel simply did not know where she belonged, or what would happen to her life. She could not for a moment imagine returning to Serpent's Nest, there to resume her duties as archpriestess of the Coil. Too much had happened, too many corners had been turned, too many doors had been opened.

"Ishbel Brunelle? Queen of Escator, lover of tyrants?"

Ishbel jerked out of her reverie, heart thumping. A bird-woman had just ridden to her side, her lovely face wreathed in smiles, her eyes in calculation, and her wings tucked in awkwardly behind her back and trailing partway down her horse's flanks. Ishbel could see they were thin, as yet un-muscled, and she knew who this woman must be.

Salome, Axis' father's exotic and somewhat infamous wife.

Ishbel didn't like birdwomen. They reminded her too much of StarWeb, Maximilian's former lover.

Salome was obviously also a very good horsewoman, and that put Ishbel at further disadvantage.

"Ah," said Salome, her smile undimmed, "you are not happy to see me. Well, at that I am not surprised. I have yet to meet a woman who *was* happy to see me. But no matter. Here it is, such a lovely day, and I am bored, and thought to make your acquaintance." She indicated the saddlebags. "On my way to you I collected some bread and cheese and dried fruits and some rather strong ale. Shall we find somewhere nice to lunch?"

"Look . . . Salome, isn't it? It is a nice invitation, and I thank you for it, but—"

"I can tell you all about Ravenna."

It wasn't so much what she said as how she said it that told Ishbel that Salome didn't want to exchange pleasant gossip, but potentially useful information.

"Why?" said Ishbel.

"Because I don't like her very much," said Salome. "Too righteous by half."

Ishbel's mouth twitched. She knew that Salome was likely saying only what Ishbel wanted to hear, but for the moment that didn't matter. Ishbel would have given her right arm rather than be forced to spend an afternoon picnicking with StarWeb, but suddenly the idea of sitting in the winter sunshine with Salome, listening to (hopefully) some sharp-tongued gossip, sounded appealing.

Salome grinned, seeing the decision on Ishbel's face. "I have two guards trailing me," Salome said. "I don't like them. Can you get rid of them?"

Ishbel looked to where the two men rode some four or five paces back. She gave a single jerk of her head, and they instantly peeled off and vanished within the general convoy.

"Sleeping with the tyrant has its advantages," said Ishbel.

"I knew I was going to like you!" said Salome.

Axis was just about to pull his horse away from those of Maximilian and StarDrifter when Isaiah rode up.

Isaiah looked between the three of them, then he nodded at a peak about an hour's ride away.

"There is something I want the three of you to see," he said. "Will you come with me?"

Salome and Ishbel found a spot on a rise along the eastern face of the pass where they were certain to get several hours of afternoon sun, hobbled their horses, and found themselves a comfortable spot among the rocks. Before them the wide pass spread for miles in either direction, its pink and sandstone walls rearing thousands of feet into the sky. The larger portion of the relatively flat floor of the pass was filled, in every direction, with slow-moving humanity and horseflesh. Wagons and siege engines trundled northward; cattle, sheep, and goats were herded in pools of red and cream and mottled gray through the river of soldiers; loose horses followed their ridden companions obediently. Salome set out the bread and fruit and cheese, and they shared a flask of ale.

For a while nothing was said. They sat companionably, eating, watching Isaiah's invasion army creep inexorably onward.

"You're having a baby," said Ishbel eventually.

"And I have heard that you lost yours," said Salome. "You can have this one, if you wish."

Ishbel thought about how she should react to that, then she saw Salome's eyes twinkle, and she thought how bizarre, yet how refreshing, it was to have someone actually make a small jest about what had been such a tragedy, and which had tarnished two lives so badly.

"Thank you," said Ishbel, "but I don't think that it would look very much like Maximilian. He might have his doubts."

Salome laughed. "And I don't think StarDrifter would ever let this baby out of his sight."

And neither would you, thought Ishbel.

"Is Ravenna sleeping with Maximilian?" she said.

"Yes," said Salome. "She has had her cap set for him, so far as I could tell, ever since she joined up with his party at Narbon. He resisted all through the FarReach Mountains, but I believe she managed to get her claws into him the night—"

"—the night he and she came to Isaiah's palace at Sakkuth, and discovered my sins. I see. Tell me, what is Ravenna?"

"*What* is she? A marsh woman. Apparently they tread the borderlands between this world and the world of dreams." Salome paused. "Not very impressive. Maximilian could surely have done better for his comfort."

Ishbel brushed some tears from her eyes. It hurt very badly that Maximilian was sleeping with Ravenna.

"Her mother is traveling with Maximilian as well," said Salome, handing the flask of ale over to Ishbel. "Venetia. I like Venetia and I think you would, too. I think she must have chosen badly for the father of her daughter."

"Why are you telling me all this? Why be so kind to me? What do you hope to gain?"

Salome laughed. "Because I like the sound of you! What gumption! What talent!"

Ishbel narrowed her eyes at Salome, as if she thought the woman was crazed.

"A woman whose arts include the ability to cleanly disembowel a man with one cut? Ishbel! I want to know how to do that!"

Ishbel smiled, unable to believe that she still could.

"And then to bed the Tyrant of Isembaard," Salome continued, "and have him set aside all eighty-six, or whatever the number is, wives for you. Meanwhile, your husband, yet another king, has abandoned both kingdom and people to embark on a foolhardy rescue mission. My dear, your skills are amazing."

Ishbel now gave a small laugh. "Oh, Salome, everyone else judges me."

"Ah, but I am a *very* bad woman," said Salome, winking. "We have a special affinity, you and I."

They sat there, grinning at each other, not trusting the other one a single inch, and suddenly a firm friendship was formed.

"Allies?" said Salome, who recognized the moment before Ishbel did. She held out her hand.

"Allies," said Ishbel, taking it. "I have never had a female friend before."

Salome laughed. "Neither have I. Oh, look, who is *this* approaching? Can it be . . . ?"

Ishbel looked up. Isaiah was riding toward them, Axis and Maximilian directly behind.

She felt cold, and looked away from Maximilian.

Isaiah drew his horse up when he got close to the women. "Will you mount your horses," he said, "and follow me?"

Then he pushed his horse forward, directly up the sloping walls of the pass.

CHAPTER THREE

Salamaan Pass, Northern Kingdoms

Isaiah dismounted at the very top of the pass, giving his horse a chance to recover from the steep, difficult climb. He let the reins trail loose, and the stallion wandered off, nosing among the stones for any stray blade of grass.

Behind him the five other riders did the same, not speaking, Maximilian and Ishbel carefully keeping to opposite sides of the group as they had done on the ride up the mountain.

Isaiah walked to a point where he could stand on a large, flat-topped rock and stare south. He could see the smudge of Hairekeep in the distance, and beyond that farther still Isaiah fancied he could just make out a black haziness that might be Sakkuth.

Aqhat he could not see at all, but he could *feel* it.

The Skraelings were changing into the likeness of their master. Isaiah shuddered. Since Lister had told him about the Skraelings, Isaiah's dreams had been disturbed by nightmarish visions of what lay ahead.

Skraelings, hundreds of thousands, if not millions of them, under the control of Kanubai.

Or of DarkGlass Mountain, and Isaiah did not know which was worse.

Where are you, Lister? he asked. *What are you doing?*

I am south of Hosea, my friend, traveling with a horde of creatures that I no longer feel comfortable calling Skraelings. They no longer tolerate me so well, and I stay out of their way.

A pause, then Lister continued. *Pray to the heavens, my friend, that they pass you by on their way south.*

Isaiah shivered, breaking off the connection, and turned around.

Axis had come up close, and was looking down into the pass at the slowly winding column as it moved north.

"Why do I get the feeling," Axis said softly, not looking at Isaiah, "that what you are about to say will shatter worlds?"

"Worlds are already shattering, my friend," said Isaiah. "Perhaps what I say now will help rebuild them."

He walked closer to the grouping of Maximilian, StarDrifter, Salome, and Ishbel.

"My lord," Isaiah said to Maximilian, "do I have permission to speak?"

Everyone, save Axis, looked between Maximilian and Isaiah in surprise at both Isaiah's words and tone.

"Better you than me," said Maximilian.

Isaiah nodded. "Very well." He turned to the others. "I need to tell you a tale. I will be as brief as I can. Some of you"—he glanced at Ishbel—"will have heard parts of it before.

"This is a tale of my land, now called Isembaard," Isaiah continued, "and of the Northern Kingdoms from Escator to the Outlands, and including Viland, Gershadi, and Berfardi. All of these lands are wedded together more strongly than you can imagine. It is the legend of Kanubai, the chaos of that time before life, and it is the tale of the Lord of Elcho Falling."

Isaiah paused, walking slowly about the top of the mountain, his boots scrunching in the loose gravel, every eye save Maximilian's fixed on him.

Maximilian had turned very slightly, and was now looking into the distance over the western FarReach Mountains.

"In the beginning," Isaiah said, "and for an infinity of time there was nothing but the darkness of Chaos, who called himself Kanubai. Kanubai grew tired of his lonely existence, and so he invited Light and Water to be his companions. Chaos and Light and Water coexisted harmoniously, but then one day Light and Water merged, just for an instant of time, but in that instant they conceived a child—Life.

"Kanubai was jealous of Life, for it was the child of the

union of Light and Water and he had been excluded from that union. He set out to murder Life, to consume it with darkness and subject it to Chaos, but Light and Water united against him in order to protect their child. Aided by a great mage, Light and Water defeated Kanubai in battle, and they interred his remains in an abyss. They stoppered this abyss with a sparkling, life-giving river, which combined the best of Light and of Water, and they hoped that Chaos was trapped for all time."

Isaiah gave a small smile, looking at each of his audience in turn. "The mage who aided Light and Water was a man they knew only as the Lord of Elcho Falling. It was he who defeated Kanubai in a major battle that raged for months through day and night over this entire land, and he defeated him only with the aid of Light and Water, who were his weapons."

Again he paused. "And who *are* his servants."

"You are Water incarnate, are you not, Isaiah?" Axis said. "And Lister . . . Light?"

"Yes," Isaiah said.

Axis took a deep, deep breath, glancing once more at Maximilian, who still regarded the far distance as if it were fascinating. "Go on," Axis said to Isaiah.

"We must shift forward in time, many millennia," Isaiah said. "To a time some two thousand years ago."

Very briefly, Isaiah told the group the tale he'd told Ishbel. How the Magi had built their glass pyramid, through which they meant to touch Infinity, over the precise point where Water and Light had placed the stopper to Kanubai's abyss. Boaz had opened the pyramid into Infinity, and in the doing cracked the stopper. Kanubai had been crawling his way free ever since.

"This is where the legend of Kanubai and that of the Lord of Elcho Falling begin to merge once again," Isaiah said. "Boaz was a magus of the land, and one so powerful he headed the entire Threshold project, but he was the son of a northerner, a man called Avaldamon, a mage the likes of which few of us have ever met."

"Ah!" Maximilian said. "We had never known what

happened to Avaldamon! How ironic, Isaiah, that his issue caused the stopper holding Kanubai to crack."

"Aye, ironic indeed," Isaiah said.

"I didn't know," said Maximilian. "No one knew where he'd got to. We thought him lost. Is that where . . ." He glanced at Ishbel.

"Yes," said Isaiah, "Ishbel is a direct descendant of Avaldamon's line through his son, Boaz."

"So *that* is where the connection happened," Maximilian said. "I could not work it out."

"Will one or both of you start to speak sense?" Ishbel said. "*What are you trying to say?*"

Isaiah looked pointedly at Maximilian, and he sighed, and stepped close to the group so that he became fully a part of it.

"Avaldamon's elder brother, named Fledge, was the Lord of Elcho Falling at that time," Maximilian said.

"Yes," Ishbel said, "I know this. I just don't understand what this has to do with you, Maximilian."

"Ishbel," Maximilian said, "the name of the House of Elcho Falling is Persimius. *I* am the current Lord of Elcho Falling. You are also of the family of Persimius. I knew it the first time I touched you. I am descended from Fledge, you from Avaldamon."

Ishbel stared at him. Her face was white, her eyes huge, and she trembled very slightly where she stood. Salome came to her, and put a hand about her waist, but Ishbel scarcely felt it.

Maxel was the Lord of Elcho Falling? Maxel?

"Kanubai is risen," said Isaiah. "Water and Light are once more incarnate. The Lord of Elcho Falling needs to assume the throne of his mountain fortress at the edge of the world."

"Really?" said Salome. "Where is that, then? I've never heard of it."

"The fortress of Elcho Falling," said Maximilian, "fell into disuse perhaps two thousand years ago, fairly soon after Avaldamon went south. It was abandoned by the Lords of Elcho Falling, who took up residence in their summer palace, now the king's palace in Escator." He took a deep breath. "Elcho Falling is Serpent's Nest."

"And Ishbel," said Isaiah, "through the knowledge gained in her training as archpriestess of the Coil, is the one who shall need to unwind it for Maximilian—to present to him his throne. She is far less an archpriestess of the Coil than she is of Elcho Falling, which is her inheritance, too."

Ishbel finally found her voice. "You've been manipulating everyone's lives for *all* of our lives, haven't you, Isaiah? My parents, my entire *family* . . . were they murdered so that I would be raised within Serpent's Nest? What of Maximilian? Were his seventeen years of hell necessary to hone him for the crown *he* needed to assume? Did you allow a child to endure a nightmare, and a youth to lose half his life, *just so that you could mold us into what you wanted*?"

"Lister and I did what was necessary," Isaiah said, "to save us *all* from Kanubai. The future rests in your hands, Maximilian and Ishbel."

"Well," muttered Axis, "thank the stars it's not up to me this time."

CHAPTER FOUR

Salamaan Pass, Northern Kingdoms

Ravenna had no idea where Maximilian was. She'd searched up and down the column, had virtually exhausted herself and her horse, and almost burst into tears of relief when she saw him, StarDrifter, and Salome riding to rejoin the column from a path that led into the mountains.

"Maxel? Where have you been? I've been so worried."

He gave her a glance, but kept riding so that Ravenna had to push her horse to catch up enough to hear his answer.

"I've been out riding," he said.

Ravenna looked at StarDrifter and Salome, knowing something had happened, but that they were not likely to tell her.

What were they up to? It involved Ishbel, no doubt. A pang, part of anger, part of jealousy, shot through her.

"Maxel?" she said again.

"We've been speaking with Isaiah," Maximilian said. "It was nothing important, Ravenna."

"You were not so very surprised at the story I related, Axis," Isaiah said. He and Axis were left alone atop the mountain peak.

Axis gave a shake of his head. "I'd heard a little bit of it from Maxel before we left Sakkuth. The rest . . . well, the details I did not know, but none of it surprised me." His mouth twitched. "And I *am* glad it won't be me to save the world this time."

"Considering you did such a shitty job of it the last time

around, Axis, I'd be hardly likely to hand it on to you."

Axis laughed. He waved a hand at the column grinding its slow way through Salamaan Pass. "And this is evacuation rather than invasion, am I right?"

Isaiah nodded. "Invasion was the only concept my generals could accept."

"The Skraelings are heading south."

"They will provide Kanubai with his army."

"Stars, Isaiah, what about the millions of people left behind?"

"We can leave the Salamaan Pass open for some weeks after the Skraelings have moved into Isembaard, but once Kanubai moves, we shall have to close it against his eventual march into the north. People will be able to flee north once word of the Skraelings spreads."

They were quiet a moment, thinking about the terror that would spread throughout Isembaard. Axis hoped that the news would spread fast, and that many would have the chance to make their escape.

"And me, Isaiah?" Axis said eventually. "I have a feeling that there is a far greater reason for you to have dragged me back from death other than to have a useful counselor for your more insecure moments."

"Aye, there is. The first reason that I, that *Maximilian*, needed you back you can see before you. Kanubai is going to invade the north, Axis. He is going to try and destroy both Elcho Falling and its lord before they have a chance to destroy him. Maximilian will need an army, and he is going to need a general who can command it for him. You are that man."

Isaiah now turned to look at Axis directly.

"The second reason Maximilian needs you is because he is going to need a friend. Someone who has been through what he now faces—the assumption of an ancient title, the resurrection of an ancient realm, in order to repel an even more ancient enemy. There is no one about him now who can provide that friendship, save you."

"Not Ishbel?"

"No," said Isaiah, "not Ishbel."

* * *

That evening, just as Maximilian and his group were finishing their evening meal, Ishbel walked into the circle of firelight.

"Maximilian? Would it be possible to speak with you?"

She looked gaunt and anxious, and held her cloak gripped tightly about her.

"Have you not done enough?" Ravenna said. "You can't just walk in here and—"

"Ravenna," Venetia said in a low voice, gripping her daughter's arm.

"Maximilian," Ishbel said, ignoring Ravenna. "We need to talk about what Isaiah said today. Please."

Maximilian gave a nod, rising to his feet.

"Maxel—" Ravenna began, making to rise herself, but Venetia literally hauled her back to the ground.

"No!" Venetia hissed as Maximilian and Ishbel faded away into the night. "You need to let them speak, Ravenna. *Alone!*"

Ravenna stared at her mother, then reluctantly nodded.

Venetia studied her, wishing she knew what to say. She'd watched her daughter work her way into Maximilian's bed, and she'd seen—clear to anyone save her blinded daughter— his reluctance to keep her there. Venetia had traveled with Maximilian for many weeks now, and she thought she knew the man. Guilt and honor bound him tightly, as did his wish not to hurt Ravenna's feelings, whom he felt he owed for his release from the Veins.

But guilt and honor and debt did not make a good foundation for a relationship, particularly when Maximilian still yearned for Ishbel.

"Ravenna," Venetia said gently, "Maximilian will break your heart eventually. You do know that, don't you?"

"He loves me."

Venetia looked across the fire to Salome and StarDrifter, both watching and listening carefully.

"He does," said Ravenna. "We've been through so much together. You just don't understand."

* * *

"Maximilian, I had no idea you were the Lord of Elcho Falling. I'm sorry."

They had found a spot relatively isolated from the camp-fires and people, but one with enough light cast from the many fires that they could see each other's faces.

Maximilian looked at her, noting the hollowed cheeks, the overly bright eyes. She looked very tense and nervous, but she also looked more open and honest than he'd ever seen her.

He wished she could have found that honesty far sooner. He wished he could have been the kind of man she could have been honest with.

"You never gave me a chance to tell you," he said.

"What I said, in the woodsman's hut . . ."

She couldn't go on, but both of them heard her words echo through their minds.

I hate him. Over the years I've had visions of him, and always I know that if ever he catches me, then he will wrap my life in unbearable pain and sorrow, for pain and sorrow trail in the darkness at his shoulders like a miasma. I know he will ruin my life. He will ruin the world.

"Do you still feel that way, Ishbel?"

She hung her head, fiddling with her hands.

"Do you still dream of me, Ishbel?"

Her head came up again, her eyes bright with tears. She nodded.

"And are they still the same?"

"Worse," she whispered.

Maximilian sighed. "What did you want to say to me tonight, Ishbel?"

"Just . . . just that . . . that I was sorry. I wish . . ."

"Don't get started on the apologies and the wishes, Ishbel. It is far too late for that."

"There is something else."

"Yes?"

"What I learned today—that you had been kept in the Veins for seventeen years—made me feel ill. I find it difficult to believe that someone could do that to you."

"I don't want to talk about it, Ishbel. It does no good. Besides, they also put you through the horror of your parents' deaths."

"But *seventeen years*, Maxel!"

He noted the use of the familiar, but was too tired to correct it.

"It is over and past now, Ishbel."

"No," she said, "I don't think it is." She paused, deliberating what to say next, knowing it could drive a further wedge between them, but wanting quite desperately to let him know she *did* know what it had been like for him.

"A long time ago," Ishbel said, "when we were almost happy, that night in the woodsman's hut, when we made love . . . Maxel, one of my skills is to uncoil memories. When you slept, I lay my hand on that scar on your left hip, and uncoiled—"

"I don't want to hear this, Ishbel!"

She was crying now, silent tears that slid down her cheeks. "I know what it was like for you, Maxel."

He half turned away, moving a hand slightly as if to wave away her words.

"What do they want of us?" she said after a lengthy silence.

"To save this land from Kanubai."

"I have no idea how."

He gave a small smile at that. "Neither do I. I fear it is a great mistake choosing me to try to save the world."

"I could not think of anyone better to choose," Ishbel said softly, but Maximilian did not hear it, for he had turned and walked away.

Five days later, Isaiah's invasion force moved into the Outlands.

They met with some minor resistance from small bands of men, but they were quelled within hours.

There was nothing between Isaiah and the north.

Nothing between Maximilian and Elcho Falling.

CHAPTER FIVE

Pelemere, the Northern Kingdoms

"Look," said Sirus, "if we attack from his left flank, we'll—"

"That's shit-talk and well you know it," said Fulmer, King of Hosea. "That's all you can talk, yes? You couldn't fight your way out of a brothel, let alone—"

"Shut up," said Malat, weariness evident in voice and posture and haggard expression. "Just *shut up*, Fulmer. You do not help the situation at all."

"And *you* can?" Fulmer said, his voice rising a little, betraying his youth and inexperience.

Malat sighed, moving away from the other two kings and pouring himself a cup of warmed wine, buying time before he had to answer. The past few months had been stupidity personified as the three kings of the Central Kingdoms pitted their armies against that of the Outlanders, whose forces were led by Chief Alm Georgdi, who had replaced the murdered Rilm Evenor as the war leader of the Outlander tribes.

In theory, the armies of the Central Kingdoms should have destroyed the Outlanders. Their combined forces were four times the size of Georgdi's, they had considerably more resources, they fought on their own territory, which meant they did not have the long supply lines that Georgdi did, and their armies were better equipped.

Unfortunately, superiority in theory did not translate to success on the battlefield.

They had fought Georgdi up and down the plains between Pelemere and Hosea and, while Georgdi had enjoyed no major victories, he had suffered no defeats, either. His army was well disciplined, highly motivated, and battle-skilled.

And it enjoyed the supreme advantage of having but one leader.

On the other hand, the Central Kingdoms' armies suffered from lack of coordination, lack of cohesion, and three supreme commanders who bickered constantly among themselves and who could barely agree on the day of the week, let alone a coherent battle strategy.

"Georgdi is in danger of surrounding us," Malat said, turning back to the other two, his wine untasted. "We've managed to get ourselves stuck in this . . ." He caught himself just before he said *nightmare of an indefensible city.* "Stuck here in Pelemere. Our supplies are low to the point of non existence. Winter settled in a month early. We don't have soldiers used to fighting on starvation rations in the middle of snowdrifts . . . and Georgdi *does.* Gods, my friends, they've fought the Skraelings in Viland for decades. Fulmer, have you heard anything from the supply train that was leaving Hosea two weeks ago? We *need* those supplies, man. Badly."

"I've heard nothing," said Fulmer. "None of the scouts have yet returned."

Malat and Sirus exchanged a worried look. No one had heard anything from the north for at least ten days. The entire area had been blanketed by snowstorms, yes, but they should have heard *something.*

"I think—" began Sirus, when he was interrupted by the door opening and one of his captains entering.

The captain bowed, excusing himself for the interruption.

"Sire," he said, "Chief Georgdi sits his horse outside the city gates, requesting a parley."

"What?" said Fulmer. "He has come to surrender?"

"No," said the captain, "he says he has come to warn of the approach of a tide of death."

BroadWing EvenBeat fought his way through the gusts of snow, his wings barely able to hold him aloft.

He was terrified.

He'd never encountered a storm like this. It wasn't its ferocity so much as *what* it was.

Not just wind.

Not just snow.

There was something *else* in the air about him.

BroadWing couldn't see the creatures, but he could *hear* them, and he could *feel* them. Whispers, cold, soft fingers brushing his face, his arms, his belly.

And sometimes, so fleeting he thought he'd imagined it, a face, an Icarii face, floating before him.

A cold smile lighting its features.

Then it would be gone, and BroadWing would be left to fight his way through the storm once more, desperate to get to Pelemere, desperate to warn the northern kings of what approached.

"Tell Georgdi he has our word," said Malat. "He enjoys safe harbor while in Pelemere."

As the captain left, Malat looked significantly at Fulmer. "He *does* enjoy safe harbor while under the parley flag, Fulmer."

"Perhaps he wants to surrender," said Fulmer.

"And perhaps you're nothing but a young fool," said Sirus, sitting down in a chair. "It might be better to allow Malat and myself to talk to Georgdi."

"If it wasn't for *my* forces and *my* supplies—" Fulmer began.

"Yes," said Malat, "and we're more than grateful, Fulmer. I don't know what we would have done without you. But I think it is important to hear what Georgdi has to say. He has fought with nothing but honor, and I don't expect anything else from him now."

Fulmer grunted, but he said no more, and joined Malat at the table with Sirus.

He hoped they would make Georgdi stand.

Chief Alm Georgdi was nothing like what any of the three men had expected. Somehow, Malat thought, as the Outlander entered the room accompanied by three of his men, all unarmed (and one looking as though he'd come straight from the battlefield, given his grubby clothing and exhausted features), they'd always imagined Georgdi as an enormous bear of a man. A hulk, rippling with muscle, and probably bristling with a full beard and curling mustachios as well.

Instead, Georgdi proved to be a trim man of good height, short of hair and clean-shaven, who looked as if he should be a scholar rather than a far-too-successful warlord. His attire was stylish, his manner elegant, his eyes bright and honest.

Malat instantly knew that whatever news he brought, it wasn't going to be good.

An approaching tide of death?

Georgdi waved aside all formalities and offers of refreshment, pulling out a chair and sitting at the table without waiting for an invitation.

"We're in trouble," he said, his well-modulated voice as elegant as the rest of his appearance.

"So you *have* come to surrender," Fulmer said.

Malat closed his eyes briefly and prayed for patience.

"All of us are in trouble," said Georgdi, ignoring Fulmer and looking between Sirus and Malat, instinctively knowing the better men at the table even before Fulmer had opened his mouth. "And all our families besides. Many of them will already be dead. Our petty little battles must be forgotten in the face of what approaches." He turned, gesturing to the disheveled and exhausted man who'd entered with him and who now took a step forward.

"This man is Jelial," said Georgdi. "Lord Warden of the Eastern Plains Province of Gershadi. Fulmer, you know him, surely? Yes, well. Jelial's hometown is Hornridge. He staggered into my camp late last night. Jelial?"

"I have been running south for these past six weeks," Jelial said, and the three kings went cold at the sound of his voice, because it echoed with hopelessness, "trying to keep ahead of death."

"Oh, for gods' sakes, man," said Malat, rising from his seat, "*what have you to tell us*?"

"Several million Skraelings are approaching," said Jelial, his voice still dead. "They ate their way through Hornridge. No one survived."

Jelial looked at Fulmer. "Hosea is no more. Everyone, *everyone*, is dead. And as they come farther south, as they feed, they're growing stronger, larger . . . *different*. Gods, sometimes I have caught glimpses of some of them who bore the heads of jackals! The creatures are now streaming toward Pelemere. They are perhaps a day away, maybe two if you're lucky. Get everyone out. *Get them out!*"

"Nothing will stop the Skraelings," said Georgdi in a tone as casual and even as if he were discussing the arrangements for a breakfast. "I know Skraelings. I fought them with Evenor in Viland. They are murderous in bands of a few score, and almost impossible in bands of a few hundred. Millions? Let alone the millions of what Jelial describes? I am not even going to attempt to stay and fight on these plains. You are welcome to your Pelemere and your Central Kingdoms, gentlemen. Within minutes I am going to rise from this chair and ride back to my army, which I shall gather about me and with all haste ride, *flee*, back into the Outlands, which I can either hope the Skraelings will ignore, or where we might have some chance of containing them in the passes between the FarReach Mountains and the Sky Peaks. What you do is your choice. If you decide to abandon your kingdoms—which, frankly I advise, because you stand no chance against these Skraelings—then you may flee with me. The more of us there are to battle the Skraelings in the mountain passes, if it comes to that, the more hope we have of standing firm against them."

Fulmer, Malat, and Sirus stared at him. For the moment none of them could speak.

"You have lost your kingdoms," Georgdi said, his voice now softer. "By the end of this week they will have vanished beneath a seething tide of death. Get who and what you can out now. You have a day, two at the most. Sit there and gape if you wish, but, frankly, I'd be *moving*."

With that he pushed his chair back and rose. "I don't have time to linger here. My armies spent the night packing, we will be gone by midmorning."

"It's all lies," Fulmer said, white with shock.

"No," Malat said quietly, "it isn't."

"The Skraelings?" said Sirus. "Millions? What is happening? They've never come this far south before. And in such numbers . . . What in the world are they doing?"

"They are led by a man called Lister," said Jelial. "He styles himself the Lord of the Skraelings. His Skraelings are swarming south. Migrating. My lords, I beg you. Flee. *Flee.*"

"I do not think news can come much worse than this," said Georgdi. "I think—"

"News *can* get worse," said a voice from the window, accompanied by a blast of cold air.

Everyone leapt to their feet, turning to face the intruder.

An Icarii man was balanced on the window ledge, one hand still on the shutters which he'd opened.

"My name is BroadWing EvenBeat," the Icarii man said. He jumped down to the floor, spreading his hands to show he was unarmed. "And I did not think I would survive to get this far."

"*What* news?" said Georgdi.

"Isaiah, Tyrant of Isembaard," said BroadWing, "has just led an army of a million men or more out of the Salamaan Pass into the Outlands. Adab has fallen. They are allied, I think, this Lister and Isaiah. And we"—he gestured, taking in everything from Hosea to the FarReach Mountains—"are all but dead, for there *is* nowhere to flee."

"How do you know this?" Georgdi said.

"For weeks I have been looking about the FarReach Mountains, scouting for Maximilian, who entered Isembaard," BroadWing said. "My companions and I had reached the eastern parts of the mountains when another Icarii warned us."

"What in the world is Maximilian doing in Isembaard?" Fulmer said.

"I don't think any of us have time for that story right now," BroadWing said.

CHAPTER SIX

The Sky Peak Passes

Malat had always thought he would not fear death when it came, but would accept it with courage and honor.

Of course, he'd never envisioned a death like this.

It was not just that death beckoned, or that death *strode* through the snow toward him, but that it was taking so damned long about it. The continuing terror, day after day, week after week, was not something Malat had ever thought to endure, and it had sapped his courage and honor and fortitude.

They'd fled Pelemere with Georgdi. Not everyone came. At least half the population of the city had refused to believe that a sea of Skraelings seethed down toward them—and who could blame them for disbelieving? They'd stayed, despite desperate shouted warnings, and now they were dead.

Malat remembered how, three hours after riding out of Pelemere, he'd pulled his horse to a halt and looked back.

Pelemere should have been clearly visible—a black blot on a hill in the middle of a vast plain.

Instead it had vanished beneath an undulating river of gray.

Skraelings.

Eating.

Malat, as all those who'd pulled their horses to a halt with him and looked back, could not quite comprehend what he saw. He could not imagine that number of Skraelings; of *any* creature. He'd sat his horse, his mouth agape, and stared, and it was only a few minutes later, when one of his men screamed, that he'd looked to his north.

A wave of Skraelings was less than five hundred paces away, and approaching fast.

Thus began the nightmare. Almost three weeks of constant battling, of bunching together, of fighting, of running, running, running eastward as fast as they could. Malat estimated that between Georgdi, Fulmer, Sirus, and himself, they'd escaped Pelemere with two hundred thousand people—both soldiers and civilians. Now Malat would be surprised if there were any more than fifteen thousand left.

Fulmer was dead, lost that first day.

Sirus also, lost a week later when his horse stumbled and then collapsed as a score of Skraelings swarmed over it.

The only reason any of them were still alive was because the bulk of the Skraelings were still to the west. Eating, Malat supposed; feeding through the Central Kingdoms toward Kyros.

Sometimes, when he managed to snatch a few minutes' rest, Malat would weep, thinking of his wife and remaining children, of all those he loved sitting in Kyros, not understanding that within days, weeks at the most, they would be eaten by these damned . . . damned . . .

Malat wanted to die. He wanted to succumb to the Skraelings' teeth, to their claws, their hunger.

But always, every time they faced renewed attack, something in Malat forced him to take up the sword again, and wield it, and somehow survive.

For another day.

They were in the western reaches of the Sky Peak Passes now. Georgdi, still alive and somehow still in control, still *hopeful*, said that if they could reach a gorge he knew of a few days' travel ahead, then they would have a chance. It had a narrow mouth, apparently, and they could defend themselves more easily there.

Malat didn't really care anymore. He put one foot in front of the other, or sat his horse staring sightlessly ahead as it somehow managed to put one foot ahead of the other, and he forced food and water down his throat as needed, and he wrapped himself against the increasingly bitter cold. About him, the few civilians and soldiers who survived bunched together for security and warmth and similarly trudged forward, defending themselves from never-ending attacks by groups of Skraelings, losing a few more comrades with each attack.

Malat thought there must be a trail of blood leading back to whatever remained of Pelemere.

That they survived at all was due to the Icarii. Not only BroadWing EvenBeat, the man who had warned them of the Isembaardian invasion into the Outlands, but several score of others who had joined him. They warned of approaching Skraelings, scouted clear routes through the territory ahead, and they were skilled bowmen and women, attacking Skraelings from above. They'd lost a few of their number, and Malat, as Georgdi, was incalculably grateful to them. They could have fled, this was not their fight, but they didn't. They stayed, and helped, and died, and Malat, who'd never had much respect for the birdmen, now admired them immensely.

But he still didn't think any of them would survive.

Winter closed in with tight, cruel fingers. Every few days heavy snowstorms enveloped them, and in those storms . . .

BroadWing said ghosts lived in them. Perhaps the ghosts of Icarii long dead, he didn't know, but they were almost as terrifying as the Skraelings, although they did not attack or maim or murder. They simply terrified with sudden appearances, their ethereal faces materializing in the snow before vanishing again, always accompanied by the barely audible beat of wings, and a constant undertone of whispering . . .

Malat could not understand how any of them would survive. If, by some miracle, they outran and outfought the Skraelings, and if these snow ghosts finally left them alone, then they still had a million Isembaardians with which to cope.

Their world was falling apart, and Malat did not think anything left within it could possibly endure.

Alm Georgdi was the first to hear the beat of approaching wings.

He was huddled in front of a campfire, his face haggard, his hands trembling from both weariness and cold.

He looked up, hoping it was not bad news.

BroadWing EvenBeat landed a few feet away, staggering a little. He was exhausted, as was everyone else.

"Georgdi," he said.

Georgdi grunted. Bad news, then.

BroadWing staggered forward, almost collapsing as he sat before the fire. His face was white with cold and fatigue.

"Georgdi," he whispered.

"What is it?" Georgdi snapped.

"The Skraelings," BroadWing said. "The Skraelings . . . they have abandoned the Central Kingdoms."

Georgdi stared at BroadWing, not able to understand what the birdman said. *Abandoned the Central Kingdoms?* "They've returned to their frozen wastes?" he said.

"No," BroadWing said, "they've swarmed into the Far-Reach Mountains. Every last one of them. The mountains are covered with them."

"What . . . *why?*"

"They are moving en masse into Isembaard," BroadWing said. "For the moment we're safe. From the Skraelings, at least."

CHAPTER SEVEN

The Sky Peak Passes

Lister stood with Eleanon, Bingaleal, and Inardle on a snowy platform high in a narrow gorge within the northern FarReach Mountains.

Below them the last ten thousand or so of the Skraelings swarmed southward.

Millions had passed by in the last day or so, desperate to reach DarkGlass Mountain. They were now moving supernaturally fast, almost *flowing* over the ground, pulled by Kanubai's power. By now, Lister reckoned, the first waves of Skraelings would be seething almost to the gates of Dark-Glass Mountain.

He could hardly bear to think of what might be happening to northwestern Isembaard as the Skraeling nation swept through.

Above them, snowflakes drifted gently down from heavy clouds, settling on rocks and clinging to crevices.

As they settled, very slowly they transformed into ice-covered lumps.

The Lealfast nation. Hundreds of thousands of them covering the FarReach Mountains. This was as far south as they, or Lister, would come. Isembaard might have a few more weeks, but then it would be Kanubai's and DarkGlass Mountain's entirely.

Lister sighed. "It comes to pass then. The Skraelings hurry to their true lord."

"Pity the Isembaardians," said Eleanon, watching the Skraelings. "They can have no idea of what is about to descend on them."

"Isaiah and I could not warn them," Lister said quietly. "Isaiah did what he could to get as many of his people out of the area as possible. The Salamaan Pass will remain open for a week or so for refugees, but then . . ."

"Then the Lealfast will do what they have to in order to keep these northern plains free, for as long as possible, from the armies of Kanubai," said Eleanon.

"Kanubai will do everything *he* can to get to Elcho Falling," said Lister. "He'll need to attack before the Lord of Elcho Falling attains his full strength."

"We will do everything we have to," said Eleanon, "but we pray to all gods above, and to the Star Dance that runs through our souls, that the Lord of Elcho Falling rises soon. Without him we are all doomed."

"Lister!" said Inardle. "What is that?"

At her alarmed voice, everyone looked to where she pointed.

A black shape climbed up the steep slope of the gorge on which they all stood. From this distance it looked half bat, half spider, and it certainly moved with the speed and agility one might expect from a creature bred from those parents, but as it grew closer the figure resolved itself into that of a man wrapped in a black cloak (albeit still climbing with the speed and agility of some creature of the night), a satchel slung over his back.

Lister laughed, and relaxed.

"It is one of my comrades," he said. "You have not met him, for he has been in Escator these many years past."

Within minutes the man had climbed to join them. Tall and spare with thick dark hair over lively eyes, the man embraced Lister, then shook the hands of the Lealfast present as Lister introduced them. "This is Vorstus," said Lister. "He has been 'minding' Maximilian."

"I have watched the Skraelings pass by," said Vorstus. "It is all happening, then."

"You seem somewhat delighted at the notion," said Inardle.

"*You* haven't been stuck in Escator these past thirty odd years," said Vorstus. "I'm dying for a bit of excitement."

Inardle gave him a strange look, then raised an eyebrow at Eleanon.

"Maximilian will need you soon," said Lister. "It is difficult to imagine that Isaiah has not yet broached the subject of Elcho Falling with him."

"Elcho Falling," Vorstus said. "I cannot *wait*."

"As he said," Lister remarked drily, "he's the one who has been stuck in Escator all these years while *we* have had the delightful company of the cursed Skraelings."

"Where is Isaiah now?" said Vorstus.

"Somewhere close to the Sky Peaks Pass," said Lister. He rubbed his hands together, as if suddenly tired of the cold, windy vantage point they occupied. "Shall we join him, then?"

Northwestern Isembaard, from the western banks of the Lhyl to the far western branch of the FarReach Mountains, was a roiling nightmare. Skraelings—or what had once been Skraelings—had seethed out of the FarReach Mountains and washed down over the northern plains of Isembaard like a rotting inundation of death. Many people had died under the sudden, unexpected onslaught, although some managed to escape west into the mountains, but within a day of the creatures emerging from the FarReach Mountains, northwest Isembaard was utterly lost.

The first wave of dog-headed creatures had reached DarkGlass Mountain a week or so after they'd crossed into Isembaard. They seethed over the glass pyramid, climbing over each other in order to reach its capstone, then sliding down the far side. Within moments the entire pyramid was covered with a writhing mass of gray, partly transparent creatures, their dog muzzles slavering in excitement.

Deep inside DarkGlass Mountain, Kanubai raised his own muzzle and howled.

The mass of Skraelings covering the pyramid screamed at the sound echoing beneath their bodies, and they tore off thousands of the plates of glass in their desperation to find the shafts that led directly into the Infinity Chamber.

Where waited Kanubai.

When the first creatures arrived in the chamber, they abased themselves before Kanubai, rolling over on the floor and presenting their bellies to him, that he could suckle from them all their life's blood.

By morning, when Kanubai would have had the opportunity to suckle lifeless a few thousand of the creatures, a devil-sun would rise over Isembaard, and it would emerge, not from the east, but from DarkGlass Mountain.

CHAPTER EIGHT

Entrance to the Sky Peak Passes, the Outlands

From the Salamaan Pass, Isaiah's vast army moved inexorably north. Adab and Margalit fell with nary a murmur. Neither port nor city had been built to withstand sieges, and they had no military defense, for all the fighting men were west with Georgdi.

No one had expected a threat from the south.

No one, for a moment, thought to try and resist this juggernaut, sweeping through like an inexorable, unstoppable tide.

Isaiah sent a force of some twenty thousand men into Adab, and some forty thousand into Margalit, to keep them submissive and to secure his own rear, but he did not enter either place himself. Instead he pushed north, north, and then slightly northeast, moving the column as fast as possible.

Isaiah's route north was accomplished with virtually no military action whatsoever. Village after village, town after town, had laid down before him without a fight. Most Outlander men were fighting with Georgdi to the west, and none who remained was stupid enough to attempt resistance.

By the time Isaiah had reached the west of the Outlands, a day's travel from the Sky Peak Pass, he had something like a third of the numbers that he'd led through Salamaan Pass. The rest he'd left at various locations along his winding trail northward, partly to guard his rear and to keep the Outlanders subservient, but mostly because he simply could not sustain and feed such a massive number of people himself. The Outlands would need to dig deep into their reserves of food, and no doubt their resentment would grow by the day, but very soon, Isaiah reasoned privately, they would have far more, and far worse, things to worry about.

The remaining third of Isaiah's column consisted of the core of his army—his best and most experienced fighting men. It also contained his five generals (irritated at the lack of fighting, but contented with the spoils in territory gained thus far), as Isaiah wanted none of them left behind to become bored and perhaps decide to embark on some military adventures of their own, as well as Axis, Maximilian and his company, and Ishbel.

Maximilian was largely content to allow Isaiah to push north as he wished. He still had to take that final step of actually assuming the mantle of the Lord of Elcho Falling, but Maximilian did not think he needed to do that until they reached Serpent's Nest itself. He was mildly surprised at the move to the northeast, but Isaiah had explained to him that they might meet survivors of the Skraeling terror in the Central Kingdoms at Sky Peaks Pass. Maximilian spent his days riding either with StarDrifter or with Axis, sometimes with Isaiah, deepening his friendship with Axis and, somewhat to his surprise, with Isaiah.

In the evenings, Maximilian generally walked the boundaries of the column's encampment. Alone. He spent the time deep within himself, returning time and time again, in his mind, to the Twisted Tower, wondering what he was going to do about its empty spaces. Maximilian had accepted fully that his were to be the shoulders to bear the burden of Elcho Falling, but he doubted his ability to bear the weight well.

Perhaps Serpent's Nest held some answers, some hope.

He saw Ishbel occasionally. Sometimes they met in the evening, as Ishbel now made her camp with StarDrifter and Salome, who shared a tent set apart from that of Maximilian, Ravenna, and Venetia. Their brief conversations were awkward, and Maximilian supposed she was as glad as he to break them off. There was no animosity between them, but there was a huge abyss of things said and done, of regret, of loss, and of that enormous weight of sadness and despair with which Ishbel claimed he would burden her life.

Maximilian supposed they were better off apart than together. He couldn't bear to watch her gaze turn to bitterness because of the grief he had brought into her life.

Besides, there was the added complication of Ravenna.

On this night Maximilian sat in his tent, one hand gently resting on the Weeper as it lay at his side, watching Ravenna and Venetia as they prepared a light evening meal. There was a tension between mother and daughter that hadn't been there when first they'd left Narbon so many months ago. Maximilian was not sure what it was—he had avoided asking Ravenna—but he did know that Ravenna had suggested none too gently to her mother that she seek somewhere else to unroll her sleeping blankets.

Venetia had not shifted from Maximilian's tent, for which Maximilian was grateful. He did not particularly wish to be left alone with Ravenna, and he did not wish to cement their relationship into semiformality by having people say *There stands Maximilian and Ravenna's tent*, rather than saying, as they did now, *There stands Maximilian and his party's tent*.

Ravenna was a problem Maximilian did not know how to solve. He'd got himself so drunk that first night in Sakkuth, both with wine and with enraged, frustrated love; he'd wanted to forget everything that he'd seen and heard over the past evening, drink himself into oblivion, and all he'd done was further complicate his life. He'd known of Ravenna's interest, she'd made it perfectly clear to him on their journey through the FarReach Mountains, but in the face of finding Ishbel again it had meant nothing.

Maximilian wished he had not slept with her. Ravenna had used the opportunity to slide completely into his life, so that now she shared his bed every night. If she had been some nameless, anonymous woman Maximilian would have welcomed the physical relief from his frustration, and he could have then thanked the woman and asked her to leave.

But he could hardly ask Ravenna to leave. Not after all she had done for him.

And most certainly not now.

At least with Venetia sharing the tent, he had an excuse to avoid making love with her. He found that difficult . . . sober.

He sighed, imperceptibly, but Ravenna heard and turned

her head to him, and Maximilian could see her tensing, readying herself to rise and come to him.

At that moment Isaiah ducked through the flap of the tent, and Maximilian rose with a too-wide smile on his face.

Isaiah saw the smile, glanced at Ravenna, and grinned in return. "Maximilian, can we speak?"

"Let's walk," said Maximilian. "The crispness of the snow will do my head good."

"The scouts report that there is a column of men, and some Icarii, less than a day's march to the west," Isaiah said. They walked the northern border of the encampment, their boots crunching through the snow.

Maximilian could not reply immediately. "A column"—all that would have been left of the fighting forces, and perhaps even peoples, of the Central Kingdoms.

"How many?" he said finally.

"Perhaps fourteen or fifteen thousand," Isaiah said, "and in a desperate state. There must be more, Maximilian, further to the west perhaps. There must be more who have survived, I am sure of it."

Maximilian did not want the comfort. "Fourteen or fifteen thousand?" *Gods, what had happened to Escator? Had the Skraelings seethed that far west?*

"They will reach us by noon tomorrow," Isaiah said. "Doubtless they shall be surprised to see their old friend traveling with the invader."

Maximilian spent a few minutes alone before returning to the tent.

Isaiah's news had shocked him. It drove home how disastrous had been the wars, and then the Skraeling invasion, for the Central Kingdoms. It particularly shocked him because he realized in a blinding flash as Isaiah spoke that the time had come to leave Escator behind him completely.

It was time for Elcho Falling.

Maximilian sighed. Then, suddenly, his shoulders straightened and he swiveled about on his feet, turning to look northeast, toward where lay Serpent's Nest.

The Mountain at the Edge of the World.

Home, as Ruen never had been.

Much later that night Ishbel woke from a nightmare, crying out in fear.

The Lord of Elcho Falling had been standing in the snow, his back to her, when he'd slowly, slowly, turned his face to look over his shoulder at her.

The Lord of Elcho Falling wore a face, and it was Maximilian's face, and the despair Ishbel felt now was worse than she'd felt ever before.

"Ishbel?" It was Salome's voice, concerned. Since leaving the Salamaan Pass, Ishbel had traveled with Salome and StarDrifter, sharing a tent and deepening her friendship with them both. Axis often joined them as well, but he was with some of the troops tonight, no doubt indulging in soldierly camaraderie and building useful friendships and alliances.

"Ishbel?"

Ishbel felt a hand on her shoulder and finally blinked into awareness.

"I'm sorry, Salome, I woke you."

"You woke half the encampment," said Salome, "but now we're all awake, come sip some tea with me, and tell me of what you dreamed."

"Oh, I don't want to—"

"You will sit with me, and sip tea," said Salome, somewhat grimly, "and you *will* tell me of what you dreamed. I am sick to death of being woken up every second night with your nightmares, and StarDrifter and I would both like to know to what we owe the pleasure. StarDrifter? Get up."

Ishbel rose reluctantly, hearing StarDrifter grumble as he, too, sat up from his sleeping roll and moved over to the barely alight hearth in the center of the tent.

Salome was all efficiency, poking life into the coals, setting a kettle to steep, fetching mugs from a corner.

Ishbel sat down cross-legged before the hearth, watching her with some admiration. For a woman who had so recently grown her wings, Salome moved with a lovely grace. Ishbel was sure that had it been her, she would have carelessly dragged a wingtip through the coals well before now.

"I'm sorry," she said to StarDrifter, who was yawning to one side.

He gave a small shrug. "No one can resist Salome. It will be *she* who rules the Icarii nation, when we discover it, not I."

Ishbel saw Salome look at StarDrifter, saw them smile slightly at each other, and felt a pang of such envy she actually felt physically ill.

Salome sat down herself, checked the kettle, pursed her lips in annoyance to see it not yet begun to steam, then looked at Ishbel. "Tell us about the dream."

Ishbel thought about trying to squirm her way out of it, but almost instantly decided resistance was useless. Besides, she trusted both StarDrifter and Salome, and perhaps they could offer some advice.

"It is about Maximilian," Ishbel said, and StarDrifter grunted.

"How surprising," he said.

"*StarDrifter!*" Salome hissed. "Go on," she said to Ishbel. "We need to do something while waiting for this damned kettle to boil."

So Ishbel told them: about her experiences as a child, locked in the house with her family's corpses; about what the corpses had whispered to her; about the dreams of the Lord of Elcho Falling that had continued throughout her life; what she had said to Maximilian in the woodsman's hut (at which both StarDrifter and Salome winced); about her horror when she realized that Maximilian was the Lord of Elcho Falling.

"I love him—" Ishbel said.

"Well, I'm glad you can finally admit that," Salome muttered, stirring a handful of tea leaves into the kettle.

"—but I have put such a distance between us and I don't know how to close it."

"Do you actually want to?" said StarDrifter.

Ishbel opened her mouth, then closed it, not knowing how to answer.

Salome waved a hand over the kettle, dissipating some of the steam that trickled from its spout. "All this talk of sadness and despair trailing about Maxel's shoulders," she said. "Very dramatic. I commend your imagination. But what do you *know* of this sadness and despair? I don't doubt that you can see and feel it, but how do you know its origins, or purpose? It could just as well represent Ravenna's desperate clutching at Maxel's shoulders."

StarDrifter laughed, and Ishbel managed a smile.

"The despair reaches out to envelop my life," she said. "It comes from Maximilian. Is *caused* by him. I wish it didn't. I wish it wasn't there, but . . ." Her voice trailed off, and she gestured helplessly.

"I have no idea what this miasma of despair means, Ishbel," Salome said, "but I see that you love the man, and he you."

"Ravenna—" Ishbel said.

"He doesn't love her," Salome said. "He is irritated by her. He feels bound to her by guilt and by the stars alone know what else, but he doesn't love *her*. You. Only you."

She took a deep breath. "For all the gods' sakes, girl, none of us can have any idea what that vision you have of Maximilian means, but this I *do* know. You have to live your life, and you need to take the risk. You need to clear the air between Maximilian and yourself. You need to make it perfectly plain to him that, despite all this talk of a nasty miasma, you want to share your life with him. Damn it, you *must*. Are you not bound by blood and destiny? Do you not both love each other? Yes, yes, I know both of you have made mistakes, and said and done things that perhaps you shouldn't have. But if you don't take the chance, Ishbel, you will shrivel up and die, and Maximilian with you, *and* everyone else with the tragic pair of you. Ishbel, this is the selfish Salome speaking here! *I want to live*. Sort it out with Maxel."

Both StarDrifter and Ishbel were staring at Salome by this stage, then StarDrifter gave a short laugh.

"I can add no more to my wife's wisdom, Ishbel. Sort it out with Maximilian. You must."

CHAPTER NINE

Entrance to the Sky Peak Pass, the Outlands

They had set out as usual in the morning. Up before dawn, striking camp, trudging forward, foot after foot—most of the horses had been eaten weeks ago. They had long since ceased sending out scouts, for the Icarii were exhausted, and as sick at heart as everyone else, and neither Georgdi nor Malat cared to hear whatever bad news they might bring.

Eventually, they knew, they would meet up with the Tyrant of Isembaard's forces. Georgdi and Malat had discussed briefly what they would do once they met: unconditional surrender and pray that Isaiah would feed them. There was not a man or woman among them in any fit state to fight, and fifteen thousand starving, exhausted, tottering excuses for soldiers and citizens would be no match for what they'd heard Isaiah commanded.

They had also discussed the possibility of retreating—to Pelemere, or Kyros, or wherever. But neither man had wanted to turn back west. For all they knew, the Central Kingdoms were utterly destroyed. West lay only rotting flesh and ruins. East lay . . . something else. They just had to pray that the something else was better than the rotting flesh and ruins.

It was, as always, BroadWing who brought them the news.

There had been some words among the Icarii traveling in a group just behind and to one side of Georgdi and Malat, and then BroadWing had taken off, lurching a little in his tiredness as he rose into the sky.

Malat supposed that with their superior sight the Icarii had spotted something ahead.

BroadWing returned within minutes, landing a few paces away from Georgdi and Malat.

"Do I want to hear it?" Georgdi asked.

"An army, massive," BroadWing said. "Stretching as far east as my eye could see."

And that was far enough, Malat thought glumly.

"Before it," said BroadWing, still unable to believe what his eyes had shown him, "sit a line of kings on their horses. Waiting for us."

A line of kings, BroadWing had said, and Malat thought it true enough. Four men sat their horses a few paces before the mightiest army Malat had ever seen, or even dreamed of.

One of them he knew, Maximilian of Escator (gods, how had Maxel joined up with this invasion?), and the others BroadWing identified to Malat and Georgdi.

"Stars," BroadWing said, "I can hardly believe it. There, that man, that is Axis SunSoar, once StarMan of Tencendor. Then Maximilian of Escator, who you know. Next to him is StarDrifter SunSoar, Axis' father, and now Talon of the Icarii. *My* king. And the final man must be Isaiah of Isembaard."

Malat agreed with BroadWing on that point. He could think of no one else save the Tyrant of Isembaard who would wear such a magnificent collar of gold, or sit a horse with such innate arrogance and power.

Malat and Georgdi stepped forward, and a moment later Isaiah pushed his horse into a walk toward them.

They had closed half the distance between them when suddenly there was a movement behind Isaiah.

It was time.

Maximilian sat his horse, watching Isaiah ride out to meet Malat and Georgdi, and he knew it was time. From the moment he'd received news of the offer of Ishbel as a bride, events had pushed and pummeled him toward this moment. Everything appeared absolutely clear, totally straightforward. The air hung cold and frosted about him, the snow crisp and solid beneath his horse's hooves.

All was so lucid, so crisp, so clean.

Maximilian took a deep breath, leaned very close to Axis, whispering, "*Back me up!*" Then he pushed his own horse after Isaiah, kicking it into a canter.

Behind him, the entire army stirred in surprise, and Isaiah's five generals laid hand to their swords and narrowed their eyes.

"What the fuck . . . ?" Armat murmured.

Isaiah heard him coming, knew precisely who it was.

He smiled a little, glad, and reined his own horse back.

As Maximilian rode past him he pulled his horse to one side, bowing his head in deference.

Malat and Georgdi halted, surprised but not particularly alarmed as Maximilian pulled his horse to a halt in a flurry of snow before them.

"Welcome to the ancient past, my friends," Maximilian said, his voice clear and strong, carrying back to those who waited behind him. "Welcome to Elcho Falling." His mouth gave an ironic twist, and he nodded over his shoulder, indicating the forces stretched out behind him.

"You are Maximilian of Escator?" Georgdi said, a note of puzzlement in his voice.

Maximilian glanced at Malat as he spoke. "No. I am Maximilian Persimius, Lord of Elcho Falling, commander of you and yours, of Isaiah of Isembaard and all his, and of this army behind me. I am very much afraid, my friends, that the war has only just begun."

He held their eyes a moment longer, then he wheeled his horse about and rode directly back to the army.

He was pleased (and relieved) to see that Axis had positioned himself slightly to one side and in front of the spot where Isaiah's generals waited on their horses, their faces masks of anger.

Maximilian met Axis' eyes briefly, and Axis gave a very slight nod.

Maximilian reined in his horse before the generals. He could feel the tension rippling from not only them, but from the entire tens of thousands of men gathered behind them. He could see, feel, *intuit*, the hands reaching for swords, the mouths readying themselves to shout out the assassination order, the mayhem that gathered itself to leap.

He was moments away from death; Isaiah and Axis as well, Ishbel and StarDrifter and Salome also. Everything, the entire world, was a heartbeat away from complete and total disaster.

And Maximilian, for the very first time in his life, felt as if he was, *finally*, right where he belonged. Purpose filled him. The Veins had not killed him, these generals did not stand a chance against him, and even Kanubai would probably lie down and cower at the sight of Maximilian atop his horse.

Maximilian laughed out loud, flinging out one arm in an extravagant gesture. "My friends, my generals, is this not the most exquisite moment? I have surprised you, and for that you have my humblest apologies . . . as also you have them for the fact that I now announce *myself* your commander, Axis SunSoar and Isaiah of Isembaard my immediate captains, to whom you shall answer and who shall speak with my voice."

All humor vanished from Maximilian's voice, and it became tight, ringing with determination. One of the generals, Morfah, had opened his mouth to speak, but Maximilian gave him no chance.

"I am the Lord of Elcho Falling. *This*"—as if it were one with Maximilian, his horse stamped one of its front hooves on the snow—"is the land of Elcho Falling, arisen from ancient memory. Know me as your lord, gentlemen."

"Fuck you," said Morfah, and he drew his sword.

Maximilian walked into the Twisted Tower. His steps were unhurried, his posture relaxed. He moved through the ground level chamber and climbed into the second level. He walked to a chest of drawers, opened the third drawer from the top, and withdrew a small block of stone. He held it, and retrieved from it knowledge.

* * *

Morfah thrust his sword into the air, opening his mouth to shout the orders that would see *him* finally take control of this army, and which would see both Isaiah and this pissant Maximilian dead in the snow.

And then he turned to stone, and a moment later crumbled into dust, his horse shying to one side at the unexpected relief from the weight of the man on its back.

Maximilian smiled, the expression grim, his eyes moving slowly over the four remaining generals, now staring at him in complete shock.

"I *am* now your lord," he said very quietly, and yet in a tone that still carried.

"Maximilian!" Axis shouted, now thrusting *his* sword into the sky. *"Lord of Elcho Falling!"*

An instant's hesitation, during which Axis looked pointedly at Ezekiel, who then thrust his own sword skyward, shouting, "Maximilian! Lord of Elcho Falling!"

Another moment's hesitation, then the shouting spread through the ranks.

Maximilian! *Maximilian*! *Lord of Elcho Falling*!

"How soon loyalties turn," Isaiah said, chuckling. He, Maximilian, Axis, StarDrifter, Ezekiel, Malat, and Georgdi were in his commodious command tent, having ridden there once the shouting had died down and Maximilian had given Lamiah, Kezial, and Armat orders to return the soldiers to camp and to ready themselves and the army for a march northeast within the next week or two.

"I wish you'd told me that was going to happen beforehand," Axis said. He was still a little shaken by the events, and didn't quite trust the three generals outside not to turn immediately to plotting Maximilian's destruction.

"I don't think even Maximilian quite knew he was going to do that," Isaiah said. "It was well done, Maximilian. It was time for you to come into your own."

"Will someone *please* explain what is happening?" Ezekiel said. "Isaiah?"

"Ah," Isaiah said, "there is a long tale behind this day, Ezekiel." He told the general, as well as Malat and Georgdi, the ancient tale of Kanubai, and of the Lord of Elcho Falling, and of all the events that had brought them to this point.

"Today," Isaiah said, concluding his tale, "Maximilian has stepped out from under the shadow of Escator and into the light of Elcho Falling."

"What the hell did you do to that general, Maxel?" Malat said. His voice was very quiet, and he looked shaken by what he had heard.

Maximilian made a small gesture with his hand, but otherwise did not answer.

"Lamiah, Kezial, and Armat will have forgotten that small trick by the end of this week," Ezekiel said. "Maximilian, I am still bemused by this tale, and I do not know whether to believe in it or not, or whether to believe in *you* or not. Suddenly my world, as everyone's, is turned upside down. Isaiah, you say that Isembaard is finished? That this . . . Kanubai . . . and his army of Skraelings shall trample it into thralldom?"

"And worse," Isaiah said.

Ezekiel gave a small movement of his head, as if to try and shake his thoughts into order. "*I* cannot comprehend this, and I wager that every single Isembaardian outside this tent, including the other three generals, will find difficulty in comprehending it. Maximilian, do not think you have won a victory here today. Do not think that you have won hearts and loyalties. Shock and sleight of hand has won you the initial skirmish . . . but . . . gods, man, how do you expect to win the respect and loyalty of a million people who shall shortly learn that their homeland, and all their relatives and friends left behind, their homes and memories, lie dying under the terror of an appalling horror? What advantage you won today with surprise will be gone within a week, maybe less."

"We have a long journey ahead of us," Maximilian said, "and we can all take it but one step at a moment."

Ezekiel made a small sound of disgust. He turned to Isaiah. "And you . . . no wonder you changed after that month you vanished during your campaign against the Eastern Independencies. Are you the true Isaiah, or did he die during that month, and you replace him?"

"He died that month," Isaiah said. "No loss, surely."

Ezekiel just gave another shake of his head, and turned away.

Axis exchanged a glance with Isaiah, then looked at Maximilian. "Now what, Maxel?"

"We wait here for Light—Lister—to join us," said Maximilian, "and then we march north to Serpent's Nest, there to rebuild the Mountain at the Edge of the World, Elcho Falling." He paused, and a look of consternation came over his face. "Gods, Isaiah, the crown of Elcho Falling! It remains in Escator!"

Isaiah gave a small shake of his head. "No, Maximilian. I think you will find that when Lister arrives, he will have what you need with him."

Maximilian grunted. "Vorstus, I suppose." He shifted his gaze to Axis. "In the meantime, my friend, while we wait for Lister, I try to win hearts and loyalties. As Ezekiel has so correctly pointed out, my small trickery today will not impress for long. A title is a pretty thing, but it will not win me allegiance."

He looked about the tent. "What loyalty *do* I command among those in this tent?" he said, softly. "Tell me, that I might the better understand the task ahead."

"Mine," said Isaiah. "I am your servant."

"And mine," said Axis. "You know that."

Maximilian gave both men a nod. "StarDrifter?"

"Mine as well," said StarDrifter. "As all the Icarii. I spoke with BroadWing briefly before I came to this tent, and I know how he feels about you. You have our hearts, Maxel."

"But can I trust Salome?" Maximilian said, with a small smile.

"Ah," said StarDrifter, returning the humor, "for her I cannot vouch."

"Ezekiel not, I think," Maximilian said, looking at the man.

"My loyalties cannot turn on a whim, Maximilian," Ezekiel said. "I admire what you did today, but the story Isaiah has told . . . it is too much. My heart remains reserved. Isaiah had my respect and thus my loyalty. You have yet to earn either."

Maximilian gave him a nod, accepting his words. Ezekiel would be a hard man to win, but once he gave his word and his loyalty, he would be true. "Malat?" Maximilian said. "Georgdi?"

Malat gave a great sigh. "Yes, you have my loyalty, Maxel," he said. "This has all been so much to comprehend, but somehow I am not surprised."

"Thank you," Maximilian said. "Georgdi?"

The man sat for a long moment, looking at Maximilian, considering his position and the words he would speak. "This is *my* land on which we stand," he said. "The Outlands. Why should I hand my loyalty to a man who comes to take it from me?"

"Because that is the only way you will ever keep it alive, Georgdi," Maximilian said.

"I am with Ezekiel," Georgdi said. "My heart remains reserved."

"I can accept that," Maximilian said, "if you can stay your knife, the both of you, until I have a chance to prove myself."

Georgdi laughed, and even Ezekiel raised a reluctant smile. "You have a great task ahead of you," the Isembaardian general said.

"Oh, aye, I know," Maximilian said. "And somehow I think the two of you shall be harder even than Kanubai."

Axis and Maximilian sat alone in the tent, everyone else having departed.

"That was some stunt you pulled today," Axis said. "Why did you do it?"

"Because it was time."

"Had you discussed it with Isaiah beforehand?"

"No."

Axis gave a small laugh of admiration. "You have balls, Maxel, I'll give you that. But how confident *are* you? There is an appalling journey ahead for you . . . for all of us. How good are you, my Lord of Elcho Falling?"

Maximilian gave a great sigh. "Axis, can I confide something to you? I have told no one this, although Isaiah and Lister will need to hear it eventually."

"Why do I feel like this is going to be bad news, Maxel?"

"Because you have experience behind you, Axis." Maximilian paused, then told Axis about the Twisted Tower. "It is our memory palace. Where is kept all the knowledge needed by whichever poor bastard had to shoulder the burden of Elcho Falling. But so much has been lost. It is well over half empty. I don't know what to do . . ." Another small pause. "I hope that when I get to Serpent's Nest, when I raise Elcho Falling—"

"You *can* do that?"

"Yes, I can do that, at the least. I hope that when Elcho Falling rises out of Serpent's Nest, somewhere within its corridors I will find enlightenment."

"Stars, Maxel . . . what if you don't?"

"Then I shall be running to you for advice, my friend."

"Ishbel doesn't know?"

"No. She has no knowledge of the Twisted Tower."

"But she was archpriestess of the Coil. You'd think that if the answer was in Serpent's Nest, then—"

"Thank you for your thoughts, Axis," Maximilian snapped. "Do not think *I* haven't worried over that as well."

"Well, perhaps Isaiah or Lister—"

"Yes, perhaps."

In DarkGlass Mountain, Kanubai turned his dog snout north and sneered.

So, his adversary had opened his mouth to spout drivel and declare himself.

Kanubai was not perturbed. The Lord of Elcho Falling was weak; the stink of his vulnerability could be smelled even from this distance.

The man might once more wear the title, but Kanubai doubted very much he would be able to wield the power that came with it.

CHAPTER TEN

Entrance to the Sky Peak Passes, the Outlands

"I watched you, Maxel. I watched what you did today in front of that army. You constantly amaze me."

Maximilian had been walking back to his own tent when Ishbel spoke. Now he stopped, looking at her as she emerged from behind a line of tethered horses. It was late at night, and Maximilian was weary beyond belief, but something in his heart lifted at the sight of her, at her beauty, and at the softness in her eyes.

How he wished he had not lost her.

She smiled, a little teasingly, walking much closer. "But I should not have been so very amazed, eh? You are the same man who walked into my chamber in Pelemere, and led me straight to the bed. You overwhelmed me, and I could not resist you."

"I wish the Isembaardian army were as easy to seduce as you, Ishbel."

She laughed. "I will try not to take that as an insult."

He smiled, too, thinking how ironic it was that now they were torn apart, how close and easy they could be with each other. Oh, to have had this camaraderie when they had shared a bed.

Her amusement faded. "Do you have a few minutes, Maxel?"

"Yes, of course. What is it?"

She hung her head, as if gathering courage, then she lifted her face, and looked him straight in the eye.

"I have been such a fool, Maxel. I have let go the one thing that could have made of my life a paradise. You."

Maximilian went cold. *No, Ishbel. Not this, I cannot stand it. Not now, when it is too late.*

"Maxel, I love you."

He made as if to speak, but she hurried on.

"I have made so many mistakes, so many ill choices. I have said so many foolish things. I—"

"You have visions of despair engulfing your life because of me, Ishbel. You cannot—"

"I am your *wife*! We have never formally ended the marriage."

He laughed, harsh and lost. "I think our marriage is well and truly over, Ishbel."

"I can accept whatever you bring into my life, Maxel. *Whatever it is,* because that will be easier than losing you completely."

"Oh, gods, Ishbel . . . I'm sorry, but—"

"No!" Ishbel literally threw herself against him, desperate for his touch and for his warmth. His hands closed about her shoulders, and she leaned back to gaze at his face. For an instant, he leaned down to her; she was sure he would kiss her, she could feel his breath wash over her face, she *willed* him to kiss her, then he pushed her away and stood back.

"We can't," he said. "I'm sorry. What was once between us must be ended."

"What *was* between us was misunderstanding and blindness, Maxel, and I agree that it should be over. What *can* be between us is—"

"We can work, we *will* work, together to raise Elcho Falling, Ishbel. I can't do that without you. But our marriage is over."

"You love me," she said. "You do."

"I—"

"He doesn't love you, Ishbel. You tore his world apart. He will never forgive you."

Ravenna walked out of the darkness, a cloak wrapped tightly about her. "Maximilian was always mine, from the moment I first laid eyes on him. I helped free him from horror— what have *you* ever done for him? What Maxel and I have between us is not something you could ever understand."

Ishbel stared at Ravenna, then looked at Maximilian, pleading with her eyes for him to refute what Ravenna had just said.

He dropped his eyes away from hers.

Ravenna let the cloak fall free, and one of her hands rested on her as yet flat belly. "I carry his child, Ishbel. His heir. Maximilian Persimius will cleave to *me* now."

She stared at Ishbel's stricken face for a long moment, her eyes gloating, victorious, then she turned on her heel and walked away. "Maxel?" she called over her shoulder.

"I'm so sorry," Maximilian whispered, staring at Ishbel. "So sorry."

Then he also turned, and walked away.

He paused, just before he vanished from the faint light, and turned his head, ever so slightly, to look over his shoulder at her.

I'm sorry.

Then he was gone, lost to the darkness and to Ravenna.

Ishbel stood, tears streaming down her face, hating Ravenna more than she could ever imagine hating anyone, but feeling above all a tide of despair and sorrow and loss wash over her as she watched the Lord of Elcho Falling walk away from her into the night.

It was then she understood, finally, what her visions had been trying to tell her: that it would be the *loss* of the Lord of Elcho Falling that would disfigure her life with despair, and she sank slowly to her knees in the snow, weeping with wrenching sobs as her world shattered into a million pieces.

GLOSSARY

Alaric: a nation in the extreme north.

Allemorte, Baron: a nobleman from Pelemere.

Aqhat, Palace of: the home of Isaiah, Tyrant of Isembaard.

Armat: one of Isaiah of Isembaard's generals.

Axis: *see* SunSoar, Axis.

Aziel: archpriest of the Order of the Coil.

Ba'al'uz: court maniac in the Tyranny of Isembaard. Ba'al'uz is pronounced "bay-uz."

Baxtor, Garth: a physician who employs the Touch (the ability to determine sickness through touch). Garth was primarily responsible for freeing Maximilian Persimius from the Veins eight years before this tale begins.

Bingaleal: one of the Lealfast.

Borchard: son of King Malat of Kyros, and friend of Maximilian Persimius.

BroadWing EvenBeat: an Icarii, and friend of Maximilian Persimius.

Brunelle, Lady Ishbel: an orphan from Margalit, raised to be archpriestess of the Order of the Coil.

Cavor, Count: cousin to Maximilian of Persimius, Cavor kidnapped Maximilian as a fourteen-year-old youth, imprisoned him in the gloam mines, and seized the throne himself.

Central Kingdoms: a loose term for an alliance between Hosea, Pelemere, and Kyros.

Coil, Order of the: an order that lives in Serpent's Nest. They worship the Great Serpent and use the bowels of living men to foretell the future.

Coroleas: a continent in the west of the Widowmaker Sea, renowned for the immorality and cruelty of its peoples.

DarkGlass Mountain: an ancient pyramid originally built to provide a pathway into Infinity. Once it was known as Threshold.

Doyle: a member of the Emerald Guard and former assassin.

Egalion: captain of the Emerald Guard, and friend to Maximilian Persimius.

Eight, the: Ba'al'uz' eight companions in his journey north of the FarReach Mountains.

Eleanon: one of the Lealfast.

Embeth: lady of Tare in Tencendor. Former lover of Axis and StarDrifter. Now long dead.

Emerald Guard, the: Maximilian Persimius' personal guard, composed of former prisoners of the Veins.

Escator: a poor kingdom on the coast of the Widowmaker Sea. It is ruled over by Maximilian Persimius.

Evenor, Rilm: an experienced battle general of the Outlands.

Ezekiel: Isaiah of Isembaard's most senior general.

Ezra: son of Salome, Duchess of Sidon.

First, the: the top caste of Corolean society comprising the Forty-four Hundred Families. The First commands virtually all of the wealth and power within Coroleas.

Fleathand: the steward of a house in Pelemere.

Forty-four Hundred Families: *see* the First.

Fulmer: King of Hosea.

Georgdi, Chief Alm: general of the Outlander forces.

Gershadi: a nation to the north of the Central Kingdoms.

Hosea: a city state of the Central Kingdoms alliance. It is ruled by King Fulmer.

Icarii: a mystical race of winged people who once lived in the mountains of Tencendor. The Enchanters among them wielded the Star Dance to produce powerful enchantments. A scattered remnant from the destruction of Tencendor live in the lands about the Widowmaker Sea.

Inardle: one of the Lealfast.

Insharah: captain of a band of Isembaardian soldiers. Friend of Axis SunSoar.

Ional: a former archpriestess of the Order of the Coil at Serpent's Nest.

Isaiah: Tyrant of Isembaard.

Isembaard, Tyranny of: a massive empire below the Far-Reach Mountains, currently ruled by Isaiah.

Jelial: Lord Warden of the Eastern Plains Province of Gershadi.

Kezial: one of Isaiah of Isembaard's generals.

Kyros: a city state of the Central Kingdoms alliance. It is ruled by King Malat.

Lamiah: one of Isaiah of Isembaard's generals.

Lealfast: an Icarii-like race of the frozen north.

Lixel, Baron: Maximilian Persimius' ambassador to the Outlands.

Madarin: an Isembaardian soldier.

Malat: King of Kyros.

Margalit: the major city of the Outlands, and Ishbel Brunelle's childhood home.

Maximilian Persimius: *see* Persimius, Maximilian.

Morfah: one of Isaiah of Isembaard's generals.

Outlands, the: a province to the east of the Central Kingdoms, renowned for its wild nomadic culture.

Pelemere: a city state of the Central Kingdoms alliance. It is ruled by King Sirus.

Persimius, Maximilian: King of Escator. Maximilian endured seventeen years in the gloam mines, as a youth and young man when his cousin Cavor seized the throne.

Prata: master of a small Corolean fishing vessel.

Privy Council of Preferred Nobles: also Privy Council.

Ravenna: a marsh witch-woman who patrols the borderlands between this world and the Land of Dreams. Her mother is Venetia.

Sakkuth: capital of the Tyranny of Isembaard.

Salamaan Pass: the only relatively easy access through the FarReach Mountains into Isembaard.

Salome, Duchess of Sidon: the most powerful woman in Coroleas, and perhaps the most hated.

Second, the: the Thirty-eight Thousand Families who comprise the second caste within Corolean society. The

Second is comprised mostly of the educated intelligentsia, traders, and minor landowners.

Serge: a member of the Emerald Guard and former assassin.

Serpent's Nest: a mountain on the coast of the Outlands.

Sirus: King of Pelemere.

Skraelings: wraithlike creatures inhabiting the ice and snowbound wastes of the far north.

Star Dance: Enchanters among the Icarii wielded the music of the stars (the music made as the stars move about the heavens, and which the Icarii call the Star Dance) in order to create powerful enchantments. The Star Dance is no longer available to those Icarii remaining alive, because the Star Gate, which filtered the Star Dance through to them from the heavens, was destroyed during the final Tencendor wars.

Star Gate: a magical portal that once existed in Tencendor, the Star Gate filtered the magic of the Star Dance, which the Icarii Enchanters used to create their enchantments. Demons destroyed the Star Gate during the final wars of Tencendor.

StarWeb: an Icarii, and lover to Maximilian Persimius.

SunSoar, Axis: formerly a hero from Tencendor and a member of the Icarii race, Axis once reigned over Tencendor as its StarMan before relinquishing power to his son, Caelum. Axis died five years ago during the destruction of Tencendor.

SunSoar, StarDrifter: Axis' father, and a powerful Icarii prince and Enchanter.

Tencendor: a continent that once lay in the western region of the Widowmaker Sea. It was lost five years before this tale begins in a catastrophic war with demons.

Third, the: the third caste within Corolean society, mostly comprised of workers.

Thirty-eight Thousand Second Families: *see* the Second.

Threshold: *see* DarkGlass Mountain.

Turmebt: father of Isaiah, Tyrant of Isembaard.

Twisted Tower, the: a palace of memories.

Veins, the: the gloam mines of Escator where Maximilian Persimius was imprisoned for seventeen years.

Venetia: a marsh witch-woman who patrols the borderlands between this world and the Land of Dreams. Ravenna is her daughter.

Viland: a nation in the extreme north. The Vilanders often have trouble with Skraelings.

Vorstus: abbot of the Order of Persimius, Vorstus aided Garth Baxtor and Ravenna in freeing Maximilian Persimius from the Veins eight years before this tale begins.

Weeper, the: a strange but immensely powerful Corolean bronze deity.

Zeboath: an Isembaardian physician.

Zeboul: the most senior among the Eight.

Continue the adventure
with Sara Douglass's

THE TWISTED CITADEL

on sale
May 27, 2008

The River Lhyl, north of Aqhat, Isembaard

Hereward stood on the deck of the riverboat, arms wrapped about her upper body, hugging her thin shoulders. Her dark hair blew into her eyes and across her face, obscuring her vision, but she made no move to tuck the strands behind her ears.

Her black eyes stared straight ahead, almost unblinking.

To the far bank.

Skraelings seethed there, staring back at her, globules of saliva dripping from their over-toothed jackal's jaws. Their huge clawed hands clenched, desperate for her.

But they would not cross the water. They hated the water.

The River Lhyl was all that stood between Hereward and a tearing, agonising death.

The Skraelings still panicked Hereward, still caused her stomach to clench in a twisted misery of fear and physical nausea, even though it had been weeks now since they had appeared on the river bank opposite Isaiah's palace of Aqhat.

Weeks since her, and Isembaard's, world had disintegrated.

Hereward had lived a relatively good life within the palace.

Her father was Ezekiel, now the most senior general to the Tyrant Isaiah, as his father before him.

Ezekiel had very little to do with Hereward during her childhood. He'd been careful to ensure that she (as her mother) had adequate housing, and that Hereward had a good schooling. Ezekiel had taken greater interest in Hereward once she'd reached adulthood, and had secured her a position within the palace. By the time she'd reached her

mid-twenties, Hereward had attained the position of Kitchen
Steward—a pretentious title for the person who supervised
the meals. It was an exhausting job, but Hereward took pride
in it. She was free, she earned a good wage, and one day, she
hoped, she might have saved enough to open a tavern . . . in
Sakkuth, perhaps. Hereward had had enough of the rigidity
and formality of palace life at Aqhat.

Then, everything had changed within the space of an hour
or two.

Isaiah had left for his northern invasions many months
earlier, Hereward's father, Ezekiel, with him. Palace life had
quietened into utter tedium as over ninety percent of the
people who had inhabited the palace left to trail behind the
Tyrant. Most of the wives had left for the eastern cities, their
children with them. There was but a handful of soldiers left.
Servants and slaves had enough time to enjoy a siesta during
the hottest hours of the day.

And then one day . . .

Hereward had been in the palace's vast kitchens. She spent
a large part of her day there, talking to the cooks, planning
menus, supervising the cartage of food from the kitchens to
wherever in the vast palace complex it was needed. It had
been a strange day, for everyone had been unsettled without
being able to pinpoint a reason. If a servant dropped a spoon,
then everyone jumped at the clatter, shooting dark looks at
the unfortunate offender. Hereward could not concentrate
on the menus—and there were so few of them by the gods,
surely she could manage *this* small task!—and kept having
to ask the cook with whom she spoke to repeat what he had
just said.

For some reason, everyone kept looking to the windows.

Just before midday there had come a shout from the
outside.

No. Not a shout. Hereward thought later that it had been
a howl of sheer terror, the sound knifing into the bright midday sky.

For an instant everyone in the kitchen froze.

Then Hereward started to walk toward the door which
led into the great courtyard beyond. Her legs felt leaden,

every step an effort, and her chest felt as if a great hand had clenched about it.

Somehow, Hereward understood very clearly in that moment that her life was probably either about to end, or to change so utterly that she would wish it *had* ended.

There was a great deal of commotion in the courtyard. People were grasping at the shoulders of others, asking them what had happened, what was wrong.

Others pointed to the gates which led to the river, and covered their faces with their hands, and wailed.

Not wanting to, but unable to stop herself, Hereward walked toward the gates. She stepped through them, ignoring the people who brushed past her—either going in her direction to see what had gone wrong, or rushing back toward the palace, faces set in masks of horror.

Hereward stopped some twenty or so paces the other side of the gates. From this vantage point she had a clear view of the River Lhyl, and the far bank, where stood DarkGlass Mountain.

She stood, and looked, unblinking.

Her mind could not process what she saw. It tried to present to Hereward various interpretations, all of which Hereward knew were incorrect.

DarkGlass Mountain had not somehow become enveloped with every billowing white sheet hung out to dry in Isembaard.

DarkGlass Mountain was not covered in a sudden storm of snowy thistle flower.

DarkGlass Mountain was not burdened under a sudden and unexplainable invasion of white locusts.

Instead, the glass pyramid was covered—*crawled*—in an undulating, horrific tide of grey wraith-like creatures. They were coming from the north. Hereward was vaguely aware that the far riverbank was covered with the creatures as far north as she could see.

People were pushing and bustling about her. Hereward thought that some of them might be screaming, or shouting, or some such. She didn't really know or care. Right in this moment, all she could do was stare.

Then someone said: *What if they cross the river?*

Utter panic consumed Hereward. She wracked in a huge breath, tried to expel it, and couldn't. She turned to run, but couldn't. Her legs just would not work.

Then came another shout (or perhaps a whisper, Hereward did not know).

Skraelings!

Hereward knew of them. Every since the Tyrant Isaiah had brought Axis SunSoar back from the dead and into the palace, stories of Axis' life had circulated about the palace staff. Hereward had heard about the Skraelings. She knew of their horror.

Skraelings?

Somehow Hereward managed to force herself to breathe, and then she managed to take a step back toward the palace. Another breath, another step, and then she was running with everyone else, buffeted and bruised by the mass panic, her long black hair coming free of its pins and half-blinding her.

She didn't care. All she wanted to do was to get back inside the kitchens and *think*.

The kitchens were virtually deserted. Hereward sank down to her haunches behind the door, instinctively finding a hiding place. Her hands were buried in her hair, her eyes were staring, her chest heaved with her huge breaths.

She didn't know what to do. She still could not order a single thought, let alone decide on a course of action.

Gradually the kitchen staff returned. Some sat or stood like Hereward, stunned and unable to think or act. Others grabbed what they could and ran . . . where, Hereward was not entirely sure, but ran.

After what appeared to Hereward a very long time, she rose, clutching at a table for aid in getting to her feet.

She must have been crouched down for hours—her legs and back were stiff and cramped.

"We have to aid ourselves," she said, to no one in particular. "No one will come to help us."

"We need to leave, then," said Heddiah.

"Yes," Hereward said.

"East—" Heddiah began.

"*No*," Hereward said. "Not east. "Where in the east? Into

the Melachor plains? Into the mountains where live the bandits? In one we'd starve or die of thirst within a week, in the other we'd be murdered before the Skraelings had their chance at us. And in both, we'd stand no chance whatsoever once the Skraelings manage to get across the river. Have you *seen* how many of them there are? Millions! *Millions!*"

Hereward stopped, appalled at the note of hysteria in her voice.

"No," she continued, now controlling her voice, and trying to inject as much persuasion into it as she could. "Not east. Even if we were left alone, or if we survived the Melachor plains, it would take us many weeks before we reached any kind of safety."

"Where then?" said a woman called Odella.

"North," Hereward said. "North, up the River Lhyl."

"But the Skraelings are just across the river!" said Heddiah.

"They can't touch us," said Hereward. "Not on a boat. We just don't touch the western shore . . . we *can't* touch the western shore, ever. Even if somehow, somewhere, the Skraelings manage to cross the river and surround us on both sides, they still can't reach us in the middle of the river. It is the safest place."

There was silence as people considered her arguments.

"We take a boat and," Hereward continued, "and with the winds driving south-westerly, we can tack upriver . . . many leagues each day. We can reach the north within . . . what? Ten days?" Hereward actually had no idea, but no one contradicted her.

"And then?" said Odella.

"And then we go wherever is safest. By the time we reach the north we will have a better idea of what is happening. There will be news." How they were going to gather news and information when they were stuck in the middle of the river Hereward did not know. But there would be news somewhere, somehow, surely. "We can make a choice then. But at least it is far away from *here*. We cannot stay *here*."

Now Hereward stood on the riverboat's deck, looking at the Skraelings hungering on the far bank. That terrible day in

Aqhat seemed a year away now, although it had only been a matter of a few short weeks. The remaining kitchen staff had eventually agreed with Hereward that the boat north would be the safest and quickest, if the most terrifying, means of escape. They had commandeered a riverboat, large enough to hold their party—some twenty-eight, counting spouses and children—and had set sail northwards. Five or six of the men had river experience, and they quickly taught the others how to steer and set the sails so they could tack into the wind and sail north against the Lhyl's gentle current.

The winds had not been as good as they'd hoped, and they had not travelled as fast as they had expected, but at least they had kept safe. They were careful to stay in the centre of the river where the water was deepest and where the riverbanks were each some twenty paces away. Skraelings haunted the western bank, hordes of them, scores of tens of thousands of them, hungering for the *Tasty! Tasty! Tasty!* that the boat held. The Skraeling whispers pervaded the hull of the boat, and everyone had to grab what sleep they could while the terrifying whispers slid cold and malicious about them.

Hereward hardly slept. It was dusk now, and Odella had called her a while ago to come and eat with the others.

Hereward wasn't hungry. She felt as if she took her eyes off the Skraelings for just one moment then they would attack.

Somehow they would find their way over the water.

If she did sleep, Hereward had nightmares of waking to find them crawling over her, their terrible claws sinking into her flesh …

She'd come to hate Axis SunSoar and Isaiah. Somehow she'd managed to associate her current plight with these two men.

Whoever had heard of Skraelings before Axis arrived in Aqhat?

And why had Isaiah deserted them? Why had he taken everyone who could possibly have saved the people of Aqhat north into the lands above the Far Reach Mountains?

The Skraelings roiled and whispered on the far bank. Their long, thin arms reached out for her, their jaws drooled, their teeth caught the last of the light and their tongues bulged obscenely from their mouths.

Hereward had never felt so alone and so hopeless in he life. She had never been able to even imagine feeling thi way.

After a moment, she turned, and walked below decks t join the others in their evening meal.

The Sky Peaks Pass

They met very late that afternoon for an early supper i the command tent. Maximilian had been out, and ar rived back in the tent once everyone had gathered. He looked tired and strained, and only nodded a general greeting as he entered. Two serving men were still bringing in platters of food, setting them down before those already seated at the table. Maximilian ignored the table, and walked over to join the four men standing at the wine servery.

"Georgdi, Malat," Maximilian said. "Are you somewhat recovered? Have you slept? How are your peoples?"

"Most are well enough, Maxel," Malat said. "They are grateful for the shelter and opportunity to rest and eat after so many weeks on the run from the damned Skraelings. But within a day, I think, they shall be rested and fed enough to start worrying about what lies behind them—how much of their homelands remains, and if any of their families survived the Skraelings horror. What I can say to them then, I cannot think."

"We can send out a scouting party back to see what is left shortly," Maximilian said, "I think—I *hope*—the Skraelings will stay south of the Far Reach Mountains for the time being. *I* want to know what has happened to Escator. Georgdi?"

"I'd like to know what Isaiah's . . . sorry, *your* . . . army has left of the Outlands, Maximilian," Georgdi said. "Once my men have rested sufficiently, I shall need to ride east to Margalit. I assume it still stands."

"It still stands," Maximilian said, "but Isaiah left many thousands of his soldiers there to secure his rear. Wait," he said, as Georgdi opened his mouth to speak, "I know you want them gone, that you want *us* gone from the Outlands, but unfortunately this province is likely to become the first to feel the full force of the Skraelings' push north. I am not going to shift men from the Outlands until I know what is happening."

"Which is what we need to discuss tonight," Axis said, standing to Maximilian's right, with his father, StarDrifter SunSoar at his elbow. He handed Maximilian a glass of wine, then nodded at the table. "Shall we sit? The serving men have left us in peace."

Salome, Ishbel and Isaiah were already seated and had been conversing in soft tones. Now they fell into a watchful silence as the men approached the table, all eyes on Maximilian.

In his turn, Maximilian watched Ishbel out of the corner of his eye as he took his seat at the head of the table. Of all of them she looked the most rested, and certainly the most collected, and Maximilian wondered at the tranquillity she appeared to have acquired after his rejection of her.

He thought of the vision Ravenna had shown him, of Ishbel crawling through the gates of Elcho Falling, and opening the citadel to the dark invader.

Then he remembered what Axis had said the previous night: *I had seen a truth, but I had misinterpreted it, so badly Azhure almost died and I almost lost the woman without whom . . . well, without whom I would have accomplished none of what later I managed.*

Ishbel's chin rose slightly under Maximilian's regard. He thought she looked very lovely, with her blue robe and soft fair hair falling over one shoulder, and very noble, with her unexpectedly tranquil and collected demeanour.

She didn't look to him like a woman who would betray Elcho Falling, but then who was he to judge?

Maximilian gave her a brief nod then acknowledged Salome and Isaiah.

"What has happened?" said StarDrifter. "Axis said something about Kanubai? That he has . . . vanished?"

"The sense of threat from Kanubai abruptly ceased late last night," said Maxel. "Both Isaiah and I, and I assume Lister, could sense Kanubai previously. That sense has vanished."

"DarkGlass Mountain," Ishbel said. "It has taken him."

"We think so," said Isaiah. "We think—"

"Who else?" said Ishbel.

"You have been in the pyramid, Ishbel," Maximilian said. "Do you think it capable of taking Kanubai?"

She looked at him without hesitation, or embarrassment. "Yes. It *hates*, Maxel, and that hate is a powerful force."

Again Maximilian contemplated her. Ishbel conversed easily with him, and he found that remarkable after the way he'd treated her the previous night. He had been sure that she'd be awkward, and embarrassed, and had spent much of the time before he'd come back to the tent trying to think of ways to put Ishbel at ease. Now all those strategies were very obviously redundant.

"The glass pyramid is a dangerous enemy," Ishbel continued. She glanced at Isaiah. "When Isaiah and I entered it . . . oh, I can't explain it, but it was almost as if the pyramid *lived*. It could reach out its walls, and touch us. Kanubai might have been powerful, but was he powerful enough to best what he thought was his ally?"

She concluded with an expressive shrug.

Maximilian gave her another nod, then looked at Isaiah. "No one knows DarkGlass Mountain as well as you," he said. "Talk to me. What is it capable of? What will it do?"

Isaiah sighed, rubbing at his eyes and using the movement to buy time to think. *What* was *the glass pyramid capable of?*

"It is hugely powerful," he said finally, "and hugely angry, as Ishbel said. That anger and hate stems from its ancient past, when one of the magi, Boaz, Ishbel's ancestor and the nephew of the then Lord of Elcho Falling, caused it to be dismantled. I think, but I have no way of truly knowing, that it wants vengeance."

"Against *whom*?" said Maximilian.

"Against anyone who stands in its way," Isaiah said, "but more particularly, Boaz and Tirzah, who tried to destroy it, and all their descendents. Ishbel definitely, but also you, Maximilian, as you are of the same blood lines and as you are powerful enough to threaten it. It may have also inherited Kanubai's feud with Elcho Falling. I don't know. I just . . . I just don't think it is going to sit there and glow in the sun cheerfully. I think it will *act*. I think it *has* acted."

He paused, the fingers of one hand tapping slowly on the table top. "I think that the glass pyramid is the greater danger. Kanubai was known. The pyramid is utterly unknown. Not even the magi completely understood it or its powers."

"So even though Kanubai may be dead I cannot go back to Escator, curl up in my bed, pull the covers over my head, and dream of happy hunting parties in the forests north of Ruen?" Maximilian said with a wry twist of his mouth.

Isaiah smiled. "No, Maxel. You cannot. There are still great trials ahead of us. None of us can afford to relax."

"And so what are you going to *do* about this?" said Georgdi. The Outlander general looked tense and frustrated. "My homelands have been invaded, and currently all you seem to propose is that your million soldiers and settlers just mill about in confusion. You don't even have true or tight control over them! I—"

"I have in no manner proposed we do nothing," Maximilian snapped. "I am here to consult and to decide, not to dither."

Georgdi shot him a look, but said nothing.

"The world is torn apart, Maxel," Malat said. "If you want to ask for the loyalty of every man and woman north of the Far Reach Mountains, then you shall need to stitch it back together again. Otherwise no one will fight for you."

"Malat makes a strong point," Axis said. "I talked among some of the Isembaardian soldiers today, and there is great restlessness. They may have owed Isaiah their loyalty, but they do not know you, Maxel. Moreover, they are terrified of what happens to their families in Isembaard. Rumours fly, and men talk of aiding their families by themselves if you cannot do it for them."

"And the generals?" Maximilian said.

"Quiet," said Axis. "I have seen Ezekiel, and the others

rest in their tents. I will talk with them in the morning . . . but they will take instant advantage of any discontent within the army. We need to decide what to do with them."

Maximilian grunted. "Isaiah," he said, "do you know where Lister is?"

"I believe he is moving north from the Far Reach Mountains," Isaiah said. "He will want to join you at Elcho Falling."

"What he wants is immaterial," said Maximilian. "Particularly with what has happened over the past day. What are these glass pyramids, or spires, that you have used? Axis has told me of them. Do you have one with you?"

"In my pack," said Isaiah. "Not with me here."

"Fetch it, if you will," Maximilian said, and Isaiah rose and left the tent.

"Axis," Maximilian said, "what do you know of Lister? What did you learn about him while you lived and travelled with Isaiah?"

It was not Axis who answered, but StarDrifter. "If I may," he said, seeking permission from both Axis and Maximilian to speak, and at their nods, continued.

"Of Lister I know little, but Axis and I know something of the force that travel with him."

"Force?" Maximilian said. "I thought he travelled with the Skraelings."

"He did," StarDrifter said, "but travelling with him, and still with him I assume, is a great force of winged peoples." StarDrifter told the group about the table about the ancient history of the Icarii in Tencendor, how, when many generations ago, they had escaped persecution into the Icescarp Alps, a group of Icarii had continued travelling north into the frozen wastes.

"We believed them to have died," said StarDrifter, "but now Axis and I believe that they survived. They must have travelled deep into the frozen wastes and there, so I believe although I cannot explain *why* they did this, they interbred with the Skraelings to create a new race. They call themselves the Lealfast, and they command great magic through the Star Dance."

"I thought the Star Dance had been destroyed," said Maximilian.

"So did *I*," said StarDrifter, "but these glass pyramids that Isaiah and Lister use to communicate were made by the Lealfast, and they use the power of the Star Dance, although anyone who commands power can use them. I don't know how, but the Lealfast still use the Star Dance."

"One of them flew down to Aqhat," said Axis, "to stage an attempted assassination of Isaiah in order to encourage his push north. He escaped before my eyes, using powerful enchantment. If the rest of the Lealfast command such power, then they may be powerful allies."

"Or powerful enemies," said Maximilian.

Isaiah re-entered the tent at that moment, and sat down at the table. In one hand he held a glass spire, about the height of a man's hand, which pulsated with a rosy light. He placed it on the table then gave it a gentle shove, sending it sliding down the table to Maximilian.

Every eye at the table followed its passage.

Maximilian stopped the spire with one hand. He studied it briefly, then picked it up.

"It is a thing of great beauty," he said softly. Then he lifted his eyes, and looked again at Isaiah. "How does it work?"

"You cannot use it?" Isaiah said, his tone a little challenging.

Maximilian held Isaiah's gaze for a long moment, then looked back to the spire in his hand.

Everyone at the table watched him, and for several heart-beats nothing happened.

Then, suddenly, the glass glowed through the gaps of Maximilian's fingers. First pink, then red, then it flared suddenly a deep gold before muting back to a soft yellow. The ascetic face of a middle-aged man appeared in its depths, his thin mouth curved in a slight smile.

"Lister," said Maximilian softly. "Well met, at last."